Illumination

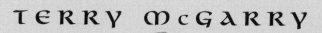

TERRY McGARRY

Illumination

TOR®

A TOM DOHERTY ASSOCIATES BOOK

NEW YORK

ILLUMINATION

Edited by Jenna Felice and Teresa Nielsen Hayden

Book design by Ellen Cipriano
Map by Ellisa Mitchell

A Tor Book
Published by Tom Doherty Associates, LLC
175 Fifth Avenue
New York, NY 10010

www.tor.com

Tor® is a registered trademark of Tom Doherty Associates, LLC.

ISBN 0-312-87389-1

First Edition: August 2001

Printed in the United States of America

0 9 8 7 6 5 4 3 2 1

IN MEMORY OF JENNA

And Galandra was born the first mage, of the union of earth and air and water, Eiden and Sylfonwy and Morlyrien; and Eiden loved her for her peaceful heart, and shaped himself in her image that they might be pledged; and in the children of Galandra the spirits of earth and air and water are united once more; and three become one.

—TELLERS' TALE

north

The Sea
of Wishes

The Isle of Senana

The Sea
of Charms

The Meri Isles

h

Maur Alna

The Knee

The Khine

The
Boot

The
Ankle

The Strong
Leg

The Heel

Maur Lengra

The
Leeward
Sea

Big Toe

The Weak Leg

The Ha

The Toes

Wiggle
Cramp
Stub
Curl

The Little Toes

The Low S

The High Sea   Crown   The Sea of Storms

(The Windward Sea)

Nape   The Head

The High Arm   The Neck

ck

RIST

The Heartlands   Shrug

The Sea of Sorrows

The Muscle

The Belt   The Low   The Thin   The Fist

The Elbow   The Arm   Wrist

Maur Aulein

Maur Bolein

Maur Gourd

Maur Sleith

The Forgotten Sea

The Dreaming Sea

Illumination

The Serpent

eblik na Lareon could no longer turn back.

The mob bore him onward like a tide that had no ebb, just flow. Thousands had gone ahead safely during the night. Now the first flames sprang up behind them, the first glass shattered, the first doors splintered under spiked boots.

Understanding had come to the king. He had set his soldiers on them.

Seblik was not of them, he bore no mark, but stragglers would be killed without a second look—or with a second look, given too late, and then perhaps a shrug of thin remorse as the bloody mistake was lost underfoot. Seblik na Lareon was a modest scribe, a translator, nothing more. The vision of himself as that trampled body fueled the imperative to flee.

Too late, too late. He must keep on, he must go faster—he was a sheep with mad dogs at his heels, the cries of the mob sounded like the blatting of ewes. But where? Run *where*?

A woman near him staggered, went to her knees. He dragged himself back against the flow, helped her regain her feet. She clutched to her breast a mangled hand, fresh crushed by a blind boot. "Too late," she moaned, the voice of his own despair. Soot streaked her mutilated cheek, embossed the old, scarred mark. Despite his urge to help, Seblik nearly left her then; his body recoiled as from contagion. He reminded himself that he knew better. He put his arm around her. His leather satchel, heavy with codices, battered their lower backs as he helped her onward, shoved this way and that by people desperate to get past.

The last of them, the dregs, the forsaken, those who had tarried. Only at dawn had the cry been raised in the vacant, squalid quarters, only by midmorning had the scale of the thing become evident. They had been leaving, in small, unobtrusive groups, for weeks before. The city had filled with them, then drained, and until today no one had been the wiser. Now the westering sun gilded their doom.

Seblik would not have been in their quarter at all, were it not for his own cursed studies. He risked his position, he risked being damned by association, but he could not resist their lore, their skills, their fluency in the old tongues. Now he would pay for his thirst for knowledge. Too late he had tried to slip back to the palace. The streets were already full of soldiers; he was forced into alleys, forced into a roundabout route, forced ever outward toward the city's edge, and beyond it; and then the fleeing crowds had engulfed him and there was no way back, there was no choice.

And wouldn't he prefer this? Whatever the cost, wouldn't he prefer their learned company to that of their enemies?

Up, up they went, Seblik and the stumbling woman, up the rocky way, scales rippling over the Serpentback, ascending the sea-bordered ridge as the hours ground past and the relentless sun sank under its own weight into black, whitecapped waves. Through the night they pushed on—no choice, as the way grew narrow and so many pushed on behind them. Hour after hour they heard the screams as the slow, the weak were cut down; hour after hour, there were fewer between the two of them and the end of the ragged column. Why cut them down, what disastrous cruelty was this, to kill those you would be rid of when they were ridding you of themselves?

There was nowhere for them to go. They could march for weeks and in the end there would be only rock and more sea. The Serpentback led to wasteland. There was nothing for anyone there but slow death.

Behind them, the stifled shrieks came closer. Behind that, the laughter of murderers. Toying with them, now; knowing, as they did, that their headlong rush was hopeless. They would have ample time to scythe this wearying field of wheat, whose slow, short roots could not carry them fast enough to land too barren to sustain them should they reach it.

I am not one of them! his useless mind cried. *See me, all unmarked! I am translator to princes! I will be missed in the merchant quarters, they will pay coin to see me spared!* But there was no coin here on the wind-scoured Serpentback, there were no powerful patrons, and they would spare neither his life nor the time to ascertain his innocence before taking it from him.

"I hurt," the woman said. Seblik had been supporting her for almost a mile. His arms ached, his legs burned. Terror was no longer enough to mask exhaustion.

"I cannot carry you," he said.

"Leave the sack."

"I cannot."

Still they walked; and then he chanced to raise his head.

"Look," he said. "Look."

Dawn was behind them, the blood of the dead seeping into the sky; perhaps a mile ahead, the rocky outcroppings of the Waste spread to either side like wings—even seemed to rise, an illusion created by moonset. Seblik's mind was beginning to go. There had been no water, no crumb of food, on this mad flight. But the cliffs were there, the land was there, asserting itself against the sea. The cliffs were crenellated by *people*. The main group had not dispersed into the Waste to buy their futile weeks of life. They were standing firm—unarmed, facing the pursuit.

Soldiers on horseback would follow the soldiers afoot. Ships would launch, must already be rowing toward the serpent's sides.

The fools *awaited* death.

The sight gave the woman renewed strength, and she walked for a while under her own power. No need, now, to cast her off, or cast off the bag of precious codices. The weight of that decision lifted from him, Seblik too found strength to go on.

The serpent writhed beneath them.

Just a shudder at first, easily dismissed as a spasm of weariness in his own flesh. Then another, and a third.

Seblik turned, and took in:

Perhaps a hundred foot soldiers backlit by dawn, silhouettes bulked by spiked greaves and breastplates; the lightening sky made shades of them, as if the damned souls of soldiers dead long past had escaped some crack in the netherworld's ceiling and rushed out to harry the marked ones. Swords catching the sunrise on tempered steel and flinging it in all directions like so many blades of light; the soldiers had let their weapons sag, milling in confusion as the Serpentback bucked again and trembled. No more than a handful of marked ones between himself, the woman, and the blades. Leagues upon miles distant, the burning city, a vicious ember under nacreous sky.

The serpent twisted, rumbled its rocky agony. They broke into a run.

He lost the woman; fell, himself; scrabbled back for her along the stony path, found her tumbled into thorn and gorse, the serpent's shale-scaled side rounding precipitously to the sea a yard beyond her. He pulled her free, thought she was sobbing—it was he who was sobbing. The other marked ones had gone past them. No buffer now. Armored death loomed over them; a sword tore free a swatch of dawnlight and dragged it toward them in an endless, sweeping arc.

Seblik hurled himself flat at death's feet. The woman half-rose to flee. The sword, aimed for where their heads had been, bit deep; her fending forearm shattered. The serpent pulled itself from the water and dropped abruptly back. Seblik, lying flat, clung like a mite to the scaly hide. The soldier, standing, was flung off. His razored armor rasped down the slope, sword clattering before it.

A liquid calm washed through Seblik then. He got to his knees, found the woman lying on the path ahead. He knotted her tunic's sash around her upper arm to stop the blood; the sword had ruined all below the elbow. Grunting, he hauled her onto his shoulders. He staggered to his feet, lost them in the next rockquake, got up again. He ran headlong for the cliffs. They were too far. He ran anyway.

With churning feet, with momentum, he rode the writhing serpent. He flew; it cast him up into the air and forward, the woman's weight counterbalanced by the bulging satchel. He came down still running, boot soles finding miraculous purchase, propelling him on until the next spasm sent him airborne.

He gained the stepped cliffside. Hands reached down, bore the woman up and away. A quake sent him reeling out of their grasp. He clawed at the bucking rock, looked up, and saw a thing he'd expected never to see again in his lifetime: marked ones plying their banned craft.

A red-haired woman, a fair man, a dark man. Six others, in a triangle around them, two to a side. Seated on rocks, passing their instruments among them, making arcane the commonplace tools of his own craft. Under the crash of the sea, the hiss of spume, the groaning rock, the shouts and cries, a low hum resonated in his bones: their chanting. The three in the center of the triangle—red woman, light man, dark man—rose to their feet with the fluidity and patience of ritual. Oblivious of the madness below, they clasped wrists with their arms crossed. They wove themselves into a tight ring. It grew tighter and then tighter still, until Seblik couldn't see where one left off and the next began—until they merged into one being, a creature of light so intense it made him squint.

They were breaking the serpent.

Fatigued rock parted. Seawater rushed into jagged fissures. Segments big as houses shifted. Straggling soldiers slid screaming into the sea. The sea itself began to boil.

A segment cracked off, scant yards from him, but the rock he clung to with torn fingers remained attached to the cliffs. He crawled toward those rescuing hands—in moments he would be safe, safe as anyone could be in the Waste, better to face hunger and thirst for a week or a year than fall to a cruel death on the hungry, tortured stone—

The strap of his satchel snapped. The bag of codices tumbled away. He cried out, turned; it was lodged in a cleft, just past arm's reach. Above him voices shouted, begging him to grab hold, climb up. He felt the reaching hands.

He dove for the satchel. With the last strength in his spent limbs, he hurled it up and over the cliff, into the arms that waited for him.

The serpent released a deafening roar and crumbled into the roiling waters. The sky cracked open. The dim stars twisted on their fabric of night; the fabric *folded*, swallowing the sunrise. For a moment, all was twilit silence. Then a great wind swept through, flattening all life. Seblik clung to the bucking rock, and screamed back at the earsplitting tumult, and it subsided.

He had survived the shattering of the Serpentback.

Like an afterthought, Seblik's granite perch crumbled too, stressed past enduring. The ocean reached for him. The waters were black, but they opened on a depthless sea of light.

Seblik fell, and fell, into the ages.

1

BINDING

unset through the high, round window draped the attic in shadows. Liath, tracing invisible designs on the floor with the feather end of a quill, had lit no lamp. Where the feathers brushed, they left a faint, shimmering blue trace. The darker the room grew, the clearer the traces.

If this were a casting, with binding materials, the phantom light would blaze around the quill. It would guide her hand as she painted kadri and inked borders along the blocks of wordsmith's marks inscribed on vellum or sedgeweave or parchment. As she filled in her lines with pigments, the blue guiders would be absorbed into tangible saffron, ochre, verdigris. When she could no longer see the patterns in her mind's eye, the illumination would be complete.

These dim echoes of her guiders were a new thing. Each movement—of hand, or foot, or quill—left a trail through the dark air as if through still water.

Every motion has a consequence.

Through the floorboards she could feel the vibration of life: tavern life, village life. Cottars and crafters, traders and herders, gathered from miles around to drink and game, gossip and dance. She had gone to sleep to the sound of sorrow and celebration each night for twice nine years. The first roll of beater on drum out front, the laughter of children scattered by the broom whisking the road clear for dancing, called her down to her celebration. For once, at least, she wouldn't be on duty; there'd be no hauling fresh kegs in from the coolhouse or negotiating the slippery cellar steps to fetch a cask of some ancient sweetwine.

When she reached for the pull string on the trapdoor, a muffled tide of laughter surged up. She eased back on her haunches. *Go, then,* it seemed to say. *Go on your journeying, as you long to. But every motion has a consequence. You will be leaving Keiler here.*

Memory cast another kind of light against the gathering shadows: the flickering of the fire in her local triad's cottage. She had sat there last night, sipping valerian tea after her three-day trial. Hanla, the illuminator who'd trained her, had left to bring news of Liath's success to her family. Hanla's son Keiler had gone to replace materials in the binding house out back. Graefel had sat with her in silence for some time, but of a sudden he'd said, "I'll tell you a wordsmiths' secret. About your name."

An illuminator—trial-proven or not—should be told no more of scribing than anyone else in Eiden Myr. Song was for binders, painting for illuminators, scribing for wordsmiths. Graefel's triad was ever mindful of tradition. Yet his blue eyes, cold and flat as an animal's, held no remorse.

"The ciphers inscribed during a casting form words," he began. "And names are words. Words that can be spoken."

This seemed a strange thing for him to point out. Wordsmiths scribed in the Old Tongue, everyone knew that. A tongue was a spoken thing, by definition. Why did he look so stern?

"Your name, unlike most, has extra ciphers in it. One might call them shadow ciphers, because they don't sound when 'LEE-uh' is said aloud. You carry them with you—a hidden part of yourself, like your innermost thoughts. Were I permitted to tell you which ciphers they are, still I could not tell you what they signify."

He was looking at the fire, not at her. Its glow carved the planes of his vulpine face, glinted in his russet beard.

"Perhaps there will be an extra portion of pain in your life, or perhaps it will be luck, or joy," he went on. "Whatever it is, Liath, you must meet it head-on. Ciphers are the strongest power in the world . . . and those will be with you the rest of your days."

Liath had followed his gaze, as if this mysterious future could be glimpsed in the embers' running, molten depths. But suggestions of pattern slipped too quickly into chaos, leaving only warmth and brilliance.

The attic trapdoor thumped open. "Why are you sitting up here in the dark?" Hanla's swarthy face was lit by lampglow from beneath.

"I see guiders without a casting," she answered. "I was trying to understand."

"Ah." The illuminator's chunky frame briefly shut the light out as she squeezed through the opening, then sent rhythmic, crazy shadows dancing on the angled ceiling when she sat on the edge and swung her dangling legs. "Second thoughts about your journeying?"

Liath blinked at the Khinish woman, at the brown eyes she had bequeathed her son and bindsman Keiler, while Graefel, his father and wordsmith, was the source of his red hair and angular face. Keiler had been a second brother to her, a brother who shared her magelight, as her birth brother Nole did not; a brother who understood magecraft, as her family could not. How could she tell his mother, her teacher, what lay heavy on her heart?

"You think I didn't feel the same way when I took the triskele? I knew the cost. I remember my trial every time I look toward Khine." Hanla's expression had softened, but her voice was brisk. "You will learn magecraft we don't know. You'll bring home skills we cannot teach you. It's the reason plants go to seed on the winds, the reason we breed stock in other towns. Magecraft stays healthy only as long as we journey. Eiden Myr is a body, and we are the blood flowing in it."

Liath refrained from mouthing the last words with her. "*You* settled down," she said.

"Yes, and far from home, just as you fear. The Neck is my home now, not Khine."

They could have been sitting in the cornfield doing lessons in the rich soil. Those sun-soaked days, the golden nights of stories and camaraderie in the tavern below, already seemed a world away.

Liath glared at the tear-blurred shapes of stored clothing, blankets, tools; a spare cot, a two-legged stool, a crate of pewter goblets they never used. Always tongue-tied and stupid about anything but tavern business, she could not speak.

Hanla gestured at the forgotten quill, still twitching in Liath's hand. "A dozen years ago we caught you doodling with a stick in the dust. Now your guiders shine without a casting, begging to be used, though you've scarcely recovered from three days of trial. That is what you must reckon with, my dear. Consider Roiden."

Liath thought of Roiden, a bitter man, hunched around a flagon of Finger wine, eyes tracking her as she did her chores. He'd lived in the village all her life, but she avoided him, ashamed of her own light; she ducked away from those eyes when they caught her listening, rapt, to rovers' tales of the wild places—the plains below the Belt, where the wind spoke in eerie song, the dark wet woods and marshes of the Legs, where weird lights burned and weeping trees were older than memory. The places she could not wait to go.

Spirits take Roiden, she thought—angry at his pain, at the guilt he'd caused her. "I've considered him," she acknowledged. Then, levelly, "I remember Pelkin."

Hanla nodded. "And your sister doesn't. That's a sadness on you, is it?" When no answer came, she said, "Your mother will bear this, Liath. As she bore it before."

All the old words, the same words, and none of them "Keiler."

"Let's go down," Liath said abruptly, rising. The quill—not a true quill, since those were stored by binders, but a shed feather from some pigeon trapped in this attic long ago—dropped to the boards in a soft blue sparkle. Liath ignored it. "An ale and a dance or two will set me right."

The greatroom was full of strangers, unfamiliar faces and garb amid the wrights, the hillwomen, the cowherds—all the folk her eye picked out with recognition. Lately there had been more travelers than usual, all going toward the Ennead's Holding—all but one runner, a slight, pale lad of no more than nine-and-five who'd come from there. His cloak, unlike the wool of ordinary folk, shifted and shimmered in the lamplight. Nine velvet colors, sewn in triangles so expertly that they seemed one piece of cloth. Weatherwarded, so the cloak was untouched though the boy looked tired and travel-worn. He sat shyly by himself, watching the celebration with dark blue eyes. He showed no sign of being a Reckoner, the eyes and ears of the Ennead. Not far from him, Liath was surprised to see Lowlanders, Southers from the look of them—thin build, dark hair, horsehair vests over shirtless brown skin, soft breeches not suited to this climate. Come up all the way from the Weak Leg? No Southers had been through in some time.

Old man Marough roared at the sight of her. "There's our little mage now!" He bulled his way through the crowd to slap her too hard on the back. "Hanla, where's that triskele? If she hasn't earned it, no one bloody has."

Hanla forced a tolerant smile. "When it's time, Marough," she said. "We have our traditions."

He snorted: *There's no countenancing mages.* But relief had made him expansive. Liath had saved him a great deal at her trial. "Drinks on me until the triskele is taken, then!" he said to the room. "You'll get that sorrel for it, Danor, that one you've been eyeing since Sweetbriar foaled. Meira's just done shoeing her."

Marough's sons and nephews left their stones games and their ales to cluster round her, clasp her arm; she stopped them before they lifted her on their shoulders to parade around the room. They were a rough lot, always headed for trouble. Liath had broken up more brawls with them at the center than she cared to count. Still she couldn't help but smile.

Then she locked eyes with her mother, standing by the pantry door. Geara n'Breida l'Pelkin, Geara Publican, stout and blond, had drunk all comers under the table in her youth. This had been her mother's tavern when she pledged Danor. The Petrel's Rest was a legacy of daughters; Liath would be the first to break the chain. Her sister Breida, who loved horses and Galf n'Marough with all the passion of her nine summers and two, might or might not be the second, though she was named—contrary to custom—for a grandmother, the Breida who had passed the tavern to Geara. It was Nole who had inherited the inclination for affable hosting. By rights he should take over when the time came, instead of helping Megenna run her family's craftery in Orendel. He would make a grand master of the house: his big frame would fill out as he aged, his beard would come in thick and red, he would be Danor all over again. Plump Breida, flirting unsuccessfully with the Ennead's runner boy when she should be collecting cups, was a gentle, fearless child who would mature into a comely woman. Liath would stay as she was—whip-thin, too tall, all gangly limbs, her only graces a pair of thoughtful gray eyes and the pictures in her mind.

Geara had not been there for the trial, though there'd been plenty of gawkers, folk hoping the prentice's luck would rub off on them. Danor had brought their youngest the first day, but thereafter they'd stayed in the tavern. Liath had seen neither of them since she stumbled home at dawn, bleary after dozing off in her chair in the triad's cottage—only Breida, snuggling close to her in their bed. Drowsily she'd demanded a full account; at full light, she'd thumped Liath as she'd gotten up, for letting her fall back asleep before the end of the tale.

Marough's middle son pushed a cup of wine into her hand. "Anything you ever need!" he said. "I owe you, Liath Illuminator!"

"Not 'Illuminator' yet," she said. "Not till I take the triskele." Geara seemed to be listening. Was that pride on her face? Acceptance, after all these years?

"But everyone knows your magelight's special. Sarse and Aunt Sharra heard Graefel say so."

Geara turned on her heel and disappeared into the pantry.

"Aunt Sharra said—"

"Tarny, your brother's won two more rounds at stones." Hanla smiled innocently, slipping in beside Liath. "You'll have a snail's time catching up."

Tarny's thick lips pursed. He looked across the room, then back at Liath, and with a cry of frustrated petulance he launched his rangy horseman's body into the crush of people.

Hanla followed Liath's gaze toward the pantry. "It's love that's broken her heart. She doesn't hate you."

"Only my talent."

"Yes." There was no more to say; there was no mending this. "Now, have your ale, eh?"

Dance rhythms drifted in from outside, local drummers joined by log-beaters from the next valley and a gourdsman from Drey. Oriane and Taemar, Danor's feisty parents, pinched her cheeks and insulted the ale, to remind her she was both child and publican still; they made ribald jokes because someone had to, they said, with Geara's merchant sisters away. Danor's brothers ran the brewery in Iandel now. They had carted their parents in late that afternoon, laughing and shouting loud enough to rouse Liath from exhaustion, and then taken over in the cookroom. Oriane and Taemar cherished all their Clondel grandchildren, though Nole resembled them most, and Breida was their sentimental favorite. They tried hard to make up for what was missing.

Burly, red-bearded Danor banked the fire against the nighttime chill through the open door, and a sweetness of birch smoke filled the room. The crowd grew boisterous as full dark came on. Demick the smith juggled winter apples while his sister played the spoons. Children crawled under tables, untying boots and goosing stonesplayers. Porl the carpenter, never easy at rest, attempted to pull a wobbly stool out from under Naragh Cobbler, who threatened to dump her lentil stew over his head if he didn't leave her in peace. The weavers, just as bad, were arranging a trade with a downriver tailor. Iandel dairyfolk complained of weeds come over from the Clondel water meadow, giving their butter a foul taste, and was Grae-fel's triad too busy with their prentice to see to important matters? Galf and the millers' younger son, trying to impress Breida, batted a bean sack around the room until Geara chased them out; Drey folk laughed uproar-iously over some mishap in Orendel. All celebrated the end of sowmid planting, the hard days of ploughing done and only warm weather ahead of them now.

Liath sat in the close, smelly tavern, and let them toast her, and raise her on their shoulders, and howl when Hanla said it was still not time for the triskele; and drank sips of the wine they pushed on her, and listened to their speeches, and table-wrestled all comers as she'd always done, with her wiry arms muscled from lifting barrels and her hands rough and strong from mopping and brewing, hands that followed the blue guid-ers in her mind when her tall Norther body had been bred for this, the keeping of a public house at the base of the Aralinns, where winters were hard and friendships easy, where no one ever forgot the magecraft that spared them illness and fire and drought, the Ennead that kept them safe from the Great Storms.

Old Drolno Teller told the story, from his choice spot by the hearth. At the first sound of his voice, pitched in ritual tones, the drummers fell quiet and the dancers clustered in, sinking cross-legged to the floor or clearing space to sit on tables. Youngsters were pulled into parents' laps. Liath sat outside with her teaching triad, on the bench below the sunrise window—listening with them, as she had done since she was six, to the story of their craft's founding. Of how sea and earth and sky, once united, could no longer abide together, and separated into three parts, begetting sons and daughters of their rage and love: fire, cloud, wind. Where skyfire met earth, the barrier between sea and sky, Galandra was born—the first mage, the peacebringer, who could soothe the contentious spirits. Earth loved her for her justice and her beauty, and fashioned itself in her image, that they might be pledged—and became Eiden, the figure of a man spread on the waters. All folk were Galandra's children, born of her by Eiden. Those who took after Eiden became caretakers of the ground and the crea-tures on it. Those who took after Galandra became mages, arranging them-selves in threes, after the first spirits. Their charge was to keep the spirits in harmony: settle the earth when it had bad dreams, persuade the sky to release hoarded water, calm the winds when they grew rambunctious or cajole them when they grew torpid. Whenever three mages worked together, the spirits were united once more. "And three become one," Drolno finished, the time-honored words.

Hanla echoed "And three become one" as she draped the triskele-heavy chain over Liath's head and called her Illuminator. Keiler winked at her over his mother's shoulder. Graefel bowed low. Hanla gripped her arms, hand to elbow, forearms tight, in the sign of friendship and respect around the Neck.

"Make us proud," she said.

When they announced that the thing was done, there in a private moment off to the side, Liath took another thumping from Breida, and had to dance with nearly everyone as consolation for the spoiled show. When she'd had enough, breathless and footsore, one more tapped her on the shoulder, and she turned to see her brother's beaming ruddy face, petite Megenna on his arm.

"You've done it," he said, unnecessarily, and gave a tug on the tuft of hair at her nape, all that was left of her long auburn braid. "And now the pea will leave the pod."

"I'm sorry, Nole." Journeying, she would not be here to illuminate at his pledging, to raise the first ale.

He shook his head with a smile. "We'll still be here, pea."

Shyly, Megenna handed her a battered cup. It was the pledgeware, she saw—they held its mates.

"To your future, then," Liath said, raising the cup.

"To all your shining days," Nole said, raising his.

"May you come safe home to us." Megenna touched her cup to theirs.

Three toasts given, they drained the cups. This was good ale of their own, none of that smoky yarrow-gruit stuff the Curlew in Orendel had traded them. A sweet taste of home to carry on her tongue through the days to come.

Breida slipped out, in a nightshift under her cloak, and hugged them all. "Galf's promised me a ride," she murmured into Liath's shoulder, "and Mother's making me go to bed."

Liath smoothed red-gold hair from her sister's face. "Then dream of Galf, and riding, and perhaps tomorrow the dream will come true."

Breida smiled, started to go, then faltered. "Don't leave without saying goodbye to me," she said, and ran inside.

"Never," Liath whispered to the empty doorway.

In a set formed by her parents on one side, Keiler and the millers' daughter across from her and Nole, and Graefel and Hanla on the other side, they danced a figure as complex as a kadra, the paths of their bodies ringing and intertwining each other to the intricate cadence of the drums. Rounding with the women in the center, Liath grasped her mother's callused, sweaty hand in her left and Hanla's broad, smooth hand in her right; she danced hard, fueled by jealousy at the way the eyes of the millers' daughter lingered on Keiler. She was swung by her bearlike father, who danced as if on air; by her tall, solid brother, who delighted in spinning her hard and fast; by Graefel, polite and precise; and by Keiler, who held her too loosely. The wine and the incessant beat, the sweet night air and whirling dance, wove together in a binding older and brighter than the stars.

The drummers took a rest, sitting on the blocks and logs that were their instruments, and the dancers trickled back inside. Sweat cooled on Liath's flesh, and she shivered. The pewter triskele lay heavy on her breast-bone—cool when she was hot, it seemed, and warm when she was cold. Three arms radiating from a central point, curving into a shared periphery: three in one.

Liath acknowledged the drummer Lisel with a smile—after the events of her trial, they shared a bond nearly as strong as healing—then paused to ladle water from the barrel by the front door. When she straightened, Keiler was leaning against the shingled wall, surveying her with wry amusement.

"You've held up well," he said. "Still on your feet and able to put two words together."

She smiled at the russet hair and brown eyes. Did he ever wish he could sing with the drummers, add melody to their rhythm? He would always sing alone. Did hearing the rousing drums and having to save his beautiful voice for binding ever make him sad?

She didn't know how to broach the question. At first light, she would be gone, time only to cut a stout walking stick, pack some food. It was too late.

"I loved my journeying," Keiler said, with that quick eagerness—as if it had just occurred to him and he must tell someone or burst. "I'd do another, if we weren't the only triad in these parts. At least you didn't have to spend the last year preparing your journey truss. I never want to work that hard again." He laughed at her expression. "You'll love it too, and you'll come back and tell me all about it and make me jealous."

Tell my mother, she wanted to say. Perhaps he would, some late evening, resting from his bindsman's labors. Binding was the hardest physical work in magecraft, all the vellum to cut and soak and stretch and pumice, pigment to grind, quills to cut, ink to mix. So many times, she'd wanted to help him, stand by him with the sun on his muscled, shirtless back and ask how it was done, how she could help. So many times, she'd tagged behind him up the bindsman's road, pretending he wasn't pretending he couldn't see her, watching him collect catsclaw sap and goldroot, oak gall and pokeberry, bugs and clay. He was only two years her senior—a year younger than Nole—but he'd taken the triskele young, trained by his aunt, his parents' binder, then journeyed till Befre stepped aside to make a second journeying herself. Would he walk with her, now, up the binds-man's road, if she asked him to?

They stood in silence, watching the moon's downward arc. Then, "I'll miss you, Li," he said, and kissed her, awkward and too quick, as if it was something he had been planning to do for some time and wasn't sure how to handle when the moment came.

Still on her feet and able to put two words together. She opened her mouth to say them: *I'll stay*—

Keiler's eyes focused past her, and brightened, and he raised a hand and drew to his side the millers' daughter. Ferlin. Liath could smell her before she saw her, that sweet dusting of new flour, and a hint of perfume, as if she washed her golden hair in blossoms.

Probably chrysanthemums, Liath thought. *Probably has head lice.*

"We're to be pledged at midsummer," Keiler said. His gentle smile made him look older than the boy she'd grown up with. It was nothing like the lopsided grin he wore around her. "We won't announce it till you've left. Didn't want to step on your celebration."

"It's not very big news anyway," Ferlin said. Too sweet, too demure. *She knows,* Liath thought. *And she knows she's won.* "Megenna and your brother are all the talk around here these days. And your trial, of course. . . ."

Liath's heart had known that she could not pledge him, not while he was triaded with his parents here. Liath's heart had known that she couldn't wait on him season after season, until Graefel and Hanla freed him to triad again; that she couldn't wish that their aging be speeded. Liath's heart had known all this. Now Liath knew it, too.

She gripped the ladle tightly so she wouldn't put a finger to her lips, searching for a memory of the last kiss she would ever have from him. Then she hung it back in the deep, cool water, and gently replaced the barrel's lid.

A tremendous crash shook the walls, followed by a roar of voices. She whirled, thinking, *They've turned the great table over,* and *It's a brawl, but something's wrong.* The tavern was a living thing. She could sense its moods. This wasn't high spirits or old surly grudges; this was something new and foreign and mean.

A jug smashed to dust against the doorjamb as she came through, and Growl the ginger cat streaked out, ears laid flat. He looked to have just escaped Melf n'Daughan's cruel hands; the boy looked up at her from a crouch, grinning wickedly. She would have cuffed him, but the greatroom was in an uproar. Marough's sons were at the middle of it, and his brother Daughan's older boys, but scuffles had broken out all around the central commotion. The great table was off its trestles, the benches toppled. Older men and women, hooting and jeering, had pulled stools, stones boards, and smaller tables off to the sides; one old couple still bent over their game. Meira and Sharra were taking bets on the outcome, but Meira swore, dumped tallysticks on Sharra, and waded into the fray. The young runner boy cowered in a corner. A sheepherd's dog braced on the floor beside him, barking. In the doorway, a grinning drummer struck up a frenetic beat on a handblock.

Straining to see who Marough's lot were fighting with, Liath made out long dark hair, vests over bare skin.

Geara was stretched up to pull sliding wooden slats down over the back shelves. "Mind yourself, Liath."

A standing lamp toppled; in the puddle of spilled oil and brandy, the flame flared up. It consumed the brandy and the oil, blackened the nearest rushes, and died away against the floorboards. The firewarding had held.

The biggest man in the central clump of bodies came stumbling backward out of it, reeling from a blow. He doubled up when he hit the wall: Danor, flung out like a rag.

Leave it, he mouthed at her, unable to get a breath.

Liath dove in.

Stop the wranglers and you usually stopped the brawl. Tarny was raising a stool over a Souther's turned back. Liath hugged him from behind and wrenched him around so that the stool came down through empty air and crashed to the floor—something else for Porl to fix, that would make him happy. Tarny twisted in her hold and tried to land a blow, but she slid her arms up around his shoulders and locked her hands behind his neck, keeping her head low in case he made a grab for her hair. Just loud enough so he would hear her over his own elaborate swearing, she said, "Calm yourself, now, Tarny, it's just Liath."

All the fight left his body. "That's it, then," he sighed.

She released him and stepped away, looking for Sarse. The Souther had turned at the sound of wood splintering, slit green eyes burning in a brown face. Below that, with a *snick* that pierced the tumult of the room and a wink of barbed metal that cut the gloom, a knife came out of a side sheath.

The others—three men and a woman, there were five in all—had also drawn knives, and now backed into a circle, with a larger, ragged circle of Marough and Daughan's clan around them. The drummer's block scraped to a stop. All shouts and laughter ceased.

"Brawls are all well and good," Liath said quietly, "as long as someone helps clean up. But we don't draw blades in this tavern." She put herself just in front of Tarny, reaching back a fending hand but not quite touching him.

"They're the cheaters," Sarse n'Marough whined.

Two of his cousins started for the Souther, but Danor, recovered, grabbed each by the collar and hauled them back.

Voice pitched to reason with small children, Geara replied, "Well, we'll never know that now, will we, with your stones and tallysticks all over the floor."

"It was never a question of *cheating*," said the Souther facing Liath. Her eyes blazed with contempt. "It's a question of who are the sheepherds and who are the sheep."

"I don't care what it's a question of," Liath said. "Put your knives away. You can kill people with those."

A grin spread slowly across the Souther's face, white against the sun-dark skin. "Yes," she said. "We can."

The moment balanced on the edges of those blades. Blades that were not made for shaving carrots or working wood. Hooked things, evil— meant to maximize harm. It would take only one more drunk, headstrong wrangler to set the lot of them on the strangers, knives or no. Behind her, a plank creaked.

Tarny's shifted weight drew the knifepoint upward—not gut, but heart. But the Southers kept their circle tight.

The woman's brow quirked, and her gaze dropped to the opening of Liath's shirt. "You're a mage?" The knifepoint lowered a tad.

"I took the triskele tonight."

An unspoken signal rippled through the little circle. Liath raised a hand, catching Marough's eye: *Hold them off, let this end.* Two days ago, her tavern or no, he would not have heeded her. Now he swept sons and nephews back, clearing a path to the doorway abruptly vacated by the drummer.

Liath caught a glimpse of trim fox-colored beard outside. Flanked by Hanla and Keiler and a score of villagers, Graefel Wordsmith stood ready to intervene.

Good, Liath thought. *Let Graefel sort this.* It was what mages did: sort out disputes, settle troubles, heal bruised pride as well as broken bones. Let Graefel clean this up; leave her to clean up her tavern.

The Southers sheathed their knives and filed out in two pairs, their back guarded by the woman Liath had spoken to. She cast Liath a final look before she crossed the threshold: evaluation.

"*Were* they cheating at stones?" Liath asked when they'd reassembled the trestle table and the players were sorting through the wet debris for pipes, pouches, stones, tallysticks.

Sarse n'Marough scuffed a foot in the rushes. "Probably weren't, most like. But they said we were!"

"That's not exactly what they said," cousin Erl n'Daughan put in slowly.

Geara handed three of them brooms and gave rags to the rest. "You have all night to worry over who said what, but not unless I see a tidy greatroom in the next few breaths."

Liath set lamps and benches to rights, Tarny pacing her like a puppy. Danor drafted him and a cousin to fetch fresh ale, sending the millers' older boy down for wine and Liath with him for a cask of the fruit brandy Geara's mother used to make. Sarse followed his brother.

From the back of the cellar, Liath could hear the voices out by the coolhouse. Sarse and Erl were goading Tarny. He was a coward, they said. That Souther could have spit Liath like a pepper on a frystick, and Tarny just standing there like a fool. The Souther would come back for Liath in the night, didn't he know that? Didn't he see that look the woman gave her on the way out? And he just let her walk away!

The cellar shadows rubbed cold against Liath's flesh. She stood the brandy cask on end and shouldered past the millers' son. It was clear, now, who'd goaded this new brawl into life. *Spirits take me for not seeing it sooner.* She flew up the stone steps and broke through the storm doors in back to see Tarny just rounding the side of the building.

Erl and Sarse were snickering, not far behind him. She caught up, hauled them back much as her father had, cursed them, and continued past at a jog. "Tarny! Stop!"

The Southers' leader was just lifting her pack from where she'd braced it against a barrel in front. Looking past her, one of the men saw Tarny. He shouted a warning, intermingled with Tarny's shout of rage. In one smooth movement, like a dance step perfectly timed, the woman drew her blade and turned. Tarny saw it—but he was too big, too lumbering to pull up once he had launched himself. The woman's eyes went wide; she saw that he was unarmed, she recognized a drunken lumbering fool when she saw one, but too late. Tarny ran up on the blade.

They stood for a moment, frozen, as if balking at an embrace. Then Tarny staggered back and sat down hard in a puff of dust. He stared at his belly, where the metal-banded grip protruded.

"You idiot!" the Souther cried. All arrogance had fled that voice; it spoke horror. As if she'd never meant to use that knife of hers. As if she hadn't really known she could.

Yet she'd turned with the lithe coordination of trained reflex.

There were screams. Some people ran away; some people ran to Tarny. "Don't pull it out!" the Souther called, straining forward against the grip of her fellows. They dragged her off, surrounding her.

What Liath had witnessed struck home. The night went very pale. She could feel the crowd's shock bloom into rage, but she couldn't summon any words against it.

When vision returned, Tarny lay on the ground and Hanla was holding a red-soaked cloth around the base of the knife in his gut. The Southers stood off to the side; why hadn't they fled? Villagers and travelers milled around, staying well clear of mages and Southers, clearing off farther as Marough and Meira and the others tumbled out of the tavern.

"You can heal him," the Southwoman said. It wasn't a question. She was looking at Liath, though Graefel stood before her, his authority a barrier between them and the villagers.

Tarny turned his face to Liath, imploring. He opened his mouth. Only blood came out.

"Our triad can heal him," Liath said. The spiritlorn *fool*—

"No," said Marough. He turned to Liath too. "You."

"I'm not the—"

"You do it, Liath," Hanla said. Her dark eyes burned.

Only a day. It had been only a day. Yesterday afternoon they had stood like this, surrounded by gawking townsfolk, as the drummer deposited shattered heartwood in the middle of the casting circle, at the end of her trial. Broken by Tarny, who rushed headlong through the world, leaving a trail of debris behind him. Trial castings were considered lucky. Marough had not wanted her to do it—he hadn't trusted an untried mage. She was the publicans' daughter, a child, beneath his notice. He'd never minded her and never would; he wanted the illuminator. His son could not afford to make reparation for this if it were not mended. But Lisel, their drummer, knew that the only hope lay in the fortune of a prentice's first castings. Then, as now, Hanla had stepped aside—not pushing Liath to test herself, but deferring to the brighter light.

Now Marough gave the order.

"You fixed his mess before," he said. "You do it again."

Keiler was running down the road from the mages' cottage, where he'd gone to fetch a sack of binding materials. He threw the sack down and with his hawthorn stick traced a circle in the dust around Tarny. It didn't matter to him who did the illumination. They must begin.

Liath walked to the near side of the circle. She sat down cross-legged. She closed her eyes to slow her spinning mind. When she opened them again, Tarny's wound was bound against the bleeding; the blade had not been withdrawn. Hanla was standing outside the circle. Graefel and Keiler sat on the dirt-scratch arc to form two points of a triangle, and Graefel was bent over a wood-backed sheet of vellum—animal skin, for an animal casting, as all flesh was animal. In the silence, his quill point scraped the leaf with the sound of a death rattle.

It was as if her trial had resumed after a brief hiatus. As if it had never ended. Perhaps it would never end.

"It was Tarny, on that blasted roan." Drummer Lisel, voice thinned by outrage. "He knows we practice down there, he knows there's no wardings!"

"He lost control." Cousin Erl, because Marough, the father, was too disgusted to bother speaking. "It's a bloody drum, is all! No one was hurt!"

Lisel laid the fragments on the casting ground. An assortment of fruitwoods— pear, bayberry, apple, cherry. Shattered by the hooves of the horse that bolted, the horse Tarny shouldn't have been trying to ride in the first place, a horse kept for breeding but famously unbreakable. Liath knew this drum; Lisel had played it all her life. A masterly piece of work, the woods cut at angles and joined painstakingly into an instrument of rich variety. It had been crafted by one of her forebears, passed down from mother to daughter. Generations of finger oils were rubbed into *this wood. The drum had sounded at rituals and celebrations for as long as anyone could remember. It was irreplaceable; a copy might be made, if Lisel had the skill, but it would not be this drum. Even Marough knew it.*

It was only her trial. They had made winter wheat grow high, cast fire without strikers, herded a raincloud overhead and persuaded it to release its burden of water. But to mend so intricate an object . . . it couldn't be done. The slightest flaw would ruin the timbre.

Hanla said, "With Liath, it can be done."

Liath backed away from the fractured wood, shaking her head. Lisel was fitting the pieces together, holding them in place. "I can't." Liath murmured.

"You can," Hanla said.

Tarny, still conscious, groaning past the bloody rag Meira had jammed between his teeth. The calm, determined scritch of Graefel's pen across the page. The rustling of Keiler preparing her brushes and pigments, the smell of linseed oil. The beating of her heart, too fast. Her fists clenched around their own trembling. The silence of a crowd too large to keep silent.

They had said she had the brightest magelight in these parts in memory. They had invested all their pride in her, all their hopes. After her trial, they believed she could do anything.

It was magecraft that made the wranglers so reckless. If they couldn't be healed, they wouldn't be so irresponsible with their bodies, with their horses. All the fights, the broken bones . . . *Every motion has a consequence!* she wanted to cry. *Let Tarny bear the consequence of his!*

It was an accident. She was a mage; she had been called.

Graefel passed the vellum on to her.

The grain of each wooden segment ran in a different direction. Each was a different size and thickness. Grain must be matched precisely to grain. The joins would hold, as they had done for countless years under countless poundings, if the grain was mended right.

Keiler handed her a selection of reed pens and the oak-gall ink he'd provided Graefel. When the kadri were outlined as her guiders showed her—the symbols for growth, for depth, for smoothness and strength, resonating into a unity—he gave her cornsilk brushes and held out a palette of plant pigments bound by catsclaw resin. A bowl of water allowed her to vary the intensity of the pigment as she laid it down—first a wash, then the coloring for depth and shadow. Water pigments worked differently from those bound in oil or wax; the lay of the sedge showed through, both symbol and background visible, one illumining the other. It was like painting with light itself.

· · ·

Keiler anticipated her needs: tallow-soot ink, a sharp goose quill, horsehair brushes, oil-bound pigment. This would be work more of intensity than complexity; Graefel had scribed only one large initial requiring historiation, and she would fill the border with a fine mesh for knitting together what was torn. She must work quickly, lest Tarny's lifeblood soak away into the dust.

Centering herself over her tools, shutting out the crowd, the smells, the scrutiny, she awaited the formation of the guiders. Her magelight would show the way to mend this horror and make a dying man whole.

Only the knotwork remained. All Graefel's ineffable words, whatever grace and power was building in Keiler's unvoiced song, would be for nothing if she did not weave true.

Her guiders led the pen. They burned so bright she feared she could not see the page; and yet she could. The world coalesced into a place of flux and stability, curve and line, the straight, strong pen and the fluid ink. In all those breaths, which were but a moment, Liath's training entered her completely, seamlessly, and she was herself no longer, but the vehicle and vessel for the patterns she completed.

Suddenly, her guiders were gone.
She could not summon them.

The circular knotwork flowed easily, down one side, across the bottom, up again, and then into the interstices between the powerful words the ciphers formed, patterning them into a wholeness that would amplify the strength of their own connections. Woodflesh into woodflesh, all in its place. How could there be fear when aiding such a thing? It was no more than the wood itself wanted, to be whole, to be as it was. There was no simpler task than to put things back as they were meant to be.

This is what I do, this is what I am, she had thought. This is what I take with me into the world.

She looked up at Hanla in a panic. *I can't,* she mouthed.

Hanla pursed her lips. This was nonsense. *Do it.*

I can't! A blinding ache spread from her eyes into her head. There were no guiders. So often she had wondered if she had any talent at all, if the magelight wasn't some other Liath existing inside her, nothing to do with the artless publican she knew herself to be. But hadn't she mended what could not be mended? Hadn't Graefel himself, the one she'd always tried to please, stared gaping at what they wrought at her trial?

All proven, all tested, the triskele bestowed, the impossible acknowledged. All fled in one terrible moment.

She had not forgotten the kadri. She knew the symbols, their deriva-
tions, their resonances. Her hand knew how to draw the borderwork, the
crossweave fillers. She was highly trained, the knowledge permanently
embedded. But it was not enough. Without the magelight, she didn't know
which of nonneds of kadri were the right ones, she couldn't feel her way
to the appropriate borders or fills. Her art was not one of intellect. A
guttering magelight might not cripple a wordsmith; she didn't know. But
without that inner light an illuminator was helpless.

"Hanla, please—" She broke off into a moan, sagging back.

Hanla shoved her from the circle, swearing, snatching the precious
vellum from her, taking her place.

Bumped off to the side, Liath watched the casting continue. She did
not know whether it could succeed, thus interrupted. Perhaps they should
begin again—cast passage.

Her dreams seeped like spilled ale into the dirt.

*They laid the sedgeweave on the broken drum and clasped hands over it, and Keiler
voiced a tune so sweet and fulfilling that it seemed to bind their souls even as the
inscribed, illuminated leaf turned to a breath of white smoke beneath their twined
fingers.*

*As the sun set and her trial ended, the drum sealed into a wholeness, and the
awed drummer took it in trembling hands and brought forth a sound as resonant
and true as any it had made through the generations.*

Tarny did not watch as his flesh worked the barbed knife out and knit
around the hole where it had been. He looked only at Liath. She looked
away, at the midpoint between his terrifying face and the wound that
should have killed him: where the vellum lay, vibrating to Keiler's hoarse,
piercing bindsong, illuminated in another's practiced hand. The vellum
became a fleshy, liquid thing, and knit into itself, tighter and tighter, until
it seemed a small scab on Tarny's ribs, and knit again into nothing, and
was gone.

Tarny sat up, and the weapon fell into the dust. The Southers had
long since slipped away.

*Liath could scarcely believe it. That such intricate mending was possible with a
casting, that such power could be brought to bear . . . why, they could heal the
very spirit of Eiden Myr, should it ever fall ill. . . .*

· · ·

You healed him, thank the spirits, she tried to say, and *I'm sorry,* and *I don't understand,* but she could not speak past the ache in her head. Keiler's supporting arm would withdraw if she did, and she wanted to savor it, just for a moment, before her failure rose up to meet her.

"You are the strongest mage I have ever met," Graefel said. Hanla beamed like a proud mother beside him. Keiler looked as if he'd never seen her before. "By rights you should go to the Ennead, not on a journeying."

Her stomach clenched. Her grandfather, Pelkin, had warned her of this. The Ennead demanded lifelong devotion. To go there, to ward against the Great Storms, was the highest calling. Few left the Ennead's holding again except as proxies, servants of the Ennead, and then they traveled for a lifetime. For nine years and three Liath had prepared for this trial, for the journeying to come. For nine years and three she had dreamed of the exotic lands she would see, the new castings she would learn. For nine years and three she had dreamed of that, and of the homecoming that would follow. She could not go to the Ennead's Holding, to that stony, windswept place at Eiden's Head. She could not spend her life in their service.

Graefel sighed. "But the Ennead call whom they will, and thus far they have not called you." The ghost of a smile might have touched his lips. "Your reprieve is secured, and you'll be on your way with our blessing."

The strongest mage he had ever met . . . His words had warmed away the fatigue of the three hardest days of her life. With Graefel's hard-won praise, she felt she could do anything.

"It wasn't perfect," Hanla said bitterly. "I could feel it. He'll always have trouble with his food now."

"We did what could be done," Graefel said, toneless. He did not look at Liath. "We'll try again, when he's stronger."

"What *happened* to you?" Hanla could be brusque, but she rarely angered.

"I don't know." Liath's voice broke. "It's gone. It's just gone."

"It doesn't go. It can't. The only thing that can cut you off from it is coring and sealing, and only the Ennead can do that. I can still sense your magelight, smell it. It hasn't *gone* anywhere."

"I'm sorry . . ."

"You abandoned a casting at a crucial time."

"I'm *sorry*—"

"You could have healed that boy properly!"

"He shouldn't have jumped on that knife!" Liath got up, staggered, shoved Keiler away. They were angry because she had failed to repeat the impossible, when she had lost the core of herself. Gone, just like that, without reason. She had only now come into her own. How could it just *go*?

Her eyes fell on the Ennead's boy, watching them wide-eyed from the edge of lamplight. He must have come out to see the casting and not budged since.

Coring and sealing. Cutting the magelight's connections to the spirit and sealing it off, as if in a cask. It could not be extinguished or extracted, but it could be contained. No one knew what happened to a mage thus sealed. Some said you lived as a shadow, without feeling or volition. Some said you sickened and died. Some said you went on as if born a child of Eiden, perfectly able to take joy from tilling soil or tending bees or spinning wool. Some said it was a story to frighten naughty prentices.

If it could be done, perhaps it could be undone, no matter how it had happened to begin with.

She opened her mouth to address the boy, but Marough's clan chose that moment to gather themselves and head off home. Tarny struggled in the grip of Sarse and Erl. He stopped by Liath. They glared at her—she heard Meira say, from up ahead, "No thanks to *that*"—and left Tarny to stand on his own.

"They said she was going to hurt you," he said softly. "I'm sorry, Li. On Eiden's breath."

Liath rubbed her face wearily. How could she mark him for a fool when he had meant to protect her? She didn't understand it—he'd never looked after her when they were growing up, in fact he'd bullied her—but she hadn't understood the wild idiocy that put him on the blue roan's back, either. It was their way to be headstrong louts, to goad each other into ever grander stupidity. Perhaps the only way to tame them was by healing them. Perhaps now he would be Hanla's pet.

"It's all right, Tarny," she said. "You're all right."

Geara stepped out of the tavern.

"I know you would have done it if you could," Tarny said.

"But I couldn't." She watched her mother warily. "And I didn't. Leave me alone, Tarny." She winced. "Please."

He sulked off to catch up with his cousins. Geara moved over to stand by the runner boy. Nole looked out an upper window, rumpled and confused, roused from sleep. Graefel's crystalline eyes bored into her. Hanla said stiffly, "It will all come right. You'll be yourself in the morning."

"Come inside, love," said Geara. For a moment, Liath thought the words were for her. But it was the Ennead's boy she drew with her back into the warmth and the light.

Graefel said, "I do not accept this." He gestured to his bindsman, then to the casting circle still etched in the dirt. "A candle, Keiler. In the center. Now."

"Don't do this." Hanla's whisper carried clearly across the new distance between them. "We'll test her tomorrow. She's fatigued, or it's the drink." But it wasn't fatigue or drink. Hanla knew that. Hanla had seen her work when she could barely stand for exhaustion. Hanla knew her inherited tolerance for drink. "Let it go, Graefel."

He would not. He ordered Liath back into the circle, ordered Keiler to hand him fresh materials. The earliest casting of all: igniting a flame. Not the simplest, but the first taught, the deepest ingrained. Liath could feel the man's anger across the casting ground—it could have lit that candle by itself. But when he ordered her to receive the leaf, no guiders would come. He could not ignite the magelight inside her.

"Draw them anyway," he said. "Hanla, tell her which."

"She knows which."

"*Help her.*"

Hanla let out an oath, but when she leaned close her words came in the measured tones of the teacher, coaching her to do what had been rote since she was nine-and-three. "What is the fire when the light has gone?" she said in Liath's ear. "What is the flame when there is no heat?"

Liath drew the distillations, candle and flame, air and earth abstracted to their essences, rendered in a symbology that flensed from flame all but its intrinsic flameness, then joined it in a weave of other symbols, other distillations. Air when there is no wind. Lightning when there is no flash. Earth when there is no substance. She made flame of its constituent elements; she joined flameness itself to wick, to wax. The materials were correct, the kadri precisely rendered, the meditation clear in her mind. But there were no guiders. Keiler sang. There was no flame.

"Try again."

"Grae—"

"*Try again.*"

She tried again, and again, and again, until tears stained her cheeks, until the reeds bent in her cramped hand. Still there was no flame. Still Graefel said, "Again."

"There are no more sheets," Keiler said. He was hoarse.

"Then bring a tallow candle. Use vellum."

He would not relent. He would grind her into the ground beneath the boots of his icy rage, he would kill her before he would see her fail.

Again, and again, until Keiler said "There is no more," and it was true, unless Graefel sent him to the bindinghouse. He seemed poised to do so. He looked at Liath as at a stranger who had kicked him in the road, without motive, without excuse. His crystal eyes burned red around the blue.

"*Graefel.*" Hanla hauled him to his feet. He shook her off and stalked away with a gesture of profound disgust. Hanla started after him, then seemed to remember Liath, sitting in the broken circle. "Perhaps it's for the best," she said, patting her absently on the head as if she were still six years old.

For the *best*?

"It's my fault, really." The Khinishwoman watched her pledgemate up the road. "I loved him so much." Then she was gone, to follow him, comfort him, Liath forgotten.

It was madness. Her teaching triad had shattered into incomprehensibility. She got up, dusted off her breeches, looked to Keiler for support when dizziness swept her. He steadied her, but Ferlin's pure sweet voice rang out down the river road, calling him to the mill, calling him away. "I'm sorry, Li," he said. His voice wove into the echo of Tarny's, and was gone.

Her father was in the tavern, as always, awaiting her return. Nole, embarrassed for her, had withdrawn from the window—a good brother, granting her privacy. Even the gawkers had drifted away. Liath stood alone in the road.

For a moment, the skin of her back itched, as if someone were watching her, and she turned, her heart racing— If it was him, if it was Pelkin, come back from nine-and-two years of exile— But it was only Roiden, bloody vindicated Roiden, grinning at her before he faded back into the shadows. Her grandfather had stayed a world away, as he was told to.

She looked toward the golden light falling through the tavern's open door as it had fallen all those years ago.

Geara stood in that light.

"Come inside," her mother said. This time the words were for her.

Liath walked toward the door, and turned: turned down the quiet alley, past the midden heap and the old copper vats, past the coolhouse and the croft; took the little path through gorse and thistle, into the trees, where it became the bindsman's road. Up into the hills the path went, branching off to this thicket or that one, where this binding plant grew, or that one. The way grew steep; exposed roots formed a rough set of steps. A faint breeze stirred the brush around her. She hiked hard, the triskele thumping against her breastbone, and at last came out at the small overlook that had been cleared when Clondel was a new village, with no triad to look after it, so long ago that only tellers knew the history.

She tucked herself into the choice spot at the base of a wind-bent tree, hugging her knees to her chest. Below her, the cluster of buildings along the road was growing dark as lamps were extinguished, the triad's cottage last of all but the tavern. Beyond it stretched pastures and orchards and fields new-tilled and newly fallow, bordered by the silvery Clon and wide Ianda, rambling sedately toward their confluence in the Heartlands. Behind her the hills shrugged into the Aralinn Mountains. At the end of those mountains was the Ennead's Holding. In good weather, it was a threeday's journey to the pass and through on horseback.

The wind that brushed her face carried the chill of a new day. The winds had names, but no one remembered them anymore.

Perhaps the Ennead did. Perhaps they would teach her.

Liath looked out over the dark village, trying to burn into her eyes the contours of a place she knew every corner of in her heart, and saw the big lantern outside the Petrel's Rest go out, leaving only the little nightlamp over the door to light her way home.

TჄORN

He shook chalk from his hair and peeled off layers of rags, putty, paint—
layers of self. The surface, carefully fashioned over years. The median
layers, somewhere in which was buried an ordinary man with ordinary
desires. Deepest within, the magelight, still burning hot. It seemed a long
time since he'd been himself.

But disguise suited him. Folk spoke true only when they believed they
were among their own. As dusk gathered, he had lingered at the fringes
of the bonefolk, but crafters were no different, or wrights—or mages.

The folk were frightened. Their parchment faces had twisted in the
firelight, their insectile bodies jittering. They spoke of shadow, of a darkness they could not name, unaware that a shadow lurked among them.
Working as they did with viscera, with skinned things, they had a knack
for seeing under surfaces, yet they had not questioned his. Too intent on
their own concerns.

His mouth quirked at the irony of it. The bonefolk came only for the
dead, were said to consume the flesh they carried off, suck the marrow of
the bones; some claimed they fed on the spirits of the unpassaged. No one
knew the location of their boneyards, but every town had a bog or a
shadowed dell that was rumored to be their stopping place. "It's enough
to scare a boneman"—the old saying was truer, now, than anyone guessed.

But the bonefolk would confide suspicions to no one outside their
circles. It was their lot to be feared, despised; they reveled in it, sad
punishment for perceived failures. Their enormous dark eyes seemed ever
full of tears. They would continue on their dogged way, plying their

grisly, necessary trade—and continue gathering information, for him, little though they knew it. Useful folk, those willing to look inside things.

They had provided him with nothing new tonight, but they circulated through a large region, trading knowledge with bands whose routes they overlapped. He would plumb them again when they returned. For now, it was enough to have seen horror on the face of fear itself.

He bathed to remove the stink of carrion. She would find it distasteful, and he had need of her tonight. She had long maneuvered to share his bed again. If she provided the information he sought, perhaps he would accommodate her, this time.

He donned fine black leggings, velvet doublet, black silk-lined cloak that fell in folds rich as shadow.

Suitable garb for these dark hours. His garments were the color of his soul.

hawk floated high overhead, a feathered speck in the blue basin of sky. Come down, hunting, from one of the blackstone peaks. The mountains were curving in, an embrace of great rock that would squeeze the foothills tight into the only negotiable pass.

Liath pulled a kerchief from her belt and flicked at stubborn flies on her horse's neck and rump. The sorrel bought by good Petrel's Rest ale, so that Marough's lot might drink themselves into a deadly brawl.

The village and patchwork fields had folded into the valley cleft. She could no longer gauge the distance home. The smells of brewing and baking, middens and livestock, were lost behind her, and even the light breeze that carried them had retracted. High above, the hawk circled round and headed down the valley. Liath's knuckles were white on the braided hemp reins. She relaxed her fingers slowly. When she raised her head, the hawk was gone.

She looked at the boy. He had a sweet face, still chubby with childhood but promising handsomeness within a few years. The eyes, under a forelock of black hair, were a long-lashed, deep blue, but gauntness hollowed their beauty. She had caught up with him in blue morning, as he was leaving; it had taken her that long to argue a sleepy Marough into making good on his debt, then to ask Danor for the loan of the sorrel— still awake, waiting up for her, he gave it to her outright, but she would not think on that—and pack a few provisions. The boy had looked pained to have her with him, but agreed to guide her. What else could he do?

She had not wakened Breida to say goodbye.

"Mellas—that's a Heartlands name, isn't it?"

"Yes, Illuminator."

It was an unfamiliar title, too new. Liath Illuminator was not yet her name, might never be; she was still Liath n'Geara l'Danor, Liath the publicans' daughter, Liath of the Petrel's Rest in Clondel in the Neck. But she didn't correct him. She still wore her triskele.

"How long have you been a runner for the Ennead?"

"Two years now, Illuminator."

"Did you grow up in the Holding?"

"Mostly, Illuminator."

"What's it like there?"

"It's very big."

"I mean, what is life like? What are the people like?"

He looked at her blankly.

She sighed, then tried on a smile. "They say the Aralinns are haunted. Didn't happen to see any mountain wraiths on your way down, did you?"

He turned haunted eyes away and shook his head.

Idiot, she thought. Better to say nothing than to say everything wrong.

They rode on together, two awkward children unable to pass the time of day. Young forest clustered in around them, lanky spruces rooted in crumbled mulch, both the ghost and the renewal of logging country. There had never been farming up this far, nor ever would be; the hills thickened as they rose, with conifers like spiky fur on a bear's back. The air grew pungent with old sap and fallen needles, the way soft now under the horses' hooves.

By midmorning they passed the second of two woodsmen's shacks, long abandoned, the haunt of flies and owls now. Liath and Nole had slept the night here once, on rotted, dropping-spattered planks that exhaled a dry decay, regretting with every creak of old wood and flutter of bats the mischievous adventure that had lured them. It was as far as one could get on foot in a day. It was as far, in this direction, as Liath had ever traveled.

She flicked at stubborn memories. There would be only strange roads ahead of her now, and then no roads at all. Only the sea, which she had never seen, and whatever secrets the Ennead pledged their lives to.

"They *will* help me," she murmured.

The boy blinked—she had not spoken for some time—but if he understood he gave no sign of it.

At dusk they made camp in a clearing just off the road. It was well used: a firepit had been dug and dug again, many nights of old ashes piled behind it. A brook sluiced through aspens, tumbling and smoothing black Aralinn stones. They let the horses drink, then hobbled them off to the side where sweetgrass grew, saving the grain. Beside a modest deadfall fire, they ate hard cheese and flatbread with bean paste.

The silence was almost companionable. This might be a lesson—to be quiet, to speak only when necessary, after a lifetime of crowds and forced conversation. She dug a hip into spongy bracken, laid her head on her balled-up blanket, and pulled her cloak up against the sowmid chill. Trying to learn that lesson, to hear wisdom in the murmurs of night, she found the deep, instant sleep of travelers—then half woke, uneasy, under moon-bleached stars. Breida's absence beside her reminded her where she was. Mellas was a shadow propped against a tree; she picked him out by the dim, doubled reflection of embers in his eyes, but slipped back into sleep before she could speak.

A scream brought her bolt upright. The horses snorted and stamped. The mountains, and then her mind, echoed the sound of that scream. It was the boy's voice.

"What?" she said. "What?"

Mellas huddled in his blankets, cringing against the tree.

"Are you all right?" Sore muscles threaded her limbs with flame, but she crawled over to him, extended a hand.

He shrank into himself. His eyes were focused past her, but nothing was there.

"I won't touch you, Mellas." Her voice dropped to the near-whisper that calmed drunks. "What frightened you?" The hills were warded; bears and wildcats wouldn't bother them. "Did you see something?" The horses had quieted. "What is it?"

"Bad dream," he managed. "That's all." He was dragging the words out. It was painful to hear. "Please. Go back to sleep. I'm sorry, Illuminator. That I woke you."

It was the longest statement he had made in her hearing. "Must have been a pretty bloody bad dream." *That'll teach me to bring up fool stories. If a mountain wraith sucked me dry it would be no more than I deserve.*

He retreated into silence and she to her bed. He was still staring into the fire as she drifted down again, her last thought that he must be trying to stay awake, that he must have these bad dreams often to be afraid of sleep itself.

In her dreams someone admonished her. The tone was urgent, agitated—but she could not understand. She woke groping, for what she did not know, and heard the boy's voice. His muttered words made no more sense than the dream words, though the inflection suggested they should; his eyes were open but unseeing. She feared to wake him. Who was he speaking to, through sleep? She lay watching him, trying to catch a comprehensible fragment. Sentences tumbled over themselves to get free of his mouth, but transformed into nonsense when released into the air.

Does all his talking in his sleep, she thought wryly. It was no comfort against the eerie half-language he spoke, the audible roiling of a troubled mind. There was more wrong with this boy than a shy tongue.

After some time, his eerie babble subsided and he relaxed, eyes closed, breathing easy. Liath couldn't find her way to dreams of home, only to a twilight realm where voices gibbered into void, ever at a loss.

When she woke for good at sunrise, the birds chattered to each other in their own language, and Mellas was dead out, pale as a wraith. She packed up everything except the blanket he lay on, filling the water flasks, burying the coals, and readying both horses before she roused him.

At the tug on his blanket he writhed and struck out.

"All right, Mellas, I was just trying to wake you. Looks like I managed, eh?" She rubbed her wrist. "It's time to go."

The day was hot and close, the air smothering. A haze had come into the sky, uncharacteristic of sowmid mornings. The sun was a bright stain behind blank white. The hills rolled off into distance, the way become steep. There was no varying the pace today; just a grinding uphill walk, step after slow step. Liath leaned forward, off the mare's kidneys. Her legs screamed, her ankles screamed, her breeches chafed—and all for nothing, for what point in becoming travel-hardened, when there would be no journeying for her?

She would not think on it. Not today.

The filly's shod hooves slipped, struck sparks off stone. They'd be safer with mules in country like this. The mountains stood matte black against the glare of sky. The world became all tumbled boulders, everything black stone and blue-gray echo of spruce. But flecks of silvery mica glittered in the stone. Flowers hid among the rocks, tiny sprays of heartsfire and snowdrop, sowmid flowers clinging, somehow, in the crevices of this hard place. The mountains abounded in lessons.

An endless, twisting, switchback climb. Eyes straight ahead, though there was no helping the horses, they had to pick their way. Drifts of pinecones. A stream somewhere off to the left, a continual watery tinkle, like a leak; when it crossed their path, they stopped to drink, rest, chew oatcakes. The curve of the trail afforded no rearward view. They were walled in immensity.

When only a casting could relieve her tortured limbs, they came suddenly up and over and around and out and *into*. Peaks in fantastic shapes carved the sky to either side, and before them a grassy sward was strewn with petals, flanked by sweet groves. How did such trees thrive here, where lungs labored in the thin air? Magecraft? It seemed arranged by design—the hard climb, with this as reward. The mother of their stream ran the meadow's length, its watery whisper echoing back to them.

Oh, she thought, *that Nole could see this, that Keiler could!*

After a breezing canter and cooldown on the straightaway, they watered and groomed and hoof-picked the horses into dusk, by a small fire built for cheer rather than warmth, in a scented glade by the stream.

"Tomorrow we go down again, and then up," Mellas said—the totality of his fireside conversation.

The haze had thickened into clouds that looked to fret into showers. Upon its rising, the full moon's glow was diffused as if through lamb's wool; they lay down under a blanket woven of light. Mellas muttered through his journeying in the landscape of dark dreams, and Liath, back turned to him, spiraled inward to a trial that never happened, a trial gone horribly awry.

When the boy's cry dragged her from sleep, she cursed him and pulled her cloak over her head. But he called again, a piercing plea. Her name. Irritated past endurance, she sat up to find him flailing on his back, something fastened to his chest, something too black to see.

"Oi!" Liath gave the cry that scared goats off the roof, deer out of the cabbages, cats out of the larder, the only cry surprise and habit allowed, then propelled herself unthinking at a thing all shadow and edge, a hole in the night, darkness within darkness. Something sprang back like moss under her fists. Mellas sobbed, and Liath shouted, and groped backward for a stick, a brand, found a rock from the fire's ring and hurled it blind into the shadow's side. It sank in; the thing lifted straight up, shrieking, and was gone in a smear of night against the sky.

Liath fell back, pushed under by the downdraft. It had been twice her size. Nothing that big could fly. There *was* nothing that big, no creature of the air. And they were warded against animals. Even beyond the triads' protection in the hills, their travelwardings should have held against attack.

Or perhaps they had. "We should be dead," Liath panted.

Mellas, curled up into a ball, whimpered.

Fury gripped her. "Spirits take you!" she cried, grabbing him, forcing him upright. "Why didn't you tell me there was danger in these mountains?" With his shirtfront clenched in her fists, she shook him, as the thing had done, and he cried out in weak protest. "Why didn't you *tell* me!"

"I didn't know!" He scrabbled backward; she held on to him a moment longer, to prove she could, then shoved him onto his rumpled blanket and turned away.

"I didn't ask you to come with me," he said. It should have sounded sullen—he was hanging his head—but the statement had the bitter ring of truth.

She slammed her palm against a tree trunk. Petals rained from jostled branches. "What *was* it?"

"A bad thing," the boy said in a hollow voice.

Liath snorted. "Yes," she replied. "It was that."

What should they do? She didn't know, and didn't want to be the one to make the choice.

"How long till sunrise, do you think?" she said.

The moon, no more than cloudglow, had gone behind the peaks. There was no way to judge. Mellas gave a helpless shrug.

At least it hadn't gone for the horses. They'd hobbled back a ways, stood with nostrils flared, ears swiveling. They mistrusted the skies now, the air itself.

"We should have made a bigger fire," she said. "Come, help me make another."

He cast a frightened glance into treeshadow. "We need more wood."

"I'll fetch it. You fan this, get it going again. Here, there's some tinder left."

The fire they built, of the damp, aromatic deadfall of fruit trees, hissed and steamed. They could have seen better without it; it created a periphery where light ended and nothing beyond was visible. It might attract more than it repelled. But they had to do something. The dew had settled on them, chilling their bones.

The flying shadow had been no natural thing; but neither could it be magecraft. Magecraft couldn't make things out of nothing. Magecraft worked with the spirits, to heal, to ward, to prompt growth. Castings freed women to bear children or not, as they wished. Through castings, milk flowed, calves and kids were born sound, crops grew tall, blight vanished. It staved off floods and accidental fires and drought, kept illness at bay, made old age comfortable, wine never turned to vinegar in the cask, water was always fresh. Castings protected life's beginning, smoothed the journey to the spirits at life's end. Magecraft turned the Great Storms from Eiden Myr.

But magecraft could not make crops grow unless seeds were planted. Magecraft could not make rain fall without rainclouds. Magecraft did not summon shadows.

"Illuminator . . ." The boy's voice cracked. "Liath . . ."

She went for her use knife, prepared this time; she had gathered a pile of stones as well as firewood. She scanned the circle of darkness, listened to the horses. All was quiet but the stream. "What?" she whispered.

Mellas crouched—in fear, she thought, until she too began to feel what he had placed palms flat on the trampled grass to feel. A low trembling, as of a herd of horses coming in for their morning grain. She could hear it though the blood roared in her ears.

She stared at Mellas. He stared back.

Earthquake.

It could not be. The Ennead tended their mountains, as all triads tended their vales and downs. They soothed the troubled spirits of earth. Had the Ennead abandoned them?

Unless it was rockfall. Liath grabbed for Mellas with one arm, the horses' tether with the other hand, as if she could gather them into the shelter of her body, as if anything could stop the crushing weight of boulders rumbling down the cliffs.

It would be over in a moment—just a moment, and they would know. The ground bucked; they staggered, the horses reared and backed, Liath could not hold the line, she should have unhobbled them, it would be their death if they could not run—

Mellas twisted away from her, snatched a branch from the fire, shook it at the thing that had reared up at light's edge, the thing that had to be a bear but was not. Stone-cold shadow become motion, it ground itself upright. The mountain, detaching a piece of itself to quest toward their fire, their heat, their life. The earth stopped shaking as the thing paused between steps. Something like a head swayed slowly to and fro.

Liath squeezed Mellas hard, a message to stay still, stay silent. She backed him up a step, with infinite care, more a shifting of weight than a step; and then another, that much farther from the flames. It could not see, it could not smell—the fire must be the lure. Another step—

Overcome by fear and tension, Mellas yelled an obscenity and flung the branch at the thing. The wood smashed into a spray of sparks. The shadow crashed to a semblance of all fours and rumbled toward them.

Liath turned and tried to run, but the ground shook her feet loose. She thrust Mellas away, or perhaps he was already running. She could not get her feet under her. She could not claw purchase from the grass to crawl. .

An eerie wheedle cut through the noise. Liath scrambled out of the sphere of light; she blundered into Mellas, and he dropped a bundle-sized rock he must have thought to heave at the thing. It was not as dark outside the firelight as she'd thought. Dawn leached gray into the frowning swirl of clouds, and the first spatter of rain dotted her face. The rumbling halted.

What stopped it? she wondered. *Dawn?* It sensed by feel, she was sure; it felt movement through the earth. Could it sense their heartbeats?

Her legs were trembling. Mellas, transfixed, was more solid. She steadied herself with a hand on his thin shoulder. Thunder grumbled far overhead, a faint cloud-echo of what they'd felt in the earth.

On its heels, the low wheedle came again. This time Liath thought she saw something—some brief, quick movement in the corner of her eye, gone when she turned toward it. Then again, from the other side of her. The rockshadow swayed, then backed off, with a rolling sound as of a nonned giant sheaves turning in their blocks.

Liath looked hard at Mellas, then into the graying air—and for a moment it seemed that a reflection of his pale face glanced back at her from the trees, elongated, eyeless. A travesty of his blanched child's face. It was gone before she could blink, her eyes retaining his pale visage, seeing its echo in the wood.

They were alone, shivering in the intermittent spray of rain, wary of their own fire. They jumped when the horses snuffled at their shoulders. Both seemed unhurt, though the boy's brown gelding had snapped its hobbles.

Good on you, Liath thought.

When they dared, when the dilute light had dimmed their fire to insignificance, they returned to their camp and packed up damp gear. Trees lay smashed where the thing had gone; they could not deny that it had been. The rain came in earnest as they mounted, dazed. Powerless as their wardings might have been against what plagued this place, their cloaks still repelled water.

Their passage seemed cursed thereafter.

Rain fell in a steady downpour, slicking the way. The trail became a long zigzag that seemed to go halfway across the mountain before doubling back; at each turn was a cliff, and a narrow, rocky path suitable for goats. Downhill, the going was more treacherous than up, but just as hard on legs and horse, a butt-end slide. Their mounts were weary, and spooked at small sounds. Liath braced tight, hands on the cantle. One slipped hoof here would be the end.

For a time the road was wider, graveled by scree. It rose and fell like waves; the horses trotted up, carried by their own momentum, then slowed at the top and walked down the other side. As they came over one of the steeper rises and started down, the tired sorrel tripped, pitched forward, and dropped out from under Liath. She hit the stony ground hard and rolled. The filly, above her, rolled too. Afraid to be crushed, Liath kept rolling until the slope bottomed out, then scrabbled over rocks to the trail's edge and looked back. The filly was struggling to its feet, Mellas reaching for the reins.

"Is she all right?" Liath called. Mellas dismounted and ran his hands over the sorrel's muddy legs.

"Yes, Illuminator, I think so." He led the horses toward her. "Are you?"

"Yes." In fact, she was quite numb; then pain flooded her knee and elbow. Mellas untangled her cloak and tried to help her up. She had to lean heavily on him; the knee would not support her weight. There was a bloody scrape where her breeches had torn, and red smeared her arms and palms.

"Your head is bleeding," Mellas said.

She put up a hand and found her short hair wet where the stones had got her. "It's all right," she told him. "Heads bleed a lot for nothing."

"Round the next turn, down there," Mellas said. "Some shelter and a stream. You could wash."

She smiled weakly. "All right."

He pushed the sorrel's rump to bring it around next to Liath. The filly's nose was scraped, but it seemed sound otherwise and unfazed by the fall.

Liath had landed on her right knee, so she was able to mount, awkwardly, with a leg-up from Mellas; but the knee would not bend to the stirrup. On the turn, she braced her left leg, held on to the saddle, and beseeched the spirits to keep her there. A fresh downpour answered her, but the spirits obliged.

At streamside, Liath rinsed blood and pebbles from the raw, scraped skin and out of her hair. The knee was purple and grotesquely swollen. All she could do for now was soak it, wrap it, and think about tonight's misery rather than tomorrow's pain.

The high peaks held on to the last of the day as the mountainside deepened into shadow.

Though laconic as ever, Mellas was quick to do all the work for them both. They finished the cheese and beans—Mellas gave her part of his half, she thought, though too deftly for her to be sure—and treated the horses to some grain. He stood with them after that, stroking them, leaning his head against the gelding's shoulder.

Liath wished fervently for a triad to nudge the rain off, refresh the weary horses, heal her knee. In a village like Clondel, with a resident triad, no one slept on injury or sickness.

As the light failed, the horses lifted their heads and sniffed the air. Wildcats would make them nervous; the big predators roamed the high ranges, and you couldn't tell the horses they were warded. But Liath expected every shadow to rise up against them. Perhaps the horses did, too.

If the earth moved to swallow them, if the fabric of sky stitched itself into winged death . . .

"That's two," said someone behind her. She twisted painfully to see a Souther emerge from between the striated skin of oak trees. Another came up from the side, holding Mellas by the scruff of the neck. "Small for a mage, though, seems to me."

Still another stood over Liath, sheathing his knife. "This one's hurt."

"Where's the third?" The woman Liath had confronted in the Petrel's Rest. Another man, shaven clean to show a long scar on one cheek, came up soundlessly from the side and shook his head.

They'd surrounded the little campsite and only the horses had noticed. They looked the worse for wear. Their breeches were soiled, their vests cinched tight against the chill; they had donned blousy shirts, but those were stained and tattered now. Their short cloaks were mantles, not even real cloaks, and ragged along the hem.

The knives were clean and honed. So was Liath's—but it was in the Southman's belt, easily found where she had laid it ready to hand, a milktooth against the things she knew might come for her, but all she'd had.

"You were wise not to try it," he said, for her ears only. He meant the knife, she realized. It hadn't even occurred to her to raise it against him. This man was trying to be kind, telling her she'd chosen well not to lift one blade against five, telling her he didn't fault her for it.

She wanted to laugh in his bearded face, but she hurt too much.

"Where's the third?" the woman repeated, squatting in front of Liath. "He took his horse, but there are no tracks."

"There is no third."

The woman spat into the bracken. "There's always a third. Tell me, girl. We're not in your tavern now."

Mellas stared at Liath, blinking.

"I tell you, there is no third, and he's no mage."

The Southers exchanged looks. One shrugged and said, "No tracks," as if it confirmed Liath's claim. "But it must have been them," said the bearded man. The woman in front of Liath raised a hand, and they fell silent. "This one's no mage either, from what I saw." She extended the hand to finger Liath's triskele. The flesh around her green eyes crinkled. "Funny, you still wearing this. Seemed to me your journey ended at your own front door."

Liath had never been a Marough, to let herself be goaded. She had been wise enough to keep her feelings for Keiler to herself, never revealing the one place where she was vulnerable. The anger that rose within her now—at the injustice of this killer goading *her*—was twisted by humiliation.

"Spitting drunks not enough for you?" she said. "Come to try children and the lame?"

The woman shrugged and stood up, one fluid movement. "I'm Verlein. We're headed for Crown. Someone keeps putting nasties in our way."

"It wasn't us."

"It was some mage hereabouts."

Liath shook her head, wearily adamant. "It can't be done by magecraft. They came from . . . I don't know where."

"It's how you did that?" The bearded man gestured to her leg.

"Tired horse," Liath said. "Accident."

"Well, you've found a nice spot for the night. We'll join you." Verlein grinned, the grin Liath remembered—more a baring of teeth than a sign of amusement.

"Are we your prisoners?" Mellas asked.

The short man released him and tousled his hair. The boy ducked away.

"We'll join forces," said Verlein.

"I'll wager they don't find mages tasty," the tall woman put in. "A mage might keep them at bay."

"One mage?"

"No mages," Verlein said. "I told you—this one's lame in more than her leg."

The woman laughed. "Strength in numbers, then. I'll hold her up, and she can be my knife hand." She raised an arm as if in salute: it was bound tight under the hanging sleeve.

"They hurt you," Liath said. *They hurt you, and not us.* The sick, hot ache in her knee ran straight to her head.

"Gadiya had a disagreement with a tree," Verlein said, grinning hugely. None of them really looked at anyone they spoke to; their eyes continually scanned the deepening shadows between the oaks, the cross-hatching of sky visible through the branches. The scar-faced man melted into the forest. Scouting. The others shifted to cover the hole he left.

What are you? Liath wanted to ask. *What business have you in Crown?*

No goods to trade, traveling light, on foot, from somewhere deep in the Lowlands. It made no sense. But nothing made sense.

"That cloak is warded, and you're sitting in wet things?" Gadiya snorted. "You're a fool. Get those clothes off, wrap up in that cloak, it's long enough. Best keep warm, after a fall."

Mellas, left on his own, went back to the horses. He didn't untie them, so no one objected. The Southers wouldn't take their mounts, would they? No point, with five of them. Unless one walked . . . but why . . .

"Show the boy how to rig a tent, we've enough blankets," Verlein told the smaller man. He had the same dusky skin and long black hair as the others, but his queue was braided with knotted string. Verlein's hair was straight and flat, tied simply; Gadiya's was a loose mass of curls. They had looked so alike to her, in the tavern.

"Here," said the scarred man, slipping back into camp. Why was he proffering his knife? "The bark, girl. I peeled it nice and fresh, you're lucky there's willows about. To ease your pain."

The rain slacked off, and somehow Gadiya got a small fire going. Liath wouldn't take off her clothes to dry them, and Mellas wouldn't help with the tent. "We'll have to leave it behind," he said. "When they come."

"Boy's right," said the bearded man. He regarded Mellas briefly, calculating.

The short man reached over to finger Mellas's colored cloak. The boy hugged his gelding's neck, pressing his face into its brown coat.

"Leave him, Torbik," said Gadiya.

"I might have a use for that cloak," said Torbik.

"I might have a use for more than that," said the man with the scar.

Mellas squeezed his eyes shut.

"You're scaring him," Liath said—stupidly, but she had to say something.

"Oh, we haven't even begun to scare him," scar-face said, very quietly.

There was a long silence. Verlein and the bearded man exchanged a look; Torbik and Gadiya watched them while watching the trees, and scar-face, eyes burning with an old, cold light, stared at Mellas. The bearded man spat on a tree and turned away.

What did they *want*? Liath clenched her teeth on the bitter willow bark; further appeal would only anger them, and there was too much between them that she didn't understand. How many days to the Holding on foot? If she startled them, created a diversion, would Mellas be smart enough to run? In her mind's eye, she could still see lanternlight shatter off those jagged blades; she could still see Verlein's expression when hers met flesh. Verlein couldn't have the heart for random cruelty. But where did a man come by a wound that scarred him in spirit more than flesh? In those long moments, Liath welcomed the gloom that drew around them like a cloak. Better the monsters of the night than these human monsters.

"Get some sleep, Ontas," Verlein said abruptly. "Gadiya too. Benkana, Torbik, with me on first watch."

Ontas turned, slowly, to face Verlein. He had more than a head on her, but she straightened, shifted forward; he thumbed his scar thoughtfully, then slipped his light pack off to unroll his blanket.

Mellas, glaring at the ground, shouldered past him—jostling him, eliciting an astonished grin—and flopped angrily down beside Liath.

"Mellas . . ." she murmured.

With a soft cry that only Liath could hear, he pulled the cloak over his head. Moments later, he shuddered into sleep. She made herself stretch out beside him, resisted the impulse to pull him into the curve of her body.

From the other side of the fire, a Souther stared at her, picking the teeth of his grin.

The others had been feelers—looking, sniffing, attacking what they found, but not intent, not focused. These horrors converged upon them with determined malice. They were bent on death.

A flock of sky-fragments shrieked razored fury. The mountainside rumbled with the approach of living rock. The night came alive; stones and sky and forest warped into abomination.

There would be no stopping it.

The Southers ringed Liath, Mellas. Liath gripped a stone in each hand, hurled them into spongy shadow whenever a Souther's stance shifted and afforded her a clear shot. The Southers' arms darted left, right, stabbed forward; their vicious toothed blades ripped and gouged. Torbik had taken a woods axe from Mellas's gear and hacked determinedly at a shapeless blackness before him. It writhed away with an otherworldly shriek, tangling with the things behind it. On the far side, more came. The circle of Southers tightened.

Mellas would not wake up. Liath shook him, shouted at him—hers the only human voice raised. He might as well have swallowed a cask of brandy as his own tears when he lay down. She sat him up and he flopped back limply. Until she saw him draw breath, she was certain he was gone, his spirit consumed by shadow while she sat helpless.

But he lived. They would not have him.

The shapes suggested forms, yet blurred past recognition. They resolved only in the corner of the eye, and then only into grotesque parodies of natural things. The harder you fought them, the less substantial they seemed. Yet they fell back from axe and blade and stone and club. They could be hurt. They were real enough for that.

Benkana, the bearded man, flung his off arm toward her and something thumped in the bracken. The use knife. Liath got to her feet. She stood over Mellas, one foot planted on each side of him. If the knee was broken, what of it? The leg propped her up. Agony was irrelevant. She stabbed at shadow over her head and it dodged away. She stabbed at shadow behind her and it shrank back.

A gap was opening in the ring of attack. They were thronging from the direction of the deep forest, downslope. The Southers, acting in unspeaking concert, had sensed the weak spot and were driving toward it. Verlein, Benkana, Gadiya led the way. Torbik and Ontas danced with the shadows at their rear—backing toward Liath, as the other three drove into the gap. They would have to move now.

Liath braced her bad leg straight so that pain would not buckle it, and heaved Mellas to his feet. He came to, shaking his head, woozy. Remembering where he was, he cast his eyes about wildly, desperate to run, hemmed by defenders he did not trust.

"Go," she urged him through gritted teeth.

"Purslane," he moaned.

The gelding. She hadn't known its name.

"They're gone, they ran," she said, not sure if it was true; they had stopped screaming, at any rate. "You go too. Run, through the hole. Run and keep going. Go."

He looked at the struggling Southers, the trampled fire, the shapes impinging on all sides, darker than darkness, always closer. He shook his head and forced Liath's right arm over his shoulders, thinking perhaps to drag her with him. She barely shifted the knife to her off hand in time: something black and fluid snaked in at them, and Liath lashed out. You couldn't tell if you'd hit the things, they either withdrew or they didn't. This one withdrew. But a rush of displaced air flattened their hair, and they looked up into the heart of night itself.

The skyshadow screeched as it dove at them, no sound a living creature would make, a sound from nightmare—a thousand outcries edged with a scrape of metal. Liath thrust her blade up at it, but it evaded easily, winging out of reach only to drop down and harry them again.

A doglike whine started in the back of Mellas's throat. It rose in pitch and intensity as he strove to drag Liath along with the Southers, as Liath hopped on her left foot to keep from being dragged, as she flailed upward with her milktooth to stave off the attack from above. Mellas threw back his head and shrieked at the thing; they screamed rage and frustration at each other until it was past all bearing.

"Eiden's balls, let us die in peace!" Torbik roared—and something vast and dark swept past his defenses and took him down into silence.

Their rear breached, all they could do was dive for the gap in the shadows and run for the trail. Terror blanked pain, and Liath lurched forward on her own two legs. She heard Ontas behind her. Mellas got ahead of her, tried to stop, turn; she shoved him hard and he staggered away. She lost her balance and sprawled in the muddy bracken. Ontas went past her. Mellas cried her name. The word cut off with a scuffle, and the last she heard of Southers or Mellas was a string of oaths from Ontas.

Cold, greasy darkness engulfed her. She could not see, or breathe; she could no longer feel the needles grinding her face, the damp soaking her clothes. *Is this what death feels like? Nothing?*

Then night returned, a brighter, softer darkness. The thing had rushed past her, or through her, and gone on. All was quiet at the edge of the clearing where their camp had been.

Liath got to her hands and one knee, sobbing, and turned back for the campsite. It had let her be. *Maybe they don't find mages tasty.* But she wasn't a mage anymore. The triskele dangled from her neck, swinging as she crawled. The pewter was warded in some way she had not been taught; only triaded mages could cast a triskele. Perhaps it had saved her, magelight or no.

Torbik lay dead. If she hadn't seen him fall, hadn't seen the others run ahead, she could not have known him—not for himself, not even for a man. The thing had scoured all skin from his body.

Hands roused her, wrapping a cloak around her where she sat. Her cloak, it seemed. Benkana.

"She's alive, all right."

"Best not wake her till this fire's going."

"Too late."

Liath counted four Southers and no horses. "Where's M-Mellas?" Her voice rattled. She was shaking uncontrollably.

"Got away," Verlein said.

"L-Lucky b-boy."

Gadiya and Ontas were making a pile of stones. They looked up at her. "That depends," Gadiya said. Under the pile of stones was Torbik.

Benkana had sorted their gear. "You can wear his pack," he said to Liath.

"She can't walk."

Benkana considered this, then moved off into the trees.

"I still say we should bury him," said Ontas.

"Like a turd?" said Gadiya. "Don't be disgusting."

"It's better than letting the rodents have him."

"Nothing wrong with that. Nature's way."

"He was my friend!"

"And mine as well. But the bonefolk won't be long."

"Up here?"

"They'll come. Why make it harder for them?"

If there weren't wraiths before—if the shadows weren't the rumored wraiths—there would be at least one now. No one to cast passage for those who died by violence. No one to cast passage anyway.

Ontas stared at the flat stone in his hands. "Always knew Eiden's head was full of rocks."

Verlein slapped Liath on the shoulder. "Well done, girl," she said, though Liath had done nothing but survive.

Verlein took pleasure in all this. Victory made her generous. She drew energy from conflict. Not enough to seek it out, perhaps; but when it happened, when it was over, she glowed with life and lust—she looked the way Liath had felt after her first casting. Castings knitted, healed, spurred growth. Verlein's talent, it seemed, was only for destruction. That she wrought it in defense of her life, or others', did not make that exultation any nobler; sometimes she wrought it by mistake, too. It was a tainted thing. Liath turned her face from it and did not answer.

"Well, we got away with cuts and bruises. They didn't mind a stationary target, but they didn't have the heart for a chase. We'll know that, for the next time." As she spoke, she picked through the clutter for the driest tinder, then crouched over it with strikers. "Did they injure you?"

Liath shook her head. Benkana returned, trailing two slender stocks, and started to strip the stocks down to poles.

"We'll take you to Crown," Verlein said.

"Maybe she wants to go home," Gadiya replied when Liath said nothing.

"She can't, on her own."

"One of us could go back, fetch her people."

"We're too few as it is."

"We owe her nothing," said Ontas. "The boy might have . . ." He placed a last stone at Torbik's feet and got up. "Well. It's too late now."

"You're the one who let him go."

"I saved his hide. He was going back for her, when she fell." He looked at the makeshift cairn. "It's more than we did for Torbik. So I sent him on his way." There was a pause. "To die, I suppose."

Verlein swore at the tinder, which refused to catch a spark. "It's done now. Let's go. We'll get warmer hiking than huddling round a fire I can't start."

Benkana pointed at the makings of a litter. "I'll need a dozen breaths."

"No." Liath got her left foot under her, grabbed a low branch, and hauled herself up against frozen muscles and redoubled pain. "Give me one of those poles," she said to Benkana.

Quirking a brow, he obliged. She got her good foot on the pole and snapped it to three-quarters length. "I'm not going to Crown," she said. It was the truth.

"You can't make it back," Gadiya insisted.

"Then I'll die."

Benkana closed his hand around her walking stick. Liath jerked it away. He cocked his head, opened his hand. She gave it to him, frowning, and he deftly wrapped the stump of a branch at one end with a linen kerchief and the cord he would have used to tie the litter. A seating for her armpit, she saw, as he returned it. A crutch. She met his dark eyes and nodded.

The rest of them had their battered packs on. Gadiya offered her some rice cakes; then they were gone, sinking back into the forest, the same colors as the bark, the soil, the morning mist that swirled in to take their place. The only sounds were Liath's breathing and the drip of condensation off the leaves. Even the birds had fled from the shadows.

It was a long time before she heard the muffled thuds behind her. She turned, and thought that she'd been mistaken—that the shadows had come for her after all. But Mellas's cloak was the color of leaves and sky; the brown and red-gold horses were a brief, deceptive touch of harvestmid in the rain-wet gloom.

"All right?" she said, hiding her relief.

He nodded. A livid welt on one cheek seemed the worst he'd suffered.

"They've gone on. Is there a clear space where we can overtake them, ride by?"

He frowned, backed up a step.

"We can't stay here; the shadows will come."

He pointed Fistward.

"No. We have to get to the Holding." She squinted at him. "Both of us, eh?"

His eyes were downcast. "I want to go back."

"But the Holding is your home. You have to go home sometime."

He gave the bracken a wan smile that made him look thrice his age. "Yes," he said. "I know."

"Look, Mellas," she said. "I can't go back. I have to see the Ennead." She closed her eyes, but black sparkles danced behind her lids and she had to clutch the stick to keep from toppling. Eyes open, at least she could balance. "I'm ill, Mellas. If I wait too long, they might not be able to restore my light."

He pondered this. "Do you really want it back that much?"

Roiden's bitter eyes seemed to glare at her through the trees. He'd shown a light, but failed his trial, no one knew why; he'd become a gnarled, mean thing. But she was stronger than that. She'd received the triskele. It was not the same.

She could be a brewer, a traveling merchant, based in Clondel but journeying afar to trade the best ale in the Neck for whatever the rest of the world had to offer. It was good enough for her aunts with their bran-dies. She could build an inn; there were always more people passing through Clondel than they had room for, they had needed another inn for years now. The only pain she felt was the injured knee, the ache of cold, the sick fatigue—there was no chasm inside her where the magelight had been, no yawning absence. She would not die without it.

But she could not truly live without it. There was simply no question of turning back, no matter the cold, the ache, the pain, no matter how badly she wished to be home.

"Yes," she said softly.

"Right, then," Mellas said, and dug a wallet of provisions from a canvas saddlebag. "It should take them till midday to make the High Ridge. If we pass them there, we'll still be in the Holding before dark."

Liath gnawed on a heel of bread and regarded the changed lad thought-fully. Perhaps he had escaped more than a Souther's threats, and regained more than the horse he loved.

The canopy of trees had obscured the hard truth of sky: black thunderheads were driving in from the Sea of Storms. Headed down into the Heartlands, where the sowmid rains were expected. The Ennead couldn't deny all rain. They were on their own.

Liath kept her seat only by clutching the cloth-covered wood of the saddle's frame; she could not grip with knees or calves, or guide the filly, just let it follow the other horse. As forest deepened around the descending trail, the way became more mud than stone. When the clouds cracked open, rain hit them like a fist.

"We've got to take shelter!" Liath called. Mellas reined in so she could come up beside him; the filly was a good girl, Liath's backshifted weight was enough to bring her to a halt. "It looks like there might be caves hereabouts. Can we find one?"

"But it's our chance," Mellas said. "They'll be taking shelter too."

Liath plumped her weatherwarded cloak back over the filly's hind-quarters to share the protection, and lifted the hood away from her eyes to peer down the trail. "Are we close?"

"We have to be. When did they leave?"

"It had just gone light."

Mellas nodded. "They'll be up there, somewhere. In a cave or under the trees."

Maybe ready to jump out at us. But they had believed she was headed home. They'd been sure the horses were dead or they'd have whistled for them, searched, rattled pebbles in a pack to sound like grain. They'd let Mellas run away to die.

Thunder cracked so hard they ducked, and lightning arced, a vivid green, somewhere toward Crown. The world's worst fool wouldn't stay out in weather like this.

"Come on, then," she said, reaching down to jam her right bootheel hard up against the stirrup. Her knee screamed when she forced the leg to bend. "Don't worry about me—if it's time to run, you run. I'll stay on somehow."

Mellas faced forward. "I'll always worry about you," he said, then bent to speak soothing words in the brown's ear as he gigged it through the sheeting rain.

They were just off the trail, under the trees, two on each side. It was only a few strides to intercept the horses. Mellas's shied when Ontas burst onto the trail, and slipped, going down on its side. Mellas kept his seat, but by the time the brown scrabbled to its feet Ontas had the reins, and pulled the rearing gelding down by its head. Liath, five lengths behind, meant to run them down if they jumped out—she had trusted weight and speed to put them off or knock them aside. But the filly balked when the three Southers blocked the road. She was a good girl. She didn't run people over. Her straight-legged skid through the mud ended with Verlein hanging on her halter and Liath clinging to her neck.

"Do you think we're stupid?" Verlein shouted. "We don't count the dead till we see the bodies!"

She hadn't seen a lot of bodies. Liath was certain of it now. Her tone smacked of rote: lessons she had learned from a teacher, not in the field. Anger didn't cover it. Liath could hear the difference; Liath had been a prentice for a dozen years.

And who would teach such things as these Southers had learned?

"Let us go! We can't help you!" She had strapped the crutch in front of the saddle, but she was lying on it now and couldn't get to her knife under her cloak. She clawed and pounded at Verlein's hands on the halter. The rain drove into their eyes, battered their wind-bared heads.

"I had no use for you, girl, but I'm blasted if I'll be made the fool—"

"Look!"

Mellas's cry carried the high, piercing urgency of childhood. They looked.

"Oh, sweet spirits," Verlein said.

The slope above the trail was moving. The entire slope, bearing down on them. Tree roots skewed at crazy angles. Big rocks were borne along like leaves in a river. They had only breaths before it hit them. Liath's feet weren't in the stirrups. She slid down the filly's neck till she was standing, but hung on, a useless instinct. She looked down, to see where it would push them, as if it mattered, as if she would live.

A wave of mud swept them off the trail. Their screams were swallowed. Liath tried to keep her head up, tried to kick out, but it wasn't water, and she couldn't swim anyway. Something hard took her in the back, then slid away. She slammed into a treetop, felt the horse's weight press on her; the tree yielded, went over. There was a sickening drop. They were still moving. It would carry them down the mountain. She shut eyes and lips tight, though she wanted to scream panic. Her head went under.

It pinned her arms and legs, pinned the horse against her, a sucking vise. There was no counting breaths when you could not breathe. She counted heartbeats instead; the blood pulsed in her ears, inside the deep silence of earth. Nine heartbeats. A lifetime ending. How much mud lay on her now? Eiden smothering his own children. This time the triskele would be her death. He would spare his own and take Galandra's. She didn't know if her eyes were open or closed, but the mud was black from the inside, a beautiful sparkling black, black and glittering as the mountains.

Forward movement subsided like a breath. The filly flailed, once, a spasm, then went still. The pressure eased on Liath's face. Rain washed the mud from her eyes. She drew breath in one long, ragged sob.

The storm passed on, leaving them in a wreckage of forest two slopes down.

The sweet sorrel was dead, the gear buried with her. One end of the crutch poked up. Liath gripped it, pushed; the forked end of it found leverage on something below. Her cloak, still tied at her neck, nearly strangled her, but when she lay back there was enough play to slip her head out of the loop. She poled herself downslope, hauled the crutch up, and poled herself forward again, and again, until she could stand. Then she foundered, unable to lift even her good leg. Everything was brown, shapeless. Drizzle pocked the surface of mud.

Verlein slogged toward her through knee-deep ooze. She was brown from head to foot, the whites of her wild eyes like something seen through sackcloth eyeholes. She reached out for the end of the crutch. It was slippery; it took several tries for her to drag Liath from the muddy trap down to the ridge below, where the long spill of rocks and sodden earth could reach no farther.

A man hung, dead, from a canted treetop upslope. They found Gadiya's broken body just above the trail. Benkana was lifting himself from the muck. He looked at them without knowing them. Then he fell back and covered his soiled face with soiled hands; mud sloughed off him like shed skin. The man in the tree was Ontas.

A child's sob drew Liath painfully around a bend where the trail skirted a low outcropping, the crutch jammed under her arm.

"Don't try," Mellas said, "don't try, it's all right, just rest . . ." His voice cracked, and he sagged onto his knees.

The gelding was trying to get up. Its off hind was shattered at the hock, a white shock of bone protruding from the uniformity of mud. It fell back, and tried again, sides heaving. Mellas pressed his cheek to its brow, cleared mud delicately from ears and nostrils. "Purslane," he murmured. Tears carved tracks in his brown face.

Liath's use knife was still in its sheath, still honed; the shadows hadn't dulled it.

She wasn't a bindswoman. She didn't know of any other way.

"The sooner the better," Verlein said, coming up behind her. Benkana followed at several paces.

Mellas heard them. "You get away from him!" he cried. Lifting beseeching eyes to Liath: "Make them go!"

"Turn your backs," Liath said, limping to Mellas.

This wasn't right. You didn't kill animals. The only people who killed animals were binders, and they put them to sleep first, some secret trick of binders, to see they felt no pain. It was done with utmost respect for the life that was sacrificed that they might have leaves for their castings. Old animals simply passed on, and went to the bonefolk. Civilized folk never had need to kill—not animals, not each other. This should not have happened.

Mellas took the knife and held it flat behind the jawbone. The gelding thrashed feebly, then quieted as Mellas eased the heavy head into his lap. "I can't," he said.

"You shouldn't have to." Liath leaned down, ignoring agony; she took the knife, gave the neck a pat, then did the thing with one deep unhesitating stroke.

The death spasms knocked them both sprawling. Liath sat up, swallowing bile, while blood-drenched Mellas keened. The sensation of blade opening flesh was a horror she would never be free of.

"We are too few now, Verlein."

"For what?" Liath said, looking up. "What are you here for?"

"It hardly matters now," Verlein said bitterly. "We're turning back."

The trail above was washed out. They had no supplies. Their cloaks and blankets were gone. The shadows would come. They would not live to see the foothills again.

"What could possibly be worth enduring what you already have?" Liath said.

Verlein could still be surprised. "You really don't know?" Then she laughed. There was an edge of hysteria to it.

Liath spat into the mud. "I deserve the truth, Verlein. After all this. Don't you think?"

Verlein didn't answer for some time. She looked out over the devastation, up at the indifferent sky. At last she said, "The truth is drawn on this mountainside, clearer than any scribing. Perhaps someday you'll learn to read it. Safe passage, mageling."

The runner and the crippled publicans' daughter wended their tortuous way down the black mountain. Where it was too steep for Liath, whose leg would no longer bend, she slid down on her rump, one rock at a time, maneuvering with the crutch. They ate what they could find along the trail, mostly peaberries this early. Before nightfall, Mellas found them a shallow cave, and they huddled in the stale remains of some creature's nest. She held him, though he no longer cried; under the ruined surcoat he was thinner than she had realized. The mudslide had swept away whatever changes the previous night had wrought in him. He was a troubled child, terrorized past all endurance. She hoped he'd sleep the night, and didn't think she could sleep at all; but he startled awake each time he began to dream, and their small, shared warmth tugged her below the threshold of waking.

Only when they found themselves whole at daybreak were they convinced that no shadows would come for them in the night.

For two days more, they went up. There was plenty of water, but nothing to eat. Mellas found bitter leaves he claimed would sustain them, something like spinach that tasted like gall. Now a sour stomach added to the grief, but it was an ailment they shared, as they shared sick, unspoken fear at every shift in the night.

They shared the walking, as well. Up was impossible for her, even with the crutch, so Mellas became her right leg, with her arm slung over his shoulders and her balancing with the crutch in her left hand. She didn't know how his slight frame bore it. She told him to go on ahead, bring help back for her, but he refused with a vehemence that bespoke more than protectiveness.

"I won't leave you," he said.

There was nothing to do but go on. There never had been.

Under a blue sky curded with white cloud, they came out of a fringe of stunted pines onto a massive outcropping of bare, black rock. Mellas halted.

Ahead of them was only sky; the dropoff must be sharp. "Which way around?" Liath asked. The trail had forked twice, and split again here.

"This is it. You don't get in from the back. There is no back. You get in from the top. Or the sides."

"We're *standing* on it?"

Mellas smiled—a brief, shy flash of straight white teeth, as charming and fleeting a thing as a snowdrop in a crevice. "Yes," he said. "Part of it, anyway. We don't usually come this way. I'll show you."

He walked right up to the edge, silhouetted against infinity. "Come on."

She shook her head, but then crutched toward him. He helped her get down to crawl the last few feet and peer over.

Her breath stopped.

Below her was a sheer cliff face flanked by a complexity of promontories. Nesting seabirds were pale specks and flutters, their cries lost to distance. Far below, something undulated and danced in the sun, something made of soft white light; when its thunderous whisper drifted up to her, she knew it for a cataract. Its runoff became a sinuous bright river, leading to a gray-sand crescent. On the crescent was what must be the village of Crown; she could just make out movement around it, boats dotting the harbor. Beyond that—stretching forever in all directions save behind her—was the sea. Travelers had described this to her, but her mind's eye had not prepared her. Bluer than her lost guiders, all motion and sparkle, its wild scent rising up the mountains' ending.

"It's so big," she murmured. The Holding, or the sea, she didn't know. Either. Both.

"Everyone says that."

He must mean all the mages he had brought here, summoned to serve the Ennead she had never wished to serve. The implications brought her back into herself, and she pushed carefully away from the precipice. Beneath her, in a place both underground and high in the sky, was gathered the most powerful magecraft in Eiden Myr. She stood at the edge of the world, crippled and unworthy.

"You could still go home," Mellas offered, almost too softly to hear in the ocean wind. "Proxies in Crown could heal your leg. You could work passage on a ship sailing to Shrug, get a ride from there in some trader's wagon."

She looked at his brown clothes stiff with blood, his spiky hair, his welted cheek, and thanked the spirits for the gift of his life. The ground-in mud had gone to dust; it suited him better than the Ennead's colors had. The lost cloak had fitted him badly, somehow. They were a sight, the two of them, ragged and soiled, injured and on foot. She fingered her triskele, wondering that the chain had not snapped.

"Show me the way in," she said.

The boy nodded, and said nothing more as he guided her back and around and down into a narrow cleft and through a great ironbound ash door, past a surprised watchman and along a torchlit entryway into the heart of stone.

IRON

After he'd seen to the evening's business, he returned to his spare chambers. Out of sorts, he went to fling the shadowsilk cloak across his sleeping pallet, then thought better of it and hung the rich garment on its peg beside the others. A meal sat cold on the sideboard, delivered while he worked. This breaching of his sanctum, though convenient, was an irritation. He aligned the silver with the square plate, centered the goblet above it, drew the linen parallel to the edge of the wood. All unsupervised entry to his quarters would be prohibited henceforth.

Not that his quarters were ever empty. He glanced up at the two stout doors at the back. He chose the leftmost one, the one it was not necessary to lock.

The chamber was dark, but a thin whiff of smoke testified to a candle just blown out. She had heard his approach. A lithe shadow on the canopied bed in the far corner, she uncurled herself slowly, opening her limbs to him. He left the door cracked; the bar of light it admitted draped itself across her calf.

"You were gone some time," she said, in the throaty voice meant to arouse him.

His foot hit something: a pile of cloth. He bent, retrieved her cast-off garments, and folded them on the small chest before disrobing and placing his own clothes neatly beside them.

"You should let me do that," she said, as he sat on the bed and drew her into his arms.

"And cast mine on the floor as well? I ask very little of you, Olna. Neatness is such a simple thing."

She ran a fingernail down his cheek, along the side of his neck, down the center of his chest. "You take your pleasure of me the way you bathe, eat, void yourself—with no interest, merely fulfilling your body's needs that it not distract you from more important things. What is it? What is more important than pleasure, than love? Share it with me. Perhaps I can help."

"Must you always speak?" he growled, stretching out beside her, not yet covering her.

"You say so little. Let me know you, let me understand you that I might please you better."

He had not yet determined whether what she desired was his soul or his power. Now it no longer mattered. He suffered her to run light fingertips over his brow, around his eyes, his lips. "You are rugged, like a mountain, and beautiful, and hard," she said. "Let me please you. Let me *know* you."

He let the frustrations of the day well up inside him, stiffen him. This had gone on too long. Her wheedling, her fishing, and her presence here. He took her suddenly, roughly, closing his fist in her hair that she might not hide her surprise or hurt from him. His body was a honed instrument. The lean muscles she so admired were forged with long hours of work, toward a purpose she would know naught of.

"You pain me, lover." Discomfort pitched her voice high.

She was so yielding. He despised softness, though he required it to slake this particular thirst. He reached for the side table, turned a trick handle thrice and back, withdrew the object inside. The tallow candle toppled and rolled to the floor with a crack.

She kept speaking even as he pierced her with his flesh, in pitiless rhythm, bringing all his weight and strength to bear. She had asked him to make it last, this time, concerned at how quickly he used her and left, hoping to wring seduction from what was mere necessity. She had sought more pleasure, more time to plumb his secrets. He obliged her now—but it was his pleasure, not hers, and it lasted for only the time it took the blade, harder and sharper than he was, to enter her as his flesh did, and for the blood to soak the mattress, and for the light in her eyes to dim.

"You are hate," she rasped, in that moment of clarity that precedes the end. He no longer had to force her to look into his face; she was speared by what she saw there, and he climaxed as he watched her see it. "That was your secret. . . ."

When he was finished, he bathed again, shaved with care, trimmed hair that had grown too long. He dressed in a loose linen robe and sat calmly down to his neglected meal, consuming it without lingering. He cleaned the plate, then placed the cloth and utensils in a tidy pile, as he'd left the body. Later, and on his order only, servants would come to remove all soiled things from his chambers. He lay down on the hard pallet under the window. There was work yet to be done before dawn, but he functioned inefficiently without sleep; he would rouse himself in time.

He never dreamed.

The mountain hummed with magecraft. Liath could feel it in her bones, a kind of itch. When she touched fingertips to the smooth wall, the rock trembled, like a struck bell as the sound tails off. The air was charged, as before a storm, though the storm had gone and the day they had left behind was clear. White-garbed triads were stationed in a row of galleries along the mountain side: wordsmiths and illuminators bent over their work, binders chanting. She could smell their magelights, with that sense that was not taste or smell but felt like both; her nose took in oils and acrid ink and metallic pigment, her ears caught quill points scritching on vellum.

Fluted columns opened, on their right, into airy cloisters. Daylight spilled in through window grates: this passage ran along a cliff face. Fountains tinkled, and fragrant herbs grew from long stone planters in bushy profusion. The passage ended at an ironwood door. On the other side was a chamber of sorts—a junction, with identical doors on three sides. A stone-buttressed, triangular wooden landing surrounded an iron stair that spiraled into darkness at their feet and over their heads. The stair jiggled in its brackets as Mellas shut the heavy door, closing the last of the daylight off and leaving them in rushlight. "That'll need tightening," he said. Oiling, too, by the sound of it.

He opened the door to their left. A cool smell of stone gusted out, damping the salty tang of sea air. This passage canted down, but the incline was gentle and her crutch didn't slip. The center of the floor was worn into a depression by the tread of countless feet. Brackets held pitch-topped torches; every fourth or fifth had burned out, and Mellas muttered something about the torchman. What light there was reflected from the mica-speckled walls in an ever-changing dazzle.

"Stars," Liath murmured. Stars, twinkling deep in the earth.

"We call it nightstone," Mellas said.

"In the Neck it's just blackstone. I like your word better."

After an interminable descent, the floor leveled and the passage rounded into a long bend. Archways appeared in the walls at irregular intervals: narrow stone steps up or down, doorless alcoves filled with darkness. The air had grown colder. When the way straightened again, the openings revealed tunnels that branched and branched again, into torch-lit infinity.

After another junction chamber, they came into a brighter section that smelled of life—food, bodies, animals—and made their way through store-rooms and antechambers, side passages and workrooms. It would take at least a season to learn her way around. Liath's knack was for patterns, and the Holding seemed to have none. No arrangement of chambers repeated; one room led into another, long burrowings into the rock. It made her uneasy, but in truth it was no less haphazard than the arrangement of fields in the valley below Clondel, or the roadside sprawl of cottages and crafteries that was the village itself. Trees and plants grew around each other toward the light, as was expedient. Clondel had started as one hos-pitable cottage along a well-traveled Headward route, the rest springing up around it to suit demand; the upper rooms and attic of the Petrel's Rest had been built on that first cottage, itself changed to suit the growing business. Addition built upon adaptation. This was an ancient place, steeped in power; she could not expect to understand it in a day.

They came through the stables. Here, at last, the activity she'd ex-pected—grooms raking out stalls, stitching tack, brushing coats glossy. It made her suddenly ill; the chronic ache of her leg spiked into pain with a vengeance. All these animals, living their lives in a hole in the ground. The stable chamber was vast, the stalls and haylofts built of heavy, age-darkened wood. There was plenty of space, and the arrangement had clearly worked for a long time. But Liath felt the weight of stone. The flames in the corridors danced, and were not smothered, and did not fill the place with smoke; there was some system of holes or crevices through-out the Holding to circulate air. The rich smells of manure and hay and horseflesh were not overpowering. Yet her body refused to believe that there would be air for her next breath.

"Sit her down, boy, what ails you?" said a gruff voice. Big hands maneuvered her onto a mounting block, helped her sink down with her bad leg straight. Liath looked up past sturdy wooden shoes and soiled apron into a beefy face. The man unbent himself with a grimace.

"You're days late," he said to Mellas, "no cloak on you, looking like death, your horse become a lame sodden mage, and come in the back way to boot. Let's have it, then."

Mellas did not even try to speak. He looked the man straight in the eyes and set his jaw against tears. Liath drew breath to defend him. There was enough air in here for that. But before she could speak, the man—head stableman from the sound of him, farrier by the look of him—pulled the boy roughly into his arms.

Mellas squeezed his face tight against the waxed canvas apron, mouth open in a soundless cry. His dark head seemed smaller than the hand that cupped it.

The man looked inquiry at Liath. She shook her head.

"Ah, that Purslane was a spoiled brute," he said, voice thick. "Knew his fool boy loved him. Took every advantage of it, didn't he."

Children stopped what they were doing, put curry combs aside, propped rakes against stall doors. Slowly, they gathered around the pair. One little girl put out a hand; then an older boy; then another. Most were younger than Mellas. They laid fingertips on him, silently, pressing close but making room for littler ones to scoot in. Even the horses were quiet, and if there were rats they made no sound; two calico barn cats watched unblinking.

Mellas was in his family's hands now.

"Fetch and return, deliver and return, that's what my young runners do," the stablemaster said, after they'd eaten, after Mellas had spoken in private with him. A gangly girl with hair like wheat had carefully cut the right leg of Liath's breeches and applied a poultice—the kind you'd put on a horse, for a strain that didn't merit a casting. The dulling of pain was soporific. She basked in not-cold and not-hungry and not-afraid. Even the ale the man had poured her tasted good, and it was mediocre stuff from the Shoulder, the yeast not settled.

"Reckoners do most of the calling, of course, but sometimes the Ennead hears about a promising prentice, sends someone off to deliver a summons and ride back with the vocate. That's a job for mine." With his mug he gestured to the children who sat with them.

So vocates were the mages who'd been called to train as proxies. He'd already mentioned what he called passers—"journeyers who visit, triads who visit, vocates who fail, all passing through. A sieve, that's what this place is! Pour vocates in the top, let them dribble through the crevices, see which ones stick."

His hearty pride in the level of craft he worked to support made Liath think twice about confiding her ailment: she herself was a passer. She could take no clue from Mellas, who had fallen asleep on a pile of saddle blankets, peaceful at last.

Putting it off, she asked instead, "Where do all the children come from?" The youngsters watched her with interest, taking her measure; thus far she fit into no category of mages they knew. Except for Breida, who was different, Liath was not good with children. She didn't see many in the tavern, except on special occasions or when they fetched a parent home. Children in the village functioned much like runners—small and quick and reliable, and no craft to be pulled away from. But these children worked harder than the ones at home, and without complaint.

"Reckoners' children, mostly," their master said. "The road's no place for a child, so they put them up here, or in the laundries and sculleries and the like. Those they don't foster in Crown. And if they show a light they go off. I hate to lose 'em, though of course it makes me proud. I lose 'em anyway, light or no. When they get too old and head off to ply the craft they learn here. Farriers, wranglers, stablekeeps . . ."

"The ones with a magelight—they prentice somewhere?"

"The proxy's home village, most often. Then later sometimes they come back. There've been vocates and reckoners and warders were grooms and runners under me. They never forget old Bron." He gave the children a stern look. "And are you warders' get, to dawdle the day away?"

"Can I take Amaranth out?" a towheaded boy said quickly. "Beadrin got to take her yesterday."

"Don't you mean the day before? I seem to recollect *you* had her yesterday."

The boy, caught in his fib, looked down, but he was hiding a grin and he elbowed the girl next to him, who was giggling.

"If Beadrin will trade her turn with you, she can breeze Betony."

The girl nodded, but the boy, sensing opportunity passing, cried, "No, I want Betony!"

"Then you shall have her, and Beadrin shall take Amaranth."

The boy wriggled and made a silly face at being outsmarted, but gave up protesting. After a round of assignments and negotiations, the older children went off to exercise the horses, the younger ones tagging behind to help tack up or just to watch.

It was still daylight out there. They would be all right. But: "Master Bron," Liath began.

"Oh, just Bron, lass. I'm Bron to my youngsters and just Bron to everyone else."

"There's something you should know. About the mountains."

He waited calmly.

"There's danger. Things. Shadows. You shouldn't send any children that way, not anymore. Not until the Ennead sees to it."

He considered this. "You know that's a rumor older than my granny's granny."

"Yes. But these things were real. They killed a man."

Nothing in Bron's position changed; he still lounged with one arm up on a row of halter hooks, balancing his mug on a meaty thigh. But Liath sat up straighter, called to attention by a spark in his dark brown eyes. He was a Khinishman. The sharpening of his aspect made it evident. He looked the way Hanla looked those rare times when Liath did something forbidden or dangerous. His skin was paler than hers, no longer flushed from his work, but the build was the same. The eyes were the same.

"The boy didn't tell me that," he said.

"The Southers weren't very nice to him," she said quietly.

"Traders?" he asked.

"I don't think so."

"Triskeled?"

"No. They weren't mages."

He nodded, and she could almost see him hanging up the information, like a frayed halter, to take care of later.

"And these shadows?"

She described them as best she could. "I have to warn the Ennead," she said.

"I'll see they hear of it."

She wanted to believe him, though he was looking at Mellas and not at her. You should look into a person's eyes when you made a promise.

"I was there," she said. "I can tell them what it was like."

This time he looked at her. "I'm sorry."

She was taken aback. "But I have to see them . . ."

He put his mug aside. "You've an ailing magelight. Mellas told me as much."

"Can't you take me to them? Or one of the children?"

He shook his head. "They'd have my hide for it. There are always folk coming up the mountain, petitioners with chilblains or a land dispute who aren't satisfied with their own triad or the reckoners. The Nine have larger matters to concern themselves with. It's why there are proxies in the first place. It's a sound method, and I approve of it."

She blew air through her lips. "Suppose you just gave me directions? If I went on my own, they need never know it was you who . . ."

"You won't find your way even with the best directions. And some steward or proxy would catch you before you made it halfway down."

Liath set her mug on an empty saddle rack, the aftertaste too bitter. "There's no one else I could ask?"

A child came running in, displaying a reddened finger—caught in a buckle, perhaps. Bron pulled her into his lap and ruffled her hair while she sucked on the finger to soothe herself. No need to cry, no need for him to fix it. She just wanted to be in his lap while the hurt eased.

"The proxies come to us on behalf of the Nine; we don't go to them. Their mounts are kept in their own stable. The vocates see proxies when it's time—the ones who test them for new reckoners and warders, see what they're suited for. Older reckoners, usually, tired of the road. They've been gone from home a lifetime, their trades taken over by those they left behind. Most times, this is all the home they have now." He looked down at the child. The hurt all better, she beamed up at him, then slipped away to rejoin her friends. "The Holding proxies keep to themselves. Out in the world, reckoners hear every grievance, suffer every thickhead with patience and courtesy. Here they guard their privacy—and they guard the Nine's fiercer still."

He waxed expansive, she saw now, when he was thinking, when he was deciding something else. He studied her as he spoke, evaluation unconnected to the words he was saying, easy words that demanded no attention from him while he made up his mind.

"You're better off going home," he said.

"I can't do that."

He nodded. "I warrant you've put more than a foot wrong somewhere along the way."

"Please help me," she said quietly.

He opened his mouth to reply, then cocked his jaw and looked away. Helping her could get him in trouble. She had to wedge something persuasive in the crack before he made a decision.

"My grandfather was a proxy. Is, I hope, still. Somewhere. Pelkin n'Rolf n'Liath. I was named for his mother," *though my mother cursed the choice.* "Perhaps you knew him?"

Bron thought for a moment. "Reckoner or warder?"

He kept mentioning warders. Hanla had told her there were warders in the Holding, mages who helped the Ennead with weathercastings, but . . . "Warders are proxies too?" she said, frowning. She had always thought that "proxies" and "reckoners" were two words for the same thing—mages who traveled on behalf of the Ennead, acting in their stead, extending their protection throughout the world. They dressed in black, wore nine-colored cloaks, and worked magecraft that the local triads couldn't: casting triads, dissolving triads, casting magesickness off binders and illuminators who worked with dangerous pigment.

"Of course they're proxies," Bron replied. "Warders live their lives here. They do the Ennead's weather work in proxy. There's far too much of it for the Nine to handle alone—they'd be at it night and day, and it would wear them out for when the Great Storms come. You must have seen some warders on your way here. The ones in white?"

She nodded. Everything came in threes. The Ennead, the warders, and the reckoners made three. If Pelkin had become a warder rather than a reckoner, she would never have seen him again—he would have spent his life here. She looked at Mellas, at the door beyond which the fostered children made what home they could. If Pelkin hadn't already pledged to Gran Breida when he was called, Geara might once have been one of those children.

But if Pelkin had been made warder, he would be here now.

"My gran was a reckoner," she said, remembering a spill of light through a tavern door, words spoken in the shadows beyond it, a baby crying within.

She looked down, but not quite fast enough to hide the sudden long-ing that twisted her face. Reckoners maintained a web of information, feeding the Holding the most recent news of weather patterns across Ei-den Myr—the only means of shepherding a world so large, from up at its windswept head. Bron, who ran the Holding runners, might be able to contact reckoners. To see her grandfather again . . . to ask for aid . . . Ca-sually, adjusting the poultice on her knee, she said, "Could you find him for me?"

Bron glanced at the door, just as she had—at the children whose parents had abandoned them to him. Pity softened the lines of his face. "Not quickly. If he's a reckoner, he's on the move. You'd get to the Nine faster than you'd get any help from your old gran." He sighed and rubbed his stubbly head. "The only way to the Ennead in this Holding is to earn your way to them. You're too old for a runner."

"But not for a vocate."

"No."

"Then pretend I'm a vocate," she said, leaning forward. "Deliver me, as if I'd been called. Do they know who's coming?"

"Only reckoners know who they call—and myself and my runners, when it's them do the fetching."

"Then one more won't make a difference."

"It might."

"But I could try."

"The vocates train under stewards, and then proxies come and choose warder from reckoner, and then they meet the Nine. But it could take a long time, that way. And they'll find you out, if you can't cast."

"Then I won't tell them. I'll find a way not to cast."

He regarded her for several breaths. Then he said, "It might work. If you're very clever about it." Pity for her, an abandoned grandchild of a proxy, had won out.

"Will it land on you?"

"Spirits willing, and you don't tell the Nine . . . let's just hope not." He slapped his thighs and rose, calling for Tazzi, the poultice girl.

"You'll warn the children? You'll keep them off the roads after dark? All travelers should be warned—"

He raised a hand. "You let me worry about the roads."

"And Mellas?" she said softly, looking down at the sleeping boy. "You know he has bad dreams."

"Ai," said the man. "But he's back with Bron now."

Tazzi paused at the end of the last row of stalls. "That way's out," she said, pointing up a wood-ramped tunnel large enough to accommodate three riderless mounts abreast. It doubled back at the far end, zigzagging upward. Liath would have preferred the ramp, but the child led her to an iron circle-stair. She had to drag herself along the rail. At least it was securely mounted.

The passages up here were narrower, and their flat walls met at a low apex overhead; triangular niches had been cut in the stone every threefoot for bowls of oil, which provided a calm, buttery light. This part of the Holding must have been a later addition—or an earlier, more careful cut. Now and then people in ordinary clothes passed in silence, intent on their business.

"Do you play with the warders' children?" Liath asked.

The wheaten head cocked to the side. "They play too much. All the time."

"Don't they have chores?"

"Some. Silly ones. We have real work to do."

Liath could hear the unspoken words: *They have parents.*

"But don't you play? Jackstraws, or hideabout, or . . ."

"With each other. Not with *them.*"

Lonely children, fostered by Bron, raised in torchlight, no talent to send them home to their village triads. Why couldn't they be sent home anyway? Surely an aunt or uncle or grandparent would look after them.

She asked. The girl shrugged.

They were born here, Liath knew that much—she knew reckoners turned Headward when they came with child. The Holding was a world of its own, neither Lowland nor Highland, not Norther or Midder or Souther; its customs were like no regional customs Liath had ever heard of. Like the passages, adaptations to the needs of various ages. A hodgepodge that found its own ways to cohere into a working whole.

But why would reckoners come with child only to foist them on others? Why cast off the first freedom? Pledgings traditionally undid that casting; people pledged in order to be parents to a child. As well be partners in trade otherwise, and bed whom you would. But reckoners didn't pledge and didn't triad.

They moved deeper into the complex of tunnels.

At last Tazzi pushed through a pair of heavy drapes that covered the far side of a deep doorway. Beyond was a long, rectangular hall divided by screens into three sleeping areas, each with several stools, chests, and a mattress broad enough to sleep oxen. Thick carpets layered the walls, even the floor, muffling the whole space in the blacks and browns of the sheep the wool was sheared from. "This is where we bring them."

"Can you tell someone I'm here?"

"They'll find out." The girl looked itchy to be away. "There's baths down there, privies over there." Before Liath could ask more, she slipped out the way they'd come: deliver and return.

She longed to prowl this deserted place, but the knee buckled as she put weight on it. It had well and truly had enough. There was no longer any mortal peril, the drive to find a safe place to sleep, to reach a destination. For better or worse, she was here now. The poultice, the meal, the noontime's rest had been only easement, not healing. She had pushed herself as far as she could.

She used the privy, a closet with a raised pinewood seat over a hole that sounded of running water below. There was a row of three on one long side of the hall, and they hardly smelled at all. A small fountain tinkled in the stone beside her, filling a gourd for rinsing. The Holding must be full of ducts. She thought of the cataract, wondered where the wastewater emptied.

Somehow she washed, in a communal pool as dark and glittering as its stone basin; two others there, a man and a woman, bathed wordlessly, dried themselves, donned shapeless gray tunics off a rack, and departed through one of the several doors with barely a glance at her. She dressed in a tunic like theirs, wrung out what she'd been wearing and left it to dry, then returned to the oil-lit sleeproom. How did they bear this eternal night?

Too tired to rewrap the knee, she lay back. It made her head spin. Should she shout for someone to come? Should she go find a steward, search for proxies? Perhaps she would just nap . . . so long since a mattress had cushioned her, warmed her . . .

"In sleepclothes in the middle of the afternoon? If they've set you night meditations, you're in the wrong hall."

Liath sat up too quickly and winced. A young man held the door hangings apart. Fine brown hair framed soft dark eyes, a long nose; of slight build, he wore gray softboots, gray wool hose, and a gray velvet surcoat over a bleached linen blouse. She understood the drapes now: you could get in without disturbing anyone by opening a door that might creak or slam.

"How do you know it's afternoon?"

He chuckled and let the drapes fall together behind him. She caught the dull glint of a triskele as he unbuttoned his coat and loosened his shirt laces. "I'm Tolivar Binder. You and Karanthe should get on well. She's fond of beds herself."

"I just put on what others did, in there."

He glanced down the length of the hall, toward the baths, and shook his head. "You should have seen me, my first day. Left off here, no in-structions. I got lost straight away. We're supposed to break each other in, but that's difficult when someone wanders off into the tunnels. At least you didn't do that."

"I need a healing," she said.

He sat beside her and peered at her knee. "Yes, clearly you do. You came through the mountains, didn't you? And at some cost."

"There are shadows in the mountains."

"No doubt—being mountains and all that."

"Shadows that can kill you."

He regarded her for a moment more, head tilted, then laughed. "They tried that on me, when I first came. A fitting prank. Blindfolded me, brought me up top, told me to ask the wraiths the way back, ran away laughing before I could tear the blindfold off. Left me out half the night, the sods—I could have gone over a cliff. But you're the first newly to haul that old story up. It's supposed to be the other way around, you see. *We* scare *you*."

She sighed. "Yes, I came through the mountains. The mountains are the only way here."

"Not true. I sailed, myself." He turned his head at the light tread of boots on carpet. "Dabrena, look! Our first healing subject since Ronim's hangnail."

Dabrena was a doll-like girl with honey-brown hair cut blunt at the shoulders, and in bangs over green-flecked eyes. She was outfitted just like Tolivar. The clothes were handsome, but you didn't get velvets that perfect dove gray without some kind of dye. Reckoners wore black under their nine-colored cloaks; gray was apparently for vocates, the called ones, and Bron said it was warders she saw in white. Such colorings wouldn't undermine magecraft—the Ennead and its proxies illuminated Eiden Myr. But it felt wrong.

"It was a hangover, and we shouldn't have healed it."

"We needed the practice."

"It was a waste of good vellum. We should have *given* him a hangnail." Dabrena sat on the other side of Liath, and drew her breath in through her teeth. "Oooh, that *is* nasty. The scrapes are festering. No one's looked at it yet?"

A stablegirl had done more for her. "It's been days since it happened. It would be nice to have done with it."

"We look after our own here," Tolivar said. "That's the point. We work together, whether it's casting or cooking or cleaning. All in the same boat. So of course we'll heal you."

"Tolivar knows his way around knees," Dabrena said, reaching past Liath to poke him.

He grinned. "I'm *from* the Knee. Seafaring family. Here, let's have a look at it." He pushed the tunic up to midthigh and laid callused fingers gently on the black-and-purple flesh. Bindsmen's hands never lost their trade-roughened skin. "It's too swollen to tell if the kneecap's broken, but if you've been walking on that leg, I'd say not. Bad bruising, a sprain. Dab?"

"We need an illuminator."

"And wonder of wonders, here's one now!" Barefoot and silent on the carpets, another mage had come up behind them. She wore sleep-clothes too; she must have been a lump under blankets, or Liath would have seen her. Tall, blue-eyed, she had the high color of someone from the Neck; she looked the way Liath would have wished to, if she hadn't long ago given up wishing for beauty. Lissome, not lanky, her braided hair a lustrous auburn, no hint of freckles across her chiseled nose. Whichever part of the Heartlands she hailed from, it wouldn't be far from Clondel.

"I said we need an illuminator." Dabrena got up and craned her neck.

"Don't strain yourself, dear," the woman said, standing beside her. The difference in height was ludicrous. "No, I don't see a soul. It appears you're stuck with me."

"Go back to sleep, Karanthe. You get those ugly circles under your eyes when you don't get your nap."

"And miss the late arrival?" Karanthe turned a look of frank appraisal on Liath. "I wouldn't dream of it."

"Well, you work it out," Tolivar said brightly. He headed for the door. "I'll see the steward."

"Steward?" Liath said.

"Wynn Miser," said Dabrena.

"Wynn n'Grump l'Niggard." Karanthe lowered herself to the bed and stretched out languorously on her side. "Keeps track of the casting materials. Bofric Steward sets us our lessons. Lenn oversees the larder. They're not mages, so there's no question of playing favorites."

"Why should there be? Don't you share everything?"

Karanthe smiled sweetly at Dabrena. "We're supposed to."

Dabrena sighed and lay back next to Karanthe. "How did you fare with Jonnula?"

Karanthe flopped onto her stomach. "Oh, she'll go for a reckoner, all right, and I'll spend the rest of my life wrangling rainclouds. I don't want to talk about it."

Two girls lying in a meadow, gossiping about villagers.

"If old Knobface weren't so decrepit, you could seduce your way into black."

"Don't think I wouldn't try it. Stone's hard on the knees, though."

"Oh, yours callused over long ago. . . ."

They stared at Liath's knee, then at each other, lips pressed tight and eyes wide. Then they rolled on the huge bed, laughing too hard to speak. Liath grimaced at the jouncing and they laughed even harder. These were mages? *Holding* mages?

But when Tolivar returned they got straight to work. They rolled two carpets back—"If the steward sees the dustballs under here, he'll have us cored," Dabrena said—and Tolivar drew a white chalk circle on the sleek black stone.

Unthinking, Liath made to sit at one point of the triad. The young mages smiled, shook their heads, guided her into the center.

Tolivar handed leather-backed vellum to Dabrena. It was odd to see this tiny creature, barely into womanhood, become a wordsmith before her eyes. They were all business now, clicking into trained routine, but as Tolivar passed quill and inkpot to Dabrena, as Dabrena passed inscribed vellum to Karanthe, Liath could sense the loose connections. They had not been cast a triad, share everything though they might. An early casting, and it showed—not in individual skills, but in the integuments . . . in the bindings. They did not anticipate each other. They did not think as one. They might make a good triad, if it was desire for Tolivar that bound the women; a bindsman bound his triad as well as their castings. Perhaps they aspired to that: rivalry and camaraderie and frustration, for a lifetime. But Karanthe wanted to be a reckoner, and reckoners never triaded. . . .

She'd like to see Karanthe's work. In all her years in training, she'd come to know only Hanla's work well. How different was Karanthe's technique? How differently did her eyes see? But Liath was in front of the illuminator, not behind her. Spared serious childhood injuries, she had been the subject of a casting only once—the first freedom. Dabrena had focused on the leaf, squinting, the tip of her tongue sticking out; Karanthe examined Liath. It was completely different from the look that had eval-uated a potential adversary. Liath, reflected in the illuminator's eyes, was no longer a person, but an object: flesh and bone to be knitted back into their proper form, liquid to be drained from a swelling.

Was that how I looked at Tarny? she thought.

Perhaps not, since she had failed.

All was swept from her mind as Tolivar, accepting the illuminated manuscript from Karanthe, stripped the vellum from its backing and draped it over the injured knee. The three moved in to clasp wrists over her. She smelled sleep and soap from the illuminator, dust and tallow soot from the wordsmith, basil and hyssop from the bindsman. Mage-light ran like a current through their joining. It was muffled, separate. Not part of her. She yearned toward it, yearned to add her own to theirs. She could feel it swell, she could taste it without tasting, smell it without smelling, it surrounded her and soaked into the vellum against her flesh but she could not be *of* it, she was trapped inside herself, a blaze behind a grate. The bindsman sang, his voice husky, gentle, heart-melting in distilled compassion; her body responded to it in no relation to the healing. Her knee burned hot, then itched. An ache grew in her chest. The vellum knit itself into a wart, and when it was gone the blessed relief of physical pain was nothing against the relief of their magelight's flare subsiding. The irrelevant jolt of lust left in its wake a languor of irony.

I will be ever smashing my heart on bindsmen, she thought, *just as my failures tighten around my throat.* The healing of the joint only made a triad of the three things.

"Try it," Tolivar said, putting his hands on her again to flex the joint. "Looks good. Feels good too."

"Come," Dabrena said, helping her up. "You haven't been the subject of a healing before, have you? It's hard, the first time."

"She doesn't look well." Karanthe lifted her feet and they slid her onto the bed. Layers of wool settled on her heavily. "Do you think we did something wrong?"

"Do you think *you* did something wrong, that's what you mean," Dabrena said. "Don't be a toad, Karanthe. Can't you remember what it's like to not be part of it?"

Their voices receded down an echoing corridor. *Going to supper*, Liath thought. *Going wherever vocates go to learn whatever the Holding teaches.* If she could get out from under these covers, she might go with them. Tolivar's eyes were so lovely. . . .

"I remember," Karanthe's voice said from far away. "I was three and touched a piece of red-hot iron in a smithy. It was so beautiful, so glowing. I had to see how that light felt. I cried for days after the healing. They finally called the triad back, all the way from Elingar. Nobody could smell the magelight in me—I was too little. But it was there. Trying to reach up. Trying to see how their light felt."

Not from the Heartlands, then. Elingar was in the Belt.

But she looked so like one of ours.

The voices were gone, and the nightstone lay heavy on her, its glittering weight pressing her into depthless caverns.

She didn't know where she was, or why she was inside a windowless place thick with the scents of sleep, or why there were bodies shoved up against her. Before she could cry out, one snorted and turned over; an arm flopped across her. Whose arm?

They shared everything. Like puppies in a birthing box, all squashed together in their big beds. It didn't matter whose arm. It was warm. It was a human arm in a world of shadows. In this lightless place, someone would be there to tell her when dawn came.

She came alert into ochre light when clothes arced over the bed to land on her in a heap. It felt like waking to a midnight emergency. The bed was empty. Dabrena and Tolivar were dressing nearby; two of the chests along the wall spilled clothes, all the same grays and whites. "My extra set." Karanthe came around the nearest screen. "It should fit you."

"We're late," Tolivar said, bouncing on one foot while he pulled a boot onto the other.

Dabrena gasped, "I was supposed to get the meditations from Bofric!" She laced her shirt on the run, coat flapping open as she plunged through the draped door.

"What happens now?" Liath asked as she dressed. It was luxury past speech to move without pain, to stand on both legs. Her crutch still lay at the foot of the bed. She'd keep it, she thought; when the Ennead repaired her magelight, she'd need a walking stick for her journeying.

Tolivar gestured her gallantly toward the door. "You'll see."

They put her to work stirring rolled oats in a huge pot. There were mages of all shapes and colors, hungry people who wouldn't get fed if they didn't see to it themselves; she could not retain half the names, though a Haunchman named Corle showed her how to help and then said nothing further, and she heard Jonnula shouted out of the cookroom.

Sitting at a long dormant table, spooning oats into themselves, the gray-clad vocates complained about everything they didn't laugh at, from the sour mood of the larder steward to the extra lessons that Bofric, the training steward, had assigned.

A swarthy mage arrived late and rumpled. Taking one look at Liath, he rolled his eyes and said, "Another? How many is enough? We have newlies coming out of our ears."

"The next sleephall got that last batch," said a tawny woman—a Girdler, from the look of her. "It *is* our turn."

"I tried to wake you, Eltarion," said Jerize, a girl with velvety black skin and eyes. "You have a little problem with discipline."

"Nothing is a little problem." Ronim, who'd had the hangover. "We all have big problems. Well, everybody except Tolivar."

A mage whose face was all freckles, where you could see it past his dirty-blond hair, gestured to Karanthe and Dabrena—and Liath, who sat between them. "He has his problems too."

"We may all have a problem soon enough," said a short mage with a crooked nose, examining his spoon with great interest. "I've heard they're sending most of us back home. Don't need us."

"They called too many," said a mage who wore a perpetual scowl. "Look at us. We're crammed in here like bats in a roost. If some of us don't go for proxies soon, we'll be bedding these newlies down in the passageways."

"We'll sleep hanging by our feet!" said Tolivar. "More blood to the head, better meditations."

"Dabrena can sleep in a lampwell," said Karanthe.

"If *some* of us came when we were *called*," said a rotund mage at the nearer end, "maybe there wouldn't be so much overlap."

"If some of us ate a little less, *Selen*," Dabrena said, "maybe there'd be more *room* for the rest."

"All right, all right. I was only saying."

"But they did call too many," Jonnula said. Out of all of them, this ash-skinned, pale-haired, pale-eyed mage's name had stuck: Karanthe's rival. One of them, anyway.

"Why, do you think?" asked a quiet, clear-eyed man across the table. He was big, and held his spoon with care, as if he might inadvertently bend it.

"How does your neck hold your head up, Terrell?"

"Well, I don't know. How will I know if I don't ask? They ask us enough questions."

"Looks like we aren't answering well enough."

"Here, you're from Clondel, Liath—haven't you seen more mages passing through lately?"

"And passing back, too. With never a word about why."

"I know what it is," said a cheerful brown-haired woman with a mole on her chin. "But I shouldn't tell you."

The table erupted; some threw scones, some pounded pewter goblets. The mage crossed her arms over her face to ward off the assault, but peeked through, apparently enjoying herself. "All right! All right. It's like this." She paused for effect, savoring every breath of attention. "What they're looking for isn't proxies. What they need is a mage to groom for the Ennead."

Everyone spoke at once, but Ronim prevailed. "They won't need another triad for years now. Vonche and Naeve are the oldest, and they're what, eight nines of winter? That's hardly old. And even then they'll only need two, to triad Evonder."

"You don't just sit down and be on the Ennead. They get trained for years."

"Maybe they're looking to start now."

"They started long ago. They must have."

"Maybe Vonche and Naeve are tired."

"You don't get *tired*. You leave the Ennead when you pass."

"Unless your mind goes first."

"That hasn't happened in a long time."

"Nothing's happened in a long time. So long that none of us know what we're talking about. We shouldn't even be talking about this. Suppose they find out?"

"We're not seekers, jamhead. We don't take a vow of silence."

"Or a vow of stupidity."

Counterexamples were pointed out.

"I tell you, they'll be short one mage. It's this special wordsmith, you see. Evonder and Lerissa are of an age, yes? This mage will triad with them. They've been planning it a long time. This mage will change the whole configuration of the Ennead."

"I'd say so. What will happen to the rest of Evonder's triad, and Lerissa's? You don't break up triads to form a new one."

"They're the Ennead. They can do whatever's wisest."

"Why is it wise? Why do they need to do it at all?"

"Because they can stop the Great Storms."

There was a full breath of silence.

"What?"

"You heard me. If you knew you had the power to do something like that, wouldn't you joggle whatever you had to? Vonche and Naeve are old enough to step aside. Why shouldn't they have a rest? Other mages do, out in the world."

"That leaves an open triad. If Lerissa and Evonder triad this word-smith, what happens to Worilke and Freyn? They're not old enough to put their feet up."

"A second journeying?"

"Then they'd need a whole triad!"

"Worilke and Freyn aren't going anywhere. They'll be short an il-luminator, that's all. One mage. It's as I told you."

"And who told you, Dontra?"

Dontra looked at the ceiling and pursed her lips. A gob of porridge hit her in the cheekbone and slid down her jaw. Wiping her face, she laughed, "Oh, all right. I heard some stewards talking. How else do we ever learn anything?"

"That's what the droplet said when it hung on the eave. The next thing it said was *splat*."

"Spirits, who cares how she found out? Don't you realize what this means? One of us—an illuminator—on the Ennead!"

"It'll take a stronger magelight than any of ours," said the short one with the crooked nose.

Dabrena sat up and Karanthe stiffened. Something happened under the table, and Dabrena startled and looked at Tolivar. So did Liath. His face smoothed into innocence.

If Karanthe saw Tolivar silence Dabrena, she gave no sign of it. Her voice was tight as she said, "Liath's is strong enough."

Liath's breath caught in her throat, and she choked on it and bent over coughing.

"That must be why she was called," Terrell said in wonder.

"Don't be so fast." Jonnula looked across the table with frank suspi-cion. "What's your game, Karanthe?"

"No game," Karanthe said flatly. Liath could feel the tension in her, once the coughing subsided and Dabrena stopped thumping her on the back. "We healed her yesterday. Oh, we all smelled the magelight, as soon as we met her. But in the healing I *felt* it."

"That means nothing," Jonnula replied. "Yours is strong too."

"Magelights *can* be deceptive," Ronim mused. "Remember Dalgir? A magelight that could smother you, but only average craft."

"That was poor training. Perhaps Liath had better. What triad did you prentice with?"

"Uh," Liath said, staring at her bowl.

"Came on your own, did you? So did Jonnula, and they let her stay."

"More's the pity."

"Who was your *triad*?"

"You must have thought a lot of your own magelight."

"Shut up! I want to hear who her triad was."

"She's from Clondel. She said. That's Graefel's triad."

"Then she had good training. And I *can* smell her magelight, even between those two."

A mousy mage on the other side of Karanthe wrinkled her nose. "All I can smell is Karanthe. Don't people bathe in Elingar? You smell like the sweat of everyone you slept with."

"She bathed—her hair's still wet. That's nervous sweat. She's nervous! The mighty Karanthe!"

"Afraid this newly will show you up?"

"Don't worry, Karanthe," Jonnula said with a nasty smile. "They don't want her for a reckoner. They want her for the *Ennead*."

Liath stared at the half-eaten bowl of mush. She'd been so ravenous when she woke, all those days of hunger to make up for. Now the sludgy porridge turned her stomach. The waste angered her.

"Aren't we due at lessons?" she said.

"Yes, we are," Dabrena said significantly, rising.

"Well, they're not really lessons, not like learning to cast," said Selen.

"They're meditations," said Terrell.

"Make-believe disputes between aggrieved parties," said crooked-nose, "to see what we'd decide for them."

"Questions," said Jonnula. "Like, What would we do if a future member of the *Ennead* sat down at our breakfast table?"

"And if we want dinner, we'd better get to them."

"If I don't get dinner I'll eat one of you." Freckle-face stuck his coated tongue out. "Who made these oats—Jonnula? They taste like sedgeweave."

"Eat sedgeweave much, Garran?"

"You can help me clean up." Ronim laughed. "We'll have the pleasure of committing it all to compost, fueling and renewing the great cycle of life in Eiden Myr."

The rest went out, grumbling and joking. It was like listening to one person think out loud in many voices—with a mind that leapt from subject to subject, easily jollied past its concerns. Karanthe and Dabrena hung on Tolivar's arms. Liath followed at a distance, trying to make sense of what she had heard.

Jonnula fell back to walk with her.

"I'll see you cast, Illuminator," she said. "One way or another. I'll see this blinding magelight of yours put to the test."

The meditations were just that: questions to meditate on, while sitting on rush mats in a carpetless chamber full of braziers burning scented cakes.

After a nonned sleep breaths, the vocates began speaking. First one, then another—eyes open but not looking at each other, in a sort of trance. What is the current when there is no sea? What is the body when the spirit fails?

These were training questions out of childhood. They drew no conclusions, for none could be drawn; the questions were meant to prompt the formation of kadri, they weren't meant to be *answered*.

What is the mage when the magelight fails?

At dinner they continued gossiping about the Ennead; they described the Nine to her, but couldn't say what regions they hailed from or how they'd come to be on the Ennead. They were Eiden Myr's most precious resource, and the vocates had to prove themselves before they were granted access. They called it earning the ring—the silver ring, the proxy ring, flat-faced with a kadra engraved in it. She had touched that ring with awe, turning it on Pelkin's thick finger, watching light burnish the flattened silver but fail to penetrate the graven triangle and circles. A kadra she never learned—reserved, she supposed, for the Ennead's use.

What is a Holding when you can find no Ennead?

After dinner they had time to spend as they pleased. Dabrena showed her the larder and the scullery and introduced her to Lenn Steward and to Bofric, whose nose did look like a knob handle.

"Must have been fun, growing up in a tavern," Dabrena said as they strolled back. The vocates never left the confines of their three levels, which were laid out in triadic triangles; the newlies tried, got hopelessly lost, as Bron had said, and were hauled back, chastened, by whatever proxy found them wandering.

Liath smiled, though "fun" was not the word she would have used. "And you?"

"Cottars," Dabrena said. "In the Fingers. We sowed at sowmid time, harvested at harvestmid, worked the vineyards, sheared sheep, marled fields, whatever was necessary, and got our stipend for it. If there's backbreaking work to be done, I know how to do it."

"But you're . . ."

"So small?" Dabrena laughed. "All the more reason to be strong enough to handle a team. And," she added with a wink, "I can handle big oxen like Terrell too."

"I thought it was Tolivar you liked."

"Why only one? The freedom's on me, and this Holding is full of pretty vocates. If I go for a warder, I'll probably pledge, but what's the rush? Anyway, I like to get up Karanthe's nose."

"Is being a warder what you want?"

Dabrena sighed. "I didn't think so, when I was called. I thought I'd be perfect for a lifelong journeyer—I can turn my hand to almost anything. But I've come to see how important that is here. The warders look after all of Eiden Myr. I know how things work, not just one trade or one craft. I was harvestmaster, the season before my trial. I was a good one, the youngest we'd ever had. I'll be a good harvestmaster for Eiden Myr."

They had passed the meditation chamber, in use now by another sleep-hall, and turned in at the next doorway. Inside were spruce benches set in a circle. This was where they would play reckoner, debating hypothetical questions that might confront them in the villages they visited. *Playing Ennead*, Liath thought—as the children in Clondel did, nine of them at a time fending off storms acted out by the others, sitting in mock council to decide grave matters they could never quite specify. All children dreamed of wearing the Ennead's colored cloaks. Most grew out of it, lightless or not.

"Question," Jonnula said, after the rest of them had straggled in. She looked as if she'd just eaten a sweet. Karanthe sat beside her, and did not join Dabrena and Tolivar.

"Out with it, Jonnula," said Ronim when she'd paused too long. "I'd like to get my ring before they're casting passage on me."

Someone across from him made a suggestive gesture involving a ring and a finger. Jonnula raised her voice over the laughter: "What would we do if we found a pretender acting the mage in a village?"

"You can't *act* the mage," Garran shot back. "You'd have to cast."

"On a journeying, then," Jonnula said. "Eating people's food, drinking people's ale, but slipping away to the next town each time before a casting was required."

"Sounds like a malicious accusation to me," Dontra said, huffy. "Something someone would claim who had a grudge."

"We'd have to prove that, either way," said Selen. "Jonnula's right, it's a valid question. It might well be put to reckoners."

"Yes," said Terrell, "because a mage like that would go to villages where there was no resident triad."

"Well, of *course* he would, Terrell," said crooked-nose, a wordsmith whose name Liath still did not know. "That's where journeyers *go* half the time, because that's where they're needed."

"They go to triaded towns too," Tolivar said, "to learn."

"Half the time, I said. Did I not say half the time? Did anyone fail to hear me say—"

"It's a stupid question," Dabrena cut in. She was tucked tight between Tolivar and Liath; Liath felt muscles bunch in her thigh.

"It's been put to us. These are dialogues. We have to answer."

"So what would we do?"

"Prove the charge first! I said that six breaths ago!"

"Prove the charge. Test the mage."

"And if he fails?"

"Take back his triskele."

"Escort him home."

"Take a switch to him."

"Find out why he was doing it in the first place."

"That's obvious—to get out of doing an honest day's work."

"What kind of a life is that? What's the point in doing nothing?"

"Herne's the lazy one. Ask him."

Scowl-face scowled more deeply and grunted.

"We don't have to know the answer to that. Just what we'd do if we discovered a pretender. Is there consensus?"

"Send him home!"

"Show him the hazel!"

"We don't take *switches* to people, you dolt."

"Let him haul carcasses with the bonefolk for a summer, he'll be glad of any other work after that."

"I'm telling you, the answer is to talk to him. Find out what went twisted inside him and straighten it out."

"I go with that. That's proper reckoners' work."

"I go with it too."

"I'd say that's consensus. Give up your hazel switch, Cinn? Eltarion, give up the bonefolk?"

"Oh, all right."

"I suppose."

Jonnula got up, staring at Liath. "Question," she said, and the rest fell quiet. "What would we do if such a mage were sitting in our midst right now?"

This time the responses came all at once. "Who is it?" "Test him and find out. Proof first." "Aren't you tired of yourself yet, Jonnula?" "Stop creating trouble where there is none." "You're such a weevil." "That couldn't happen." "That one *is* a stupid question." "Send him to the stewards, have him thrown out." "Proof first!" "*Who* is it?"

"It's me, Terrell." Liath relaxed her fingers where they'd closed on the hem of her coat. She met the triumph in Jonnula's ice-colored eyes. *Eiden strike you,* she thought. *I've twice your magelight, and I'll prove it.*

"I felt it," Karanthe said softly. "You were so tired, after the healing. It shouldn't be like that. It was your light, trying to reach out, but . . . *past* something. I felt it, Liath."

"She has a light, she's wearing a triskele, she's a mage," Dabrena said. She looked to Tolivar for support, but he was frowning at Liath thoughtfully. "This is absurd!"

"Proof first," said Ronim, more quietly than before. "The accusation's made."

"A malicious accusation," Selen said. "I disregard it."

"No one cares about *you* here," Jonnula said. "*We* is what counts." She turned to Liath. "I dare you."

Liath rose from the bench. "Go to your steward. Get your materials. I'm waiting." Inside her, voices cried out, like the vocates' voices—her mind speaking all at cross purposes. *Don't be a fool! Tell them the truth!* one said. *It was an aberration, I'll be all right,* another replied. *You tried!* said the first. *That was at home. This is the Holding, steeped in magecraft. It will be different here. I will make it be different here.*

"I'll do it," Jonnula said.

"You're not a binder," Tolivar pointed out.

"Then you come with me."

Dabrena grabbed his hands. "Stop this, don't encourage her, she's a snake, we all know that."

"The accusation was made," Tolivar said, in mild mockery. "I would see it disproved."

They brought the materials, inscribed the circle.

"Give me Herne, and Annina." She did not look apology at Tolivar or Dabrena. Ruthlessly she picked the brightest of them. Without pride, without relief, she sat on the chalked line. This was where she belonged. Not in the center.

They chose a simple casting, making mist from a bowl of water. Herne scratched minimal ciphers that carried an extraordinary power. Unassuming Annina, the mousy girl, handed Liath exactly the materials she would have requested, an uncanny talent.

Herne passed her the vellum.

To the spirits with the guiders, she thought. Magecraft was a craft, and she had mastered it. A dozen years you prenticed, drawing in the dirt for season after season before ink was permitted, or pigment; chalking on tree bark, on old canvas, for seasons more before using imperfect, throwaway sedgeweave. Then one day your triad sensed some swelling in the light within you, and the mage you'd prenticed with concluded she had no more to teach you. Only then was your power unleashed in a true casting, only then would they run the risk of what you might do if you erred—only then did three days of trial begin.

And then you were a mage, and pewter shaped by magecraft was chained around your neck, and you were never not-a-mage again.

I am a mage, she thought, laying the illumined leaf by the bowl. *I will be a mage, though all the shadows rise to meet me.*

The silent air in the room was charged; sparks snapped against flesh as the binder and the wordsmith took her hands. Liath closed her eyes. Annina's song was ornamented, but not like Keiler's, and fluid, but not like Tolivar's; she modulated with her throat instead of her mouth, an eerie ululation, like water singing.

The song ran off in rivulets, and ceased.

The leaf lay where she had put it, beside the bowl of liquid.

"It was true," Selen whispered. "Illuminator . . . I'm so sorry."

"What *is* it?" asked Dontra.

"I don't know." Liath got up. Her voice had no tone. "I can't . . ."

No one spoke. They waited, staring at her with every expression from disgust through discomfort to amusement. They were all her age. All poised on their journeying, but called here, instead. Mages, but untried, untriaded; mages only in name.

"I can't cast," she said. "There's something wrong with me. That's why I came here."

Two breaths passed. Then the questions peppered her: "When did you find out?" "How did you pass your trial?" "*Did* you pass your trial?" "Why are you still wearing a triskele?" Before she could answer, they answered themselves: "She found out by failing, of course." "She wore her triskele to get in here, to trick us." "Why didn't she tell us right away?" "She was hiding it, if we hadn't asked her she'd never have admitted it." "If she's crippled, she's crippled." "I've never heard of such a thing." "But I can smell her magelight!" "Magelights don't just stop working." "It's absurd." "It's a lie." "She's only trying to get attention." "Nobody would do that." "You poor thing . . ."

Dabrena regarded her with profound pity. In the midst of all the crosstalk, her quiet words surfaced. "That's why it was so hard on you. The healing."

Liath looked helplessly at the tiny young woman who had come closest, so far, to being her friend. *I'm sorry,* her look said, and Dabrena shook her head firmly, opened her mouth—

"Come with me, please."

It was a new voice. Liath looked up to see a man in ordinary clothes. Jonnula stood behind him in the doorway.

"He'll be sympathetic," Tolivar murmured. "Wynn's all right."

Silently, Liath followed the steward. She barely felt the brush of Dabrena's hand. Jonnula stepped aside with a mocking bow, savoring the downfall she'd seasoned and stirred.

"If you failed your trial, you have the choice of trying again with another triad, or resigning yourself to continuing in your family's trade," Wynn Steward told her. He was a hard-looking man, all bone and angle. His chamber felt spare, despite being filled with tall cedar lockers, piles of vellum and sedgeweave, shelves of bottled ink and cakes of pigment, boxes of reeds and quills. He played with the catch on a locker, avoiding her eyes. "The failures come from time to time, looking for something to do with a magelight that can't work castings. There is no accommodation for them here. The Holding is a place for mages."

"I passed my trial. Something went wrong. *After* the trial."

"Then your trial did not last as long as it should have."

"Three days! As they all do!"

"Your trial did not adequately try you. It did not ferret out this flaw in your magelight. Therefore it did not last long enough." He opened the locker and rummaged within for some item he probably did not need; he didn't find it.

Liath hissed in exasperation. "Rules are rules. A trial is a trial. I passed mine. Then something happened. The Ennead can't choose whether or not to help me if I can't ask them!"

"I won't have you wasting their time."

"Is saving a mage a waste of time? A dozen years of training will be wasted if you put me off."

"Contrary to what you may believe, the Ennead does not exist to be an appeal of last resort to aspiring mages."

"I'm not aspiring," Liath said through gritted teeth.

"There is nothing wrong with your magelight. It is merely inadequate—or you are."

"You're not a mage. You can be no judge of that."

"Ah, the old cry. 'If you were a mage, you'd understand!' You come under my purview precisely because I am not a mage, and cannot be swayed by emotional appeals to solidarity. My duty is to the Ennead. I provide them with the best new proxies. I weed out the false claims. And the hubris."

Liath's jaw was cocked, her fists clenched. She had gone about this all wrong. This man purported to serve logic and duty, but he required humble pliancy. She took a deep breath and relaxed her stance. "I beg you," she said.

He snorted and slammed the locker shut. "You failed, and you seek to avoid the consequences. Go home. Prentice again in some other town, with better masters. Or settle down, pledge a pretty boy, and spin threads or whatever it is your people do."

He didn't care what her people did, only that it wasn't magecraft. The cut bit deep. "You'd be hard put to run a tavern fine as the Petrel's Rest in Clondel, and Graefel's triad would cast rings around you. But I forget. You're not a mage."

"Graefel n'Traeyen?" he said, frowning. "I knew his illuminator. Hanla n'Geior. Long ago. . . . Did they ever pledge?"

Liath let the corner of her mouth pull up. So quick, so easy, to see into this man's heart. "And have two sons to show for it, as handsome as their father."

He closed his eyes. "I still cannot help you."

"Nor would I let you if you could." She left him with the lie, and called her petty cruelty an honest answer.

Tolivar awaited her around the turn, pacing.

"Your steward wasn't sympathetic."

He frowned, perplexed. Poor Tolivar. The steward *should* have been sympathetic. He probably tied the steward in sailor's knots with a wave of his hand. But Tolivar was a vocate, and things were not always as they should be.

She tugged at the tight lacings at her neck. She'd tried to look presentable, but Wynn hadn't liked her wearing vocate's gray. "He's tossed me out."

"Only if you leave. You belong here."

He had forgotten that she had come on her own. He was quick, articulate. It obscured an odd quirk: that when he got it into his head that something was one way, it took a while for him to accept that it was another. "I wasn't *called*, Tolivar. I was supposed to go journeying."

"Reckoners are journeyers. You'd have that choice. Karanthe's a lifelong journeyer. She'll be a reckoner if it kills her."

"But she was called."

"Well, yes. The reckoners got one whiff of her magelight and sent her Headward straight away."

The Ennead calls whom they will. And thus far they have not called you.

"I wasn't called," she said again. Testing it in her mouth. She had not wanted to be called. She had avoided reckoners—their black velvet, their colored cloaks, their mirthless faces. They passed through Clondel but never stayed. Was it hubris, to hide herself? Was it an insult that they had not somehow found her anyway? She could have been one of these mages. She could have made Jonnula and Karanthe compete for *second* place.

But Pelkin had told her not to. Come back for Breida's birth—Breida, born nine moons after Liath had prenticed with Hanla—he had been banished forever by Geara, told never to return to the home he had abandoned, never again to see the granddaughter named for his pledgemate, who'd died of a broken heart.

The infant reached out to him from across the room, as if she could see him. "Her name is Breida," Geara said. "And she will never love you."

Liath ran after him, out into the summer night, away from the baby's wails and her mother's staunch, dry face.

"I've been prenticed," she told him. "I showed a light since you were here before. Hanla is my teacher."

"Yes," he replied. "I can taste your magelight." He knelt in front of her. "You'll be an illuminator, spirits willing." She nodded gravely, sensing that he would tell her something wise, something important. "Liath, you must make me a promise."

She hesitated. "What?"

He laughed heartily. "Ah, you are your mother's child, and your granny's too, Liath Publican! Never agree to a trade until it's clear. Good on you, pet." Then he sobered. "What I ask of you is this: Whenever mages come dressed as I am dressed, wearing rings like this one, I want you to hide from them."

"Why?" she asked.

He pulled her flame-colored braids around in front of her and tugged on them.

"Because your light is very bright, my little love. Brighter than mine by ninefold. The other mages like me are in the business of finding little girls like you and . . . Spirits, I see I've frightened you. There's nothing to fear. No reckoner will harm you, triskeled or no. But if they see you, and smell you, they'll mark you, and someday they'll come back, when you're grown, and ask you to go with them. And then you'd have to leave your mother forever."

Tears came to her eyes. "Like you left Granny Breida?"

"Yes," he said softly. "Exactly like that. So you stay away from them, eh? Don't break your mother's heart again. Do you understand what I'm asking and why?"

She nodded. She was crying.

"Do you agree?"

She closed her eyes and nodded again.

"Open your eyes, then." He spat into his hand and stuck it out. Watching him to confirm that it was what he meant her to do, she spat awkwardly into her own palm. He slapped his hand against hers and clasped firm. "A pledge of flesh and humors," he said. "Those are all I can bequeath you in the end, child of my child."

And he kissed her on the head, and slipped away into the shadows, and she couldn't see him in his black tunic and hose, though she thought she could still catch a ripple of the colored cloak flung over his arm. She turned and went back into the spill of light through the tavern door. . . .

"I'm just a mage," she said. "I was proud at my trial, I admit it. I was proud to make Graefel's triad proud. But the rest . . . it has nothing to do with me."

"I don't think it's your choice," Tolivar said quietly. Liath startled; for a moment she had thought she was still talking to Pelkin, through the years. "You haven't gotten a whiff of your own magelight. Didn't you hear what they were saying, before? They practically had you on the Ennead. It's *that* strong, Liath. You're a catch. They can't toss back something like you."

He had not forgotten that she wasn't called. He was seeing things as they should be.

"Thank you, Tolivar," she said. "But I have to go." Into the tunnels. Not back to Bron, but down. Bron had said down, they'd catch her before she was halfway down. *Proof first,* she thought. She would put that claim to the test.

Tolivar looked down the passageway. "We can't talk here."

"There's nothing to talk about"—but he had looped his arm through hers, was drawing her toward the stairwell. *Find out what went twisted inside him and straighten it out:* Tolivar was the one who made them agree to that. He was playing reckoner now. But she could still hear his bindsong in the back of her mind, the sweet compassion, the bitter sympathy.

She went with him.

He ushered her down the steps that Wynn had led her up, then down yet another level. Good. Down was where she'd be going.

"This is all storage down here, larders and so on—we had to ward them once against rot. But we grow things too . . . here, here it is, see for yourself."

He opened a door on an unlit chamber. A loamy, fungal smell came from within.

"Go in," he said. "Trust me."

She took a step inside, then another. Her eyes were slow adapting to the darkness. Long streaks of dim light seemed to hang in the black space. It wasn't torchglare. She took another step in. Veins of rock, in the walls. Glowing.

"What is it?" she breathed.

Tolivar came in and latched the door behind him. The glow increased, a silvery light like moonlight, like reflections off the bits of quartz or mica in the nightstone, but not reflection—internal light. It was enough now to illuminate the chamber, which was filled with long, raised gardener's beds, each at least two threfts wide, planted with some kind of white heather. Frilly and thick, it took on an unearthly cast in the weird glow.

"Isn't it beautiful? It's mushroom heather. Not much taste, but we could live on it, if something cut us off. Dabrena tends it; she misses her toft at home. She comes here when she needs to be alone and think. I prefer to get out and smell the sea, myself."

White heather, planted in darkness, thriving on soil and damp alone. It was a wonder, but not the wonder she had meant.

"The *walls*, Tolivar. What *is* that?"

"Oh! This is the first time you've seen it? The veins run all through the mountain, though more down below than up here, I'm told. It's magestone. Vocates are brought in through a huge archway of it. Only magelight makes it glow. Impresses the new arrivals, proves we're meant to be here."

"It glowed for me," she said.

"Of course." He sat down on the wooden side of one of the planters. "Now, listen. There are nonneds of mages here. We have to take care of ourselves, be resourceful. That means we do work under stewards' super-vision, instead of the stewards doing it for us. But sometimes it means we do things without the stewards knowing, or against their wishes. Our duty is to each other. That's what being a vocate is—that's what being a proxy is. Away from the Ennead, spread across the land, reckoners can't go running to them about everything. We're trained to sort problems out among ourselves."

Another person spouting rote words. She was disappointed in him. Then he said, "I think that might include you."

"How do you mean?" she asked cautiously. But she sat down be-side him.

"You should have told us yesterday. We'd have helped you." He meant himself, Dabrena, Karanthe. For all his talk of duty, he was most loyal to his friends. "We'll still help you. We'll all help you. That's how it is here."

"You can't. Jonnula won't."

"Jonnula can go to the sharks. We'll heal you. Or we'll hide you till we know how."

"Why, Tolivar? I'm no one."

"I like you. I'd like you to stay. We could be friends. Maybe even a triad, who knows? Karanthe will sail off on the first breeze she gets. That leaves Dabrena and me for warders, yes? Dabrena will settle down in a few seasons. As warders, we'll triad. We'll need an illuminator."

He was older than any of them. It came to her slowly, as she studied him away from the others. He had a youthful face, a boyish way, but there were years behind it, if you looked.

Was that what drew those two? "You don't want either of them, do you," she said. Then, guessing: "The magelight came late . . ."

He shook his head. "No, it came right on schedule. My sixth summer, there I was, trying to sing wind into the sail of my little boat on a calm day. I fostered winters with a triad in Glydh, when the sea was too harsh for children. The same as spending middays in training year-round. I was called five years ago. I just didn't go."

No one declined a summons from the Holding.

"A woman?" she guessed.

He shook his head. "No. That's not my way."

"But Dabrena . . . Karanthe . . ."

"I care for them both, Liath. Karanthe dallies, and Dabrena's a child, but they're my friends and I stick by them."

"They both want you."

"Well. They're very pretty. It's a kind of control they like to exert. I don't mind it. And I'm . . . fond of Dabrena."

"Do you not like girls?"

"Girls, boys . . . oh, Liath, the body's such a wonderful thing, but you see—what I love is the craft. When I sing . . ." He looked down into the heather, blushing, but continued evenly, "When I sing, I make love with the spirits. Binding, joining in a triad, joining with flesh and vellum and magelights and spirits . . . it's the only true pledging for me."

"Then why didn't you come when you were called?"

"And spend my life inside a rock? I was raised a sailor." He smiled. "Well, that was how I saw it then. Now I know that it's the winds and the waters *inside* that matter—inside this place, and inside me. I journeyed, I plied my craft under the sky and the stars, but it was never enough. There is such power here, such . . . ecstasy. In the end, I had to come. I just went round the far point."

"I don't know where I'm going," Liath said softly.

"Back with me, I hope. To supper. I'm starving." When she only quirked her mouth, he said, "Liath, you don't have to know. We'll get you healed somehow. We'll get you to the Ennead. See what they say, when they get that whiff of your extraordinary light." He chuckled. "Maybe you'll go for a proxy before Karanthe, and drive her spare. Then you can find boys like me and talk sense into them. Maybe you'll go for the Ennead itself . . ."

His bindsong twined through the back of her mind. He wove dreams in her ear, all the ways things *should* work out. The magestone poured light on his silken hair, softened the mischief in his eyes. He smiled until she smiled too; then he pressed his smile to hers, or she to his, she would never be sure. She drank in sweetness without promises. Ecstasy and power . . .

He eased her back into the springy heather, magegrown heather pale as moonbeams, and parted surcoat and shirt to cup her breast, bring his dry lips down to it. Her hands sought laces without fumbling, slipped the loops. The remembered languor of his healing song made her movements slow, unhurried. The soft hose slid down, and she stroked him before guiding him into her. He moved only a little, watching her to be sure, one strong arm supporting her back, the other hand cupping her head. "That's it," he said, voice hoarse, when she arched against him, and doubled unsurpassable bliss with a flood of warmth. In his mouth her short name made the sound of a song.

"Another first?" he said, after he'd produced a handcloth and wiped the residue from her and they'd fastened each other's clothes. She sat in the circle of his arm, head against his neck, just resting. Not thinking of the layers of stone that lay between her and the Ennead's chambers.

"There was a journeyer," she said. "At home. He gave me that kind of pleasure with a touch, a kiss. But they hadn't yet cast the first freedom on me. I'd never seemed interested in boys." Only the one who was a second brother, the boy no parent could have guessed. "And in the morning he was gone."

"Such is the way of journeyers. Did he teach you to respond in kind, at least, before he went?"

She kissed the corner of his wicked grin and drew away. "He didn't have to. Mages learn by example."

"Then I've learned a sweet thing from you today."

It startled her to remember it was day.

"Come back with me," he urged.

She sat up. "We did that because you want me to stay?"

"I don't know about you, but I did it because I wanted to. Your light . . ." He smiled. "How could I not crave you? I wanted to do that, I want you to stay. They stem from the same source."

"You can't hide me. Your lives are wide open here."

"Let us try to heal you. We never finished the dialogue, Liath. Jonnula betrayed you to Wynn before we had the chance. Come back with me, and let us try. They'll surprise you."

And the steward was going to be sympathetic, she thought.

But she went with him.

The vocates looked up from their supper in amazement.

"I see you've heard Wynn's thrown her over the side," Tolivar said.

Liath stood by the door, ready to bolt, humiliation washing over her afresh. She didn't belong here. Spirits take them all.

Dabrena took one look at them and said, "Oh, Tolivar, you didn't." Before Liath could stammer apology, she began to laugh. "He's a moth to a flame!"

Karanthe smiled. "I'm glad you came back. I never meant for that to happen. I hoped we could heal you." She was not sitting with Jonnula now.

"Your little fugitive is safe here for now," Dontra said with a chuckle.

"She should have been called," Tolivar said. "Something went wrong. This is all wrong. It's down to us to patch it."

"We can't keep her hidden from the stewards."

"Then let's find a better way."

"The better way is for her to leave, as she was told."

"We worked hard to get this far."

"We can't break the rules for her. Rules are for a reason. If the steward felt she should go, she should go."

Dabrena uncurled herself and came to stand by Liath's side. "If she goes, I go with her."

"Don't do this," Liath said. "They're right. I'll go."

"And I'll go with you," Garran said.

"I'll go too." Eltarion.

"And I." Selen.

"And I." Ronim.

"And I." Karanthe.

"No." It was Jonnula, rising. As if the taste of her own words was a strange enlightenment, she said, "We stick together."

"*Jonnula?* Are you well?"

She ignored the gibe, but her tone dripped honeyed venom. "Let's try to heal the poor ailing wretch. Why not? Why not do what Dabrena wants, simply because she wants it?"

Dabrena held her tongue—she was getting her way—but she watched Jonnula with narrowed eyes.

The mage made a show of tying her pale hair back, as if rolling up her sleeves. "Someone get the casting box."

"Jonnula!" Dontra shot her a withering look. "She's a newly!"

"She's not a newly," said the tawny woman. "She's not a *vocate*."

"Tolivar had it last," Karanthe said.

He nodded. "I'll fetch it."

He'd never gone to Wynn Steward that afternoon, or the day before. They'd used hoarded materials, probably stashed piece by piece in pockets, down shirts, over ninedays. Of course. There were castings they didn't want the stewards to know about.

Ronim, Eltarion, Terrell, and Jerize were already struggling with the heavy table, pushing it out of the way.

"We could do more harm than good," said Herne.

With the same expression of savoring a strange new flavor, Jonnula said, "Splitting up would do more harm than anything."

"Should I stand watch?" Garran asked her.

"That's all right. Nothing we can do about it if they come."

Tolivar returned through the cookroom, bearing the box Liath had barely noticed the day before. He had to tilt it to get it through the door, but it didn't look heavy. "Who's binder, then?" he asked, looking for someone to hand the box to.

"You," said Jonnula. "With Dabrena and Karanthe. You healed her before."

It was a different room, a different day, but the same three mages, the same awkwardness for her in sitting in the center. She hadn't asked these people to save her. She'd been no particular friend to them. At least one of them despised her. Yet they would risk all for her—break rules in this place where rules were everything. Their group mind had decided, despite its doubts, to back her. It put a debt on her that she could not discharge.

But she sat, and let them try, and tried not to hope too hard. Of course they failed. Dabrena's spirit burning into the page before her; Karanthe's eyes drilling into Liath, as if there were some hope of glimpsing her ailment's essence; Tolivar's husky voice breaking into exquisite surf on the rocky walls—none of it was sufficient. Of course others tried. By consensus now, they chose the brightest: Herne Wordsmith; Jonnula Illuminator, reeking of magelight; Annina Binder, whose voice filled every scratch in the stone. But there was nothing broken for them to fix. There was nothing trapped for them to loose. Her magelight burned bright as ever. It had simply ceased to serve *her*.

"Enough," she said when the rest had tried, when the casting box was nearly drained, when the mismatched hodgepodge of mages called from every limb of Eiden Myr had made triads of themselves and failed, and failed, and failed.

They were strong. But they were not the Ennead.

"Yes, it is quite enough." A moment overlaid on a moment, a voice overlaid on a voice. "You have earned your rings."

He stood in the main entryway, where Garran had not kept watch.

"Wynn Steward—we were just—"

"I know what you were doing, Karanthe. I watched it from beyond the door."

In the shadows. They had risen after all.

"Old Knobface was with me, but he's gone off to make the arrangements."

The vocates were stunned silent. Liath did not turn. Where was Jonnula's leadership now?

"You're supposed to say, 'Arrangements? What arrangements?' " She could hear the thin smile in his voice. "Come now, Terrell. Do me this last pleasure."

"What arrangements?"

"For your new chambers. You'll have to move your own trunks to the middle levels, of course, but that will burn off all the excitement. Close your mouth, Dabrena, that expression ill becomes you. You've *earned the ring*."

"All of us?" It was crooked-nose's voice. His name was Loris. Not that it mattered now.

"Yes. You had only to think as one, to resist fragmenting under stress. They wouldn't have called you if you hadn't the power. Oh, the meditations and dialogues are important—so they tell me—but the real training was when you cooked, cleaned, slept. All together. Until you could work as one."

"But we failed." Though Jonnula affected puzzlement, Liath caught the undertone: she was only prompting, only making sure. She had known. She had deduced that the way to what she wanted lay in rallying the rest of them. Now she would get it.

"The castings were of no matter. What ails this girl cannot be healed. You succeeded as you were meant to. Mages aren't made into proxies; they make proxies of each other. All that remains now is detail—learning to cast a triad, choosing who will ward and who will reckon. A day's work, and not my concern."

"But . . . teachers were supposed to come, proxies, to—"

"We only led you to believe that. Proxies have no time to mind vocates."

Terrell was looking from Ronim to Dontra and back. "But it was the Ennead we were competing for . . . that's what you . . ."

"Hush, Terrell. It was a rumor, nothing more." "Forget about it. We weren't competing after all. That was the trick. We did it!" "But they were going to send us home." "They can't need this many proxies." "Maybe they just need warders." "But I want to go for a reckoner. So does Karanthe." "Well, when they *do* need reckoners, they'll turn to us, won't they, the newest proxies?"

Wynn did not answer them, and Liath did not say, *You're doing it again. You're all doing it. You're seeing it the way you want to. You're filling in the words for them, and someday they'll say other words, and you'll stand gaping while your dreams sift through the sieve and away.*

At the other end of the hall, the older steward's bearded face appeared in the door that led through the baths, back to the sleeproom. His gaze caught on Liath, his brow furrowed; then his eyes slid away as if she were a chair left out of place.

"Ah, Bofric," Wynn said. "I believe they're ready now."

"Well, come along then," he said irritably.

"We earned the ring!" The repeated phrase grew into a shout. They cheered, laughed, hugged each other; Terrell whirled Selen in a dance that took them down the length of the long hall. Karanthe and Jonnula walked past together. Liath rose, that she would not impede their passage. She turned, locking eyes with Wynn.

"I was fond of Hanla," he said quietly to her. "I did her the favor of letting her prentice leave here with dignity. You failed me as you failed her."

Two mages dressed in pure white came to stand just inside the doorway. Surprised sounds from behind her made her turn; another had entered past Bofric.

"No!" said Tolivar. Karanthe held him back.

Dabrena slipped past. "You can't do this," she said. "We're not vocates anymore. We chose to help her. That choice stands. We're the equal of warders and we're higher than stewards."

Wynn smiled down at the petite girl. "Not until those rings are on your fingers. You're still in gray, girl."

"You're not a mage, Wynn Steward, and you never were," Dabrena said, standing her ground. "I'm wearing color."

"That can still change," he said mildly.

"Leave it, Dabrena." Liath looked up at Tolivar, including him, and smiled to smooth the agonized frustration from his boyish features. "Rules are rules," she said, and turned to Wynn, cocking her chin, lifting her brows, opening her hands. "Eh?"

The warders surrounded her and headed for the corridor opposite the inner door that would take the vocates back to collect their belongings, move on to the next stage of their lives.

"We'll bring you back!" Tolivar called after her.

Liath did not turn again.

"Go to Crown!" Dabrena's voice receded as she joined the others. "Stay there! We'll find you!"

The door at the other end of the hall closed firmly.

"She has a strong magelight," one of the warders said to Wynn.

"She claims it does not work," Wynn said dryly.

"I've never heard of that," said another warder. He stopped, and the others did too. "Explain, please," he said to Liath.

She did, watching them carefully, answering their questions honestly. "I came hoping the Ennead could heal me."

The warders looked at each other. "This smacks of petition," one said. "Yes," another answered. "And that business of the shadows is a joke in poor taste." "Though it's petition, still she may have cause," said the third.

"I'd say not," said the first. "It's not a matter for healing. She is blocked. She must find her own way past it." The second said, "If we bring this to the Ennead, then every mage with a weak light will come traipsing up here looking to have it bettered." "And if the Ennead can better them? Doesn't that serve all Eiden Myr, as they were meant to? We protect them too much, I think." "And leave too much power in the hands of the reckoners." "This is not a moment for debating internal reforms." "True. What shall we do then?"

Triads were not meant to think as one. Triads were sturdy stools that stood on three separate, individual legs. Always a third to break a dead-lock. Always a third to mend a falling-out. These warders were three, but not a triad. Only part of a greater whole. Too easily distracted by their own thoughts.

Every motion has a consequence, she thought. The world was a peaceful place. Yet Lowlanders carried barbed knives, and drunken fools impaled themselves on them, and shadows came in defiance of them, and came, and came. Some motion was too fast to be seen. Some motion was too unexpected to be prevented.

"She must go," a warder was saying. One was short, one tall, one dark, one female, one thickset, one plain; in their snowy velvet and hose they were all the same person.

"As I said," the testy steward agreed, "two ninebreaths past."

"She must go on her journeying," the warders continued, "and seek the crack in whatever has encased her magelight. It cannot be broken from without. It is as a shell, and the chick must peck through from within. She must try this before the Ennead will receive her. Only when all else has failed—"

Liath drove for the gap.

Two of them stood closer to each other than to the third, who stood closer to Wynn Steward. In speaking of encasement, they had not encased *her*. Mages were obedient to custom, tradition. She was meant to stand quietly and await their judgment.

Well, she thought as she launched her rangy body past them, giving just enough shove to knock them off balance, *I did*.

Surprise cost them strides, and she had enough head start to pull off one boot, and then the other, hopping as she ran. The steward stood shouting after the warders. There was a junction chamber at the far end of the passage; they would catch her there as she wrestled with doors. The nearer stair was stone. She slipped through the triangular opening and onto the landing. One flight went up, one down. Silent on stocking feet, she went down. Her eyes adjusted to the dim glow of oil lamps. Above her she could hear their single voice split: two up, one down.

The light increased as she descended, brightened in streaks along the curving wall. Magestone. It would lead them to her, she thought, they could follow its fading glow wherever she went. But no—they were mages too, it would glow for them.

She passed the next landing and slipped, her feet numbed by cold rock. Landed flatfooted on the next step. Caught her balance back from the air and continued down, gauging her lead by the quick tap of the warder's boots behind her. He called for her to stop, they meant her no harm, she must wait, they would talk.

They would talk, and she would listen. No. She had had enough of their whole-cloth truths. She could not batter down the walls of protection surrounding the Ennead. But she could burrow through those walls. Magecraft had carved the tunnels for her.

At the next landing she slipped back into the glow of corridor, ran hard until she found another stairwell, ran down that. The warder had stopped calling to her, but his bootsteps still followed. She went down another level, caught a glimpse of white velvet in the passageway there, went down again, and again. This time she pulled her boots on, emerged into the corridor. Two women at the far end wore ordinary clothes; they questioned her with no more than a look as she passed and went down again. On the level after that an elderly, black-garbed proxy called her vocate, asked her business, clearly expected a lie. Proxies hauled lost vocates back. She backpedaled, but this one was ready. He caught her arm in an iron-banded grip.

Where was the warder? Paused somewhere above, she hoped, asking others if they'd seen an errant vocate.

"Wynn Steward told me this would happen," she said in peeved tones. She had never been a facile liar, not like Keiler or Ferlin when they were caught where they shouldn't be. Yet she found herself saying, "He *told* me if I didn't change clothes I'd have trouble in the upper passages."

The reckoner was impatient to be somewhere else, but unwilling to believe her. "Who are you?"

"We've just earned the ring, we brought our things down, but I'd left a trinket under the mattress, and—"

"You're nowhere near the proxy chambers," he said. "Why don't we try the truth?"

All right.

"I'm running away from warders. They want to throw me out because I wasn't called. I came on my own because my magelight's"—not *blocked, that was their creation*—"ailing, something went wrong after I passed my trial. I thought the Ennead might help. I came through the mountains. I was attacked by shadows. They're real. Somebody has to do something." She drew breath for the despised plea, and calculated the leverage required to break his grip. "I need to see the Ennead."

"How did you get into the Holding?"

A strange question, after what she'd just told him.

"I might put someone in it if I told you."

He smiled. She blinked; it had the charm of Mellas's smile, the wickedness of Tolivar's. "I see," he said. He released her arm. "That's quite a trinket, to leave under a mattress. I suggest you see to it."

It took her a moment to comprehend that he'd let her go. Only when she was two levels away did she think to wonder why.

Perhaps he was just amused by whopping lies.

She followed the shadows: the places where the torchman had been negligent. She kept to the older tunnels, looking for light that flickered, sniffing out pitch. The levels widened as she descended. Rounding a curve in a tunnel where every fifth or sixth torch had burned out, she came not to a stair, as she expected, but to a blank wall. Doubling back, she passed what she thought was the stair she'd come out of, then passed another just like it, and a third, and still no way down. She split the difference and went up the middle stair, but footsteps somewhere ahead sent her back down, and up one of the others. From that level, the only other downward stair curved and descended gradually, a long lateral move out of her vertical orientation.

Down was down. There would be connections, somewhere, in the lower levels. She would sniff out the Ennead as she'd sniffed out the torches.

It grew difficult to ignore the weight of stone. One shudder of earthquake and these tunnels would be crushed like the hollow shafts of quills. Nausea rose in her as it had in the stables. She'd eaten little at dinner, and there was no telling how much time had passed since then. Somewhere outside was air, light, space. But they would do her no good if she could not reach them. There were no doors now, no chambers—no fountains, no larders. Without food and water she would grow too weak and confused to find her way back if she gave up.

It was already too late to find her way back. She came to another dead end, went up two levels and down another stair, and met still another blank wall. The passages curved around, curved back, curved down, sometimes curved up again; she ended up in a corridor she was sure she'd passed through before. Going up again—up was up, somewhere above her was a place she could start from again—she found herself in darkness, no lingering scent of pitch. The stair had not been lit, and the glow from the corridor below had not followed her up the spiral.

She felt her way back along the wall, and could not find the stairwell.

It had to be there. She was not so faint or fatigued that she would miss it. The tunnel had curved; she had come out on the inside of the curve and felt her way back along the inside wall. Yet surely she had passed where it had been.

She turned back, counting steps. At two nines she turned again, and went twice that many steps. Still there was no opening in the wall. The darkness was total. Phantom torch flames danced across her eyes, but they were only memories of light. Here there was no light. She could not find her way back.

She stopped, collected herself, willed her heart to slow. Somewhere there was a stair, up or down. Something in the air suggested space, or distance. A long tunnel. How long? How far before there was egress? She could be here all night.

Here, it was always night.

A few steps farther and she paused again, keeping her hand on the chill stone, as though she might fly loose into darkness. She reviewed every step she had taken. It was possible to reason this out. Once she got back into the light, she would take a torch, carry it with her, never mind if it drew attention.

Eiden's spleen, why were there no doors? What point in passages that led to nothing? And where was all their bloody magestone now?

In the silence, she thought she heard words.

She moved toward the sound. Voices—proxies or stewards, it didn't matter. They were far away, barely audible. As she approached, she re-alized they weren't distant; they were whispering. Behind a door, per-haps. A little farther and she'd be able to tell. She groped along the wall, took baby steps, irrationally afraid that some chasm would yawn open at her feet.

Her foot fell on empty air. She shifted backward just in time, before she had her weight on it. The whispers rose abruptly in pitch. A breeze caressed her face, then died away. The whispers subsided.

A hole. A ventilation hole. But she had come so far down into the mountain . . .

It was not wind whispering in the crevices. The chasm breathed. Every exhalation carried the echoes of voices. Every inhalation swallowed them again. A rise and fall of conversations from below, or conversations that never were. In the darkness, she might have been listening to the deepest thoughts of the mountain.

The rise and fall of whispers called to her from the abyss. It had the cadence of Mellas's dream language; it was the snatches of muttered words heard just at the edge of sleep. It contained all knowledge and all sadness, all memory and wisdom. It blew across her mind like a dry, dusty wind.

She turned from the precipice, with deliberate care, and retraced the last few steps, clinging to stone that afforded no handhold. This accounted for the sense of space. She'd found one end of this benighted corridor. Now she'd go find the other.

A low wheedling raised the hairs on the backs of her arms.

Spirits shield me, the shadows are here too.

In darkness, shadows were invisible. Black lay on her eyes like velvet. Her fingernails bent against rock. The strange crooning echoed on stone. Where was it coming from?

Ahead of her. She backed up a step. Nowhere to go.

When the sound stopped, it was worse.

Now it could be anywhere.

A whine crept up the back of her throat. She stood very still. She breathed shallowly, tried not to breathe at all. Time passed in breaths. Movement occurred in time. Stop the breaths, perhaps the movement would stop.

"Ooooh, you smell *delicious!*"

The voice came from directly behind her right ear.

She flattened herself against the wall.

"I could smell you from two levels away. Deathfires and incense and boiled blood. You smell of love, and lavender." The voice floated through the black air until it hovered in front of her face. "Oh, come closer. Let me smell the world."

Liath squeezed away along the wall, questing with her toe. Where was the drop? How far? Was there a lip around it?

"No no no. Oh, no. No fleeing, no falling. Consigned to wind and whispers—no, Portriel will not have that."

Flesh closed on her hand and she bit her lip to stifle a shriek. Haunts were said to feign flesh at times, to lure folk to their doom. The hand on her hand drew her forward. She resisted; it yielded. It was an old hand, bony, callused. Fragile.

"Who are you?" she whispered, and wondered if it seemed the whisper came from the abyss.

"Portriel! Silly old fool. Why must you bring her up? Come *along*. It's a long way down to the heart of the world. When you fall, you fall forever."

The voice didn't want her to go over the edge. Fingers plucked at the back of her hand, brushed her knuckles. If this was escape, she would take it. She turned her hand and closed it around the fingers. They twisted, and pulled her after them.

Now there was no crabbing along the wall to find the way. Ahead of her was a rustle of fabric, the soft padding of bare feet; it was like following a whisper. Except for the firm, even stone her boots trod, she might be gliding through a black lake. Currents of air brushed her face. Without sight, all sensation was intensified. Any moment her foot might come down on nothingness again; she didn't know who led her, didn't know where she was being led. She was mad to follow the mad. But the breath of stone receded behind her; the mountain whispered only to itself. Her mind began to clear.

"Portriel?" she ventured.

"Poor 'Triel," the voice agreed. "Poor, poor 'Triel."

It led her to chambers as dark as the passage. They were filled with pillows, thickly layered with carpet.

"Nothing to break here," Portriel said, as if it delighted her. "All the breakables have already been broken! Move as you will, fear no harm. Worst you can do is stumble. Fall on your face! The stone will catch you. Here there is no forever."

Liath sat for some time with the old woman, sharing her invisible wine, listening to her soothing nonsense. But at last she said, "How do I get back to where I came from?"

"How do I know where you came from?"

"The parts of the Holding where there's light, where people are."

"There are people here. There is light here. You are a beacon in the dark." She sniffed. "A smelly beacon."

"I mean where the other mages are. The proxies. The Ennead."

"It's the Ennead you're looking for, is it?" The words were so lucid, so quietly serious, that Liath thought there was someone else in the chamber. But Portriel continued, "People are always looking for the Great Trines in history. It's a fool's errand. What is, is. Though come to think of it, some things are that aren't too."

Like Mellas asleep, Portriel sounded as if she should make sense. But neither she nor Portriel would be waking from this.

"Is there a way out of the dark?"

Portriel laughed for a long time. Then her voice dropped, and she said conspiratorially, "Can you take me to the stars?"

"I don't know."

Portriel moved toward her eagerly. Liath was surprised at how she sensed the eagerness through the shared medium of air, without seeing an expression or a hunch of shoulders. It was a relief not to have to see. She was always intensely staring, watching her step, picking her route, gauging the distance to things. "Take me to the stars," Portriel said. "With you, they'll let me stay."

"What are you talking about?"

"The stars! Outside! Oh, please . . ."

The word "outside" was enough for Liath.

It was Portriel taking her, not the other way around, until they'd come to an iron door. Liath could smell it: rust and weight. When Portriel pounded on it, something clinked and jingled, and Liath reached out to feel the tail ends of a broken knocker. Reaching down—she had to nudge Portriel aside to do it, and the woman scurried around her to continue pounding—she found a latch, and slipped it up. The door locked from this side.

"It's open, Portriel," she said quietly, and pushed.

A gust of salt and indigo swept over them. They stood on a walkway, iron-railed, carved in the face of an outcropping overlooking the ocean. After the long dark, it was not strange to emerge into blue evening. She was only surprised that she had spent so little time lost. It had felt much longer.

The walkway curved away out of sight to either side. Someone was coming around the left-hand curve, swearing. "Oi!" he cried when he saw them.

Liath was tensed to spring back through the door. But it was only a steward, in ordinary shirt and breeches. "What in all the spirits you think you're doing?"

Portriel had moved forward, arms outflung, to grasp the railing. Except for her clothes, she looked exactly as Liath knew she would: long, wild gray hair, age-spotted hands, dressed in the frumpy off-white comfort of lambswool robes. She had turned her face up and outward, to drink in sea air, or first starlight.

"She wanted to come out," Liath said.

"She's not permitted out here! Look at her!"

An old, mad woman; were they afraid she'd hurl herself over the rail? "She's all right. She wanted to see the stars."

The steward made a strangled noise. "*Look at her.*"

As if in response, Portriel turned her joyous face toward them. Over the gummy grin, her eyes were sockets as black and empty as any tunnels in the Holding.

"Sweet spirits," Liath said. She moved toward the woman slowly, taking care not to startle her. She could feel the rail; her hands gripped it securely. But Portriel was not afraid to fall—and down there the stone *would* catch her, and catch her hard.

"You're using your eyes again," Portriel scolded.

"Yes," Liath said. "It's not safe here."

"And it's safe within?" Portriel released the rail to wave a hand in the steward's direction. Both he and Liath swayed forward. "You can't bring me in this time," she said. "Steward Steward. I have my own steward now. She'll *watch* me."

"If she watches you fall to your death, it'll be my skin," he said.

"And what do *you* do out here, Steward Steward?"

"Look out for you," he grumped.

Liath, baffled, gestured at the door: Why not just bar it? He raised his brows and gestured at Portriel: From *her*?

As if she'd been listening to a conversation, Portriel explained reasonably, "I get through the doors, when I'm myself. When they're not locked, I forget they're open. But when they're barred I forget they're locked. It's a puzzlement, yes?"

Liath blinked at the steward, shaking her head. "Yes, Portriel," she said. "It is that."

The steward glanced behind him, as if someone stood ready to chastise him. "She can't stay," he said weakly.

Liath turned to the rail and put an arm around Portriel's shoulders. The waist would have been more secure, but she would have had to bend down, as if to hold a child. "I've got her," she said to the man. "There should be an attendant for her. Then you wouldn't have this problem."

"Wouldn't need *him* then," Portriel said.

"And you think I don't have better things to do than worry all night are you there, are you coming through just as I've looked away? Frail as a bird, you are. You'd be over the edge in a blink, did the wind sneeze." He appealed to Liath: "I'm the oilman, I've important work to do, seeing to all those doors. I can't be worrying about the likes of her."

Clearly he *was* worried; he had moved closer, not farther, as he complained.

"I'm here now," Liath said.

"And who are *you* when you're at home? You belong with the ones above." He was standing right behind them now. "You want to know her secrets, don't you. You think there's something she can tell you to give you a leg up over the others. Well, she can't. She's old. Leave her be."

Portriel no longer seemed to be listening; she had pushed up her sleeves and stretched her arms out, and was turning her hands over in the starlight. Bathing in it.

"*She* found *me*," Liath said. "Wandering lost in the tunnels. I'll go back as soon as she's had enough."

"Go back, don't go back, it's no skin off me."

"Galandra was Earth's bride," Portriel said dreamily. Her soft words silenced them both. "I would be Sky's bride. Sylfonwy could come to me as a weave of winds. They say in ancient times there were weavers like mages, and what they wove were the elements and their children. Mistweavers, flameweavers, stoneweavers. It's a windweaver I would wed. I would drink the breath of the sky."

The oilman watched her in awe. When she lapsed back into wordless reverie, her cratered face lifted into the gloaming, he said, "She was one of them, you know. She was the best of them. And beautiful. I saw her from afar once, as a lad. I heard her laugh. Never thought to see her like this."

"She was on the *Ennead*?" Liath whispered.

"Ai. And now she's dafter than dustbunnies, and no matter what I do she finds her way here and tries to look at the stars."

Liath really saw him for the first time. Spare and drab, he was all gnarled crafter's hands and wistfulness. "No one told you to look after her, did they," she said. "No one looks after her at all. Except for you."

He shifted uncomfortably, scowling. "I've got affairs to attend to," he said. "You say you'll watch her?"

Liath smiled gently. "She's safe with me. It'll be too cold soon to stay out. It won't be long."

He looked her up and down, tonguing his front teeth thoughtfully.

Seeming to find her acceptable, he returned the way he'd come, looking back only once to reassure himself that Liath still held the old woman safe.

"Tell me what you see," Portriel said.

Liath startled at the commanding tone. A member of the Ennead, in her day . . . "A bit of Crown, down below. Rocks and shadows. The sea. The sky." Somewhere below them and to the side, the cataract hissed. The sea was a deepening blue, surf breaking on a jagged tumble of rocks. In her wanderings she had come a good ways through the Holding, and perhaps halfway down. The sea was much closer here, much louder. She was transfixed by immensity; the sea never stopped moving, as if it were alive, as if it breathed. Half the world was this wildly scented, surging thing that she had lived entirely unaware of. The rocks at its edge were green with moss, glowing with the last traces of day. Crown was obscured by the angle of stone; only the lights of a few outbuildings were visible. How did they live, down there, with heaving eternity at their doorstep?

"The sky," Portriel said. "Tell me more."

"There's no moon yet."

"No? It's a big mountain. Look at the sea."

Silver glints struck off the wavelets. Portriel was right: the moon was rising, somewhere behind the massive rock.

"What else?" Portriel demanded.

"The evening star. It's twinkling."

"Only one?"

"There's another bright one a little below it, to the side."

"Galandra's Tears. The evening stars are tears of sadness for the day that's gone. The morning stars are tears of joy."

The stars were Eiden's spirit, only visible in darkness. Shooting stars were Eiden's tears; so was rain. Those were just figures of speech. The land was his body.

"What else?" said Portriel.

"Other stars. More every breath. There are no clouds."

"And their configuration?"

"Their what?"

"Their configuration," Portriel repeated irritably. "What patterns do they fall into, girl?"

"Uh . . . I'm sorry, I don't . . ."

"What do they look like?"

"They look like stars. Like . . . grain, I suppose. Scattered at random."

"At random?" Portriel jerked back so fiercely that Liath had to close her fist on lambswool to maintain her grip. "And do they rise at random too, each night a different arrangement?" Her tone was scornful.

"Well, no, not night by night. But over the seasons. It's the sowmid stars, now."

"And how do you know?"

"I . . . just know. I don't know. I'm not a steerswoman, Portriel."

"And how does a steerswoman steer?"

"By the stars. It's a craft. I'm a publican."

Portriel's arm shot up. Pointing. Her head did not follow it. "What color is that one?"

"White."

"And that one?"

"White. They're all white. Stars are white."

Portriel made a phlegmy sound in the back of her throat. "Two good eyes in your head, and you can't see a thing. Look again. That one there. Is it the same color as that one there?"

Liath looked. It wasn't. She'd never bothered to notice. "It's more red. The other's more . . . blue, I suppose."

"Yes yes, good girl. Now look again. How do you know they're sow-mid stars?"

"There's a little group by the horizon, you don't see those in summer. In summer there are three very bright ones in the middle of the sky. They're dimmer in summer, in winter they're all very bright. They reflect Eiden's moods."

Portriel moaned, as if Liath were hopelessly dense. "Look," she said. "Stare. Don't blink your eyes. Just stare. Keep staring. No cheating, Portriel will know. Do your eyes water yet?"

Liath nodded, then remembered and said, "Yes."

"Now what do you see?"

The stars had begun to seem black on a white background, blurred by her running eyes. "Swimming stars," Liath said wryly.

"You must look with better eyes than that."

"*Look past it,*" Hanla said. "*Not at it. Through it.*"

Liath had not eaten for a day and a half, had slept only in winks when Hanla wasn't vigilant enough. The warm summer evening was cold, she was that weary, that hungry. But the kadri would not come. "They're just mountains!" she wailed. "I want to go home!"

"*What is the mountain when there is no stone?*" *Hanla asked again. She was relentless. She was horrible. Liath hated her.*

"*It's not a mountain!*"

"*Then what is it? Draw it for me.*"

I can't, she tried to say, but she knew it would be no use. I'm only nine-and-three. I'm so tired, Hanla. I want to go home. Home was only two fields away, up the rise and over the little bridge and across the road. But there would be no going home until she had done this. Nine-and-three: halfway through her training. Six years from showing a light, six years from taking the triskele. There would be no triskele if she could not form kadri. Kadri were integral to the illuminator's craft.

Graefel had said she would have trouble with this. Graefel had said she was too hardheaded, the daughter of hardheaded publicans. But Graefel didn't have to form any bloody kadri.

She let herself go soft. It wasn't difficult. She was exhausted, broken under Hanla's merciless demands. Tears sprang to her eyes, humiliating; she couldn't wipe at them or Hanla would know she was crying. She stared through them, at the black mountains against the indigo sky, the first stars hanging among the peaks. The mountains were as hard as Hanla. You couldn't budge them. They were always there, looming, protective and inescapable. She would not let them defeat her, she would not . . .

"That's it," Hanla breathed, as the chalk moved in her fingers, squeaking on the slate. "That's it, Liath!"

She looked down at what she had drawn. Triangles, with dots between them; it was more childish than any scrawl she'd made at six. Yet she saw them with new eyes. The lines were not a picture of mountains. They were not mountains at all. Only the essence of mountains. The thing that mountains represented.

"That's Endurance, Liath," Hanla said. "You've drawn the kadra Endurance."

"Don't you see?" Portriel said. "Don't you see the kadri in the sky?"

She didn't. She saw only points of light, like so many magelights, too far away to reach.

Portriel's sunken, lined lips cracked into a grin. "It's all right," she said. "I only hoped. I couldn't see them, either."

They stood that way for a long while. Full dark came on and was not dark at all, lit by a myriad colored fires overhead. When the moon rose past the barrier of rock, the glare was unwelcome. Galandra's Tears were long fallen into the sea. The air grew chill; Portriel shivered in her soft robes.

"It's time to go in," Liath said.

The old woman nodded. She would never have her fill of stars. But she was old, and thin, and the ocean blew a remembrance of winter at them. Whatever fire inside her yearned toward the fires in the sky, it was not enough to warm her aging bones.

"Who'll take you out there, when I'm gone?" Liath asked, relieved that the latch had not slipped down and locked them out.

"That pesky steward, perhaps." She chuckled. "No. No one will take Portriel to feel the sky. But I thank you, child. Portriel thanks you for the gift of the stars this night."

As the darkness of the tunnels enfolded them, she slipped her arms around Liath's arm. "I did it to myself, you know."

Liath stiffened. She did not want to hear this.

"It was the madness. One by one, tooth by tooth. Oooooh did it hurt. What I wanted. The pain."

It wasn't age that made her toothless, then; castings could keep your teeth in your head until your passing day.

"And the eyes," Portriel said. "But I felt much better when they were gone. They didn't have to do what they did."

Liath grew cold inside. Portriel, insane, had blinded herself, plucked out her own teeth, some paroxysm of madness. Certain diseases of the spirit were incurable. So they had taken extreme measures. "They cored and sealed you, didn't they."

"Ai. That they did."

Liath had sensed no light in her. It was cut off that completely. *I'm sorry,* she wanted to say, and *Do you miss it?* She wanted to ask what it felt like—compare it with what she felt. But she felt nothing. You couldn't sense your own magelight. You couldn't feel it swell within you. Guiders were different for everyone. Liath saw scintillating blue lines; some people saw diffused luminescence, or a faraway point of colored light pulling them toward it. Hanla said she saw a crystalline fragmentation, Graefel a lambent golden outline around objects and people and ciphers. Keiler heard a faraway ringing in his ears. But none of them *felt* it—not like colic, or heartache.

"It is a bag of sand in the belly," Portriel said. "It is a sack of ashes. It is a cask of spring water from which the parched may no longer drink."

But you no longer harm yourself. Was it a worthwhile trade?

They were turning in a place where there had been no turn before. "Where are we going?"

"To the spirits. To the bonefolk. To the worms."

Suddenly very weary, Liath wished only to rest, eat. "Portriel—"

The small woman was intent now, determined. She had gotten something else into her head and would drag Liath behind her until they'd done it. "Portriel has more to show you. More stars. Stars in the deep rock. Faster!"

"Please stop, Portriel. I thank you for your rescue, and your hospitality, but . . ." Would she want to do all the things her blindness had prevented? "I can't keep track of these turnings."

"The labyrinth changes," Portriel replied. "The labyrinth lies. The labyrinth tries to trick you. The stone dreams . . . and in its sleep it shifts, dreaming itself new."

Down, and down. They were in some sort of spiral now, the tunnels circling back on themselves and down the way the iron stairs did. Then it bottomed out. There were still no torches.

"Where are we going?"

Cackling now, Portriel rubbed her hands briskly and leaned forward. There was a shift in the air. A door opened.

The light beyond was dazzling. Liath blinked, staring without seeing. The shapes inside stared back.

"Portriel," one said, in a rich low voice. It spoke forbearance, irritation gentled into patience, as toward a beloved child ignorant of its own intrusion. "Welcome."

"Well come?" Portriel said. She looked around sightlessly. "I see no well, though we are in one."

"Who is your young friend?" another asked. They were seated around a triangular table, each point of the triangle flattened so that three could sit in a row. They wore robes of simple cut but luxuriant fabric, silk that rippled like honey in the serene light of oil lamps. Magestone marbled the walls around them. It glowed.

Liath swallowed.

"I don't know," Portriel said. "But she's a rank one, eh?" She slapped Liath on the rump.

"We'll summon a proxy to see you back to your chambers."

"A proxy, a doxy. All women are all things in time. I need no guiders. The light's too bloody bright in here as it is."

With that, the old woman hunched back down the corridor, unerring in the dark she couldn't see.

"Well, child? Speak up. Your name, at least."

"Liath n'Geara l'Danor," Liath managed past the knot in her throat.

"Liath . . . ?"

It was her mage name they wanted. She was wearing vocate's gray, though it was soiled now from a day's wear and all the scrambling in the tunnels. Her triskele had flopped to the outside of her loosened shirt. She stood up straight, tugged the borrowed surcoat down, shrugged the shoulders back into alignment. There was nothing to be done about the sagging hose.

"Liath Illuminator," she said. "If you can restore the name to me."

She bowed to the Ennead.

They were garbed in triadic colors. Between that and their ages and genders, it was fairly easy to match them to what the vocates had described. Gondril, Landril, and Seldril, the triplets, were the leading triad, dressed in shades of red—rust, scarlet, rose; Gondril was heavier and kindlier than the other two, and each wore long raven hair in a different style, but the features were identical. Worilke, Freyn, and Lerissa were the weather triad, two middle-aged women—one dark, one olive—and one pale younger woman; they wore saffron, amber, and brown. Vonche and Naeve were elderly, Evonder unmistakably their son; the balance triad, they wore purple and indigo and robin's-egg. Their triskeles were pewter, the ones bequeathed them when they passed their trials, but where proxies wore silver rings the Ennead wore gold. Nothing else distinguished them, except perhaps the nightstone table, which seemed new-cast though it must be immensely old. Like the walls, it was veined with magestone, but the veins had been persuaded to flow straight along the edges. The chairs they sat on—what she could see peeking out from under their ample robes—were plain wood, uncolored and unadorned.

"Well, it's a most unorthodox way of heeding a call," Vonche Illuminator said, "but we never do specify *how* to come." He chuckled amiably and gestured Liath to a bench against a wall.

"I'm not a vocate," she said.

"Of course you are. We called you."

Liath could only stare.

"We called you. Bron sent a boy. Apparently he did his job."

"But . . ." Bron had bent rules for her. She would not betray him. "There was a boy," she said, comprehending it as slowly as she said the words. "But he witnessed my failure. He . . . must have decided not to deliver the summons."

The nine mages exchanged looks.

Liath winced. "Please don't punish him. He saved my life, in the mountains. I made him guide me."

"There will be no punishment," Freyn Binder hastened to assure her. She was a plain woman, with the dusky skin and light eyes of the Weak Leg. "Now and then, though rarely, our information is inaccurate. Runners have leave to use their judgment. They would not wear Ennead cloaks if it were otherwise."

Seldril Binder, her quick black eyes missing nothing, said, "What failure?"

Miserably, she told them. She had longed to explain, but in the event she found herself mealymouthed, inadequate. Her head was still spinning: Mellas had been in Clondel to call *her*.

Gentle, coaxing and prompting when words failed her, they drew her story out. They were astonished at the paralysis of her magelight, keen to know what happened in their mountains. At her description of the shadows and the Southers, they exchanged looks of triumph, outrage, chagrin. She could interpret none of it. It was hard enough to spit out the unembellished truth. When she'd finished, she said in a meek voice, "Why did you call me?"

Vonche and Gondril cast her sharp looks: it was a stupid question. Then it came to them what she meant. "How did we know about your strong magelight?" Vonche rephrased.

She nodded. *I hid from reckoners for nine-and-two years.*

"Your wordsmith sent us word, when your trial was imminent. In a sense, Graefel called you."

Liath didn't understand. Graefel was a village wordsmith.

Vonche fumbled for something in an inner pocket, held a silver ring out on his open palm. "He sent this, in case we had forgotten." When Liath blinked, dumbfounded, he added with a touch of irritation, "Graefel n'Traeyen l'Brenlyn was a proxy."

It came to her in a rush, before she even knew she understood: That was no smile of pride playing on Graefel's lips, when he told her she should be sent here instead of on a journeying. "*But the Ennead call whom they will,*" he had said. What she'd seen was the beginnings of the cold smile he produced when things were not going his way. He'd been angry that the Ennead had not heeded him.

She tried to remember how he'd treated Mellas, if they'd had words before it all went wrong. The celebration had been so crowded, so wine-soaked, and her memory of it was hazed with the smoke of time and hardship. There were so many runners and proxies, always passing—passers, old Bron had called them, and it was true, they never stayed for longer than it took to get a good meal and a night's ease in a bed. "*I didn't ask you to come with me.*" Truer words than she'd known when Mellas spoke them. He'd been sent before her trial had ended; it was a threeday's journey from the Holding. They'd had that much faith in Graefel's word. Yet Mellas had never delivered the summons. When he saw her failure, he'd chosen not to. Graefel must have known. Bron must have known. What had Mellas said to them? Why?

She closed her eyes. The world was tilting. Yet the world was not changed; only her understanding of it.

He was so angry . . .

It only meant that she had lost more than she'd known, and disappointed them more deeply than she could have guessed—and come closer than she'd realized, all those long years, to what Pelkin had warned her against on the night of Breida's birth. There had been a proxy in their midst all that time.

Graefel had betrayed her.

"Are you all right, my dear?" Freyn asked. "How long has it been since you slept?"

Liath waved the concern away—then remembered who she was with. "I'm sorry, Bindswoman. . . ."

Freyn laughed. "Oh, child. If you knew how we tire of the constant deference, everyone on tiptoe—"

"You didn't know about your wordsmith?" Landril Illuminator asked.

Liath shook her head, afraid now to be too deferential.

Evonder Bindsman snorted and leaned back with his arms crossed, his first contribution to the discussion. He had a sulky mouth, and astonishing eyes under tousled sandy hair—eyes the green of a sky about to storm. He would have been handsome, if not for the chip on his shoulder. "She's a child," he said.

"Graefel Proxy was a brilliant mage, in love with an equally strong but more stolid illuminator who was also made proxy," Landril said curtly. "He would have liked to continue a proxy, I think, but the urge to pledge was too strong between them. It disrupted their work. Their fellow-reckoners cast them triad with some relative of Graefel's in Clondel."

"Befre," Liath said. Befre had stepped aside for Keiler when he passed his trial, that he might triad with his parents. She went on a second journeying, as soon as reckoners came who could dissolve the old triad and cast the new. Befre had never wanted to triad, really—she did it for her brother, though her heart lay in journeying. That's what Keiler had said. Liath hadn't understood. She wondered now if even Keiler knew.

"The illuminator never truly wished to proxy," Landril went on. "I suppose it only seemed fair, as well as sensible, to triad in Clondel, which had no resident triad at the time—a sop to Graefel, for relinquishing his position."

"It wasn't a sop," Naeve Wordsmith said. She was a powerful light, and beautiful, too, though age had padded and sagged her somewhat. "I remember Hanla. Her family were mages—and, worse, ambitious Khinish. They pushed her strongly to succeed. She heeded the call for their sake, and could not go home again having forsaken the ring."

"At any rate," said Gondril, "we saw no reason that Graefel's talent should be wasted—he was an excellent judge of light, and climate, and he helped cast some strong triads. But he ensconced himself in his roadside village and had no contact with the Holding for years. Until suddenly word came that he had found a remarkable mage. We sent a runner to arrive at the bestowing of the triskele." He smiled. "I presume he arrived on time."

"Yes." Liath made her voice level. "Right on time."

Gondril slapped the table lightly. "And now," he said, surveying the faces around him, "that remarkable mage is ailing. Shall we see to this?"

"Please," said Evonder, with heavy sarcasm. "The anticipation torments me." Liath concealed a flash of resentment. He was a member of the Ennead, though he didn't act it. His magelight burned. He deserved her respect even if he didn't return it.

Lerissa Illuminator laid cool hands on her, as if Liath's skin would give some evidence of what ailed her, feverish or clammy—as if Lerissa could sense through touch what others sensed as a scent or a taste or a light. She smelled pleasantly of rose oil. Her hands were smooth, soft, the hands of an illuminator who had never plied any other trade. She shook her head, raised slim dark brows at Freyn. Freyn tried—matronly, gentle, her hands a healing all by themselves. Then Worilke, muscular, dark as nightstone, with fingers competent as a crafter's; and lastly Seldril, reserved and chill but redolent of authority, vitality.

"I can feel nothing amiss," she said.

"Nor I," said Freyn.

"No one has ever attempted to heal an ailing magelight," said Naeve. "There has never been, as far as we know, an ailing magelight at all. Vonche?"

The illuminator shook his gray head. "I've never heard of it."

"Magelight is a torch that never burns out, a candle that never melts," said Worilke.

"Not even when your hands are too weak to mix pigment or hold a quill, not even when your spirit wearies of this world and looks toward the next," Vonche added.

"But we must try to heal her."

"Of course."

"Layered, or trebled?" Evonder asked, impatient.

"Trebled, I think. Each triad finding its own way."

There was a depression in the center of the table, a place for items to be set, but to her surprise they did not cast around the table. The binders—Seldril, Evonder, and Freyn—chalked a large casting circle on the chamber floor, then a triangle within it, and their own, smaller circles at its triadic points. That, Liath realized, was the kadra on the proxy rings. They fetched materials from a side chamber, and the mages of the Ennead sat on the floor like any vocates, like any village triad. A triad of triads.

Liath sat in the center. She did not think the stone could contain the overwhelming power she felt building as they cast. The magestone blazed brighter than flame, silver-white glare bleaching out the lamplight. Three leaves they created, and laid them one atop the other at Liath's feet, and they melted into one another, three becoming one in the most powerful of all magecraft.

All this for her . . . but to no avail.

"Layered, then," said Seldril brusquely. They shifted position with practiced ease. Masters at work, efficient and precise. When one thing failed, you tried another. Just mages, just good mages . . . yet so much more.

The illuminators sat at one point of the triangle, the binders at another, the wordsmiths at the head. They passed the vellum from one to the next, each adding a unique touch of power. The binders sang together, three melodies that echoed and twined around each other but did not touch until the final note, which combined into a deep drone—a resonance, a kadra made of sound. The single manuscript, thick with pigment, wilted and faded away. There was no change in her. She stared at the floor where it had been for so long that the air seemed to sparkle, but it was not her guiders, just a trick of the eyes. She was as she had been. Whole, not cored; yet bound somehow, barred like the windows. Other mages could see the light through the bars, could smell it burning . . . but it could not spill out.

Even the Ennead could not heal her.

"That was embarrassing," Landril said dryly as they returned to their seats. Gondril scowled at him: "Our pride is the least of what's wounded here." To Liath he said, gently, "Well, you see that even the Ennead can fail. . . . No, clearly that's no consolation. You're a good mage, Liath. Not concerned with pride, but with lost potential."

"Am I still a mage?"

The question hung in the silver air.

"There is a possibility," Seldril ventured, in measured tones.

Gondril and Landril looked at Liath, and then at Seldril. Something passed among them, an unspoken and complex interaction of like minds. It was eerie to behold. A bit like listening to the vocates think aloud; but their communication passed in silence, among three people more alike than any mages ever were.

"Quite brilliant," said Landril.

"Quite mercenary," said Gondril, a caution and reproof.

"Would you care to enlighten us?" Worilke said—and the wry twist in her voice reminded Liath that they, too, were once vocates, and in their youth suffered the same testing and molding as the ones above. They had probably ribbed each other the same way, slept like puppies in the same bed. It was hard to imagine.

"Quite simple, really," said Seldril.

"We can smell her magelight," Gondril said. "*But she cannot cast.*"

Landril added, with emphasis, "Nor could she be enticed to cast."

Worilke's brows went up. "Ah," she said. "I see."

Liath felt their evaluation like hands probing her, searching for weaknesses, points of stress—wranglers checking a horse for faults at a trading fair.

"It might work at that. And it is manipulative. She will have to agree to it."

"I don't know that *I* agree to it."

"Explain."

"Too great a sacrifice, too great a risk."

"But if she agrees? Volunteers, as it were?"

"Well . . . yes, I suppose so. For something like this."

Liath bit the inside of her cheek. Lerissa noted her distress, and gave a tinkling laugh. "Why don't we *ask* her, then?"

Gondril smiled apology, then pursed his lips, debating how best to present the thing. "If there were a threat to Eiden Myr," he began, "and you found yourself in a unique position to thwart it . . ."

". . . at some potential cost," Landril put in.

". . . and at no small risk to yourself," Seldril added.

". . . would you be willing to try? Would you give it your very best try?"

Liath frowned. "Of course I would."

Gondril nodded and looked to Vonche.

The old man shifted in his seat, rearranging his robes with long, fine fingers. "There was a very powerful mage," he said. "Brought to the Holding by mage parents when he was very young, raised here with Evonder and Lerissa. Two seasons ago, he left when he was discovered . . . doing wrong. We tried, with him. He was very valuable to us. . . ." He faltered.

Naeve took up the tale, smoothing her short silver hair, turning the flat ring on her finger. "He was beloved of us. We don't know why, or how, but something twisted inside him. Perhaps we indulged him too much; he was so very brilliant. He collected tales of ancient magecraft, and in secret he created permanent manuscripts, never meant to dissipate in castings, to preserve his forbidden knowledge. It's dark magecraft, you see. He is using magecraft to do harm. To do evil. *He* sent your mountain shadows—that has his mark on it."

"The runner must have a latent talent, a magelight that never blossomed," said Worilke, thinking it through as she spoke, her sculpted face darkening. "It manifests in his sleep, but can cause no harm of itself. Somehow our errant mage worked a casting *through* his mind, knowing he was sent to fetch you. He wished to stop you from reaching us. But how did he know so much? The boy?"

Evil indeed, to abuse a little boy so badly he feared sleep, and touch. Liath's dismay must have shown, for Gondril said, "The boy was not at fault. We should have shielded him better. Who was to know that remote manipulation was possible? Such cruel invention . . . it is difficult to reconcile with the child I taught to cipher."

"There is no doubt that it was his work," Worilke said sharply. "But whether the strike was aimed at Liath or at us remains to be discovered."

"Either way, it rose up to bite the agents he *did* send to strike at us. Darkcraft will do that."

The Southers, Liath realized. Their vicious blades were aimed at the mind of Eiden Myr. But if the Ennead knew . . .

Gondril regarded her sadly. "We did not send the storm that nearly killed you," he said. "But our mountain is well warded. The mountain defends itself. And us."

"All irrelevant," said Landril. "What matters is bringing an end to the darkmage's work."

"He's building a stronghold somewhere," Lerissa said. "In the Belt, we've heard, on an enchanted island in one of the lakes—such rubbish collects around the proxies' stories of this man. I think it's in the Fist, myself. But it seems he travels, as well—the better to evade us. He passes himself off as a plain wordsmith, unassuming. He might be anyone. Anywhere."

"If I were collecting mages for a rival ennead, I'd go as low and far as possible," said Worilke. "He's in the Weak Leg."

"In a holding woven of marsh grass—oh, no question." Lerissa smiled to dull the bite of the words. Worilke didn't smile back.

"Reports up the proxy chain say that his influence is thickest in the Lowlands," Gondril put in as compromise. "The Ennead has relied on the proxy chain for a nonned generations. If word comes of a Lowland sighting from a proxy as trustworthy as—"

"There are no longer trustworthy proxies," Freyn put in. "Any of them could be his agent. This *must* be stopped."

"The point," Landril snapped, "is that he is gathering mages. If he had his eight, we would know it, so there is still time. We've done all we can in calling the brightest to us."

"His tongue is silvered with lies; perhaps it is some casting he invented, to bind mages to him," Naeve explained to Liath. "We ward our proxies, but it is not enough. Many have been lost."

Vonche sighed. "Torrin Wordsmith had the strongest magelight of us all. Not the experience, perhaps, and not the craft, but he had the dedication and he would have been ready when it was time. We need him. We need him so much that we were prepared to change the triadic configuration of our ennead to accommodate his talent. We eldest would step aside, and a new mage would come into our ranks. But we are stymied at every turn. Torrin corrupted, working dark magecraft. Our head reckoner lost, perhaps dead, in pursuit of him. Strong mages in the Midlands and Lowlands bonded to his dark purposes. Liath Illuminator, our best hope, unable to cast. Even that may be his work, for all we know."

"So it was true . . ." Liath breathed.

"So what was true?"

That they'd wanted her for the Ennead . . .

"There was a rumor," she said, taking care with her phrasing. "In the dining hall. About a mage who might . . . change things here. But it was a lie . . . planted to trick them . . ."

"Rumors, eh?" said Freyn. "Oh, go on, child, tell us what you heard. We encourage the gathering of information; it's the first duty of reckoners, to be our eyes and ears in the world before they are our voice and hands. And we're familiar with the methods some of the stewards use. Disfavor will fall on no one."

"They said there was a mage who was strong enough that you could stop the Great Storms forever. But the triads would have to shift members. And it meant the illuminator vocates were competing for a . . . to be on the . . . to be the one to fill the gap."

"What an interesting concatenation of truth and conjecture," Lerissa said. "But vocates *will* draw their own conclusions."

"That's the way of it," said Naeve. "With time, they learn to draw the correct ones."

But they *had* drawn the correct one. They had deduced that she was the one called in hope she'd fill the gap.

"Who will you . . . consider now?" Would they ward poor Mellas against being used again? Were there others with such latent talent, other unknowing weapons? Would they post guards against the next assassin Southers? There were too many questions.

"Jonnula n'Devra l'Jonnel is difficult," said Worilke slowly. It would be her illuminator. "Calculating, manipulative."

"But brilliant," said Freyn, who shared Jonnula's complexion.

"Yes, there is that. Not Karanthe n'Farine l'Jebb; her rover's soul would never forgive our keeping her here." She turned to Liath. "The answer is that we don't know."

"The whole point may be moot. Torrin n'Maeryn l'Eilody may not be redeemable."

"He must come back to us, or be cored and sealed permanently."

"Yes. It was ever extremes, with Torrin, was it not? If he returns, if his heart can be softened, he can bequeath the world the greatest gift since Galandra. If he does not, we must seal him, or he will plunge the world into darkness."

"What will he do?" Liath asked. She sounded like a vocate newly. But the question remained. "I mean . . . what does he gain from doing evil? What's the point?"

Seldril managed a thin smile. "He ruins us."

"That's all? That's all he wants, to . . . to see you fall?"

"To bring down the current Ennead, yes," Landril said. "Isn't that enough? He would be the most powerful mage in all the world; and he would see our downfall. It isn't a difficult notion."

"Spirits forgive whatever we did to anger him so," Naeve said softly. She made a point of looking just past Gondril. "Push him too hard, perhaps. Praise him too little."

"He's a spoiled child," Worilke snapped. This was plainly a sore point. "Children care only for what they want *now*, and have no concept of consequences. Torrin seeks to avenge a slight. He is testing us, and the moment he finds he can best us he will destroy the peace and plenty that Enneads have guarded and cherished since time began—for the pure, perverse pleasure of hurting *us*."

Gondril turned to Liath, and asked her again the question that was already asked and answered. "Will you aid us, Illuminator? Though we have failed in aiding you?"

"With Torrin," Freyn broke in, "we can put an end to the Great Storms. Who is to say we could not then free Liath's magelight?"

"It's all right," she said softly. "You don't need to promise me impossible things. I want to help. I've seen the shadows."

Gondril clapped his hands and squeezed them tight. "Then I can see no better match, nor nobler intent at its forging."

"Show her the fragment," Worilke said.

From the binding chamber, Evonder brought a strange thing: a scrap of vellum, hardened by time, inscribed with glossy black ink.

"What *is* that?" Liath breathed.

"Part of a permanent manuscript," Freyn said. "One never intended to dissipate in a casting. Created of materials that do not fade, or run."

It was a marvel, and a terror. Such a thing would undermine all magecraft.

"It's safe," said Naeve. "We've destroyed the rest of it. This one piece can't do much harm. But see the formation of the ciphers. See the flowing hand, the ornate ascenders, the tilted crossbars, here and here. Watching him cast, you will know him by his hand."

These wordsmith's marks would not go to dust or dew at the completion of a casting. They seemed alive on the vellum, almost wriggling. They might crawl to the edge, crawl off onto the hand that held it, burrow into the skin. She flinched from the dark sentience that lurked behind those ciphers, but could not tear her eyes away. The twists and curls of that scribing led into oblivion.

Evonder removed it and Liath exhaled, unaware that she had held her breath.

"You will go on your journeying," said Seldril. "Like any journeyer, you will observe the castings of the local triads you meet. Observe all the castings you can, though you cannot participate. When you have found the man who scribes like that, you have merely to bring us some hair, some skin, some scrap of his flesh. It will enable us to core and seal him from afar. He will have no choice then but to return to us, to be unsealed."

"Spirits willing, we will be able to lift the darkness from his heart," Gondril said, and Naeve added, "And make amends for whatever harm we did him, to twist him so."

"What does he look like?" Liath asked.

"Dark," said Naeve, and "Pale," said Worilke. "Young," said Vonche, and "Aging," said Evonder. "He's rather a study in contradictions," Gondril concluded wryly.

"How to picture him for you?" Lerissa Illuminator said, looking inward, to memory. "Lean. Your height. Dark hair—though he might have cut it or let it grow, or treated it with bleach or dye. Narrow eyes, hooked nose, thin lips. He's seen three times nine harvests and five, but the years—or his own darkcraft—have etched his face, and he may look older still by now."

"There's no telling what he'll look like," Landril said. "You'd do better to forget what they've told you and keep an open mind. He might be anyone. With his darkcraft, he might have had any sort of glamour cast on him."

"But magecraft can't . . ." Liath began.

"Darkcraft can."

"You'll have to ride," Gondril said, "though perhaps you'd planned to journey afoot?"

The loss of the gentle sorrel pained her afresh. "I would have walked. But I rode here, or tried to. I can ride back out."

"It will serve the interests of time." The mage nodded as if she had proposed something sensible. It was part of their appeal—making everyone feel included, important, even a crippled mage. She understood now why the Holding shielded these people. It was not just what they were. It was who they were. "You will have your journey year to accomplish the task—if Torrin Darkmage isn't stopped by Ve Galandra next, he'll be too powerful to stop at all. But the sooner the better, for all of us."

"I'll send for a mount," said Landril.

"I'll see to clothing and provisions," said Seldril. She and Landril made their exit through the door to the materials chamber. They walked, unthinking, in step.

"We will renew our wardings in the Aralinns," Gondril said, "and add a casting that will thwart those particular manifestations, now that we know what form they take. We've had the washout repaired. But I suspect you won't want to travel that route again."

"Not that route, no," she said quietly.

"It's for the best. After he left us, Ve Eiden last, we were fairly certain of his movements for a time. The Fist, the Low Arm, then into the Lowlands. He might have gone to ground anywhere along that route, perhaps doubling back to folk who welcomed him. You should retrace it. Evonder?"

The sandy-haired bindsman startled from a slouch and took his legs off the table. "Yes?"

"A ship from Crown." Irritation nipped the corners of Gondril's words. "*Oakwind* can transport horses, can it not?"

Evonder shrugged. "Coaster. Not much of a draft. But she can stable a mount on deck if the weather's fair. To Caragil?"

Gondril allowed himself a small smile. "I suspect the weather will hold a day or two. It would be best if she left at dawn; she can sleep on board. *Oakwind* to Caragil, overland to Bosk, a riverboat downland to Koeve, and thence along the Low Arm and through the Lowlands until he is found. Liath? What say you?"

Liath's heart was beating very fast. A journeying was one thing—wandering from place to place as whim or village needs took you—but this discussion of itinerary made it suddenly real. She would have to make real decisions. She might make real mistakes.

"Won't he know I'm coming? Like in the Aralinns?"

"Not without the boy," Gondril said.

"He'll smell my light, as you and the vocates do. . . ."

"We're counting on that," Landril said. "He'll crave your light. He'll want you close to him. But you will be unable to cast on his behalf."

"Will you do it?" said Seldril. "Whatever may come?"

"Yes," she said.

Their approval was warm as a hearth after a long cold time on the road. But she knew better now. Graefel's approval had warmed away the exhaustion of her trial, when there were only harder days to come, and his approval was a victory for him, not for her. She recognized ambition now, and manipulation. That these mages were straightforward about their use for her did not negate the fact that it was use. But what else was there for her? Her magelight was locked away, beyond the reach of even the Ennead. She would never again see her paintings knit into the wonder of a casting.

Be an alemonger, or save the world, she thought as the Ennead bade her fair journey and put her in the hands of aides.

She donned the plain clothes they provided and went wearily where the warder led her, down to the Crownside gate. The sharp sea air cut her lungs, the immensity of purpling sky swept her with vertigo; the plaintive calls of returning seabirds reminded her how far she had come. Standing between steward and warder, she felt that all the past days culminated in this moment, in this place. The Ennead; daft, tragic Portriel; the vocates and their ambitions and allegiances and ignorance; Bron and his fosterlings; the Lowlanders' pugnacious secrecy; Mellas dreaming in tongues; Tarny and the blade, Hanla and Graefel and the surfacing of an old, alien grief, sweet Ferlin lighting Keiler's eyes, Geara's low voice saying *Come inside*. All the tunnels and the shadows, the clefts and peaks, the tavern and the stony bindsman's road.

They put reins into her hand; the mare was the color of sunrise. The steward said, in the gruff cadences of Khine, "This is Amaranth. They say she'll go nicely for you."

The children's favorite horse.

ash

He nearly cast his tools across the room in a rage. Thinking better of it, he laid them carefully on the worktable. He had been patient for a lifetime. Trial and error could not be expected to yield immediate results.

Yet results he must have, and soon.

Dawn would not be long in coming. He loathed the daylight, the corrosion of sun. Darkness made all things opulent: torchlight caressed the richness of fabrics, the creamy texture of blades; firelight flickered on ciphers and made them dance. He craved what was rich and opulent and complex. He would consume it all, see it go dark, until his grandeur was the only light that shone in the world.

He would rend the world, as in the beginning. He would see it sundered. He would shred spirits of earth and air like parchment, like the thinnest strand of spiderweb. A mist of web stretched across an upper corner of the workroom, its maker patiently working; in another corner, her sister fed. So would he feed. He would suck Eiden's body dry, leaving a husk as this fat spinner had done. He would feed and grow fat, bloated with power. And then—

He swept the intricate weave of silk away, catching the spinner in his hand and closing his fist on fur, on wriggling legs. Viscera squeezed through his fingers.

Like this. Like this.

"Bring me another," he said to a stooped figure in the shadows. "A stronger one, this time." The servant scurried away, cowed, trustworthy in tongueless silence.

He turned to the wet hulk of the one he had used up. It had not lasted long enough for him to scry what he sought. Time, and raw materials—those were always the considerations. He did not have an endless supply of these creatures; waste was inefficient. But he must see for himself whether the whispers were true. Whether they were, in fact, maneuvering to strike at him.

He had woven his plans with care, these last years. He did not like to think that he was running out of time.

2

Illumining

The coaster boasted its own triad, three mages who loved the sea too much to be parted from her. They warded the ship, cast wind and fair weather in a pinch, offered their services at each port, and otherwise took joy in being sailors—hauling lines, tarring seams, stitching sail with arcane tools. The wordsmith reveled in salt spray and plunging deck; he would stand at the prow, head flung back, arms spread, hair streaming, and laugh into the wind.

In her mind, she had pictured Torrin Wordsmith like that.

The darkmage wouldn't venture so close to the Holding, not unless he'd completed his ennead, and even then he'd strike from afar, unless he was mad. These sailors were unquestionably mad—to ride a splinter on something that never stopped moving, that had no end, no sense! What seemed mysterious and profound from atop the Holding was a terror of motion from the surface. Anything might lurk in the fathoms beneath the fragile craft. Any whim of wave or weather might sweep them under.

Morlyrien was hard on his children.

They drew their casting circle in seawater on the afterdeck. Liath wouldn't cast for wavesickness—couldn't have even if she could. But the wordsmith's long, raked ciphers were arrayed like so many masts. His hand was as sweeping as sail. He was not Torrin Wordsmith.

The sun sank into the Aralinns, limning them in blood.

She disembarked at Caragil, whose hills rose and fell beneath her even when she stood still, and encountered only female wordsmiths on the hard uphill road to Bosk. The river barge that plied the Koe through the wooded hills was a stolid craft and rocked hardly at all, even when drenched by a brief, hard sowmid rain—but slewed, instead, which was worse.

Spirits help anyone who tried to put her on another boat.

She led Amaranth off onto a wet landing as the shower tailed off. Forest swallowed the cries of the boy driving oxen up the towpath to return the barge to Bosk. The flies returned ninefold. The mare had a good shake, then nosed Liath's pack for a treat. She had a mind of her own, this Amaranth, used to thwarting the whims of children, and made her own decisions about when she'd earned a reward. But she knew how to charm too. She mouthed a handful of grain with winsome pleasure. A lamplighter passed them, tugging his hood in anonymous greeting, and touched flame to wick, and went on; Liath stood beneath the docklamp as the first moths flittered toward the glow.

Such a search as she was charged with could take years, and if he had warded his stronghold she might ride right past it. The pattern of his scribing had burned into her eyes like the glare of sun off water; she could not blink its black afterimage away. When she saw the man who had scribed those lines, she would know him. But the memory of pattern was the only tool she had.

No. There was one more. Her own bright, useless light.

If she couldn't find him, she'd see that he found her. They were looking for each other, though only one of them knew it.

She left the viscous pool of yellow under the moth-battered docklamp and walked Amaranth into the gloaming.

In the deeps of night, she was startled from her bracken bed by a painful flash of light. Another came hard after; Amaranth whinnied, and strained at her tether. Liath gathered their things, shivering; in these heavily timbered hills there had been no safe place to build a fire. More lightning arced across the sky, casting a stark tracery of black limbs on the forest floor, as if a shadow forest dwelled beneath the real one.

"It's all right," Liath soothed. "What's a little skyfire, eh? These woods are too wet to burn, and they must be warded."

But the ferryman had complained of a dry sowmid, blaming Liath, as if as Norther or as mage she had some hand in the Ennead's management of the weather; and the rain had not lasted long enough to soak woods as thick as these. She'd found dry bedding only a handsbreadth down. There was not so much as the scent of rain now.

In the gloom under the clouds, she could not find the road.

This time the lightning came with a crack of thunder that jarred through Liath's legs—but it was not thunder, she realized, as Amaranth reared, as she clamped the bight of the reins just before they slipped away, as the rising wind blew the first whiff of scorched wood to her. Somewhere, nearby, a tree had split, and the whole forest had felt it. How much deadwood was there? She hadn't paid attention, the light had been nearly gone, the woods had swallowed them so quickly, there had been only one road away from the landing. She should have disembarked at Koeve as she was told to, it was a real town with real roads, she shouldn't have stayed on till the turnaround, greedy to make a few more miles.

"We'll go back to the river," she told Amaranth, but the stench of burning made the horse frantic. Would it help to bind her eyes? That was how you were supposed to get horses out of a burning barn, but no barn had ever burned in her lifetime, no barns ever burned, everything was warded, were there no mages here, was everyone gone, had the world gone mad?

He's found me, he's found me, he's already found me—

She cut the thought off hard.

Something big crashed through the trees to one side of her, and all around was the skitter of small creatures, fleeing.

It would be left, along the road, back to the river, to the water, to air and safety, but she could not find the road. Then, in another day-bright flash, she saw the break in the trees, and dragged Amaranth toward it, hauling with her whole body canted forward. There was room to mount now, though Amaranth danced away sidelong just as she'd grabbed the saddle. "*Mark* you, horse, hold *still!*" She got aboard, tried to rein around, but Amaranth was having none of it, and even Liath could smell it now, the smoke borne on the wind off the river.

She let the mare turn, but she could not rein back, the mare's poll would not flex, Liath couldn't get her nose down. They plunged onto the black road at a gallop.

If the forest burned behind her, she could not hear it over their hoofbeats. But the air was better now, as long as they didn't break a leg perhaps they'd be all right, perhaps it was best to let the animals decide which way, how fast. They ran headlong from flames they couldn't see, paced for a time by deer before they darted off into the living trees, there in one flash of lightning, then gone. This must have been a logging road, a way down to the river to load timber on barges, but for some stretches it had not been maintained, and branches whipped her no matter how low she hunched over the mare's neck. Then abruptly they were out of the trees, and houses clustered around them, lights were on, there were people in the road. Liath reined the winded mare in easily, then let the ropes out as Amaranth hung her head, sides heaving.

"Come on," someone said. "Walk her awhile."

Liath slipped to the ground on shaky legs.

"Are you all right?" said someone else.

"Fire," Liath said. "A fire, in the forest."

Looks were exchanged. "Yes, we saw the skystorm," said the first person who'd spoken to her, and the second said, "Yes, I expect there is."

"And well past time," said another.

Liath shook her head. "You have to *go*," she said. "What if it reaches here?" Someone took Amaranth's reins, continued the cooldown around the triangular commons.

"It won't," said a placid voice. A triskele gleamed. A mage; and two more, flanking him. As calm as if this happened every day.

"*Don't you ward these woods?*" she burst out.

"These woods, yes," said the frontmost. "But not the ones you rode through. Jiel Wordsmith."

"Liath Illuminator," she replied wearily. "Why? Have you too much forest to attend to yourselves?"

The mages laughed, and one—the binder from the look of her raw hands, though in logging country who could tell—said, "Ward the world too closely and you do more harm than good."

"Swaddle the babe too tight and it suffocates," said the wordsmith, and the illuminator added, "Don't quench a fire only to drown what you save."

"I don't understand," Liath said, struggling to be polite.

The mages looked beyond her, their smiles hardening, and she turned. A curtain of flame rippled beyond the screen of nearer trees. Large branches crashed to earth in a shower of spray; the canopy blazed up into the night, heat bending the air, and a thunderous crackling echoed off the wooden structures. But the trees and brush that bordered the little village were untouched. The fire stopped at the edge as at an invisible wall, pressed against it, then spread to the sides: a pool of flame stood upright, its surface flat and still, its depths churning with molten crosscurrents. A few slower animals lumbered out of the forest, coats smoking, unhindered by the warding, and were captured in wood-and-wire traps by waiting townsfolk.

"We have work to do," said the illuminator. The binder retrieved her sack from a doorsill and slung it over one shoulder.

"Some of them aren't going to make it," Liath said, seeing a badger stagger and fall.

"No," the binder agreed. "And the ones we heal will be homeless now, and strain the resources of the others' territory."

Liath rubbed her face, dazed by flight, by fireglow. "*Why?*"

"Because it's as it should be," the wordsmith said. "The forest ages. Fires burn the old and make way for the new." Pinecones had collected in drifts around the cottages; he picked one up and presented it to Liath like a tallystick. "This bears the potential for many trees, but let it fall and decay into mulch and it will grow nothing. In high heat, it opens like a flower, and seeds the ground with the future."

"Skyfire has its purposes, just like rain, and wind, and light. We can shepherd, but we must not deny."

With their faces rounded and hollowed by flame, the mages looked half mad. Liath tried to hand the pinecone back, then dropped it on the pile when they would not take it.

"Cast with us, journeyer," the wordsmith said. "To better understand."

Liath shook her head, backing away. She spotted Amaranth being led back around the commons. Her muzzle was dripping. They shouldn't have watered her so soon. *No,* she thought, *no, I've got to go on.* But the mare was blown. And Liath too had work to do.

"I'll just watch," she said.

Afterward there was dancing, to the dull drumbeats of softwood, and ritual words were spoken to the spirits of forest and fire. The villagers cobbled together a feast. Fire cast strange shapes up the sides of buildings; toward dawn the blaze died down, and a spatter of rain steamed into smoke as the mages made their final, bark-scribed casting, calming the spirit of seared wood—casting passage for the forest that had died this night.

This was not proper use of magecraft. If they could ward, they should ward; if they had to coax new growth to keep their forest healthy, they should do that. Yet compared with darkcraft this was a minor thing— lapse, not abomination. The wordsmith's charcoal marks were square. He was Jiel, not Torrin, Wordsmith.

"Is it safe to go on?" Liath asked. She was grateful for the food, but she would not sleep in this place.

"The forest is warded Heartward," the binder admitted. "And skyfire like that is unusual in sowmid; these are strange times. But you're weary. Force a night and you lose a day."

It's your bloody fire that's lost me a night, Liath managed not to say. "We'll be all right."

"Safe journey, then," they bade her, and rejoined their folk. Somewhere an infant was crying. Liath led Amaranth past the cottages and tiny crofts and into the cool balm of living forest.

The smell of burning clung to her for days.

"Ailanna Binder," the woman said. "On your journeying long?"

The forest had seemed endless, all its villages tucked away in the trees, with little traffic on the soft-mulched road: a family of tinkers, in a rattle of tools and tin; tradesfolk porting their wares; a pair of seekers with the silence on them; a weary journeymage who barely acknowledged her. Once she thought she caught a pale glimpse of bonefolk through the trees, but when she peered carefully there was nothing. For a while, the rhythmic drone of two-handed saws came to her; then the path forked and forked again into the deep quiet of tree rustle and birdsong. When this friendly mage came up to water her horse at the same spring, it was a relief to speak, a relief to see a human smile.

Liath said, "Not very long. Where does this road lead?"

"To Logard. I've just been to a pledging in Chandry—spirits, I envy you the coming year. I'd all but forgotten what a big town looks like.

You'll rest with us awhile, of course. Let my pledgemate show off his cooking. We've plenty of castings for you."

"Is your illuminator away?"

"Well, no . . ." The woman gave a bemused smile. "But he's got a new grandchild, and he'd be glad of the time with her."

"I usually like to watch first, before I try casting with . . ." Liath faltered. ". . . with unfamiliar mages."

"Do you? It's better training to dive right in. But as you prefer." She turned in at a rough-hewn stile, and brought Liath home to the cheery flicker of a hearth in a slope-roofed longhouse that was not hers. The first of many non-homecomings.

Ailanna's pledgemate, Bordill, spoke barely a word, but cooked eloquently: brown-sugar squash, smallbeans mashed in butter, threespice pudding, a delicious drink he blended from a secret combination of root and bark. "What is your journey wish, Liath?" Ailanna asked as they cleared the table and Bordill settled by the fire with some carving.

So in these parts they made a wish, before they went. *To find a mage named Torrin. Tall, dark, with a queer style of scribing. Perhaps he's passed this way?* But she could not say those words, not to anyone. If he didn't know she sought him, he mustn't find out. Instead she must watch, and learn, and volunteer nothing—and lie. She had become Jonnula's hypothetical mage, accepting hospitality she could not repay. When she leaned down to replace plates in their cubby, her triskele caught on her shirt and twisted. She freed it as she straightened, and said, "For an end on it, so I can go home again." And even that was not the truth.

"Ah." Ailanna swabbed out the last mug and hung it on a hook. "What would you most like to see, in all Eiden Myr?"

What, indeed, if she had her druthers? The weeping Lowland trees, Galandra's fire lighting the swamps, the Memory Stones in the Heel, the Haunch's sucking tides . . . sunrise over the Dreaming Sea, sunset in the Sea of Wishes—

"I grew up in a tavern. I've heard the stories. I've seen all Eiden Myr in my mind. I don't need to see it with my eyes."

Oh, lie after lie, lie layered on lie, and now she was creating untruths from angry facts that were worse than lies. She found a rag and turned to wipe down the dark, whorled table.

"Journeying should be a joy," Ailanna said slowly.

"Yes, well . . ." She wanted to please this woman, but invention failed her. "Where did *you* go? What can I expect?"

Ailanna's face shut down. "Oh, I journeyed long ago. The world is different now."

Liath had failed to feed some hunger she had for the anticipations of youth. She hung the rag over the hearth, where the cookfire had died to embers. "Where should I . . . ?"

After decks and fields, the horsehair-curl mattress in the guest loft felt soft as sheddown. At daybreak the illuminator fetched them: the triad was called to heal a logging injury that had festered. "They're a stubborn lot here, tell us to save our vellum, they'll mend on their own," Ailanna said. "But there's been more call for wood than usual. They need all their limbs intact." Liath rubbed her knee absently as she watched the logger's greenish, purpling finger flush red, and then pink, and whole.

The illuminator was polite but vague, his heart no longer in his work; when Liath said no, she was not yet looking to settle into a triad, he lost interest in her entirely. The wordsmith was gentle and frail; it hurt to imagine him plying darkcraft in secret. Liath pleaded an itch to put more miles behind her—a patent lie, after what she had said the night before—and winced as she rode away. She had made no friends of the Logard mages.

The frail man's ciphers had been exuberant, full of open loops that arced obliviously into the other lines. The spirit of a youthful mage dwelled within that aging shell. She would have liked to know him better.

He was not Torrin Wordsmith.

In the Arm, the hills gave way to gentle, stream-delved downs. The landscape looked like creased gray-green sedgeweave. Along the rivers, around the millponds, villages were rendered in the ochre and charcoal of thatched and shingled roofs. Around each village lay a sketchwork of ridged and furrowed fields, waste and woodland, meadows dusted with wildflowers, pastureland dotted with livestock, the pink fluff of orchards in sowmid bloom. Every third field lay fallow; the others were striped with young vetch, oats, beans, or awaited harvestmid planting. On the nearest ridge, a man was breaking ground, still training his oxen to the plough; they wouldn't mind him at the headland, and one of two children breaking up clods behind him had to run ahead to turn them. A scent of wild thyme drifted from an upland pasture.

Rose madder for the fruit trees, alizarin and antimony for the wildflowers, vineblack and burnt umber for the tilled fields, viridian for—

She squeezed Amaranth into a trot.

In the Muscle she met a phlegmatic mage who people said could speak to haunts. He was closemouthed and suspicious of her—but his hand was small and guarded. He was not Torrin Wordsmith.

In the Fist there was no one, just tumbled rocky crags and grassy patches that looked like mold, and the wind came lonely off the Forgotten Sea. Archis the Spiderkeep took her in—an old woman, crooked and bent from collecting the silk she spun into thread fine as the webs she harvested, her black hair streaked with white like the fine hairs on her spinners. "Aren't they lovely?" she said, stroking the agile, furred creatures. Magecraft had warded her hands; the spinners nibbled but never bit her. "They say a storm is coming . . . you can tell by the way they curl their legs." Liath wrapped tight in her bedroll, and still woke convinced that things were crawling on her. Yet Archis was right: they were deliberate and graceful and somehow wise, and beautiful cloth came from their work. She rode halfway back along the steep downland coast before she found a triad and, because they looked after Archis, was glad to see its word-smith's plain scribing.

In the Elbow the mages demanded she cast with them, but their word-smiths were all women and she passed through with lame excuses. It was just as well; the rocky country was a haven of goats, and all the houses reeked from the dripping cheesecloth hanging from the rafters. In Hoge she heard of a wordsmith prenticing nine at once; but his prentices were all young Elbow women who could have been taught at home, and the at-traction was his melting smile and emerald eyes. She didn't even have to watch him cast—merely tuck her triskele away and attend a crowded lesson as if she were just another smitten prentice. His marks on the parch-ment offcut were poised and facile; an impressionable prentice could fall in love with a man who scribed so deftly. But he was not Torrin Word-smith. She rode on, clutching her fist around the itch deep in the bones—the itch to hold a quill as he had held one.

In Bowdrin she stayed with a wordsmith's family—pledgemate, children, and a brother who had shown a light but failed his trial and chosen to run their craftery instead. After supper, they discussed magecraft, and he withdrew into a corner with some mending, glancing up now and then with no expression. He reminded her of old Roiden, in his corner of the Petrel's Rest, swigging the Finger wine they stocked just for him. "Roi-den's man," the wine trader was known as—Liath had never heard his real name. No one else could stand the stuff he sold, bitter wine for a bitter man. The thought made her uneasy, and her sleep was troubled; in the morning she rode off as quickly as politeness allowed, and left the last of the hills behind.

Where the road bottomed out, it swung into a bend. Around the bend were three reckoners.

They greeted her with measuring looks. "Quite a light you have there," said one. "We're Holding-bound," said another, and the third said, "You'll come with us."

Liath pretended she was Sarse n'Marough, cock-a-hoop about some idiot thing, and said, "At my trial, I helped cast the best rainshower my training triad said they'd ever done!"

Rainshowers were absurdly simple, assuming the clouds were there; you had only to squeeze a little, and out the rain came.

They traded looks and cleared their throats. "Never mind," said the first. "Safe journey," said the second. The third said nothing at all. She rode past them, nodding and smiling, and the tension in her legs prompted the mare back into a jog before she'd asked for one. Best not let them think about it too long. They might change their mind.

There was no avoiding reckoners—no pantry she could disappear into when black walked through the tavern door. She told the next group she'd already been called. If their colleagues had given her leave to journey awhile before she turned Headward, that was good enough for them. The third group she had to beg, but duplicity came easier now, and they too let her go. By the time she'd rounded Maur Aulein and come into the flat terrain that was the true Lowlands, she was expert at turning their calls, and she no longer flinched when she spied black tunics and silver rings.

Pelkin never told her that all she had to do was *lie* to them.

When she caught herself nodding off in the saddle, she picked a field at random and bedded down in a clear space between cow pats, with the mare on a long tether. Cattle shifted and grunted on the other side of a thin hedge. The shard of moon was ringed by luminous cloud. She might paint this sky, had she a handful of moondust to bind into pigment. She drifted down into a great expanse of white land, mountains bright enough to blind, and her shadow lying black before her. It was not the shape of her body, and did not move as she moved. When deep chill woke her, sometime before dawn, a fog had obscured the sky and clung to the bushes, and she rose, stiff, and walked the next three miles to warm her aching bones. No shadow mocked her in the dregs of night.

Toward daybreak she gathered with folk in a village whose name she didn't know, to greet the dawn for the first of nine festival days that would culminate in Longlight. At home they would be linking arms along the road and turning their faces, one by one, toward the light. Here she knelt with strangers on stony ground, waiting for the sun's creeping rays to touch the tips of solstice stones in a little cairn. In a nineday the spear of light would reach their base. Longlight had been her favorite holiday; suddenly she despised it. Spirits take the bleeding climax of the bleeding light.

In every town there was a public house, and in every public house there was information: who was coupling with whom, which fields were producing best, who was slacking off . . . but never a word about a man named Torrin. She saw big scribing and small scribing, thick scribing and thin, ornate and dull. She heard bindsongs that grated and bindsongs that gentled the air they flowed through. She saw illuminations she yearned to try, and could not. She met mages kind and mages distant, mages young and old, and none of them Torrin, nor any with rumor of him. Had the

Ennead been fed some monstrous lie? If this man was so dangerous, why was there no word of him? Could he have warded himself that well?

A man with such a gift, a light so strong, a light that *worked*—she could throttle him for misusing it so. Bloody fool. Didn't he know what he *had*?

Halfway to Maur Bolein there was a mage with a hand remarkably like Torrin's, but his light was dim and he was very old; at the top of Maur Sleith there was a mage named Torrin, but his hand was nothing like; on the coast road to Maur Gowra there was a dark, mesmerizing mage revered by his village, but he was a bindsman.

None of them was Torrin Wordsmith.

She began to see the shape of his ciphers in the crooks of trees, the twists of rivers. Without this man to find, she would have had no mage's journeying, even a mock one; she would have brewed bitter ale at home and traveled the world a merchant, all her training reduced to a mental tally of trades. She wandered alone, hating the man she had to thank for belaying her fate, repaying hospitality with suspicion and lies.

The Lightmid sky was hazed, the air sticky. True to the nickname of their largest bay, the Lowlands seemed the armpit of Eiden. The accents thickened, as if each speaker were trying not to lose a mouthful of soup; the food grew bland, then sour.

It was easy to forget that she had been maimed, yet she never forgot. It was easy to forget what she had been sent to do—easy to fall into the rhythm of the journeyer, easy to believe she was what everyone she met took her to be—yet she never forgot. If she took a bed where there were no mages, or where mages had no pending work, she earned her keep by scrubbing a cookroom floor or digging post holes or forking hay down to livestock, and on those mornings she was only journeyer, not mage at all . . . and yet in every task she undertook was the wince of the task unfinished, in every floorboard was the feel of that hardened vellum, in every washline were the dark, alien lines of that scribing. It seeped into her flesh, downward from her eyes and out to her limbs, and everything solid she touched reminded her of the taint, the threat.

Ease and safety only made the threat more poignant.

On summer bonedays, you could smell the binders' harvest. On behalf of deceased relatives, offerings were left for the bonefolk, beyond the binding carcasses that were their province: cloth, blankets, tools, wines and ales and brandies, things it was assumed they did not produce themselves but that no one knew if they cared for, either. In the evenings, villagers gathered in the commons or the tavern, and there was no drink or dancing, just the drums beating a low drone. No tellers spoke on bonedays—only plain folk, remembering their dead. Children tore eyeholes in sackcloth and went begging sweets from door to door, pretending to be bonefolk; at home such behavior would have met with a scolding or worse, but Lowlanders were amused. Liath sat alone in a darkening hemlock grove and remembered Gran Breida as best she could without the family stories to fill in the gaps. Her own memories of her lost grandmother were scant.

An impossibly tall figure detached itself from a tree trunk and regarded her for what seemed a long time. She sat very still, staring at the bone-white face, the dark, brimming eyes. She had heard that they seemed ever on the verge of tears, that their fine, pale skin sagged on their elongated frames, as if they were melting, and it was true. There was both feminine and masculine in the peculiar face, but it suggested maleness to her. He cocked his head, blinked slowly; raised a long-fingered hand in a spindly wave that curled into itself as his wrist bent nearly double and brushed his chin. A mantis—an albino mantis was what he looked like. Each graceful motion seemed to be a calculation of leverage and tension. When he didn't move, she could barely see him; he blended with the dusk as if made of air and the memories of trees.

A troop of children crashed through the brush, their torches bobbing and smoking in the haze of stillness. They stumbled over Liath, and squealed and shrieked and then laughed with nervous relief. "We thought we found the boneyard!" one cried. Children, scaring themselves silly on the customary boneday hunt. Liath didn't tell them how close they'd come.

The boneman was gone as if he had never been there.

Mages rounded the children up and sent them on home, it was getting late, they should be in their beds, they'd find it next boneday. The children groaned.

"No harm done," she assured the mages. They took her back with them, let her watch them cast a gentling on the unpassaged spirits that bonedays made uneasy. They were haunt hunters, they told her; they followed the bonefolk, as best they could guess, and tried to cast passage for those who'd had no triad at their deaths.

"Do any of them manage to go on?" Liath asked.

The wordsmith answered, "It comforts me to think they do."

He was not Torrin Darkmage.

In Horm, six reckoners surrounded her, and no promise she made about obeying the call when she was ready was good enough for them. "Why can't it wait?" she said at last. The world was an endless obstacle course of bloody reckoners. "I might spend my whole life in the Holding—can't you grant me this little time?"

"There is special need of lights as bright as yours," one of them said at last. "This is not an ordinary call."

Yes, yes. To keep us out of the Darkmage's clutches. They thought they knew so much. She'd like to rub their noses in their ignorance until they promised her no proxy would ever harry her again. "I might as well tell you then," she said. "I *was* called, I told the truth about that. But . . . I went, you see. And they—" She saw again the triumph in Jonnula's eyes, Wynn Steward's condescension. "They threw me out."

They grilled her on details of the Holding, and she supplied them readily. She told them stories and half-truths, barely conscious of the lies that came so easily. In the end they had to let her go. She knew more than they did. That gave her power.

That night she dreamed in shadow, and in her dreams her shadow pooled around her, and spread, dissolving the ground beneath it; she sank into it slowly, helpless. She could not swim. She could not scream. There was nothing to hang on to.

In Umbril, near Maur Gowra, she met a wordsmith with sable eyes and a face so handsome it drove the breath from her. He claimed to be separated from his triad for a time, but wouldn't say why. Even the name he gave, Elfinnin, was beautiful. She followed him until he grew angry with her, then followed him further. "What do you *want* of me?" he snapped, and when she said, "To know you better," replied, "I'm traveling to see the girl I fathered on someone else's pledgemate. The situation is difficult enough. Would you leave me in peace?" She believed him, and mistrusted her belief—he was imposing, powerful, and could talk the sap out of a catsclaw tree. Still she dogged him, until they came across a journeying binder, and she contrived to pay their night's keep with a warding. The wordsmith had no choice but to agree. Liath had never felt so low as she did when the parchment came to her, filled with Elfinnin's scribing, and she had to hand it to the binder and flee. Leaving a casting in the middle; leaving a necessary casting undone; leaving the publican in the lurch. Running, like a coward.

He was so beautiful, and so talented, and she had so wanted to impress him. But he was not Torrin Wordsmith.

Nor was the man the locals complained about in Oeral, too big for his own triskele; nor the wordsmith said to have a queer hand, in Jedim; nor the one in Hoida, or in Ait, or Sask.

I'm here, she thought, weary and hot and desperate. *I'm here, Darkmage, with my bright extraordinary light.*

Find me.

"You're afraid to cast, aren't you."

It was Solly, a prentice boy the local illuminator had told her showed little promise. She'd seen him berated for attempting some pattern that was beyond him, and backed away, hoping not to embarrass him. She was embarrassed enough herself. The illuminator had taken grave offense when Liath declined to cast with her triad. But Solly had followed her around the bindinghouse, still holding his practice sheet.

"I was afraid to draw in the beginning," he confided.

"I'm not afraid," Liath said. She tried to turn the subject. "Where I come from, they didn't scold us for trying new things." *Not all of them, anyway.*

"It's not a new thing! I saw a journeyer do it. She called it knotwork. She was a Highlander. She was nicer than you."

Liath sighed. So that's what he'd intended, with his skewed scribble. "I didn't know illuminators don't do knotwork here."

"They don't. But you can show me, and then they will!" He plumped down beside her and leaned against the warm, weathered wood of the shack. "You're a Highlander."

"Well, yes, I am." She looked over what he had done.

Liath's knotwork specialty was long-curve-over-long-curve. It gave the effect of spiraling in without destroying continuity. The over-and-under, the continuity of path, the intentional breaking of continuity for effect—she loved knotwork. Spiraling felt in the hand the way it looked to the eye, a headlong rush down a turning hill, and was a joy to draw; but then you had a spiral, and that was that. Knotwork absorbed the gaze in the doing of it and afterward. The most challenging work to do well under time pressure, it afforded clever inventions while maintaining strict dimensions and constraints.

Kadri were work. It was the patterning she loved. Looping knots, executing weaves, fitting angles. Intertwining birds and beasts, making them wind around each other without losing their identifiable shape. Discovering the patterns in the scenes around her and painting them: drawing the world through her and re-creating it, filtered through her own eyes, in color and texture. Freezing one moment of time, one tableau, before the manuscript dissipated and returned it to the transformed world.

She showed the boy her knotwork tricks, scrawling in chalk on the back of a discarded piece of bark. The chalk left crumbles against the hairy surface, and her lines went wiggly over bumps, but it was such pleasure to draw again. . . . "Will you let me try already!" the boy burst out. She blinked, and surrendered chalk and treeskin. It took practice to make the trick work without a grid; when at last he got it, his eyes shone with fierce delight.

He showed his teacher, who used it in a casting that afternoon. Liath's throat tightened, and she had to walk away. By evening she was back on the road.

She showed the illuminator in the next place, and the one after that. She showed them other tricks and knacks and techniques; she learned how fine her training had been by comparison with the plain craft she saw. She had been taught by a proxy, after all; it was hard to believe even now, but Hanla had been a mage at the Holding, she and Graefel had undergone the same trials of passage, and had gone on to learn whatever higher castings the Holding taught them after they went through that inner door. Holding mages steeped in techniques and styles from the wide world over. Now Liath brought Hanla's training back into the world. In return it showed her new castings—how to break fieldstones, soften a stump's roots, clear a tainted well—but she was denied the practice of them. She had to be content with the one new knack she could use: the knack of showing others her knacks. Most illuminators' craft was quite basic—two dozen kadri, a handful of weaves, familiarity with only local materials. The limited contents of most binder's sacks appalled her.

"You can trade, you know," she told a bindswoman in Strall. She had woken late in the triad's cottage, to the pitiful cries of a dozen late weanling lambs milling in the binding pen. The wordsmith and illuminator had gone off on some errand. The binder, busy in the yard, was never still; she put Liath to work rubbing pumice powder over scraped calfskins. "Our binder was always after any binders who passed through, pestering to see what their journey trusses held. I saw him trade an entire lot of sedgeweave for one beetle once. It made a powerful iridescent paint."

The binder stirred some goatskins in a lime barrel, then took up a whetstone and a thin, curved blade. "I'm sure your binder was very special," she said. "Our triad serves three large towns, and it's all I can do to supply the basics. Swap meets and travel are a luxury few can afford."

"But if it improves the craft . . ."

"Craft is craft. It works as is; what would I do with shiny beetles, and strange songs I can't get my throat around? I have work to do, girl. Come hold this lamb for me, or grub for beetles, it's up to you."

Liath stared at the trembling lamb. Keiler had never let anyone near him on the days he took skins. Befre had taught him not to. Befre had said that death was a private thing—a terrible, somber ritual. Befre had said that no one should be permitted to witness murder. Keiler had told her so, before he stopped sharing his binder's lore with her, when they got older and the triadic separations became important. Some of the light had gone out of his eyes the day he first assisted Befre in harvesting vellum. "There's no other use for a bull calf," he'd murmured, on the overlook up the bindsman's road. "It would never have been born, and anyway it was asleep, it never knew it was dying." He was trying to convince himself. When she came out to offer comfort, he shouted at her for following him, and it took days for them to make it up. He was harder after that.

"I'm not a binder," she said.

"I have no prentice. You're a mage with a strong pair of hands. It'll go easier if you hold him still for me. Pet him, talk to him. You don't have to stay for the cut."

The lamb knew. He strained to the end of his tether, squealing in a panic for his mother; the lambs in the pen renewed their frightened bleats. Liath could not keep hold of his wriggling, downy body.

The woman swore. "You're right, you're not a binder." She cupped the small head firmly, bringing her eyes down level with the lamb's. Liath could not make out what she did, but after a moment the little body sank limp to the ground. His eyes slid shut, his breathing slowed to the rhythm of sleep. The binder trussed him by the back legs over the cauldron and retrieved her long knife from a worktable. Liath remembered the feel of knife biting flesh, and her gorge rose, but she made herself stay as the cut was made, and the blood flowed down the pale woolly chin and into the cauldron, and the rise and fall of the lamb's sides ceased.

"You see?" the binder said. "Not so horrible. No pain. Pain would seep into the skin, make the parchment unusable."

"But he was afraid," Liath said. Phlegm clogged her throat. "Won't that be in the parchment?"

"It was only for a moment. He might feel as much in a thunderstorm. Now leave me. I've got to do the rest before the wind shifts. I don't want them to smell the blood."

After a time, her hand ached more than her heart; the absence of the motion of drawing was a pain deep in the bones. She craved kadri. She yearned to grasp the delicate hollowness of quill, to caress the flesh of page with wet black ink, to feel the muscles in her hand bunch and flex. She let her hair grow out that she might plait it, something to do with her fingers. She dressed Amaranth's mane and tail till the mare nipped at her in irritation. Like a cottar, she wove baskets, braided hemp—she took up any craft that would let her feel, for just a few breaths, something like the feeling of her own. A still pool after a rain showed her the face of a hard drinker on a Darkmid spirit day: pallid, pinched, desperate for a draught of what made her feel alive.

Alone, resting beside a dusty road, she found a stick in her hand, deadfall blown from an ash grove threfts behind her. Her fist tightened on it, then relaxed; her fingertips slid down, took control of the point, braced the shaft against her knuckle. Lines appeared in the dirt, overlaid on a memory of childhood, her inability to abstain from the forbidden.

Those are patterns, Liath. You know better than that. Patterns are for mages, not for little girls.

They are not! They're just lines!

That's the sun, isn't it? And clouds? And cottages?

Don't be angry, Mother.

I'm not . . . angry, Liath.

Then why do you look so mean?

Oh, Liath . . .

Don't cry! I won't do it again, I promise! . . . Mother?

Rub it out, right now. Rub it out, tell no one, and never, ever do this again. Do you understand me? Never again! And tell no one!

Liath looked down at the figure in the dirt. She had drawn the kadra Hunger.

She cast the stick away and scrubbed the figure back into dust. Hot tears spilled from her eyes as she covered her face with her soiled hands.

Mud: the essence of Eiden. It was not her element. She was not his child. When her hands came away, they left a mask like the ones naughty children wore on bonedays. She had worn such a mask as a shroud in the Aralinns; perhaps if she wore this one long enough, she might begin to believe it was her true face. There was no water to wash it off. By the time she came to a stream, wind and sun had dried the mud, and the mask had cracked.

A mage she met in Kepil claimed to be on a second journeying because he felt like it, but the words did not ring true. His light was middling, his eyes shifty. It turned out that his binder and illuminator had distrusted him so much they'd had their triad dissolved.

His hand was cramped and jagged. He was not Torrin Wordsmith.

In Yorl, a mage exhausted from weathercastings cursed the Ennead and all magecraft. But his hand was spidery and sprawling. He was not Torrin Wordsmith.

A wordsmith in Ginsk called her aside before a casting and asked her to leave with him and find a binder to make a new triad. He was in love with his pledged illuminator, he said, and could no longer bear to work with her. When Liath told him that no journeyer would do such a thing before his current triad was dissolved, he grew despondent; but he brightened when she said she'd consider it, only she'd have to watch him cast first. His hand was blotted and muddy, and she thought he might cry when she bid them farewell.

A man like that would not be Torrin Wordsmith.

"You must do this casting," said an illuminator in Bessef. "It's the only way you're going to learn."

"I'm too tired. I've been casting everywhere I went."

"I'm tired too. We've been shearing by day and rolling by night. When you're triaded you'll have to cast whether you're tired or ill or in a foul mood. Sit down, dear. Now."

Liath looked at the wordsmith. He was a nondescript man, perhaps five nines of winter, with sloping shoulders, thinning hair, and a dull light. She never wanted to see another wordsmith's work. She could not cast with every triad in the world.

"I'll do the next one," she said weakly. "Just let me see you work first. Please?"

The illuminator threw up her hands. "Have it your own way. But if you don't pull your weight, I'll have you listening to the fleece breathe while I cuddle in bed with my pledgemate."

Liath took her now-accustomed place behind the illuminator and waited through the endless scritch of quill on vellum. She couldn't even remember what this casting was for.

When the wordsmith handed the inscribed vellum on to the illuminator, Liath gave it only a halfhearted glance. Tight, overcareful marks; the wordsmith had never relaxed into his work. Then she blinked, and looked again. The ornate ascenders, the tilted crossbars, the odd cant . . .

It was Torrin's hand.

She rubbed her eyes. His light was not that bright . . . it could not be him . . . yet the ciphers squirmed on the page, black maggots burrowing into the calfskin, an infestation of marks, a living pox. They grew invisible, insectile legs and crawled to the edges of the leaf, migrating, multiplying—she had to stifle a warning to the illuminator, she must not give away that she knew, but she could not hold back, if the things touched her hands the woman was lost—

"Stop!" she cried. "Don't let them touch you!"

"What in Eiden's name . . . ?"

"He's not—it's not—don't—" He was staring at her, his bovine eyes widening. The binder had risen to take her arm. She shook him off, transfixed by the wordsmith's gaze.

"It's not *what?*" the illuminator snapped. Swearing, she got up and held the vellum to Liath's face. "It's a piece of calfskin, girl. He's my wordsmith, Bayle. What is *wrong* with you?"

Liath gaped. The wordsmith's marks were tight, confined. There was no life to them. He was lucky they worked at all.

"I'm sorry . . ."

"As well you should be! Interrupting a perfectly routine casting. Go on with you! Are you sick in the head?"

Liath put one foot in front of the other: back to the binder's house, to the barn beyond it, where her gear was stowed, where Amaranth's serene presence would make the world right again.

"I'm not done with you!" the illuminator called as her triad sat down to salvage the casting. The binder said something about looking after her, the wordsmith mumbled agreement, but the illuminator was tired and cranky and planned hard words for her.

Liath leaned her head on Amaranth's neck for a long time, inhaling the sweetness of hay and living flesh and rich manure.

"I'm seeing things now," she told the mare. "I'm seeing his ciphers where they aren't. They've poisoned me. What will I do?"

The mare whuffled gently and bent her head to the hay bin.

She bedded that night on short straw in an empty herdsman's shed. Its withy roof wanted thatching; starlight leaked in and stained the rough walls with dim blue figures. Ciphers wormed along the floor, marched like ants over her tight-wrapped sleeproll, crawled into her nose and ears and the corners of her eyes, became an undulating, blacker black against the darkness behind her lids. She lay whimpering until dawn breached the tattered thatch, and found her blankets soaked with sweat. Her hands would not stop shaking.

"I'll find you, Darkmage," she said into the puff of dust her rising made in the flail refuse. "I'll find you and I'll stuff your cursed ciphers down your throat."

The Lightmid days shortened on their inexorable journey to Ve Eiden, to equinox, to balance. Everywhere she passed the summer drudgery of weeding, but she could not uproot the foul things that had seeded in her mind. Haying time came, and she cut and rolled and raked and cocked with the rest, from morning dew till evening; she welcomed the noonday sleep, when the golden glow diffused the writhing shadows behind her eyes; she drank barley water and herbal brews and ate the bread and cheese and onions distributed by the haymasters, glad to have earned her food with honest labor. She gave ordinary lights no notice; if he could mask his light, he was beyond her finding. Her search thus quickened, she fell into a routine: harvest or dress some flax or hemp, enjoy a meal and the anonymous companionship of workers, inquire after the local triad, sniff for magelight, and go on—or stay, if there was a bright light, and suffer the brief indignity of the observer, just long enough to see the scribing, then away with no explanation.

His ciphers were muddled. He was not Torrin Wordsmith.

His ciphers were jittery. He was not Torrin Wordsmith.

His hand was slanted backward. He was not Torrin Wordsmith.

His hand was thick, his hand was thin, his hand was exacting, his hand was sloppy; his hand was this, his hand was that. . . .

Dogged resolve was not enough. Hard travel was not enough. She looked, and looked, and looked. But they were not Torrin Wordsmith.

Summer lay heavy on the land as she came into the Haunch.

Because its members were all pledged into local crafteries, the Ardra triad had no cottage, but kept a large post-and-beam bindinghouse staffed by family members, at the end of an oak-lined lane not far from where the Vrea rambled down past the millhouse. Haunch folk took pride in tending their trees, perhaps because the empty grasslands of the Girdle were a stone's throw away. Their arbors were a balm to the spirit, and all the fields and buildings were framed by stately elms, shaded under the spread of walnuts, encircled by tulip trees or fringed with dogwoods. They pruned and watered their gentle, crafted landscape, and this morning the bee drone and birdsong was cut by the firm, arrhythmic smack of tight-rolled linen on bark—a tree tender on his nineday rounds, whacking the trunks to get their sap moving. Linen was the other pride of the Haunch. The flax had come in a nineday past, and scents of ash and urine and droppings hung in the still air: folk were leying bucks, pouring lye through deep-packed barrels of linen folds.

It was a listless morning under a heat-hazed sky, a day for sitting in shade and sipping juice fresh from a coldcellar. She had watched the triad cast, ascertained that its wordsmith was not the Darkmage—no surprise, for he was a genteel family man with a long history here—and left them. She hitched Amaranth by a trough outside the Golden Swan and surveyed the dappled commons. How sweet to rest here, even for half a day . . . The half-timbered buildings were framed of hardwood, three and even four stories high, with roofs and moldings in the familiar triangular patterns, the exteriors plastered with bluish river clay. A far cry from the three-bay stone cottages common in the Neck. The haying was done, the corn not yet ready, and townsfolk had taken as much of their work outside as they could. A man had filled two buckets from the central well in the triangle and was porting them on a yoke over his shoulders. Children rolled hoops or frolicked with the quick, compact brindle dogs favored by dairyfolk in the region. Two women had hauled a row of saddletrees from their workshop and were sanding them preparatory to padding them and stitching on the heavy linen. A pair of young boys worked an enormous quilt, no doubt a pledging gift for an older sister. Young people called to each other across the green; a man walked sedately along the edge, sprinkling water on the street, and two horses slowing from trot to walk raised hardly a puff of dust.

Two men in black rode the horses.

With a soft oath, Liath turned, slipping her triskele inside her shirt lest the light catch it, and walked into the public house. They were probably bound for the triad's place, or to lay in supplies. She'd sample the ale here, find it wanting, and be on her way while they were still engaged in their business.

The tavern was quiet. Muted sunlight illumined the knots and swirls in burnished walnut. The stools were cushioned, the pewter tankards polished to a silken sheen; each small, round table sported a bouquet of herbs and flowers, angle-bound to stand on end like barley stacks, and the rafters were festooned with fragrant garland. She breathed deep, and caught only the faintest tang of sour ale. The clear hardwood floor was streaked with damp.

She was so, so far from home.

She offered the publican a tallystick she'd earned in lieu of supper, bundling hemp in the last village; he knew the roper who held its long end, and it bought her a pitcher of his own ale and a deep bowl of chilled tomato-and-celery soup. She settled into a corner by the window, to the back of the propped-open door.

By the cold hearth, a teller droned to her prentice, a wide-eyed girl of seven or eight. Lone drinkers were scattered at tables, brooding or resting. A handful of rumpled, travel-worn folk who could only be seekers sat in silence by a raised dais, contemplating the depths of their ale.

As she raised the spoon trembling toward her lips, she looked across at the wan face of a man bringing a tankard to his own lips with hands that shook as badly. He met her gaze and gave a sympathetic shrug. She looked down, quelling a flash of anger. Were their maladies so different?

Would that drinking deep of the lush colors of summer could soothe her ache as fresh ale soothed his—or that freeing herself of something as simple as drink would banish the shadows that stalked her.

". . . and the man who could not die," the teller's prentice said, her voice rising as she lost hold of the end of the story, "despairing in his loneliness, sailed off into the land beyond the mists, because . . . because . . . Oh, I don't remember why, it's such a long sad story."

"He sailed off into the land beyond the mists because he believed that if he lived alone, he would never again be brokenhearted over the passing of a loved one." The teller had shed the incantatory tone and was explaining now, gently. "Was that a good idea, do you think?"

"Well, if no one lives there. But people must live there. People live everywhere."

"That's right. But what did we just talk about? The different kinds of stories, yes?"

"Oh! I see. That's one of the teaching and thinking stories, not one of the real ones. Are any of the faraway lands real ones?"

"No. And that is your introduction to adulthood, my pet. Some stories we tell to enthrall and entertain, made-up stories about made-up places that give people something to mull over, or dream about. Other stories we tell because they're true and important and must be remembered. We are Eiden's memory, you and I and the other tellers. But we're also amusement for Eiden's children on long winter nights. Tonight you're to make up a story of a place that could never be, and tomorrow you'll tell it to me. Put it in the same form as the funny one we did earlier."

"A tall tale?"

"Very good. Eldrinda's first tall tale. Well, aside from the time you told your mother a freak wind knocked the clothesline in the mud. Now tell me something about the land beyond the rain."

"It *can't* be a Great Storm!" The seeker erupted from silence so violently that he upset his little table and had to wrestle it level again. "We have those all the time."

"I wouldn't call three in a generation 'all the time,' " another shot back, as if they'd never stopped talking.

"Perhaps there's a particularly big one coming," said another, more calmly. "There's *something* coming. All the signs point to it."

"Galandra is not going to sail back on the wings of a storm!"

Seekers' conversations seemed to be the same conversation, continued over lifetimes, all across the world, among all their members. This debate made no sense to Liath, but their debates never did; usually they only gave her a headache, as logic failed them and they compensated with volume.

Outside the window, someone said, "Hold up a breath."

Liath paused with the spoon lifted.

"What's wrong?"

"Besides warders who don't do their cursed job? Phlox."

The soup spilled back into the bowl. She slurped the remainder quickly, and tried not to cock her head. If only the bloody seekers would shut up.

"Is he all right?"

"Just a stone—here, that's got it. Look, these rings are good for something!"

It was the reckoners. Their errand concluded, if they'd had any, they'd stopped in the alley when the horse pulled up.

"Looks all right. He's got his weight on it now."

Good. Go on your way. I've had enough of lying to you people. She had to strain to hear them, as the prentice girl raised her voice to be heard over the seekers.

"I'm still bothered about that hail," one reckoner said.

"Must we discuss this now?" said the other.

"We have to rest sometime."

"They have to be told. You know that."

"But it's such a long hot way to have to go. Why not—"

"—stop in this tavern for a mug of cool ale?"

Liath held her breath.

"Well . . ."

"No. I know you. One would become three."

A chuckle. "And three become one . . . in my belly."

"Let's go."

"But one of us should go back. I tell you, this stone in his foot is a sign. The spirits are telling us something!"

"Eiden wept. What seemed amiss?"

Liath took a sip of ale. It was cool and touched with mint, a fine job of brewing. She barely acknowledged it.

"Their wardings should have held."

"Shoddy magework. It happens."

"They were good mages, solid lights."

"So they made a mistake! Time is wasting. We can talk while we ride. Mount up."

"But to go all the way to—"

"I'm certain our reckonings aren't getting through. I don't trust the chain anymore. We go ourselves, and that's that."

"Do you smell something?"

Liath squeezed herself between the window and the wall, trying to peer out from the shadows. The angle was wrong.

"Besides this midden heap?"

Inside the tavern, a seeker said, "If the world will be transformed at the third coming of Galandra—"

"There has been no second!" said another seeker.

"We don't know that."

"—then what better agent to transform it than a storm? Or a trio of Great Storms?"

Shut up! Liath beseeched them.

"No," she heard through the window. "I don't smell a thing. You will not lure me into that tavern with a fabrication." At last they came into view: two fair figures in black, riding down the alley and away.

Liath slumped back into her seat and poured the rest of the ale into her tankard. The shaking drunk raised a feeble toast to her, having observed her actions with bleary amusement.

"We have no way of knowing whether the second coming has happened or not," a seeker said, rehashing an argument Liath had overheard countless times before. They believed Galandra would return in times of great need, and that her visits, three in all, would form a Great Trine. Their hopeless question was whether the next time would be the second coming, or the third. *Now would be a good time, Galandra,* Liath thought.

"It might have already happened, and no one remembers, not even tellers," another seeker said.

"Ask this one! Teller, have you no tale of ancient upheaval to tell us?"

"For you to pick apart and use as fodder for your deafening debates?" the teller snapped. "We're in the land beyond the rain here. You know where you can put your Great Trines."

"Folk rely on you to tell their past truly," said the first seeker, "and you stuff fairy tales in their mouths like sweets."

"We heard what you told your girl," said the second.

"I will not argue with you people," the teller replied. "You come here, you collect my stories, you whine at me how you must have more to work with. I've given you all I know!"

"Not *us.*"

"You're all the same. I'm training a prentice here. Is this to be her first tale? How a pack of seekers drove her poor old master berserk? 'And the first seeker he bashed with an iron from the hearth; and the second he did choke with fragrant garland; and the third, to make a Great Trine of it, he—' "

"All right!" The seekers laughed. "All right, old man!" They raised their drinks and called for a humorous tale, and it was at least a dozen breaths before they lapsed into an argument over the origin of jokes. The debate grew so heated that the teller's prentice had to shout to be heard; her child's voice was piercing, and the man with the shakes gave Liath a pitiful look and buried his head in his arms.

Under the cacophony and the publican's helplessly polite attempts to intercede, their words braided with the proxies' in Liath's mind. She remembered Gran Oriane, sitting in the Petrel's Rest, regaling them with her experience of the last Great Storms. The sky going dark, the wind rising, the sea thrashing; Lowlanders fleeing the coast and taking refuge as far upland as Iandel and Clondel and Drey. How they knew the Ennead had split the Storm and sent it safely around because the roiling black clouds overhead separated and boiled off Armsward. Of the unnatural calm that followed, all the breath sucked out of the sky.

The Great Storms came because, despite all Galandra had done, Sylfonwy and Morlyrien would never be at peace. What was it that Torrin Wordsmith could do, or empower the Ennead to do, that Galandra could not? And what havoc would that power wreak, if he bound enough strong mages?

The purpose of the Ennead—the true purpose, beneath the organizing tasks that had accrued to them—was to thwart the Great Storms. Facing into the Windward Sea, ever vigilant against the Storms that boiled out of that sea without notice, they sheltered all Eiden Myr in the lee of their powerful Holding.

What better vengeance, what better flaunting of raw power, what better way to clear the field of competition, than to invoke the Great Storms at will? If Torrin was the key to stopping them forever, was he not the key to engendering them too? He could prove his might and ruin the Ennead all in one blow. If he could summon, without warning, storms of that magnitude, he might sweep away the ancient stone fastness of the Holding itself.

Now you're thinking like some crackpot seeker, she told herself. *And yet that must be how Torrin plans to destroy the Ennead—and the whole world with them.*

The seekers were up, shouting in each other's faces.

She downed her ale and slammed the heavy tankard down. "Oi!" she cried. "This fellow keeps a spotless house and brews a fine ale. Mind your bleeding manners!" Then she hefted her pack off the seat next to her and left the stunned seekers, the astonished prentice, the laughing teller, and the gaping drunk behind.

If she did not find the Darkmage, there would be no gentle, crafted towns; there would be no reckoners to worry, or seekers to puzzle it out, or tellers left to tell the tale. If the Great Storms were not diverted, they would sweep away all life and memory, and there would be nothing left at all.

The commons was as she had left it, but over every calm, beautiful thing she saw was the traced outline of catastrophe. The buildings tumbled shells, the trees uprooted and strewn like tallysticks, the children and little brindle dogs lying dead . . .

She mounted Amaranth and reined her Legward.

The two reckoners were hiding behind a dovecote. They converged on her before she could turn. The shorter one took Amaranth's reins, and snapped down hard when the mare tossed her head.

"You'll come with us now," the taller one said.

She protested, and they told her to mind her place. Every subterfuge and persuasion that had worked on previous reckoners failed on these. She asked their names, sought to soften them, to make it personal—but Jimor and Laren would not be softened.

She had underestimated the thing that reckoners did best, the thing that reckoners existed to do: pass information. "You've carved a trail of lies over half of Eiden's body. You've been called time after time. You've said no or you've claimed you'd go, yet here you are, still journeying."

"I'll go tomorrow," she said, but there was no hope for it—she had exhausted their collective patience. Given time, the Ennead might hear of her, and send back some excuse for leaving her in peace. But she didn't have that time.

"No," they said. "You'll come now."

She heeled Amaranth hard and the unsettled mare gathered her hindquarters and drove forward. But the smaller reckoner was prepared. He'd looped the rope around the horn of his wrangler's saddle, and his cutting horse had braced. Amaranth was tugged around hard, and Liath, who was not, came half out of her seat.

She loosed her off foot from the stirrup and slipped down the rest of the way. Laren tried to hoist her back into her saddle, but she made herself dead weight. Swearing, he dismounted and called for Jimor to help him.

Liath drove her elbow into the soft cavity under his ribs and left him gasping. Jimor was off his horse before she came around, but from the corner of her eye she saw him swinging and ducked. No way to know if he'd meant to hit her or grab her. But she would not run. If they wanted to take her, they would have to fight her.

For a moment she dared hope that would end it. No reckoner would physically force an unwilling mage into the Ennead's service. But Jimor faced her, balanced, ready—accepting her challenge.

He was heavier and stronger. When they grappled, she threw him, but he recovered in an eyeblink, rolling onto his back and tangling her ankles with his. She writhed to keep from going down, and hit the ground hard instead of taking the fall. Laren had his breath back and his feet under him. If they got on top of her it was over. One she might wrestle into a body lock, but not two.

She kicked viciously at Jimor, giving him no choice but to pull back to cover himself, then did what he least expected—launched herself at him. He tried to use her own momentum to flip her over him and away, but as she hit him she clutched hard, blind, and got a solid grip on shirt and hair. They tumbled, both struggling to come out on top. With a sickening thunk, his head hit the dovecote. Pigeons burst forth in a scatter of sheddown.

She disengaged her limbs, staggered to her feet, turned to look for Laren. He crashed into her from the side. They went down. He pinned her, tried to capture her wrists. She looked into his dirt-streaked face and said, "Is it worth all this?"

"You *must* come with us," he grated.

She could not get her leg in position to knee his crotch. He had one of her hands now and was bending it back, trying to make her give up the other one. She stopped fighting. Startled, he looked down at her, and she cracked him hard between the eyes with the top of her forehead.

The impact dazed her so much that she had trouble rolling him off her. He was still breathing. So was Jimor. The spirits had been kind— she hadn't killed either one.

Not yet.

She stood on shaky legs and leaned against the limewashed wall of the dovecote. She'd have to fetch the triad; a few sleepbreaths might make the difference between life and death. But after a brief hesitation, she stripped them of clothes and rings and stowed them in her saddle pack, put their cloaks in Jimor's saddlebags and laid them across Amaranth's withers. Two men in their underclothes would find it hard to persuade anyone they were proxies.

Only after she'd ridden around back of the bindinghouse, told the girl there that an urgent healing was needed at the dovecote in the linden grove, and put a good three leagues between herself and the mess she'd left did her shaking ease. She pulled up short.

The reckoners in the alley had been fair. Jimor and Laren were dark. She had seen only the black clothes, thought only of getting free. They were not the reckoners she had heard talking.

Ennead proxies would not abduct a mage.

She wheeled Amaranth and ran full-out back to the bindinghouse, but the triad had been to the dovecote and come back alone. "There was no one there," they said, measuring her, not sure yet whether they should be angry.

At a loss for an explanation—even a false one—she turned and left, following the river slowly now.

They were Torrin's men. She should have let them take her.

She stopped by the dovecote and tried to track them, thinking that they would have to return to him, to report, to resupply themselves, and she could trail them there. But no sign remained. She dawdled the rest of the day, riding in a loose circle, rehearsing apologies. But she'd had her chance, and let it pass. There was nothing to do but go on.

That night she took the rolled-up clothes out of her pack and poised to fling them, and the saddlebags, in the Vrea.

Then she looked at what she held. Jimor was of a height with her, but thicker; Laren was half a head shorter, but of comparable girth. With the sleeves rolled up and the hose tucked in her boots so the shortfall wouldn't show . . .

It was like garbing herself in shadow. The ring was loose on her finger, the silver chill. She rolled Jimor's cloak behind her saddle, and consigned the rest to the river current.

She journeyed, then, in the darkest times—a black-garbed shadow on a sunrise-colored horse in the depths of night. Deep into the Weak Leg she rode, through rushy, bird-strident marshes, over roads that were little more than planks laid across sucking bogs, into jungles where tin-roofed houses were set on stilts or braced around the trunks of great-canopied trees. She saw the weird flicker of Galandra's light; she saw vibrant flowers, as big as her head, that smelled of rot; she saw trees that wept. She heard the nightlong screech of strange animals, inhaled the miasma of perfumed decay that was the lowest of the Lowlands, where everyone looked like lost Gadiya and Torbik, where everyone eyed her as if she were one of their vaporous swamp haunts. Inland, they warded their jungle from wildlife and burned it for charcoal; on higher ground she passed the furnaces rendering the ore dredged from the splayed rivers between the Toes. Dug and lined and domed, the earth belched searing fumes.

Separated from the group mind into which she'd never been initiated, a lifelong evader of reckoners, she had to guess at how to behave, how to persuade. When she found a bright light, she observed him scribing, and no one questioned—she was a reckoner. In strange airy inns and public houses, she inquired after shifts in trade; if he was marshaling mages, he would need supplies. She could ask them anything, and they would believe it was information the Ennead required. She could tell them anything, and they would believe it to be double-checked, Ennead-sanctioned. A ring, a cloak, dyed clothes . . . it took so little to bestow so much power.

A rogue proxy was a dangerous thing. Only now, a rogue mage herself, and so easily duped by rogue mages, did she begin to understand the depth of the Ennead's fear—and the depth of the Darkmage's desire.

A picture was forming, but it was incomplete. More of this product than usual going here; more of that product coming out of there. None of it pointing to a central location that might be his fastness. There were anomalies in trade, just as there were anomalies in weather, but none of it jibed.

More information than could be had in a tavern would come from only one source: the reckoners themselves. She grit her teeth. She had banished the spectre of her childhood by inhabiting it. This last step—to join them—could not be that hard.

Her hair cropped short and bleached with stolen soapmaker's lye, she looked nothing like the travel-worn, red-plaited journeymage who'd lied her way across the Lowlands. She said little, let them assume what they would; like the vocates she had known, they answered their own questions, and explained her appearance for her. An offhand mention of strange weather or unusual shifts in trade brought a torrent of opinions. But in the end they had only pieces, just as she did, and their group mind was spread over too wide a world to make a reasonable whole of them.

Casually, always so casually, and never by name—she let them supply that—she mentioned the Darkmage.

"Oh, steer clear of him," they told her. "You've a bright light. He'll be wanting that. Stick with us, don't travel alone."

"I was a vocate when he was coming up," someone said. "He was Holding-born, or close enough, always intended for the Ennead . . ."

"He was to pledge Lerissa, I heard, but Evonder stole her from him. Some triad that would have been!"

"No no, they couldn't stand each other. You think vocates are competitive? Try being groomed for the Ennead."

The more she learned, the more she learned they didn't know. They knew the Torrin of the past, the bright scion of Holding mages, the great hope; they knew a youth or a man who kept his own counsel, went his own way—in other words, knew him not at all. They knew he had fallen, but had a dozen reasons why, and no two the same—all guesses, rumors. They knew he would seek to bind them, if he found them—but it had become a kind of contest to see whose light burned bright enough to attract the Darkmage, and no one she met was missing a friend or colleague. Some of them were probably his agents. Some of them, she suspected, secretly hoped to be found, the potential of a second ennead resurrecting long-dashed hopes. Many were half in love with him, or at least with the idea of him, even the ones who didn't bed men.

I'm the one he has to find, she thought. *And he won't find me among these people.*

The proxy chain was more a mesh of links: groups of reckoners who circled, in small parties, over an area, passing regularly over the edges of the nearest circles and exchanging news at the intersections. But there was always a need to pass information outside the scheduled overlaps. Several times she had been mistaken for a proxy rover; now she assumed the role, as real reckoners did who'd fallen out with their groups, or who hungered for harder and more varied travel.

"Is there any word of the Darkmage's whereabouts?" she would ask after delivering a message, sitting with reckoners around a driftwood fire near the coast, or a turf fire in an inland tavern, or a fragrant birch fire by a river. "No one knows," they would reply, or "If we knew where he was, so would the Ennead, and put a stop to him soon enough." Derisively, they would list the rumors they had heard and heard debunked: He was holding mages prisoner in the Fist. He was underground in the Girdle, or on an island in Lough Isil or Lough Grendig or Lough This or Lough That, or in old mining tunnels in the Blooded Mountains . . . He was everywhere in Eiden Myr at once, and if he wasn't then he had been there, or was on his way. There was no countenancing any of it.

The messages were all panicked weather reports, complaints against lax warders. If he had been in the Lowlands, he was gone now—she had traveled them all, and there was not a breath of word in the humid air. And if there had been, could she have made sense of it? Fragments told her nothing. Only the Ennead, where all information came to rest, could see the shift and swirl of patterns across the world. She had bogged down. There was no firm place to dig in here, no stone to fashion into a holding that would protect and conceal. She began taking messages bound upland, and made her way, leg by leg, back along the flat coast of Maur Lengra, toward the Crotch and the Girdle. *This is the last one*, she thought, as she accepted a Head-bound message from another rover, repeating it back to him word for word. The phrasing of the message was everything; if any reckoner along the chain garbled it even a little, incorrect information would reach the Holding. She took care to pass exactly the words that had been entrusted to her. But she had acted, for too long, on precisely the words that had been said to her at the outset. That would no longer serve.

The information the Ennead had given her when she left was at least two seasons old. Now she understood the timeliness of reports, the uselessness of the outdated. She refused to fail the Ennead by clinging to their information past all reason. Suppose they had learned differently by now, but had no way to tell her? He was not in the Lowlands—not in the Fist, as Lerissa believed, or in the Weak Leg, as Worilke believed. She would deliver this report to the proxy circle that met near Rikka, then strike off for the Highlands. The Fingers were gnarled with rock, the Strong Leg ridged; from Head to Boot, Eiden's body was one long series of mountain ranges. He was up there, somewhere. He had to be.

She got past Kark, nearly to Rikka, before she was waylaid by local mages. It was an isolated village, as were most in this dark, vine-choked leg. Their relief at finding her was profound, always a bad sign, a sign that something important wanted doing. She tried to ride past, but they trailed her, pleading. The illuminator was down with a raving fever. Her triad couldn't cure it without her. "Tell us you were trained illuminator," the binder begged. *No*, her mind lied as her head nodded reflexively. "But

I can't—" "There's a baby coming. Her last birth was difficult. Come. We haven't time." Anguished, Liath followed to their cottage, a mud-caulked osier weave among brittle bonewood trees. "I can't cast with you," she finished, trying to stop them chalking the casting circle around the birthing stool where the woman sweated and moaned. Children and aunts and cousins stared at her; the pledgemate, gripping the woman's hand, supporting her back as she arched in agony, blinked at her, uncomprehending. *I should have run. I should have lied. I should have ridden on and let them curse me.* The woman screamed. The wordsmith strode to Liath, dug fingers into her shoulders and shook her hard, said through gritted teeth, "You *must* cast with us. *Now.*" "I can't, it's not permitted, a Holding edict, I can only observe . . ." While lies came pouring from her mouth, too late, blood and fluid poured from between the woman's legs. Her ragged cries filled the air. They were all just *standing* there! Liath knelt by the stool, reached out, but the pledgemate struck her aside. "We need a *mage!*" he shouted, and at last the others crowded in, took action. Liath pulled herself off the floor, stumbled back against a wardrobe, watched in horror as the infant emerged limp, a mottled blue under the birth fluids. "Don't be dead," she breathed. "Oh, spirits, don't let him be dead. . . ." A knife flashed, the cord was cut, someone bent to the tiny mouth to pass breath to the lungs—

"It's no good," a voice said, an interminable time later. The room had grown dark. Someone was sobbing. A nearer voice, the binder's, said in her ear, "Get out. Get out before I strangle you with that chain around your neck." She groped for the beaded entry, and her toe caught a wicker-work cradle and sent it spinning into the wall. She fled through the dark-ened common room.

The wordsmith emerged as she stood gripping Amaranth's saddle, unable to pull herself aboard.

"There's been enough death here today," he said, "or I would send you to join that poor babe. You go to your Ennead, and give them the story of what happened here, in return for their *edict.*"

It was a lie, there was no edict, it's not their fault—it's not my fault, if I had not come here it would have been no different, you would have had no more illuminator than you do now—

Liath dragged herself onto the mare and rode into the onset of night, unable to close her ears against the deafening silence of the child's cry that had never come.

She blundered onto the gathering of the proxy circle: a dozen reckoners, who met in this wooded campground once a moon, then dispersed to guide their local triads, meeting the members of other circles at the other triadic points. Liath delivered the report of flooding in the Toes with dull precision. Another rover repeated it back to her and, at her nod, headed out.

Liath took the proffered food, but when it was gone she could not remember having eaten it. They tried to jolly her out of her daze, said there had to be *some* gossip from downleg. Drought still plagued the Heartlands, while the Haunch was smothered in fogs and the Girdle had seen more rain in one summer than all the previous year; it was nothing new, and they were bored, looking for something unusual to occupy their group mind. From habit she alluded to the Darkmage, but they seemed disappointed, as if this too was a tired subject. They droned a list of sightings— in so many places so widely spaced that they could not all be correct, and were probably all wrong.

"What difference does it make *where* he is?" someone asked. "What matters is what he does, and the Ennead will see to that."

"But proxies *are* the Ennead, out in the world," Liath said, her bent head coming up slowly.

"The Darkmage eats proxies for supper," someone else said—

And they laughed. The rest of them *laughed*.

Such power these reckoners wielded, such authority, when the whole world was at risk, and they spent their time gossiping, bedding each other, anticipating festivals, their next meal. Complacent in safety. Laughing at what would destroy them.

And I was frightened of this, she thought. *They don't deserve those rings they wear.*

And you don't deserve that triskele, said Jonnula. Liath looked dully at the treeshadow that had spoken. *No*, she thought. *No, you're right. I don't.*

Never lie, Pelkin said. *The day mages start lying is the day the world begins to end.* Was Pelkin here? She was among reckoners. It made sense for Pelkin Reckoner to be among them, too. Yet it was only in voice. That was not enough. *I'm sorry*, she told him. *There wasn't a choice.* But it was not Pelkin who had spoken after all; those were no words that he had ever said to her. It was Graefel Wordsmith, become Graefel Proxy once more, gathered here with his own kind. He had spoken with Hanla's voice. And they had lied to her, by omission, all her life.

She saw Roiden's bloodshot eyes in the trees, felt their baleful glare. What was it Roiden had said? He was saying it again now, his words nestled in the soughing of leaves, but everyone was speaking at once, and she could not untwine the tangle of words.

I'm afraid, she told them, but only wind and crickets answered.

They were all around her, the shadows of her past mixed into the shadows the fire cast and the shadows that were the black-clad reckoners, and she was utterly alone—no one to cry out to, no one to assure her it would be all right, no father waiting in the tavern with arms full of forgiveness, no one to steady her when she staggered. No one to give advice. Tell these reckoners that Darkmage creatures lurked among them, and the proxy chain might dissolve in an acid bath of mistrust; if the Ennead wanted them to know they would have told them. Admit her ailment, ask for help, and she risked revealing her secret to Torrin, either to one of his spies or, through the chain, to some far-off proxy who would then be turned and pass the information on to him. That secret, that blunted magelight, was the only hope of an Ennead that had rallied its best proxies against the Darkmage and lost them. Only these fools remained. Nothing—neither truth nor lie—would help her now. Great Storms were coming, an infant lay dead in the bonefolk's cold white arms . . . She could say nothing, do nothing but go on, and she could not go on, she could no longer see the way, she couldn't find a man she couldn't see, the shadows crowded around her, she had become a shadow. Ciphers writhed in the reckoners' clothes, danced in fire ash, slithered through the bracken under their sleeprolls, dangled in the foliage, leaked like sap. The air swirled and eddied with symbols she was not trained to know. In their black clothes the proxies themselves were ciphers, ink-black ciphers arrayed in ever-changing combinations to form words she could not read, saying things she could not understand. Their words became gibberish in the air, sound condensing into incomprehensible symbol and flying off on the breeze, insubstantial as feathers. Where did the words go? Did the Darkmage, the Wordsmith, the master of lies, summon them, collect them in dark barrels of thought, reach in and sift through them with his fine, long-fingered hands, his scribe's hands . . .

In the dark, in the night, in the unfathomable air, they were all Torrin Darkmage. She would never know him. He was everywhere, everyone. He had wormed inside her like his cursed ciphers; she would never find him, never thwart him, never be free of him.

She felt her foot go into the stirrup. Somehow she had saddled the mare and was about to mount. A hand fell on her shoulder and she writhed away from it, mumbled incoherent protest. *Don't touch me*, she had said, but what came out of her mouth was only a gush of black ink that evaporated into the black air. *Don't touch me*, she said again, *I'm tainted*. They did not understand. She caught a glimpse of concern, a brief flare of orange from the fire's light before the shadows closed in again. She settled onto Amaranth's back, felt the mare shift nervously, urged her forward. Direction, direction . . . it didn't matter. She could no longer see the road. Let the animal choose her way.

They walked through the dark wood, Liath swaying in the saddle; branches groped her black clothes, ripped her stolen tunic. Was there a trail? She didn't know, couldn't see. A shadow dropped noiselessly in front of them and winged away; as Amaranth shied and Liath felt the saddle jarred from beneath her, she recognized the cut-off squeal of a mouse caught in razor talons, and she was the mouse, too, caught in something so much larger than herself that she could not keep watch for it, could not avoid it, could not hear its silent wingbeats or see its looming shadow in the darkness. She flew through black, endless air. She had been falling for a long time.

The ground slammed the breath from her. Brush sprang back over her face. When she managed to crawl free and find the reins, she could see again. The night wood was not impenetrably dark. Moonlight dappled a mossy rock near her right hand. Amaranth tugged at foliage to her left. She was favoring her near hind foot. A moment's search through moonwort found the thrown shoe.

A farrier. A farrier, she could find. She had neglected her mount. She should not have done that. A simple, practical task: Find a farrier. She could do that. She could get up, and find the trail—there had been a trail, Amaranth would not wander through thickets—and walk the horse in the direction she thought they had been going. The night yellowed with moonset, but before the light returned she came on a silent village, and a symbol she could understand: an old, bent iron horseshoe nailed over a stable door.

She drew her fist back to knock, then looked at her black tunic and hose. No. No more reckoning. Another simple, practical task: Open her pack, find her plain shirt, her travel-stained breeches. In the lee of the stable, pull off boots and replace her shadow garb with ordinary clothes.

I'm Liath, she thought, stamping back into her boots. *Liath Publican, from Clondel, in the Neck.* The loose ring slipped easily from her finger, and she knocked on the door with flesh, not silver.

The door rolled open on wooden casters. A monstrous face, lit grotesquely from below by a swinging lantern, peered out.

She stood rooted to the spot, unable to speak. Was this another seeming? Had the whole world truly dissolved into deformity? On a head at least a head above hers, the face was half man, half abomination: mouth twisted into a formless smear, cheek discolored and so puckered that it pulled the flesh around it out of alignment, a shapeless lump where the ear should be; scarred, crusted scalp. Worst of all were the eyes: one regarding her with patient intelligence, the other crusted shut. The flesh on the left side of the face oozed a clear liquid. The smooth flesh on the right contracted into half a smile.

Come in, the man gestured. It's all right.

The motion of his hands made sense, as the words issuing from the reckoners' mouths had not. She went in.

The terrible damage extended down his neck and probably under his shirt, although his arms moved freely as he pointed her to a bench, hung the lantern on a hook, and crosstied the mare in the aisle between empty stalls. He ran expert hands over her legs and checked her hooves. She had always been finicky about lifting her feet for Liath, but she relaxed into this stranger's hands as if she had come home.

Only when a stablemaster—a youngish man, squinting in the light, mussed from sleep, smelling of brandy—fumbled in through the back and said "What's wrong with *her*?" did Liath realize that her face was soaked with tears and that she was rocking back and forth on the bench.

I've had a hard night, she tried to say. *I've had rather a long, hard time.* But her mouth opened and closed without a sound. She could taste her tears.

Leave her, the big man said with a curt gesture. He had unsaddled Amaranth and was brushing her down, picking out burrs with deft, gentle fingers. Liath rose unsteadily and made her way over to place a hand on the mare's chest. *Oh, Amaranth, I'm so sorry. I should have taken better care of you.*

It's all right, the man motioned. No harm.

Only the good half of his face was turned to her. It smiled before he went back to grooming.

"Eiden's balls," said the rumpled man. "Now I have two of them who don't speak!"

Liath wiped her face on her sleeve and tried to pull herself together. "My apologies, sir," she said. It came out a croak. She cleared her throat. "She lost a shoe, in the woods. I should have just bedded down, I suppose, but I . . . I . . ."

"Oh, never mind, business is custom. I'm Folle, I own this place. A mage, are you?" He looked critically at her triskele.

She tucked it into her shirt. She had meant to take it off. Why hadn't she taken it off?

Folle's hand slipped off the crossbeam he had leaned on. He caught himself and stood up straight. "Well, you can't pay with a casting. But if you've a trade you might find daywork tomorrow."

"Magecraft is a trade," Liath said quietly.

"Yes, of course it is, but you're all born into something, aren't you?"

"I'm a publican," she said.

"Very good! Beilor can use you at the Lark and Sparrow. There's a market tomorrow and we all expect a good deal of custom. You'll have to pasture that mare out back, I've reserved the stalls for the merchants as usual."

"That's fine," she said, wondering why he assumed she had nothing to barter now. It was true, unless he wanted a set of soiled reckoner's clothes and a twice-stolen ring, but an odd assumption to make about a mage.

Better not to ask. She had her own answer for that question.

The scarred man turned and moved his hands in a complex set of gestures—touching the horse, pointing, waving a flat hand back and forth, circling a finger off to the side.

"I have no idea what you're on about, Heff, but you're the one let her in this time of night—you see to the rest."

"She needs all four shoes, and he doesn't have her size now," Liath said. "But he can make them tomorrow."

Folle stared. "Some knack of mages, is it, making sense of the likes of him? I can't make front nor rear of him most of the time, though he never stops flapping his hands. Doesn't matter to me, he does his work and minds the place and leaves me to my leisure, but still." He turned to go, then turned back, scratching his head. "What kind of mage did you say you were?"

"I didn't say." She dearly wished to leave it at that, but his brows went up and his shoulders squared as he prepared to take offense. "I was trained illuminator."

"Oh. Well, good on you. I'm off home. Don't let her sleep here, Heff, I'm not a hostelry."

When he was gone, she looked at Heff, who was pitching fresh bedding into a box stall for the mare. "He's not very nice to you, is he?" she asked quietly.

The big man shrugged, then propped the pitchfork against a stall door and explained, He took me in during a time of distress. He's lazy and selfish, but he means well.

Liath laughed at the wordless joke, delighted that she'd understood it from the movements of his hands, amazed at the sensation of laughter itself. Untying her sleeproll from the saddle, she drew breath; instead of speaking, she touched the mare's shoulder and her own chest, and pointed to him.

He nodded, gave his half-smile, but brushed his lips and gestured to her in turn. Speak, he was saying. He tapped his ear. I can hear you.

"All right," she said. "Again, my thanks. I've been . . . remiss. Just watch your pockets, eh? She's got quite a nose for treats."

She turned to go, to find a place to bed down for the slender remains of night, but he belayed her with a light finger on the sleeproll and pointed to the hayloft.

"But Folle said . . ." She grinned at the gesture he made then. "Well, in that case."

When the mare was tucked in her stall and Heff had extinguished the lantern and gone off to his own bed—a cot in the back, from the sound of it—she laid her blanket on the bales and watched the slow circling of the ciphers, black on black.

That was a near thing, she told them. *But you haven't got me yet.*

In the darkness, she made to them the gesture that Heff had made, and rolled over on the hay, and slept, dreamless.

At daybreak he shared food with her—pickled cucumber, a hunk of bran-bread, cold peppermint tea.

Folle's sleeping in, he gestured, eyes twinkling. The publican too.

"Don't talk with your mouth full," Liath replied, deadpan.

It was clearly painful for him to chew; he should sip broth, she thought, so as not to work the muscles under the burns. They had to be burns, though she'd seen the like when a Marough put a foot through a stirrup and was dragged a dozen threfts. Some accident at the forge?

"You need a healing," she said quietly.

His good eye blinked slowly. Then he reached out and gently brushed the fringe of bleached bangs off her forehead, thumbing the mark that head-butting the reckoner had left. So do you, his free hand said. His gaze looked past the bruised skin and bone.

She nodded, and his meaty hands dropped into his lap. Then: Come along, they told her. It's time for work.

His small forge was set up under a scaffold of raw lumber in the dirt yard out back, as if a shed was intended but incomplete. She could smell the resinous cuts in the wood. There was hardly elbow room for her, let alone for a man his size. The tools looked secondhand; the handles of some of the hammers were black.

Many farriers worked in tandem with the public stables, especially if there was an ironsmith in town, but that only meant their smithies were set close by. Heff was in Folle's back pocket. "Don't you have a workshop of your own?" she asked.

I did was all he would say.

"I'd hide that, if I were you," the publican, Beilor, said as she came in through the back with a sackful of wood chips. When she looked at him without understanding, he reached for the chain around her neck; she raised a hand as to a forward customer, and he took her meaning. "All right," she said slowly, and flipped the pendant around to hang down her back. "Better?"

"It'll do," he said.

"Why are there no mages in this town?"

"Best not ask that, love."

"I'm asking."

He pulled stools off tables and flipped them upright. "Well, because what mages we have are at Sauglin, for one thing. I suppose it's where you're headed yourself."

"But there's another reason."

"We go it on our own here. What you people do keeps us weak and indebted all our lives."

Let it pass, she thought, but said, "The Ennead keeps you safe all your lives, and magecraft keeps you healthy and fed."

"Our crofts and farms keep us fed, and left alone the weather would see to itself. The Great Storms . . . well, there hasn't been one in my lifetime, and if you ask me they're an exaggeration. No storm could be that bad. Our buildings don't burn down because we're not stupid enough to set them on fire, and those who are deserve what they get."

"And if you're hurt, or sick?" Liath struggled with what she was hearing, but it explained a great deal of what she had seen—and not seen—through the Leg. Reticence, averted glances. As a journeymage, perhaps, she would have borne more brunt of it. She had been too long a shadow.

"We do the best we can," Beilor snapped. "And that's all I'll say. I'm taking a risk with you as it is. Don't make it worse."

Liath chewed her cheek, then shrugged. "Those mugs in the back room?" she said, strewing a handful of fragrant cedar chips across the floorboards she'd swept. "I'd re-stack them, if I were you. If someone breathes on them, they'll go over."

Trade was brisk from midday on, and she was run off her feet until suppertime. Beilor offered her a meal if she would work through the evening. She'd earned Amaranth's shoeing and her keep and half again as much, a nice profit for Folle—and judging from Folle's general state, the publican would have his tallysticks back in short order. But she agreed, to get some of her own.

The stableman came in as Beilor was closing the shutters against the mosquitoes the new-lit lamps would bring. The publican nodded at him, and two men vacated a table as Folle moved to sit. Then the publican stiffened, and Liath saw the farrier in the doorway. He *was* startling, backlit by the queer glow of dusk, lamplight flickering on his mutilated face—as big as the biggest men of this region, where folk grew tall and broad; big enough and scary enough to give a Marough pause. Beilor took a step toward him, the cant of his body threatening. She looked at Folle, but he had turned his head to make small talk with someone next to him.

"You're not wanted in this house, blacksmith," Beilor growled, loud enough to still all other conversation.

Folle abruptly pounded on the table. "Where's my brandy?"

Liath made no move to fetch it. Instead she examined the crowd for assurance that the publican's grudge was his own. The expressions were outrage, disgust—fear.

So they would not let him drink in their taverns.

We'll see about that, she thought, and took a step toward the front, ignoring Folle's renewed, louder demands for his drink. But Heff caught her eye and shook his head. Returning his calm gaze to Beilor, he waited just long enough for the man to gather himself—then made a small bow and faded back into the fading day.

He was checking on me, Liath realized. She served Folle his brandy, but the man contrived to be deep in conversation whenever she approached him, even though she saw several people look for excuses to move away. After a time she heard the name of another tavern in the town, and saw him jovially embrace two reluctant men and urge them toward the door. At the last moment they extricated themselves and went back to their friends, whispering and shaking their heads. Folle's shoulders slumped for only a moment before he squared them and went on, with a jaunty, in-effective wave to a round-eyed woman by the door.

At darkfall drummers came, and there was strange, heavy-footed danc-ing, all jumps and stomps and flailing arms. The stacked mugs collapsed with a spectacular crash. Liath served the traders cranberry brandy and tart red ale and kept the men in line, though most of the women were well able to fend for themselves. One youth was determined to whirl her across the floor. She handled him all right—no daughter of the Petrel's Rest would do less—but when he froze, gaping at her collar, she found that in the commo-tion her triskele had flopped around front. He slurred apology and slunk off, leaving Liath with one hand covering the warm pewter symbol, the other still holding a cool pewter flagon of Haunch sourwine.

And not a drop spilled—an old pride.

"Don't mind him," said a soft voice from the chair behind her. A ponytailed, freckle-faced girl. "Daglor's pining. He's hoping she'll be in tonight so he can make her jealous."

"He won't impress her with how well he holds his ale." Liath felt exposed, an unwelcome stranger, though no one was staring.

"You're a mage?"

Something in the girl's tone got her attention. She set the flagon on the table and said, "I'm wearing this, eh?"

The girl pushed some bread crumbs into a little pile. "I wonder if you can help me."

"That's what mages do."

"My brother . . . he's a mage too. Maybe you know him, or you've met him somehow, or . . . His name is Jann."

"I'm sure he'll send word soon," Liath offered. "He's journeying?"

"Well, you see, it's not—" The girl broke off and stood. Liath followed her gaze to the door. Where Heff had stood, another man was scanning the room. He saw her, started in, then hesitated; dancers blocked the view, and in the next glimpse he was gone. "I've got to go," the girl said. "If he comes in, please, put the pendant away. I'm sorry." She weaved away through the couples.

Liath hid the pendant anyway.

She served till closing and helped clean up—did most of it, in fact, working faster and better than Beilor. The routine calmed her, reminded her who she was. She might go on, she thought as she rinsed mugs in a back-room bucket—there was no cookroom, the Lark and Sparrow hosted only drinking and dancing, drinking and gaming—and stacked them so one heavy footfall wouldn't topple them. She might just manage, if she remembered that she was an honest publican from the Neck, if she steered clear of lies and reckoners.

She heard the creak of the floorboards behind her, but not in time. An arm snaked round her neck, squeezed off her outcry. Someone, a man from the size and smell, dragged her backward. She kicked out at the stack of mugs—the crash would bring Beilor—but missed. She jammed her elbows back but they slid off his sleek vest. The back door went by; he hoisted her around before she could reach out to slam it. He was strong, but he was trembling. She stabbed her heels down, feeling for his insteps, not connecting—a spastic dance.

He shoved her against the clay-plastered wall and put a knife against her throat.

"My Leskana talked to you," he rasped. The man who'd been at the door—father, brother? There was no smell of liquor on him. She tried to answer, but his left forearm pressed into her windpipe, and the breath would not come.

"My son is gone," he said. His voice broke into a higher register. "They took him. Before he'd even left, they came. He had talent, that one. Had his granda's gift."

"Th—" she choked. *They called him, that's only natural, they're calling a lot of mages now—*

The knife bit harder, a row of little pricks. A toothed Lowlander knife. Against it, the flesh below her jaw felt absurdly tender. Her mind's eye flashed on blood gouting from a horse's neck, oozing from Tarny's gut. Her use knife was with her gear. She rested fingertips on his horsehair vest, waiting for the knife hand to relax. An eyeblink of inattention was all she needed.

"But I've gift enough," he said. His skin was damp. His eyes darted. The blade held firm. "I've gift enough to know he's—"

The arm, the knife, flew away from her as a figure loomed behind the man and flung him almost casually against the coolhouse wall. Liath gasped and doubled over.

There was silence for many labored breaths.

The man sheathed his blade. "All right, Heff," he said. "I've no quarrel with you. But why you defend one of them, after what happened to you—it's made you funny, Heff."

Heff reached behind him to push Liath toward the street.

"And I'm telling *you*, Head louse. If I see you here again, in a breath, in a season, in a year, I'll cut your throat. I'll cut your throat for Jann."

"Ach, I knew there would be trouble," Folle said. "I must have been legless last night, to do business with a mage. Should have sent her off straightaway. Don't look at me like that, you. You're softhearted—and I'm softheaded. We both know better."

Liath came into the lanternlight. She'd washed the thin, shallow cut the knife tip had left as it was pulled away, and rinsed her collar as best she could with shaking hands. "Tell me why they don't like mages here."

Folle looked at Heff. Heff pointedly turned his head. It presented the good side to her—shaven smooth, cheek and scalp. A rounded jowl, prominent brow, flat nose and chin.

"They don't like *Norther* mages."

Liath remembered the scornful rake of Souther eyes in her own tavern. But there had been hesitation, a glint of respect . . .

"Too many are called," Folle explained. "Charvisk—Jann's father—he's less angry than some you'd meet. They're called and they never come back. Some are never heard from again."

"How long has that been going on?"

"Years. Always. We've always bred bright mages in these parts. But more lately."

The Ennead could be trying to beat the Darkmage to the better mages; or the Darkmage could be the cause. Either would explain the weather problems—but not the attitude Beilor had described, or why Jann's father would attack a journeymage. If she'd had the black on, it would have made sense. "There's more to it."

"Why should there be?" Folle said—nervous, striking out in defense. "They call our brightest to the Head and return nothing. We learn to live without, we take pride in it, but we can't have them reaping our children season after season. You're one of them, with your accent, your fair skin. Charvisk . . . he's been saying he'd start taking theirs if they didn't return our own, and there are many here—not myself, mind you, I'm just a hardworking businessman—who wouldn't protest."

Liath rubbed her eyes. The bone bruise on her forehead was throbbing, and the cut at her throat, which she hadn't felt when it happened, stung now. He'd meant to carve her a second necklace, a bloody shadow of the one her triskele hung on.

"Tell the proxies," she said. "That's what they're for."

"We did. They don't like us. We're too independent, and we have no triad for them to order around. They don't come anymore."

"Send someone to the Holding."

Folle laughed outright. "Do you think we haven't?"

"They have . . . some concerns, right now," Liath said.

"Oh, I'll say they do!"

Liath examined him more closely. "What do you mean?"

"They're losing the Feet, and the Weak Leg. The Midder Lowlands, the Norther Lowlands, haven't felt it yet, but the Souther Lowlands are chafing. Folk are angry."

This needed mending, but it was not her task. If she found the Darkmage, the Ennead could stop calling so many mages. If it was the Darkmage's doing, then that would stop too. You didn't put buckets under a leak—you plugged the keg.

"The Head's a long way from here," Folle said wearily. "The Ennead neglects us. It's always been that way. It's not your fault. But it's not mine either. You should go."

"They look after you," she said. There were powerful forces at work, things Folle couldn't understand; there was more at stake than he knew, or should ever have to know. "You take for granted what you get from them. You forget yourselves. I'm not surprised the proxies lost patience with you."

The brandy bloom was fading from his cheeks. Clearly he wanted to be in his bed. "Go," he said. "Go to Sauglin with the rest, and make a nice triad for yourself, and go home, where the only angry fathers will be the ones whose sons you bed too young."

Had the shadows aged her so much? Dully, she asked, "What's Sauglin?"

"Sizable town a morning's ride upland. Where the untriaded go this time of year."

The untriaded. Mages who had journeyed, and found no one. Mages without allegiance, without triadic roots. At home, such mages found each other eventually, at festivals, at markets, visiting relatives in other towns. But a regional gathering . . .

"I'll get my horse," she said. The mild mockery of her abrupt acquiescence was lost on Folle. With the relief of her departure imminent, he became again the voluble stablekeep: he hoped the shoes wore well, if there was any problem she could see his cousin in Gloir . . . *Just don't come back here*, she heard between the words.

Heff followed her down the aisle between the stalls—full now, Liath realized, with traders' horses; there had been no local mounts awaiting shoeing when she arrived—and out back past his cold forge to the paddock where Amaranth dozed among a score of oxen. A huge fluff-footed gelding trotted over to the split-rail fence of the next paddock and pressed its head into Heff's chest.

You are going into hard places, he said.

A pain went through her. He'd done more than look after her mare and rescue her in a back alley. He'd reminded her that words were not the only power in the world, that a kind man could live behind a monstrous face—that her eye for pattern could still recognize good. Nothing could banish the shadows—but he'd neutralized them with his gentle presence. He would come with her, now, if she asked him to.

"You have a shop here, a trade."

He expelled a harsh breath more bitter than a bitter laugh. This? his hands said scornfully.

She opened the gate and led Amaranth out. "I think I understand a little what happened, Heff," she said. "Your smithy wasn't warded. You were burned in a fire. I don't know how you could have been injured by halves like that, but I respect that you don't want to tell me. I hope you didn't—lose anyone."

The stillness of his body, his steady gaze, told her he had.

"No one brings their horses here now, do they?"

He shook his head. He was watching her, waiting.

"Why do they shun you? Afraid your bad luck will rub off?" "*Our buildings don't burn down because we're not stupid enough to set them on fire, and those who are deserve what they get . . .*"

Ignoring the question, Heff said, You need protection.

She had been alone a long time; the prospect of companionship made her aware of the ache's depth. Even at home she had been alone—a mage among publicans, a prentice among mages, and to self-exiled Graefel no more than a belated victory, a prize to send the Ennead to prove he was still their brightest proxy.

"You might bring Folle's local custom back by leaving, but then who'll shoe his horses for him?" she asked.

In a complicated set of gestures, which he had to repeat, he said, I've been training him. He'd do all right.

"He'd sit in the tavern all day!"

Not if there's work to do. He drinks because this place is going under. He'll go under with it unless I leave.

"But . . ." she prompted, seeing his face twist into something between pain and dismay.

He turned away and didn't answer. She looked where he was looking, across the paddock, into the deeper darkness under a spread of dogwood. It took a long time, but at last she made it out: a pile of stones, a smaller version of the cairn the Southers had made of Torbik's body. She'd seen them, here and there, through the Weak Leg. Abruptly she understood that they were memorials. The bodies were long gone to the bonefolk, but the cairns remained.

"I see," she said softly. "That's why you've stayed?"

To her surprise, he shook his head; then, as if frustrated for the first time at the inadequacy of his language of gestures, he sketched something with his hands that she took to mean *That's only part of it*, and something else that looked like *I don't want to get involved.*

"I don't understand," she said.

"How could you?" came Folle's voice from behind her. She turned, and found him offering a wallet of provisions, a kindness completely at odds with his bitter tone. "You still believe in magecraft." He shoved the linen wallet at her. "Take it. It's for both of you. Go with her, Heff— she'll have you when no one else will. She needs a bodyguard now, Charvisk made that plain. Do it, you fool. Go!"

Heff backed against the paddock rail. His piebald draft horse nuzzled into his hand, and he anchored himself on the warm flesh, as Liath had so often done with Amaranth.

"I'd welcome you beside me on the road," she began, though she had dismissed the notion of protection. His presence would raise questions she could ill afford, yet she was so tired of being alone, and this place caused him only pain. . . . Perhaps the spirits had guided her to this town to help him break free of grief's bonds, and she could do a good turn in the midst of darkness.

"You see?" Folle said. Heff shook his head, his fist clenching in the gelding's mane, and Folle swore. "Stubborn *fool*. You think to teach them a lesson. Remind them of their folly and they'll mend their ways, ward their homes, embrace the Ennead's mages . . . You're a reminder of no folly but your own!"

Heff went very still.

"A mage cursed him," Folle told Liath, every word a blade aimed at Heff. "Could have healed him, owed him a healing, owed him his *life!*—" His voice broke. "But he left him looking like *that*. He'll never heal now. The dungspawn saw to it."

Heff was still shaking his head. He looked to Liath, as if she could refute the words, but she was helplessly confused, and desperate to know if the grain of truth in Folle's harsh words was one very simple word: *Darkmage.*

"Magecraft doesn't traffic in curses," she managed, grasping at neutral fact. "And if it did, it would still take three."

Folle turned on her with a horrible grin as wide as the night. "A mage came here to Gulbrid, thinking to find favor, speaking against the Ennead. Oh, he was tolerated for a while, but he pushed and pushed, didn't know when to stop, he forced them into it! They ran him to the edge of town, and still he spouted his gibberish, on the road, to merchants, to children. Children! Did he think they would allow that?" His smile had become a rictus; his voice dropped to a vicious hiss. "But Heff took him in. Heff *defended* him. Never spoke much even when he could, but oh, he had a way with him when he chose to, stopping fights, calming troubles. Saving people like you. Only that time it wasn't one heartbroken father. It was a whole angry town, and they were having none of it, not even from Heff. He wasn't one of us, he should have known that—why didn't you know that, Heff? *Why?* Why did you do it?"

Liath was speechless in the face of whatever agony had gripped the stableman. He looked exhausted, all the drink worn out of him, bags under the rings under his eyes, yet those eyes burned with a fierce, desperate, incomprehensible light.

Heff gestured—slowly, as if exhaustion was sapping him too. Folle nearly sobbed: "*I can't understand you.*"

"Because it was right," Liath translated softly. Then, when Heff motioned to correct her, "Because he was right." She frowned and shook her head to clear it. It had to be Torrin Darkmage. Heff was a good man; he could not have thought the Darkmage was *right*, and anyway it didn't matter, what mattered was that he had been here and she had to find him, she had to go. She wanted to grab them and shake them and shout "*Where is he now?*" But something terrible was passing between these two men, something that went profoundly deeper than a lazy, posturing stablekeep hiring an ostracized man out of pity. The tension between them was a fine wire that would cut her if she tried to pass through.

Again Folle addressed her—respite from the intensity of facing Heff. "They took him in, gave him refuge in the smithy. They could have let him go on, fend for himself, but no, they had to *shelter* him. Did Serle want that, Heff? You never told me. You never told me!"

Heff raised his hands; let them fall; raised them again, and motioned. "You didn't want to know," Liath translated. Of her own, she added, "You wouldn't have understood his hands—"

"Oh, you're not light, are you, little Norther," Folle spat. Liath backed up a step, raising her hands peaceably. "You're smart enough to suss it— burned farrier, no shop of his own, smithy, no wardings. But you're wrong. They were fine ironsmiths, the both of them. Good craftsmen don't let their shops burn, wardings or no. That's our pride, here. We don't need your bloody wardings. But folk wanted that mage dead. When Heff wouldn't give him up, they *burned* him out."

Liath glanced across at the dogwood tree.

"Serle was his brother. He was always laughing, that one, full of mischief, quick to turn a joke. He was everything this one wasn't. He was light itself! He was light and life!" Folle's face contorted. "Your little brother, Heff. Of all the people in the world, *he* was the one you had to protect, and he *burned!*"

Heff was on him before Liath could blink. They crashed against the stable wall. The horses backed nervously, and in the paddock the oxen jolted out of a drowse. Liath dropped Amaranth's reins and threw herself on Heff, but he was solid as stone, immovable. He had Folle by the collar, pressing him hard against the shingled wall.

"Heff, don't," Liath said, unable to haul him away. "Heff, he's not worth it! Don't be Charvisk all over again!"

Heff shoved away from the man, took three steps, then whirled to gesture angrily, You don't know all of it.

"No," Liath said in a low voice, reaching to help Folle up, then backing away herself when he swatted at her.

He scrambled to his feet, brushing at dust in angry futility. "Perhaps I'm being unfair." His reasonable tone was crueler than the harsh one. "Heff *tried* to save him. But the roof caved in on him, didn't it? Serle saved the mage, and Heff tried to save Serle, and failed, and the mage saved him. Off they went, the two of them, the mage with Heff out cold over that piebald's withers. And three days later he rides back home. Just staring. Just staring at everyone staring at him. As if they'd be *sorry!*" He cried out, slamming his hands on empty air. Someone shouted out a window for quiet. "Why haven't you healed, Heff? All these moons and it's as bad as the day you rode back in. What did he do to you? *Why did you come back here?*"

"Because the alternative was to go with him," Liath said as Heff's hands moved. "Because this is home. Because *he* lies here."

"He's dead, Heff," Folle said through tears. "If he's here, he's a haunt. And this is no home for you." There was a long silence. Finally, Folle whispered, "I loved him too. Never forget that." He went back into the stable, closing the door firmly behind him.

Heff stood with his back to her, breathing hard, fists clenched.

"Heff . . ."

Don't, he gestured. Just go.

"What will it serve you to stay?"

He turned slowly, looking at the stable door. Making a pair of door and dogwood—unyielding, inadequate wooden symbols—he said, They were pledged.

Liath had gathered as much. Folle was grieving, hard. "You may only be making it worse for him."

He sighed. Maybe, he gestured.

"Come with me. Just a little ways. You wanted to see me safe. I accept. You're an ironsmith—"

Just a farrier, Heff said. *He* was the smith.

"A farrier's welcome anywhere. You can make a new start. Leave the heartbreak behind."

He thought about it for a long time, but in the end he shook his head. Whatever bound him to this place—Folle, the memory of his lost brother, the ongoing silent rebuke of his presence in the midst of murderers—it was more bond than he could break.

"All right," she said. She'd like to stay, herself. Don her reckoner garb and dispense some kind of justice. But what Folle had described was unthinkable; if it was true, it was beyond the scope of proxies, or mages, and she was neither. The justice she concocted would be no more than retribution. And she could not be certain that Folle's anguished, raging account was correct. Easier to believe that the Darkmage had set the fire, or done something hideous to goad the townsfolk into it, cast some glamour over the ironsmiths' minds—even that the fire *was* an accident, during the chaos Torrin had engendered, in a shop they refused to ward.

Whatever had happened was down to the Darkmage. Her only course was to continue. Stop him, before he caused any more horrors like this one.

So she grit her teeth against the inconsiderate, necessary words, at all that they implied that she could not afford to imply, at the questions they would raise in Heff's mind, and said, "Which way did the mage go when he left you?"

Heff stiffened. Why? he asked, turning to her.

There were a dozen lies she could tell him. Very softly, so that no one not standing between them could overhear, she said, "Because I'm looking for him."

It was a long time ago, Heff said. The direction won't help you.

"You never know."

After some consideration, he said, Would you do him harm?

Truthfully, because if the Ennead could not core and seal him they would have to destroy him, she replied, "I'm supposed to keep him from harm."

Heff pointed upland. Toward Sauglin.

"Thank you, Heff." She picked up the linen wallet, which had fallen into the dirt. "Thank Folle for me too." Amaranth stood with her head stuck through the fence rails, cropping the paddock grass. Heff backed her out with a hand on her chest, and Liath took the reins. "I wish . . . there were something I could do."

He gave a sad half-smile, and offered her a hand to clasp. She stepped up on the bottom rail to leave a soft kiss on his undamaged cheek instead. "Spirits guard you."

And you, he waved—then moved not at all until she had mounted and reined Amaranth around the paddock and onto the upland path.

A mist was gathering at the edges of the outbuildings, settling on the pastures, drifting like loose fleece around the quiet sheep. For a league or two, Liath listened for the muffled tread of Heff's big gelding, but it did not come. She wiped condensation off her lashes, and settled in for the night ride.

She should make Sauglin by dawn.

Sauglin: the ideal place for a minion-hungry darkmage to find fodder.

But it was not. Wordsmiths and binders sniffed her light like rutting dogs; some offered their beds, some their crafteries, anything for her promise to triad them, even to consider it. They were untriaded for a reason—dull lights all, or inadequate crafters, or unpleasant. A paltry lot, stinking of desperation. And among them her light was a beacon. A smelly beacon.

If you only knew, she thought, as she fended them off. *If you only knew what you wouldn't get if I said yes.*

Yet the Darkmage might come. He might need mages badly enough to scrape the dregs, and there were such easy pickings here. He had been just downland of here, only a few moons ago; he might have holed up somewhere close enough to make a foray. This was the last of three days. She'd see it to the end.

It won't kill you, she told herself, sitting in a humid tavern that stank like a bad dream of home—then reconsidered as she took a sip of warm, watered beer that tasted of cat spray. The nervous untriaded were drinking hard. Soon the taverns would be selling midden drainage. She watched shadow scribing warp the rafters as magecraft's misfits eddied around her, and put off men who wouldn't have given her lanky body a first look in the Petrel's Rest.

Good thing she's a publican, Ferlin giggled to Nelis, the fullers' older daughter, in the corner. *Getting them drunk's the only way she can get them at all!*

Liath sighed. The haunts of her past had returned on the mist last night. She was going to have to live with them—Ferlin and Nelis, for now, with their scented hair and curving thighs and generous breasts. *That journeyboy was so snockered he was flirting with Liath!* Charming. That was one of the cobblers' cream-skinned daughters, a matched set of pouting lips and sapphire eyes.

"Ah, and if you knew what pleasure I'd had of him, and how wonderfully sober he was," she told them. Of course they did not reply. Here she was more coveted than a Clondel cobblers' daughter, and their galling gibes melted in the drenched air, just as her smart retorts had, unformed, in the real air of home.

They're only jealous of your light, Hanla said. She was not ugly. Keiler had loved her large gray eyes, claimed they reflected the changing colors of the sky. *I can read the weather in your eyes,* he'd say, and try to count the freckles across her nose.

"Who?" asked a horse-faced, pockmarked boy next to her. She smiled at him and downed her putrid beer. If Clondel girls could gossip in the shadows, this boy could look attractive. Perhaps there were other ways to pass the time.

"Not you, boy-o, I'll tell you that!"

In the dimness and mediocrity, Liath was pulled straight in her seat by a light that was more than ordinary. She twisted hard to see its owner and found tilted eyes in a wedge-shaped face, smooth ebony skin, glossy hair piled in a complexity of braids.

"I've had my eye on you, Gill *Wordsmith,*" the mage said. "I knew you were up to no good. I thought, Ah, that's not fair on the fellow, he can't help being uglier than the worm side of an old stone. But then I realized what it was: *This.*" The woman reached a muscled forearm around Liath and jerked the triskele from the boy's neck; he shouted an oath as the chain snapped.

"Are you daft?" Liath shoved her chair back. The woman said, "Undoubtedly—but here," and pressed the triskele into Liath's palm.

It felt as dead as the pewter flagon of wine she had held while her own triskele lay warm under her other hand. The edge bore a slight seam. This triskele had not been cast by a triad.

"Good pewterer's work, though," the woman said. "I come from the Heel. It's crawling with metalsmiths."

"But his light . . ." Liath said. It wasn't bright, but it was there, a waxy yellow warmth.

"I've light enough," the boy said, rubbing sullenly at the burn on his neck. "I lost my triskele, that's all, and I'm too far from home to get another."

The woman smiled with her tongue in her cheek and shook her head. "You're from Pange. There's something in the water there—when mages don't clear it often enough, the children come out with bulgy throats like yours. A threeday's ride downland. Six days round trip and you would have missed this? Don't bother. You didn't *just* lose your triskele. The wear on this chain, the dulled finish on the pendant's back . . . You've sweated on these for more than a nineday."

The boy had begun to sidle off partway through the examination. As the woman finished, he bolted into the crowd.

"How did you know all that?" Liath asked in awe.

"I'm a seeker. That's what I do. Figure things out."

"But——" Liath gestured helplessly at the woman's triskele.

"Oh, I'm a mage now, but I was raised a seeker. It never wears off. Nerenyi Illuminator."

"Liath Illuminator."

"Two of a kind. And if we drink much more of this swill, we'll triad each other, with that sackhead for wordsmith."

They left the tavern and strolled among the market stalls set up in the commons. "What did he hope to gain?" Liath asked. She had one tallystick left from Beilor's payment—tallies seemed to have a wider radius of value in the Lowlands—and traded it for a pair of frysticks and ginger brews.

"Who knows?" Nerenyi said, nibbling an orange pepper from the side. "Three days of camaraderie with triskeled mages he couldn't join? A pretense of importance before going back to his family's trade? The closely guarded secret of how to pass a trial? I shouldn't have been so hard on him, but seekers abhor deceit."

Liath froze. *For the best, it's for the best——*

The illuminator folded into herself cross-legged on a clear patch of brown grass. "On the other hand, I'm hard on everybody, and I'm a mage now, so up Eiden's rear with it."

Liath laughed, half-drunk on relief, watery sunlight, cat spray, and this woman's ludicrous bluntness. Nerenyi laughed too, and the shadows faltered and contracted, cowed by the brilliant white of her smile, the dancing lights in her black eyes.

"They only started this gathering last summer," she explained, gesturing broadly with her stick. A chunk of eggplant flew off the end and hit Liath in the eye.

"What prompted it?" Liath asked, recovering.

"Well"—Nerenyi swallowed and wiped her mouth with the back of her hand—"they finally clicked to the fact that the Holding won't call mages out of a triad. Took them long enough, didn't it?"

Liath made a face. "No one I've seen here has to worry about being called."

Nerenyi bent over laughing, somehow not impaling herself on the frystick.

"Except for you," Liath added.

"Oh, I'm not that bright. The faintest ember looks bright in an ash house. You, on the other hand, should be a proxy by now, or better. Are you on the run from reckoners?"

Liath blinked. "Well . . . yes, I suppose I am."

"Good on you! Follow the rules, do what you're told, never question. I may have to journey all my days, but by Eiden's teeth I'll never do it on their behalf."

"Don't you want to triad?"

Nerenyi stacked their wooden cups to return to the market trader. "Illuminator," she said, hoisting Liath up, "I want to triad more than anything in the world. But spirits save me if I do it here."

Neither of them had the wherewithal for a bed, or for a stall to share with their horses, so they took mounts and gear and camped on a rise just outside of town. The hillside was dotted with the campfires of other journeyers. Those who could cast for their board had done so on the first day, leaving nothing for the others.

"What is it seekers seek, Nerenyi?" Liath asked, feeding their modest fire, watching sparks fly up at the hazed stars.

"The truth. The past. The future."

"I don't think they're making much headway."

Nerenyi thought for a breath. "How do we know that the moon and the sun are worlds like our own?" she said. "We see two luminaries in the sky, and we know that all the most powerful things come in threes. Thus, the world is the third luminary. If you could stand on the sun, you'd see Eiden Myr—Eiden all brown and green, and the bright blue water around him. I think the triskeles must have been fashioned after that concept, a little. If you look at them edge-on, they're flat. But if you look at them straight, they're round, and made on a pattern. It's the same with the flat, round faces of the proxy rings. I'd like to talk with the first mages to cast one, and find out what they were thinking." She lay back against the hill's incline and looked over at Liath. "We can't dig up the past and examine it. Tellers only remember back a few generations, and the longer their tales have been handed down the more has been lost and garbled. All we can see is how things are now. If we listen very close, and think deeply enough, we can deduce the past and guess the future. It's all there in the details—but it takes a lot of looking. We've—they've—made plenty of headway, considering. Give them time."

Liath was unconvinced, but the answer whetted her appetite. "What do you know about the Great Storms?"

"I'll tell you, if you tell me why there's a reckoner following you."

She sat bolt upright and looked around so fast she nearly rolled down the hill.

"Steady, steady. He took lodgings in town. But he was watching you the way I was watching Gill. Blond fellow. He knows we're up here. And he knows *you*."

The way she watched Gill . . . suspicious of a pretender. Had they found out about her crippled light? She swore.

"We'll let the fire die and go at moonset. If we don't trip over some sorry mage and break our necks, we'll lose him."

Liath tried to relax the muscles that had tensed for flight. If it was one of Torrin's people . . . if it was *him* . . . she wanted to be found. But a fair-haired man, who knew her—if it wasn't someone who'd seen her playing at proxy, it had to be one of the vocates. Bloody fool Ennead, to put one of them on the road!

"Are you sure?" she said weakly.

Nerenyi cocked a brow.

Liath sighed, and tossed away the wood she'd been holding. "I'll wake you when it's full dark."

They picked their way up the hillside, trying not to laugh when Nerenyi's horse, Coriander, dropped not far from a sleeping journeyer. Then they slipped into a screen of trees, and onto the upland road. "I was headed for the High Arm when I heard about that cesspool," Nerenyi said, after they'd cleared the hill and put a good league behind them. "I've seen eight of the nine seas. I want to see the Sea of Wishes, before my journey's over."

The High Arm, muscled with rock, led to the gnarled Fingers. A deduction so simple a seeker would laugh at it: a fastness required mountains. But she should try the Blooded Mountains, too, and the Strong Leg, and the Oriels, which ran alongside the Heartlands. . . . There was no knowing which way to turn until she got there. "I'm just wandering," Liath said. It was too much to hope for companionship now. Journeymages didn't travel in pairs unless they were two legs of a potential triad. Heff had chosen not to join her; this mage was an illuminator, and convention decreed—

"Then we'll wander together until our paths fork," Nerenyi said. "And the sooner we wander into an inn or some nice warm high corn, the happier I'll be."

In the end, they bedded in a ditch because the wind had picked up, wrapped in waterwarded cloaks but chilled just the same. Rough hands woke Liath at dawn, a triskele dangling in her face. She rolled away, scrambling to untangle her arms from her pack, but it was a mage in ordinary clothes. "He's a binder," Nerenyi said, laughing at her. "An overenthusiastic binder."

"Two of you!" he cried, clearly not for the first time. "Good thing I saved you from freezing to death! Our illuminator's just pledged and gone off to make a child." He rattled off a list of neglected castings as they followed him to his cottage. Liath swore when she saw how close they'd been to shelter.

Nerenyi eagerly pitched in to ward the village's waterlogged potatoes against blight. Liath watched long after she dismissed the wordsmith's plain marks, fascinated by Nerenyi's painting. It was all muted colors, and yet carried a subtle intensity, playing tints and hues against each other to build a tonal weave.

Halfway through her border, Nerenyi began to speak.

"This pigment is far too dilute—have you no binder, bindsman? The substance that binds the pigment to itself and to the leaf, yes?" Then, "And this scribing—could you have filled any more of the leaf, or made your initials any smaller? Small ciphers, small mind, the saying goes. Well, your manhood must be adequate, anyway, given what they say big scribing is compensation for . . ." It went on and on, leaping from the personal to the craft-related and back, a random stream of commentary. Some of it was complimentary; but the damage had been resoundingly done.

Too much work remained for the outraged mages to send them away. "We'll use your friend this time, if you don't mind," the wordsmith said, tone dryer than a kilner's hat. "Now I see why you're together."

"You take both of us, or neither," Liath said, and rode off with Nerenyi—but when they were out of earshot she cried, "What *possessed* you?"

"Now you know why I was in Sauglin," Nerenyi said. "I'm as untriadable as the rest of those louts. Embarrassing, isn't it?"

"But your craft, your light . . ."

"My light is fine, it's such a shame, what a pity, what a waste"— her voice lilted derision. "Can you *imagine* how tired I am of hearing that?"

As a matter of fact, I can.

Nerenyi t'Galandra Illuminator—born Nerenyi n'Jheel l'Corlin among the tin and copper mines of the Heel, where all who showed a light took Galandra's name at puberty and all who didn't took Eiden's— came of seeker stock. That was unusual in itself; most seekers were born into normal families, and sought kindred minds only once they realized they were different. Nerenyi was the child of pledged seekers. Aware of her light, they'd kept her from the mages until she was nine-and-four, old enough to choose her own path. She'd chosen magecraft. Her training triad's delight paled when they discovered her flaw: when she•was aroused, by a casting or anything else that opened her to strong emotion, she was prone to outbursts. What she said was always the truth as she saw it; seekers were trained to speak truth or say nothing. But Nerenyi, when excited, was compelled to vocalize her thoughts, no matter what they were—and those around her did not appreciate the candor.

"It's also why I've never pledged," Nerenyi added with a wry grin. "One night in my bed is more than enough. Of course, the truth would never hurt the perfect lover. . . ."

By afternoon they had come upon another casting opportunity—two other journeyers, a wordsmith and bindswoman committed to finding a third. Nerenyi was desperately hungry to cast; now Liath understood why.

This time she gave the requisite glance to the wordsmith's work—assured, but too even—and, when the truths came on Nerenyi like a tic, walked around the casting circle to whisper conciliation in the journeymages' ears. "She can't help it," she said. "Just ignore her, eh? It's nothing personal. She doesn't even know what she's saying." It worked: she had not watched her father soothe ruffled customers for nothing all those years.

The wordsmith was strong, arrogant; he could have easily been Torrin. But without Nerenyi—unless she dressed again in shadow—she would not have been able to see him scribe. When the chance came to turn to-ward the mountainous Strong Leg, she contrived not to turn. She would not bring this mage into danger; but the opportunity was too valuable to lose.

"I can never repay you for the service you are doing me. But do you not want to cast, yourself?" Nerenyi said when they'd been on the road a sixday. "Your light's brighter than mine, yet you defer to me. Is some-thing wrong with you?"

"I can go without for a while," Liath replied. "I like you. I like making the way easier for you. Let me keep doing it."

Nerenyi nodded at the evasion. "With a light as bright as yours, your castings would attract notice." She threw Liath a sly look. "Either that, or you can't draw a line to save your life."

Liath returned a wan smile.

The seeker looked like a river-smoothed blackthorn tree, a frozen twist of current plucked from a flow of black water, all curve and turn and grace, lithe and powerful. Liath felt anemic and ungainly beside her, yet they made a compelling pair: one fair, one dark, both tall, from op-posite ends of Eiden's body. Her illuminations were subtly different—odd shapes, somber colors, kadri that were never quite the same ones Liath had learned. She saw the world through alien eyes, and Liath came to understand that the colors she saw were not exactly the same colors Nerenyi saw.

When she looked through Nerenyi's eyes, she saw no shadows.

She couldn't smooth other mages' anger enough to interest them in triading her friend, but she harbored the hope nonetheless. It was a bright hope. It cheered her.

Nerenyi never stopped questioning. She was a seeker still; she'd thrown over the life, but couldn't shake the habits. "Why can't we cut our own quills?" she asked one night. "Why must we be dependent on binders?"

"I don't *know*, Ner," Liath said. "Because it works, that's why." Ner-enyi gave her a sour look. "Because when they tried other ways, the castings were no good."

"When who tried?"

"I don't know! The mages who came before us, long ago!"

"And who were they?"

"That's something for tellers to remember."

"And they don't."

"Then it was so long ago it doesn't matter."

"But it does matter. It matters very much. How can you be you if you don't have all the history you carry?"

Liath wasn't sure she wanted to be whoever history had changed her into. "I'm a person. The world is bigger than me. Eiden remembers, if he needs to."

"Mystic blather."

Liath propped herself on her elbows. "Look around you. With your mind's eye, the one that sees kadri. Nobody's sick, everybody has enough to eat and always has. Isn't that enough for you?"

Nerenyi sat up. "No, Li, it's not. I have to know why too."

Like a little girl, asking why why why until it drives her father spare, Liath thought. "Being a seeker and mage seems a . . . hard combination. Mage-craft is an ancient tradition."

"Must you blindly follow that tradition to be a good mage?"

"Yes," Liath said firmly. She had disobeyed proxies, and thus by extension the Ennead. She wore a triskele that proclaimed her capable of things she could no longer do, a physical blasphemy. She had lied, and lied, and lied. But she believed in magecraft no less for it. With Nerenyi's insidious logic, she might rationalize her lapses: she was *not* a good mage, because she was not a mage at all. "Trite sayings are common because people keep finding them to be true. Magecraft works because it's old, because it's been tested and improved year after year since Galandra's birth."

"And if I don't believe in Galandra?"

Liath groaned. "You don't believe in *anything*, Nerenyi. You don't believe the night will follow the day, no matter how many times you see it happen."

"No." Nerenyi was smiling; Liath didn't have to look at her to hear it in her voice. "But I'd like to know why it did all the times before."

Summer's waning was adrift with wishes—fluffy white seedlings that Southers claimed would carry your words to the spirits. The air was filled with sound: the swell and subsidence of eggbeetles' whirring, like surf in the trees; the sandy whisper of rattleseed stands stroked by a breeze. At night, in stillness, fireflies hovered—called midderbugs here. She watched their little glowing arcs and wondered if that was how mages looked to the abiding spirits of rock and sea: brief lights that flared and were gone.

"You parrot your training, no more," Nerenyi said.

Liath took a deep breath. Nerenyi couldn't help being the way she was. "I had excellent training," she said. "If a mage had to parrot someone, they could do worse than my training triad."

"And they taught you never to question, didn't they. Whenever you asked why, they said 'Because,' and that was that."

"It wasn't that way at all!"

"You didn't ask why?" Nerenyi misinterpreted sweetly.

The fact was that she hadn't, not really. She had loved magecraft and devoured all the training she was given. She had believed totally in Hanla's wisdom and authority—Hanla, who had been a reckoner once. Why couldn't they have gone for warders? They could have pledged, then, and lived together in the Holding, and satisfied Hanla's family. Why did they forsake the ring?

Why. She laughed. She had been asking why for four moons. Why was Torrin the way he was . . . how could simple coddling produce such a monster . . . why had he turned, why did all rumors end in blank walls, why did those ciphers haunt her sleep and warp all shapes into their shape . . . why . . . why had her magelight failed . . .

"It's not that I don't ask," she said at last, to the stars. "It's that there are no answers. Not for me. Not yet."

"At least you're asking the right questions, then."

Liath snorted. "You seekers love unanswerable questions, don't you. It puts you in a drugged state, pondering the impossible." Illuminators trained with such questions, but they answered them with kadri. Some things could not be logicked. Some things could be rendered only in symbol, in essences that linked directly with the spirits they represented. Some things were too profound for the mind to explain or its words to define. "I'm an illuminator," she said, forgetting. "You know as well as I do that our craft is of the spirit. The mind is for wordsmiths, the heart for binders. They think, and feel; we sense. I can't answer your questions in words. Some things just are."

Though some things are that aren't, too. . . .

"Yet you no longer claim there are no answers," Nerenyi said gently. "Only that you apprehend them in a wordless way."

Liath's head hurt. "I can't best you at this, Nerenyi. You're the seeker. I'm a publican."

"It's not a contest."

Liath shrugged. "All right. But I'm awfully tired. Don't take offense, but I think I'm going to sleep."

Nerenyi obligingly bundled down. "I'm not offended. I'm disappointed. I like talking late into the night."

"You like plaguing me, that's all."

"That too. Sweet dreams, publican."

Sleep crept over her like a shadow, but the haunts had gone, and Nerenyi's casual blessing kept the darkest dreams away.

• • •

The Girdle was a place all wind and distance. There were few roads and many rivers; you rode straight across the flats on a sun reckoning, then hit a tributary and looked for a ford. The wind sang in the grass, a continual, mournful melody of time and loneliness. Long-bodied horses thundered past in wild herds. There were a nonned different grasses, from purple and silver to a green so intense it was blue; and stands of low-growing flamewood, like eternal prairie fires. Sod houses lined the rivers, feathered by nodding broom and fangrass. Storms swept through sidewise; you could see them coming for miles, drawn like bristle brushes over the landscape, scrubbing it clean. The sky, when clear, was the blue of deep ice, so broad it could crush you.

"I've never seen the like of it."

"What?"

"I've seen the reverse, when someone had a great shock . . . but truly, that is astonishing."

"*What?*"

"Your hair! You're going red!"

"Oh, Eiden's bloody—"

"I don't think there's enough yet to cut the white off . . . you'd only have a spiky sort of fringe, it would stick straight up . . ."

"Stop laughing! We haven't done it yet."

"But I can just see it—"

"Here."

"It's not sharp enough!"

"Yes it is. Believe me. I keep it sharp enough to slice shadow. And I don't want you to cut it. I want you to shave it."

"What joy! I'll be journeying with a potato."

"Take the knife, Nerenyi."

"Wouldn't you rather let it grow out? Perhaps the colors will alternate. You could braid it like mine and create the most blasphemous effect."

"Just . . . do . . . it."

"All right, Illuminator—but remember, this is on your head!"

"Shut up and shave."

"Hold still then . . . ssss, I'm sorry, it's just a nick . . . hold *still*, wench . . . there. Turn around and let me see—"

". . . Nerenyi?"

"Oh, my."

When the Oriel Mountains were a ghostly line on the horizon, Liath said from her bedroll, "You didn't want to leave the seekers. But you found magecraft too interesting to resist. Did the rituals of forming kadri help you answer your impossible questions?"

"I thought the rituals were inane and childish. Such queries as seekers waste no time on. 'Why is the day sky blue'—I might answer that, someday, since there has to be a reason. But 'What is the mountain when there is no stone'? Ludicrous."

"But you passed your trial. I've seen your kadri."

"Yes. It surprised me. There were answers to questions I thought should never have been asked."

"I thought that was what seekers liked. Going into a daze by contemplating the absurd. Or shouting at each other in taverns."

"So you've said. You're wrong. We—they—we honestly believe the answers are there. The questions seem absurd only to people like you."

"Thank you so much."

"My pleasure. Go to sleep."

"My pleasure. Good night, Nerenyi."

"Don't let the questions bite."

Much later, as an afterthought, after rising to relieve herself, Nerenyi whispered, "I'd like to see your kadri, Illuminator."

Liath pretended to be asleep and did not answer except by the deafening throb of her own pulse.

"And where I come from, this is Glee," she said the next afternoon, drawing the exuberant kadra in the dirt with a stick. Her pleasure in the motion must radiate from her like body heat. *I'm not doing this to cheat,* she told herself, again. *Just to quiet Nerenyi's questions.*

But what had begun as a curious comparison of their respective techniques became an endless query-and-answer. How did this knotline work? What foliage did she prefer for borders, and how stylized? How did she get those elements to align so well?

There was so much Nerenyi didn't know. She made up for it with talent and invention, but she'd started seven years late. Nothing could compensate for adequate training—and there was nothing like the Holding training Hanla had received and passed on. Holding mages came out—or stayed in—knowing the techniques of all their colleagues. They increased their craft a nonnedfold. The random movements of lone journeyers could never spread the variety of craft the way the close quarters of many mages did in the Holding. Why didn't all mages spend time there? Instead of journeying, or in addition to it, why not require a stint in the crucible of magecraft? Or establish central places, like Sauglin, where journeyers could go and share what they had learned while they were hunting potential triads, where homebound, world-lorn Ailannas could go to refresh their spirits and their craft?

"Why, why, why," Liath grumped, then closed her mouth hard.

"Because," Nerenyi said placidly. She did not ask what Liath had meant. Instead she said, "You should be a teacher."

"I have no triad. You've got to be triaded to train a new mage, or you can't cast a triskele."

"Because because because," Nerenyi said, with an edge to it now. "You have shown me so much. I envy you your teacher, and I pity others for lack of your teaching."

Showing others her knacks. She hadn't thought it through; Nerenyi had condensed it into possibility by giving it a word. *Teacher.* Could there be an alternative to alemongering, a way to draw even if she couldn't cast? It wouldn't be enough—drawing was nothing without a casting to give it purpose—but it would be more than she had now. It would appease, a little, the nagging ache. Might she suggest it to the Ennead? A special dispensation, for service rendered? She might become a new kind of steward. . . .

The twisted ciphers rose in her mind's eye, a grotesque shadow of her lost guiders, like a weave of black bars before her, abomination and confinement.

She blinked hard and focused on Nerenyi's beautiful face, horrified at the pleasure she found in the illusion of guiders, the joy in seeing something *like* them again. If she surrendered to this, she might never be free of them. She might never be . . . a teacher.

"That's a—a nice idea, Nerenyi," she managed.

"I'm glad you like it," Nerenyi said, and wuzzled the new fuzz on Liath's head. "Now show me that twist of the leaves again?"

Their progress through the Girdle had been good, but as they came around the foot of the Oriels, which shielded Eiden's heart and lifted Midlands into Highlands above the Belt, the harvest came on. They moved slowly from village to village, helping cut and stack the rye and wheat and barley that all would eat. Liath's arms and back ached so she couldn't sleep, but with hillfolk and mountainy folk come down for the harvest, news poured like grain from a bag. She heard, at last, of a strange, dark mage who spoke in this village commons or that one—always against the Holding.

"What happened to him?" she would ask. And always the same answer: "Oh, he went on." Sometimes they said he'd been run out of town for his crazy talk. Sometimes they said he'd taken mages with him. He was an attractive man, well spoken, but never said where he came from or where he was headed. And if he'd said what he wanted, they hadn't understood it. Most of them shook their heads, dismissing the incomprehensible as a passing oddity.

Then, one morning, someone disparaged the Fingers, and someone else said that's where that queer mage had gone, and the first said good thing, they deserved him. It made each hard swing of sickle worthwhile thereafter. Twice each day, harvest mead was distributed in wooden hoggins. She never got the knack of laying each graspful of stalks on the sickle and binding them with the other hand, as Nerenyi did, so the harvestmaster always positioned a child in the stubble behind her, holding a handful of headland grass ready for ties. This reminded her with some frequency how little she liked mead and how badly she got on with children—but nothing dulled her fierce satisfaction. She would have him yet.

She no longer knew what she would do when the ciphers on a leaf matched the ones scribed behind her lids. She had lived with those ciphers for two seasons now. She had built an image of their maker so vivid she felt she knew him. A tall man, as tall as she; strong of body, hardened from traveling, perhaps enhanced by his dark craft; ablaze with magelight. A sharp, savage face, cruelly handsome. He would draw her to him, make her forget everything but his own dark imperatives. His eyes were velvet black, the eyes she felt on her in the deepest part of the night, when she woke terrified that he would find her and terrified that he would not.

While the stacked crops were left afield, they made their way along the track between the Oriels and Maur Alna, coming around the head of the long bay as the first of the oats were being stacked on carts for transport to the village barns. Nerenyi was about to lift the celebrated last sheaf when she flamboyantly pretended to a cramp in her leg, letting a gaggle of children bring it in between them. Then they joined the feast to mark the harvest home, and joined the barn dances to stamp the threshing floor firm.

"You're in love," Nerenyi said suddenly, her face darkly flushed from dancing and a good deal of barley beer. "With someone you're angry at."

Liath, engrossed in a fine custard, was caught short. "Well . . . there was a boy at home. He . . ." It was done by now. He was to pledge Ferlin in midsummer, and midsummer was gone. Life at home, frozen in her memory as she had left it, had moved on.

"No," Nerenyi said flatly. "Not him. Someone else."

"There is no one else."

Nerenyi cocked a brow.

"I tell you, there's no one. A dalliance, in the—early in my journeying. A sweet moment, no more." She examined the lingering memory of Tolivar. Sweet indeed, as the first should be. But only that. "I'm not in love with him, Ner. I'd tell you if I were."

"I don't think what I sense in you has much to do with your body—though I won't say you couldn't have used a tumble with one of those Sauglin magelings."

Liath laughed, but her palms had grown moist. *She knows. She doesn't have to deduce it. She can feel it.*

"It's something to do with your light, I think. Changing its flavor somehow."

Wary, fascinated, Liath said, "How do you mean?"

"It's smokier. More bitter."

Tainted. Changed. Even her magelight smelled of shadows now.

"As if you've wanted something more and more the longer you

couldn't have it. It tastes the way people look when they've been pining for someone."

"I'm over Keiler," she said—and, abruptly, no longer cared if it was true. "He's pledged by now, lost to me, and I always knew I couldn't have him. It's nothing." She was mouthing the words, and she saw the ironic moue Nerenyi made, but all she could think was *Good. Good. Let her believe I'm lovelorn. Let her seek no farther into me than that.*

And, *Spirits, I wish she knew.*

There was something else, another truth under the truth Nerenyi told. But Liath didn't know what it was.

Summer's end was a watery gold trembling in the air as they negotiated the rocky terrain of the High Arm. News of strange mages was gone with the corn. Each day Liath said to herself, *Today I will leave her.* Each day she placated mages who would have thrown Nerenyi out or wouldn't have scribed for Liath Journeymage, or worked beside Nerenyi in croft or cookroom, or braided Nerenyi's silken black hair, and thought, *Tomorrow.* They were nearly to the coast. Even when they came into the company of seekers, and Nerenyi spent an afternoon in subdued discussion with them, she lingered despite the excuse to be on her way. Nerenyi's journey year would end on the middle day of Ve Eiden, the equinox, the change of season from summer to midder; the three-day festival would begin to-morrow, and everywhere were preparations for the day of balance. Liath watched her with folk like the folk she'd left for a craft that had not yet provided a home. Would she return to the seekers, untriaded, a failure? She wanted to look on the Sea of Wishes before the end. It was just a little farther. No darkmage would spring from the road between here and there, to steal her soul. . . .

In the midst of idle conversation that night, when it was just the two of them again, Nerenyi imposed a silence on herself. Only when it lifted— apparently of its own accord—did she explain that seekers did that not as penance, but when they were stuffed with food for thought and had to digest it.

"You could have told me that before I spent two nights thinking I'd wronged you some way."

"You probably have. Or you will. So there, you've paid in advance."

She spoke without enthusiasm, as if needling Liath had become rote, and she would not look at her as they rode.

At a casting later that day, to ward barrels of seaweed against rot, she said, "These lines are terrible. Why do you scribe them so close, and so near the leaf's edge? And hardly room to historiate the initial. Have you no consideration for your illuminator? And why do you put up with it? Because the binder is your unpledged child? I don't know what your pledgemates look like, but it's clear he's the product of a union between you. He's already got your thinning hair, your tendency to go to fat. I suppose you've never told him. Are you really so thick that you never guessed? . . ."

This was more than Liath could mend. "You go too far," she said when the betrayed mages had sent them off and turned to confront their changed relationship. "You did harm this time!"

"I can't help it," Nerenyi said. Her eyes were hard, her mouth a grim line. "It just comes out."

"It's an illness. You should have it healed."

"It can't be healed. Many have tried."

The words struck to Liath's heart, but fear twined in too.

"Nerenyi," she began.

The seeker bent, then straightened in her saddle. "Your reckoner's been here."

"A lot of people have been here. It's a well-traveled road."

"No, it was him, and recently. Those tracks . . . his horse had a notched shoe, just like that, as if he'd dented it on something. I noticed it in Sauglin."

"You did not."

"I did."

"You couldn't have noticed a detail like that!"

"I did, Liath. It's what I do. But why is he ahead of us now? Unless he's . . ."

Liath saw Southers lunging at her from the trees. She swayed back, and Amaranth halted.

"You stay here. I'll ride up ahead. If he's there, I'll flush him out."

"I'll come with you."

"And let him see you?" Nerenyi reined around to face her. "Why would you do that if you're avoiding a proxy call?"

Because she wasn't avoiding the call. Because Sauglin might have been coincidence. Because he might have a message for her—that made more sense than the Ennead sending a vocate who knew her thoughtlessly into the field—she had to see him to be sure—

"What's in that pack you never open, Liath?"

They stared at each other across the settling road dust.

"What did those seekers say to you?" Liath countered.

Nerenyi grinned. "You're learning. But you haven't answered my question."

"You haven't answered mine."

Nerenyi's tongue went into her cheek. "Do you know what Gill Wordsmith really was, back in Sauglin? Do you know the real reason I was so hard on him?" She didn't wait for the reply Liath didn't try to give. "He was a scryer. A false mage, sent out to gather information. They usually have dim lights, enough to pass. I think now that sometimes they may have very bright lights too."

"Sent out by *who?*"

"Show me what's in your pack, and I'll tell you."

"You said you'd tell me what you knew about the Great Storms," Liath said, casting back desperately.

"You never told me why there was a reckoner after you."

Liath's knuckles went white on the reins. "What if the same thing answers both? Do I still earn both answers from you?"

"If you want them."

She slipped the straps from her shoulders and drew the pack around in front. She had not opened it since the night by Folle's stables. Now she unlaced the flap. Drew out a hunk of black tunic, linen threaded with silk. Dug down to find the silver ring at the bottom. Displayed it on the palm of her hand.

Nerenyi was not a vocate, not a proxy; the seekers, though they sometimes sounded it, were not a group mind. Nerenyi waited for Liath to tell her what the reckoner trappings meant.

Don't make me do this, Liath pleaded silently. *Don't make me lie to you. Please, just conclude the obvious: I'm a lapsed reckoner, I'm fleeing humiliation. Please, Nerenyi. Say it.*

The black eyes were hard and glittering as agate.

Liath's hand closed around the ring. She spread the pack wider, lifted it pointedly.

"Yes. You've shown me. Did you kill him?"

The suggestion shocked her—yet she nearly had. "No."

"All right. The Ennead sent Gill. They know the Lowlands are chafing, and their proxies are failing to maintain control. The Ennead exists to serve Eiden Myr, not to control it. The tellers remember that, and the seekers rediscover it as they question the reasons for everything. Many seekers go in search of the Great Trines of history. They believe that once there were three enneads. There have to have been; logic dictates it, based on the unassailable strength of threes. One mage cannot cast; but if she could, she might do anything. Three mages balance each other's flaws. A single ennead is precarious. We don't know why there is only one, now. We don't know what evil or cataclysm winnowed it to that. But we question the authority it exerts. Fortunately, we're crackpots, so the Ennead pays us no mind. In truth they have nothing to fear. From us. But they fear Lowlanders, Southers most of all. They send these dim-lit, dispensable mages to spy on them."

A vast disappointment seeped through Liath. Nerenyi—as disfigured in spirit as Mellas, as wounded as Heff—had failed to become a triaded mage, and now, just as Liath had, she was seeing shadows where there were none. "The Ennead is three triads," she said, in the voice she used to calm insulted mages. "That is all we require to divert the Great Storms. That is their purpose. How could they control anyone, from up at the Head? Their failure has been . . ." She struggled to articulate, and grew angry at Nerenyi's patience. "They've only failed to give as much information as they get, and let common folk know what sort of information is passed. They're *weather reports*, Nerenyi. You're enmonstering people who are trying to control the *weather*!"

"Common folk," Nerenyi echoed, as softly as Liath had begun. "You see? Do you see your bias?"

Liath shook her head hard. It was too much. She struggled to find her way back to the point. "Sauglin. You sent Gill off. And you attached yourself to me because . . ."

"Because I thought you were another."

"And am I?"

"You carry reckoner's things. You watch wordsmiths with a kind of hunger. You're looking for someone."

The lie came to her so easily that she nearly groaned. Lies brought the shadows. Lies were the shadows. But she and Nerenyi had used each other since the day they met. Was their friendship a lie, too? Did it matter more than finding the Darkmage—or keeping Nerenyi clear of him, despite it all? Nerenyi had put the lie right in her hands. "My grandfather. My grandfather is a proxy. My mother banished him when her mother died of a broken heart from his abandonment. Now she's—repented. She begged me to find him. It meant leaving my post as a reckoner. If they see me, they'll drag me back. But I have to find him. I never met him. I was a baby then. But they told me his hand resembles our village wordsmith's, who was trained by him." One by one, she felt the loose planks of her story and nailed them true. Her throat had thickened as if she'd eaten something rancid. She pushed the words out. She would despise Nerenyi for believing them. "I know he's dark. I favor my father. He might not know me either."

"Well, that reckoner is fair, and we've been here too long." Nerenyi wasn't convinced, just pragmatic. "We'll cut through here. We're near the sea anyway, it's what I came for. Come on."

Liath closed her pack and followed through the thinning trees, over clumped hillocks of juniper, through sharp, shiny dune grass.

"I don't believe you, Liath," the seeker said. The sun had slanted low, off to the left, and made it hard to see.

"And suppose I was lying? Your ill-considered truths ruin mages' lives."

Nerenyi seemed to wince, but perhaps it was just a squint against the angled glare. "Yet still you ride beside me."

A salty tidepool blocked the way. They turned sunward to skirt it. There was no path here. It was the spirit days—if they lost the light, there would be no moon to show their way.

A publican with a crippled magelight; a seeker who alienated every mage she cast with. Liath regretted leaving the mute farrier, the nightmare-ridden boy, behind. What a troop they would have made. Was that itself indication of the Darkmage's insidious influence? The wounded, the disfigured, the maimed? Did all darkness radiate from him, wherever he was? Charvisk, and Verlein's blade, and the floods and drought? Gill must have been one of Torrin's people; she had half-suspected it all along, but it made no difference once he was gone. With all Nerenyi's talk against the Ennead, she could very well be one, too, tracking Liath in case she was tracking Torrin. Their friendship had mattered to her. Now it was dissolving into no more than manipulation.

"The Great Storms come in threes, once a generation," Nerenyi said, answering the long-ago, never-answered question. "But the words of magecraft, of ritual tales, suggest an ominous possibility. Tellers have stories of such storms as would wipe the world clean. Such a storm was supposed to have brought Galandra into being. Seekers who believe the myth of Galandra believe she will return with such a storm, perhaps to start anew. Three become one—one storm to end all storms. The erratic weather may be a portent. No doubt the Ennead is nervous. I don't blame them for sending you, really, or Gill. But they are exerting themselves in the wrong direction. And they did send you."

Liath started to speak, but Nerenyi raised a gloved hand.

"There's more, Liath. The reason for the Storms. Some seekers, myself among them, fear it may be magecraft itself. We have tampered with the weather to our own ends for time immemorial. We don't know how things were before. I know you don't believe in before—I know you observe the old ways, I respect that, I do . . ." She hissed air through her teeth. "I wish we had more information. The Ennead has called all their brightest mages back to them, all their best proxies. To form a new Triennead? To ward against the weather that is coming, they will need the strength of three nines of mages, and even then they may fail. Magecraft may have cast itself into a deadly corner."

"*You're* a scryer," Liath said suddenly, the moment it occurred to her. Not one of Torrin's—and yet the duplicity of it enraged her. "You've never really been a mage. You trained, you took the triskele, but what difference does your malady make? You only cast to find out more about magecraft, so you can report to your seeker folk! I'm surprised you didn't try for the Ennead itself. What happened, Nerenyi? Your light is bright enough, for all you disparage it. Were you called? Did you ruin proxies' lives, belching your truths, and bar yourself from the Holding?"

"No!" Nerenyi reined up at the foot of a crumbling dune as the sun slipped behind it.

"And you accuse *me*!" That Nerenyi had been perilously close to the right answer made it worse. "You don't know *anything*, Nerenyi. There is *so much* you don't know."

"*Then tell me!*"

Liath threw her head back to the sky. "I can't," she said through clenched teeth. "*I can't.*"

"Then go on," Nerenyi said. "Ride on."

Liath stared at her, not trying to disguise the pain. "I can't," she whispered. "I can't leave it like this."

"I want to be a mage," Nerenyi said, hoarse. "I gave *everything* to magecraft, even though it couldn't heal me, even though it would make my ailment more obvious. Seekers are nomads. Their only home is with each other. I would give anything to triad, anything to pledge, to settle. Anything but . . ."

The shadows lengthened around them. "But what?"

"But the truth."

Liath bit down on a bark of laughter. "Well, we've neither of us given the other much of that, have we."

"No." Nerenyi's voice was hollow. "But if we had, imagine what we might have learned."

She was right. Nerenyi, set to finding Torrin, would have found him, while Liath floundered in darkness. But Nerenyi would blurt anything when aroused. Somehow she had kept secrets; but no secret was safe with her. She could not be asked for help.

Fatigue weighted her voice. "We have to part, Nerenyi."

"Yes. I know."

Of course. "Then come on. You wanted to see the sea."

They rode side by side to the top of the white-sand dune, and looked down at a village curved like a shell at the water's edge. The sun slipped into the sea in a spreading crimson stain. She had seen the sun go down in the Sea of Wishes after all. She shut her eyes, and a pinpoint echo of the light burned there, the color of her guiders. Instinctively she looked to Nerenyi, to drive the hurt away, then caught herself, and made a pained sound.

Nerenyi stared at the leagues on leagues of water, stretching past the eye's ability to see. "It's so big," she breathed. "I always forget."

"Everyone says that," Liath replied. "Let's go down."

The cottages were tiled with opalescent shells and faced the sea. No one stirred as they led their horses down a shadowed alley, though the crunch of hooves on shells was loud. They came out onto a last ridge of dune, and walked down a boat ramp and onto the ruddied sands. A nonned threfts to either side, quartz jetties ran from the ridge out into the sea, calming destructive force into a roll of ordinary breakers. The little village seemed deserted, but coracles were tethered to spikes driven into the pale sand, lined up where the tide would bathe them in seawater.

Liath remembered a dream she'd had, great expanses of white, and for a moment the sea seemed a fluid shadow lapping at the edge of the world.

Nerenyi dismounted, sank into the sand, breathed deep—and Liath saw through Nerenyi's eyes for one last time, and shared her wonder and exhilaration at the infinite water.

Then it became again the terrifying sea, whispering threats. She walked back up to the tideline, rearranged dry seaweed with her boot toe. "Where will you go?" she asked softly.

When the illuminator did not respond, Liath thought the surf had swallowed her words, and braced herself to repeat them. But Nerenyi said, "On."

"Your journey year is over."

"I have no home to return to. Seeker parents, wandering, please goodness alive and well. I'll keep traveling. It suits some, to journey their lives long. It will be enough." She looked up, her velvet eyes bereft of all betrayal. "I regret that I won't get to learn the truth of you. If a time comes when you can tell me, I hope you'll find me, somehow. Don't forget me, Liath."

Liath shook her head: *Never.* But before she could speak, or reach out, Nerenyi got up and brushed the sand off and said briskly, "It would make the most sense if I took Amaranth. That way the proxy might follow me instead of you. But . . ."

"But you can't part with Coriander," Liath finished for her. "I would never ask you to."

A shadow rose from one of the coracles. It turned into a gangly youth. He stared at them, then scrambled out, gave three piercing whistles, and ran for all he was worth up the dune, head down and arms pumping. He darted between cottages, and whistled again. Liath and Nerenyi watched helplessly. Did he think they were going to steal a boat?

The sea washed the last tint of sunset away, and the sky faded to moondark. Nerenyi sighed and gathered Coriander's reins.

A clatter of hooves became a fat little man clinging desperately to a pony skidding down the boat ramp, trailed by the boy and a handful of other seafolk.

"Mages!" he cried. "Please wait, please wait for me!"

They waited. The pony trotted up and deposited him. "Mages!" he cried again, then lowered his voice and smoothed his clothes—sleep-clothes, a linen nightshirt and felt slippers. "They need mages. I've just been to Ondree and found none and here you are, sent by the spirits in my foolish panicked absence!"

"Who does?"

"The other mages, of course. The ones who sent Korelan."

Liath backed away; Amaranth snorted as the surf tickled her fetlocks, then turned to sniff it, tossing her head when froth got up her nose. "We're only two," she said, "and both illuminators. We'll be of no use to anyone. You need to find a triad."

"No no no, you don't understand—spirits calm me, I can't get a straight word out of my mouth. It's illuminators they need. And here, now, two at once! Sent by Sylfonwy, there's no doubt of it!"

Nerenyi made a face at his personification of the wind spirit, but her eyes were bright again. The man's arrival had roused others, and he directed them to unmoor the boat the boy had fallen asleep in while waiting. "Where?" Nerenyi asked.

"Out *there*," he said, and pointed at something they should be able to see and could not. "Senana. The isle."

"Not very big, is it?" Nerenyi said skeptically. Then her eyes narrowed, and Liath looked again, and there was something—a bump in the straight seam between sea and sky.

"Big enough for two nonned to live there still, though it's a hardscrabble life and many have left. Big enough for its own triad, once. Big enough to die on."

He was ushering them toward the boat; Liath scuffled with a stubbornfaced girl determined to take Amaranth's reins.

Nerenyi had unscrambled the man's words. "Their triad's illuminator has passed, and now someone else is about to go," she said. "Someone's got to cast passage."

This was it, then. The mages on that island would have to take Nerenyi as they found her; they'd have no choice. It wouldn't poison the casting. If it did, there'd be nothing Liath could do anyhow. Let her go. It was time to go on.

"Liath!" Nerenyi said, and gestured with her chin.

Liath looked down the long crescent of shore.

Cloak an otherworldly ripple in the cool sea air behind him, blond hair flung back, gray horse flowing over pale sands like mist—the black form had to be the reckoner from Sauglin.

Liath strained to see his face.

"Come *on*, you fool," Nerenyi said. "He'll have you in a breath."

"Wait—"

"I don't care what's passed between us. You could be wrong about him. I won't let him have you. Not while I can stop it."

Nerenyi was stronger than she was, and Nerenyi was convinced this reckoner meant her harm, and nothing she could tell her short of the truth would make her listen. She could have twisted the grip back and been free, but it would have meant breaking the wrist. If she fought Nerenyi, she would hurt her. Nerenyi hauled her into the boat. She flailed for a handhold when the craft tipped under her weight, then sat down hard on a wooden seat.

Not a boat. Not again. Not a boat one-ninth the size of that coaster. Not a tippy little boat. The blasted thing was made of nothing, layers of tarred canvas over a frame of willow laths stuffed with moss. "No," she said.

Nerenyi stepped lightly across three seats to position herself toward the far end. Liath tried to get up, but a girl tossed a heavy coil of wet line at her. Others gave the boat a great running push into the surf and hopped in. The youth in the stern seat was sliding a steering oar into place and trying to show respect for her triskele instead of amusement at her distress. Korelan, who'd come from the island. She craned to look past him.

The reckoner was closer now—cantering, not galloping, but gaining. She couldn't see his face. There was still time to get out—the water couldn't be over her head yet. Again she tried to get up, but felt the boat sway under her; a hand on her shoulder pushed her firmly down, and the girl beside her said, "Please, mage, that's very dangerous." Nerenyi was dipping a smooth ashwood oar into the water as if she'd done it all her life. All Liath could do was clutch at the seat, like a child clutching the pommel on her first ride, as the craft seemed to go straight up the next wave and drop, leaving her stomach to roll in on the crest.

The reckoner didn't hesitate at the tumbled jetty; his mist-gray horse sailed neatly over and continued on to where the fat man stood with their mounts and a handful of villagers. Someone swung a light back and forth in a long arc, a signal to the island.

The coracle broke through the last of the shorebound surf, Korelan began a rhythmic chant, and the craft shot out into the sea, leaving the village, and the reckoner, behind.

When the crescent was itself a smudge on the water and no other boat had followed, Liath squeezed around on the seat to face front. Leagues of darkness lay between them and the island shouldering out of the sea, and nothing but black water all around, nothing to cling to but this nutshell, so weightless that she could feel in its frame every swell, every pull on the oars. Heartbeat on heartbeat later, the rising shadow before them resolved into sheer cliffs and a long slope down to the ocean.

For a moment, her eyes widened. The island was the perfect place—rocky, craggy, isolated, not well known or much thought of—for a dark-mage to carve out his fastness.

Then she swore.

After everything, Nerenyi was rowing straight to it.

Dawn was breaking over the Hand as they reached the Isle of Senana. Two figures waited at the stony landing. Both tall, spare, their long hair tossed by the wind—one iron gray, one black. A flock of gulls wheeled up at the coracle's approach. As the rowers stood their dripping oars on end and the frontmost reached a fending hand out to the white-spattered dock, Liath saw that the figures were both women.

"Welcome," said the gray-haired one. Her accent was strange, guttural. "Imma Binder. My daughter, Gisela Wordsmith." Liath looked at the wordsmith, at the salted, sun-browned skin, the grave sea-colored eyes. She had lived on this hard, windswept place all her life. Had she welcomed Torrin Wordsmith onto her island?

Korelan got out first and made the tether line fast to a rusted cleat.

Nerenyi hopped out and greeted the mages, while Korelan and two others helped Liath step up onto a seat and across to the relative safety of weathered wood.

The small dock was mounted on a stretch of sea-blacked limestone, fissured into blocks like loaves of bread. The barren expanse gave onto brief, sloped fields, high with rye that needed cutting and binding. Beyond a fringe of trees at the far end, one path threaded up a rugged incline to a plateau that must end in the sheer cliffs she had seen from out on the water. The whole island couldn't be longer than a sixmile. A handful of straw-thatched, moss-grown stone cottages stood within sight; the others must be up on the plateau, or round the turn of the headland. Three donkeys, twitching flies from mangy coats, waited by what must have been a dockman's shack, now sagging, its warped boards no longer plumb.

"How close is it?" Nerenyi asked as Korelan unhitched the donkeys. The five youths who had rowed the coracle had flipped it over their heads and were porting it onto the limestone flat, their bare toes finding unerring purchase. "They're needed for the harvest anyway," Korelan told her, as the bindswoman replied, "She's hanging on. Either for us, or for her grandson." She smiled at Korelan, the seams in her weathered face deepening. "We've time yet. But thank the spirits you're here."

Liath swayed a little on the uneven stone, making her way over to the donkeys. If she ever got her hands on whoever invented boats . . . "Can they carry two?" she asked. Korelan nodded. With herself and Nerenyi aboard the gray one, the mages on the white, and Korelan seated sideways on the black, they began the long, weary journey through fields and sparse, unfamiliar trees and up. The plateau was a wilderness of unmortared stone walls, bending to join each other in a patternless welter, some protecting vegetable crofts, some nothing but cattails and burdock. And still the ground was full of stones, as if all the generations who had scraped a life from this unforgiving earth, building homes and fences, cairns and byres, had failed to use them all.

They stopped at the second cottage along the high road. An old woman sat in the dim interior, stroking the forehead of the older woman in a truckle bed that had been dragged from another room to be closer to the hearth. The peat fire had burned low; Korelan set about feeding it, while Imma flung the window hangings back to let the air and early sunshine in. "Good morning, Werka," she said. "This is Nerenyi t'Galandra, and Liath n'Geara. It seems Sylfonwy and Morlyrien both heeded our calls. Now you have your choice of illuminator."

"It's Nerenyi will do the casting," Liath said quickly, humbled by their pragmatic approach to death. Let there be no misunderstanding. Her dark visions of a rocky fastness, her bitter hurt over Nerenyi, were insignificant here.

The woman on the bed was past speaking, but she turned her ancient face a little toward the sunlight, and Liath thought a name was trying to form on the thin, spent lips.

"I'm here, Granna," Korelan said, squeezing her hand briefly before resuming his household tasks with the ease of old habit. He had been looking after her for a long time. The other woman—a sister, Liath thought; the same pointed chin and turned-up nose—made ready to go.

"We've said our goodbyes," she told Gisela, in a thicker accent than the mages'. "She knows I can't bear to watch her go. I'll be off now. There's water in the kettle and tea in the tin."

Gisela walked out with her. Nerenyi found stools enough for them all to sit on, while Korelan swept the room, sending dust motes dancing in the sun, and Imma checked her binder's sack.

"Is she in pain?" Liath asked softly. The woman seemed to go in and out of a dream; now and then her eyes flew open and she strained to speak, but a comforting word would lull her back into a half-doze. Her bony fingers clutched and released the knit coverlet. Somehow Liath knew that the fine, straight stitches were the work of those hands, in younger days.

"No," Imma said. "She's not ill. She's old. A nonned hard winters and another dozen glorious summers. Werkarel n'Dalrien was an oyster diver, in her day, and a good earthcrafter besides. Lost her daughters to the sea long ago, one by one; her pledgemate stayed with her as long as he could, but last winter the chill got into him, and no illuminator came in time."

"What happened to yours?" Nerenyi asked. Liath winced at her directness, but Imma smiled.

"It was her time too. She was my oldest sister."

"Who cast passage for her?"

Liath threw Nerenyi a sharp look. Imma caught it, and said, "Here on the isle we don't tiptoe about harsh truths. Life is harsh, here, and sometimes short, magecraft or no. My sister's prentice cast passage for her—it was her trial. Crafting her triskele was the last casting my sister did."

"And the prentice didn't want to triad here?"

Imma shook her head. "Most of our young folk leave. She was bereaved, and bored with island life, and she had ambitions to be called for proxy. They would not have found her here."

The old ways were all about them in the small common room. No weaver's loom had fashioned any of the cloth; all was homespun or hand-knit. If there were carpenters, they had not learned the knack of joinery, and the furniture was lashed driftwood or woven rye straw. The iron pots and tools in the fireplace were simple and very old. A place outside of time. The thought gave her a chill, and she gratefully clasped the warm wooden teacup Gisela handed her.

"And your pledgemates?" Nerenyi asked, blowing on her tea, not used to taking it hot.

"Gisela is not pledged," Imma said, "and her father is in his sailboat, or awaits me in our cottage, a good, patient man who'll be too polite to express his disappointment if we find another third and take up a triad's responsibilities again."

Something passed between Gisela and Nerenyi then, Liath thought; some kind of look, either recognition or evaluation or both. She quelled a jealous pang. Absurd.

"As you may have noticed," Gisela said, speaking for the first time, in a voice as gravelly as the island's road, "many castings want doing. Perhaps you'll stay awhile and help us catch up? Between the two of you it would be half the work."

Nerenyi looked at Liath, who struggled to hide her reaction, and her eyes narrowed. "Perhaps," the seeker said for them both.

Morning shifted into afternoon and wore on toward evening. The mages told them island stories, thick with love of its wild beauty and respect for its rugged endurance against weather and time and the sea. Toward evening Liath curled up on the braided hearth rug and slept, intending to stand watch in the night. No one roused her, and she woke to the sound of wind questing into chinks in the stones, rattling the shutters. A lantern was set near the bed, wick turned very low; Korelan sat with his grandmother, alert and still. Her breaths were regular but wheezing, a steady counterpoint to the wind's moan; someone sprawled in a chair near Liath's head, snoring softly. The space smelled of peat smoke and tired bodies, and onion stew someone had warmed. Two people were speaking behind the closed door of the end room—Nerenyi and Gisela. She resolved to get up, offer to spell Korelan. In the next moment it was morning, and she was shivering under a scratchy throw someone had tossed on her, and Nerenyi was offering her a cup of thick black tea.

Ve Eiden. The balance day.

They watched, and waited. Conversation came sporadically. Korelan was older than his thin face and shy manner had suggested. What little he said conveyed an abiding dedication to this island and its ways. He'd prenticed to a cheesemaker in the Fingers, but brought his skills back home with him, and tended the scruffy goats that roamed the rocks. "Ah, she'd flay the skin off me if she knew I wasn't binding the rye," he said, but his voice was gentle, regretful. He hovered over the old woman, saw to the bedpot, pressed a moistened rag into her mouth when she could no longer drink. The nights collected under his eyes in puffy rings. Liath, her mind a blur of Gran Breida's last days and the Ardra tree tender, suggested they turn her for a bit, rub her arms and legs. Korelan's grateful glance—the only time his modest eyes met hers—was almost enough to make up for the service she could not do his grandmother.

Gisela, a mystery of sea-distant gaze, said little to her, but seemed to have become the late-night debating partner of Nerenyi, who said less. Liath and Imma made tea, fetched water, cooked what they could. Conversation died under its own weight. The world contracted into the small space of the common room, the short walk to privy or rain barrel, brief stints pulling vegetables from the back garden. Outside, the relentless wind; inside, the labored breath, the sedgeweave and pigment and quills laid out on a sideboard.

"Why can't we live forever?" Liath whispered, after a nonned heartbeats with her back to the hearth, hugging her knees and watching the strong old woman fade in the afternoon light.

Imma overheard her. "Think how much we'd miss," she replied.

Liath had not meant anyone to answer; it was the kind of dialogue she and Nerenyi would have had, but Nerenyi was out walking with a silence on her, and Gisela was asleep in the darkened side room. Still, she'd brought it up. "Magecraft can cure so many ailments. Why can't it cure old age? We could smooth wrinkles, if binders wasted vellum on vanity. We cure stiff joints and bad backs all the time, bring failing eyesight back . . ."

"Part of life is the leaving of it," Imma said.

Because because because, Liath thought.

"But that's not good enough." Liath looked up in surprise; Imma was smiling. "You've spent a lot of time with your seeker friend, I see." When Liath nodded, Imma thought for a moment, then said, "No one can know what it's like in the spirit world. Pethyar, we call it here, though I don't think mainlanders have a name for it at all. Some claim to hear haunts, but haunts are unpassaged, they never completed the journey. They can't tell us what it's like. It seems to me that pethyar is a place of infinite potential, unfettered by the boundaries we struggle under in the world. That doesn't mean there is no flesh there, or sacrifice, or effort. But I think . . . I think that in that place, if that's an adequate word for it, one can blossom into a true, full self. I can't say this very well; I'm a binder, not a wordsmith. But I feel it as a flower. The flesh is a bulb in the earth, and sprouts a white stalk, and takes nourishment and pleasure from the earth . . . but there comes a time when the plant needs air and light, and it grows up, and green, into a freer space . . . that's the best I can describe it. Would you have magecraft lay a board over that ground?"

"There's too much life in your example. This is death."

"Yes. I don't understand it myself. That's how I feel it to be. It's all I can say, besides tell you that death is just a fact of life. Magecraft can't cure death. We could wake Gisela right now, and form the casting circle, and draw the fluid from Werka's lungs and heal her aged flesh and strengthen her bones . . . but she would still pass on. I asked your question, when I was a prentice, and my teacher said that mages had tried it, and failed, and were horrified by what they'd done, and learned the lesson."

Liath wondered what they had created in their attempt. "You don't cheat the bonefolk"—it was an old saying she'd taken to mean that you couldn't put unpleasant tasks off forever. Now she heard a different meaning in it, and shuddered.

"It's gone cold." Korelan frowned.

"I'll stoke the fire," Liath said—but Imma stared hard at Werka, and in two long strides was rapping on the sleeproom door.

"No," Korelan said.

On her way back, Imma touched his head gently, then fetched her white chalk from the sideboard. "It's time, love."

Liath ran to the door. A gust of wind pulled it from her and banged it on the stone; a dash of rain hit her face. Charcoal clouds were racing to fill the sky. Gales came up quickly on the island, Imma had said, but often blew as quickly out to sea. If Nerenyi had been here, they could have warded off the weather . . .

"Nerenyi!" she called into the rising blow. "Nerenyi, it's time! Come back!"

The wind carried a biting silence.

"Close the door," Gisela said. Liath obeyed, and turned to find them assuming the triadic points. The third stool sat empty.

A whine rose in the back of her throat. She saw again the blue skin of the strangled infant.

I can't, she heard herself say, to Hanla, to the vocates, to mage after mage after mage on her long false journeying. I can't, she would say to these mages, and they would answer, You must. You're a mage. Sit down. It's time.

She groped for the latch again, wrestled to keep the door from flying back, wrestled it closed behind her, pitted her lungs against the insurmountable wind: "NERENYI!"

Korelan opened the front shutters, leaned out into the rain. "Please, Illuminator," he said—not loud, but the plea carried.

She went in. She sat on the third stool. Gisela was holding the wood-backed sedgeweave—sedgeweave, not vellum, not parchment—plant fiber, not animal, no death for a death, there's been enough death—sedgeweave, to ease the stalk through the packed topsoil—

Nerenyi would come in time.

Imma handed pen and inkpot across the dying woman. Gisela scribed in sure, fluid strokes—too fast, too sure, let her ponder, let her think. But she'd had three long nights to formulate whatever words a wordsmith scribed. Nerenyi would come. Nerenyi would come. But Gisela had filled the leaf. Imma was readying a sharp quill, and pigment pots, and brushes—

The door crashed open. Liath's heart convulsed in relief, and she turned to see Nerenyi stagger in, soaked to the skin, a beacon of magelight in the dark of storm. But no one was there. The wind had sucked the door open, or she hadn't fastened the latch. Korelan rushed to close it.

Gisela handed her the leaf. Imma offered her choice of brush or quill, unfamiliar with her preferences.

Nerenyi would come. Nerenyi would come. She would go through the motions, a placeholder, just not to upset the rhythm. Nerenyi would come in time. She laid the binding board on her thighs and took the quill. If she were doing the casting, she'd start with the border, make it a full-circle panel: a circle filled with a circular knotwork pattern with a continuous cord path. No, three cord paths, for body, mind, and spirit—the strands of life forming an unbroken whole around the scribing. Triple-interlacing was the hardest but the most potent; Liath was good at managing three cords. The quill was already inked, Imma holding the pot ready for her to dip again. She *would* start with the border. Werka breathed—there was time yet. She would teach Nerenyi this final pattern, sketching the start of the illumination that Nerenyi would take up, infuse with her light. She breathed with Werka, felt her heartbeat through the mattress her knees pressed. There was no sense of pain from her at all— just readiness, a push toward release. Gisela was at Werka's right hand, the side of intellect and memory; Imma was at her left, the side of emotion and courage; Liath looked into her lined face. The lines formed a pattern— why hadn't she seen that? Each season, each love, each loss, graven into the visage she presented to the world. Who would think to smooth such lines away with magecraft? Werka had earned this passage, every exertion written into her flesh a triumph. Liath's eyes absorbed the lines until they burned with their own light, then bent to the leaf, touched fragile quill to the laid weave . . .

The lines burned blue. Coldly, magnificently blue. She trailed them with ink, echoed them, rounded them and braided them, long curve over long curve for all the long years. Werka dove into depths of water, and when the oyster beds were spent she broke her hands on the stony ground, digging roots to live the winter. Brined from the sea, sanded by the hemp lines of her little sailboat, split open once, twice, thrice to release new lives into the world, salt tears draining back into the salt sea that took them from her. *Oh, Korelan, she does love you, she loves you past speech. . . .* Into the initials she painted the wild sky and all the colors the sea drew from it, the sea where Werka's heart lay though her proud body had worked the land, the mother sea that bore the wake of her brief passage through the world. The kadri formed and inked themselves, glowing turquoise and azure and cerulean and indigo and slate, all the hues and tints and shades of the sea and all the losses returned to shore on its inexorable tides. *This line is for peace; this line is for acceptance; this line is to remind you not to be afraid.*

The song of the wind was Imma's song, the whisper of surf and the memory of stone, ebbing and flowing over the colored leaf set on the woman's failing breast like a window. The song and the light focused in the weave of images and words, swirled around, and up, and for one blazing moment she could *see*—

The wind died against the stones in a last spatter, and a rattle came from Werka's throat, and her face went blank, her open eyes fixed on a far point.

The leaf was gone.

"I couldn't cast," she said.

They didn't say *Of course you could, we saw you do it*. Gisela nodded, and Imma said, "But now you can."

Nerenyi was standing behind her. "I should have known," she whispered. "Selfish, blind seeker." Liath groped for her hands, pulled them in front of her, held them tight. Nerenyi's night-black hair spilled down around her, freed from its plaits as she raced the driving wind. She had not returned in time.

"I saw . . ." Liath said, and could not go on.

"Yes." Imma got up, gestured to Korelan; he shook his head, shrank farther into the corner, unable, after all his caretaking, to do the final tasks. Imma pulled the coverlet up, slid Werka's eyes closed with her binder's hand. "Go in joy, old friend."

Liath got up, walked with Nerenyi to the fire, stared at its pale light. "I *saw* . . ."

"You saw," Gisela confirmed, standing on Nerenyi's other side.

Liath looked at the seeker. "You'll be staying."

Nerenyi nodded. "They've asked me. Gisela asked; Imma agreed. Liath . . ."

Liath put a finger to the seeker's lips. "Nerenyi," she said in answer. After all the words, that one word was all.

Then she left her friend with Gisela, and went to Korelan, and put an arm around his shoulders, and guided him softly to Werka's bedside, and sat with him through all the dark hours and all the long blur of tears.

She bade them farewell at dawn. A brief, hard hug for Nerenyi; a blessing on the triad they would be. A promise to return, in better days. No thanks to these mages could be enough. They saw her back onto the steep harbor path—just a quick, doubled handclasp, and they were gone.

From the top of the path she could see past the fields of bound rye and around the foot of the island. A village coracle awaited her at the landing, summoned by the light Imma had lit, at midnight, to signal that Werka's had gone. On the other side, toward sunrise, tall, tattered figures stood on a narrow shell beach. Backlit and distant, still as plant stalks. No boat was in evidence. There was no telling how they had gotten here, or if they had been here all along. The angle of their heads shifted as they gazed up at her. She shivered, and started down the slope.

Artesal, the rotund village man, was alone in the boat. He said little as she clambered in, except to talk her through the handling of oars. With only the two of them aboard, the craft bobbed high in the water, and the slightest motion of an ashwood blade sent the sharp prow in an unintended direction. But Artesal was tolerant, and at last she coordinated her movements with his. The sea was calm in the still, light-blue morning. They rowed facing backward until the halfway point; then, for luck, or to use different muscles, or because she had the hang of it now, he turned them to face their destination, and push on the oars instead of pull.

The rhythmic motion left her mind free. Three seasons gone, and she had acquired nothing but rumors. Anything could have happened in the meantime. He might have gone back to the Ennead of his own accord. They might have found some other way to him. He might have completed his counter-ennead and be preparing to summon the Storms. He might have had a change of heart.

He might be dead.

She could continue on her journeying, whole, able to participate—all was redeemed for her now. She could go *home*, and prove to her mother that you could show a strong light and still not abandon the ones who loved you. Graefel had forsaken the proxy ring, and Hanla with him. There would be no punishment. The Ennead would understand; her light had returned, she was no longer of use as a blunted knife. If she went after Torrin now, he would turn her as he'd turned the others. She could go back to the Holding and show Jonnula and the rest how bright her light really was. She could feel Tolivar's callused hands on her again— but no, he was Dabrena's, that had come clear to her at last. She could train for a place on the Ennead . . . visit home and look at Ferlin in Keiler's arms and smile hollow victory at her . . .

All the doors that had closed to her when her light shuttered were open again, but now they opened on blank walls. She whirled from one to the next. She could not have Keiler, as mage or pledgemate. Her mother's hurt would not be healed by her staying there. That hurt predated Liath's birth, and Breida had taken her place in their mother's heart, and nothing Liath could do, or not do, would change any of it. Watching Eiden's side rise and spread on the horizon, she understood that, too, with luminous clarity. How many miles it had taken her to comprehend that simple thing. . . .

The final realization was that neither time nor experience had provided these insights. Casting passage had.

Artesal spoke again as they felt the pull of the shorebound tide. "That reckoner left, all right, so I suppose you're in the clear, whatever the problem was. Didn't want to interrupt a vigil, nor wait for it to be over either."

Liath had forgotten about the reckoner. No matter. She had the use of her light again. She'd cope with whatever mess she had left behind.

"But he told me to give you a message," Artesal went on. There was reproach in his voice; the reckoner must have taken it out on him. "He said: 'I warned you too well, child of my child. I neglected to remind you there was one reckoner you needn't hide from.' "

The coracle grounded up hard on the shore, and Liath shipped her oars and stepped back onto the mainland.

The reckoner had been Pelkin.

ᚦ U S T

He negotiated the back passages of his fastness with practiced ease. He loved the complexity of its interstices, the dank odors exhaled by the living stone. They had chosen well.

The vault he entered was completely unlike his own spare chambers. He had piled the periphery with the ephemera of his studies, as some deep-earth creature might line a burrow. The scents of erudition clung here: spent candlewax, lime-soaked vellum, powders, warm metal—power. But the center was clear. He could still make out the casting circle scored deep in the stone. He could still make out a tang of blood, if he sniffed for it; a knifepoint run along the circular gutter would pry up thick brown flakes. The desiccated humors of confinement. As long as they lasted, the triskele that hung on its original chain from an eyebolt in the vault's low ceiling— gleaming dully in the light of the lamp he set in its usual niche, to complement the two set at the other triadic points—would remain warm, and viable. The fine pewter, shaped by three of the most powerful mages of their time, was alive. It was heated by the magelight of its erstwhile wearer.

"Good day," he greeted it cheerily. "Not that you know whether it's day or night, here. You'll never again know the warmth of the sun you so adored, the silver bath of moonlight, the touch of the stars. What a child of Eiden you were, in the end. You did not deserve the legacy of Galandra. But you will earn it after all. Doesn't that please you? You will earn it for me."

The pendant revolved slowly on its chain in the draftless chamber, turned by the heat eddies of the oil lamps.

He could feel the hatred the shade bore him, and the pity. The pity enraged him; he stilled his trembling hands with a calculated self-restraint. His own fault, for taunting it. Yet he could not resist. The plans he had sown were so close to fruition.

"Bet-jahr," he said, savoring the syllables of eternity. "And no, you will not know that either. In the event, you will remain here, trapped in the trappings of your craft until time wears your lifeblood away, and then released only to become a haunt of crumbled stone. But never fear. You'll have ample company, Daivor. Nothing will remain alive when it's finished."

The shade's soundless, unearthly howls raised the hairs on his arms, made his blood run to ice. He had heard the same silent cries the night they captured it—casting passage not into the next plane but inward, maneuvering the life force into a spiral, tricking it into the endless curve of the triskele around its own neck. The body had gone to the bonefolk, as it must—couldn't have them battering at the walls to get at it, that would draw attention. But the blood remained.

"I will be so much more than you ever were," he said, to punish it. "I already was, as it goes. So easy to lure you here. So easy to bind the bindsman. One wordsmith, one illuminator—your own dying moans were our bindsong. Your blood ran down the stone for ages, collecting in the gutter. I'd cut your throat and not the wrists, had I to do it again, but we thought we needed your song, and who knew how long the casting would take? Binding a spirit. It had never been done before." He realized he was talking to himself, and shook his head clear. He never ceased to be awed at his own invention. Armed with ancient knowledge, freed from the constraints of tradition, he had created more brilliant castings in these last seasons than the world had known in all its history. His only regret was how few there were to laud him.

It would not matter, where he was going.

Bet-jahr.

He applied himself to the work he had come here to do. The flesh was dust, but the spirit could still experience pain—and this bindsman still had a great deal to tell him.

The world had burst into color, everything rarefied and new. Sand that had looked white resolved into individual grains of pink and lime and aqua. Roan Amaranth was gold layered into rose; the girl who held her, Artesal's daughter, was the brown of fresh-turned earth after a day in the sun. Was this how the world had looked, before her guiders left her? Why had she never noticed?

There was no sign of Pelkin n'Rolf.

Bidding the crescent villagers a fair Ve Eiden, she went back to offer restitution to the mages Nerenyi had wronged. All seemed quiet from the road; no smoke rose from the chimney. But as she walked Amaranth down the front path she saw that the yard hosted a small crowd. Had festival competition resulted in injury?

"That's her!" the young binder cried, pointing.

The seekers, the ones Nerenyi had spoken to—and two mages reeking of light, one strikingly beautiful. Too early in the season he wore a silk-lined cloak; his felt hose and velvet coat were not dyed, but they bespoke fine Holding tailoring. His triskele was cast in gold.

"I believe you've been looking for me."

His eyes were black wells of promise and power. She groped under her paralysis for some memory of instructions, and came up with only Nerenyi's voice: *"You watch wordsmiths with a kind of hunger. You're looking for someone."* Nerenyi—dangerous Nerenyi, who'd never meant her harm— had betrayed her to these seekers, and these seekers belonged to him.

She forced one foot to follow the other toward them, when every instinct told her to run. The seekers regarded her as they had from their huddle with Nerenyi—like traders presented with some unfamiliar but intriguing item, trying not to show their keen interest. One Haunchman from the look of him, two Midlanders, and a woman from somewhere in the Boot.

"From the binder's cry it sounds more like you're looking for me." She kept her tone breezy. "Should I know you?"

"You do know me."

After so long in the thrall of those shadow ciphers, she should know him on sight. "I'm afraid I don't. At any rate, I'm here to see them." She lifted her chin toward the family of mages. "It's the festival of balance. I've amends to make."

"They are my people," he said. "You can make them to me."

The triad stood nervously in front of their cottage. They belonged to no one; they had no idea what was going on. The four seekers had tightened into a knot, whispering among themselves. Oh, she should have known it, should have known he'd turn seekers to his cause; it must have been so easy, the promise of ancient lore, the past unraveled. Nerenyi had nearly won her to their quest; now she saw them as pathetic, so desperate for a crumb of knowledge that they'd devour lies.

A good solid publican from the Neck wouldn't brook any nonsense from a stuck-up, overdressed mage. She let some irritation show. "And who are you when you're at home?"

He smiled, long and languorous, and she dug nails into her palms. "I am a very long way from home, as I think you are aware."

"I think you've spent too long with those seekers. It's one of their kind that's brought me back here. Never gave a straight answer, for all she couldn't keep her mouth shut." She addressed the triad. "If there's a good turn I can do you, in recompense for my rude companion, please tell me. I'll cast for your illuminator, or mind your cottage while you enjoy the festival . . ."

The wordsmith, mute, shook her head.

Liath shrugged. "Then I'll be on my way." She sketched a mocking bow to the other mages. "And a fair Ve Eiden to you, whoever you are."

"Wait."

The simple word carried a binding authority. It stopped Liath's hands halfway to the saddle. The reins slipped from her fingers and she turned.

"Illuminator, are you?" he said, his voice low, compelling. She nodded despite herself. "And with a remarkable light. Very good. We are wordsmith and binder. You will come with us."

The lank-haired binder hefted his bulging sack.

Moons she'd had, most of sowmid and all summer, and she'd never considered how exactly she would take what the Ennead needed. "*You have merely to bring us some hair, some skin, some scrap of his flesh. It will enable us to core and seal him from afar. He will have no choice then but to return to us, to be unsealed. . . .*"

As the binder fetched their horses, scattering the resident binder's indignant geese, the wordsmith glanced back. Liath reached into the side pocket of her saddlebags. Her hand closed on her use knife. Blood was part of the body. It would have to do.

"Why aren't you wearing a normal triskele?"

"Don't be disingenuous," he said. "Mount up."

She'd have to run for it the moment she'd blooded the knife. Her stomach clenched. Reduced to Souther tactics. But she wouldn't kill him. The triad could heal whatever minor wound she inflicted. She'd have to wrap the blade quickly, cloth would hold the precious substance better than metal between here and the Holding. . . .

The triplet hoofbeats of cantering horses resounded heavily in the earth beneath them. The wordsmith and binder exchanged a frown, and the wordsmith looked to the triad; they shrugged, hands spread, straining for a glimpse of the road.

Heff rode into the yard. He was mounted on his piebald gelding, with a packhorse, bearing his farrier's tackle, tethered to the saddle horn.

She bit down on an outcry: *What are you doing here?* But he read it on her face, and gave the slightest shake of his head.

Just a few moments more and she'd have the material the Ennead required. Heff might help her get away, but not thundering in like this, why couldn't he have waited, *how had he found her?* And what would the Darkmage do to him—the man who'd cursed him to a face that would never heal? Would Heff demand a true healing now? Could she gift him with that and still do as the Ennead had bidden?

The wordsmith gazed on him with no recognition.

In the extreme clarity of fear, Liath saw the wordsmith in a new light—from the side this time, as they had both turned. Her eye caught on his gold triskele. On the seam along its edge.

"How did you find me?" she breathed to Heff as he dismounted. He waved the question away and said, He is not the man you seek.

She nodded. The triskele had just told her that. Some impostor, sent to divert her—or whoever the Ennead might send. She was intended to take what she needed from him and go back, thinking her task complete. Did the Darkmage know who she was? Or was this trap not set specifically for her?

They'd had no time to send a runner to him—this was only the third day since Nerenyi had spoken with the seekers. This man probably worked independently, an advance diversion. She and Nerenyi had been too odd a pair, had invited scrutiny.

If Heff hadn't ridden in out of nowhere, she'd have given herself away. Her actions would have told them exactly what they'd wanted to know, and spoiled her for Torrin permanently.

This was a test. So far she had not failed it. Though she'd thought it was in vain, she'd given no indication that the game was up. She might still salvage this.

"What is he on about?" the binder demanded.

Liath bared her teeth in a smile she had learned from the Southers. "He says," she began, and her hand snaked out to jerk the fake triskele from the man's neck, "you're not a real mage." She tossed the gold medallion at the resident triad; the illuminator caught it. "Not cast. Ordinary metalwork."

He stepped back, hand flying to his throat as if she had yanked off a limb. She pressed on before he could regroup: "You mark me, pretender— I'll have the reckoners on you!"

"But he said . . ." Then the resident wordsmith's bafflement twisted into anger. "You said the Ennead had sent you! He said they were a new kind of proxy, sent out to find damaged mages . . . your friend . . . you . . . we told him . . ." She swore.

"And what did he tell you lot?" Liath asked the seekers. A risk—but she had to quell suspicion, buy herself time. As quickly as that, between one word and another, she had decided that nothing would stop her finding the Darkmage. "What did you say to Nerenyi? She hurled every sort of wild accusation at me. None of it made sense. Can't you people ever make sense?"

The seekers looked at the pretender, as if awaiting orders; then they turned, without a word, and walked away.

Liath swore. "Now they've put a silence on themselves and we'll never sort this out. Well, it's the reckoners' problem."

"It's all of our problem," the resident illuminator said quietly. "I hear there's a rogue mage on the loose. I hear the proxy chain is breaking down. I hear mages are cursing Lowlanders. I hear reckoners are refusing to do necessary castings. I hear children are dying."

Liath faltered. "What did you say?"

"You heard me." He examined the golden triskele. "Pyrite," he said, with a bitter laugh. "Not even gold. What a fool I was. But my pledgemate . . . my son . . . it was a difficult time."

"I know," Liath said. "I'm sorry."

The false Darkmage drew himself up. "You can smell my light. Who are any of you to claim I am not what I say I am?"

"I knew a man with a good light," Liath replied thoughtfully. "At home. He failed his trial. Got stuck a cottar for the rest of his life. He never forgave any of us. I suppose there are a lot of ways to take out that kind of hatred. And you're not the first pretender I've met. I don't suppose you have a friend named Gill, from Pange?" She turned away before he could answer. "Come on, Heff. If you still want to come with me."

He made half a face and said, I followed you, yes?

"Who is this man, who shows no light?" the binder cried. The older man tried to belay him, but he was furious and confused. "How does he claim to know who is mage and who is not?"

Liath was amazed at how lies fell into place, inked patterns following guiders. "He doesn't," she said, mounting her horse. "I only told you that once I got a good look at that 'triskele.' "

"You couldn't have known whether it was him," she said to Heff as they rode Fingerward, trailing the packhorse laden with the tools of the journeysmith he'd become in order to follow her. "He can disguise himself."

I'll know, Heff replied.

She was trying to regain her saturated vision, but the shock of reality had bleached it. Heff's good eye was the color of dew-wet moss in the first dapple of morning. His stubble of hair was chestnut with gold flecks. His burns were a mauve smear, as if his lips had melted over half his face—not healed, but no longer leaking fluid. Beside Amaranth, dwarfing her, the gelding was old snow on charcoal, and the packhorse was brown as Norther tea, with three inky legs and one forefoot dipped in cream to the pastern. The world was still full of colors. But there was no color without light; and there was no light without shadow.

"You don't know why I'm looking for him."

It doesn't matter, he said. I will see you safe.

"How did you find me, over all those long miles?"

He mimed tracking her.

"It's too far. You couldn't have trailed us that far. We'd have seen you. Nerenyi was too good at that."

She was the other mage?

Liath nodded.

Why did she stay on the island?

"She triaded, and pledged too, I think, or will if they ever get three reckoners to do it. I wish you could have met."

He laughed silently. We did, he said. She called me "half-face" and said if I ever harmed you she'd take off the other half.

"She what? When?"

While you were telling mages you were sorry. She saw me before that, I think, but I wasn't close enough to concern her. I couldn't make her understand.

"No, I imagine not." She shook her head. Nerenyi, unable to comprehend Heff's handsigns; was it really something only Liath could do? Nerenyi, protecting her from the protector. How close had Pelkin gotten? Had she warned him off, as well?

I should never have thrown my lot in with hers. But Nerenyi had taught her things, and smoothed her way when her light was ailing, and hauled her off to the island sanctuary that restored it—but most of all, Nerenyi had been her friend, no matter what misguided choices she had made.

"You could have let me know you were there. I'd have put her straight."

You had her to watch you close. You needed me to watch from a distance.

"I wish you could have been friends, then," she amended, and this time Heff agreed.

A little later, she said, "I don't suppose you saw a blond reckoner on the same trail, eh? An older man on a gray horse?"

Are you looking for him also?

"No. But I dearly hope I find him."

Too many false rumors, some with her own clumsy, light-lorn misadventures as their source. Too little trust in proxies, too easy acceptance of pretenders. The world was coming apart, in a nonned subtle ways. Soon he wouldn't need to summon a Storm.

Heff had come by some tallysticks, and treated her to a meal and several flagons of the local wine at a roadhouse.

The taste of it recalled Roiden, what she'd said of him to the Darkmage's man, and the words she'd thought his memory had tried to tell her when the world had gone dark at the reckoner encampment. The old sick feeling seeped into her stomach. But even the shadow ciphers had color now—greenish black and midnight purple. They were no match for the blue lines that would blaze the next time she cast. Her own magecraft would banish them. Her light was too bright for the Darkmage to tarnish.

The Ennead would call her in if they knew—but they didn't know. She had seen enough of proxies to understand how some were twisted. But she could not be twisted. She had lived too long under the overlay of those dark symbols. The Ennead might have shown her the fragment not solely to identify but to confer immunity. She would not fail them.

"To Eiden Myr," she said, raising her cup.

Heff pointed at her, and raised his.

It was only a pair of toasts, not enough to make it count, and where she drained her cup to seal it, Heff drank his in three measured draughts, some custom of his folk . . . but still it sealed a new beginning. The innkeepers had taken them for pledgemates, and asked Liath why he didn't have his face healed. She said she didn't know and left them to wonder. They served a fine stuffed pepper, with mollusks and butter-drenched mushrooms and hard, tangy goat cheese on a bed of bitter greens, and after a while even Roiden's wine tasted of light.

They took a room, as if they'd traveled together all their lives. She dragged the mattress out of its frame and slept in the sling while he turned restlessly on shedfeather. In the dark, he could not speak to her, and he dreamed in silence.

· · ·

They began the long climb into the granite ridges along the back of the Hand. This was where he had disappeared—gone to ground, somewhere in this rugged region, she was certain of it.

Every time she cast, her light would be a beacon. He wanted mages. She was a mage again.

Yet when she sat on the thin line of a casting circle scored in the hard gray stone, and collected herself, eyes closed, in preparation for her first intentional casting as journeymage, a bolt of cold fear shot through her bowels. Suppose her guiders did not come? Suppose the urgency of the vigil had pushed her past the malady, but this routine warding did not?

No warding was routine, no matter how often it had to be renewed. If the stonewarding failed, this quake-prone area would shake itself to rubble.

The guiders formed, chill and blue. She accepted the sedgeweave. She inked the kadra Stability, drew rocks and mountains with holding kadri embedded firmly within them; she connected the kadri with earthing lines, fixatives that bound kadri close. With stone-ground, oil-bound pigment, she painted a checkered border of thick blues and grays, to hold fast the words of integrity the woman across from her had scribed. She drank in pattern and color with fierce relief . . . and furtive pleasure. She laid the page down, linked hands with the others, sensed their magelights unify within the binder's modulated drone, felt joy . . .

Her magelight had deserted her once. Who was to say it would not again?

Again and again, as they picked their way over gritty outcrops and around the thundering white weave of stepped rapids, through damp stands of yew and hemlock and around dense dustwood brakes, she found mages, and cast with them, and her magelight did not fail her. But each time she wondered: *Have I taxed it? Have I drained a limited store?* Her trial had drained her deeply; perhaps the price of a lamp that burned so bright was that its well must be refilled. If she exhausted her powers again, would she have to wait another two seasons before they recovered?

Again and again, she told herself it made no difference. If her light went null, she would be protected from the Darkmage's manipulation, and would have that much more time to fulfill her mandate. It didn't matter.

But it did matter. She had to admit that every time she sat down to a necessary task, with mages who depended on her and the people who depended on them. It mattered a very great deal.

Liath pulled peas until the late-midder vegetable harvests were in, and Heff, who claimed to be only farrier, set himself to any ironsmithing he was asked for, borrowing tools as needed to make other tools. He was quarrysmith, forestsmith; he could craft a wood-and-iron harrow with a carpenter, help with repairs on a mill, then fashion whatever was needed in cookroom or field. His packhorse's panniers were bottomless boxes of treats. Invention never failed him, and Liath enjoyed seeing the delight on the faces of those whose small problems he solved with an ingenious tool. When she asked him where he'd come by so much specialized skill, he said, I journeyed too—but would not say when or why. He had an irritating habit of pretending he couldn't convey what he wanted to, when in fact he just didn't want to. But she had her secrets too. She tried not to begrudge him his, though her head—blast Nerenyi—was a continuous spin of questions. One of them was always needed, wherever they went; what Heff couldn't mend, Liath could. Their alliance forged itself into a solid partnership.

Halfway across the back of the Hand, the trees aflame in harvestmid color, she was called to help heal a mare down with a bad case of colic. The wordsmith and binder were ready, but Heff stepped between them and would not let them cast.

"Maybe the farrier can work some earthcraft on her," the owner said doubtfully, then looked down at his daughter. It was her beloved horse. "What do you think?"

Her big eyes fixed on Heff, the little girl nodded.

Liath rubbed her head. Earthcraft . . . Imma had used the same term. As if the ordinary work of daily life were equivalent to magecraft. "Heff, I don't think . . ."

Heff made an angry chopping motion with his hand.

"But if she—"

I will take care of this, he said.

It was a long, difficult night. Liath helped him when she could, but dozed off, at last, half-slumped over a straw mounting block. When she woke, it was to a sound eerier than Mellas's nightspeech. She thought it was the wind, at first, but the night was still; she thought it must be the mare wheezing, and roused herself.

The mare was up. Her head hung wearily, but she was on her feet. The little girl, who would not go to bed though even her father had given up after sending the mages away, stood by her. Heff, his back to Liath, dipped his fingers in a water bucket, then rubbed them inside the mare's lips.

Heff was making the sound. It was a tuneless, tongueless crooning— an alien sound from a throat that no longer worked. It had breathed life back into the spent spirit of the animal.

When lightless children were caught singing or humming, they were chastised—such things undermined magecraft unless done by binders in the course of their work. Heff showed no light. Was this, then, the earthcraft the wordsmith had mentioned?

"Common folk," Nerenyi had said. "You see? Do you see your bias?"

In the subdued lanternlight, Liath felt she saw Heff for the first time.

And Marough's clan, for that matter—rough and coarse, unmanageable as their wildest horses, yet deft healers in their own right. Marough had never paid the publicans' daughter any heed, not until the night she failed him—yet she had paid him no heed either. He was not a mage. He was an ordinary man, working an ordinary craft, with his farrier pledgemate and his roughneck sons.

Common.

Not a mage.

The barn door rolled open to admit a draught of sweet dawn air, and the father took in the scene with palpable relief. "Come on, love," he said to his daughter. "Come get some sleep."

The first birds began to call through the lightening air. As father and daughter went off, Heff said, You should not have considered sacrificing an animal to cure this mare.

Liath said, "She could have died, Heff. We would have healed her quickly, saved her a night of agony. That's what mages do."

He moved to put the lantern out, but before he'd turned the wick all the way down he said, What I do is better.

Dying leaves drifted along the road, flitted past like ash; rain, when it frequently came, was slanted and cold, and then the air smelled of loam and ungranted wishes. But the clear days were fresh, the sky a blue so solid you might carve a piece to suck on, and the horses were full of vinegar. Down each Finger they went, and back again; the turn of the moon found them scouring the Meri Isles, drinking hard fresh cider, laying turf in for the coming cold. The trees grew tattered as bonefolk, and when the bonedays came binders across the isles harvested the last of the goats bred for parchment.

They interrupted one just as he was readying the blade—a young man not long triaded. They'd been arguing over direction—Liath thought they should sail for the Strong Leg before the weather worsened, concerned at the lack of word, afraid she'd erred in forgoing the Blooded Mountains, and Heff was opposed but would not say why—and were halfway across the harvest circle before they realized. A spacious clearing in a hornbeam grove, with goats in a roofed pen at one end, screened from the dark-stained slaughterground by a slatted baffle.

No sooner had the binder finished swearing at them than a child came to fetch him for a casting. "Eiden's bloody bollocks," he said, looking at the goat struggling wildly to back out of a hemp noose. "Will you mind that one for me? I can't put him back or I'll have the others loose again and be another threeday gathering them up."

"Of course," Liath said, to head off any response Heff might make. He was already on the ground, calming the maddened goat.

When he was free to use his hands, he made an untranslatable gesture toward the path the binder had taken, then said, If he treated them more kindly they would not fear him.

"Not everyone has your gift," Liath said, reaching to scratch the other goats through the willow bars of their enclosure.

They should be taught, Heff gestured curtly. The goat bent its head to gnaw on his boot. He said, This is a young animal. These isles are full of fodder, yet they begrudge it the little it would eat over the winter, so they take its life.

"It would happen sooner or later," she said helplessly, and bowed her head at the look he returned her. Nothing she could say would persuade him this was necessary.

When the binder returned, she pulled Heff toward his horse. "They won't feel it," she said. "I've seen this before. Let's go, Heff." But he looked at the binder approaching the goat, which renewed its twisting bid for freedom, then shouldered past him to kneel in front of the half-strangled beast.

"Don't ever tie them by their necks," Liath translated as his hands spoke. Her tone was far milder than his gestures. "You can't train them to it. Goats are clever and . . ." What was the word? She understood Heff in concepts, not words. Words were not her craft. ". . . irrepressible. They need special handling."

"He doesn't know what he's talking about! This is magework—"

"I wouldn't interfere," Liath recommended quietly. "Watch him. Maybe you'll learn something." In fact, she was not certain what the farrier would do; but she tensed for a sharp jerk of his muscled arms as he broke the goat's neck rather than let this peach-fuzzed bindsman bungle the cut.

Heff gestured again.

Omitting the vulgarity, Liath translated, "Get your blade."

When the bindsman complied, shaking his head, still talking a streak, Heff drew him down by the animal. Watch, he said, clear enough for anyone to understand. Be ready with that thing.

He held the goat's head up, big hands cupped like blinders so it couldn't see the blade. He stared into its eyes. It went completely still, then sank down onto knees and hocks. Liath thought she heard him crooning, though the bindsman might have taken it for a moan. It was like what the bindswoman in Strall had done . . . but the goat's eyes never closed. Mesmerized by Heff, it just stared at him. There was a human look in its wide-spaced eyes, as if it had just witnessed the most astonishing thing. Heff nudged the bindsman, who seemed equally mesmerized. He slid a stone basin over and made the cut.

The goat never moved as the blood drained. Its eyes locked on Heff's until all the light had gone from them. Then a spasm rippled through Heff's frame. The binder didn't notice. Heff laid the goat's head down gently. Its tongue lolled. He stood, still looking at it, his limbs loose, as if they'd fallen asleep—as if he had gone from his body and had not yet quite returned.

"That was brilliant!" the bindsman cried. "I've heard of them doing something similar on the mainland, but never like that, only to put them to sleep. The mage who trained me just gave them a conk on the head. Some binders drug them, but she said that's no good, that taints the parchment. . . ."

His babble of words continued as he sealed the container of blood, put it aside for later use, then prepared the carcass for skinning. "That's a remarkable knack you've got. Spirits, if only you were a bindsman! If only you showed a light—I could prentice you, wouldn't that be funny, a big man like you my prentice? But of course if you showed a light you'd be triaded long since. I don't suppose you'd consider staying to do the rest of them? . . ."

Heff stared at him. The binder's voice trailed off and he backed away—as if he'd seen in Heff's eye the death he had just wrought, as if it had come home to him at last, echoed in that ruined human face. He mumbled something about having work to finish. Liath, very quietly, said again, "Let's go, Heff." This time he came.

He was quiet on the road after that—mourning that small, brief life, and the others he could not save. In deference to it, she gave up the notion of shipping for the Strong Leg. There was still the Pointing Finger to search, the little stub of the Thumb. The idea of sea travel had turned her stomach anyway.

What he had done was what that bindswoman had tried to do but only partially succeeded. In a kind of vigil, he had taken the animal's death upon himself. No sleep to sweeten the bitter moment, no illusion that death was easy. Heff had borne the brunt of that passing; his body had been wrenched by it. The "trick of binders" was a borrowing from another craft—earthcraft—and they had not fully assimilated it, or could not.

What else did earthcrafters know, and do, instinctively, that magecrafters could not? What details had she missed, over all those years of paying them no heed? How could her training triad, so wise in so many things, have missed conveying this to her?

"Do you want to be a publican all your life?"

She startled. Graefel had bent to peer over her shoulder, regarding her work with his icy, critical eyes. She'd been concentrating so hard on the pattern that she hadn't heard him return to the cottage. Hanla was on a visit, and Keiler was with Befre in the hills, collecting.

He'd scared her, and she knew the border she'd scrawled on the sedgeweave offcut was no good, and that made her angry.

"No," she said, "and that's why I'm practicing. I won't show Hanla this till I've got it right."

She knew what the wordsmith was thinking. Practice makes perfect only with perfect practice. He wanted her to do everything just right from the very start. He never gave her a chance to learn from mistakes. If it wasn't perfect he just walked away. He froze you out. She knew he was annoyed that she wasn't his prentice. Keiler had gone to Befre and she had gone to Hanla and his other son, his older son, hadn't shown a light at all, and somehow that made all her faults worse. He thought Hanla was too easy on her. Hanla, who'd starved her for days until the kadri came! Hanla, who rapped her knuckles with a stick when she made lazy marks. But Hanla knew when she'd reached her limit. Hanla would sigh and pat her head and say, "All right, child, we'll start fresh tomorrow." Graefel would have kept her at it till her fingers bled and her eyes shriveled into dry prunes. Nothing but perfection was ever good enough for Graefel—and Graefel did not abide backtalk.

"At least you have a family to go home to," Keiler said later, after she'd finished digging the midden under and Graefel had released her from her punishment. They were lying by the river, hands behind their heads, chewing cattails. "Imagine if your training triad was your family."

She flopped over to look at him, and he gave her a lopsided grin. Graefel's triad never stopped being a triad. They were mages over supper, mages in their baths, in their sleep. That was part of the enchantment of it, for her. To really be a mage, instead of just someone who learned magecraft in the afternoons when work at the tavern was slow. She saw Keiler's life as charmed—a life of pure magecraft, where everyone he lived with shone.

"My family doesn't understand anything," she said.

"They're not supposed to. They're not mages."

"Yes, but I mean . . ." She stripped her cattail down to a thread of green stem, flicking fuzzy seedheads into the Clon. She didn't know what she meant. Father was all right. But Nole teased her all the time now, as if she'd gotten snooty or stuck-up or something, and she hadn't! It wasn't fair. And Mother was always too busy with Breida to be bothered with her, and sometimes when she offered to mind the baby for a bit—she adored Breida, her chubby cheeks and cuddles, her fierce determination to be into everything—Mother would hesitate, as if Liath couldn't be trusted with her own sister!

Or as if her magelight might rub off.

"You're lucky," Keiler pronounced. "When you get sick of pigments and inks and quills and reeds and your back hurts and your hands burn and you want to puke from the smells, you can go home where nobody's testing you all the time. Father plays tricks on me. I never know when he's giving me a regular chore and when it's some mage thing my whole bleeding future depends on."

"Befre's training you, not him," Liath said angrily—really meaning "Hanla" and "me."

"Don't try telling him that." He propped himself on an elbow, dark eyes going wide. "Spirits, you didn't, did you?"

She nodded. "And now I can go home and haul kegs till my back aches and scrub vats till my hands burn and mop up drink spill till I want to puke."

Keiler burst out laughing. He cast his chewed-up cattail into the river and *rolled on his back, kicking his feet in the air, until Liath threw herself on him and they tumbled over each other in the rivergrass, earth and sky spinning around them, two children ablaze with a light that nobody passing them could see.*

She looked at Heff. No light there, nothing of the heat and glow one mage could sense in another. But what might earthcrafters sense, one in another, that she could not? A scent of sage or coriander, a sharp sweetness, a tingle?

Seekers said that there had to be a third power. Everything that mattered came in threes; all true strength derived from three. Eiden Myr was the third luminary, the balance of moon and sun. Galandra was formed of the union of Sylfonwy, Morlyrien, Eiden. Even the strength of one person was a product of three: body, intellect, and spirit. If magecraft was one of the powers they had meant, and was complemented by earthcraft . . . what was the third?

And if mages were children of Galandra, earthcrafters children of Eiden . . . *who* was the third?

The Darkmage was not in the High Arm. As the sky went hard and the wind bared its teeth, she could no longer avoid the truth. If he had been here, his passing had left no sign.

"The Oriels, then," she said. *An enchanted island in the Belt. Tunnels in the Blooded Mountains. A mine in the Heel. He's out there somewhere.*

Heff reined Heartward with no objection.

The Aralinns were blackstone, the Gerlocs of the High Arm all gray and pink granite veined with quartz down into the Fingers; the Oriels were white. Their peaks, the highest in Eiden Myr, looked snowcapped whether they were or not. The mountainsides took on the hue of whatever grew there. When Heff and Liath entered the range, they were evergreen shadfjing down into flame and gold; by the time they were halfway to Mulard the landscape was subsiding into grayish brown. In contrast to the rugged terrain of the Hand and Arm, here the going was easy: a river had carved a sinuous path down the center of the range, and well-kept roads followed it to either side, connected every ninemile by chain ferries. No one plied the treacherous river itself. Villages were staggered, Armward and Heartward, and trade was brisk all up and down the line. In daylight the glare off the peaks gave the narrow river valley a strange extra glow; at night the numinous reflection was eerie, accompanied by the river's gurgling hiss. Even at moondark there was a ghostly suggestion of presence, a light as much sensed as seen—a memory of the day, clinging in the porous stone. Galandra's mountains, some called them, or the Spirit Range, the tangible ghosts of a mountain range long gone. Here there were no haunts; here the mountains were their own haunt.

The riverfolk lived much as anyone else, though they traded upriver and down for the crops they had no land to grow, so bread was unusually scarce. The lumber trade was brisk, with many a sawmill running off the strong current, and upslope the mountainy folk mined silver and tin. Liath ate mosses and truffles and mushrooms, and slowly developed a taste for lichen; luckily, their crofts were fertile here, and there were always vegetables when she couldn't bring herself to sample any more local fare. She drew the line at a jelly-like freshwater barnacle they picked raw from the shell, or boiled and ate shell and all, but Heff would munch happily from the mounded bowlfuls of the things that graced all tables. They ate communally, and charged for nothing but imported food; everyone shared the work of the river, so you had only to enter during a meal and you were seated and handed a tin or holly plate and spoon. Fragrant needle mattresses were as easy to come by, in common rooms where the hearth logs burned all night—but you were expected to stay long enough to complete a task before you left. Liath swept a lot of chimneys and laid up a lot of compost when no castings wanted doing—and so did Heff, for iron was a trade good here, and repairs were all he was called to do.

"There's no beer," Liath said yet again, staring at the fermented goat's milk they'd given her in what looked like a thimble, and the cup of brambleberry wine Heff had barely touched.

There is beer, Heff said. But it costs.

"There are no tallysticks," Liath said.

There are tallystones, Heff said. But we haven't earned any.

"There are no taverns," Liath said.

They don't need any, Heff said. They don't serve beer.

Liath laughed. She could read humor in his hands now, and reticence, and brusque irritation, and gentle prompting. Often his hands said one thing and his face another. His hands never lied.

"We could have some of that firewater they pretend is brandy. I think they flavor it with scorched moss. And I saw one of those barnacle things in the bottom of an empty cask. *Gah.* There's still smoke coming out of my ears."

Drink any more of it and you'll sound like me.

She looked up sharply. "I'm sorry. I should have thought."

He was laughing in silent huffs, lips pulled half back over white teeth that shaded into brown where his lips no longer worked. Someday, he said, you'll believe me when I tell you I welcome it.

They were sitting up late in the common room of a triad's house; riverfolk came and went freely in each other's common rooms, here where all houses were public houses. The white glow of night seeped through the louvered shutters and grayed the arch of the cruck roof, leached the yellow from the pinewood table, made the rushlight an extravagance. Liath could smell the heather thatch overhead, but it was quiet, warded against spiders and mice.

"Wouldn't he heal you, Heff?" she asked quietly.

He would have, Heff said, unperturbed. I stopped him.

"Why?"

He pushed his noxious drink away and gestured to the burlap beds they'd hauled in for themselves from the storehouse; they'd be warm enough now to sleep on. Liath settled herself into the scent of forest and pulled her travel blanket partway up, watching as he did the same. She knew he'd answer her, before he went to sleep. And finally he did, echoed by flickering fireshadows on the walls:

So they would see me and remember.

A cold wind from the Head swept them out the bottom of the Oriels and into the Belt. The first of the lakes appeared as the last of the brown leaves crumbled away.

"I should go Legward," Liath said. "There's nothing here. He's got to be there. It's the only place left."

There's the Belt, Heff said. And that's where we are now.

"I heard something about the Blooded Mountains."

Haven't you had enough of mountains?

"We'd have the Girdle first."

The Girdle will be a misery to cross when snow comes.

"I really think . . ."

You think he's in the Strong Leg. But if we go there, and he's not there, you'll curse yourself for not looking in the Belt.

Liath sighed. He was right. He was right, and she was cold, and they had to go somewhere they had a chance of earning winter gear for themselves—the riverfolk had offered, but she'd stuck it out with her own thin cloak, as unwilling to take their charity as she was to wrap herself in the warm velvet reckoner's cloak that still lay folded at the bottom of her pack.

"The Belt, then," she said, and urged Amaranth forward.

Lough Isil, Lough Mur, Lough Elin . . . one after another, lake after lake, with no end on them, as midder chilled into winter and the stark trees slept bare and the nights expanded. In the summer the lakes were colored—one rust, one emerald, another crimson—but in winter they went to a uniform gray. The flow of their journey slowed with the approach of Longdark; they guested longer in each triad's house, and Liath worked hard casting preservation on food stores, forming temporary triads with other journeymages whose travels, too, had run hard as winter sap.

Yet they did push on. He'd be holed up in his fastness, shoring up his defenses, preparing his attack. He would not expect the Ennead to strike at him in winter.

As they rounded a turn and crested a rise and another lake spread itself before them, she drew breath to tell Heff that—to begin the cautious process of confiding in him. But she was cut off by a shout from up ahead.

"The fowl pest on you! May you be afflicted with the itch and have no nails to scratch with!"

She thought she must be mishearing. Despite the long nights, they'd gone short on sleep, roused each of the last eight days at dawn for Longdark observances, watching the sun climb over some ancient tree grown at winterrise, or its light creep toward solstice stones at water's edge; at nightfall they held candlelit vigil wherever they found themselves. Where Heff came from, folk put great significance on the phase of the solstice moon, and he seemed uneasy that it was just going to moondark. There hadn't been a solstice spirit day in years. It soured his mood.

"Fling it back! Fling it back or you're a horse's ass!"

"You're an ass's ass! I've flung all I plan to, you besotted spawn of a dungmonger. Fling it yourself."

The scene came into view: two men just after facing off across a muddy field, one of them stalking away, and a crowd of at least a nonned folk jeering and hissing.

"Forfeit!" cried a young man ankle-deep in mud in the center. He wore a gigantic floppy felt hat and baggy trousers, and was clanging two pitchforks together. "Official forfeit!"

"His forfeiting shot was better flung than all Pierren's combined!" someone in the crowd yelled, and someone else added, "You couldn't judge a flood if your house floated off." "Give it to Jalthe, you putrid wretch of a turnip!" said a third.

The youth held firm. "The forfeit stands, the round goes to Pierren n'Larr—tally a win for Caragar. Next pair!"

Two women detached themselves from what seemed to be queues to either side of the fallow field the crowd surrounded. So many people—a whole cluster of villages. All the village elders were here, participating— and at least three triads of mages.

"May rabid hens devour you one limb at a time!" cried the first woman, who had positioned herself at a sawhorse set at one end of the field.

"Noxious boils on each of your toes!" the second woman threw back, leaning on the opposite sawhorse. "On the underside!"

"May you fester unpassaged and unmourned!"

Back and forth the insults flew, until the youth in the ridiculous hat clanged his pitchforks and declared, "The round goes to Gintha n'Dorn. Next pair!"

Liath and Heff dismounted and led their horses up behind the spectators on the near side. All wore stained shirts and torn trousers and breeches—clothes patched and mended until it was no longer worth the thread to sew them up, then left to fray. A dozen mages, in decent clothes, stood in a loose group to one side. At least four villages gathered here, then. A few turned and acknowledged her with a nod. Beyond them were blankets bundled on a handcart, and donkey carts filled with splintered beams and dried woody weeds. Down by the lakeshore, three huge stacks of deadwood stood waiting to become Longdark bonfires.

Two men came forward—both burly fellows, and if the prize was for shabby attire, they tied for the win.

"The snot cat and death-strangling to you!" called the man at the farther sawhorse.

"May your sores get sores!" the nearer man flung back.

"A sated wolf in your field and the ewe-pest in his belly!"

"The white scourge on you!"

"Downpour and drenchings, storm and fog and ill vapors rot you!"

The nearer man turned red and slammed a fist on the wooden crossbar. "A death without a mage to you in a town without a triad!"

"Oooh," one of the mages said, as the crowd murmured disapproval, "genuine loss of temper. Arbitrator will deduct for that." He moved to stand with Liath. "This is the last round."

"He seems to be really angry now," Liath ventured.

The first mage grinned. "That's only because he's losing."

"Verne loses every year," another mage said over her shoulder. "Which is why you, Chinda Binder, will see nary a winceberry cobbler from me."

"It gets a little heated at the end sometimes," a third mage explained.

"Don't you have reconciliations here?" Liath asked, thinking of the Neck, where her training triad would have rounded up anyone with known, outstanding grudges and presented them to each other for a polite resolution.

"This is it," the older mage said with wink.

"Gets it out of their system," said the mage next to her. "You can make people say they're sorry when they're not, or they can lance their own boils." He grinned again, wider this time, and punned with pointed intent: "We're making light of it."

In Clondel we have brawls for that, Liath thought, but she grinned back at him.

"Go on," he said. "Get in line."

"Me?" She stared stupidly. "I don't even know these people."

"You don't have to." He cocked an ear, as a young girl flung "A swarm of flea bites on your pimples, you obese turd!" at her opponent, a clear-skinned, rail-thin boy. "Inventiveness and originality are what count. You'll feel better for it."

Liath shook her head, wishing Nerenyi were here. She'd be perfect for this, if she could get exercised enough.

Me, Heff gestured. I'll do it.

She blinked at him. But you can't even speak . . .

He grinned his half-grin, cocked his hat at a jaunty angle, and sauntered to the end of the line. His turn came up quickly—there were only a couple of people left. Liath cringed to think what his opponent might say about his face.

"Aches and agues and itches on you, puny lout!" cried the woman opposite Heff.

Heff responded. It was nothing like speech, nothing like the way he spoke to Liath with his hands, but his gestures were completely unmistakable. It was like a dance—an eloquent, beautiful, astonishing dance. Liath gaped. The crowd burst into wild cheers and applause. The mages cried, "Well flung!" The arbitrator awarded the round to Heff, and his opponent had to be helped off the field because she was laughing too hard to stand upright. Two more took their places as Heff returned to her side.

"Oop, best stand away," said the older mage, sweeping them back with open arms. "This pair's the last of them now."

The arbitrator rang his pitchforks, cried "The fling goes to the village of Haringar!," and threw the pitchforks as far from the crowd as they would go.

A great shout went up from one side of the grounds, the other side echoed it, and then all the onlookers were converging on the center, hurling the arbitrator into the mud, hurling each other into the mud, grappling in it, hurling themselves into it. Toddlers, the very old, and women with child stood off to the sides, scooping up great gobs of muck in double handfuls to fling into the melee, urging it on.

"That's two of your winceberry cobblers, Salda," the mage behind her was saying, and the one beside her told someone else, "I'll have the other half of that quilt you still owe me from last year's fling"—they were laughing, settling their bets, and then fanning out to heckle the wrestlers.

A mudball exploded against Liath's shoulder. She stared down at the long smear of brown, watched a clump of old roots slide off, then lifted her head. No telling where it had come from. Heff was laughing, holding out clean hands—it wasn't him.

She drew a long breath, let the mare's reins slip to the ground, and shouted, "Oi!" Then she dove in.

Blast the Ennead, blast the Holding, blast the shadows and the bloody blasted Darkmage! She landed with a spectacular squish in the freezing muck of the fallow field. Inspired by her arcing dive, someone dove on top of her, and then someone else; unrecognizable, anonymous, she rolled and wrestled with the folk of these villages she did not know, and flung mud gleefully at whoever flung it at her, and after a long, mad time lay exhausted with everyone else and laughed until her belly ached, then followed them as they dragged themselves up and staggered down to the lake and plunged in, rinsing clothes, cavorting and splashing. They *were* mad; the water was frigid. Yet wrestling in the mud had overheated her, and the shock was how invigorating the shock of the water was. Couples danced and fell, young men and women did handstands, parents scrubbed children and each other. Their skin shone with health and joy; they almost outshone the waxed-linen lanterns the older folk were setting along the shoreline, whose soft glow reflected from the water in a luminous chain. Ringed in light, they sloughed off the old year, the old hurts, and one by one emerged naked onto the shore to rub each other dry.

When only a few well-padded souls remained in the water, Liath spotted Heff on the far side of them, and splashed her way over, jumping and bobbing in the water to keep her circulation going. They stared at each other in the glow of dusk, dripping, skin stippled. The burns did stretch down the right side of his body, the rest of which was furred with chestnut hair, but he endured the icy water calmly. He had not yet rinsed his face; the mud made one even surface of it, and she saw it for a sweet, serene face, gentle and well proportioned. He was a child of Eiden. His element had rendered him beautiful.

"The burns don't hurt, do they?" she said. He shook his head. Some kind of healing *had* been cast on him, then—a healing that left the wounds themselves, as a message to those who'd caused them. Heff had made vellum of himself, his own burns the inscription of condemnation. Verlein had been right: there was scribing everywhere, if you knew how to read it.

She took the shirt he'd been rinsing and brought it to his face, gently sluicing the mud away.

The day balanced between light and dark. On dry ground, the mages lit the three bonfires, and the flames roared and crackled and tossed sparks high into the moonless sky. The revelers sat by them through the night, wrapped in blankets as their old clothes dried, then ritually burning the clothes themselves. They passed food and jugs of brandywine until some fell asleep where they were and others rose to walk the ethereal ring of light at the lakeshore. Groups of adolescents tended the fires in shifts, hauling in cart after cart of junk wood and dry weeds, a year's worth collected from all the villages for this night. One of the mages had taken their horses to stable at his family's place. Liath slept soundly, happily, through what remained of the longest night, head pillowed on Heff's thigh, and woke at dawn to the sound of sleepy laughter as the hardiest revelers rose to welcome the return of the light.

Their mages cast a cleansing on all assembled. She moved from triad to triad more from fascination with the unfamiliar magework than to check each wordsmith's scribing. A mass casting, for health, renewal, the purging of ill humors. The illuminations were joyful—bold strokes of primary colors. The melodies the binders sang were clear and morning-sweet, and the manuscripts dissipated through purest dewdrops.

"May all your roads be firm and dry, and the foul crippen never afflict your milch cows," one of the mages bade them, in grinning inversion of a fling, as they took their leave.

She was still laughing as they topped the next rise. The triads had cast with smiles on their lips and dawn in their eyes, all their shadows trampled in the mud. Their wordsmiths' marks were clean and straight. There was no darkmage in this place.

She smelled snow on the wind as they crossed the wooden bridge that spanned the Gow, which drained into the marsh flats above Maur Gowra, and swung upland again along the lower lakes. The fields were kept warm with a layer of manure, and Liath was kept warm helping to cart it—and marl, and lake mud, and cheesewater, and soap lees, and malt waste, and wood ash and wine waste, and binder's waste as well, the refuse left in the lime vats after the mage had pulled the hides. Ironwork kept Heff busy, though he pitched in to clear ditches. It was a relief when they failed to note a turning and found an unpopulated stretch.

We could turn back, Heff gestured, eyeing what looked like ice patches on the hill to their right.

"That's a woods up ahead." Liath squinted against the glare of white sky. "Perhaps that's where the village is. If not, we're travelwarded. Nothing will bother us."

As they came slowly into the silent shelter of forest, they saw that nothing had lived here at all in a very long time. The canopy was a close weave of branches. The ground was an even smoothness of fine grains, no bracken or leaf mold or undergrowth. The trees—ash and alder and black walnut, uniformly spaced, like a planned grove—were pale as bonewood, and harder than bone.

Liath touched fingertips to one of the trunks. "They're made of stone," she breathed. "This is the Stonewood. I never believed the stories." All the rough striations of the bark were there, but rendered in a substance not their own—or replaced by it. *What is the tree when there is no wood?* She moved through kadri made manifest, tangible responses to unanswerable questions. "Who would have made something like this?" she asked.

Not mages, Heff said.

It had to be magecraft; something like this would not happen naturally, not smack between Belt and Girdle, hilly lakeland and flat grassland. Now and then, in digging the bogs, folk came across small animals whose bones had dissolved while their flesh was replaced by earthen elements. The bonefolk would not take them, and in a matter of breaths they disintegrated. But these trees had not been buried in stone, to absorb the quality of it. They had to have been crafted.

Perhaps it was your people, long ago, she thought, looking at Heff. It was too farfetched a thing to say aloud.

The forest was strangely temperate, as if the stone trees sucked all the cold from the air. The road narrowed to a path, then died; no one had trod a route through the fine soil that lay like a deep layer of dust. As if

no one had been here in a nonned years, or a nonned nonned. This was
an incalculably ancient place.

"I say we sleep here," Liath said. "It's warm, and we may have a
long ride to the next hearth."

No firewood, Heff said with a wry twist of the fingers.

"We don't need it. I don't even need all this thrice-shrunk wool. Let's
go on till we lose the light."

Heff seemed uncomfortable, glancing about as if the haunts of this place
flitted just outside his field of vision. But it did not feel haunted to Liath.
Just very old, and very quiet. Their brief presence in this wood would
not disturb its long sleep.

"It must have been sacred to someone, once," she said when they had
bedded down on the soft earth in the timeworn silence.

It had come moondark again. She could not see if he replied.

She did not remember dozing off, but she surfaced from sleep to hear
Heff's blankets whisper into a heap, then a farther sound of him making
water. In a moment she'd call out to him, help him find his way back.
She had to go herself, but in the pitch blackness one of them ought to stay
where the gear was.

No, spirits take that, she thought—she could call to the horses if they
got lost. She was bursting.

She sat up, and heard the horses startle awake, and something fell
heavily where her head had been.

She rolled away, tangling in her blankets, then Heff's. A hand
clamped on her shin. She twisted free, then kicked out hard, expecting
another grab, and connected solidly with flesh and bone. There was a
grunt. "Heff!" she yelled, scrambling up, shedding blankets. If she could
be silent, she could not be found. Please Eiden it wouldn't go for the
horses—

She wasn't moving fast, but she collided hard with a tree and bounced
back dazed. Her body convulsed, expecting another attack. The sound of
the impact had betrayed her location. But her boot must have done more
damage than she thought. She groped ahead for the tree and felt her way
around the massive trunk, bark the consistency of stone, neither warm nor
cold. When she judged she'd put it between herself and whoever was
there, she flattened her back against it. The attacker was a mage. She could
smell the magelight. She could still feel the hard grip on her shin. That
had not been a lucky grope. It was someone who could see her. But the
magelight didn't outline you, and he had seen her body clearly enough to
catch a limb. Some kind of nightsight? That was well within magecraft's
purview, an enhancement of the eyes. . . .

He was still on the other side of the tree. She held her breath, strained
to hear him. The powdery soil muffled his tread—or he was down, she
might have knocked him out—she couldn't risk calling Heff again—

She heard something. Just a swish of fabric, moving from left to front.

She held her breath. It had to be Heff. He had better ears. If she called to him when she sensed the magelight move—

It came around the tree so fast that there was no articulating a name, she just yelled as she rolled away from it, trying to maintain contact with the tree—stumbling away blind would only invite another collision. Then she heard a grunt and a crunch of bone, and the thud of a body in the soft ground. The whisper of wool on wool, someone walking. Heff, it had to be Heff, feeling his way back to where he thought the camp was. He could not call out to the horses. But if it wasn't . . .

She could no longer smell the magelight. But calling to Heff would do no good; he could not call back. She was trembling so hard she had to hold on to the tree. She was afraid to move. She could no longer think straight. She needed her eyes.

There was more rustling, then a pause, then the flare of a small light, and the yellowed halo of Heff's face, the shadow of his hand shielding the flame. He had a lit a stub of candle.

She breathed his name in relief.

He made his way through the trees to where the body lay and knelt to hold the light by it. Liath joined him. The mage lay on his side, head canted horribly back. The blue eyes were glazed and sightless, the pale skin sallow in the candlelight. His face was long, his hair lank. By his hand lay a binder's blade.

"He looks like the one from the high coast, the one who was with the pretender," she said. "But he's not." She bit back the obvious conclusion. Heff had lost a brother too.

He looked up at her, stuck his free hand out hard and flat: he'd straightarmed the man in the face and his head had snapped back. Liath nodded, watching the hand clench into a trembling fist, then relax and reach to slide the man's eyes closed.

Heff rose and went back to the little campsite. The horses would not be calmed with the smell of death so near. He set the candle on a thick root and started rolling up his blankets.

We'll leave him for the bonefolk, he said, after Liath had gone to relieve herself, glad that she hadn't wet her warm winter breeches. But we should move camp.

"That candle won't last," she said. "Wait for daylight."

Heff looked toward the anxious horses.

"There's no helping that," she said. "The bonefolk will come."

What if there are more of him? Heff asked.

Liath had been wondering the same thing. She laid her rumpled blankets out closer to Heff and said, "I'll see the magelight." She made no mention of nightsight.

Heff sat with his back against hers. She centered herself in that solid warmth as the candle guttered and died. Despite the proximity of the corpse and the terror of the dark, she nodded off, but woke to feel Heff sitting straightbacked and alert. She wondered how long it would be before he slept peacefully again.

"He would have killed me," she said. They had both seen the prybar that lay where her sleeping head had been.

She felt Heff nod, but only when dawn had grayed the forest back into existence could he turn to her and say, I killed him.

For a moment Liath felt very old, though he had a good nine years on her.

I could have crippled him, Heff said. I could have left him whole enough for mages to heal. I killed him.

"You couldn't see him, Heff," she said. "You struck out. You connected. You were lucky. He wasn't."

Half of Heff's face twisted.

She could not wash this act from his eloquent hands, or the reflexive efficiency with which he'd performed it.

The corpse was gone. The bonefolk had come, silent in the night. Where it had been lay a pile of tallystones, a use knife, the binder's blade, a buckle, and a triskele. The bonefolk always left things of heavy, earthen elements. Heff left them too.

They fed the horses grain from the panniers, then packed up and mounted in silence. Now it was Liath who glanced warily around, wondering how fast the next attack would come, what shape it would take. By noon the air had chilled enough for coats and cloaks again, and by midafternoon they had emerged from death and timeless trees back into winter, and the relief of a village and warm beds and work to be done. Yet it was no relief at all. Even with the big farrier to guard her back, she felt completely exposed. They knew she was coming. He knew she was coming.

Heff wanted to turn Headward. The plains are too cold and the footing treacherous, he said, and villages few and far between. Better to save that journey for sowmid.

"Sowmid?" she burst out. Sowmid was a lifetime away. The Ennead had only given her till sowmid. She had to find him now, while he was curled in his burrow for the winter. She said, "In sowmid the Girdle rivers will flood and there'll be no fording them. I can't wait till sowmid."

But you neglected the Heartlands, he said.

"He won't be in the Heartlands," she told him, but couldn't say It's too near the Holding, with no mountains for a fastness. So again she said, "He's in the Strong Leg," and again Heff countered, That is a bad way to go. You're thwarting me on purpose, she thought; and he must have seen it on her face, for he said, I am just trying to keep us alive and keep you safe.

She reined around to face him, across the snow-dusted ground, as she had reined to face Nerenyi on a sandy road at Ve Eiden. To one side, the ice lake glittered dully in the afternoon light, fringed by leafless trees, snow collecting in its frozen ripples. To the other, the rounded silhouettes of the last low hills framed a wedge of white-gusted plains. He was right about the plains. There would be no orientation on a gray day in the Girdle. They would have to dig in against snow, and the horses might not survive it. She couldn't bear to lose another, not after what happened to the sorrel; she'd grown to love this rose-roan mare. And the death of a horse was your own death, on those plains in winter.

"He's a bad man," she said, speaking more to herself than to him. "I have to stop him. I have to go the right way."

Heff shrugged. Better alive, and a season late.

The wind swirled snow into her face, bit through her fleece-lined cloak and gloves and boots, stung her eyes. Amaranth stamped against the chill, her breath misting in twin plumes. Every human instinct told Liath to seek a sheltered vale crowded with inns and taverns and triads' cottages, full of logs and peat. There'd be nothing to burn for fuel on the plains; only the droppings of wild elk and horses, if they hadn't all migrated downland. The grasses would ice into brittle blades, cutting the horses' feet.

Yet Girdlefolk wintered somehow. The herd bands survived, in their layered tents; they found something to burn in their braziers and firepits; they protected their animals.

Girdlefolk die, Heff said. Winter culls the weak from them, just as it does from the herds, and the ground owls, and the plains rats. Perhaps there's a reason bonefolk don't feel the cold.

For a moment, deep inside herself, she gave in.

Home, her heart cried: the long, sustained cry it had been making since she left. She had ignored it, but it had never gone. Like a half-heard bindsong, it was the undercurrent of all her days and nights. She had her light back and she had journeyed and she could head home. But everything had changed. She had changed. She could not go home, now, and sit complacent in her safe tavern, and wait to make a safe, complacent little triad.

"I won't sit by a fire while someone tries to destroy the world," she said, too softly for Heff to hear. Then, louder, "I'm tired of things trying to kill me. The weather's tried before—tried its best, by all the spirits, and failed. It culls the weak, eh, in winter on the plains? Then let it. It won't cull me."

Please don't go, Heff said. His face was unreadable, but his hands pleaded. They are set on killing you now. If you turn Headward, they'll leave you alone.

"Who?"

The ones who protect him.

"Then I'm getting close. The harder they try to kill me, the warmer I'm getting." And the more of them who tried to kill her, the more of them Heff would have to kill. She had come to love the farrier too. Dragging him Legward would cripple his spirit; every death would kill him a little. The mare she could look after. She could not prevent Heff from harming himself on her behalf.

She could not prevent him from following, either. He had found her before and would find her again. But she could outrun him. He had the packhorse, and his piebald was bred for the plow, for hauling up stumps, no match for her light mare. Without his protection, she might not make it through the circle of protection that was tightening around the Dark-mage. But for whatever reason—fear of the man, fear for her—he did not want to go where the Darkmage had to be, and that was where she had to go.

Even if they kill you? a small, terrified voice asked her, the voice that wailed to turn for home. It was the voice of weakness, and she detested it—yet it was the voice of wisdom, too. This was real. This was not some game at home. But all Eiden Myr was home, and there were killers in it, the killers who had come into her tavern, and worse, and she would step in front of their jagged blades before she let them hurt anyone else. Even Heff, and even if he was only doing the same for her.

"I'm going Legward," she said through the bitter air. "I'm going alone. I won't put any more deaths on your hands, and I won't have you always pulling me in the wrong direction. Go Heartward, Heff. Find a safe, warm place with good folk and start a new life and leave the killing behind you. You are such a good man. Go do good, with your marvelous, mysterious craft. I owe you my life. Spirits willing, I'll find a better way than this to repay you, when it's all over."

Before he or his hands could move, she had turned the mare toward the wedge of plains and nudged her into a gallop.

There was plenty of daylight left, and the sky was only spitting flakes, a taste of what was to come. The innkeeper had said there was a town a sixmile below these hills. In the town would be folk who knew the herd bands' routes. There would be clear days between the snows, travel days. Winter might slow her, but it would not stop her.

The world became a blur of white. White sky, white air, white plains; white fields clustered around isolated villages. The herd bands' encamp-ments looked from afar like manure mounded in the snow, but it made them easy to spot. Their ash-and-willow-frame tents were portable huts—layer upon layer of wool, canvas, horsehair, deerhair, and puffy quilts stitched into triangles to keep fleece or sheddown evenly distributed. Their mages could clear land for grazing, but the next snowfall quickly undid the work, and they could not force grass to grow in frozen soil; the bands moved from cache to cache, feeding themselves and their stock on warded supplies put by in good weather. Winter culled only those who struck out on their own. Though the bands moved independently, they were a tighter-knit community than even the riverfolk of the Oriels or the fiercely tribal folk of the Weak Leg. They had no interest in the Ennead one way or another, and had no use at all for reckoners, who only noted the erratic weather and sent their reports on Headward.

"There's no predicting it," a teller complained as Liath fell in with her on the road. Girdle tellers were rovers, like tinkers and journeysmiths. "One day like sowmid, the next a blizzard the likes of which we haven't seen since my gran's time. You ask me, those warders up Headward are playing a game of stones with us."

She said it without rancor, and Liath couldn't tell her it was more likely a rogue mage playing a game of stones with the warders.

"The fellow in this camp we're coming to, he'll set them right," the woman said.

Liath went still. "What fellow?"

"Some odd fellow who's taken the children in hand. He's gone from one band to another this last fortnight. I heard he's with the Jhardal band, thought I'd have a look for myself. See if the rumors are true."

"What do the rumors say?" Liath asked as casually as she could.

"Oh, that when he's done with them the proxies will have no more secrets. They hoard their information, you know. They know things about the weather that could save our lives, but do they tell our mages? Do they guide our triads, as they're supposed to? Not anymore. Just look around and move on. Waste of space, the whole black lot of them, but you can't miss them on a snowy day."

"He's a proxy?" Liath tried, wondering if this teller's tales were as jumbled as her conversation. "He's giving away proxy secrets?"

A mistake; the teller raked her up and down with eyes suddenly wary. "Couldn't say. They're only rumors. Going to see for myself, as I told you."

It was all she could do to keep from spurring Amaranth ahead. When they finally arrived at the sprawling village, they found a storm of activity: people moving entire huts up against each other, pounding stakes into the hard ground. "Blizzard coming," someone stopped to say, acknowledging the teller with a shake of two fingers. "Stakedown tonight, hope for the best."

The teller snorted. "Blizzard coming, so he says. Last time I heard that, it rained for three days." As she dismounted, she glanced sidelong at Liath. "I suppose you'll want to find your people. You have your choice here, Gart's triad or Porick's. They're both taskmasters, I warn you."

"Then I'd better stay with you," Liath said with an ingratiating smile. The woman scowled, but there wasn't much she could say. The tents all looked the same to Liath; the teller walked without hesitation down a series of aisles until she came to one she knew, and the family that lived there made them welcome. Everyone in the Girdle seemed to be a distant relation of everyone else, by blood or pledging or as little as a passing friendship three generations before. After seeing the horses sheltered, Zelada, the young mother, gave Liath directions to the mages, but Liath stuck to the teller like a burr. In the end the teller's curiosity was stronger than suspicion: she whispered to the mother, with a conspiratorial nudge, "So where is *he?*"

It was the same tone Liath's mind used when it spoke to itself of him, and she felt abruptly like one of those smitten girls in the Elbow, back in sowmid, or one of the reckoners enamored of a mental image—sharing a fantasy with fools.

The young mother chuckled. "In Sira's tent." To Liath, she said, "They're already jealous of him, the tellers. Afraid you'll be out of a trade, Lheriz?"

The teller scowled, and hustled Liath out as if they were conspirators now. Did they all switch allegiance so quickly?

Liath's heart beat very fast as Lheriz drew back the thick, layered hangings over the entry of yet another identical hut. This one smelled of incense, a cake of something thrown on the brazier, and the teller muttered something about memory aids and stealing her teaching tricks. The interior was divided into two chambers. In the frontmost one, brightly lanternlit, three mages sat preparing a casting, and two Girdlefolk sat off to the side chatting in low voices. Liath blinked, thinking she'd been tricked, that Lheriz was scraping her off onto mages after all.

"Hello," said the nearest one, and waited.

"I'm Lheriz Teller," the teller said, puffing herself up.

The mage laughed gently, much as the young mother had. "I don't doubt it. You're only the second since sunrise. Slow day."

"The wordsmith's busy, as you can see," another mage said, "but we've a man covering."

"Go on through," said the farther mage, speaking to Lheriz though he held Liath's gaze, with dark blue eyes under a shock of blond hair. Another Girdler, one of the fair ones, but triskeled. He wore undyed woolens and a Lowlanders' horsehair vest, and his light was brighter than either of the ones around him, or the one Liath sensed in the back room. He was waiting on her.

"Liath Illuminator," she said quietly.

He nodded. "Porick Wordsmith. This is Mirellin Illuminator, and Jolia Binder. That's Kazhe over there, and Sira."

Mirellin was a Heartlander, beefy and florid, Jolia a lean, plain woman who might be from anywhere save the Legs. Kazhe and Sira were towheads like everyone else here—locals waiting for a healing or freedom. Only the wordsmith was of any interest to her, and she could not decide whether she should sit down and watch, or contrive to go through. She could hear children giggling in the other chamber, and Lheriz's voice going cranky, then wheedling.

"We've come on a . . . personal matter," Porick said, glancing at Sira, "but we have to solve this blizzard first. You've quite a light there—we felt you through nine layers of tent. If you're a journeyer, I'm bound to invite you to sit in."

"That's all right," Liath said, and made up her mind. She was no threat yet, and there was no back door. Whoever was inside would have to pass her coming out. "You know what you're about, I don't want to interfere. Could I just observe?"

"Of course."

Mirellin had been returning parchment sheets to a binding sack, and as she set out sedgeweave and changed her selection of ink and pigment she said, "On your journeying long?"

Liath's coloring screamed her origins, which were very far from here, but it was a customary question. "The better part of a year now."

"Takes courage to brave the Girdle in winter," said Sira.

Liath shrugged. "Magecraft should shepherd the weather. Judging from what I see here, I was right."

The other illuminator laughed nervously. "It's been troublesome lately. No pattern to it. Hard to control."

"If you divert the blizzard, won't it dump twice the snow on some other band?"

"We used to send the bad storms up into the mountains, triad by triad," Porick said. "A casting here, a casting there. We sent them where they could feed the rivers. But lately . . ."

The binder looked straight at Liath and said, "Someone's been sending them back to us."

"Well, it's not me," Liath laughed, no longer on sure footing. She'd felt that she was being tested, but she couldn't determine why, now; these mages struck her as a seamless part of their environment, just trying to do their job, nothing to do with whatever was going on in the far chamber. If she could only edge around them, she might get a glimpse through the beaded hangings, but by tradition she had to sit behind the illuminator, and it was the wordsmith who had his back to the inner entry.

As the casting began, she glanced across at the two women. Probably wanted a freedom cast or cast off; in the Girdle they didn't wed the freedoms to pledgings. Sira was picking her fingernails with a splinter of wood, and Kazhe was slumped, resigned to waiting through the casting. Whatever was going on inside, it was unremarkable to them. She strained to hear, but caught only a drone of children's voices, and now and then something querulous from Lheriz. He was teaching them something the smell of incense would recall for them later, something a teller would want to know, something that might put a teller out of a trade and leave proxies no secrets. *What?*

She clutched her shins to suppress the fidgets as Porick made some interminable inscription with his scratchy reed. She wondered which way they'd send this storm, and if it might threaten Heff, if he'd followed her. If this was the Darkmage's lair—this fragile hut in the middle of nowhere—she'd have her scrap of flesh and be gone before Heff caught up, or she'd be dead, or in Torrin's thrall. If it wasn't, which seemed the likelier, she'd have to see that she didn't ride *into* a storm, or he'd catch her up for sure. The children in the other chamber were murmuring in unison now, short sounds that didn't resolve into words. The sedgeweave was passing to the illuminator. Soon she'd be inside, and then she'd know.

The inscribed lines were Torrin Wordsmith's hand.

Liath stared at them for a long time, waiting for them to fade back into ordinary lines. Waiting for the hallucination to pass. The illuminator linked and ornamented the lines with a complexity of kadri woven into knots and patterns and historiations; it was craft at a very high level, higher than Liath had seen since she left the Holding. *These are proxies,* she thought, *and they're not diverting this storm, they're dissolving it.* There was almost no need for the wordsmith's lines; what the illuminator had constructed would collapse a sandstone cliff into a dune. But the lines were there, they were in Torrin's hand, they were not a dark vision. No shadows detached from the marks to swarm and scuttle off the page. The black ink stayed nested within the white and silver illumination, and as the mages entwined their fingers and the binder began a stuttered, rhythmic song, the leaf dissolved into a frozen mist and dispersed with a crystalline sparkle. Liath felt their unified magelights as a ring of warmth, excluding her, then subsiding back into three discrete lights as the casting concluded. These mages were triaded. With the Darkmage.

Porick, Torrin . . . not such different names. Close enough that someone calling "Porick!" would catch Torrin's ear. His light was not as bright as she'd expected. He was much younger than they'd told her, closer to her own age than to three nines and five. But it was his hand. "*You will know him by his hand.*"

It was his hand.

Another trap. He must have trained them to copy him. He would be in the other chamber, he had to be, this young, ordinary man could simply not be him, there was no scent of glamour on him, there was nothing, nothing but a lapsed proxy in a triad of lapsed proxies hiding in a backwater just as lapsed Graefel and Hanla had ensconced themselves in their roadside village . . .

"Shall we go admire our handiwork?" he said.

Liath sat frozen as winter stone while they rose from their places to go have a look; their exit admitted a billow of frosty fog, and Liath glimpsed only glittering, diaphanous white air, a blizzard disarmed into a mist. The two local women were watching her curiously. She got up, as if in a dream, and parted the beaded curtain, and went into the rear chamber.

A dozen young faces looked up at her, then back down at their work. They held oblongs of chalk, and slates such as prentice wordsmiths practiced on. A dozen prentices? From one place? Or had they collected them from different bands? But there was only one magelight in this room besides her own, and not a bright one. Their teacher was a graying man, triskeled, in ordinary clothes, the owner of that ordinary light. "Is it time?" he said, looking up. Then: "Oh, I thought you were Sira come to tell me we had to move the tent. Hello."

"Liath . . . Journeymage," she said. In her mind's eye, she searched Porick's face for any sign of deceit or darkness, and found none. It was a trap. Another trap.

"Have a seat," the man said. "All mages are welcome."

"And all tellers too!" Lheriz piped up. She sat to one side at the front of the group, holding slate and chalk like the rest.

"What are you doing?" Liath said.

"Take slate and chalk, and I'll show you."

"You can have mine," said a little girl. "Mother told me to be home early, she said we've been getting out of too many chores."

"You never did yours anyway," said another little girl.

Liath accepted the proffered implements with nerveless hands as the child showed the other her tongue and slipped out, leaving clacking beads in her wake. The squeak of chalk on slate continued.

The child had been inscribing ciphers. Every child in the tent was scribing. In the Darkmage's hand.

"What in all the blessed spirits is going on here?" Liath whispered.

The teacher lowered himself to the carpets beside her with an audible pop of knees. "You say your name is Liath?"

She nodded, numb.

"A name is a powerful thing," the man said. "It's something you should own, completely, yes?"

"I do own it. As did my grandfather's mother before me." She didn't know what words were coming out of her mouth. He had taken the chalk and held it over the slate. She watched it as if it were a hot iron poised to sear her own flesh.

"In the High Arm a name like yours is not uncommon. But you're from nearer the Head than that."

"The Neck."

He nodded. "Then your name is very precious indeed, because it carries a particular history in it. A silent history, a memory of a longer name, a transmuted word. What are names, Cherl?"

The named child answered promptly as he erased his slate with his sleeve to start again. "Words," he said.

"And what are words, Osk?"

"Sounds that mean things."

"So what is a name?"

All the children answered, as he had clearly coached them to. "A sound that means something."

"And what did we learn about glyphs, Shalana?"

"They're sounds, and when you put them all together in a row they make bigger sounds, and those are words."

"*The ciphers inscribed during a casting form words,*" Graefel began. "*And names are words. Words that can be spoken.*"

"*Longer sounds,*" Osk corrected. "Cherl makes big sounds when his father won't let him have seconds."

"You make big farts."

"You make big boogers!"

"Can you scribe that, Osk?" the teacher asked, and the children dissolved into giggles.

"So a glyph—a cipher, if you will, most mages call them ciphers, though that's another story entirely—is part of a sound. Here's a glyph for 'lee.' " He chalked something that looked like a drastically simplified kadra on the slate.

"No," she said.

He cocked his head. His eyes were amber, like a cat's, but kind; and hollowed, as if he was very tired. She shook her head, unable to articulate a lifetime's prohibition. "I'm not a wordsmith," she managed at last.

"Then draw this kadra," he said. "Glyphs came from kadri, once, a very, very long time ago."

Among children, Liath became for one moment of weakness a child again herself, obeying the teacher, copying the mark as she had been trained to do from age six.

"Ah, but of course you form it beautifully, Illuminator," he said, and an old pride flickered to life at the sound Graefel's praise had made in her ears.

"*I'll tell you a wordsmiths' secret. About your name.*"

"Try this one, 'ah.' Good. Lovely."

"*Your name, unlike most, has extra ciphers in it.*"

"And now here's the trick, here's the beauty. . . ."

"*One might call them shadow ciphers, because they don't sound when 'LEE-uh' is said aloud.*"

"Your name is an artifact of a word that meant 'gray.' But to mean a fair kind of gray—no way of telling if 'fair' meant pleasant, or just, or light—the last sound was softened."

"*You carry them with you—a hidden part of yourself, like your innermost thoughts.*"

"It would have been modified with another word at the end, but over time it absorbed just a whisper of the following word, dropping the rest. So this glyph, which would be 'tuh,' is erased, as it were, so gentled that it doesn't sound at all."

"*Were I permitted to tell you which ciphers they are . . .*"

"We indicate that with this mark here. And there you have it. You've scribed your name. Now it's yours, in its very essence."

She stared at the blasphemy in shale on her lap.

"... still I could not tell you what they signify."

"You were named for something as gray as the sea, or storm clouds, or neutrality, or a dove's wing, but softened by fairness—beauty, or justice, or light."

"No," she said again. Her voice had gone very flat. The nearest children looked up warily. "You're wrong."

"I am?" He smiled, brows arching, and crinkled his lower lip. "How so?"

"My name has *two* extra ciphers in it. They're shadow ciphers, and I can't be rid of the forsaken things. I already know what they mean. They mean I'll be plagued by people like you, puppets of a man who wants to undermine all magecraft by teaching common children to mimic word-smiths."

She rose to her feet among children who knew they had been slighted but couldn't follow the thread of her anger.

"This is a sacrilege. You're a traitor to your craft."

"I am a teacher. I am practicing my craft."

"You're weakening magecraft!"

"Does a weaver teaching you to spin yarn undermine the craft of weaving?" he asked, rising stiffly to look her in the eye. "Are you not bettered by knowing how to spin yarn for yourself?"

She paled. "I see it now. Words and sounds and meanings. You're teaching children to run his messages for him. Scrawled on bark, or linen, or *slate*—" She snatched the tools from the nearest child, who cried protest and then shrank away from the look on her face. "How can you do this? How can you train your whole life long to be a responsible mage and then do *this*?"

"How can you train your whole life long to draw patterns of significance and beauty, and not share them? How can you draw a picture of what today looks like, and see it dissipate in a casting, so that you can never look on today again?"

"To save lives and preserve food for tomorrow!" she cried. "You're a child, crying over what castings cost. And meanwhile you pour precious ciphers out across the carpet—you'd pour grain into a river because it was pretty, and let children starve!" She was so angry she was shaking.

"Passing messages in ciphers is a very clever thought. The tellers thought of that too, didn't they, Lheriz?"

The teller had been remarkably silent, her eyes saucer-wide, yet another child in this chamber of children. "We could pass our tales along to the future," she said, in a soft tone.

"She's parroting you," Liath spat. "And you're parroting *him*. You're a *teller*, Lheriz, for spirits' sake—it's your craft to remember, and teach your prentices to remember!"

"Some is always lost along the way," Lheriz said. "Tales I learned as a girl at my master's knee . . . gone now, and never passed to any prentice of mine. I grieve them."

Liath made a sound of disgust. "You deserve him, the lot of you. You're playing with precious materials as if they were toys, while you won't give the time of day to proxies who are trying to keep you alive. Do enough of this, and your mages won't be able to turn your blizzards into mist anymore, and what will you do then?"

"Learn to survive them better."

Liath whirled—it was Porick, come in behind her. They'd have her now, wouldn't they—no way out, and the Darkmage at the door.

"Torrin Wordsmith, is it?" she threw at him, enraged past any hope of caution, exhausted from her search and the hurt of leaving people behind, stressed beyond endurance by too many things she couldn't understand, threat after threat to the world of safety she cherished. "Torrin *Darkmage*, come to steal my soul?"

"I know no Torrin Darkmage," the wordsmith said quietly. "But I fear for him, if he's incurred your wrath." He regarded the disrupted scribing lesson. "Time to go home, I think, children."

"Is there going to be a blizzard?" one asked hopefully.

He laughed. "I'm afraid not, love. We've sent the blizzard home, and that's where you're all to go, as well. Scoot now."

The children scrambled up and out, grateful to be away from the cracked journeymage. Liath stood regarding the wordsmith and his folk. The teacher and the binder were nothing, but the illuminator presented an imposing obstacle, and the wordsmith was a compact Girdleman with a low center of weight. She couldn't bowl him over and slip past with one swipe of the use knife she'd taken to wearing at her belt, and she'd have to get it free of her cloak.

It might not be him. She could not be sure. She could not afford to strike too soon. Sense advised her to wait until she had a clear avenue of escape and a certain target—or until they cornered her into it. Spirits, she needed Heff now. But if he were here she'd only do something foolish. *Wait*, said the voice that restrained her at home when she was angry enough to break a jug on someone's head. *Wait and see what they do first.*

"We should all be getting home, as it goes," the wordsmith said. "Have you accommodation for the night, Illuminator? You're welcome to a bed and a meal in our tent if you like, but I presume you've left a mount somewhere—there's none outside."

The perverter of her craft, offering her food and rest. To get close enough to him to find out the truth, she'd even take him up on it. "I left my horse and gear at Zelada's place," she said. "I'd have to fetch them."

"But better to eat mages' food than commoners'?" Jolia said.

They would not be pleasant company. Good. If she irritated them enough, the mask would slip, and confirmation would drop at her feet.

Or they'd kill her once they had her alone.

It had to come down to this sometime.

"Yes," she said. "Mages should feed mage food only to mages."

Mirellin snorted. "How subtly spoken. I might have missed it, if not for the glaring metaphor in the center."

"Can you find your way?" Jolia asked. "It's going on sunset."

Walking alone down darkening aisles past tents that all looked the same was a risk. But she remembered the route Lheriz had walked—it was a simple configuration of turns, to a mind accustomed to keeping track of complex knots and weaves—and she wanted to be away from these people, get hold of her temper.

"Don't be a toad, Jolia," the wordsmith said. "She's only misguided and well trained, and you'd do well to believe so fervently in your own ideals." He gestured Liath through the beaded entry with the slightest suggestion of a Holding bow. "Ask anyone the way to Porick's tent, they'll see you right."

Liath gave the slightest suggestion of a nod and stepped past them, through the waterfall of beads and the heavy front-entry hangings, into the alley between tents. Most were still clustered tight against the wind that had never come. The sky was a wheeling sparkle of crystalline particles in the last rays of sun, the air damp and thick. She was too angry to appreciate the beauty of the weathercasting and its effects, and that made her angrier.

They were warders, not reckoners. He had triaded two Holding warders and escaped to a place all wind and distance, where few dared venture in the cold season. She didn't sense any other lights, but unless you had a knack for it, or the light was very bright, you couldn't sense a magelight past four threfts or so, less if a wall or other solid thing stood between. This encampment sprawled over nearly a mile, not counting the enormous staked tents where the stock sheltered. He could have a legions of mages tucked away on the far side. Tomorrow she'd take a stroll and find out.

Warders, who thought and spoke as with one mind, expert in weathercastings, sleeping lumped together in their big beds.

But Torrin Darkmage had been raised in closed passageways, on steep cliffs, not running wild over grassland. He'd refused to triad Lerissa and Evonder; he would not triad warders. The hair could be bleached, the age cast from his visage, but Lerissa said he was Liath's height, not compact and stocky like these plainsmen. Porick was not the Darkmage, no matter how badly she wanted her search to end here. Porick had been taught to scribe like that, by the Darkmage or someone the Darkmage had taught. Spirits, the bloody *teacher* looked more like Torrin Wordsmith—but he would not be sitting in a hut full of six-year-olds in the Girdle, a worn-out mage reduced to training common folk. How many had his minions passed their craft to? How much damage had been done?

She called through the covered entryway of Zelada's hut. No answer came. She stood outside as the air chilled and the settled mist frosted on the ground, and dusk made shadows of the huts under the graying sky. How many children were returning home even now, showing their parents what they learned today? No wonder the warders could no longer control the weather. Their tools were weakened from within, the power leached from them as their use, preserved for magecraft, spread into ordinary hands. She had learned respect for earthcrafters, but that did not make them mages. It did not entitle them to mages' lore. They could not be permitted to drain strength from the craft that sustained them.

She unlaced the door and went in to get her pack, wondering where Zelada's family was and how she'd find Amaranth. The pack lay on a pile of carpets at the far end of the first chamber. She moved around the glowing brazier to fetch it.

The teacher, she thought again. The teacher had not given his name. The teacher had called her Illuminator, though she had not told him she was one. The teacher . . .

A sound made her turn. Heff was standing to one side of the entry, face ruddied by the embers' light. He held a finger to his lips as she opened her mouth. She didn't know whether a curse or a cry of joy would have come out. Something launched itself through the loose tent flap.

Heff caught it in midair. It was a Girdler, short and hard-muscled with a cap of white-blond hair—Kazhe, it was Kazhe, spitting and twisting in Heff's grip. She broke free and came at Liath, who stood stupidly half-holding her pack. She was reaching in one fluid motion behind her neck with both hands, and something metallic arced red in the glow. A blade as long as an arm. Light ran down it like blood as Kazhe leapt over the brazier; then blade and woman went to black, backlit, one great shadow limned in death.

Liath flung the pack in front of her and drove for the midriff, reflex trained by countless brawlers staggering toward her with heavy objects over their heads. But Kazhe wasn't there; she had eeled away as Liath shifted, responding to Liath's movement before she made it. The pack flew onto the brazier in a crimson spray of firestone. Liath stumbled after it. Heff brushed past her. There was a huff of air; an oath. Liath turned, expecting to see the farrier run through. He had thrown a cloak around the blade and was struggling to wrench it from Kazhe's grip.

Kazhe released it.

The coals had sprayed smoking onto the warded carpets. The chamber was nearly dark. Liath braced herself for the smaller woman, sure it would be no contest. But a knife had come into Kazhe's hand from nowhere. She bristled with blades. Take one away and she'd produce another. Liath groped behind her, managed to get the pack up again and between herself and the underhand lunge; the knife sank in with a muffled tearing sound. Liath pushed, to send the woman off balance, but Kazhe's fist smashed into the side of Liath's head before she saw it coming—the knife had become a decoy. She was fast, too fast, unstoppable. Liath went to her knees. Kazhe had wrested the hooked blade free of singed canvas; the battered pack spilled open. Kazhe's icy eyes blazed red. The knife moved.

Heff's big arms came around Kazhe from behind and swept her off her feet, then brought her down hard by the wall as he smashed her knife hand against a support pole. The weapon bounced on the carpets. Liath tried to go for it, but her limbs wouldn't respond. The dark air was a wheeling sparkle. Carpet-layered ground heaved up and slammed her flat. She pressed up off it, dragged her knees forward. She had to get up. Heff was stronger and bigger, but Kazhe was a nightmare of blades, fast, trained.

Trained. Southers. Verlein. Blades.

Liath pushed the floor away, got her head up, her torso up, over-balanced on her haunches but didn't quite go over backward. Blood seeped warm from her cheekbone where the blow had split the skin. Kazhe and Heff were locked in struggle, shadows writhing, staggering from one side of the tent to the other. Baskets tumbled and stored items went rolling. They broke apart, breath rasping, and stood crouched, maneuvering for an opening. They were equally matched, size against speed, implacable protector against murderous intent. Liath had to change the odds before they locked again.

Her use knife was sheathed at her belt. After all that had happened, still she did not think to use it as a weapon. She drew it now, and held it by the point, remembering sultry summer evenings by the river with Nole and Erl and Sarse, flipping knives into tree stumps and straw bales with no more thought of a living target than when they skipped stones on water.

Kazhe was watching Heff, not her. The woman's chest was a clear expanse, if the little blade could penetrate the woolen coat.

"Kazhe."

The authority in that deep, sharp syllable pulled them all up short. Liath's blade sank into the carpet at Kazhe's feet. They turned toward the entry. A lantern came in, Porick holding it.

The teacher slipped in behind him and took two steps into the smashed-up chamber. "Enough, Kazhe. Stand off."

Kazhe, who was nearer, moved immediately to stand in front of him, glaring daggers at Liath until Heff interposed himself. The blades were in reach of none of them.

"Hello, Heff."

Heff nodded in somber greeting, helping Liath up, his wary eye still on Kazhe.

"Hello, Illuminator."

The stars had ceased to wheel around the room and collected in her limbs instead, a sparkling tingle. She sagged; Heff's arm held her firm to his side. She looked up at him, a question in her eyes that she could not get her lips to form. Heff, with barely a glance at her, nodded.

She looked back at the teacher, at his shoulder-length black hair shot with gray, at his sleepy cat's eyes ringed with weariness, his tall body stiff with cold and long, hard travel. Just a man, flesh and blood, battered by whatever battles he was fighting. An ordinary light; she couldn't countenance it. Perhaps it had weakened even as her own returned. Perhaps he was no threat to them at all anymore, and she could leave him and report back to the Ennead that their great hope was reduced to chipping away at magecraft's base by teaching children forbidden craft.

But Heff had identified him. The rest was details.

"Hello, Torrin," she said softly.

f l a m e

He would give her immortality. Or, more precisely, she would take it from him.

Oh, they would *go* together. She would use his intellect and life force as she used his body—as a tool. Where they were headed, his dusty codices could not aid him.

That he recognized her manipulation made no difference. He believed he had foreseen all contingencies. Overconfidence was such a handy flaw. She fostered it in everyone, with subtle flattery and admiration, with her own retiring façade. She would exploit it ruthlessly when the time came.

Her self must continue no matter what. Some were addicted to drink, some to love; she was addicted to life. Or, more precisely, to identity. There was much she could do to prolong the service of her flesh, but eventually it would fail her. She refused to go on, when nature decreed it, with ignorant mages for blind guides, to join some roiling, undifferentiated mass of spirit in loathsome communion. She would go at the moment of her choosing, and she would go entire—with all her memories and strength of will.

How many years had she sought immortality through the flesh? How many years had she wasted in her cravings for young men, for the life they exuded? Much pleasure it had given her—but in the end all fleshly pleasure paled in comparison with the ecstasy of eternal life and infinite power.

His forbidden scholarship would give her that.

It was a delicate thing. She had to bind him with threads so fine he could not feel them, or see them. She was aware of the use some women were put to; long ago she had herself warded against *that*. No blade could pierce her. Her body was as inviolable as any flesh could be.

But flesh was limited. Where she was bound, where he would take her, there would be no threat of drowning, or suffocation, or aging. All the cosmos would be hers to control—and control it she would, because in that place the strongest will would prevail, and hers burned with a passion that dimmed his light to insignificance.

urning his amber gaze on Kazhe, Torrin said, "I gave you an order. Should I have scribed it for you?"

"I didn't like the order, and I don't like these creatures the Ennead sends." She turned contempt on Liath. "Did you flatter yourself you were the only one? They sent a stream of assassins—we sent them back in pieces, until *he* forbade it—and then beautiful women, to seduce and betray. You're obviously neither."

A cut worthy of a Clondel cobblers' daughter. "I'm just a mage," Liath said.

"Scraping the bottom, to send their journeypups now. You wouldn't give up, would you? You really do want to die."

"That's enough."

"She killed Roshain!"

Heff stiffened.

"Then you must have sent Roshain to kill her. What else have you done, Kazhe?" His voice was mild.

"We set a few traps. Nothing you'd disapprove of. No one tried to hurt her until she didn't turn Headward after the Belt."

"We'll speak further about this."

Kazhe threw her hands up, defeated by Liath's thick head and her master's weak stomach, and moved to retrieve her blades. Heff set Liath aside, just a firm grip on her upper arm to keep her on her feet. She shrugged out of it. The dizziness was passing. She wouldn't droop like a wet kitten in front of these people. She hadn't finished with this white-blond spitfire of a guard who had sent a man named Roshain to murder them, to die at their hands.

"Hmm, what's this?" Kazhe said, prodding Liath's torn pack with the end of her long blade, coming up with a hank of nine-colored cloak on the point.

Porick stared at her with new eyes. The Darkmage was unmoved.

"So you're a proxy too—or pretending to be one. Steal these, did you?" Kazhe's laugh was a feral baring of white teeth.

Liath dismissed the guard to address the master. "What now?"

"Now Kazhe will leave your things alone and start cleaning up the mess she's made."

"And us?"

"Porick offered you a meal. And myself as well."

It was an invitation, but with a bite. Liath evaluated her prospects of escape if she went for her scrap of flesh now.

The Darkmage barely suppressed a weary sigh, reading her eyes. "I'm afraid we're substantially more than three," he said. "Come out and see."

As he and Porick left the tent, Liath made an unsteady grab for her pack, then let Heff stuff the clothes back in and bundle it up for her. "How is it you're here?" she whispered.

He'd caught up gradually, coming here just behind her and the older woman. He'd seen the little blond one come out of where Liath was and post herself near this tent. The family inside had gone to a neighbors'. He'd gone around the back, pulled up enough stakes to slip under, and stood guard, waiting to see if the little one would do what he expected. She did. But he had not known what the sheathed blade was. If he'd known that, he said, he'd have made sure to have some kind of bludgeon.

"You *couldn't* have caught up with me," she said.

He looked away and stilled his hands.

"All right, don't tell me. But I'll have it from you later, Heff, I swear it." Then she softened. "It's good to see you. Thank the spirits you didn't kill for me again."

After she embraced him, he said, I may have to yet.

"You won't. I'll see to it." She glanced at Kazhe, who had righted the brazier and a couple of baskets, found a broom, and then stopped to regard their exchange.

With lazy ease, Kazhe bent to retrieve Liath's knife and offered it to her hilt first. "Someone should teach you how to handle these."

Liath sheathed it. "All I need is a target to practice on."

Kazhe laughed and turned her back, lifting the broom.

Zelada was standing outside with her family. Heff shrugged apology at her. There was a crowd, scattered with mages. All but three moved to stand near the wordsmith. The pretender from the high coast, and his bindsman, who must be dead Roshain's brother. Gill, the false mage from

Pange. Jolia and Mirellin. At least eight in addition to Porick. And some who weren't triskeled, like Sira—who disarmed her, taking the knife Kazhe had returned.

Snow swirled in the air like a risen ghost of the blizzard as the Dark-mage's cadre escorted Liath and Heff to Porick's warm tent and a meal so heavily spiced it brought tears, ginger tea so hot it scalded. Kazhe joined them late, setting an array of weapons just inside the entry. She jammed herself in beside Torrin, sitting cross-legged with the rest of them around the communal stewpot. Her blue eyes burned hotter than the food. A jug of liquor was passed around; Liath declined, as did Torrin, but Kazhe took a good long swig, throat apple bobbing, then wiped her mouth with the back of her hand and exhaled with a hiss. But she held her tongue.

Conversation was stilted; outside, it began to snow in earnest. The mages discussed options in low tones. Liath turned to Torrin. "What will you do with us?"

"What would you do with me?" he countered calmly.

Liath let out a harsh laugh. He'd watched her throughout the subdued meal—never rude, but considering, waiting. What did he expect her to say? "I would stop you," she said.

"From teaching children to scribe?"

"From working against the Ennead. From doing darkcraft."

He smiled, a closemouthed curve of lips that was nothing like the blinding smile of the pretender. The pretender had looked like a darkmage. "Darkcraft is the Ennead's invention. You'll have to kill me to stop me fighting them. Would you do that, Illuminator?"

Kazhe, who had been only half listening, drilled her with a glance. She ignored it. "If that's what they asked of me."

His brows went up. "And it wasn't?"

"No. They don't want you dead. They want you to come back."

Kazhe broke in. "Tell that to the dozen who—"

Torrin stilled her with a raised finger. "And how did they expect you to effect my return?"

"Maybe they want me to talk you into it."

Kazhe gave an ugly snort and turned her attention back to the mages. They were debating the disruption of moving the tents in close this late in the evening, or another weathercasting.

"You aren't trying very hard."

"I'm tired. Maybe tomorrow."

"And suppose I put you in my thrall tonight? My tongue is silvered with lies. Suppose I demand that you cast with me? Ostensibly to send this storm back to the warders, but in fact to enslave your light."

Liath swallowed but kept her expression flat. "You can't. I can't cast. Something ails my magelight."

He seemed taken aback. Then he said, "Of course. They would never have sent a light so bright if they knew they were delivering precisely what . . ." He regarded her closely, a frank stare that would have made her blush if she hadn't clamped down hard to keep fear in check. "Yet you don't look like someone blocked, or sealed. Those who forsake their light cripple themselves—but triskeled mages who cannot cast generally go mad. You look quite well."

"I'm handling it," she said, remembering shadow ciphers swarming across the ceiling, her hand cramping in pain for lack of brush to paint with, the hollow-eyed stare of a heavy drinker.

"I suppose they made a pretense of trying to heal you."

Liath clamped down harder. "A lot of mages tried to heal me."

"I haven't."

Two simple words, and there it was: the crux of his power. The offer they implied, the blessed relief from pain, from desire. She did not need a healing, yet every fiber of her cried out to be put in his hands. "Your light isn't bright enough. I don't see what they were so concerned about, truth to tell."

He laughed, and she looked away—looked down at the thick slice of black bread that had been her trencher, at the center stain where pepper stew had soaked into it. When his white smile had faded from her mind's eye, she looked up to find him regarding her almost fondly. "What a grave misjudgment they have made," he said. "That's three. The number of power. Let's hope they all come home to roost."

Liath felt Heff straighten; then she heard it too, a horse, slowing to a stop just outside. The tent flap opened to admit a whirl of snowflakes and a man bundled against the cold. Kazhe was on her feet before the flap fell shut, a long knife in her hand. As the figure unwrapped a wool muffler to reveal a bearded face, she stepped toward him. Liath frowned, recognizing the man but unable to place him. Kazhe, two-thirds his height, grabbed him by the back of the neck and drew him down for a fierce, brief kiss, then moved out of the way. The man glanced at Liath, blinked and looked again with no expression, then said to Torrin, "You've got to come back. Verlein says they've been located."

It was Benkana.

Torrin, to Liath's surprise, turned to her. "It seems everyone's eager for me to come back. Strange, isn't it?"

The scathing reply she would have liked to make did not come.

"All I wanted to do—aside from find you, Illuminator, though I didn't know it until tonight—was teach good folk to scribe and read each other's scribing. It made sense to start with the children. Things learned in childhood are never forgotten, not if they're learned well. A literate generation, to grow up and train the next. A world where nothing would be lost, where the past could be read by anyone and restored to all."

"Torrin," Benkana said quietly.

"Yes, Benkana. I know it's very urgent. I'm not going."

Objections filled the tent. Kazhe prevailed: "You have to."

His eyes were cold. "That was ill phrased."

"You must come back," Benkana said—the same words but in a more reasonable tone. "The Ennead is throwing everything they have at the camp. They need you."

"Verlein has plenty of mages. They can defend themselves. Some of the warders are concentrating on us, here. That splits their attention. They're only guessing Verlein's whereabouts. Probably they're attacking everywhere I've been, or everywhere they think I've been. It's nothing the local mages can't control."

"Verlein needs you. She needs your voice."

"I'm afraid I have other plans."

"I know your work is important to you," Porick said, "but there are others who can carry on. You've seeded all the scribes you can. You are no longer required. It has a life of its own now."

"It is my work, Porick."

"This is more than just your work," Kazhe said. Her face had lost its pugnacious glare; she was genuinely beseeching him. It made her look very young. "You've been in danger since Gulbrid. But now you're a danger to everyone around you. They're not attacking everywhere you've been. I pay close attention to the reports. They're getting a bead on you, Torrin. If they find you, for certain, in a place like this, they'll kill everyone."

"Come back where we can shield you better," Benkana said.

Torrin raked a hand through his hair. "You can't have it both ways. Either Verlein needs my magecraft to defend her stronghold, or the stronghold is safe haven for us."

"It's both," Benkana said. "You know it can be both. There's no one there who isn't part of this fight, there are no children. Add your light, and your mages' light, to what's already there, and it will be a place of safety. You can't defend yourself adequately, cut off like this. You're endangering innocents, and staying on the move is no longer wise. You *must* come back."

"All right," Torrin said. He seemed abruptly weary. "All right. Porick? What about the weather?"

"An ordinary snowstorm. But I wouldn't travel in it. Wait till morning, at least."

At Torrin's nod, Benkana gratefully began peeling away layers of wool. Kazhe, smirking at his ineptness with the heavy clothing, moved to help him. Porick asked Sira to see to the man's mount. Torrin tilted his head back to ask Benkana something. The flesh of his neck was pale, as if the sun had never touched it.

Heff moved too late to stop her. Liath's boot crunched on condiment dishes as the other leg propelled her up and forward. She raked her fingernails deep into the expanse of white skin. In the same motion she was driving for the entry. She flew through the hanging tent flap into a blast of snow. The horse, ground tied, backed away. She caught the reins, swung aboard, and dug her heels in. The tired horse startled into a run. She hauled him around to her best estimate of Headward.

Pain exploded in her left shoulder and arm. She cried out, clutched at the pommel of the saddle, reeled back to sit down hard and was jarred up by the horse's pounding gait. Her left arm was pinned to her. A stained wooden point protruded from her coat. Her vision went dark. The horse slowed to a lope and she sank into the saddle, letting it rock her. She would not fall. She would not fall. The snow had closed around her, would fill the trail as fast as the horse left it. They had to keep going.

But the horse could not. He'd been ridden hard to beat the storm. She let him slow to a trot, then a walk. *Just a little farther, boy,* she urged him. *Give me another half mile.*

How much he gave her she could not judge, but the cold was seeping into her as blood seeped out, and the pain was very bad. The jouncing of horseback hurt too much to bear. She stopped him and got off somehow, though she banged the shaft on the way down and had to grab hard for the saddle and consciousness.

"All right," she whispered, draping the knotted ropes on his withers. "Go on back now. Eiden guide you." She slapped him on the rump, and prayed he'd find his master before the cold got him.

The snow was knee-high, and would soon be to her hips. She slogged through it for perhaps five threfts, then swayed back and sat down hard. She had not taken her shrunkwool coat off in the tent; the gloves were in the pocket. She fished them out, pulled the right one on with her teeth, sobbed as she forced the left one on.

The thing in her shoulder was an arrow. Was there nothing these cursed folk would not turn into a tool of murder? Archery was *sport.* Yet someone—Kazhe, pulling bow and quiver from the gear she'd stowed by the entry—had thought to use it for this.

It was bloody fine aim—in the wind, in the dark, a moving target. How proud they must be of their proficiency. But they'd missed her heart by a hand, got her shoulder and upper arm as she balanced over her knees at a gallop.

The cold masked the pain but made it hard to think. She had to find cover. She had nothing for her face, nothing to protect her head. Just till morning. They had to go back to wherever it was. The camp. The fastness she had searched for, moon after moon. It no longer mattered where it was. Inside her glove, under her fingernails, was the flesh the Ennead required. They had found the camp anyway, Benkana said. It had nothing to do with her. Now all she was charged with was bringing these scraps of flesh and humors Headward. Outlive the storm. Outwait her enemies' departure.

There was no shelter on the plains in winter. But soon she would get sleepy and just lie down to rest, to die. No. There *was* shelter—she just had to get under it.

Down. She must go down. She pawed one-handed through the drift as the storm dumped new snow into the hole she dug, then dug faster. There was no feeling in her left arm at all; a nauseating ache spread from her shoulder into her back. She kept digging until she hit something half brittle, half springy.

Grasslands grass, two threfts high, bowed by the weight of snow. A pocket of air and relative warmth. She stopped digging when she hit hard-packed earth, and shimmied inward.

The snowfall filled her tracks, hid the blood trail. She curled into her makeshift burrow. Plains rats survived in underground tunnels. The Dark-mage's lair might be in tunnels. It didn't matter. Nothing mattered but staying alive.

She felt for the protruding shaft with her good hand. She didn't think she could yank it out of herself, and if she did a gout of blood would follow and she'd be dead in minutes. Nothing for it, then. Leave it in, hope the arrow itself stanched the worst of the bleeding, hope shock didn't . . .

Consciousness returned with a bitter jolt. Cold, she was so cold. . . . How long had she been out? The wind howled overhead. Was the storm getting worse? Was Porick wrong, was it a full-fledged blizzard? She'd be buried alive here, no air, no warmth. She shook uncontrollably. Cold, cold, so cold . . .

Voices brought her back again. They were looking for her, calling through the storm. She hoped the horse got through all right. Then the voices were gone, receding down a tunnel. She would sleep just for a little while, just till morning, and see if the weather had cleared, see if she had suffocated or bled to death, see if she could dig her way back out with a useless arm.

It hurt so much, and she was so cold. She could barely open her eyes. There was nothing to see. Just let them slide closed—

No. She hauled her mind up from leagues and depths of white silence. She groped for the arrow shaft, the alien wooden thing that had invaded her flesh, and twisted. Agony radiated from the hole it had made in her. Pain would keep her awake. Pain would keep her alive. Don't think about the damage, don't imagine the torn muscle and shattered bone. Embrace the pain. The pain was searing. The pain was fire. The pain was life.

One more thing to do. She got the glove off her left hand, fumbled a small linen cloth from her pocket, spread it. With her right glove in her teeth, she dug under her nails, depositing flecks of skin and half-dried blood into the handcloth. Then she folded it, thrice, and stuffed it back deep in the pocket. Replacing the gloves took the last of her strength.

Pondering agony, she fell into a trance. Above the muffling grass and snow, the wind moaned for her.

His voice came as out of a dream.

"You'll be dehydrated," it said. "You should take a handful of snow . . ." Reasonable, sensible advice. Why was it coming in the Dark-mage's voice?

It was a soothing voice. She hadn't noticed that before. He should have been a bindsman. A gentle baritone, never raised in anger. It sang her a bindsong, through the wind and the snow. A song of life, so she wouldn't submit to the cold, the pain, let the long sleep take her away.

"Porick's triad is diverting the storm for you. Don't worry; it's hidden you quite well. My people were unable to find you. But you're out of sight of the Jhardal camp. You'll need a star reckoning to find your way back. Do you know how to reckon the heavens? It's a lost art, even to steersfolk. Perhaps you'll be able to follow my footprints. Not what you had in mind, I know."

A dream. Her own mind telling her what she wanted to hear. But it sounded so real. It sounded as though he was sitting in the snow just outside the mound of her hideaway.

"If you stay where you are until dawn, Illuminator, you'll die. I know you can hear me; I can see your light. I could see your light from the encampment, just as Heff can."

Heff! She had abandoned him, left him in their clutches. They wouldn't hurt him—it would serve no purpose—but Kazhe would be livid, who knew what she'd do—

"Like Heff, once I see a light, learn to recognize it, I can find it again wherever it is. He's a good friend; he cares for you. That credits you—that you found a way into a heart so blackened. When I left him, he was nothing but anguish and rage. Somehow you made him feel something else. He did his best to keep you from me, diverting you like a triad diverting a storm, whenever you turned in my direction. If I'd known you were coming, I might have sent someone for you. My people, I fear, protect me too well—a flaw of the Ennead's that I inadvertently replicated. I didn't know it was you I sought until I saw you. But there's time yet. Time, I hope, to explain all you need to know."

Go away, she thought. *Go away and take your voice with you. Stop plaguing me.* It was hard, staying alive. He was distracting her, making it harder.

"Did you know that Heff can see magelights, over any distance? His world is a sea of lights, each with its own color and smell. Most are an undifferentiated mass. But once he knows one, he can always find it. He could have brought you to me at any time. Don't be angry with him. He knew your road would only get harder once you found me. He sought to protect you. How the spirits brought you together I don't know, but I thank them for it. I hope you'll stay with us, that he might stay as well."

She stuck gloved fingers into her mouth and bit down hard to keep from groaning. The pain was so much worse when she surfaced to pay attention. Why couldn't he have left her in peace?

"It's getting colder. You've got to get up, and walk. The snow's tailing off; I can see the stars. It's very beautiful. I'm going to leave you now, Illuminator, and go back. If you stay where you are, you'll die. If you turn Headward, you'll die. There are no villages or bands for many miles. You're very brave, fighting for what you believe in. But what you believe in is a lie. Don't die for it until you know it for what it is."

There was no sound of hoofbeats, no horse's whuffle in the cold air. He must have walked, if he had ever been there at all.

It was quiet for a long time. The storm had gone, as promised, or of its own accord. She struggled free of her lair, whimpering in pain, then growling, forcing her stiff legs to unbend, forcing her right arm to clear the snow. It was that or sleep forever. She emerged into a wonderland of frozen stars, ice crystals blued by starlight, an enchanted snowy silent world.

Large oval prints lay on the snow like a scribing—partially filled, but visible. He had been here. He'd gone back, wearing the bent-willow snow-shoes the Girdlers used.

He'd left a pair for her. They lay canted in a drift. She'd dug her way out right underneath them.

Move. Go. Somewhere. Anywhere.

She fumbled to fasten the awkward shoes to her boots, and fell twice trying to stand on them, twice more trying to walk in them. The arrow, driven forward, protruded nearly half its length from her upper arm. Sobbing in pain, she grasped it and nearly pulled it free, but stopped herself at the last moment.

He had to be lying about how far the next village was. The Girdle was threaded with rivers, and the rivers were lined with villages. But she could not be sure, and she didn't have the time or the life left to be wrong. She should turn Headward. But the only certainty was the Jhardal camp, where those shoeprints led.

Live, or die.

She put her feet in them and followed.

Halfway there, or a third of the way, or more, or less, a figure grew from the whiteness ahead of her. She had collapsed twice; now her knees gave way for good. The face was muffled in scarves. The eye looked like Heff's. Strong arms lifted her, put her right arm around broad shoulders. She tried to hold on and couldn't. The stars were so bright, like blades in her eyes.

"No guard," she said. They had freed him, sent no one with him . . . he could take her home now . . .

Holding her, Heff could not answer. His swinging gait in the wide shoes jarred the arrow. She moaned once against his shoulder, closed her eyes against the knife-bright stars, and slipped away.

Fever racked her. She thought they traveled, but she flew through a windy wheel of stars and snow, flew up over them into the disc of sun, burned in its searing light. She tried to pull the arrow out, anything to stop the pain, but the shaft was gone and her arm and shoulder were bound. "Don't let him cast on me," she babbled, until someone snapped at her, and someone else said to leave her alone, she was raving. She woke with no pain and a taste of bitter herbs on her tongue, and retched. She woke in agony to Heff's big hand smoothing the hair from her brow, and slept again. Sometimes she thought she heard him humming, but it was only the wind. The winds had names, but no one remembered them anymore. Perhaps the Ennead did, but they hadn't told her. Was this the wind of healing, or the deathwind? "Don't let him heal me," she begged, and Heff smoothed the hair from her brow, and she slept.

Up. They were going up. She sat a horse, with Heff's arms around her. Its neck looked like patches of snow on ashy ground. The piebald. Heff leaned them forward, off its kidneys.

"Take this," someone said. She sat up abruptly in a pile of scratchy blankets, knocking soup from a spoon. Benkana swore, then said, "All right, try again." She looked around at a campsite. Jolia and Mirellin and Porick were casting. Gill was watching them. Kazhe stood near Torrin by a fire pouring smoke. His back was turned. There were unfamiliar trees all around them, strange pale trees, like bonewood but weeping like river willows. A rocky outcrop to one side was veined with gossan: a scored face that bled rust. Heff came out of the trees at its base, and smiled.

"Maybe you'll have better luck," Benkana said, handing bowl and spoon to Heff as he crouched down on his haunches beside them.

Heff gave them to Liath and said, Eat. You've been sick.

"We're in the Druilors?"

The Blooded Mountains. Yes.

A bitter laugh tried to bubble up and came out a rasp of air. "I knew it," she said. Her voice was as rusty as the mountains.

She spooned saffron soup into herself with trembling hands, then gave up and slurped from the bowl, but could only manage half of it before she had to lie back. "Where's Amaranth?"

With my horses, Heff said. I brought all your gear.

"Thank you." She meant more than the horse and the gear. Still she had to ask, "Why didn't you come sooner?"

He wouldn't let me. He wanted to talk to you. He hoped you'd come back with him. When you didn't, he allowed me to fetch you. He didn't want you to die.

"No, I'm sure he didn't." She glanced at the fire, but met only Kazhe's hot eyes; the Darkmage was involved in something. He would want the use of her light. He would assume he could heal her, if he believed her story at all. He had been waiting for her, looking for someone like her. How much of that had been dream, how much had he said? She looked at Heff again, felt a flood of warmth at the sight of his scored face, his one kind eye. "You can see magelights," she said. "Better than I can."

He nodded.

So it had not been a dream. "That's how you followed me, over all those miles. Blessed spirits, Heff. Over *all those miles*."

It was dim from that far away, he said. But it was yours. There's only one light, anywhere, brighter than yours.

He had gestured toward the fire. "His light isn't bright at all," she snapped. What a disappointment he was, this aging man, this *teacher*.

Still, it's his, Heff said. No two smell alike. From here, it's like . . . He leaned close, outlined her body at two finger widths. Like that. Surrounding you.

"You could see that mage. Roshain. In the Stonewood. That's why you were so hard on yourself. It wasn't a lucky blow in the dark. You could see all of him."

Heff looked away, but nodded.

Liath closed her eyes, trying to think. "But you were up . . . when he came . . . he must have been tracking us . . . couldn't you sense him?"

It's what woke me, I think, but he came very fast, and I was half asleep. Before we bedded down, he was far enough that it seemed like all the other magelights.

All the other magelights. It was as Torrin had said. He moved through a realm of lights, like stars across the plane of the world. Probably he disregarded them most of the time—the way the sea of faces in an unfamiliar crowd ran together, so that the eye saw only crowd until it lit on someone it recognized.

Heff showed no light; he was not a mage by any stretch. He was earthcrafter through and through, as he had shown her. Could there be something latent, something like what Mellas had?

He must have been able to see as well as I can, Heff said, still unraveling it himself. Or he must have had special eyes . . .

"Nightsight," Liath said. "Magecraft could do that. It wouldn't even be darkcraft. Spirits, eating a bushel of carrots would probably do the same thing. But Torrin can see magelights that well too. So maybe Roshain could." She paused, and then said, "Could you really have found him for me, any time?"

He nodded. That's how I caught up with you at Jhardal. I didn't follow you. I took a shortcut to him. I knew you would find him, and where he was I would find you.

"You could have saved us both some trouble."

You could have saved us both some trouble by going home.

She sighed. "I can't argue with you there."

They wanted to heal you, Heff said. You wouldn't let them. You screamed whenever they tried. You should let them now.

"I've made it this far," she said, glancing at the mages.

I wouldn't let him heal me either. But I had different reasons, and it doesn't have to be him.

"I'd rather trust in your earthcraft, if it's all the same to you." She fingered the mossy poultice that padded her shoulder.

"You understand him, then?" Benkana said. He had gone off to talk to Kazhe, but had drifted back to watch them.

"Yes. Can't any of you?" She wanted to know if Torrin could. Benkana shook his head. "So you survived the Aralinns," she said then, glad to be off the subject of healings.

"Just. It got worse after we turned back. No shadows, but a small quake, more rain, wind knocking trees down. The land had turned against us. We shipped out by sea as soon as we could."

"And now we're going to meet Verlein."

"Things have changed, since sowmid."

"How?"

"It's not my place to tell you."

He moved away. There was no sense of malice from him. He was a man doing a hard job he believed in. What lies had Torrin fed these people? It was more than just scribing, she knew that much.

The pretender from the High Arm sat with his bindsman on the far side of the fire. Yerby, his name was, and the still anxious-looking binder was Kael. Yerby's light was bright as ever, but he'd shed the pyrite triskele and wore a real pewter one in its place, and his winter clothes were plain wool, off-white and beige and gray like everyone else's. No dye, no fakery now. Yet he was brighter by threefold than the man named Torrin. Again she suspected some elaborate ruse. Heff said Torrin had the only light in the world brighter than hers . . . but maybe brightness was relative to him, maybe he saw mages as he wished to see them, bright only in proportion to their significance in his life . . .

Had she gouged flesh from the wrong mage?

She groped in her breeches, but felt the lump of cloth right away, folded linen against her fingertip.

It was Torrin Wordsmith's flesh. That was all that mattered.

The triad had completed their casting. Yerby and Kael sat with another mage, an illuminator, with the quiet familiarity of long association—they were probably another triad. He'd need at least two, to balance with magecraft the physical protection of his bodyguards. Sira had stayed with the Jhardal band, as had its own triad. Two Lowland Southers, Ashara and Indar, carried blades like Kazhe's on their backs, and various knives, and yew-and-horsehair bows; Indar had an axe tucked in his belt. Benkana, also armed to the teeth, made a dozen of them. Two triads, four guards, Gill, and Torrin.

She could not quite fathom Gill. He wore no triskele now, real or fake, and he was armed, but not as heavily as the others. His magelight was dim, nearly scentless. Was he mage, or guard, or both? Had he run straight back to Torrin after failing whatever his task was in Sauglin? Or was he, as Nerenyi believed, a spy for the Ennead, someone who might help Liath get back to them?

She let Porick's triad heal her. If there was a chance, she'd have to be ready to take it. But the healing hurt more than the wound had, and when it was over she fought tears.

They rode another two days, out of the foothills and into a steep mountain pass. Caches of supplies had been put by, in caverns that the guards checked thoroughly before anyone entered. Liath had an uneasy sense of enterprise—foresight, planning, contingencies. The proxies he had turned had to have gone somewhere. How big was this encampment, how well supplied, how well defended? He'd had a year to prepare his fastness.

At night they posted lookouts.

"Are they to keep me from running again?" she asked Torrin, coming up next to the rock he sat on, contemplating a poisonous fall of water. "Or can't you travelward your own mountains?"

"Are you planning on running away again?"

"Do you always answer a question with a question?"

His lips curved up. "Most questions lead to others. No, they're not guarding you. You can't get out of these mountains now. The mouth of this pass is the only way in or out, and fighters are stationed there out of sight. No one leaves without my permission, or Verlein's, and by now those orders will have been modified, so even my permission will not suffice."

"I don't understand."

"I know." He gestured to the flat rock beside him; after a moment, she sat, awkwardly. "The mountains are besieged, in their small way. Many have joined us, but a few we lost again. They remain loyal to the Holding. We would not let them leave, and so they banded together to harry us. There are only a few of them left now, but they grow desperate as winter wears on."

"You'd make a good hostage," Liath said.

"Indeed. And to kill me, they believe, would knock the fight out of the rest of them. Would that it were true."

She started to ask him something else, but he turned and said, "Explain to me what ails your magelight."

She blinked to find the gold eyes so close. "I don't know. It just stopped working."

"When?"

No point in keeping it from him. She wanted him to believe her. Her blunted magelight had been her shield. Now only the illusion of it would serve. "The day after my trial. The day I took the triskele."

"Was your trial more arduous than most? Perhaps you only depleted your strength."

She shook her head and said carefully, "I kept trying to cast, even after a rest."

"Try now," he said. "I'll call a binder."

"No."

He nodded. "All right. What were you doing when it failed?"

This answer she was bitterly glad to give. "Trying to heal a drunken fool your Verlein stuck a knife in."

"So you are the same one."

She paused, afraid she'd divulged too much. But he knew she'd been to the Holding. "I suppose so."

"You were traveling with a remarkable young man."

Her head came up. "What did you do to him?"

"Shhh. Nothing at all. But I wish I'd known of him earlier. I would have gotten him out. He's been ill used."

Liath tried to find the trick in this. She had learned too much and distrusted too much of it. It would be easier if the Ennead *had* sent her to kill him—then she could be done with it, and if Kazhe gutted her or shot her full of arrows, at least Eiden Myr would be safe.

"The Ennead has harnessed the power of pain," Torrin said into the darkness, with no preamble. "It's not a difficult deduction—that if mage-craft can heal, it can harm. Perhaps you've met one or two adequate lights who were rejected as prentices, or failed to pass a trial despite good train-ing. Few speak of it, but most of those were folk deemed insufficient in compassion. To be a mage takes more than talent and skill. When proxies cast triads, their one, crucial instruction to the mages is to foster compassion and deny the use of magecraft to those who lack it. The prohibition against doing harm is deeply ingrained. But not insurmountable."

Liath opened her mouth. Nothing came out.

"The basic tenet of compassion is stressed most firmly to binders, who are charged with taking lives. Some of them nonetheless treat roughly with their stock, out of ignorance or poor training. But it took a cruel, canny mind to realize that vellum or parchment harvested in agony would harbor a malignant strength. The spirit clings hard to life. Tremendous power is unleashed in the severing of spirit from body. Terror and pain linger in the flesh, like a binding substance, absorbing and holding that power. When such vellum or parchment is used in a casting, what we consider a taint can be used to . . . advantage."

He was describing his own activities. No wonder the Ennead hadn't been more specific. *It's dark magecraft, you see. He is using magecraft to do harm. To do evil.* She might not have believed even the Ennead if they had told her something like this.

"Worst of all is a casting done on a subject who is dying. I don't know if you've ever cast passage, but there is a moment of indescribable vision. It never stays, afterward, beyond a brief depth of personal understanding. The Ennead seeks to plumb that vision, to scry into the unseen. Though they had not perfected the technique when I left the Holding, they've been learning to use the pain of the casting subject—the pain, the fear, and the passionate tenacity of a spirit fighting not to leave its dying flesh—to increase the strength of other castings."

Liath remembered the colorless blaze of light at Werka's passing. Was he trying to tempt her, knowing how she had yearned to prolong that moment of clarity, to see past it, through it? What was next—a declaration that he'd been the clever inventor of this horror? An invitation to join him in using it?

"For years this work was done in secret, as its proponents maneuvered to create an ennead sympathetic to its motives. Ours is that ennead. They are protected by the Holding hierarchy; they work and live completely unseen, save for a few cowed or ambitious souls who serve them. They have not yet reached the height of their powers. But it won't be much longer."

She looked for some sign that a human being and not a monster sat beside her. But he was no longer talking to her. He was addressing the darkness beyond the firelight, or inside his own mind. He presented a stony profile, pale skin limned in shadow.

"How does one fight something like that? Work from within? Undermine their efforts, maneuver to relieve them of power as they did their enemies? That could take years. They are hard to kill, and their power is entrenched. Those who stayed to try will never forgive me leaving them. Does one stay, and fight, and fail, and die brave and alone and in vain?" Finally he looked at her again. His eyes were yellow in the firelight, expressionless, like those of a wild animal at forest's edge. "The alternative is to work from without. That is what I've chosen to do."

"You're turning your own misdeeds back on them," Liath said, struggling to articulate horror and outrage. The hypocrisy of him, to claim that the Ennead— "I've been in the Holding. I've been a vocate. I've spoken with the Nine. *None of what you say is true.*"

"Can you be sure?" For a moment she thought he might take her hands, and she drew back. His eyes searched hers, as if the question weren't rhetorical. "Can you be utterly, incontrovertibly sure, Illuminator? The Holding is a mountain. Did you search every crevice, every passageway, every chamber?"

She shook her head—refusing him, not answering. "You're wrong," she said. "I don't have to prove it. You're just wrong."

"And if I introduce you to people who escaped?"

"I won't believe them. I don't have to believe anything you say. You could tell anyone to say anything—"

"Calm yourself, Illuminator." In his voice she heard her own speaking to Tarny, to a lumbering, desperate, misguided fool. "You've already seen it for yourself. You didn't recognize what you saw. Your young runner— I'm afraid neither Verlein nor Benkana remembered his name—"

"Mellas," she murmured. "His name is Mellas."

"The things that attacked you in the Aralinns were the torments of his mind."

"He had bad dreams . . ." *He had bad dreams, and then the shadows came.*

"He would have been a powerful illuminator, or binder. Whatever horrors the Ennead inflicted on him, or in front of him, stunned his light into hiding. But it would have tried to manifest itself, fighting to be used."

"Mellas doesn't show a light."

"Of course not. The Ennead banished it to the shadows. And so it used shadows to strike out."

She had told the Ennead about Mellas. If Bron had been keeping him from them . . .

No. He had come too close to weaving her into his nightmare. She shoved herself off the rock, getting her feet under her, putting space between them. "You're much smarter than I am," she said. "I can't poke holes in your fabrication. I can only deny you. The Ennead protects us. The Ennead represents lifetimes of tradition and safeguards and training. It could never be turned the way you describe."

"The Ennead is inbred and stagnant, and the current Ennead is the product of manipulation by forces who came to power over generations and eliminated anyone who was a threat to them."

"*To what purpose?* What in Eiden's name could it serve any of them to do the hideous things you describe? *No one* takes joy from such things. *No one.*" She faltered at a brush of memory, something old and mean that turned her stomach, but she fought it off, whatever it was—another of his dark compulsions—

"Oh, Illuminator," he said, his voice very hollow. "Loyal, naive Illuminator. I would give my life to make that so."

"Tell me why they're doing it." When he didn't respond, she seized him by the shoulders and shook him hard; he was limp in her grasp.

Kazhe was there in an eyeblink, twisting an arm behind her, dragging her out of reach. "When will you stop trying to convert these pustules?"

"When will you stop trying to kill them?"

Liath submitted without struggle, her gaze still locked on Torrin. "*Tell me.*"

"They want to destroy the world," he said, his eyes looking straight into hers, and through them.

"You're talking about yourself," Liath said. Her voice broke as Kazhe bent her arm higher behind her back. "Yourself and the cataclysm you'll summon to flatten the Holding. You're a spoiled child who wants revenge.

It's madness to destroy the world. You *live* in the world. Do you hate them that much?"

"Not this world," he said. "Not this island that we have learned to call the world. The world outside it. And yes, they hate it that much."

"The sun? The moon? The land beyond the rain? Those are teller's tales. Everything you've said is just a story to frighten naughty children. It's the kind of thing my brother used to whisper at me late at night, only in poorer taste. They were wrong about you. You're not twisted. You're cracked."

"I envy you, Illuminator," he said. He gestured for Kazhe to let her go, but an amazed huff was the response. "If belief were enough, your belief alone would make Eiden Myr the paradise it once was. On the day that belief is shattered, I will grieve."

Kazhe's body clenched behind her, then released; Liath turned to see Heff's hand releasing Kazhe's throat. They stood for a moment, speechless in stalemate.

When Liath looked at him again, Torrin had turned his back and hugged his knees to his chest, resting his chin on them. Surveying the darkness, and whatever phantasms he saw there.

They placed her far from both Torrin and Heff the next day, on her own horse at the end of the line, but only Indar was behind her, guarding the rear. Benkana, in front of her, rode the horse she had stolen. The triads were in front of him, with Kazhe and Torrin between them; then Heff, and Gill, and Ashara leading. The sky, a matted gray, sputtered icy rain, but the footing wasn't bad yet and for a while the steep trail opened up. Only thorn and brambles grew in the rusty soil. The peaks glinted gold— deposits of pyrite, like what Yerby's fake triskele was cast of. These were hard mountains, mining mountains, nearly impassable from the Girdle side and sparsely inhabited. She would not have thought he could supply his encampment in such a place, but still she kicked herself for not searching it sooner. Hindsight was clearsight.

"We're running out of water," a mage called, up ahead of her, as they entered a narrow defile. "We'll have to stop and do a casting soon." Without purification, the water was deadly.

"We're nearly there. It can wait till tonight."

Something whistled, and Benkana toppled from his saddle.

"Down!" Kazhe shouted.

Liath was slow responding; she flinched reflexively from a bite on her neck. An arrow flying past. Indar, already afoot, dragged her down and into the spiky brush behind a boulder.

"Benkana—" She started toward him.

Indar hauled her back. "First we stay alive." His long bow was in his hand; he shoved her aside to make room, then nocked an arrow between beads, his eyes scanning the clifftops. Movement flickered, and he let fly; the arrow arced through empty air.

Ahead and across, she could see Kazhe's white-blond head through the brush, and the occasional streak of an arrow from Ashara beyond her. All was quiet. "Give me a knife," she whispered to Indar. He hissed for silence.

I'm with you, she wanted to call out to them. *I'm on your side. I carry the means of stopping him.* But it would only locate her for them, if Indar's arrows hadn't; and Kazhe had arrows too.

She picked up a rock.

Shouts and a strangled cry came from the front as two men came running low along the trail from behind. Indar got two shots off before one fell. The other was still coming fast, his long blade before him. Indar reached back and drew his from its scabbard. With a twist of his arms, he brought it down across the other blade. The attacker recovered. Iron clanged as they bashed at each other. Liath stayed in the boulder's shadow, wary of arrows, then realized they'd stopped coming. But the archers below were engaged hand-to-hand; this was the attackers' chance for a clear shot. A length of rope fell from above, slapping her hard on the shoulder. A woman was coming down fast, gloved hands sliding on hemp, nothing to belay her—running backward down the face of the cliff. Others were doing the same. How many? Four?

Indar's opponent made a horrible sound as iron entered his chest. Liath smashed her rock at the descending woman, felt a kneecap crunch, then sprang out of the way as Indar brought his heavy blade around in a sweep-ing arc. Liath's eyes snapped shut just before the impact. Hot blood sprayed her face.

"*Down!*" Indar cried. This time she dropped like a lead weight. The blow meant to cleave her struck chips off rock. The woman wielding the blade stepped back as Indar closed with her. Liath squirmed around and embraced the woman's ankles. The woman fell backward. Indar planted a boot in Liath's back and plunged his blade downward; the legs jerked hard, cracking Liath in the chin, then went limp. She tried to get up, but Indar's weight shifted onto her, crushing the breath from her lungs. Then he cried out, and collapsed on top of her.

Indar's killer took her for dead; she heard him move through the brush, back up the trail. Then came a sickening thunk, and he was knocked back onto his dead comrade. His neck was almost severed; his head flopped back, his face toward her, his glazing eyes fixed upside-down on her own.

She was buried in the dead, soaked in blood. Someone was screaming in bursts, over and over. Iron rang on iron, crunched on stone; if it made a sound when it met flesh, it was a sucking whisper, lost in the tumult. Liath struggled to get up. Her arms were pinned and she could not lever the weight off her back. It was an effort to breathe, and then she inhaled the scent of blood and urine and feces, the reek of a punctured intestine. She pulled one arm out from under the woman's legs, but the other elbow jammed against the rock that had shielded her. She twisted onto her back, scraping flesh off the elbow but freeing the arm, then pressed her torso upright and wriggled out from under Indar's body.

There was blood everywhere. The screaming choked off. She staggered up, caught a boot toe on Indar, went down, and got up again, bracing on slippery stone. She lifted Indar's blade—it took both hands. Either it was heavier or she was weaker than she thought. But she had done nothing. Nothing but survive.

It was over. Kazhe stood across the trail and up, torn and bloody, wild-eyed, blade still held before her, watching for the next attacker, protecting Torrin. Liath walked up the trail, reeling drunkenly, dragging the heavy blade. Heff, stained and spattered, moved slowly to take her arm, then pull her against him. He held a blooded knife in his off hand. Up the trail, others staggered out. Jolia, Gill, Mirellin. Yerby was unscathed and unstained; the red on his clothes was trail dust. Liath moved toward Kazhe, who brandished her blade with no recognition in her eyes. Behind her, Torrin slowly pushed a corpse forward and off him. A small knife protruded from its chest. The Darkmage stared at the man he had killed. He mouthed something. A name. Coll. "He was a good man," he rasped.

"Spirits—Benkana." Liath let the blade fall and ran downtrail. Benkana lay where he had hit. He was breathing in short "puh"s. The arrow had gone through the junction of neck and shoulder, severing neither artery nor windpipe.

"Binder!" Liath shouted.

"Kael's dead," Yerby called back in a high, surprised voice, as Kazhe came running and cried, "Don't pull it out!"

"I'm not, I'm not doing anything. Get Torrin, get a binder, Kazhe, now."

"Kael's dead," Yerby said again as Porick's binder ran up the trail to find her horse and the binding sack it carried.

"Illuminator, here." Torrin's voice cut through the rest. "Leave him. Porick's triad will see to him."

She obeyed that voice without thinking, though it carried no bark of authority. He was on his knees next to someone—Yerby's illuminator, covered in blood. Heff had chased down two more horses, and his own were trotting back at his triple handclap. Porick's binder and illuminator went past her, one leading the horse, the other untying the saddlepacks. Yerby's illuminator was battered and bleeding; the worst of it was an axe gash in his side. Torrin had stripped his coat and shirt back and was pinching the lips of the wound together.

"Kael's dead," Yerby said.

"Get his bindsack."

When Yerby didn't move, Heff searched the horses he'd recovered and came back with the binder's gear.

"Hold this," Torrin said, and Heff put his big earthcrafter fingers on the wound, pressing against the renewed spill of blood.

"We have no binder," Liath said.

"I'll be binder." He was scoring a circle in the trail dust with the edge of his hand. "Wordsmith," he said to Yerby. "Sit."

Yerby stared, uncomprehending. "Kael's dead."

Muscles bunched in Torrin's jaw. "Give me the gear, Heff."

Liath watched, equally uncomprehending, as Torrin drew vellum and inkpots and quill from their waterwarded compartments. He sharpened the quill, spat in the dish, shook ink powder into it, then dipped the quill. "Take the dish," he told Liath. "I need more ink. Bleed into it if you have to."

"I'm not a b—"

"Do as I tell you."

She obeyed him, mixing spit and blood into the dish, reaching for more powder, all the while trying to center herself, to summon her guiders. She would need pigment, was the pigment mixed, should she look? *Concentrate*, she told herself. *One thing at a time.*

A casting would not work without three mages of the correct triadic disciplines. This casting could not succeed. But if it didn't, this man would die. Torrin must expect Porick's binder to finish with Benkana and join in here. She would come before Liath had to give the lie to her claimed ailment. She would come in time.

Torrin scribed across the vellum in the hand that had scribed across the backs of her eyes. This was no simplified lesson, no scrawling on slate. The ink trailed his hand in a glossy flourish, fluid and confident; he scribed faster than any wordsmith she had ever seen, even in the Holding, and glanced up often to check Liath's preparations, the other triad, the rest of their party, as if the work required only part of his attention. The lines, impossibly straight, began to form a larger pattern across the page. His scribing was an illumination. Yet that brilliant craft was dimmed to nothing by the magelight that blazed from within him.

Liath closed her eyes and could not shut it out; its molten glow suffused the air, warmed her own numb flesh through blood-damp wool, lit her mind.

When he cast, he shone brighter than the sun.

"*Illuminator.*" His hand on her leg was a shock. Her eyes flew open. He was holding the quill out to her. Ink glistened at its tip. He had dipped it for her, like a binder. "Start with this," he said. "I'll prepare brushes while you work."

She took the quill, felt the wood-backed vellum settle on her knees. Guiders. She had to center herself, let the guiders come. Guiders were a light in the mind, like magelight, but one would not pale in the other's glow. She took deep, rhythmic breaths. *What is flesh when there is no wound?* Knotwork would knit the torn body back together. Kadri would ease the pain, confirm the unity; illumination would put things back where they had been. The flesh wanted to be whole. She would paint life and health into it. . . .

Her guiders would not come.

"No . . ."

"*Now*, Illuminator."

"I can't."

"This is necessary. Do it."

"I can't—I can't—I could, I cast passage, I cast wardings, it came back—oh, spirits, not now!"

Torrin swore, and took quill and vellum from her.

"What are you d—"

"Quiet," he said, and began to draw.

Jolia's bindsong filled the canyon trail, a plain, pure melody of healing, and died away in echoes as Torrin Wordsmith illuminated the vellum with intricate knotwork and precise kadri, painted wholeness around the large initial that he himself had scribed, with pigment he instructed her to mix. His border was too ornate, his colors darker and more intense than were called for, but it was impeccable craft. . . .

It was a picture of his spirit. Liath, stunned again by failure, mind seared by the flare of his light, appalled to see a scribe play illuminator and do it well, somehow found room to recognize what she had always known but never *thought*: that what an illuminator painted turned her inside out, baring her deepest self to the mages she cast with.

He removed the completed leaf from its backing and laid it on the wounded man, then held his hands out. Liath stared stupidly at them. He shook them, throwing her a sharp look. "But I didn't . . ." she began, and he said, "It doesn't matter. Your magelight is in there. *Give me your hands, Illuminator.*"

She touched light. Her hands fit into his, bone to bone, palm to palm; he did not clasp, but laced his fingers through hers, a knotwork of flesh. Her magelight and his became seamless. The light of three mages formed a circle; their light formed a bridge. Under it, the vellum glowed, and the wounded man arched his back and moaned.

The wordsmith sang. Bindsongs had no words, but his did. They were no words that Liath had ever heard. Annina Binder had modulated her song with her throat, a complex ululation; other binders angled lips and tongue to control the flow of air. This, too, was a shaping of sound with lips and tongue, but in his mouth the sounds had significance. He was a wordsmith. He sang words.

Like Heff's handsigns, the words formed patterns. Like Mellas's nightspeech, they sounded as though they should make sense—they sounded as though they made vital sense to the mind they came from. Her patterner's mind caught the repetitions and subtle rhythms, isolated the phrasing, recognized the echoes of sounds in later sounds, understood how that linked the phrases. Her painter's ear heard the shifting colors in the melody. He was painting with sound, scribing with sound. His voice was a weary sweetness, hoarse and gentle. It painted the same picture his illumination had, and in all the darkness that haunted it, there was not one whit of evil. But *words* . . .

The glowing vellum sank into a thinness and melted away, and the wounded flesh was whole. Scarred, not perfect, but whole. The man sat up, shaking his head, and Torrin's fingers slipped from hers. She folded hers over her palms, as if she might preserve that bridge of light. But she could not hold on. Cold aloneness closed around her.

"Your light . . ." she heard Torrin say, but when she looked up he had risen and was turning to stare up the trail.

"It failed," she said to his back. "I'm sorry."

He shook his head, but did not speak until the dead were laid out and the horses tethered and Liath was standing. Then he turned around and said, "Well, at least we have identified your problem."

She rubbed her face and realized she was crying. The tears made runnels in the caked blood on her cheeks. Her clothes were stiff. She reeked. She hurt. "I'm alive," she said, looking at the carnage along the trail. The Blooded Mountains were, now.

The two of them had formed a small pocket in the midst of the regrouping. Heff handed Liath a wet cloth, gesturing that it was mountain runoff, so she shouldn't get any in her mouth. Even the water here could kill you. This was a place of death. She scrubbed her face with the icy flannel; it came away red. Fresh tears ran hot down her cheeks, then cooled in the winter air.

"You can't cast through another's pain," Torrin said.

He was still talking about her light, about what was wrong with *her*, when he and his people had made a blood-soaked slaughterground of their mountains, as they would make of the world if they were permitted to. His light and his paintings and his song had the flavor of pride, and love, and burning intellect, and deep hurt, and no evil at all; yet his deeds resulted in *this*.

"Your light deserted you at two healings," he went on.

She regarded him with pity and disgust. "You're surrounded by the dead, your own folk, and you're . . ." She couldn't finish.

He closed his eyes briefly, but persisted, "It is some sort of empathy, perhaps—"

"Stop it! Just stop it! Eiden's bloody balls, what *are* you? A one-man triad . . . spirits, the danger of it! And your binding song . . . a blasphemy . . ." She groaned. As she'd raised her voice, Kazhe had moved to Torrin's side, and she felt Heff's touch on her back. "*People have died here. What difference does my magelight make? You didn't even need it!*"

"It makes a very great difference," Torrin said quietly. He was watching her instead of looking at the dead; there was something distracted in his eyes, a sense of enforced focus on her. Was he doing this to avoid confronting the horror he had made? "I did need your light, Illuminator. A casting never works as well with one as with two, or three. Pain blocks you from using your magelight as a tool. But it does not block your light itself."

"We've got to go, Torrin," Benkana said, offering the reins of his dun gelding. He was whole, as if no arrow had ever pierced him, but looked drained. "Seven of them are dead, three ran away. We lost Indar and Ashara, Gill and Kael. We'll leave the others for their own folk, or the bonemen—but their folk will come, and we can't stand against a second attack."

Torrin ignored him, pointedly awaiting Liath's response.

She gave up and addressed the issue so they could move on. "It's not *other people's pain*. I couldn't cast the whole time I was in the Holding."

Torrin waited a long time, watching her. Then, accepting the reins at last, just before he turned to mount, he answered her.

"Precisely," he said.

Ragged and stained, packing their dead, they came into the Darkmage's fastness: an encampment and foundry in a caldera atop the only scalable mountain in the Druilors. Cupped in a rounded yellow ridge, the caldera was a rock-strewn expanse of red earth with a lake at its center; around the lake's edge was a village of tents in all shapes and sizes, bramble-thatched huts woven of thorny branches, scrapwood lean-tos and earthen hovels. Loads of charcoal and firewood had been carted in, and the muted ring of hammers on anvils filled the air. They were making weapons from the iron that was the one thing these mountains had in abundance. And they were learning to use them: around the hodgepodge of temporary dwellings was a regimented efficiency of drills and practices and marches.

They were equipping and training a horde of killers.

Liath saw again the vision of ruined Ardra, broken children in the streets, but now it was a human storm, sweeping Headward to crush everything she loved. The gentle folk of the Belt flinging their insults. The rolling Heartlands quilted with farms. The Neck, where they'd be cutting timber and breaking sod, preparing to build and plant in sowmid. Folk would not stand by and watch a horde ride on the Holding. But peaceful farm folk with farm tools couldn't hold against trained fighters armed with tools of death. Eiden Myr would bathe in blood, on the word of an insane man.

"Sweet spirits," Torrin said, as if he'd never seen the place.

Several figures detached themselves from working groups and came to meet them. Liath recognized Verlein's long stride. They dismounted and walked the last dozen threfts. Behind them, sentries she hadn't seen were now skylined on the rim, directing guards below them to lever boulders across the opening.

Verlein clapped Kazhe hard on the shoulders, then turned to survey the rest of them. "Hello, Torrin," she said. "It's good you're here." She looked older, harder; she had lost the swagger, and held herself in the relaxed stance of someone accustomed to command. "Benkana. You lost too many on the way in. Unacceptable. Take the bodies to the bonefield." Her green eyes flicked to Liath. "Hello, mageling. I understand you've been a bit of trouble." When Liath made no reply, she turned to delegate the care of the horses and the preparation of sleeping quarters, fresh clothes. "We'll feed you in the big tent," she announced with a smile that hid more than it showed. "I'd say your return calls for celebration, don't you?"

"What have you done, Verlein?" Torrin said.

"What had to be done," she snapped.

"I left you to guard my mages. I left you assembling a small band of fighters, with the suicidal intent of attacking the Ennead, as if you'd learned nothing from your first foray."

"There weren't enough of us in sowmid," she said. "We lacked mage-craft's protection. I won't make that mistake again."

"Where did all these people come from?"

"They volunteered. Folk are angry. They listened to you, Torrin, wasn't that what you wanted? You should be pleased. I'm quite proud of them. They'll pull down your Holding for you."

"They will die."

"Not all of them."

"They will kill."

"Only the people they're meant to!" She got hold of herself. "This is not the place for this discussion."

Kazhe's hand was on the blade at her belt; she looked pained, uncertain. But she had moved closer to Torrin and away from Verlein. Benkana, the reins of the corpses' horses gathered in his hand, had put himself behind Kazhe.

Their positions were clear. Verlein grinned to see it. "My senior folk, arrayed with a mage too weak to make good on his promises. Magecraft will defeat magecraft, he said. Yet here we stand, the Holding's darkcraft battering at the walls, and the Ennead cozy in their mountain. Push has come to shove, Wordsmith. Defeat them now, with the mages you have, or I will do it for you. My way."

fROST

Light angled off the sharp facets of the sapphire she turned in her hands. The walls danced with light: lamps and candles were surrounded by quartz, firestone, emerald, opal. All the castoffs and tailings of the mines, bagged for tallystones or gamepieces, worthless.

Worthless because they were pretty, and being pretty didn't plow the fields or milk the cows or shear the sheep.

But they were hard, and they were glitter-bright, and they would last forever. Cut properly, they would concentrate light into a burning point. Some, like carnelian, absorbed light, filled themselves with a suffusion and released nothing. Some split light into a spectrum of color; the ceiling was awash in rainbows. Some soaked up magelight and gave it back in a moon-silver glow. One of those she'd had set in a pewter ring. It would be the sigil of the new order, the first of its kind, and she the first to wear it.

Deluded peasants, she thought, drawing the edge of a clear stone along the wall, idly fingering the groove it had left. This stone, a shard of petrified ice, was the hardest of all. The stone that cut all other stone. How could they not see the vast potential in such a thing? Ignorant fools. They did not deserve to rule the land, though they'd earned the honor of grubbing in it.

Magecraft was power. Magelight was power. How absurd, to use it to help farmers live their sorry lives. Mages were the world's elite. It was time they began acting as such, and past time they were treated as such. The proxies were a start, with the Ennead over them and the stewards to serve them. But even the Ennead was a bad joke, with its hidebound traditions and requirements.

I'll show them, Father, she thought. *I'll show them how things ought to be run. And I'll show you.*

She scooped up a handful of smaller stones and let them fall in a sparkle through her fingers. They were light crystallized, a symbol of all that magelight could be—light and color compacted to a brilliant hardness, without warmth. She would be like them: the brightest and most impervious of all things.

She herself would be the stone that cut all other stone. Nothing would stand against her, nothing would shine brighter, and nothing, nothing, would ever break her.

hey ate Girdle-style, lined up cross-legged along planks set in
the middle of an enormous canvas tent strung on ropes and
warmed, minimally, by braziers. The food was simple and
bland—potato stew, dried fruit, oatcakes, grass jelly—but there was
plenty of it. That Verlein kept this inaccessible place supplied, fed and
warmed and clothed all these people, provided casting materials for a nonned mages, was a miracle of organization, and she was proud of it. "But
it only has to last another moon, two at most," she said. "Winter's wind-
ing down. Soon we'll march."

Liath and Heff sat across from Torrin, who treated them as guests; this
galled Kazhe, who wanted to truss them up somewhere. Torrin was framed
by Kazhe and Benkana. To Kazhe's left was Verlein, and to Benkana's
right was an albino named Jhoss, a former beekeeper who seemed to be
some sort of advisor to Torrin. Fighters were seated all around them, blades
strapped to their backs even at supper; mages sat at the other plank table.
She'd seen Torrin exchange hard words with their leader, a woman in
reckoner's garb. Afterward the woman had reported to Verlein. The mages
here, it seemed, backed the fighters who had originally been stationed to
protect them. But they did not sit together.

"Your blades will avail you naught against the Ennead," Torrin said.
They had argued about this, sporadically, all afternoon. "They have
warded themselves."

"Not possible," Verlein replied. "Can you ward me against blades?
By all means do it."

"A blade may be the only way to stop you from killing."

Verlein grinned. "You can't cast such a warding. Nor can the Ennead."

"It is not in my power. But believe me, Verlein, they can. They possess power that I do not."

"Then your magecraft can never defeat them, and staking everything on it is a mistake, as I have always said. This is our job now, Torrin. You've done your teaching, you've shown us all the truth. It's time to put the future in our hands."

"You are a fool."

"Perhaps; only a fool would rush in where she's fairly certain to be killed. But it's worth it to me if it puts a stop to them."

"It will be for nothing. Your good, strong, decent life, extinguished for nothing."

"Extinguished? Like a light? I'm not a mage."

"Every life is a light."

"Then the world will be a ninefold dimmer when I'm through."

"Your plan is a waste of resources and lives," Torrin persisted. "This is not the way. With the darkcraft at their command, the Ennead will wipe your forces away with one storm, one earthquake, one brush of ink on parchment."

"Not with your mages to counteract their castings."

"They're not my mages any longer. If they ever were."

"Our mages, then. Or mine. It doesn't matter. They'll keep the Ennead off us on the slopes of the Aralinns."

"As they've kept them off you here? Your message said you needed my help against their attacks."

Verlein glanced at Benkana. "It won't hurt. But what I need is your presence. I need Torrin Mage. You are the reason these people have rallied to me. It's *your* words they believe in."

"I am ill suited to be a figurehead."

"I'm ill suited to care how you feel about it." She leaned forward to shout down the length of the plank: "Eshadri! How about that brandy you smuggled in!"

"You will get these people killed, and do it in my name."

"The fighters are willing to die for you. Most have lost a family member or friend or lover to the Holding; the others believe completely in your cause. We'll see the mages safe."

"Not against that kind of power!"

"Our mages outnumber them nine to one. We'll make up in sheer volume what they have in concentrated power. Our magelight will burn them from their black keep, and all their dark power with them. Blades will do the rest."

"*It doesn't work that way.*"

Verlein would not heed him. His mages backed her now. He had lost control—if he'd ever had it.

"I *will* stop the Ennead," he said quietly.

"How? By teaching people to read your little squiggles? That will stop the flayings and the deaths?"

"If you would tell us," Jhoss said. His voice was a soft hiss. "If you would describe precisely what you plan to do."

Torrin seemed to struggle with himself, but said, "The time is coming. You must be patient."

"*Patient?*" Verlein burst out. "We must regain control of this world, Torrin. We must take control back from the Ennead, now, or we'll never *get* it back."

"And is that all you want, Verlein? Control? Does it matter to you at all who you kill that you might *control* things?"

Verlein swore at him in disgust and rose to her feet, but paused when Jhoss said, almost too softly to hear, "There *is* reason for haste, Torrin. At this very moment, Ennead victims are screaming, dying in agony."

Torrin flinched. "Yes," he said. "I know."

"We'll march as soon as the ground firms up," Verlein said, and left the tent, a group of her fighters falling in behind her.

The ambient noise took on a strident hilarity as the brandy casks were distributed and tin cups filled.

"There isn't time," Torrin said to Jhoss. He looked very alone in the midst of the revelers. "There isn't time to teach them all they need to know."

Jhoss said, "Leave it to us. There will be lifetimes for such teaching, when it's over."

"But who will remain to learn?" Torrin rose wearily and made for the exit, Kazhe on his heels. At the tent flap he shooed her away. She objected, and lost, and returned smoldering to her place.

"I'll watch him," Benkana said, touching her arm lightly.

She nodded, staring at the plank, then downed the brandy someone had poured in her cup.

"He is safe here," Jhoss said when Benkana had gone.

Her eyes fell on Liath. "As long as he stays away from *her*."

Heff nudged Liath and said, It is time to go.

As Liath started to get up, Kazhe said, "Oh, no, Illuminator. You haven't even touched your brandy. Eshadri nearly killed himself getting that cartload up here. It's not often we celebrate with a drink. A toast, before you go. Sit."

Liath hesitated. Heff said, She wants to keep you in view.

She's angry, Liath thought, *and she wants someone to take it out on.* But better to sit than cause a ruckus. She could hold a few brandies. Eventually Kazhe would be compelled to check on Torrin, and by then it would be time to sleep.

She inclined her head, sat down, and raised her cup. "To Eiden Myr."

"To Torrin Wordsmith," Kazhe said, and looked around for a third—

but Jhoss was sitting with his arms folded, observing them with eerie pink eyes, and the others had moved off. After a moment, Heff made a gesture and raised his own cup.

"What did he say?" Kazhe asked.

Liath resisted several urges and said, "To life and safety."

Kazhe drained her cup. Heff and Liath did the same, Heff in three measured draughts, Liath in one. Immediately Kazhe filled the cups again and lifted hers. "Go on," she said, prompting with her free hand. "A toast doesn't count unless you drink three."

"Where Heff comes from, three sips is sufficient," Liath said, "and where I come from, one is sufficient." It wasn't bad stuff, unsweetened, distilled from a good vintage, but one *was* sufficient.

Kazhe's face darkened. "Drink, I said."

"And I said no. But don't let me stop you."

"Afraid of what you'll do, *eh?*" Kazhe said, mimicking Liath's accent. "You Northers never could hold your drink."

Liath smiled very slowly. She ignored Heff's cautioning hand on her arm and tossed the brandy at the back of her throat. It went down a smooth burn in the wake of the other, filling her sinuses with a redolent tang. Eyes locked on Kazhe, she refilled the cup and downed that, then poured for them both again. "Just so you don't get ahead of me," she said sweetly. This one soaked into her limbs, tingling in fingers and toes.

"Maybe you're not such a pathetic mageling after all," Kazhe said. "But I'll still drink you under the table."

"There is no table."

Kazhe leaned across the plank and hissed, "Then I'll drink you under the ground."

A fighter nearby took note. "Benkana will have your skin."

"Spirits take Benkana!" Kazhe cried, slamming her empty cup down. The tin dented in her fist.

"Is that who keeps you in line, when you're not being Torrin's lap-dog?" Liath said. Heff elbowed her hard, and when she rolled her eyes at him went for the cask; her hands and Kazhe's tangled as they reached to stop him.

Fine, Heff gestured, rising. I won't be responsible for this.

"What did he say?" Kazhe demanded, watching Heff's exit.

"He said that Liath Illuminator thinks you're a toerag."

Kazhe froze, then roared with laughter and poured another.

The cask emptied steadily, and an audience formed. Another cask materialized to replace the spent one when the time came. Their impromptu fling grew more heated and less intelligible as the evening wore on. Bets were laid, and a grunting chant went up as they lifted cups to lips in unison. *Brandy*, Liath thought at one point. *Brandy. I must be mad.* At another point she looked around to see only hard-muscled people wearing blades on their backs, at their belts, in their boots; all the mages had gone, and she had a dim memory of some look of revulsion, as if she had betrayed them. Betrayed *them*! She drank, and said, "Why do you follow him?"

Kazhe's red-rimmed eyes seemed to have trouble finding Liath's face. "Because he is very precious," she said, enunciating with care. "Because he won't stop going into dangerous places."

They drank, and Kazhe said, "If you touch him again, I'll take your arms off and stuff them down your throat. If you break his heart, I'll take your *heart* out and stuff it down your throat."

"If I *what*?" But Kazhe had already forgotten, or couldn't hear her, and someone was filling her cup again, and Kazhe was still upright, still able to bring her cup to her lips, so Liath did too.

"To Indar!" Kazhe cried suddenly, lifting her empty cup, then letting someone steady her hand and pour for her. "To Indar!" the crowd echoed. Liath drank to the man who had fallen dead on top of her, and felt abruptly ill.

Kazhe grinned the fighters' feral grin. "Would you like to lie down, mageling?" she said. "You were good at lying down while brave folk died around you."

"You were brave yourself, when you ambushed an unarmed mage with that big blade of yours." She surveyed the sweating, laughing fighters. "Did she tell you Heff disarmed her with bare hands?"

Kazhe had her knife out and pressed against Liath's throat before the next breath, unerringly, as if she'd had not a drop—as if the blade were a part of her that drink couldn't affect. "You've had this coming, Ennead pus," she rasped.

"So brave," Liath said without budging. "So brave with your little knife in your hand."

Kazhe jerked back with an oath. She thrust the knife into the plank, then shrugged out of the crosswise belt that strapped the long blade to her back. Piece by piece, she divested herself of weapons, until an array of blades lay on the plank and she could display her empty palms.

"If only I could get the rest of you to do that," Liath said in astonishment, and then Kazhe was on her.

They wrestled loosely, drunkenly, in the center of the tent; then strong arms lifted them, propelled them into the dirt outside, and they scrabbled to their feet as the crowd poured out, laughing and drinking, shouting encouragement. Liath's eye was distracted by a lantern someone set by. Kazhe's fist caught her in the jaw. The ground slammed up. But she saw the boot coming, and grabbed it, and took her down. Again they wrestled, neither able to get a lock; then Liath's hands got a good grip in Kazhe's clothes, and she flipped her hard, scrambling up just before Kazhe did.

They circled warily, hands spread, knees flexed. Kazhe was a head shorter, but she was all muscle, with a low center of weight. She moved beautifully, fluid and relaxed with drink, but she trusted too much in her own skills. Liath waited until Kazhe bared her teeth, thinking that Liath, overmatched and on the defensive, would never strike first. Then she feinted left and landed her right fist in the center of Kazhe's flat nose.

Kazhe staggered back, stunned, but caught herself up fast and lunged at Liath while she was still overbalanced. Liath got her arm up and blocked the blow, then jabbed at Kazhe's midriff, but she had twisted away, anticipating again, and her elbow whipped into Liath's face. Liath let herself go down, then kicked hard as Kazhe came toward her; the boot meant for her groin caught her hip and spun her around. By the time Liath was up she had her balance again, like a wooden children's toy that couldn't be knocked over.

Three more times they grappled, slowing as the pain of broken bones reached past the brandy blur and blood ran into their eyes. Each time they came up even, or evenly dazed. The fuel of the liquor had run out. Someone suggested they call it a draw, and someone else protested that the bets weren't decided yet.

"Someday, Illuminator, I am going to have to kill you," Kazhe gritted through a split lip—then keeled over like a sawn tree.

Liath looked blearily at the shocked-silent crowd. "I win," she slurred, and went to her knees, blood roaring in her ears.

Heff hauled her up by the armpits. He had been there before. She remembered now. He had let them fight it out. She tried to shake him off, but her legs weren't working. As he dragged her into the clear night, her eye caught on a pale face at the edge of the circle of lanternglow.

The face was there when she woke, and there again when she woke again later, but only in her mind's eye. She probed at her jaw, the ridge over her eye, her nose—all whole. Only scrapes and bruises remained. He had been there, then. He had healed her.

Heff rose from a stool in the corner of the tent and said, It wasn't him. I wouldn't let him. Others came. They wouldn't do the hangover. You're on your own there.

She took the mug of tepid tea he offered, and sipped gingerly. It tasted bitter—an infusion of willow bark, like what they'd given her in the Aralinns—but it cleared the lint from her mouth. "I have a hard head," she said. "I'll be all right by midday."

You have a stupid head, Heff replied.

She looked up in a panic, then winced. "What did I say?"

"Nothing you shouldn't have, from what they tell me," Torrin said, ducking under the entry flap. "Feeling better?"

"I will be."

He smiled.

No, she thought, at the sight of that smile. No.

He was not the man she had been sent to find. There was no evil in him. She had tasted his light, through the bridge of their hands; it was bright, dangerously bright, impossibly, wonderfully bright, bright enough to change the world, destroy it, save it—but there was no dark taint to it.

"Go away," she said.

He nodded. "All right. But I'd like a word with you, when you're up to it." He paused at the entry to say, "Quite a right cross you have there."

She didn't watch him leave. "So," she said to Heff. "How do we get out of here?"

We don't, he replied. You wanted to find him. You've found him. You're stuck with him.

"There has to be a way."

It's too well guarded.

"With mages?"

With fighters. They won't have to smell your magelight. They'll hear you, see you, sniff you out. They've been training hard since summer.

"I can't be trapped here," she said. "I have to get back."

He shrugged: You should have thought of that before.

She glared at him, but he was unmoved. She'd won no points with her behavior last night. But spirits it had felt good.

"Then come on. Let's see what other trouble we can make."

She looked for work with the mages in their tent, as large as the meal tent but filled with casting circles. There was no question that someone knew where the camp was; the castings were almost continuous, wardings and diversions, day and night. The mages were overworked, short on sleep, haggard and irritable. But they would not let her cast with them. She couldn't blame them. She *couldn't* be trusted; she'd do anything she could to undermine their work, to let bad weather through the cracks.

"You had only to express doubt in the Ennead, mistrust of them, anything," the leader said—Serafad, in reckoner's clothes. "Anything but the blind allegiance you exuded. There were always sympathetic proxies. You could have come to us at any time."

"But I was too loyal," she said.

"Yes." She dismissed Liath with a cool glance.

Heff was in demand at every forge. She found him standing like a prentice beside Auda, a big-breasted, jovial woman who claimed to have resurrected the art of bladecasting.

"Kazhe knew how to use blades, and Verlein knew how to use blades-men—but *I* knew how to make them. The blades, not the bladesmen, though I've made a few of them as well. I don't have all this muscle on my arm for nothing! Tireless, I am."

"How did you come by such a craft?" Liath asked. The woman reminded her of Geara's sisters.

"Handed down to me. Hadn't ever done it—never saw the point, ah ah—but I heard it described at my mother's knee, and as soon as I saw that beautiful warded thing of Kazhe's, I knew what to do. Not that I didn't innovate a little here and there, and I'll never make a piece like hers—whoever cast that blade used magecraft in some way long forgotten. But when Verlein asked for more in summer, and told me why, I was quick to oblige. I'm always quick to oblige," she said, leering at Heff.

With Liath to translate his questions, he learned quickly. Auda kept up a bawdy patter—"Look at the size of him! I'm covered now!"—but she and Heff shared a love of working metal, and seemed to bond over the forge. "I've been with plenty of men who should have had a sack over their heads," she said. "Balls, I should have a sack over *my* head!" But she took Heff's good-natured rebuffs with good humor of her own, and was impressed with the blade he crafted on first try.

Heff ran a strop along the edge, lifted it and turned it to catch the light, regarding it thoughtfully—then brought it down hard on a chunk of firewood, making a cut as neat as an axe's.

And this kills? he said. That's all it's good for?

Liath translated, and Auda, giving him a funny look, nodded.

He thanked Auda for the lesson; then, without fanfare, he tossed the blade on a rubbish heap and went off to find a forge where they were making something else.

"I guess that's what he thinks of your battle blades, eh?" Liath said.

Auda could have laughed it off, or cursed Heff for an ingrate, but she turned very seriously to Liath and said, "Yes. And he's right. But someday one of these might save your life." She retrieved the blade. "Best keep it out of the midden heap till then, wouldn't you say?"

Liath took the blade. A battle blade, a longblade, saved her life in the mountains, and might save it again.

Auda, as she might say, had a point.

The woman let her take the weapon, but Kazhe came from nowhere and relieved her of it. Liath looked for Torrin, then cursed herself and turned her attention to Kazhe, who was saying, "You shouldn't be playing with things you don't understand."

"I thought we settled this last night," Liath said, looking down on the towhead from her full height.

Kazhe grinned up at her. "That was only round one. You scored on the drink, but the fight was a draw. If we'd been using these, no contest."

"No argument. I don't use blades."

"I'll teach you," Kazhe said.

Liath snorted.

"Come on. I'll teach you. It will let me keep an eye on you while I drill."

"That's very convenient. No."

"I dare you, publican. You're pretty good in a brawl. But next time, we fight on *my* terms."

"You'd teach me badly so I'd lose."

Kazhe laughed. "I wouldn't have to."

"If I wanted to learn your bloody craft, I'd be better off going to Verlein."

"I'm the one who taught Verlein."

Liath blinked.

"When Verlein met Torrin, she was a harvestmaster grieving a cousin lost to the Ennead and arguing with reckoners who wouldn't listen to her troubles."

"And who taught you?"

"My father, out on the plains, far from sight. His folk believed it would come in handy one day. It did. Verlein wanted to bring down the Ennead. I taught her how."

"And now she's a deathmaster. You must be very proud."

"I am. She's good. No one will train you better, mage, I promise you. And then we'll see who ends up in the dirt."

He was there. She sensed him, as his magelight came in range, and glanced over her shoulder. He was frowning.

"All right," she said. "You're on."

"Good. You'll start with the last arrivals. When you're ready to have me alone, I'll let you know. In the meantime, I've set Lannan to guard you. He's right over there. Make friends with him. You're going to be sleeping together."

The blades were not hard to lift, but tiring to wield and hard to control. Bladework was endless pounding at another human being until you'd found a way past his shield to do him grievous harm. It was a matter of whose arms got tired first. Liath hated it. She understood tavern brawls; she understood anger so strong it made you want to pulp another person's face. She understood the pure enjoyment of fighting, the release of tension built up over weeks of tedious hard work. But she did not understand this. What harm you could do another with your fist, your boots, was the harm dogs or squalling cats could do: nasty, but natural in a way that these blades were not. What harm you could do with what came to hand—a stool, a jug, a paring knife—lacked the vicious forethought of these weapons. They were meant to dismember, disembowel. There was no grace or honor to them. They symbolized the end of the world.

But she learned to use them. Day after aching day she wielded the wooden practice blades of increasing weight. Her pain was less than some others'; years spent hauling barrels put more muscle on the arms than years spent chasing goats or wrestling sheep, though the chasers and wrestlers had wind and agility she lacked. She scrabbled to her feet each time she was knocked down, reminded that were this real she would be missing a leg or a hand, as if that would frighten her into better performance, or inure her to the horror of what they played at.

"And who will you be fighting?" she asked Verlein, when she came to observe for a while and Kazhe was correcting someone else's mistakes. "People loyal to the Ennead that protects them, loyal to their way of life. Those are the people who will go back to their hoes and their shears and their milkbarns missing legs and hands, if they go back at all. How can you contemplate such evil?"

"To stop a greater evil," Verlein said coldly. "And if the farmers have any sense, they'll get out of our way. We'll be fighting the Ennead's forces. You didn't think they overlooked the power of iron, did you?"

"You underestimate those farmers," Liath said. "They won't get out of your way."

When Verlein shrugged, Liath wondered if the Ennead had set her the wrong task. Perhaps it wasn't Torrin they should fear.

To fight a greater evil. She refused to believe; but still she learned. If there were going to be folk running around swinging blades, she would be bloody sure to meet them blow for blow.

And she learned because Torrin frowned on it. She took up weapons to spite him. When her arms ached their worst, when her back screamed and her legs shook, when she itched all over from ground-in mud and could not see her skin for the bruises, she sought him out, and raised her blade, and smiled.

This is what you've made of them, her smile said. *And because you hate it, I'll become one too.*

Her own cruelty shamed and stung her, and she lifted the blade higher, every time, in defiance of it.

The most repulsive was Lannan, raving about the glory their battles would bring them. "There were songs about such battles, in olden times," he said. "Songs with words, that told stories, before the binders took all the songs for themselves and forgot the words. Those songs are lost now, but we'll make up new ones, to celebrate our courage and our victories."

"*Glory?*" Liath was appalled. "You call it *glory*? There's more glory in turning a midden." He would glory in ending as many human lives as he possibly could—would glory even in the end of his own life, as long as he'd killed enough to die with honor. It turned her stomach. It terrified her.

Kazhe, noxious as she was, at least didn't suffer from the delusion that killing was glorious. To Kazhe, the *craft* of it was glorious. She respected the blade, and took very seriously what the blade could do—but she didn't take pleasure in it.

"Then step in, like this—come, you step in to me—and catch the crossguard there—right—now twist—harder, you idiot, *twist*—"

Kazhe's blade sprang away into the dirt.

"Very good," she said, bending to retrieve it. Her bangs fell forward over her eyes. "And if I hadn't been wearing gloves, that would have taken a finger or two with it." Liath stood holding the blade Heff had forged. Suddenly she was down, a sharp pain in her leg, and Kazhe stood over her. "And that's what your opponent would have done had you hesitated in finishing it,, the way you hesitated just now."

"I wasn't going to—*finish* you," Liath said, wincing. She ignored the hand Kazhe offered and got painfully to her feet.

"You should have been. You hate me. You hate Torrin. I've put a real blade in your hand."

"*I don't want to kill him,*" Liath snarled.

"Good," Kazhe said. "But somebody, someday, is going to want to kill you, and you'll have to do a lot better than that."

Verlein was the most frightening one. There was a grim satisfaction about her, as if the world was finally being set right. *Now we'll be able to handle things,* she seemed to say. *Now we'll be able to run things properly.* And Liath thought, *There aren't enough bonefolk in all the world to clean up after you've handled it.*

Then there was Jhoss, ethereally pale, like a creature of mist or moonlight made stark and grotesque by the light of day. Jhoss believed that death was a regrettable necessity. As if "I'm sorry" would make up for the crippled and the dead. His cold skin, his cold eyes, his cold, pragmatic heart were worse than Lannan's sickening excitement. Jhoss—calm, slight, easy to overlook except for his white skin and pink eyes—was a being out of nightmare.

"I frighten you," he said, coming upon her silently where she sat watching fighters drill in formation. It had the pattern and rhythm of dance.

"*That* frightens me," she said.

He sat beside her on the damp log, plumping his cloak behind him, and set a wooden case at their feet. "I frighten you because you think in colors, and I have no color. You work with pigment, and my flesh has no pigment."

"You're white and pink," she said—*like the rats that have bred in our coldcellar so long they've gone pale as slugs.*

"Then those are the colors we all are, underneath." He opened the case. It was filled with sedgeweave offcuts and tattered quills. Practice materials.

"You're not a mage. You shouldn't have those."

"You're not a fighter. You shouldn't be learning bladework. Yet it is a tool you know may serve you someday. So is scribing."

She sat back, tonguing a back tooth with an *uh-uh-uh.* "You are not going to teach me to scribe. Haven't you heard? I'm a loyalist."

"You are a traditionalist. Who made the traditions?"

"I've had this conversation with seekers. I'm not going to have it with you."

He squeezed an inkpot between his skinny thighs to warm it, and dipped a quill. Liath winced as he scribed something across the top of the sedgeweave.

"My name," he said. "In Celyrian, the standard glyphs we use. Is that not remarkable? And yet no mages run screaming from their casting tent, crying that their castings fail."

"They would if everyone in the world did it."

"Superstition. Understandable. But unfortunate." He scribed another word; even Liath could see that scribing was relatively new to him. She'd seen prentices do better in their third year. "My name in Ghardic, a system of glyphs developed to represent a different tongue. Even more remarkable, yes? And proof that wordsmiths should not be entrusted with such a precious thing. They have lost an unknowable number of these systems over the ages, until only Celyrian remains. In the process they weakened their own power. Celyrian was a language of healing. Other languages, other poetics, were more effective for other tasks. Would you not wish your wordsmiths to have that power restored to them?"

"I don't understand a thing you're saying, and I won't be a party to *that*."

He plugged the inkpot and changed the subject. "Your friend is doing well. He has fashioned a sort of tunic out of iron links, not easy for a blade to pierce. He hammered metal bands across a wooden shield. Now they're all doing it. An inspiration."

"That will only keep them alive longer so they can kill more."

"Surely you don't mean that."

"No. Not really. He's protecting them. That's what he does. I wish we could protect everyone."

"That is what Torrin wishes."

"It's not the same. And he's deluded."

"I believe him."

Liath forced a laugh. "Good on you."

"The Ennead would harm a great many folk who don't even know they exist. Torrin wishes to stop them. The Ennead does harm in their practice of magecraft. Torrin would stop that. Wordsmiths reserving a powerful means of communication for themselves harms us all. Torrin would see words freed for everyone to use."

"We all use words. No one's stopping us."

"But most cannot scribe them. Imagine, Liath. If all could scribe. The messages we could send. The records we could keep. The business we could transact—accurately, across wide regions. What we could build. What we could learn. What we could become." His pink eyes burned with a fervor that made Torrin seem sane. His thin fingers curled tightly around the quill.

"Travelers carry messages. Tellers remember. Merchants do business the length and breadth of Eiden Myr. Without magecraft to preserve them, your records would rot in a matter of years."

"But imagine that we could have both."

She had begun to get a glimmer of the visions that populated his febrile imagination. She blinked hard to clear her mind of them. "We can't," she said. "And that's an end on it."

His waxy cheeks sank inward when he smiled; he looked like a bad imitation of a boneman. "But we can, Liath. We will."

One after another she came to know them. Fighters and thinkers, mages and crafters, willing to die for what Torrin told them. Their faith was fierce and profound. How could they all be wrong? She had seen how the Ennead's stewards manipulated the vocates. What did she really know of the Nine, after all, but what she had wanted to believe in the first place?

Sometimes she wanted to kill them all—stop it, right now, by running each one through with the sharp, shining tool they let her play with. That was when the blade felt heaviest of all.

"A word, Illuminator, if you will," he would say, every few days. "A word, when you're ready." "A word, when your work is done." She spent her spare time in food preparation, which Kazhe seemed to think was some kind of punishment. She would nod at him and continue peeling or stirring. But she would not meet his kind, sad eyes, or let his quiet voice into her mind. His story was too well crafted to disbelieve, his gentle words too horrifying to countenance. If she listened, he *would* turn her. If she looked, he would steal her heart. Perhaps he already had.

If he held out his hand, she was afraid she would take it.

She would never go.

The moon turned and the air began to smell of sowmid; bitter cold became damp chill, and the ground went to mud. Supplies ran short and tempers grew taut.

My journey year is nearly over, Liath thought. *I left within a nineday of Ve Galandra. When the moon turns, Ve Galandra will come again.*

Gondril had told her, when she set out, "*You will have your journey year to accomplish the task—if Torrin Darkmage isn't stopped by Ve Galandra next, he'll be too powerful to stop at all.*"

It didn't look that way from here. But they had access to information she didn't. They'd given her an assignment. They were the *Ennead*.

But they had kept things from her. It was possible that everything Torrin said was true.

They'd warned her. They'd warned her that better mages than she had been turned by him. They'd *expected* him to turn her, and only sent her at all because he couldn't use her light. To enable her to make it back to them, they'd depended on her strength of will. On her faith in generations of Enneads doing whatever they must to protect and serve the world she believed in.

Or on her blind, pathetic allegiance.

She pressed the heels of her hands hard against her eyes, until she saw stars. But there was no enlightenment in them.

It was Torrin's word against the Ennead's.

The only way to know for sure was to go back.

That night, before he turned the lamp down, Heff said, Do you know why blacksmiths often work in near-darkness?

Liath, distracted, shook her head.

Because the color and brightness of molten metal tells them when it's ready to be worked and where the weak spots are.

She didn't understand.

Some things, he said, can be seen clearest only in the dark.

"I know you're planning something," Lannan broke in. He hated her one-sided conversations with Heff. Sometimes they laid bets on how long he could hold out before he started whining.

"I'm planning the glorious song I will sing when I kill you, Lannan," she said.

She had beaten him the last three times in the practice ring, with wooden blades and iron. He blanched and shut his mouth, taking up his nighttime post outside the tent.

Liath waited until Heff was snoring; when he snored he was nearly impossible to wake. "Lannan!" she whispered sharply at the tent entry. When he stuck his head in, she knocked it hard with a rock she had smuggled in under her coat the last time she used the latrine, and caught him as he fell. He was only dazed; she hit him again, her body recoiling. He checked on her several times a night, shining a lantern on her face. She needed his blades.

Verlein had stepped up the production of weapons, itchy to be ready. Across the encampment, hammers would pound on anvils till dawn. The glare of their fires created pockets of deep shadow. She had memorized the pattern of her route; darkness made it unfamiliar, but she found her way to the lake, and around it, and to the fissure that crossed to the sloped caldera wall. There were handholds, footholds—precarious but manageable. Up was easier than down, but she would worry about that later.

Sentries patrolled the entirety of the rim. They carried lanterns. She'd almost pointed out the flaw to Verlein. As one approached her, she slipped to the other side of the rim, dug her feet into crumbling redrock, and hung on. The footsteps, the lantern, did not pause on their way by. She pulled herself up, wincing as loose debris fell away down the far side. The lantern didn't bobble. She had a dozen threfts before the next one.

Don't notice me don't notice me don't make me fight you, she beseeched each sentry silently, and three more passed her by unknowing. After the fourth, when she had almost decided to make her way down, her foothold crumbled.

She slid into darkness. Stones gouged her. How far? Spirits, how far down? She slid, and slid, and slid, spinning around headfirst, raking the heels of her hands in a desperate attempt to brake, then spinning again and beginning to roll. They had denuded the slope of brush. They needed fuel for their forge fires. She would fall, and fall, until there was only empty air and no rock at all anymore—

She fetched up hard against a stand of thorn trees. They bent, and held. Dirt and pebbles went skittering past. She stilled her breath against her thundering heart. One sentry called to another. The lanterns neared, converged at the top of the slope. One of them came partway down; the other cautioned against a trap. "Ach, too bloody loose here anyway," the first said, scrambling back up. "You go on, I'll watch."

He was patient. Liath dared not move. But finally the lantern moved off to resume its lengthy to-and-fro. When it was out of view, she turned, got her heels into the coarse soil, tugged free of the thorns that had scored her, and edged down into the blackness. There was no going back up.

After an eternity, the slope bottomed out. More trees blocked her path, less stunted. Soon they were tall enough to walk under. She got up, trembling with cold and the effort of concentration. It was pitch black, but she'd keep feeling her way to the left. Somewhere up there was the trail to the pass. More sentries to avoid. She'd have to burrow down when dawn came, and move again at nightfall. She had no water and no supplies—but there were folk out here who did. The trick would be finding them. Otherwise she'd have three days, at most, to make her way out of here. If she was lucky, the Ennead would send her rain.

Arms closed around her from behind—groping, finding her mouth, clamping down. After the first jolt of surprise, she put up no struggle, even letting herself be disarmed.

This was better than she had hoped.

She was led a long way, past snagging thorns and brambles that caught at her feet, by someone who knew this area well. Then space opened up around her, filled by a dank scent of sulfur. The one who'd captured her gave a low whistle. A torch flared.

Two men—one behind her, one inside the cave. Both thin, drawn, with bulging eyes over unkempt beards. The life of outcasts had been hard on them.

"Look what I found," said the one behind her. "Making more noise than a rat in a barrel of wood chips. And this!" He hefted Lannan's blade admiringly.

"Where are the others?" The one inside moved forward, wary, staring at Liath as if he'd never seen a living thing before.

"I let them go on. All the racket down there, too good an opportunity to miss. Looks like you thought so too, eh, little mage?"

"She'll fetch a good ransom. Maybe even water."

Concern began to edge out relief and satisfaction. "I'm with you," she said. "The Ennead sent me. I carry the means of stopping Torrin Darkmage."

For one breath of complete silence, the two men stared at each other, eyes wide. Then they burst out laughing.

"Stop the Darkmage!" one roared. "The Ennead!" cried the other.

Her mistake cut through her like a blade. They were starved, halfwild, probably poisoned by water they couldn't help but drink. She should be angry at Verlein's people for letting human beings come to this. But she was only frightened now.

"Help me get around the guards on the pass," she said, firming her voice, "and I'll—"

"What? Give us food? Clear water? Warmer clothes?" The man behind her came up close, reaching around and under her cloak to pat her down. "No food in here," he said. His hands slid up to squeeze her breasts. He laughed as she elbowed him, and gave her a shove that sent her spinning into the grip of the other one. "But you do have a something we'd like now. Advance payment. Then we'll see you safe past the guards."

She was twisted hard onto her knees, then facedown against the damp stone of the cave. The man's full weight slammed onto her, pinning her. She reached up for his hair, got an ear instead and twisted. He yelped, and banged her face hard into the stone. When her vision cleared, the one standing had his pants open. The one groping at her breeches said, "No one gets past those guards, little fool. *Do you think we'd be here if we could get past those guards?*" He shoved her again, slapped her head, kneed her hard in the back of the thigh when she made a last-ditch, snarling effort to break free. "I *hate* you!" he cried, pummeling her—less interested in rape than in his own rage. "I'll kill you all!"

"Hey now, don't damage her till I've—"

The man straddling Liath gasped. His grip loosened. She shoved him away, crabbed backward, got Lannan's knife out of her boot. His face contorted. He flung himself at her. She hesitated, unable to plunge the knife into flesh. He squeezed her throat with one hand while the other fisted and drew back to crush her face.

In the next eyeblink, a bonewood knife hilt protruded from the side of his neck. He clutched at it and toppled. She staggered to her feet, her own useless knife dangling from her hand.

The man who had captured her lay on his face, an identical hilt sticking up just inside his left shoulder blade. Beyond him, outside the cave entrance, stood a shadowy figure. Liath sensed a magelight. She squinted past the sputtering torchglare, then took a step forward.

"You cannot get out of these mountains," came a boyish voice. He moved his body into the torch's light. "You must go back."

"Who are you?" she said as he retrieved his blades and handed Lannan's back to her. The crazed man's dying gurgles still filled the cave. The youth did not spare him a glance. He had spiky hair and a fuzz of beard over sunken cheeks that should have been plump. He wore a long-blade on his back and a triskele around his neck. His clothes were stained and ragged. His face was flat and cold.

"I was one of them," he said. "With you gone, I can cover this, perhaps, when the others return from their thieving expedition, which should cover you. But you must go now."

"I can't . . . find . . ." Nothing made sense anymore.

He took her by the arm without a word, so fast she barely saw him move, and pulled her into the darkness as if he could see. When she tried to speak, he dug fingers into her arm. They went past where she thought she'd slid down. He stopped at the foot of a tumble of rocks that looked almost scalable.

"Up," he said against her ear, without breath, and was gone.

There was no choice. She went up, gauging the movement of lanterns—it was easier here, he'd picked a good spot, that should tell her something but she didn't know what—slipping up and over the rim, then bellying over the other side, groping for a toehold.

Down was much harder than up had been. But it wasn't sheer. The bottom curved away. The worst she could do was slide again. A long way. She was shaking nearly too hard to hang on. It was hang on or lie broken on the caldera floor. She hung on, and edged downward, and then flat ground came blessedly under her feet.

And bucked. She sprawled into the rockface. Her smashed cheek exploded in pain. She tasted blood. The ground bucked again; a low rumbling rose up from below, intensified until it couldn't get any louder and then grew louder still, the vibration of rock shaking the air all around her. Stones the size of her head jolted loose and bounded down the slope; one hit her behind the knee and she went down. Getting up again, she turned toward the foundry fires, the shouts. The ground tilted, and she reeled back into the rockface—then pushed off from it, drove herself into a bounding run, crossed a few threfts and went spinning into mud. On all fours, she made it to the lake. Water crested the lip and drenched her. The whole lake sloshed like brandy in a cup. Terror gripped her. The world was shaking apart. There was no safety. Lean-tos were collapsing, horses screaming. She crawled the length of her own body, once, again. They'd need mages.

Someone was racing toward her—then past, plunging into the lake, as if water meant safety when the earth was beyond control. She crawled farther, then came up more from momentum than intent, running low. She had lost all orientation. Where was the mages' tent? Was anyone even on duty? What were the fools *doing?*

People were running everywhere. "The horses!" someone shouted, flying past. Her feet went out from under her. She saw Heff near an intact lantern, scanning the darkness for her magelight. He fixed on her, started toward her. Shadows shoved past him, knocking him back.

The earth opened like a weak seam, a great gaping fissure. Steam hissed into the cold air. Two silhouettes dropped into it and were gone. Heff teetered on the brink, arms windmilling. Liath got to one knee, planted a foot, screaming his name. Wiry arms enclosed her. A mage. She roared inarticulate protest and flung her hands out, reaching for Heff across the abyss. He went down on his rear and sat dazed. The mountain convulsed, shaking him toward the edge; his heels dug furrows in the earth, then slid loose into open air. She could only just see him through the gouts of steam. She was screaming. The arms around her tightened. Torrin said, "*No.*" She struggled viciously, broke free, sprawled at the rim of the fissure. Heat seared her face. Heff threw himself flat, rolled over, and scrabbled away from the edge. Torrin lifted her to her knees and away. "Casting tent," he said. He lost his balance, veered toward the edge, caught her coat and hauled himself back. "*Now.*"

Geysers of steam sprang up all around them. Trying to look back at Heff, she stumbled as Torrin forced her along; he didn't let go, kept dragging her against the endless rumbling that made sound and motion indistinguishable. They burst into the tent, which was skewed on its poles, half down; materials lay scattered, pots broken. Binders were groping to collect what they needed.

The rumbling ceased.

"Keep working," Torrin ordered. "Now, while you can scribe." He pushed mages into triads; Serafad was doing the same. He shoved Liath down across from a binder clutching an armful of vellum and sedgeweave, a handful of quills. She took them so he could gather ink and pigment. Someone snatched the leaves from her, then the quills. "Not you," Serafad said.

"I need her," Torrin said, helping the binder.

"I will be your illuminator."

"Go to your triad, Serafad." He was already scribing, though they could barely see; most of the lanterns lay smashed, flames sputtering against warded canvas.

"She can't be trusted!" Serafad said, grabbing handfuls of her coat, trying to haul her out of the circle. Liath endured it for a moment, then snapped an elbow back into the woman's shin. She hopped away on the other leg, swearing. Liath couldn't take her eyes off Torrin, the stunning transformation of ordinary light as he scribed. He was made of light, his flesh subsumed in a glow that was all colors blending into gold, all scents of hope and loss blending into longing. Her hand twitched, lifted, as if she could touch it. Like Karanthe. She had to know how that light felt.

"I trust her," Torrin said, inking the bottom of the leaf and putting it in Liath's outstretched hand.

What if it fails me again?

Torrin read her face. "Try," he whispered.

She couldn't see, no matter how she angled the leaf. But her guiders blazed cool blue in the dimness. She followed them by feel. A block pattern, for stone. Earthing lines. Kadri for control, balance, peace. She used the pigments the binder handed her, hoping he knew the pots by shape. Just like in the Hand, she thought. She had done this casting before. Just follow the guiders, and the image that her mind filled in around them. Any moment the aftershocks would come, or the next onslaught. She couldn't paint any faster. Her heart raced, but her hand was firm. *This is what I do, this is what I am.* She closed the last kadra and set the leaf in the middle of the circle, on the hard-packed dirt floor of the casting tent, on the skin of the mountain.

Torrin's hand was cool and dry, clasping her wrist instead of her hand, a surer grip. The binder's hand was slick with sweat; he echoed the grip, and his hand tightened as he began to sing, forcing the quaver out of his voice, forcing a pure soothing melody from his throat.

The lines of scribing ran together like molten metal. The kadri, the borders flared into liquid flame. The glowing ciphers joined with the illumination to form a latticework over the leaf, taking on a life and dimension beyond the materials. They burned.

Liath had never seen anything like it. Her eyes rose slowly to Torrin, and met the reflection of her own awe.

They had worked faster than the others. Their binder's song ended; there was a silence before the others' began. The blazing leaf crumbled into the earth. Then the tent filled with voices, a discordance that felt its way into a unity. They were listening to each other, keying to each other. Torrin did not release her wrist as the bindsman's hand dropped trembling away. For a moment, the current of magelight still flared between them. The binder hugged his knees and rocked. Torrin's light was sinking back to plainness; Liath crushed his flesh in her callused hand, trying to hold that light fast. She felt the wiry hairs on his arm, the pulse in his wrist. It was timed to her heartbeat.

With a moan, she opened her hand, rotated her forearm.

He let her go.

The ground rumbled, threatening. Liath braced. The combined bind-songs trailed away together as if on some unseen signal. In the linked circles of mages, leaves sank into the earth.

The rumbling subsided. The earth went still.

Outside, dawn was coming. Verlein barked orders in the midst of devastation. Heff hammered tent pegs into the ground as if to punish the mountain that tried to swallow him. Torrin gave her into his keeping and went to Verlein. She could still feel his arm around her, still feel his light mingling with hers.

"*Unacceptable!*" Verlein shouted. Torrin turned in disgust and came face-to-face with Benkana, stumbling, carrying Kazhe limp in his arms. They rushed her to the casting tent.

Heff was fingering the rips in Liath's clothes, pushing her coatsleeve up to reveal the long gouges left by thorns.

"Don't ask," she said.

I don't have to ask. You left me.

"It was a mistake. A very big one." She took his hand, pressed it to the cheek the outcasts hadn't smashed. The mountain might have done that; in a way, perhaps, the mountain had.

No apology could be enough. She only wanted to anchor herself in his solid warmth for a moment. Then she said, "But I'd do it again, given the opportunity."

I know, he said one-handed. But next time take me with you.

Verlein's voice rose on a note of raw fury. "I don't care! We *will* be ready!" She stepped away from a group of aides and cupped her hands around her mouth.

"We ride in a nineday!"

By late morning their tent and gear were packed up, Liath's pack stitched, their horses checked, their preparation complete. At noon she and Heff sat on their gear, eating greasy brancakes that were going rancid as casting materials were rationed, watching the rebels regroup and prepare to go on the offensive.

"Eight more days of this," Liath said.

Heff grunted. When she looked at him, he said, A child has a bad cinder in his eye. His parents send him to the blacksmith. The blacksmith says, Of course I'll see to it, just let me finish this. The child presses close to see what the smith is doing, attracted by the forge fire and glowing metal, blinking at the hammer blows. Steam rises from the quenching barrel. The child's eyes tear. When the smith has finished, he turns to the child and says, There, all better now. And the cinder has gone.

"Sometimes problems are solved in unexpected ways," Liath murmured, watching one group pile debris out of the way while another patched the salvageable tents and a third loaded a cart. "You're full of parables lately, eh?"

Heff tapped her. You can get free of them when they move, he said. They will take you out of these mountains themselves. You can ride faster than they can march.

She nodded, her eye catching on Torrin as he emerged from the casting tent and walked with Kazhe toward Verlein's. Jhoss left off a conversation with the horsemaster and joined them as they passed the corral. They slogged through the mud with determined purpose. A last-ditch effort to dissuade Verlein.

"That child's father would have done as well to set him chopping onions," she said vaguely to Heff, and in the tail of vision saw him reply, That's true. There are always choices. To go, or to stay and find another way.

Torrin did not feel her gaze on him, or turn if he did.

Porick came for the third time to offer her healing. Her face was in agony. She accepted, following him to the casting tent now that Torrin had left. Porick's triad awaited them. When it was done, Porick drew her aside to say he'd healed a crack in Lannan's skull. He told her Lannan had said some things. He told her he'd regarded them as effects of the head injury. She was absurdly grateful. He was a good man, a handsome mage. She felt diminished when he went back to his triad, and confused.

When she came out, Lannan said, from just to her left, "This is more warning than you gave me."

She sprang to the right as his brand-new blade cleaved the air she had stood in. She heard a shout—her name—as he recovered. "Catch!" the voice yelled. A fighter, a woman. Something flickered in the corner of her eye. A scabbard thunked into the dirt a threft behind her. She got the blade unsheathed just in time to bring it up under Lannan's second blow. She twisted, trying to force his blade into the dirt, but he danced back.

No shields. No quilted, padded coats. No master barking instruction. Lannan was quick, and strong, and had trained longer than she had, and he wasn't drilling.

Once, twice their blades smashed together. The impact jarred Liath's arms numb, but her hands were welded to the grip. She feinted away from the next blow, and the next, letting him tire himself, then swung at him; he deflected it easily and lunged at her. She hopped back like a startled cat, and saw the point of his blade come a handsbreadth shy of her belly. Her blade was already coming up, as if someone else wielded it, someone with strong fresh arms and a good eye. It nudged his blade aside. She stepped into the space it had made and brought the flat of the blade down hard on the hilt of his. His hands flew open. The blade dropped. He bent to retrieve it. She stepped on it, and lifted his chin with the edge of her blade. His eyes were wide, shocked. "Yield," he said, a practice-ring word.

She nodded and took a step back, lowering her blade. She would never know how he moved so fast, how one of his many knives came into his hand without her seeing, or what instinct raised her longblade again. But she was the one who angled it away. It sliced deeply into his side but did not run him through. He cried out. Liath looked down. His knife had snagged in her coat. She writhed away and thrust the longblade into the dirt as mages came running. Everyone was running; a crowd had been running toward them through the whole thing, which had taken only moments.

All except the fighter who had armed her.

Verlein.

"Good job!" she said, clapping Liath on the shoulder. Her face looked more alive than it had since the Aralinns. "And you didn't even cost me a man."

Blood-soaked Lannan screamed in agony as they carried him to the overused casting tent.

Liath spat at Verlein's feet and strode away.

His tent stood, unaffected by the quake, not yet broken down and packed. There was no way to knock. In Girdle style, she opened the flap and stuck her head in.

"You wanted a word with me," she said.

He was bent over a miniature sheaf of parchment bound between velvet-covered boards. "Yes," he said. "Kazhe?"

"I will not leave you alone w—"

"Kazhe."

With an oath, the blonde stalked from the tent, shouldering Liath hard on the way past. Liath took Kazhe's place by the cold firepit. She stared at the bound sheaf.

"Sacrilege abounds," Torrin said with a smile.

Liath didn't smile back.

"A permanent record," he said. "Rather precious, as it happens. A man died to preserve this, and others like it. Mages warded it for many lifetimes. Galandra wished it."

"I hoped catastrophe might have knocked some sanity into you."

"Alas, no." He put the bound sheaf aside and let his hands fall loosely on his crossed legs. They were bony, competent hands, but smooth, as if they had never done a day's plain work. "Do you truly believe that skyfire quickened a windy whirl of earth and water into the first mage? Or that the earth then shaped itself into a consort for her?"

"Yes," she said irritably. "I do believe it. You and the bloody seekers. What did you want to talk to me about, Torrin?"

"Precisely this. Traditions. History. Myths."

"The spirits are real. Galandra was real."

"I don't deny it. The spirits are quite real, and Galandra was a real woman, with a real triad, a real family. Metaphorically, yes, she is a child of the elements, bonded to the earth. Metaphorically, she also created the world."

Liath shrugged. "That's what they believe on Khine. They're entitled to it."

"It's all true, Illuminator, your beliefs *and* theirs—but far more true than you could possibly have known. You've seen a smidgen of the old languages, Jhoss tells me. You wonder who originally developed the craft of death—who taught Auda to forge a blade and Kazhe to wield one. Such craft seems alien to our world, doesn't it. Because it is. It came with us from outside, and was abandoned as needless—abhorrent. But some never forgot, and believed that those skills might be required again some-day, and passed them down through uncountable generations. It's extraor-dinary, really."

He had been receiving reports about her. It annoyed her, but every-thing he said annoyed her. "Extraordinary," she echoed. "A craft of death."

"I despise it."

"Then stop it."

"I can't—and might not even if I could. They will need those blades someday."

"To kill each other."

"To defend themselves. There is a world out there, Illuminator, a vast world of seas and continents, nations, lands with histories far older than ours. Eiden Myr is not the world. Eiden Myr is an island. The words themselves mean 'barren land,' in an ancient language called Ghardic. It had suffered some cataclysm in ages past, and was unlivable. It was con-nected to the mainland by a strait known as the Serpentback. In the coun-tries of that mainland, mages were the keepers of the old languages, the old codices—bound books of permanent manuscripts, histories meant for all to share—and the old magecraft. Though they harmed no one, they were persecuted for their knowledge and their powers, driven into hiding, murdered. Those who lacked magecraft feared that those who had it would rule them, and sought to destroy them all. Galandra na Caille le Serith lived in the wizards' quarter in the capital city of a country called Ollor-awn. The wizards' quarter was a squalid dump for the downtrodden. She suffered the loss of her pledgemate; she foresaw that a purge was coming. She organized the mages, rallied them. It took her years, working in secret. Ships sailed with livestock and supplies, carrying mages from every port of the continent. Others went on foot, gathering in Ollorawn City for one mass crossing of the Serpentback. At the last moment, they were found out. Mages were hanged in the streets; the wizards' quarter burned. Riots erupted as the ruler's armies were sent out to strike the mages as they fled. Many were killed—but many more made it over the Serpentback, to join those who had come by ship."

She had wanted to ask him about the burning thing the leaf had become when they cast. She had wanted to know what that was. That was all. A simple question. Perhaps it would stop this onslaught. But she could not draw breath to ask it. She knew she had come to find out so much more than that.

"When the last stragglers were across, Galandra's triad invoked a very old, very powerful form of magecraft, all but forgotten even then: the *hein-na-fhin*, in which the flesh and mind and spirit of three become one in literal fact. They used that power to break the Serpentback, shattering it into the sea and cutting Eiden Myr off from the continent to the east, and then to ward it, with a magecrafted barrier that no human could cross. Eiden Myr would remain forever protected from persecution. The mages who now inhabited it would use their craft to coax farmland from the barren, rocky soil, then work that land with their sweat and tears and smuggled seeds, set their animals out to graze on it. It was Galandra's great experiment, scribed out in a codex long lost to us: mages living among mages, fostering the old knowledge, living without rulers, without war, without violence, maintaining the balance of the spirits with their craft. Her experiment succeeded for more years than we have a way to measure. But at some point her successors sealed the codices away, locked up the records of the early days and Galandra's own covenant. Over the generations, memory faded into myth; the past went into the land beyond the mists."

The hammers would not stop pounding, since they'd righted the forges. His words became a great weight, pressing her toward the ground. She tried to sit up straight, to shake them off.

"Magecraft contracted into itself. At first was the division into triadic disciplines. With so much time required to shepherd the land, they could not all learn the three crafts, so they began to specialize—into scribes, and limners, and chanters, the precursors of our wordsmiths and illuminators and binders. Castings had always worked best with three, never well with only one; Galandra believed in triads, in their checks and balances, their stability. As time passed, it seemed to make sense for each of the three to use the skill he or she was strongest in. Some were better at painting than scribing, and became limners; some with a talent for words could not draw well, and became scribes. Preparation of binding materials became a full-time occupation, and fell to the chanters. Scribes and limners forgot how to mix ink and pigment and cut their own quills; chanters ceased to learn to read the words of what was scribed, and sang wordless melodies instead. Division of labor, born of expedience, codified into tradition, and after long enough the mages believed that their craft would not work unless the divisions were respected."

The camp always smelled of warm metal, and smoke. A blue pall lay over it, day and night, the smoke from the fires of those foundries, pounding out weapons. She could barely breathe.

"In the meanwhile, the light was fading. The first mages had come with pledgefolk, friends; the mageblood was not pure. It was so incremental as to be almost unnoticeable, but in each generation fewer showed a light. The lightless took on the full burden of farming, crafting; the mages increasingly reserved the tools of their craft for themselves, suspicious, jealous of it, afraid of it weakening. In the ancient lands, folk wore colorful dyed clothes, carved decorative patterns into their walls and saddles and furniture, sang songs with words, painted pictures for the joy of looking on them. They made medicines of roots and bark and herbs, far more powerful than the few poultices and teas we remember now, so that healings were not necessary for small maladies. Theirs was a world of color and pattern and beauty, and their magecraft was none the weaker for it. Isolated here, in this perfect wasteland, we have taken on strange ways—unnecessary and unfortunate ways that diminish us. I could teach every child in Eiden Myr to scribe, and wordsmithing would be harmed not a whit."

"The world is full of color," Liath said dully. The sun had tilted past the zenith and angled against the tent walls, suffusing them with gold. "The world is full of beauty, and patterns, and . . ."

"And magecraft is harmed not a whit," he said, leaning forward. "Is dancing not a pattern? Is drumming not a pattern of sound? Does the braid in a rope weaken your painted knotwork? Those are superstitions."

"The seekers would have figured it out."

"Perhaps they have, and didn't tell you."

Nerenyi would have told me. But Nerenyi had kept secrets of her own. Anger roused her out of the heavy suffocation. "They'll grab anyone by the collar, given half a chance, and spout whatever's on their mind," she snapped. "They're worse than the gropers in my tavern. They're almost as bad as you."

"Perhaps it was too frightening an idea, even for seekers. Or perhaps none of them has any inkling at all." He scooped ashes from the firepit into a bucket, then set three sticks in a tripod over kindling. Before he filled in around them with what firewood remained on the pile, he pressed them down, from the apex, into the layers of all the previous fires. "You ran a tavern?"

She bit her tongue, her eyes going wide. *Stupid, stupid Liath.* An image flashed across her mind, of bladed folk in the Petrel's Rest. She couldn't know if they'd make good on it, the threat would be enough—*Don't make me choose—*

"Easy, easy." He struck sparks into the kindling until it caught. "I don't know where your family lives."

"Verlein knows. Benkana knows."

"And what threat could they pose from here?"

"You pose the threat! Mages at the Head nearly tore your mountain apart. You might do anything, scry anything—"

He stiffened. The small fire caught in earnest and flared up, smoking into the ill-vented space. "Never accuse me of that," he said in a very soft voice.

For a moment they sat in silence. She would not apologize, would not placate him. But he was angry. She had finally made him angry. How far could she push him, if she had to? How far would he push back? Could he reach all the way to Clondel?

"Do you know what they do, in attempting a scrying?" he asked at last. "Or when they cause harm over great distances?"

"No. But you're going to tell me."

His gaze was lost in the flames; his lashes lay sooty against blanched cheeks. "They cut the skin of a living subject—two cuts, a triangular pattern—and peel it slowly back, in sections. They believe that it symbolizes the unveiling of secrets, the revelation of inner truths. It takes rather a long time to die, that way. When the subject threatens to slip away, they heal him. They let him rest a bit, perhaps; they administer a reviving draught. Freyn is a master of potions. They can keep a subject hovering between life and death for days, while they push, and push, attempting to extend their reach." He drew breath. "If we were practicing such a craft of pain, would you not know it, Illuminator? Would you not hear the screams, the moans of despair, see the mutilation?"

Liath felt ready to throw up. She grit her teeth. "I would have heard it in the Holding."

"The Ennead's Holding is a mountain. The victims are kept in the lowest levels. Leagues of stone muffle the cries."

"This is a mountain too."

"And I've been gone for long hours, wending my way through secret passages to my dominion of darkcraft, yes."

He was always accessible here, always on call or in view. "You've got mages doing it for you."

"And they cut the vocal cords so their victims can't scream, and leave the bodies far from view so you don't see the bonefolk hanging about, yes, yes." He pinched the bridge of his nose and closed his eyes. "Anything I tell you, you will find a way to counter. You are very stubborn. I suppose I should admire that."

The tripod of burning wood collapsed into the firepit in a spray of sparks. Liath beat embers out of her coat.

"What do you want from me, Torrin? Why did you think I was the one you needed? There are brighter lights than mine."

"Not many." He smiled a little, poking the fire into a better shape, adding wood. "One or two on the Ennead, perhaps one other. But the mind that guides the hand that guides the arrow has only to be smarter, not swifter. The stone that deflects the shaft has only to be more solid."

"Stop being insane and *answer* me!"

The smile widened—blossomed, into a full, genuine smile, not just a flicker at the edge of a closed mouth. Her heart twisted inside her. "*You're in love*," Nerenyi murmured in the back of her mind. "*With someone you're angry at. . . .*" She thought, *No. No.* She averted her gaze, but she could still see the curved lips, the straight white teeth, the smile lighting the amber eyes, the weary creases subsumed in laugh lines, nostrils flaring in the aquiline nose. A nineyear sloughed off him when he smiled. No sharp, cruel features, no depthless black eyes. An ordinary, good-looking face, worn by hard times, lit by a heartbreaking smile.

Then it faded, losing the battle with fatigue. "When the time comes, if I have to, I will attempt to stop the Ennead alone. But I will fail as likely as succeed. I haven't the power. You saw Yerby's illuminator's wound; I healed it, but imperfectly. One is never sufficient, no matter how bright. Good magecraft requires three. I need a triad. I would have you for illuminator."

Afternoon had waned into evening, no longer lighting the tent walls; the canvas looked worn, and the space closed in. A chill was coming on. He had lit the fire just in time. "I feel sorry for you. You truly believe in what you're doing."

"And does that excuse the deeds you've accused me of?"

"Of course not."

"Good. You would excuse a great deal of harm, if one has only to believe what one is doing is right. There is always a reason."

"That's what I've been *saying!*" She groaned. "The Ennead has no reason to do what you claim."

"Of course they do. But what you want to know is *my* reason."

Watching him carefully, she said, "You were a spoiled child. They coddled you. You got mad at them, but they don't know why. They want to bring you back. To redeem you."

He laughed outright. "And all my darkcraft is merely vengefulness?"

"They wronged you somehow. Tell them how. They'll make it right."

"Oh, Illuminator. It's so perfect; I wonder if they knew, or if it came out unconsciously. Yes, I'm angry at them. I rage at their perversion of a sweet and peaceful craft. Magelight made a paradise of wasteland, a safe haven for the persecuted. Galandra built a world based on compassion, and this Ennead is its darkest inversion. But no one does anything without reason. The current Ennead is bent on vengeance. Exactly what they accuse me of."

"Against *who?*"

"Against the world we fled."

"The land beyond the mists. Of course."

He nodded, as if he couldn't hear sarcasm. "The lands beyond Galandra's shield. They dare not break the shield; it's what keeps us safe. They seek a way to work through it, or under it, to destroy those who tried to destroy us. Somehow Auda's family, and Kazhe's, retained their bladelore all that time. There are others who retained the thirst for vengeance. We brought seeds with us, animals, tools. We also brought the seeds of our own destruction: we brought hatred with us. Galandra might have seen it, had she lived, and snuffed it out. But it took root, and grew, a vine of hatred through the generations. Now it has blossomed."

Liath buried her head in her arms.

The soft baritone continued, oblivious of her. "No one does anything without reason. For some, unlimited power would be enough incentive. It's what Lerissa wants. But they all have their motives. Vonche craves unlimited knowledge; Naeve wants to live forever. Worilke is a staunch disciple of Galandra, but she would do anything to preserve Eiden Myr as it is. Seldril hungers for pain, Gondril hungers to consume. Freyn I could never gauge; some hatred of men drives her, though it's more than that, I think. But the story they fed you was a beautiful concatenation of Evonder and Landril. Evonder is the sulky child. Landril, by far the most dangerous, seeks retribution. He is the true heir of that first mage who would never forgive. The triplets were bred for vengeance; they are a creation of darkcraft themselves, identical triplets of different genders. They work in unison to wreak the revenge of their creators. But only in Landril does the flame of rage burn pure. Like Gondril, he hungers; like Seldril, he has a taste for pain. But neither distracts him from his true course. He is the arrow. The rest of them are fletching."

I'm going, she thought, but she did not get up. *I can't listen to any more of this.* But she raised her head slowly in the smoky gloom and said, "How would you stop them?"

"I will break the shield."

There is no shield. There are no lands beyond this. Eiden Myr is the world. There is no shield. "And let the outside world in to destroy us? Let what's left of those frightened people bring their fighters here to kill us off at last? Or—or let a storm in, a greater storm than any we have ever—"

"The Great Storms are a by-product of the shield. The shield is a warding—a twistedness, a thing of spirit, turning a piece of the world back on itself so it seems there is nothing. It has strange effects on the elements. I do not entirely understand it myself; perhaps only Galandra did. But three times every nonned years, some kind of balance of air and water must be restored, and the Great Storms come. I believe they come through a gap in the shield—one that opens each time, or one that is always there, I don't know. The enneads were formed to keep the unbalanced elements in balance; the ennead at the Head was charged with diverting the Great Storms when they came. They established their holding in a preexisting fastness, some ruin of an ancient race, whoever lived here before the cataclysm that made the land uninhabitable. Like the holdings in the Haunch and the Knee, it was meant to be a center of learning, a place of vocation and renewal. Over time, as magecraft contracted, it became a place of secrets. That was the beginning of the end."

"What happened to the other holdings?" Nerenyi had been right. A Triennead . . . *No. I'm humoring him. It's a lie, all of it, the fantasy of an ailing mind. He's a teller, that's all, a teller who makes up his own stories. He will not turn me.*

"I don't know. No one knows. They had ceased to keep records by then. Another mistake. They thought they were protecting the craft, I suppose."

Every line of his body bespoke exhaustion. She pushed again, just to see. Just to see how far she could get. Not because she wanted to know. Not because she believed him. Just to see. "Say you broke this shield. Wouldn't that only give them easier access to the people they want to hurt?"

"It would," he said, reaching for his cloak, drawing it around himself as if the fire he had built could no longer warm him. "Its breaking will disarm them."

There was a long silence. Conversations drifted in; Kazhe cleared her throat; a supper bell rang.

"What *are* you?" she whispered.

"A man," he said quietly, "with flaws and desires like any other. Not the evil creature you were sent to betray to the Ennead, casting horrors in some dank mountain cavern. Not even the dangerous, hypnotic wizard you doubtless thought you'd find. A disappointment, I imagine."

"No," she said softly, and looked away.

She would return to the Holding, and this complex, intricate delusion would fall to pieces. It would disperse into a mist, like a dream, and be gone, and the world would be as she had known it, safe and comprehensible.

She started to rise.

Kazhe pushed the tent flap back to admit a dark-haired boy in a nine-colored velvet cloak. *Mellas!* Liath nearly leaped to embrace him. But it was not Mellas, or any runner boy she knew.

"You have a visitor," Kazhe said unnecessarily, "and about nine breaths before Verlein comes in."

The boy drew a piece of sedgeweave from his coat, stained and creased. Torrin unfolded it close to the fire. Liath groped at her ragged breeches, thinking her secret lost and recovered by them somehow, but the soft triangle was there. The blood had probably been leached out of it by now, in all that had happened. But the flesh was there. His flesh, in pale, dried flakes. She could see the three old marks on his neck—he hadn't had them healed. His eyes scanned the message quickly; then he relaxed, drew the sedgeweave away from the flames, and permitted himself a small smile, which he raised to Verlein as she barged in.

"Well?" she said. "They hustled the lad in here quick enough. Didn't want me waylaying your message. Let's have it, Torrin. What did he say?"

He offered the sedgeweave.

"You know I can't read that."

"Yes. You never took the time to learn."

"Kazhe, get me a wordsmith."

"Most wordsmiths cannot read the language this is scribed in."

"Then get me Jhoss! Eiden's dung!"

Kazhe did not move.

They stared at each other for a long moment, an old friendship realigning itself into something else.

"No need," Jhoss said, eeling in between Verlein and Kazhe. "I saw the runner." His eyes fell on the sedgeweave, then flicked to Torrin. Verlein didn't see it. He took the leaf and bent toward the fire. Haltingly, he read a long series of syllables.

"Translate it," she said.

"It's . . ." He blinked. "It's gibberish."

"But it means something to *him*."

"Undoubtedly. If he will tell you."

"And he won't."

"Of course I will."

Verlein's jaw tensed. He was toying with her.

"It is a coded message, an old rhyming code I developed with a . . . friend, who remains my ally in the Holding. It says, rather belatedly, that the Ennead has fixed our location and come by local materials that they can use to destabilize the mountain."

"Belatedly." Verlein rubbed her fist against her forehead. "Is that all it says?"

Torrin stared straight into her eyes and said, "Yes."

Verlein glanced at Jhoss. "Is he telling the truth?"

Jhoss nodded, impassive.

"Bloody waste of time." She shoved out of the tent, pushing the startled runner boy ahead of her, then turned back to say, "Have this broken down by tomorrow morning. Half the camp is sleeping rough. I've granted you enough liberties."

Torrin's brows went up, and he and Jhoss shared a look. Then Torrin said, almost too low for Liath to hear, "It's time."

They waited until the sentry shift changed at midnight, then bundled Liath and Heff across the caldera floor. Kazhe stuck close to Torrin, her blade unsheathed; Benkana stuck close to Kazhe, and Jhoss kept up as well as he could. All four were armed. In a tent across the camp from Torrin's, there was a crash and a scream. "A few remained loyal to me," Torrin murmured.

But not enough. Not the guards on the pass. Not even all the sentries on the rim. And none of the outcasts.

A clash of blades rang out. "It's a diversion," Torrin said as she tried to turn and look. "Mind your step."

They had no horses, minimal provisions, no water. Amaranth was in the corral—they would take that gentle mare into battle. But she went; it was easier than thinking, at first, and then it seemed six of one and half a dozen of the other—leave now, with Torrin, or leave in the custody of Verlein's forces, without Torrin's protection. She was no more valuable than an outcast to Verlein, and possibly inconvenient enough to kill. Torrin wanted her light. He would keep her alive. He would get her out of here.

As they came up onto the rim, a sentry lantern approached but did not shine on them. Kazhe whispered something to the sentry, who continued along her patrol. In the brief flare of light, Liath recognized the tumble of rocks. This was why she had gotten over the rim. They'd thought she was one of his.

Was she?

It might be better to raise the alarm now. . . .

No. He did not believe in Verlein's fight. She would not put him in Verlein's hands. There had to be another way.

She made the awkward descent when her turn came, picking her way by feel in the dark over gaps and irregularities in the stone.

They moved single file through stands of thornwood, each with a hand on the person ahead. As if on cue, the crescent moon peeked over the rim behind them. A bank of cloud engulfed it, but there was light enough not to die by, now. She could see the brambles reaching out for her feet, and stopped tripping on them.

"Where are they?" Kazhe whispered over her shoulder, hoarse, from in front. She was waving her blade ahead of her, a dangerous way to stave off branches. She expected attack.

"I don't know," Torrin whispered back. "Keep going."

They walked for a long time. Only when the trail ran out did Liath realize that they had been on a trail. Now Kazhe bushwhacked through thickets, fighting her way forward. When it seemed they were permanently mired, they emerged abruptly into an open, windy space—stone underfoot, dark in the intermittent moonlight. Liath's eyes had trouble adjusting to distance, but it came clear to her in the next flood of silver that she was looking out from a high ridge onto an uncrossable expanse, a fringe of trees on the far side.

She looked at Heff: *Now what?*

Kazhe had sheathed her blade and was clearing brush off to the left. She revealed a set of iron cleats driven into the rock, and began reeling in the ends of the line threaded through them. Benkana knotted one end under his arms and looped the bight around himself, gathering the coil in his off hand. Then he was over the cliff, belaying himself with the rope.

"Oh, spirits . . ." Liath whispered.

Kazhe gestured for her to go next. Liath closed her eyes, beseeched Sylfonwy for sufferance, then moved forward and let Kazhe knot the line under her armpits.

"Don't look down," Kazhe said with a grin.

The descent was endless and aching. Her feet got too far below her. Her worn soles slipped on the rock. For a heart-stopping moment she dangled free, her life in her off hand. She scrabbled for a foothold and kicked herself out, then banged back hard against the rockface. Fighting panic, she positioned her feet, then could not make herself let out more line. Her fingers had a death grip on the rope. She took deep, regular breaths, then unclenched her hand a little—slipped too fast, clenched again—and regained the balance of friction and play, continuing down. It seemed to get easier. Her mind wandered. The belay slid away from her, her feet slipped, and she went plummeting into space—for two threfts, thumping into brambles, the wind knocked out of her.

"You took your time," Benkana said, untangling the rope and loosening the knot to slip it over her head. He gave three quick jerks, and the line began reeling up. "Except for that last bit."

She sat on a patch of stony ground, trembling, as the others came down one by one. It took forever, but even Jhoss did it more efficiently than she had.

Someone had already hacked a trail through the thicket they were in now. They came out of it onto a path that was more gnarled roots and boulders than trail, parts of it sunken and mired in mud. It led to another cliff, another set of cleats and ropes. *Not again, I can't do that again*, she thought, but she did—even slower this time, but without slipping. The third time went better. Down, and down, through ropes in the night, rappelling down the stepped side of the mountain into darkness. They had planned it all, set up the points of descent, maintained the lines through the long winter. But it was still a very long way back. They were on foot. They had already eaten half the food. Liath was so thirsty she could barely move her tongue in her mouth.

The graying of predawn revealed a screen of trees, bonewood and weeping mistwood among the stark black thorns. Their steps sucked in a mulch of leaves. They emerged into the bed of a drywash gully threaded down the center with mud. Kazhe struck off in the direction Liath thought was opposite from the pass. Half a mile on, someone waited with eight horses and two pack mules. She recognized the once-plump face depleted by hunger.

"You lost two?" he said, eyes hard.

"Serafad and Porick stayed with their triads," Torrin said. "They will join us later, if they can. Liath, Heff—Boroel."

"Where were the others?" Kazhe asked, dispensing hoggins of water from the mules' panniers. Liath drank greedily.

Boroel was staring at Liath with no expression. He turned to Kazhe. "I had to kill two of them. The rest were in the camp when the quake came, or near it. They didn't come back."

"Just as well," she said, and took the reins of a horse at random. "Let's go."

They mounted, trailing the mules, and followed the ghost of a river out of the Blooded Mountains, toward pink-and-gold sunrise.

"Boroel," Liath said, falling back to bring up the rear with him. "That's a Head name, isn't it?"

"Crown," he said. His blank eyes scanned the trail around them, never lighting on her for more than a moment. "I'm proxies' get, fostered out. They taught me to kill before they taught me to cast. I'm a binder, and an assassin. The Ennead sent me to murder a rogue wordsmith—just a year ago, now."

"Kazhe didn't kill you?"

"She dealt me a killing blow. Torrin healed me. He saved my life. Now I shield his."

"Any mages might have saved your life. Why follow him?"

His mouth twitched. "If you had seen what I have seen at the Holding, you would not ask that question. If the spirits are kind, they assume I died like all the others, and my family is well."

"Your parents?"

His gaze fluttered across her. "They killed my parents long ago. I barely knew them. I was referring to my family in Crown."

For three days they traveled thick woods. Few words were spoken. Torrin seemed lost in thought; an expert rider, he sat easy in the saddle, hands quiet on the reins. Did they teach them to ride, in the Holding? Or had he learned since? Liath looked at those hands and this time could not stop herself from wondering how they would feel on her body. He was of an age to be experienced, considerate, deft, but reckoners had said he'd kept to himself, and he'd kept to himself in the camp, conferring now and then with Jhoss or casting with the mages, but otherwise watching, strolling, thinking, or sitting alone in his tent. Perhaps he'd never . . .

He might be awkward, embarrassing them both, breaking the illusion of restrained power. She cringed to imagine him humiliated in bed. Or he might say, in his low voice, "You must show me, Illuminator . . ."

Such thoughts were not only dangerous, but absurd. She had been with all of two men: Tolivar, and a journeymage no older than she was now. Lovemaking had come easily to her, but she was not practiced at it. Accustomed to the practiced ministrations of older women—Holding women—he could have no interest in someone like her.

She must not think on it.

Yet she worked it like a loose tooth, tormenting herself with fantasies.

Her great talent was conjuring pictures in her mind, and her fervid imaginings were intensified ninefold by the very desire that fed them. Eiden's spines, they called it at home. It felt as if something had hit her; in one breath he was her quarry and her enemy, in the next a tired heretic dispensing blasphemies, and in the last, as if the angle and quality of the light on him had changed, he was . . . he was . . . It was like being drugged, like being blindsided by some unstoppable engulfing thing, like being swallowed. She ached for him so badly she didn't know how she endured it; there was no relief, no release. The curve of his mouth, the indescribable eyes . . . just the thought of the way his spare body moved, the vision of what it must look like under his plain, travelstained clothes . . . the glimpse of ridged thigh muscle against a trouser leg's thin wool, the angle of a linen fold on a lean forearm . . . Would the skin under his ear, where the dark hair curled in, be as tender under her lips as it looked? She had to taste him, she had to *know*, she had to see him unmasked by passion, swept clean of brooding thoughts by a surge so powerful it made him cry out—

How many women had hungered for that? How many women had sought to wend their way inside him through his flesh? How many had he turned by making them want him in exactly this way?

She knew nothing about him at all. What had his life been like, in the Holding? What were his tastes, his interests, his irritations? Where had he gone when he wanted to be alone? Who had he sought when he was hurt, or lonely? He was one of them, for all he fought them. His voice was cultured into accentlessness, the Ennead accent of no accent at all; his manner bore the reserved dignity imparted by a Holding upbringing. Torrin was a Midlands name, a Heartlands name, but Maeryn was a Head name, and Eilody no name she'd ever heard. Who had they been? What had they looked like? Whose name did he bear? *Where had he come from?*

The difference in their ages was the span of Mellas's life. He was vastly more learned than she, and far more clever; she was a thickheaded tavernkeep with a talent she couldn't control and visions she couldn't articulate. He'd never called her by name. Did he see only light when he looked at her, and no Liath at all?

She would gaze on him, wondering those things, watching his quiet hands on the reins, and he would sense her regard and glance over, and her face would burn.

He couldn't read minds. He didn't know. He must never know.

She must not think on it.

The second night she bedded down early, her back pressed against Heff's for warmth, deeply fatigued, yearning. He was there, two threfts away. She had memorized his sleeping face in the firelight the night before, could see it with her eyes closed now. But she would not. She would not dream of him. She would not permit herself the luxury.

She had to think, make plans . . . they would have to pick their moment . . . there would be no slipping away under cover of night, not with lookouts posted, but they could break away on the plains. . . .

She woke in darkness to the sound of low voices.

"Don't stop me. I don't care how cursed bright her light is. I don't care if you're smitten, or if it's just the same old blighted compassion. Don't stop me this time."

"She cannot harm me, Kazhe." His tone was pitying.

"She carries your flesh!"

"I know."

"I saw what they did with one handful of mountain dirt."

"And they can do the same with three fingernails of flesh. I know, Kazhe. Let her be."

"I'll find it," Kazhe said.

"She'll have hidden it too well, perhaps inside her body."

"I'll hack her apart."

"You cannot be sure of finding it all." Torrin's voice grew muffled. "Let me sleep, Kazhe. We face a long ride."

The forest thinned; lakes of sunshine replaced dappled shade. When the wintering Girdle grasses were a shimmer through the trunks ahead, they stopped for one last night under cover of trees.

"Who is your ally in the Holding?" she asked Torrin after they'd eaten, while Benkana stood watch and Boroel had his own meal. Jhoss, exhausted from travel, was curled tight in his blankets, and looked like a corpse. Kazhe never left Torrin's side now, even when he went to relieve himself, and never slept.

"A childhood friend." He smiled, remembering. "For a time, the last Ennead took the children they were grooming to replace certain of their members and set them to copying historical codices. Bound volumes," he explained, when she shook her head, "like the one you saw me reading in my tent. Vonche had unsealed the warded chamber where they were kept—no faulting him for that, it was the right thing for the wrong reason—and set up a scriptorium where they could be reproduced. Each is precious, and unique. Copies *should* be made. But . . . another child saw me slip a copied leaf into my pocket to keep, and tattled on me. I was punished rather severely. Seldril was already quite adept at it. But I didn't mind. It was all a clever diversion—I had slipped the original into my coat and hid it under a loose stone in my chamber. At any rate, the child repented, seeing me so badly used, exhibited as an example to the others. We grew . . . close. And remained so, even through the difficulty when I left."

She grit her teeth against jealousy. She would not allow it. So his voice caressed the memory of a lover. It was no more than useful information.

"What will you do now?" she said. "Where will you go?"

"To stop the Ennead, as I promised. There was more in that message than I let on to Verlein, as you may have gathered."

"How? You said you haven't the power to break the shield."

It was the one question he would never answer. "Come with me," he said, "and I'll show you."

They were heading into the Girdle on an angle that might take them to the low end of the Belt, or Maur Bolein or Maur Aulein, if they continued on a straight course. She could make no sense of it, though something niggled at the back of her mind, something she should have understood. If only Nerenyi were here. Please Eiden the fighting would not reach her little island.

"The only way to stop the coming war," Torrin said softly, "is for me to stop the Ennead first, with magecraft. It is a bloodless solution. Come with me. Help me, Illuminator."

Come with me. . . . The quiet plea on his worn face was too much. She looked toward Boroel, his straight sentry's back, his emotionless mask. She looked at Jhoss, sleeping like the dead, dreaming of the marvels they would create when all could read and scribe. She looked at Kazhe's narrowed eyes, intent on her; looked at the left hand resting on her knife, the right free to draw her blade in the fluid motion that would cleave through Liath's body. She thought of Verlein, of the horde that followed her, people so angry they would tear down the walls that protected them. They could not all be lying. They could not all be insane. He could not have turned them all.

But it simply could not be true.

She looked at last to Heff, beseeching. I will back you, whatever you decide, he gestured. But I cannot choose for you.

"I believe you, Torrin," she said, barely audible. For a moment, in the fire's glow, his golden eyes filled the world. They were the color of magelight. "I do believe you. And I *can't.*"

Kazhe had seen it in her eyes before she spoke. The blade was coming over her head in a silver whisper—and sinking into the grass, digging a thin trench as Torrin swept her out of reach.

Liath backed into the center of the clearing. A horse whickered protest; Heff had gone to saddle theirs. With a yowl, Kazhe strained toward her. Torrin put his full weight into restraining her, and when she spun away he nearly fell. The hand he flung out failed to snag her arm. "*Kazhe!*"

His word froze her.

"Stay on watch, Benkana," Boroel commanded sharply. "It's nothing." His blade was poised before him, but his eyes flickered from Torrin to Kazhe. His allegiance lay with Torrin. He would follow orders whether or not he agreed with Kazhe. But Kazhe knew that Torrin would not set Boroel on her. And Kazhe had never reliably followed orders she did not like.

"The safest course is to kill her," Jhoss said from where he lay. He sat up slowly. The dead rising.

"I need her," Torrin said. There was no modulation in his voice. It might have meant anything.

"Then by Eiden's flaming *bowels* why would you let her go?"

"Because she wants to, Kazhe," he said.

"I'll run her through," Kazhe said raggedly, "and you'll heal her. I'll cleave her in two, and you'll heal her." Her body was trembling, but the blade she lowered was steady. "I'll stop her, and stop her, and stop her, and you'll let her go."

Torrin laid a hand on her shoulder and squeezed. Kazhe's face was stony around burning eyes.

Liath's pack came into her hands. She slung it on.

"I'm sorry, Illuminator," Torrin said, stepping past Kazhe.

Heff put Liath's hand on a stirrup, then moved around her horse to mount his own.

"Sorry?" Liath echoed.

He came to within a breath of her. His eyes were level with her own. "To let you go back there," he said. "You will not thank me for it, even if you live." He took her chin in his fingertips. His gaze searched her face, as if burning its contours into his mind. He fixed on her mouth, lifted it; his lips were cool, polite. She swayed toward him, her mind an inarticulate white blaze, and felt some iron restraint inside him break. He probed her mouth open, molded her body to the length of his. She inhaled acrid sweat, a scent of oak gall; his tongue tasted of mint. She clutched his coat, pulling his hips hard against hers. A shivering heat sang through her nerves that had nothing to do with magelight. Kazhe made a strangled sound. With a moan, Torrin broke free of her mouth and crushed her to him, hand in her hair, lips on her ear.

"Live, Liath," he breathed, and thrust her from him, and turned away.

She fumbled a foot into the stirrup, got aboard the horse, reined around without looking at the rest of them. Until they were out of the circle of firelight, she half expected to feel a blade in her back. But there was nothing. Only a pool of shadow ahead, then moonlight silvering the sea of grass.

The last thing she heard was Kazhe's low sob: "You bloody, benighted, spiritlorn *fool.*"

Then only the creak of the saddle Heff was too heavy for, the sigh of boughs overhead, the plaintive cry of a nightbird in the forest behind them, and the rising wind.

MIST

Poison, Freyn thought. *Poison is the key. And I hold it in my hand.*

She sank back into the downy, mounded bed, idly caressing the flesh-like skin of the banewort root that perfumed the chamber with its particular scent of rot. The body was not all that could be poisoned. Spirit-leaching contamination, as a concept, extended far beyond ordinary ingestion or absorption, the application of substance to skin. She was so pleased with her own cleverness that she didn't know if she could keep it to herself. But she would not sell the idea cheap. She had sold herself far too cheap before.

"Pledge me," he'd said. A man who had been forced to send his common lover back to her common folk, retaining only the child. A man Freyn had adored since girlhood—the jet-black hair forever falling across his blazing eyes—and thought she, the wildling daughter of the lightless, could never have. "Pledge me," he said, in the child's sixth year, when her light swelled to visibility. "Imagine the power we will wield." Freyn had imagined: she had imagined giving him a child who would put the other to shame. The fruit of her womb would eclipse his pride and joy so thoroughly he might send her the way of the mother. No longer would he sit staring at the sleeping child, dreaming of the woman he had lost, dreaming of the power his daughter would inherit, the future he would carve for her. No longer would he shrug off Freyn's caresses, ignore Freyn's sultry voice, her body numinous with youth and light. She had imagined it with so much passion that it had seemed real.

Perhaps she had taken liberties. Perhaps she had caressed him too much. Perhaps she had longed too fervently for his touch, clung too tightly to his hard, cold frame, fought too hard to melt his indifference. So what? He was hers. He had asked her to pledge him, and she had.

Happy now? he said. Time had worn the tone of voice to a smoothness, a neutrality, it hadn't had when he spoke; like the dry husk of a leaf, it was only the outline of his voice, only the words, none of the resonance. *Happy now?* he said again. He spoke over and over again in her memory. The past was a great echo chamber, a crevasse of whispers in her own mind. She could never shut it. She could never make memory speak differently, or kindly.

This is what you wanted, isn't it? he said. *Isn't it?* His rigid body on hers, his iron arms crushing hers into the bed. No, she said, no, this wasn't what she meant, she wasn't prepared, no, he was going too fast—no and no, but to no avail. Only moments later, it seemed, moments and lifetimes, it was over, an act of brutal efficiency, and her blood and her sobs engendered not pity but disgust. *Happy now? Happy now? Happy now?*

There had been no child. He had gone back to his daughter's chamber, and sat dreaming of his lost love, and went off each dawn to prepare the way for her ascension, the way that his pledging Freyn had paved, and as the child grew the only consolation was that he couldn't bear to look on the image of his lover that was her face, and praised her only for her light, cared only for her craft.

Funny, Freyn thought, tickling the limbs of the man-shaped root until they flushed dark rose, that he never saw the most direct path to the girl's success.

Well, she had a new pledgemate now. He would never spurn her attentions, never fail her, never betray her. He throbbed with life and power, and he was her faithful servant.

She smiled her thin smile, drawing the tumescent plant across her lips, savoring the touch, the taste, of death.

STONE

Worilke's mother, though also a mage, had first been a teller, as her mother had, and her mother, and all the mothers before them. Worilke detested tellers, their stories made of dreams and air. Tellers' tales dissipated like cast sedgeweave. Nothing endured. All but one of those women had forsaken the light in order to ply their hereditary trade. It was a betrayal of generations.

Over time, tales mutated and decayed, each one bent and soiled by the teller before, until the straight line of truth had twisted and darkened past recognition. It had to be set right. No one knew this subject as she did. Only one man had access to the relevant historical codices—she had delivered him a binder's life to obtain them, and he'd thought it a bargain, the fool—and even the codices lied, for they themselves were scribed by tellers of a sort, imposing their own perversions on what they chronicled.

She was not by nature a scholar. A wordsmith, yes, but that work was rote and poetry; this combined the teller's way and the seeker's, and it took all her patience to sift through the ancient tales for scraps of fact, to compare with other scraps and synthesize into a coherent narrative. But the truth must be recorded. Through all the ages, she knew this woman better than anyone, better perhaps than her own contemporaries; and she would peel away the layers of myth and absurd elaboration.

She was continually interrupted. A single leaf was a night's work, between castings, the incessant questions of aides, the continual maneuvering. Never enough time to meditate on the life of the woman who had been the greatest of them, the mother of them.

Ironic, that it should fall to her. She could hear her mother's laughter in the back of her mind: *You could not escape your heritage in the end.*

It could not be helped. Once her volume was complete, she could devote her full attention to matters of the present.

She sanded a fresh leaf with care, caressed it with pumice to smooth the surface and prepare it to receive ink and hold it fast. She shaved the quill end to a fine point and moved it to the bloodred ink in the little pot. Red was Galandra's color. Red for the blood of mages, red for her mane of red hair, red for the color of her rage. The liquid was magecast for permanence. Even its surface resisted the quill; the circular membrane trembled as the shaft touched it, and a tiny ripple spread from the point of penetration. When she blotted it, what looked like a spot of moonblood stained the absorbent, unfinished sedgeweave. A sign of fertility. Words must pour from her hand as lives had from her body. Her womb had done its work and was exhausted now. But her hand was strong, and her shoulders were stronger still. Strong enough to bear the burden of the world. Strong enough to set the past right for the future.

B L O O Ɗ

Born of pain. Born of death.

Linked forever to brothers—though "brother" was a convenient misnomer for the one. Hatred for them surpassed hatred of all others. Hunger
to feel them suffer surpassed hunger to feel all others suffer—all others but
Seldril herself.

Does that hurt, little one?

Yes.

Do you like it?

No.

Surprising that not all children developed the hunger. All children
were born of pain, though not ripped, perhaps, from a dying mother's
womb. All children were born hungry, though suckled on milk rather
than blood—but that could be a little family myth. Symbolically, at least,
it was true. They'd suckled at the teat of history, and history was engorged
with blood.

Childhood—if it could be called that—was a shadowy blur of manipulation, figures coming and going, looming, fading. Only the others
were clear, the ones who were like. The first mirrors.

Do you want to cast, little one?

Yes.

Do you want it very badly?

Yes.

You know you cannot cast unless I hurt you.

I know.

Their makers had locked them together for ninedays at a time, with limited provisions. Later, the manipulation was obvious, but it had already succeeded. Perhaps they had also done so in order to see who would devour the rest. Wild dogs bore litters of three, two stillborn; black-winged predators hatched three into nests from which only one would fly. If such was the intent, thus far it was a draw. The stated purpose, of course, was to forge them into one being, teach them to depend only on the others. In that they *had* failed. They had not taken into account the hunger, or the blood.

They had not reckoned on what the pain would produce.

Does that hurt, little one?

Yes.

Do you like it?

Yes.

Or perhaps they had.

3

INSCRIBING

"She was in the mountains with them. Naeve's spies at the pass saw them carry her there."

"Yes, and did not ride out again with the armed horde."

"Perhaps she died on the way, or in our attempt to drive him out."

"A sorry attempt."

"We had little to work with."

"Suppose she does come back? We might still retrieve him."

"She will not come back in time, even if she survived the winter. The journey is too long."

"But if she does?"

"The day is too close."

"Then we must make other arrangements."

"I already have. I always do."

Liath n'Geara l'Danor Illuminator came alone to the Crownside gate of the Ennead's Holding as a late-winter dawn broke runny over the Sea of Sorrows, the Fist, the Forgotten Sea.

"Too early for petitioners," the bored watchwoman said. "Go break your night's fast, return at midmorning." Her slouch straightened when Liath's stride did not falter, bringing her fully within the periphery of the watchlamps. What had approached from out of the tail end of night was a tall, spare figure wreathed in shadow. It resolved into a hard-faced mage, gray of eye and red of hair, pewter triskele lying prominent on her chest, a nine-colored velvet cloak swirling around her calves.

"Forgive me . . ." The watcher's eyes dropped to the ring on the hand Liath hooked in the belt of her black tunic. She blinked at the glint of silver, and relaxed. Not gold. Not an Ennead member. She did not know them by sight. ". . . Proxy."

Liath nodded, and gestured at the gate.

The watcher reached to turn a key in her side of the iron contraption, then grasped the bottom crossbar and raised it. Badly oiled chains gave an unearthly shriek inside the blackstone.

Liath stepped inside.

She remembered the way. It was not a pattern, but it was a shape, a path branded on her mind as were all paths she had ever taken. Portriel had shown her that she learned such paths by sight; the route they'd negotiated in the darkness was a blur of movement to her, inaccessible to her mind's eye. But the aides had led her through lamplit passages, to clothe and provision her, to send her out on her search for the Darkmage.

She wondered how many feet had trod that route and never returned to retrace their steps.

Mages and stewards went about their duties as if it were noon. Snow-white warders spared her not a glance; ink-black reckoners inclined their heads with an air of restrained curiosity. She had the smell of travel on her. Her clothes, though care had been taken to mend them and lampglow was kind, bore a sheen of road dust and sea salt. "In the field quite a while, eh?" asked one as she approached the junction that would offer her a downward choice.

"Quite a while," she said in a low voice, moving on.

The presence chamber was empty. One lamp held watch in a wall niche, a negligible ochre sphere in the ghostly shine of magestone. The stone table was the shape of a blunted arrowhead. She trailed her fingers along the moon-bright inlay, and reached across its glow to caress the central depression in the tabletop. No stain of blood; no sense of pain. They had cast no horrors here.

She felt eyes on her. Her head came up. A door that had been closed was newly open on darkness. A bent, ragged figure floated on shadow.

"Stinky one. Good to smell you. You taste of stars."

"Do you know where they are?" Liath asked.

The blind woman snorted. "Don't want to know. But you know where Portriel is, yes? You can go to her, stink up her chambers?"

A rank whiff of unwashed, aged flesh came off her, borne on a dank draft through the doorway. Her robe was filthy and torn, her hair an unkempt mass. Her chambers were no doubt stinky enough.

"I couldn't find the way again," Liath said.

"Bring your light to the crevasse of whispers. She will find you." She sank into the pool of darkness behind her, and the thick oak door swung closed with a muffled click.

I will always find you.

Heff was stitching the stolen reckoner's clothes with a hand too thick and meaty for such deft work. He had beaten them cleaner than water could have rinsed them, some knack of Haunchmen, and now was working his earthcraft to make them whole and presentable again. They'd originated in the bodies of living things—silk from spinners, velvet from sheep. He crooned over his darning and his mending, and something in the fibers remembered where they came from, and became willing and malleable in his hands.

"I can't put those on again," she said. The black dye had poisoned her spirit.

You must, he said, his tone choppy, irritable, because he had to break the rhythm of his work to speak. It is your chance to make good speed, to arrive with a reasonable lead on Verlein's forces. You will not pass up the chance.

In the end she had donned the loathsome garb.

You will travel unseen at night, he said, and by day find proxies you can talk out of fresh horses for your urgent report to the Ennead. They will not refuse you.

"And it will help me get inside."

He did not reply until he had finished with the soft hose and handed them to her. Then he said, Yes—wear black, and the ring, and they will not question you at the gate.

"But I'll have to leave you. You said not to, next time."

You take me with you in your heart, he replied. And I will always find you.

A steward entered the chamber, bearing a taper to light the other lamps. She caught sight of Liath and fled.

It was not long, after that. They had been coming anyway.

They filed in one by one, a procession of silken color, and took their places around the table. Their eyes never left her; the implications of her return rippled through them with a visible surge of hope and reevaluation.

"Did you bring us what we asked for?" Seldril said at last.

She took her time, and took their measure.

The seasons had changed them, even here inside their mountain. Seldril had grown thin and severe, the bone structure of her face prominent, hawklike. Gondril had fattened, as if storing fuel for a long fight; pendulous breasts hung over a mound of belly under his silk robes, and eyes black as Seldril's peered out from folds of flesh that seemed to hide his own face. Landril had put on muscle, growing harder, handsomer, more rugged—what his twins could have been. Lerissa looked harder, too, her eyes shards of blue ice in the sculpted, perfect face; Liath tried not to look on her too long, imagining that chiseled beauty in Torrin's arms. Vonche and Naeve had aged more than three seasons; Evonder had a downcast, shifty-eyed air, the chip worn off his shoulder. Of them all, only Freyn and Worilke had bloomed, the binder rosy-cheeked and youthful, the wordsmith tall and centered, like a fighter, like Verlein—prepared to set the world to rights.

"I can't," she said, staring at the black clothes. "I can't put them on."

It's just fabric.

"The color is evil—"

No color is evil! You're an illuminator, surely you know that. Think of the peace of deep night, restful shade on a blazing day, the spill of long black hair, the color of your friend's face. You see these clothes as evil, because you see your fears in them. But they're just clothes.

The Ennead sat before her in all their dyed finery—Gondril's triad scarlet, rose, rust, Vonche's indigo, violet, azure, Worilke's citron, saffron, cinnamon. But color was only symbol. Inside the vivid silks were human beings. No one would have done the things they were accused of, or the things they accused Torrin of. They painted each other with their own fears. Torrin only wanted people to learn; the Ennead only wanted him back, so they could control the weather better. But they misunderstood, and imagined the worst of each other, and out of their dark imaginings sprang longblades and earthquakes and shadows. The Ennead called too many mages, and mages' families, misinformed, turned concern for their loved ones into belief that the Ennead had harmed them.

It had to stop.

"Yes," she said, and drew the stained, wadded handcloth from a belt pouch. "But he's already broken with his supporters. I don't know where he is. It's them you've got to stop. If you closed the pass out of the Blooded Mountains, they couldn't ride."

"We'll see to it." Gondril held his hand out.

"But they'll starve," she persisted. Her fist closed around the linen. She would not give him up until it was on her terms. "They're short of casting materials. You'll have to send proxies. Maybe go there yourselves. Explain to them. Send their mages home, show them that nothing ill befell them here."

"We'll *see* to it," Gondril said. She was impertinent to tell them their business. But they were too sheltered. Someone had to.

"You've got to go out," she said. "There's so much going on that no one's telling you. The proxy chain has broken down."

"The rebels have weakened it. They insinuate their own folk into it and send us false information. Give me the packet."

"It's not just that," she said. "There were problems before." She drew breath through gritted teeth. They wouldn't like this. "You've lost support in the Lowlands and the Legs. They never see you, they don't understand. You're too far away. You've got to change that—you can't leave it to proxies anymore, it's gotten too serious. *This isn't all Torrin's fault.* Those people have legitimate grievances that won't go away, Torrin or no."

"What sort of grievances?" Worilke asked.

"You call too many mages. The reckoners treat local triads badly; they've lost respect for each other, there's only resentment now—they're supposed to work *together*. The warders direct the weather in ways the triads don't understand, and it makes them angry." Evonder sneered at her, but the others seemed as though they might be listening. There was a chance . . . "It's no one's *fault*. But it has to be mended. You can mend it; Torrin can mend it, if you can work with him, persuade him. Send him back as an emissary, your most important proxy. . . ." There was too much to say, and she was only a publican, she didn't know how to explain what was taking shape inside her mind. Jhoss would know how, Nerenyi, Torrin. They would be able to articulate the effective workings of authority on such a large scale. All she could find to finish with was "Please. You've got to mend this. It's worse than you know. People are going to get hurt."

Gondril had risen; his bulk was substantial, and his eyes glittered. She wanted to wilt under the commanding weight, but she still clutched the folded handcloth. "Your advice about the rebel encampment is well taken, and I have told you we will see to it, and we will. The weather problems below the Belt are an unfortunate side effect of our attempts to curtail the rebels' activity, but also an augury of Great Storms brewing. We must retrieve Torrin and reconfigure ourselves to stop them, or there will be no question of rebels or unrest or anything else." He held out his hand. "Give me the packet, Illuminator."

"You won't harm him?" she said softly, desperately, staring at the stained, ragged linen.

"I would be lying to you if I said that coring and sealing was not painful," Gondril said gently. "I would also be lying if I said that we will not endeavor to relieve you forcibly of the packet if you will not surrender it. He has lied to you, or you would not be hesitating now. It's his word against ours—the word of a madman against the history and integrity of this Ennead and the countless ones before it. You would not have come back here if you didn't know in your heart what was right. Don't betray the triskele you wear, Illuminator. Don't betray the very foundations of the world you believe in. Don't allow that world to come to an end, when you could have saved it."

The tunic was mended; there was no helping the fact that they were summer clothes, that there was no velvet coat to wear over the silk in the chill of winter's end. The cloak would have to do.

As she pulled the tunic over her head, she said, "You don't want to go there, do you."

I would slow you down.

"It's more than that. You believe Torrin's stories."

His hazel eye flashed, and he got slowly to his feet, reminding her how big he was. She had been unfair. Heff feared very little except harm coming to her.

I would slow you down, he repeated, and pointed at the ring.

The last part of her disguise. She slipped it on, turned it so the flat silver circle faced outward. It warmed to her hand, then cooled. Magecrafted metal, cast for someone else—yet now it fit her finger, where before it had been loose.

Liath gave the linen packet, and Torrin's life, into their keeping, and turned away.

"Come," Lerissa said, hands sliding smoothly over Liath's shoulders to enclose her upper arms. A silken touch. "I'll show you to a place where you can rest." It was a favor; she could have summoned an aide. Liath was meant to understand that Lerissa was stooping to it.

Such a minor detail. The woman was doing her a kindness. But the condescension spoke in a deafening whisper: *You are nothing. We are the Ennead. Come away like a good girl and leave us to the things you don't understand.*

She looked at the handcloth Gondril held. Was that triumph in his eyes, or only her fear of it?

"You have our most profound gratitude," Seldril said. "You've done well, Illuminator. Be proud."

They bowed; Liath bowed back; they turned away, to confer in low voices. It was a dismissal.

Lerissa led her out the door opposite the one she'd entered, and up, into a part of the Holding she had not been in. "You say you don't know where he is?" she asked offhandedly.

"I left him at the Girdle," Liath said. "He might be anywhere by now. Does it matter?"

"Our work would be facilitated if we had an exact fix on him."

"Like on the Blooded Mountains?"

Lerissa flashed small white teeth. "It's difficult to move a mountain. We needed two things: material from the mountain, and the ability to visualize it in context. It will help if he's still in the Girdle. It's much the same, one league to the next."

"Have you been there?" Liath asked, as they came into a chamber remarkable for one thing: a window, small and barred, that looked out on the sea.

"No. I was raised here. My father was an Ennead illuminator before me. But others have." She fluffed the bedding on the pine-framed mattress and sniffed the water in the basin on a maple nightstand. "Stale," she pronounced. "I'll have it freshened."

The room smelled of the sea; it captured a faraway sound of surf like a conch. "You don't journey?"

Lerissa cocked her head. "We're the Ennead."

"Perhaps you should." She dropped her light pack on the bed; a puff of sheddown blew up by the wall. "You'd have a better idea of how the people you shepherd live and think."

"He did turn you, didn't he?" Lerissa said, her sapphire eyes bright with interest. "Just a little."

Liath's voice went flat. "I brought you what you wanted."

"For which much thanks. I'll have clothes sent. He didn't cast you proxy, did he?"

Liath frowned.

"No, I didn't think so. A plain village girl like you. Who did you steal the clothes from?"

"Who did you steal your place on the Ennead from?"

Lerissa regarded her mildly. "My dead father," she said. "And still he made me earn it, even cold in the bonefolk's arms." A tilt of head, a quizzical smile. "Remarkable. A roadside village. Who showed a light before you? In your family, I mean."

"My mother's father. His brothers. Their mother."

"And they named you for her. She must have been very bright."

"So they said."

"No one in your father's family?"

"An uncle of his. What does it matter?"

"So it skipped generations on both sides. Worilke will be fascinated. Lineage matters a great deal. And you matter a great deal. You must know that, though you hide it. If we retrieve him, you'll join us. You and he could push out Vonche and Naeve and leave my triad unbroken. That's what you want, isn't it? To be healed and ascend to the Ennead? It might suit me as well."

All Liath wanted was to know she had been right in delivering Torrin Wordsmith to his enemies—and then to go home and crawl into bed beside her sister, immersed in the smells and sounds of safety.

"*Can* you heal me?" she asked.

"We couldn't a year ago. But Torrin would change all that. Surely you've seen him cast. It's like strong drink, isn't it, soaking in that light? Inebriating. It makes you yearn for things you never knew you wanted."

They stared at each other for a long time. Liath was aware of being baited. Lerissa wanted to know how many ways Torrin had turned her. This slender, cool creature could not be the memory that gentled his voice and warmed his eyes. If this was what his taste ran to—this imperious cobblers' daughter, with her generous breasts pressing invitation through saffron, her rich dark hair, her silken skin and belittling gaze—he could never have kissed Liath the way he had. Not even to insure against betrayal.

"He mentioned a lover, in the Holding," she said, then shrugged. "Apparently she wasn't enough for him."

Lerissa laughed. "Perhaps we can help each other after all, Illuminator. Let me see to your comfort. I'll return with news of the sealing, and we'll move on from there."

She swept out of the room in a graceful rustle, leaving Liath to wonder: Had she found the ally? Could Lerissa's airs be an act?

She pushed her pack against the wall and lay on the sheddown mattress, her body screaming its relief to be in a bed for the first time in moons, and a bed finer than any she had slept in. No more chasing after convolutions of motive, veracity, proof. She had made her decision. It was the right decision. That she desired him couldn't be helped. It was immaterial. She had done what she must. She had done what they ordered—because it was right, not because she harbored ambitions of joining the Ennead.

Her body grew heavy, weighted with lethargy, but tides of thought and vision washed across her mind.

They had taught Boroel to kill before they taught him to cast. What had they taught Lerissa to do?

Torrin, sharing Lerissa's light, Lerissa's bed—

She would have to live with that. She had wanted things, before, that she couldn't have.

They had only to cast together. It was clear she was meant for him. The lattice of liquid flame their joined work had become . . . no one could see that and not recognize that Lerissa should stay where she was, letting Liath and Torrin displace Vonche and Naeve—

Ambition planted in her by Lerissa. Lerissa sought to retain her dead father's place, and would use Liath to assure it.

Power, Torrin had said. Lerissa wanted power. Lerissa had looked at her, touched her, like any dim-lit Sauglin mageling. Lerissa wanted her light.

Of course she did. There was nothing nefarious in that. Pelkin had tried to protect her; so had Geara, in her way. Mages had always lusted for her light, and sought to use it, right back to Graefel. It didn't mean they practiced darkcraft.

They would be doing the casting now, mixing the dried flakes of skin into ink and pigment, binding him. If they succeeded, he would come here to be unsealed, and she would see him again—

She must not think on that. She must rest, confident that she had completed a heroic duty, managed something that no one else had, out of all the ones they sent. She had done it. It was over.

But she knew. In the deeps of her mind, as the walls she had constructed around and inside herself crumbled with fatigue and the onset of sleep, she knew.

Insistent knocking jolted her out of a restless doze. Midmorning sun slanted through the window, barring the door in shadows. She staggered up, bleary, and turned the polished brass handle. Two warders, in snowy velvet, silver glinting on their ring fingers. One of them carried a baby swaddled in fleece.

"Liath?" whispered a husky voice. "Don't you know us?"

For a breath she still did not. Then she gasped, and would have embraced them, but Dabrena was already shouldering past her into the room; Tolivar shrugged wry apology, but followed quickly and shut the door with care. "Have you the use of your light?" he asked, glancing at her proxy garb, the cloak cast over a stool.

No greeting, no smiles. Liath blinked. "Yes," she said, "it came back while I was casting passage. But it's not—"

"Thank the spirits!" Dabrena breathed.

Liath gestured to the baby. "You and Tolivar?" she asked, and Dabrena nodded. "Oh, Dabrena, what gift!" With a flicker of doubt, Dabrena offered her the bundled infant; Liath hesitated, then took it, her arms filling with warmth and weight. It was a beautiful child, but oddly subdued, unbabylike, and Dabrena looked furtive, as if the child had brought her not joy but terror.

The dread she had felt at Lerissa's touch grew stronger.

Her friends were much changed. Tolivar, who loved the sea, the open air, the sky, had been living in a rock for over a year. It had left him blanched and drawn, and the warder's white gave his skin a grayish cast.

Dabrena had always looked at you straight-on; now her gaze shifted, furtive, watchful, as if something might come lunging for her out of a corner.
The longer Liath held the baby, the more Dabrena fidgeted, until finally
she scooped it against her, then put a wall at her back.

"You heard I returned?" Liath asked, unsure what to say to these folk
made newly strangers.

"You passed Ronim without knowing him," Tolivar said. "By the
Crownside gate. This level is where they bring vocates to meditate before
they're cast proxy. It's been empty for a moon now. We tried doors until
we sensed your light."

"We're fools," Dabrena said.

"We had to see her." Tolivar faced Liath. "We need you."

The caress of fear ran up the back of her neck, raising hairs.

"She's still loyal to them, or she wouldn't be here," Dabrena said,
but her eyes said she hoped to be wrong.

Liath was trying to reconcile the baby with the Dabrena who was in
no hurry to pledge. Dabrena tucked the fleece under its chin, defensively.
"Worilke's triad casts the proxies. They remove the first freedom from us.
We were all with child within a moon."

"Worilke fears the thinning of mageblood," Tolivar explained. His
tone had not changed: forced calm as his patience raveled. "Fewer in each
generation show a light. She won't abide childless mages when so many
lightless have two or more."

Liath thought of her sister, born nine moons after she showed a light;
of the stablemaster's fosterlings, and Boroel.

"Her name is Kara," Dabrena murmured. "For Karanthe."

The caress grew colder. Custom was not to name babes for the living.
"Oh, spirits—"

"We don't know for sure," Tolivar said, in a soothing tone that frayed
into uncertainty. His sweet voice, a fraying lifeline to how he'd thought
things ought to be. "She was cast reckoner with some others. They went
into the field in summer."

"So we were told," Dabrena snapped.

Tolivar rubbed his face. "There isn't time for this. We need your
help. Our illuminator refused. No one else will do it."

"Afraid of flouting the bloody Ennead," Dabrena said, with a spark
of her old defiance. But she hugged the baby close.

"It's bad here, Liath," Tolivar said. "They rule us harshly. There are
rumors . . . We don't know. We don't really know what's happening. But
we can't keep the baby here."

"Leave!" Liath burst out. "What's wrong with you? If it's so bad,
if—"

Dabrena was laughing, a horrible laugh that choked off as she heard
how loud it was. "We can't. You can't. No one can. There's a warding

on this place, a shield. It admits you but won't let you through the other way. Not if you show a light. Ever since harvestmid."

"That's——"

"Not impossible," Tolivar said. "Not for them."

She had been about to say that it was like the shield Torrin claimed surrounded all of Eiden Myr. But that was delusion . . .

"It doesn't *stop* you," Tolivar said. "But it makes you ill. It burns you inside, as if it uses your own light against you. No one's gotten through it."

"Pass her to someone outside," Liath said. "I know someone . . . a steward . . . he looks after children . . ."

"If there's a light inside her," Tolivar said, touching the fleece with a fingertip, "sending her through would kill her."

"There is a light," Dabrena said. "I know it." She looked up. "Help us, Liath. Please."

Liath frowned at the bindsack slung over Tolivar's thin shoulder. "What is it you need to do?"

"Core and seal the baby."

"*What?*"

"It's the only way to protect her," Dabrena said, quick and harsh.

"We've got to try." Tolivar kneeled to open the sack. "If she's sealed, someone can get her out."

"It takes nine to core and seal a mage. It takes an Ennead!"

Tolivar looked into her, at the light that had once stirred him to passion. The passion was gone, replaced with battered desperation. "It takes power," he said. "She's only a baby. You might have enough. *We have to try.*"

Liath hissed frustration. Lerissa would return at any moment, or send stewards with food, clothes. She was hungry, exhausted, in no shape for the simplest casting, much less this.

Tolivar chalked a white circle on the stone and seated himself. Dabrena followed suit, setting the baby in the center. She kicked out a little against the swaddling, then stilled.

Liath sat. Tolivar scooped a fingerful of saliva from the baby's mouth and mixed it into tallow-soot ink. Dabrena scribed, and passed the vellum to Liath.

The guiders would not form.

The Holding is steeped in pain . . .

"I'm just tired," she said in a low voice, staring at the calfskin vellum, the Celyrian marks that Dabrena had made in her small, orderly hand. "It will come. *It will come.*"

They tried for a long time. They tried past all reason, far past the point of safety. At any moment someone would barge in. The child lay calm in the circle, never crying, never burbling. But Liath's light was null. She could not seal the child. She could not save the child. She was as good as sealed herself.

Her friends rose stiffly, gathering baby and materials, standing with shoulders pressed close as they told her it was all right, they had done what they could—as their despairing eyes told her that she had been their last hope. She had left them nothing.

"You don't need a triad," she said, as Tolivar grasped the door handle. "You don't need me. You've seen illuminations, Dabrena, you could copy what you saw. You're both bright—you're *warders*. Try it yourselves. Your love for the child might be enough. Wanting it badly might be enough. I've seen it done—"

They recoiled, as if she had become the threat.

"*Try*," she said to their backs as Tolivar turned the handle.

They left quickly. Fearless, competent Dabrena, watching the shadows with a wince engraven in the skin around her eyes. Tolivar boyish no longer, the wicked grin pressed into an anxious frown, his joy in the light—his ecstasy—extinguished. Tolivar, who would never again believe in how things *should* be.

She could not cast through pain.

The Holding was steeped in pain.

It was true. It was all true.

Sweet spirits, what have I done?

She had her pack on, the cloak fastened around her neck, a daft plan half-formed in her mind, when the door opened.

Landril glanced at the chalk circle on the floor, read the defiant fear in her eyes. "You can cast now, can you?" he said.

"No," she replied. "I'm blocked, here. If you want to use my light, you'll have to let me out."

"None of us can go out. Not even the sealed."

Her failure might have saved the baby's life. It was scant consolation for the life she had given away.

"We will still find a purpose for you," he said. "The sealed can be quite useful."

"I'm not sealed."

He waved that off, then said, "And stop gauging the speed and leverage required to get past me. You cannot."

"Why should I want to?" she said. "I want you to break the block on my magelight so I can join the Ennead."

"Was Torrin so unpersuasive?" He smiled, a shifting of muscles in a face like a stone. There was no mirth in it. "I doubt it. And you're smitten. You reek of it." He stepped abruptly toward her, and had her forearm in an iron grip before she had fully shifted her weight to eel past him. He twisted it up behind her, pressing her body against his. "Your casting hand, yes?" Her weight shifted again. "Knee my groin and I will break it. Move your off arm and I will break it." He was inhumanly strong. Enhanced by darkcraft somehow, bones and muscles strengthened. "Not darkcraft," he said, as if reading her mind. "Hard, punishing work." His right hand came up; he traced the curve of her ear with callused fingertips. "It is tempting to spoil you for him," he said, "perhaps make you un-beddable. But there would be no pleasure in it if I had to let you live. And at any rate, you'll never have him now." He spun her away from him. She hit the wall, catching a hip on the nightstand and an elbow on the sill. The dual pains lanced through the ache of strained bones and tendons in her shoulder. He stopped expertly short of damage.

"What do you want, then? You're here for *some* bloody reason."

"Smart, sweet mageling." His voice was a velvet insinuation; he might as well have been groping her. "They would all have come to you in time, each of them wanting something, each of them seeking the way in which this prize can be used to advantage. I came to see you for myself. I came to look in your eyes and find out the truth. Gondril would have tossed you aside once you delivered the materials. Others would see you join us in order to push their rivals out, but it was only a matter of time until your loyal heart discovered its mistake. As I see that it has. You backed the wrong horse, my dear. You distrusted the wrong man."

You're seeing it the way you want to. You're filling in the words for them, and someday they'll say other words, and you'll stand gaping while your dreams sift through the sieve and away.

"You might still acquire some minor leverage, if you could discern what each of them wants and make them believe you could provide it. But I'm forbidding access to you. My armed stewards will stand outside that door. You, and the marvelous power in that contained light of yours, are mine alone. Think on that, as you sit starving and cold in this chamber. Despair, if you can. It will make you easier to manage when the time comes."

The oaken door opened out.

He would have to wrestle her for it.

She launched herself at the door just as he was through it, before he could turn, get his weight behind it, force it closed.

He let the door crash open and grabbed her. Fast, too fast—or she too slow. He thrust her to the floor of the chamber. "You are so fragile." He'd kept hold of her right hand. She heard a brittle crack. Agony blinded her. "You won't be needing these," he said, and broke another finger. Her outcry tailed off into a sob. "You won't be casting again." A third snapped. Her body jerked. "For luck," he said, and stepped away, and gently closed the door.

A bolt shot across the far side, through iron braces, across all her hopes.

Seldril made the initial cuts, keeping close watch on the subject lest he slip past Freyn's potions into unconsciousness. He had a sturdy, broad body, and a satisfying bewilderment that the early agony only intensified. He did not understand why they were doing this. He did not understand why his throat produced no sound. It was charming, and aided the casting. His confusion had seeped into his blood, and would help daze the casting's object—keep him from realizing, until too late, what was happening to him and why. When there was sufficient blood, she mixed it with the other materials in clay pots. She used a small bone pestle to grind the flakes of skin thoroughly. Then she set out the ink and pigment, laid brushes and quills beside them, and returned to the more interesting work. One of the joys of these castings was that she need not sit idle through the endless inking.

Gondril scribed as Seldril made the median incisions. Their custom-made vellum had a delicious smoothness, and he took pleasure in the flow of ink across its unusual weave. A shame, really, that his prentice must be wasted; it should have been him on this table, not some disposable proxy, and his coy, evasive light would have been a pleasure to control at last. But he would not come to heel. There was no time now; there was no choice. *These are the glyphs I taught you,* he thought, across the miles, across the water. *Would you had heeded me better, boy. Didn't I tell you that words are the most powerful thing in the world? Now I consume you with the words you cherished, and all your righteous rage will avail you naught.*

As he accepted the leaf, Landril had the face, the body, fixed in his vision; his mind alone could crush the spare frame, extinguish the light in the eyes. *You defied me,* he thought. *You should not have done that.* But the image kept wavering, sliding back into that of the child who'd been brought here when Landril and his siblings were in early adolescence. The slit golden eyes, the shock of black hair; even as a boy he'd had a disquieting composure. Seldril had been quick to break it, once they were triaded and had rid themselves of their masters. But the boy refused to stay broken. Irritating. And irritating that he remembered the boy, the youth, so much more clearly than the man.

No matter. Killing either one would do.

Seldril felt the casting coalesce. The moment of ecstasy was not far off. She made the last of the low incisions, and watched with bright eyes as Landril laid the illuminated leaf on the subject's chest. She clasped Landril's stony hand on one side and Gondril's fleshy hand on the other, waited for them to grip her hard enough to hurt. Their magelights linked, focused through the spirit struggling to free itself from the casting table. Surprisingly, there was resistance; then it crumbled, and they were in. Seldril closed her eyes. The darkness was glorious. "Sweet passage, Terrell," she murmured, but her rich, dark bindsong was a song of farewell not to him, but to the man they were touching even now—a man who would never again cross the waters of this world.

Gondril swelled with pride and satiety as he left the casting chamber and returned to his own windowless quarters. He had much to congratulate himself for, he mused, as he turned down the lantern the steward always lit, and lifted a roasted lamb's leg from the sideboard. As the oldest by three breaths, as the one unhindered by gender's particularities, he had been charged with forging these bright, untrustworthy folk into the most powerful Ennead ever to grace Eiden Myr. His elders, though they had paved the way, had left him no easy task. Half of them were mad, the other half obsessed with their own irrelevant goals. But still he had made them work together. Dispensing with Torrin na Maeryn le Eilody, the spawn of storm, had brought them within sight of the end. Only one task remained; then he could indulge his private desires unhindered and undistracted. And how delectable that last task would be.

The chambers seemed empty, with the workroom dismantled. But it was no longer needed. They had come so far since the days of their individual explorations. Could it be only a year ago that he was attempting to scry across the known world with his subjects? A failure, in its way, for it could not be done—but scrying was not their optimal use. Working *between* worlds was what mortal tools were designed for. In establishing that, the Nine had functioned as a true Ennead for the first time, each contributing—intentionally or no—some vital element of the plan.

He and his siblings had perfected the techniques dubbed "darkcraft"; a misnomer, since they worked entirely with light, the light of life and the light of mages. It was a joyful craft. While working through a subject correctly prepared, one could drink the light. It was like opening a fount of purest elixir. Seldril never truly savored it, too busy feeding on their pain; Landril came closer, severing the light from their bodies as he climaxed on them, but still his taste was anchored in the physical. Gondril had gorged on the physical and found it insufficient. Only magelight itself assuaged his hunger now.

Vonche had come upon the means of binding spirits—he'd finally gotten some use from his endless labyrinthine journeys through those old records. With the flesh on the brink of death, the spirit was unstable, but Vonche's binding technique provided the time required to work an effective casting.

Weak-willed Evonder's obsession with haunts had made them think to work through bet-jahr, the spirit world; and Worilke had developed the casting to do it, using one of Vonche's bound spirits, unmoored from the body by Seldril's ministrations. Worilke, determined to keep them from breaking Galandra's precious shield, had provided a way to cast through it.

Freyn, pathetic lovelorn Freyn, enamored of her noxious potions, had at last—and with only a modicum of persuasion—surrendered her own secret. It was clever, he must admit that; it was sublime in its cruel invention. They could not destroy the land that neighbored their island home, for they possessed not a grain of its earth. But if they could send through bet-jahr a draught of the most succulent, virulent poison . . .

It was Naeve who, almost offhandedly, broke them free of the constraints of flesh. They could send no matter through bet-jahr, a domain of spirit, a domain of light. But Naeve, brilliant Naeve who was never interested in her own intelligence beyond preserving it, had uttered the charmed words: Send a spiritual poison. Send despair. Send a plague that will sap their will to live, a plague that will rot love and hope the way leprosy rots flesh, until there is nothing in their hearts but putrid, blackened gel.

He had enjoyed the thought of a flesh-eating disease; he respected the idea of something so ravenous that it would consume all matter. But the plan was complete, unassailable. Landril would have Luriel's revenge. Naeve would have her immortality; Evonder would be united with the haunts who haunted him; Vonche would achieve his unlimited vision, for in bet-jahr all was visible, all was known. Worilke would rest content that the external threat to Galandra's crucible was nullified—and achieve, in the bargain, her heart's desire: to know the truth of Galandra, to know the woman whom history had obscured. Lerissa would contrive to remain here to rule, in her narrow-minded pursuit of earthly power; she would have no choice, since the alternative would be to rule a wasteland. Mad Freyn—there was no telling what she would do. Poison herself, perhaps, or succumb to the effects of years of handling poisons. Perhaps Lerissa— if she was not already dead at Worilke's hands, for Lerissa was a threat to Galandra's demotic way—would discover the truth about Freyn and her father, and kill her. It would be no concern of his.

His siblings would be his immediate reward. Hein-na-fhin: the ancient ritual in which three mages became one in physical fact. They thought they would merge in body, but remain discrete in spirit. Seldril expected to bask for all eternity in the spiritual pain of uncountable hordes. For Landril, vengeance was sufficient gratification. He had no other purpose. Possibly he would not even fight his own consumption. Nor would Seldril; the only thing she desired more than others' suffering was her own. Gondril would be happy to accommodate her, and offer death as a bonus.

He would consume them whole, make them part of him, as they should have been from the beginning. They had acquiesced to his dominance from expediency. Soon they would discover that he was dominant in fact.

He would subsume them into himself. Thus fortified, released into bet-jahr, he would be all-powerful. There would be no stopping him then, or denying his hunger.

What would it taste like, devouring a world?

Beyond the bars, the sky darkened, lightened. Liath bound her broken fingers tight with strips of sheet. She slept. She relieved herself in a chamber pot, bathed herself with standing water. She turned the solid bedframe on its side, then on end, and toppled it with a crash into the door; the oak held, and the bedframe jarred apart. She smashed the boards into arm-size flinders against the nightstone walls, then made a pyre of pine against the door and, with strikers from her pack, set it alight; the oak was left blackened but intact, and she hung from the window bars, gasping for air, skin gritty with soot. She drank the stale water. She looked out the window and down: a sheer nonned threfts to jagged blackstone and the grasping sea, and she couldn't fit even her head between the bars.

Voices murmured outside the door. Change in shift. But there was something different this time. The bolt rattled in its braces. She stepped to the middle of the room. There was a pause. The bolt scraped free, and the door opened.

Two burly male stewards. One whistled as he took in the devastation; without a word they gripped her by the arms and escorted her into the eternal lamplight of the passageway.

She wouldn't walk for them. They had her off the floor, skimming along on her toes. Just outside the doorway, she balked, then pushed off as they hauled forward, and swung her feet up onto the passage wall. It broke their grip; she drove herself into the one on the left. He broke her fall. She was away—but he had hold of her ankles. She kicked out, felt flesh under her boot heel, heard an oath, got free again, got to one foot.

The other man wrapped her in a crushing embrace, pinning her arms to her sides. The one on the floor got his wind back as she struggled and kicked, and captured her legs in his own thick arms. They hefted her like a rolled carpet. She writhed and bit, to no avail.

Then she saw the bodies. Two other stewards, blades sheathed at their sides, knives sheathed in their chests.

Someone who didn't like Landril had sent these men.

There had been only grunts and hisses in the silence. They were Khin-ishmen, she could tell from the coloring and build—she didn't have to hear an accent. Fair-minded folk, the swarthy Khinish, but rigorous and hardheaded. They would fight to the death for whatever they believed in. Verlein's horde was full of them—and so was the Holding. If she could invoke Hanla . . .

They took her up, and across, and around, and down, through dim passages no one seemed to use. Into none's-land, the land beyond the shadows. They were taking her to be used—to be killed. Whose men were they? Which Ennead members opposed Landril?

The thick redolence that came into her nostrils made her head spin. Warmth and effluents, sweetness and offal . . .

A small door opened on darkness. They minced through it and set her on her feet. Her boots rustled straw as she balanced. She knew where she was even before she winced in the blaze of an uncovered lamp and saw the rows of tack, the piled blankets.

"She put up a fight," one of the stewards said, stacking bales of hay where they'd come in. "Smashed and burned the door half down. Left quite a mess."

Bron chuckled as he hung the lantern on a hook. "Good on you, girl." He glanced at the other Khinishman. "Do they know?"

He scratched his head. "Hard to say. We used Ennead-commissioned blades. They might believe it was their own."

"The guards were two of the dullest," said the first steward. "That had to be Wynn's doing. We misjudged him."

"Perhaps." Bron was frowning at the ring on Liath's left hand. "May I have a look at that?"

She brought up her bound hand to show that she could not pull the ring off. He hissed and bent to rummage in a box, coming up with all manner of stoppered jars, but not what he wanted. "Oreg, get something for her pain."

"I'm all right," she said as the man left. "Maybe some food. Fresh water." Her legs started to go. Bron caught her and lowered her to the pile of saddle blankets Mellas had slept on, dreamless, such a very long time ago.

"We can't heal you," Bron said. "I'm sorry. No mages can be trusted."

"Dabrena . . . Tolivar . . ." She took a breath. "Never mind. Bron . . ." He leaned close. Apparently her voice was very weak. ". . . Mellas."

His brown eyes shut briefly.

"Is he all right?"

A pause. Then: "Spirits willing."

"If the spirits are kind, he's dead," said the other steward.

Liath turned her face away.

"See if those urchins left any supper," Bron said. She heard the other steward leave, heard him mutter at children clustered around the inner door.

"I put him in their hands," she whispered. "I told them . . ." Something was choking her. "Eiden forgive me."

"You should not have come back here," Bron said.

"No," she told the wall softly. "I should not have come."

"But you're here now," Bron continued, brisk. "What is, is. Did you set those bones?"

She shook her head, but said, "Don't."

"I won't," he said, "till you've got some food in your belly and some fire in your eyes. There's still a long way to go, my girl. A great deal to do. Might I see the ring now?"

Surprise roused her. She offered the hand. He got the ring off with some difficulty and peered inside. "That's Jimor's mark, right enough," he said. "You kept it all this time?"

"Jimor." She looked up at the Khinish stablemaster. The webmaster, fostering his loyal, loving, indebted children here at the nexus of runners—of information. "Did they live?"

"They did, though Laren cursed you roundly. There was no other way. You couldn't be allowed to succeed, we didn't want to see you dead, we couldn't reveal ourselves to you. We'd have tucked you away safe, probably on Khine."

"Did he follow me, after Ardra?"

"A ways. But our folk down there are too few. We couldn't keep hold of you once you joined the proxies."

They had been watching her—the reckoners, the seekers, Torrin's folk, Bron's folk. All watching, reporting; even herding her, in Heff's case. And Pelkin . . . she would never know what he had wanted, which side he was on. All waiting to see which way she would turn, calculating the effect on their respective causes. As if she meant something. As if she could do anything besides—

Besides fail, and err. She gritted her teeth against self-pity. She had failed. She had erred, grievously, unspeakably. Unforgivably. But she was alive. This wasn't over yet.

She sat up with an effort and thanked Oreg for the herbal draught he brought, shoveled good plain stew on top of it, then drank as much water as she could hold. Bron chuckled when she was through. "Like a wilding child you are."

She forced a smile through a sucking weight of fatigue; it turned into a yawn. "Don't let me sleep," she said. "I have to—"

"You have to heal," Bron said, rising. "Anyway, it's too late. That snort'll have you out for a good while."

They'd drugged her. "No . . ." Her tongue wasn't working. "I have to set it right," she slurred, fighting to stay above the heavy drag of sleep. "I have to . . ."

". . . wake up. Wake up, miss. Now."

She surfaced blurrily. There were two Oregs. "How long?"

"It's evening. We changed your clothes for you and Bron set those fingers—nasty job, that. He's out front answering questions now. I'm afraid Mellas might have said something he oughtn't, poor lad. Or it might be you. You've got to go."

He had cleared the hay bales from the secret door. Liath slid her feet into the straw but could not sit up after two tries. Oreg got her arm around his shoulders and maneuvered her through the low doorway, swearing at his own shoddy herbal. "Bloody forgotten lore," he said, propping her against the passage wall. "We've a lot of ground to make up, when this is over." He turned and snagged a lantern, setting it on the floor just past her. "Stay hidden," he said. "Eiden guide you." Then the door was closed, and she heard the rustle of bales restacked, and voices in the tackroom. Oreg's, Bron's . . .

Wynn's? ". . . destroy this place and your younglings with it."

"How could he know?" There was an oath, the stomp of boots, the clatter of hooves beyond, frightened children's voices.

"He turned one of Seldril's, the man was coming for her, the whole thing was meant as a trap and you sprang it too soon and he saw your Khinishmen carry her off. He's working both sides, he'll run to her next, you have only breaths. Get out, send the signal, cover yourself. This will be my death. I owe you nothing now . . ."

Liath got hold of the lantern's handle on the second try and sidled along the wall, not trusting her balance in empty air. She weighed twice her nine stone. A turn, then another, and another—they wouldn't see her light now, lantern or magelight. She slid to the floor and let darkness reclaim her.

When she came to, she was freezing, but the lantern was half full of oil, and she still felt no pain from bruises or brokenness. Bron had splinted the fingers and bound them together, a tight, even wrap, and perhaps rubbed in some painkilling liniment. The clothes they'd put on her were good sturdy linen and wool—tunic over shirt, breeches, silks. New boots with good soles. And an apron. Making a steward of her. Despite everything, it felt very fine to have fresh clothes against her skin. She wiggled her toes in the soft stockings, and felt a pressure against her left calf.

They'd put a sheathed blade in her boot, by her good hand.

She smiled.

The end of the passageway narrowed sharply, and before long she was on hands and knees. At last she came up against a dead end—but there was wood under her palms. A trapdoor. Had she come up, as well as around? She hooked the iron ring and lifted.

Below her was the horse ramp.

She blew the lantern dark, listened awhile to silence, then lowered her feet through, holding her injured hand out of harm's way, and dropped. Her legs were still rubbery and absorbed the impact too well; she landed on her rear.

She could leave the Holding—go up this ramp, find her way to the pass, get home on foot. Aralinn water was clear; there would be peaberries to eat, greens that tasted like gall, temperate caves.

She went down the ramp. All was quiet, the stalls empty. Bron had gotten them out. Seldril's folk must have been and gone. She found the circle-stair and went up. The way to the vocates' quarters was clear in her mind. She nodded at young people in gray as she passed them, just a steward on some business or other. Then she was in the stairwell she had used in fleeing the warders.

Coming up the stairs was old Knobface. She did not remember his name. She kept her face down, but he cocked his head, touched her arm as she tried to pass.

"Do I know you?" he asked, frowning.

She looked him straight in the eyes. "You never bothered."

"What . . . ?" he began, but she was past him, continuing down. "Wynn will know," she heard him mutter as she turned the landing.

Wynn was dead by now, in payment for some long-ago debt Liath could not imagine. Roots went too deep to see, in the Holding.

Her route had doubled back on itself, dodged this way and that, but she retraced every step of it, the only way to follow the memory. She felt the lack of the lantern keenly as she came into the unlit section. But she could hear the whispers. She moved toward them. They didn't frighten her now. The horrors in this mountain were flesh-and-blood. Whatever haunted this passageway was very old, and no longer had power to harm, unless it hypnotized you to the edge of the abyss, and she knew better.

"Phew! Odorous one! Smelled you coming for breaths and breaths. Now I fear to take a breath."

Liath laughed. "It's mutual, Portriel."

"Follow Portriel, as before," she said with a chuckle. "Away from wind and whispers. Away from the old words, the old lives. Many lives, in the crevasse of whispers. Many memories. What woke them, I wonder? Ages and ages they slept. Now they mutter in the dark. Mutter, matter. Did you know I was a mage once?"

"The steward told me. The one who doesn't like you going out to see the stars."

A snort came from the darkness ahead of her. "Steward Steward. An oily man."

They came into her chambers, pillowed in cushions and darkness. This time there was no invisible wine; just the yeasty, sour smell of age, incontinence. Portriel rustled around to no purpose that Liath could make out with ears alone. "Can you tell me about the Ennead, Portriel?" she hazarded at last.

"Bad people," Portriel said. "Cruel. Hurt Portriel. Sealed her, when she would defy them. Portriel was old and foolish. Then they took her light away and drove her mad. Poor 'Triel."

Suddenly she was next to Liath, moving unerringly in the dark to sit in the cushions beside her, her bony hip against Liath's. "They will heal you," she said conspiratorially, "but not the way you think, and you cannot ask them for it." She reeled off a list of people to beware of, secrets Liath could use against them—but none of the names were familiar. She could do nothing against Rontifer or Yelwyn, whoever they were. She could not restore those Portriel grieved, though she listened patiently to the keening of memory. "They killed Jaemlyn," Portriel said, "and Jaemlyn was the best of us. Oh, I fought them after that. I was a brave girl, canny, quick. But not quick enough, or smart enough. You cannot fight them from within. Someone must fight them from without!"

"Someone is trying," Liath said. *Someone tried. They've killed him by now. They were never going to core and seal him. What a fool I've been. You and me, Portriel.*

"Good," Portriel said wearily. "That's good. There was a boy, once . . . a beautiful dark boy . . . Portriel had hoped. Portriel will rejoice when she hears." She straightened. "But now."

Liath startled as the woman groped across her for her right hand. When Portriel felt the bandages, she went very still; then she explored the configuration of fingers, and grunted.

"It's time," Portriel said.

"Time? For us to go?" She had expected more information: where they did their dark work, how she could get there unseen. She had hoped the blind woman would guide her, as before.

"For *me* to go."

A draft seemed to chill Liath's skin in the airless chamber.

"Strong girl. Strong hands. I will not fight you. My neck is old and scrawny, my lungs are old thin sacks. It will take only moments. Or you could use a pillow. Plenty of those."

Appalled, Liath started to rise, but Portriel put a light fingertip on her chest.

"A hard thing I ask of you. Portriel knows. But listen—*believe*: I am an old madwoman, but Portriel is not. Portriel knows exactly what she is doing. Portriel is the sanest woman I have ever known—and I knew myself, once, so that's saying quite a bit, yes?" She took Liath's left hand in a viselike grip. Liath flinched, her body remembering recent pain. Portriel leaned in close to Liath's ear and commanded, on a fetid breath, "*Do it. Do it quickly.* Portriel has mourned her dead." It was the other voice, the voice of the rational woman. The voice of the mage Portriel must have been. "Portriel has told you what she could remember. I can be used— the brightest light on my Ennead, sealed now for long years, a loose, neglected weapon wandering their dark passageways, an old blind woman cruelly used, afraid to wrench her freedom from them. They will destroy the world with my grief and madness. Do you understand that?"

Liath shook her head, squirming.

"*Listen to me.* Look with mind and heart, not eyes. Your eyes are no good here. Darkness demands more of you. Portriel demands more of you. Kill me. *Set me free.*"

This was too horrible to contemplate. "I can't cast passage for you," Liath said desperately.

"It doesn't matter," the clear, firm voice replied. "It's better that way. I'll haunt the stars. . . ."

The hand drew Liath's to her throat, closed her fingers over cartilage. Liath snatched the hand away and bit back a whimper. This was unthinkable.

Portriel said, with dreamy sadness, "Steward Steward. I will miss him. . . ." The sane woman said, "Nowhere to hang a noose in this cave. No knives. They sealed the balcony door as securely as they sealed me. I've been starving myself for a nineday, but it takes too bloody long. Get it over with!"

The knife in her boot . . . "Don't ask this of me," Liath begged.

"Don't be a child," the sane voice said. "Do as I tell you. Would you have them use me to kill countless innocents? Would you leave me trapped in this failing shell? My body grows putrid, my brain jellifies in my skull; I'm dying anyway. Grant me this kindness—grant me this final vengeance. I will try not to fight you, but you must be quick. The spirit will struggle to stay with this blind, rotting flesh. I would be free of it. *Do it.*"

As if in a dream, Liath got to her knees and turned to face the invisible mage. She moved her hands toward Portriel's neck, then cupped her face instead, exploring with the pads of her thumbs the pits and folds in the skin, the ripples of flesh that radiated outward from her toothless smile. Liath remembered that smile; Liath remembered that face bathed in starlight.

"Go in joy," she whispered—and twisted, before the shift in her grip could register. The crunch of the brittle spine snapping would echo in her mind for the rest of her life.

Panic drove guilt and grief away as a light grew in the open doorway and soft footsteps neared. There was nowhere to hide. In the growing light, the chamber resolved into a cave, chipped and carved into crevices in which Portriel had kept a hoard of castoffs and trinkets—a sparkling hodgepodge of items lost or stolen from all over the Holding. A jay's nest of objects whose odd shapes and textures must have painted pictures for her ravenous mind.

The intruder was the steward, the oilman. He looked at Portriel, shock and pity warring in his face.

"It's what she wanted—" Liath began.

The oilman loomed over her—then dropped to his knees and kissed Portriel's dead hand. "Oh, my lady," he whispered. "I served you as I could." He raised a tear-streaked face to Liath. "Galandra shine on you in all her mercy. I couldn't do it. A dozen times she asked me, while she wasted away. Got as close as touching her, but I ran away, didn't I?" He smoothed the matted white hair. "I loved you my life long, Portriel."

"She knew," Liath said, hoping.

He nodded, and rose.

Liath bent to brush the lids down over the empty sockets. The steward belayed the movement.

"Let her go to the bonefolk with eyes open," he said.

Before they left the chamber, the steward groped through Portriel's voluminous, tattered robes. He came up with a gold ring, strung on the chain that held a pewter triskele, though mage chains had no clasp. He draped them on a cobwebbed wine jug.

"Leave that for *them*," he said darkly. "Remind them what they lost."

As he guided her down the black passageway, sharing the sphere of his lanternlight, he said, "You should hide, now, somewhere. I'll hide you. If you like."

"Hide? Because of . . ."

He glanced into the darkness behind them, then shook his head. "They won't know who did that, or they'll look to me. Not that."

"Then why?"

He raised his brows, jerking his chin forward, as if she should be able to sense the answer in the very air around them.

And then she did. A faraway, stone-muffled roar—shouts, thuds, a scream. It sounded like the ghost of some battle long past, some battle for control of this mountain fastness before there ever were mages in Eiden Myr, when those who carved the fastness defended some unknowable realm of their own. It sounded like an exhalation from the crevasse of whispers, and what was that if not the past, echoing forever inside the heart of stone?

But this was not happening in the past. It was happening now.

"Stewards' revolt," Steward Steward said matter-of-factly. "Been planning it, oh, nigh on forever now. Not sure what broke it. Thought we were waiting till the rebels came."

Maybe the rebels aren't coming.

"Come on," he said. "I'll hide you. You'll be safe in my little nook, it's not far. At least I don't have to worry about *her* now. Not afraid to die . . . but I didn't know who'd mind her, with me gone. I'll just see you safe and go on."

"No . . ."

"It's all right." He gave a beatific smile of cracked, stained teeth, a smile that hadn't let magecraft touch it in long years. "I'm not afraid. I've got duties. Important duties. I'm to—"

"No, I mean no, I won't hide. Come on. Come *on*. They need us."

She lost him in the first melee. Plain stewards were driving dyed vocates and proxies into the upper levels. She and the oilman—she would never know his name—fought their way down past a panicked, fleeing crowd of vocates and warders into a knot of angry reckoners trying to beat the stewards back. Liath dove in, flinging proxies after the crowd, and before she knew it she was on the stewards' side of it. A wild-eyed woman raised an andiron to strike her. Reeling back, Liath glanced at her own arm with a jolt of fear, thinking she still wore the black. "Sorry, sorry," the woman said, lowering the andiron. They turned; the resisting proxies had been driven past the junction door, and the oilman was locking it with a skeleton key. That was the last she saw of him. The stewards swept her off to the next set of passageways, to join another group herding a milling, objecting group of vocates. The vocates didn't know enough to resist. Liath and the woman and a handful of others went on. That group needed no help.

"We've got most of the middle levels in this section," the woman panted. Probably a cook; she was as broad as she was tall, her doughy face sheened with perspiration under a linen wimple that had been knocked askew. "Come on." She ducked into a stairwell and went down, then over, and down again.

"What started it?" Liath asked when she caught up—raising her voice over a roar from around the next landing.

The woman shrugged. "Someone gave the signal, I suppose. Wasn't me!"

"Dispute in the stables," said someone behind them.

"Bron gave the signal," said someone else. "Had to be. It was always down to him."

Stewards and proxies came crashing around the turn, beating each other bloody. Liath had no right fist, but she got along with her left, and spent most of her energy ducking ill-aimed blows by untrained, inexperienced proxies and tearing them off stewards. The Holding had become one massive brawl. There had to be a plan to the uprising, a strategy, but she could not discern it, or get a straight answer from the stewards between blows.

There was opportunity here, but she did not know how to use it, or how to find her way. She kept fighting, side by side with launderers, carpenters, lampmen—all the crafters and laborers who kept the complexity of the Holding in working order. She was only publican now, not mage at all. She stopped the mages when she could, made them run when she couldn't stop them, fought them into the ground when they wouldn't run. Mindless, she saw only dyed and plain, black and white and gray against a sea of tan and beige and dun. When they came at her with fists, she met them with boots and elbows and knees; when one slit her forearm open with a knife, she drew her knife with practiced ease and stepped inside her opponent's killing lunge. *He shouldn't have done that*, she thought, and pivoted, looking for the next one.

He was behind her, and he was a steward—with a longblade.

Trained reflex saved her: she ducked, then charged under the arc of the longblade. It struck sparks off nightstone, then fell. Her knife was between its wielder's ribs.

"Loyalist stewards!" she shouted, picking up the nicked longblade. She couldn't get the knife out of the man's body; she startled as he twitched. *Spirits, I didn't want to kill anyone!* She drove the thought away. The Ennead had armed their folk with longblades. "*You didn't think they'd overlook the power of iron, did you?*" They would kill her if she hesitated. "Ennead stewards!" she warned again. Would anyone understand what she meant? How would they tell enemy from friend? The folk with the longblades were the enemy—but she had a longblade now.

There was no more time for thinking. She beat back two longblades, blow for blow, holding her splinted fingers against the bound grip of the hilt with her left hand. A third blade came up behind them, and there was a sucking thunk to one side of her, and someone fell. A crushed wimple came under her feet, stained red. She roared, driving forward, cleaving arms, deflecting blades, cleaving a shoulder. It was hard to wrench the blade free when it sank into bone. She pivoted and drove a heel into the sternum of a woman who was just raising her blade, and dropped her where she stood. Another came up behind her. Liath fell back under a rain of blows; from nowhere, someone darted under the onslaught and stabbed her opponent twice, then was gone before he'd hit the floor. She looked around wildly, trying to get her bearings, a sense of who was where, but saw a blade about to come down on a steward across the passageway, and lunged to stab the attacker. People ran past her, some without blades, one dragging a blade too heavy for him. Retreat. They were running. Instinct drove her to follow, but she fought it, looked down the passageway.

A solid wall of stewards, bristling with blades, moving fast.

She joined the others, hurdling bodies, skidding on blood. Into a stairwell, and down. The door to the next level would not open; they crowded against it, screaming. Liath went past them with a shout and tried the door below. Also locked.

The stairwell ended there.

She waved off the people who'd followed her and began hacking at the old wood. Fatigue had burned the pain from her arms, but her blows weren't as strong as they should be and the longblade didn't go where she meant it to. Someone yelled at her to stop, then moved past her and shoved a prybar between the planks. Wood splintered but didn't give. "Help me!" he called. Others added their weight and strength. One plank snapped out of the door; no light showed through from the other side. Someone swore. "Iron," he said. "Iron inside."

Longblades scythed through the people on the stairs. Shrieks reverberated through the stairwell. Bodies tumbled down. The dying piled on the dead. Liath was jammed against the wall. Over her head was the landing lampwell. She groped up, got her hand around the lamp, and flung it into the attackers. Someone cried out; but it was a futile gesture. She'd lost the longblade in the crush. Now the landing was dark. Backlit from above, armed stewards were still coming down, slipping on blood, swearing.

"Give it up," someone said. "They're all dead down there."

"Then who threw *that*?"

"It doesn't matter. Come on. Back, everyone! Back up!"

Liath struggled free and climbed over the drifted dead, and made the stairs. Bodies lay everywhere on the way up. The passage she had fought in was lined with them. She found a longblade, picked it up, and kept going, dragging it behind her to save her strength for the next time she had to lift it. The battle had moved on. But she could not find it. Only passages of the dead, no telling anymore which side they had been on. Bile rose in her throat; she spat, and kept going.

Soon neither up nor down was possible anymore. Everything was locked. The middle levels had been secured, but everyone inside them was dead. The Ennead had waited until the stewards had herded the mages out of harm's way, then unleashed their armed fighters.

The stewards' uprising had been quelled. It probably suited them: that many fewer lightless reproducing in the world. They couldn't run their Holding without these people, but they would find other people, or perhaps it didn't matter anymore. Perhaps they didn't even plan to stay here, when they'd achieved their great goal of revenge. The Holding might be expendable. Who knew what they planned, for when this was over?

She dropped the blood-slicked longblade to the stone with a dull clang, and looked for knives and sheaths. Two in her left boot, two in her right, one on each side of her belt. She found an empty sheath attached to a thigh strap, and fastened it under the skirt of her tunic, then found a knife to fit it. The rush of battle heat faded, leaving her deathly cold. She had wounds that should be wrapped. Her right hand was a shapeless throb of agony at the end of her arm. Blood was running into her left eye, but heads bleed a lot for nothing. She had told someone that, once.

Mellas.

"The Ennead's Holding is a mountain. The victims are kept in the lowest levels. Leagues of stone muffle the cries."

Down. It had always been a matter of down—a year ago, and now. Down, past the dead, the dismembered; down, past the dying she could not heal. In someone's open chamber, where a cheerful fire still burned and a meal waited to be eaten, she found a jug of water. She wrapped an arm here, dispensed water there. Some would live. Some asked her what happened, where to go. She shook her head. She didn't know. When the water ran out, she kept walking, until she'd passed where most of the fighting was. She smelled pantries, and privies, and mushroom heather. She didn't pause.

Down. For every locked door, there was a passageway leading to one that was open. The levels descended in columns: three columns, she assumed, although the makers of this place might not have believed in threes. No stair ever went all the way down, but every few levels one connected to a deeper stairwell. People began to come out; mages were confused by her combination of bloody apron and bright light, and let her pass. One steward tried to kill her, and died for it, in the shadows. Three tried to help her; one she vaguely knew. He wanted to take her to Bron. "He's alive. I know where he is. We're going to regroup. This isn't over. They didn't get us all—"

She shook him off. If he couldn't tell her how to get to the lowest levels, she wasn't interested.

But he knew. This one knew.

"You don't want to go there," he said. "You go there, you won't come back."

"Is that why you never have?" she said. "Is that why you let them rot down there?"

"We fought back!" he cried.

"Too late," she said. "Tell me how to go there."

It was a complex combination of arounds and backs. She asked him to draw it for her, carve it in the stone with a blade, but he only blinked, stupefied by the request, and kept talking. Words were not her strength; she worked hard to form a picture in her mind, but there was too much. When he saw he'd lost her, he said, "Follow the magestone. The farther down, the more there is. Cursed, haunted stuff. The most of it is in the center, where the . . . where they keep them. You'll come to passages that aren't nightstone at all anymore, just magestone. Then you're close. It's the best I can do you."

"Thank you."

He stopped her as she turned. "Let me fix you up, get you a meal. Let's go to Bron first. He'll want to see you. He told us about you, said to fetch you if we saw you. He'll skin me if he knows I've let you go down there."

"I'm through being fixed up, and I'm through being fetched." She looked at his hand on her arm. He removed it.

"Don't go down there," he hissed as she walked away from him.

"Mellas is down there," she said, not looking back. "You tell Bron that. You tell him I've gone to set things right, or die."

"I may kill you for this." Landril kept his distance from the steward; the threat required no illustration. Wynn feared him more than he despised him, and longed to please him more than he feared him, and longed to best him more than anything. Poor lightless Wynn, dethroned so young from the monarchy of the eldest. King now only of lightless stewards— and even they had failed him.

Wynn glanced at the door. They could just hear the clash of blades, from somewhere down the passageway. "I had my hands full."

"Your hands are empty. You have let control slip through your fingers. Bulling into Bron's domain with armed men—what possessed you? I told you to retrieve her, not force their hand!"

"The blades that killed her guards were magecrafted! It wasn't stewards! Stewards killed by Ennead blades—how could you think they would not rise up at that? I had to protect myself."

"That was a ruse, and you are a fool. If I had not broken you years ago, I might suspect you of duplicity." This time he did step forward, closing his hand on the older man's throat.

"She was seen near the vocates' sleephall," Wynn offered, choking, as if the slim report of a sighting could make up for losing the illuminator, for throwing a lit torch on the kindling of rebellion. Yet if she'd returned to the vocates . . .

An illuminator, inking over chalk—retracing all her steps.

Between her stint with the vocates and her appearance in their chambers had been a sojourn with Portriel. She did not know what they planned, she could not have the stomach to free the old woman. But Portriel could get through any door that wasn't welded shut. Portriel had long ago lost the heart for escape, but the prospect of rescuing such a bright light might rouse her—

He released the steward. "Send men to the lowest levels. Arm them well. I will meet them down there."

"But the uprising—"

"Not my doing. You see to it, brother. You're a steward; control your stewards. I should never have entrusted a mage to you." He left the chamber, shoved past proxies who saw his gold ring and begged for guidance, elbowed panicked vocates aside. He heard a skull crack against the wall. No matter. They would not be needing this last harvest; there were plenty below. No more vocates would be cast proxy by this Ennead, and what Worilke did with them afterward—breed them, probably—would be no concern of his. A rebel steward saw him and screamed to his comrades— part terror, part warning, part hunting call. He slipped into a junction chamber and was gone. Let them slaughter each other in the passageways. He had no need of them any longer. Up, over, down, over, a torch to light his way . . .

She lay dead in the bonefolk's arms.

He jabbed the torch at them. They did not like fire. But they drew the body back with them. Already it was dissipating, like a leaf in a casting. He could see that the neck was broken. There were no signs of struggle in the cushioned chamber. He cursed mercy and the bonefolk in the same breath.

I needed her! He brandished the torch. They were to ride her sealed light between worlds, and release it into the old world, the hated world— and all her sick despair with it. He might do something, they might bring her back, the spirit might still linger, if he could salvage some scrap of the flesh . . .

He pulled up. It was too late. She was dissolving. The green glow was acid on his eyes. No point now in fighting them for her. Better to retrieve the illuminator. She was as good as sealed, and bright enough to stand for Portriel's light, though there was far too much hope and courage in her still. He could change that, once he had her in hand.

There were reserves. The sealed mages tucked away in his chambers, behind the door that no steward ever opened, kept in darkness and filth and despair, used by him until even he found them too repulsive. The boy who dreamed shadows, though Seldril had claimed him. But they were paltry thirds. He had wanted to use Torrin. He would have settled for Portriel. He would not trust the vengeance of the ages to a lesser light.

The illuminator would have to do.

As he strode down the passageway, he felt the blind eyes on him, the empty sockets regarding him with gleeful malice from the bouncing shadows his torchlight cast.

Very well then, he thought. Watch me, haunt. Watch your prentice burn your hopes to ashes. Watch me the way you watched me as a child. I grew up, Portriel, and I grew stronger than you, and I became your nightmare as you were mine. I may never be free of you. But you will never be free of me.

Seldril looked down at the blade lodged in her forearm, then raised a smile to the assassin who had wielded it, a genuine smile of gratitude for the agony radiating up the bone and into her shoulder. He drew it out, but faltered before delivering the blow that would finish her. She had turned too fast, as if she could see him sneaking up behind her, and moved her arm unerringly to protect her throat. Clearly he had expected the one jab to kill her, and her smile drove from his mind the resolve to strike again. She disengaged the blade gently from his hand and made another cut, a languorous caress, across the angled wound. At her soft murmur of pleasure, he staggered back, tripping over a stool and sprawling, paralyzed by horror. She couldn't help but laugh as she moved to neatly hamstring him. A lovely boy.

"What a gift!" she said, binding her arm to stanch the blood, but not before the delicious light-headedness had crept in. "And what pleasure we will have, you and I, in discovering together who sent it to me."

he Ennead's black mountain hunched around a heart of light. It had swallowed the moon—and the moon spoke, in ancient voices.

Liath scrunched on elbows through a tunnel fit for large rats while small ones fled into crevices. There had been no torch or lamp for what seemed like leagues, a long, slow swim through rocky depths. But now a sphere of silver-white light surrounded her, moving as she moved. The tunnel was carved through solid magestone. There was no more nightstone at all. Her own light made it glow, startling the vermin, easing her way.

The magestone spoke. This, then, was the secret of the crevasse of whispers: that its bottom, if bottom it had, was magestone, and the circulation of air carried the magestone's voices up the shaft. It did not speak to her. It murmured to itself, from a dream of days long past. It might not be sound at all; she didn't know if her ears heard it or only her mind.

The glow of magestone cast no shadow. No phantom hands crawled along under her scrabbling fleshly hands. Her triskele, dangling, scraped dully on stone; it was black, as if dipped in ink. Beyond the bubble of silver, darkness closed in, and as long as there was darkness ahead, not the light of a dead end rising to meet her, the tunnel must continue. She kept on, a pale worm slithering through moonsilver earth. The air would not run out. The stone would not squeeze the life from her. She would not have to back up the way she had come. She could no longer maneuver well enough to go backward, and the tunnel was slanting down.

Something changed in the conical darkness. In the center—a subtle flicker, a sweep of something grayer than shadow. The tunnel narrowed still more, and she could no longer raise her head. She eeled and elbowed, forcing her body through as if shouldering the weight of stone to either side. Her breath came faster; her heartbeat grew painful. Any moment she would wedge herself permanently into the impassable. *Turn back, turn back!* But there was no turning, or backing. She groped forward—and her good fingers bent over a ridge of stone. A current of air washed over her knuckles. She hauled her head into the open.

The tunnel let out high in the wall of an oval chamber. On a stool in its center sat a lone watchman, fidgeting. Warm torchlight sent his shadow dancing across the floor. She could not wriggle back into the hole. Its lips were a luminous circle that would betray her if he chanced to look up. She could not let herself quietly to the floor. The only way out—the only way to move at all—was straight out, then straight down. The drop was three threfts. The stone would catch her hard.

The watchman rose. He jingled a set of keys, absently, and strolled to the far gate. Seeing nothing of interest, he turned and strolled to the nearer. Then he began to pace the confines. A bored animal in a cage, as much a prisoner to his duty as the folk he guarded were prisoners of the Ennead. On his first brief circuit, Liath was too surprised to do more than freeze. On the second circuit, she gauged his idle, rhythmic steps—and straight-armed the wall, propelling her body out of the hole. She tumbled down headfirst with a flailing half-backflip, through smoke and shadow, and landed sprawling on the watchman. The air went out of him. The hilt of the longblade sheathed at his hip gouged Liath's back as her elbows gouged his ribs and thigh. She scrambled off him. His mouth worked soundlessly as he tried to suck breath, and his hand fumbled toward the skewed longblade.

Finish him, Kazhe hissed—but it was the magestone her tumbling light woke. She bristled with knives, had one in her hand without knowing she'd drawn it. The magestone walls had come to silvery life, leaching color from the watchman's flat face, but torchlight glittered in his panicked eyes. In a moment he would have breath to raise the cry. He did not think he had time. He looked at her and saw his death. She had killed, in the passages above, killed and killed; she was soaked in black blood. But she could not drive her weapon into this helpless man. He staggered to his feet, hunched over, still struggling to loose his blade. He dragged breath into his lungs like a sob. She dropped the knife with a clink and stepped back. Her calf bumped the stool he had sat on. Every tavern brawl she'd ever been in came rushing back like blood into numb limbs. She lifted the stool and swung it. It caught him in the head as his mouth opened. He flopped to the stone.

Alive. She gagged him with his shirt and buckled his arms behind him with his belt, bound his legs together with his breeches, retrieved and sheathed the knife, found the keys. Knife and keys were charcoal in the magestone's glow. She strapped his blade belt around her, pausing at the alien texture of the scabbard, flexible and sturdy as a boot sole, yet not fibrous.

Beyond the farther gate was a torchlit passage, silent and empty, an oaken door at its far end. Beyond the nearer gate was a fathomless argent radiance. There were three keys. The third one turned the oiled lock. She went through.

Without shadow to suggest contour, there was no telling the shape or distance of the chamber walls. A circular cage floated in a moon-white expanse. Its close-set, upright bars, sunken in magestone floor and ceiling, ended in nothingness. They looked black, too; the magesilver did not reflect from metal, but curbed it to a matte darkness. The ancient whisper was an incessant, muted roar, like wind or surf, rising and falling. Inside the bars were lumps and shapes, some resembling human beings. Human voices moaned, an erratic drone under the maddening whisper. Someone was crying. The sound of it floated within the rushing hiss the way objects and figures floated in the shadowless light. Everything unmoored, suspended. Past the pen was another gate, a floating square mesh, indicating a wall. This was too large a chamber for her magelight alone to light it so. The pen was full of mages.

The second key unlocked its gate. "Go," she whispered to them, then raised her voice when her whisper melded into all the others. "You're free. Go on." She recognized none of them. They weren't moving. Some stared blankly at her; others mumbled to themselves, or covered their heads, or shrank against the bars. With an oath, she swung the gate wide and moved to the next chamber. Her steps were uncertain in the confusing, shadowless light. Too long in this place would drive anyone mad. She could only hope they would recover their wits and their courage in time to get out before a guard came to relieve the one she'd bound.

The next chamber held another barred enclosure full of mages. She opened the gate and reached down to shake one, to wake her up—and found she had no arms. All were missing limbs, or ears or eyes, or were badly scarred. No blood, no gaping wounds—the flesh had been sealed clean by magecraft, but not healed, and dismemberment could not be healed. Icy fluid sluiced through her stomach. One looked at her through a full set of eyes and clutched rags around herself with whole arms. "Here," Liath said. She worked a scarred hand free and pressed a knife into it. The woman did not resist. "The cage is open, but they'll come. Those who can fight must defend the others." The woman's fingers closed around the knife, but her stare was soulless. Liath searched for someone strong enough to give the guard's longblade to. A sucking sound cut with awful familiarity through the magestone hiss. She turned as the woman crumpled. Blood spread slowly around her in a pool as black as an iron blade. She had cut her own throat.

Someone shoved against Liath—a weak push, but trembling, near panic. Others were limping, dragging themselves to the dead woman. A man whined when someone quicker snatched the knife up as he reached for it. With a cry, Liath went for the weapon. The man brandished it at her, lurching away. There were only two fingers and a thumb on the hand that clutched it. In two steps Liath had it back. He lunged at her with a feral snarl. She retreated through the gate as comprehension and outrage rippled through the others. They followed in a slow surge—but stopped at the gateway as if it were warded. One extended an imploring hand, then snatched it back and bared broken teeth.

The gate was not warded. They could not bring themselves to cross the threshold of their prison. Pain had lain beyond it for too long. If they still had tongues, they had forgotten how to use them. They clustered at the opening, growling, moaning. Enraged at her for denying them the only escape they trusted.

She went on. There would be three chambers, or six, or nine. The same key opened the gates, another the pens. The next was the largest, and the last. Three cages in its center made mockery of triadic configuration. In the wall around them, alcoves were hewn in the magestone, perhaps six threfts by nine, discernible only by the objects floating within them—tables, stools, crates.

She entered the nearest as in a dream, knowing she must not, knowing that horrors lay within, unable to control her dreaming movements. The magestone whisper rose to a howl; in their pens, the living mages wailed.

"Eiden's eyes . . ."

The wooden table was etched with arcane symbols, neither kadri nor any glyphs she'd ever seen, vertical lines with diagonal hash marks jutting from them in various configurations, a horde of little symbols marching along each leg and around the randomly scored top. Where a mage's arms and legs would go were restraints of the same strange material as the guard's scabbard, with black buckles on the end that might have been silver in real light. The table was slanted; a groove down the center would empty blood into a basin at the low end. In bins to either side were the blackened tools of a binder's slaughterground. The crates must hold casting materials. She could not bring herself to open them. She knew where the materials had been harvested, and how.

Liath wheeled and staggered from the alcove, a hand over her mouth. She unlocked the cages, barely seeing their occupants, barely hearing their inarticulate cries over the thin keening in her own mind. They would come out, or they would not; and they would not. They would be Mellas, or Karanthe, or Pelkin, or they would not; and they were not. Those she loved, those she had come here to save, were past her saving now. This place was unspeakable, beyond comprehension; it had made shambling, groveling monsters of men and women who had been eloquent, dexterous, compassionate. It had reduced bright, healthy mages to a binder's tithe penned for slaughter. The bars were no longer necessary. Terror and agony had taught them to pen themselves. When she opened the gates, they clustered at the brink but would not cross, and it was only worse for them, to offer the taste, the temptation, of freedom that would be snatched away if they chanced it. They were smarter than she was. They had learned the cruel truths of this silver place.

Eight alcoves lined the periphery, but there was room for nine. Where the last should be was a triangular doorway on darkness. An alcove they had lined somehow, perhaps with iron, to muffle the magestone's glow? It might have had a curtain across it, so total was the gloom. When she moved toward it, the penned mages howled. Two or three pressed against the closest bars and stretched their arms through, waving wildly. Waving her off. What could possibly lie inside that curtain of darkness that would be worse than what they had suffered already?

"Ah-eeveh-*eh*-oh-ih-air!" She could not look at the man whose mutilated mouth had produced that sound. But she understood it.

Not even they go in there.

She paused at the threshold. This was how freedom must seem to them: in a torment of maddening silver-white that defied all orientation and never offered night's respite, a black maw in which worse horrors dwelled. The seam between dark and light was a smoky haze, tallow-soot ink bleeding into ill-finished sedgeweave. Her hand came back unstained, though it had dipped into shadow.

She stepped in.

The shadow screamed.

Screamed, and shattered into a dozen, a nonned shadows, razor shards of night scattering in revulsion. The metallic shriek of their horror stunned the magestone silent. For one heartbeat, three, only the rustle of prisoners behind her and the ragged, rhythmic gasps of the boy huddled beyond the glyph-scarred table.

"Mellas," she whispered.

Though his eyes were open, he did not see her. Uncut, he was emaciated, his eye sockets purple hollows; he'd had a growth spurt, but his limbs were more spindly than gangly, and facial bones pressed stark against pale skin that had been rounded. His chin and upper lip were trying to grow hair. His poor, battered body, striving for manhood in this place of horror. His wrists showed old bruises from the table's restraints. But alive. He was alive.

The shadows struck.

The first sliced her cheek to the bone, the second the forearm she flung up to protect her face; droplets of blood flew black through the silvery air. She groped left-handed for a knife, ducking low as more shadows darted in. Thin, cold lines opened along her shoulders and back. Dark wingbeats buffeted her, talons plucked at her hair, her tunic. Their tortured-metal shriek was like a dozen honed longblades drawn edge-on across each other. She swept the knife out in an arc, felt something like wet moss yield under the blade and spring away. The magestone mutter rose to a fevered hiss. The table's wood jarred her hip, anchored her. She drew a second knife, with her right hand, and jabbed at the ragged, night-dark thing that flew at her eyes, then down at something gnawing on her knee. Her clothes were going to tatters. Soon there would be nothing to protect her but her own skin.

Twisting, bending, flailing out blindly behind her with both knives, she staggered to Mellas. "It's me!" she shouted. The roar of the magestone's voices nearly drowned her out. "Liath! I've come back for you, more fool me. Wake up, Mellas. Wake up, blast you! Your bloody nightmares are going to kill me!" She rose, turned, slashed wildly at shadows, beat them back. Then she would have slapped him, to snap him out of it—but the movement gentled into a caress, her fingers combing the tousled hair off his brow. "Don't touch me!" a little boy cried in her memory. She could not strike the harrowed youth huddled at her feet.

He stirred, nosing toward warmth and life. A blur of mumbles came out of his mouth. His eyes focused on her, past her—went wide at the sight of the whirling, massing shadows.

The shadows dove straight at him. He covered his head, screaming her name. She tried to haul him up but he jerked his limbs in tight. She dropped both knives and drew the watchman's longblade from its alien scabbard. She drove into the shadows.

The iron blade cut swaths through the flying things that mobbed her, hewed them into ribbons, sliced the ribbons as they warped back into flying things. In the corner of her eye she saw Mellas jab at them, a blade in each hand. He was crying, but he was fighting. Gradually they began to draw back. The luminous walls absorbed them; the ones she felled drained into the floor like water into limestone. She looked at her arms, where the fabric had shredded, and saw raw welts around the wounds. What she had felt as razors was more like strong lye. They had burned her, as they had burned all the flesh from Torbik.

"Are you all right?" she said, crouching to examine Mellas's face, hands, arms. He nodded. He hadn't taken too much damage. "We have to go."

"The only way out is the front," Mellas said, in his clear, slow way, each word an effort. The crack in his voice, caught between childhood and youth, was the only life in it.

"Then that's how we'll go, and hope there's only one—"

"Hide!" Mellas hissed, a moment before she heard the voices, the gates slamming shut, the heavy tread of boots.

She cast a panicked look around the chamber, then out at where penned mages stared at her with no humanity. "Where?"

"Under," he choked, and pointed.

She peered below the table and saw the stained hole he meant. So that was why the chambers reeked of blood. But they collected the blood in basins. And why was it so wide . . . ?

Merciful spirits. She dropped the longblade in ahead of her, and did not hear it hit bottom until she had lowered her body in to the ribs, her elbows braced. Then blade and scabbard thwacked into something thick and wet. Too far a drop, and at the end of it whatever the bonefolk wouldn't take after the Ennead harvested their materials. The stench was unspeakable. Her gut spasmed.

"Where is she?" came a voice harder and smoother than timeworn stone. Boots floated past the chamber entry. "Some of you still have tongues. Tell me, or lose them now."

Silence answered. The boots moved to the bars—two strides, then a *snap* that nearly tore a cry from her, remembering. The mage's cry would have covered it. That hadn't been a finger. "Tell me now please," he said, another murmur in the murmurous surf. "Louder. I can't hear you."

"Gone," the mage moaned, a woman's voice. A man said, "Gone into the dark!" Another said, "The boy's shadows took her."

Brave lies from folk she'd thought broken—but it only drew attention to Mellas's chamber.

"He's awake," said another voice, and Landril's boots moved toward her. Gritting her teeth, she lowered herself to hang by her fingers. The lip of the hole was pitted, affording just enough grip, but three fingers on her right hand could not bend. She jammed the pointing finger into a crevice.

"Mellas." The voice smiled. Mellas's heels scrabbled on stone as he recoiled. "But you never speak, do you. I see she's dispersed your little guardians. Where is she? You need only point." A pause. "Out there? I don't think so. The watchman's conscious. He would have seen her pass, yes?" Mellas must have nodded. "Very good. Now try again. Where——"

More noise from the outer chamber. Bootsteps striding away. Liath tried to pull herself back up and could not. Her arms were fatigued from wielding heavy blades. She could only dangle there until her fingers gave out. From the loss of feeling as the stone leached their warmth, it would not be long.

"Hang on," Mellas said, just loud enough for her to hear over the rushing whispers. "Please hang on."

"I can't," she said. Her right hand gave way—

Mellas caught it. He gripped her right arm in both hands, his chest braced on the stone, his bloodless face pasty in mageglow. Her left fingers slid toward the lip. The sounds from the outer chambers were incomprehensible. The mages were chanting, a rhythmic drum of voices; a clash of blades rang out, someone screamed "No!", others were swearing. Landril's voice barked orders. Mellas begged her to hang on. A drop of sweat or tears fell on her jaw. Her left fingers slid over the edge. Somehow she clung to Mellas, and he to her. She shut her eyes tight, putting every ounce of will into their joined arms. He was sliding toward the edge. His body was insufficient counterweight for hers. "Let go," she rasped. "Let go!"

Then her stretched, screaming tendons were strained past bearing. She was going up. Someone was hauling them up. Heff, it was Heff, his great strong arms lifting them as if they were nothing—

Bron cast them sprawling on the stone and turned in time to take Landril's backhanded blow on his cheek. He reeled back and fell over a crate. The table had been angled away. Stewards were fighting in the outer chamber, blades arcing black. The mages howled. Landril looked at her across the slaughterhole. Liath's right arm was numb, but with her left she groped for one of her discarded knives. Mellas pressed her fingers around a hilt. She was right-handed, but her throw was dead perfect, the point taking Landril in the chest.

He smiled as the blade bounced off him and spun down into the hole. "Iron," he said, almost affectionately. "I'm warded against it, of course." He didn't look behind him, or call for help. He just held his hand out, palm down, as if to a child. "Come along, Illuminator. Someone's deprived me of Portriel. But you're as good as sealed, aren't you?"

Liath nodded, rising unsteadily. She reached for the hand. He moved it to one side, seeing what she planned; when she tried to pull him off balance anyway, he twisted her arm expertly and brought her to her knees. But Bron was up, rushing him. He let go of Liath to spin Bron toward the hole. Bron went past it, but he had hold of Landril's velvet doublet. Landril straddled the hole and smashed his fist into Bron's face. Liath planted her boot in the back of his left knee at the same moment Mellas shouldered into his right. The knees buckled. Landril went down.

"Blast," Bron said, rising slowly. His face bled black where Landril's ring had laid it open. "I've wanted to put a knife into him since we were five years old."

He looked out at the chamber. The clash of battle had become the thuds of retreat. Around the cage stood armed stewards; on the floor were dead stewards, including the watchman she'd spared. Two mages in soiled white stood by the pen. Dabrena had pressed herself to the bars, stretching her arms through to embrace someone on the other side. Tolivar's slim body was stiff, shocked.

Liath peered into the hole, but there was only darkness below.

"He might have survived it," Bron said. "Our assassins are in the Nine's chambers now. He'll elude them, too, most like. The timing could have been better. They were to strike when the Nine thought they'd won the battle, and the battle wasn't to begin till the horde made the pass. My fault. But they would have had you."

"He'll be a while getting out of there," said Oreg, coming over to look.

"The ones who fled will bring back enough to kill us for him," said the man who'd tried to talk Liath out of coming here—the man who must have fetched Bron immediately after.

"Ai," Bron said. "All the stones have been thrown."

"We can't risk going out the front," said a tall woman. "That's how they'll come. Lafe and Vaeron won't be able to hold."

"The front's the only way out," Oreg said.

"We should have known he'd be warded against blades!"

"We didn't," Bron snapped. "And now we're in a corner. We'll make the best stand we can."

"Keys," Liath said. She groped around the floor, then found them down her shirt, no memory of having put them there. "Lock us in. Trade for some time."

Bron nodded to Oreg. "Do it." Oreg snatched the keys from her and trotted away. "There are air holes, tunnels, the place is riddled with them. A few of us can get out. The smaller ones."

"You need every blade arm," said a short, tough steward who could have been Kazhe, but thinner—thin enough to escape the way Liath got in, with a boost up to the tunnel mouth. "We won't go."

"You and the boy then," Bron said to Liath. "We came here for you. Those warders helped us for your sake. Don't waste our deaths."

Liath was leaning on Mellas as he leaned on her. He was taller than he'd been; he'd be her height by the time he was done growing. He had to have that chance. But she would not leave these people, or the captive mages. What lived could be healed. Her eye fell on the warders—friends so true that they had left their infant child in order to escort these stewards down here on their own authority, brazening it out. She had told Bron their names; he had found them, and offered safe haven for the baby wherever he had stowed his fosterlings.

"There's an alternative," she said.

Bron snorted. "Hack our way free through the base of the mountain? We'd drown in the sea."

Oreg came back with one of the sentries; between them they were herding the mages from the outer pens. They moved like sheep in the hands of new jailers—docile but wild-eyed, ready to bolt—and milled into the open cages almost eagerly.

"Most of these were proxies together," Bron said. "Some were mine. They don't even know me now." He swore, and turned away.

He did not even want to hear her idea. He'd taken a chance, and lost, and now he was waiting to die. He would give them a good fight, but in his mind it was already over.

Liath walked past Tolivar to Dabrena, who gently disengaged her hands from those of a woman on the other side of the bars. Something about the fall of honey-brown hair—

"My cousin," Dabrena said, and turned to face Liath full on. "What is your alternative?"

"We need an illuminator," Liath said. "You need one. You and To- livar. These chambers are full of casting materials. We'll cast our own way out. But I can't do it. One of them . . ."

"They can't," Dabrena said.

"*They have to.*" Liath walked through the open gate, mastering her horror to offer them calmness and determination. "You lied to Landril, knowing he would hurt you. You were that strong. One of you can do this!"

"They can't," Dabrena said through the bars, as mage after mage turned away. "Don't you understand what I'm saying, Liath? Do I have to draw it for you? Do words no longer make sense to you?"

The materials . . . they, too, knew what the leaves and inks consisted of. Perhaps it was too much to ask of any mage. . . .

"They're crippled, Liath. Every blessed one. They took the illuminators' hands, the binders' tongues, the wordsmiths' eyes."

Liath backed out of the pen, staring at silver air, magestone walls. A nonned bright lights here, and none of them able to cast.

Very slowly, she turned and looked past the broken mages, past the warders, past the nervous stewards gripping their blades, past Bron braced against moon-bright stone as if leaning on mist, past the impossible, shadowless glare to where a cowed little boy sat hunched, trembling, in a young man's body. No light, no warmth, no scent of mage on him at all. But Torrin Wordsmith was an ordinary light, and when he cast he burned brighter than the sun. He had been a dark, beautiful boy, a boy that gave one woman on the Ennead hope; but something had happened to that boy, something that taught him to hide the core of himself, as something had happened to this one. There was no shadow without light, and this child's angry dreams cast such shadows as could kill. Where was the light that made those shadows? What would happen if the young man cast?

"Get the materials, Tolivar," she said, eyes fixed on Mellas. "Maybe those deaths need not be wasted."

With a glance at Dabrena, he went into one of the cells. A choked oath followed the sound of a crate opening. He came burdened into Mellas's cell as Liath lifted his chin with the one good finger on her broken hand. "Will you try?"

Behind their screen of tousled hair, his dark blue eyes seemed to regard her from a depth she could never plumb. "I can't draw," he said, one slow word at a time.

"I'll help you," she said softly.

Mellas nodded, and got to his feet.

"You can't teach him on the spot," Dabrena said. But she cleared stewards out of the way. Bron would not move; he thought this was absurd. Dabrena stared at him—the tiny harvestmaster and the burly stableman—until his stubborn despair gave out and he made room for their attempt. Tolivar drew the circle in charcoal, black on silver, and Dabrena seated herself, establishing the head of the triangle. "I tried what you said, and it didn't work. I'm no illuminator. Neither is that lightless boy."

"He's more than you think," Liath said.

Tolivar sat and offered vellum and inked reed pen to Dabrena. "It should be sedgeweave," he said, "but . . . ."

"But mageflesh is all we have," Liath said quietly, sitting behind Mellas. "And what those mages wanted more than anything in the world was to be free of this place." Pitching her voice low, the voice that calmed outraged drunks and the angry pledgemates come to fetch them home, she said, "Sleep, Mellas. Sleep, and dream of freedom. . . ."

He let himself be lulled. He could sleep at will—she'd seen him do it to spite Southers. In a few breaths he was a warm weight against her, head lolling. She nodded to Dabrena.

The ink was black; blood was black in the silver light. The leaf was pale as Norther flesh, pale as Holding flesh. It was abomination, yet Dabrena worked it gently, each glyph a caress. Celyrian was the language of healing. She filled the leaf as if it might live again for one brief moment in her hands. Then she passed the leaf to Liath. Tolivar offered brushes, pigments, the hair and bone and humors of human souls, and Liath took them, with Mellas dreaming in her arms. The pigments Tolivar had chosen were the color of dreams. The air itself was dreamlike, shimmering, and a ripple seemed to pass through the magestone underneath them, and run up the walls in a silvery shiver. She closed Mellas's fingers around a brush. His dreaming hand smeared pigment across the page, and the leaf filled with colors, swirling and eddying, alive. The dreams were the illumination.

The whispers modulated into a low drone. The sealed mages were leaving their pens, like figures underwater; they gathered around the casting circle, engulfing the stewards, pressing in close like weary travelers around a campfire. Their hair and rags were limned in silver, their battered faces numinous.

Everyone around her was blurring, and with the logic of dreams she knew that they were becoming more than they were, or perhaps becoming truly visible for the first time, in the light of a place beyond the place they knew. Dreams reached into that realm; she saw that now with the clarity of vigil. Dreams reached questing tendrils through the packed topsoil. It was nothing to dream passage through leagues of stone. The passage was there now, an extension and lifting of the chamber where Mellas had been kept. The passage had always been there.

It led up on a gentle incline, into diffused light. Light streamed from it, bathing them in lambent peace. Silver mages made their way to the threshold, stepped over, were gone—risen into the sweet light. The silver mages had not been visible before, but they had been here, lingering, unpassaged. Now they were gone. Now the living could follow.

It was done. Tolivar had been singing, she realized; his husky voice had blended so gently into the magestone's voices that she had only felt, not heard, its piercing beauty. Mellas had begun to speak, in a hoarse murmur, dream words that accompanied the song and became all the words it could ever have contained, if bindsmen remembered them. In the shifting equivalence of dreams, the words were the song, the song was the scribing. The boy in her bleeding arms was filled with light.

The passage was open, carved through magestone as surely as if a cadre of miners had worked the stone for years.

But it was not done. The leaf had not dissipated. There was still a warding around the Holding. Even sealed mages could not pass through. Wherever their crafted passage led, it did not bypass the warding. They were failing. After all this . . .

She could not wake the boy. She could not shake off the dreamy lethargy, or blink away the soft distortion. It had been such a pleasant dream. But it was turning. Mellas was angry, deeply angry, and he could not control his dreams.

"*Tchatitoch!*" he said, rising.

The chamber was gone, dimmed and faded like smoke. She looked for Dabrena, Bron, for anyone she knew, any steward to reach out to, for someone to haul her back. But there were only the shadowy figures of the mages, receding down endless tunnels where they stood. "Wait!" she cried. But they were alone.

Mellas was trembling. He spoke to her. She said, I can't understand you. He jabbered insistently, his face turned to her, expressions flickering across it, but his eyes were closed, and the words he said made sense only to him. Inside himself, he dreamed within the dream, both waking and sleeping. She could not reach him. They stood on a platform of shadow within a vast, roaring space, stillness within rushing void. She took his hand; if she let go, they would spin away into the abyss. This was the birthplace of shadows. Liath's knives were gone. Inside Mellas's mind, they had no weapons but themselves.

I'm here, Mellas. I won't leave you.

His terror was a shroud. Existence was a roaring void where shadows dwelled.

Far in memory's distance, a runner and a crippled publicans' daughter wended their tortuous way down a black mountain.

Liath stamped her feet on the black stone they stood on.

This is it, she said.

Mellas's face deformed in anguish and confusion.

This is it, she said. You don't get in from the back. There is no back. You get in from the top. Or the sides.

There is a back, Mellas said, though his lips had not moved.

Show me, she said.

I'm afraid.

We'll go together.

They'll come.

Let them.

They spun free, whirling into the abyss. It was stained with terror, rank with cruelty, all warped and twisted things, gibbering griefs and pulsating hatreds. In the center of it all, drawing them in, was one malevolent sentience. Liath knew it; it had a name, but the name could not be spoken here, or thought, or even recalled. It was the source of all hurt, and laid the threat of hurt on every decent impulse, every generous thought. Mellas shrank from it, but Liath pushed on. It was stuck like a burr in the flesh of spirit, so that any movement would tear—a chafing grain of black sand implanted there and muffled over years in layer upon layer of shadow, layer upon layer of fear.

I can't get it out of me, Mellas said. I'm inside it.

Crack it open.

How?

By remembering what it did to you.

There was an eternity of roaring silence.

What did it do to you, Mellas? What did Seldril do? Tell me.

The forbidden name was invocation and release. She held on tight as the memories roared past them, a thundering blackwater of anguish and terror. What he had seen, and how they'd threatened him, that Bron's life would be forfeit if he ever told or ever ran away. He was contorted past bearing by secrecy's demands, and the only modicum of safety was the road, but the road always led back, there was no getting free—they would kill what he loved if he left it. The worst secret of all was his own power to harm—a secret he would not even tell himself, so that the shadows, when they came, were a horror to him. The shadows made him just like the Nine. But the shadows weren't strong enough to kill them.

I hate them! he screamed, into the howling, soundless void.

The shadows coalesced from nothingness, all razor edges.

I hate me! Mellas wailed, and all Liath's words of comfort were drowned out. He slipped from her grasp.

The shadows swarmed in—and down, down to the tight-packed core of pain and secrets.

Mellas shrieked a lifetime of rage into the void.

The shadows converged on the center.

An explosion of blinding light engulfed them and spread outward. It spun them wildly. In glimpses Liath saw the heatless conflagration run up against a barrier, the great shield that surrounded the stone that surrounded the prison that surrounded the bodies they had left behind. The barrier absorbed it, forming a sphere around them. They drifted inside a bubble of power.

Then the bubble burst.

It dropped them gasping back into the chamber. The mages had fallen back. Dabrena and Tolivar sat with hands clapped over their ears. The stewards stood with mouths agape. The illuminated leaf was gone. Bron was gripping Mellas as if to pull him back from a fall. Mellas covered his face.

He shone with a delicate, saffron warmth.

"There's a passage now," Liath said, gesturing at the back of the cell. "The warding's gone. Mages can leave."

"I can't see any passage," Bron said.

"That's the mageglow. You won't see it. But it's there."

"Can *we* get out?" Oreg asked, and Liath nodded.

Mellas sobbed, once, then got slowly to his feet. "I should have tried to kill them with it."

"It was more important to kill the thing they put inside you."

He nodded—a sharp, grownup nod, the acknowledgment of a man who has made a bitter decision and must live with it. In that moment he looked exactly like Bron.

"Come on," he said to the ragged mages. "It's this way."

They would not have followed Liath, or the stewards, or the warders. But Mellas was one of them. "Come *on*!" he called, from inside the passageway he had made. His voice was low, triumphant, and did not crack. "It's this way! Follow me!"

Mellas strode into the light, and slowly, too slowly, limping and staggering, carrying each other, the mages filed in after him.

"They're coming," Lafe called from the gate. "They've got keys, they're getting through. There isn't time!"

Bron drew a curved Khinish blade from a sheath at his belt and gestured to his handful of surviving stewards. "We'll give them time," he said. "Oreg, Vaeron, take the mouth of the passage. You're the final defense. Make it last. The rest of you to either side of the gate. Take down all you can as they come through." As the stewards got into position, he said to Tolivar and Dabrena, "Choose your weapons," and gestured at the dead and the longblades by their hands. "Or follow the boy. But choose now."

Dabrena looked at Tolivar. "The baby."

"Go," he said. "If we survive this, we'll meet you by the old stewards' gate."

"All right." Her voice was doubtful.

Bron touched her arm. "Mind my fosterlings for me, eh?"

She nodded, started to go, then hesitated. "Come with me, Tolivar. Please."

He closed his hands around her head and pulled it close to kiss her brow. "I've never held a blade like theirs, but I have good strong sailor's arms still. I'm needed here. I'll come to you, Dabrena. I won't die inside a rock."

With a soft cry, she tore out of his arms and ran to catch up with the last mages entering the passageway.

Across the chamber, the booted footsteps halted, someone gave an order, a key turned in the lock, and the gate swung open.

Liath took up a longblade. It was so heavy . . .

They came fast, too many for the front stewards to get them all, though many fell and the ones coming up from behind tripped over them. Blood spattered the magestone walls. The Ennead's stewards had longblades, but not Kazhe's training; though Liath's muscles were limp and her hand was broken, still she parried their blows and sent their blades spinning. The Ennead's stewards were strong, and fresh, but they had not grown up with tavern brawls; though Liath was exhausted, still she dodged their lumbering attacks and took them down with boot heels to knees and knees to groins. Two came at her with longblades raised over their heads; she braced her blade and let one run up on it while the heel of her hand slammed the other's nose into her head. A part of herself slipped away for good—the part that cringed from doing harm. These stewards knew what went on down here, and still they fought for their Ennead. Perhaps it was under threat of harm to their own. But she killed them without flinching.

The Ennead's dogs had backed desperate prey into a corner. They hadn't reckoned the ferocity of those who had nothing to lose. Bron and his curved blade danced among them, and the dead marked the steps he'd taken. His stewards fought tirelessly, protecting Tolivar where they could. Little by little, they found themselves driving forward, toward the gate they had never thought to pass again. Opponent by opponent, they cleared the way, until only a handful remained, and those turned and fled.

They looked at each other in disbelief. They were not supposed to win.

"Let's go," Bron said. "We'll just have time to make a junction and split up, make it harder to run us all down. You and you, take that magecrafted passage, guard their rear."

"Landril wasn't with them," Tolivar said, frowning, as they climbed indiscriminately over the dead and dying and made their way through the forward chambers. "Or any of the Nine . . ."

"Maybe our people got them after all," Oreg offered.

Bron shook his head. "We made our play and failed. There's no telling how things stand now."

"I should go . . ." Liath began vaguely, still moving with them. Down Mellas's passage, she meant, and out; but she was having trouble thinking clearly, and no one had heard her. She had to find Torrin—but Torrin was dead. The horde had been crushed; they couldn't have been more than a sixday behind her, there would have been news of their approach. Mellas was free, and the land beyond the Holding shadows was harrowed, its haunts released. What was left for her to do but see the Ennead destroyed?

She followed Bron and his stewards without speaking further. They grew confused along the way; the tunnels were unfamiliar, and Bron claimed they shifted. Tolivar took the lead, guiding them with some sailor's sense, like a seabird that always knows which way land lies. At last they came to a junction chamber—an iron spiral-stair up, and three unlocked doors.

"Here we part," Bron said, sending three of the stewards through one of the doors to find their own way, and the rest of them up the stairs ahead of him. "I'll go see what remains of my uprising." To Tolivar, he said, "I'll relieve your wordsmith of my sprats and send her to meet you. You take care of this one—see she gets out. She's still too valuable to risk them getting hold of her again. Spirits forgive me for not knowing it a year ago."

That rough commendation was his farewell—but he paused a moment more, and said, in the cadences of the stablemaster, "Saved my boy, didn't you, in more ways than one. Old Bron won't forget."

Then he went up, his sturdy wooden shoes heavy on the iron treads, his weight shaking the wrought frame.

He saved himself, Liath thought, but she said, "Which door?," and Tolivar shrugged and pointed to the nearest.

The route up was a twisting, tiring climb, broken by furtive flights through corridors, ducking around corners and into doorways to avoid being seen. There was no one they could trust. After a while Tolivar seemed to know where he was. Liath had trouble caring. They had to fight. She had to keep fighting. Portriel had kept fighting. There were still things to fight for. The fosterlings. The world. But she had lost so much blood, and gone so long without sleep and food. The next step was almost more than she could take. Tolivar was limping; he'd taken a bad wound to the thigh, a lesser to the ribs. They had to get out, to rest. "*You can't fight them from within*," Portriel said. "*Someone has to fight them from without. . . .*" But there was no one to do that anymore. Mellas might have . . . No. Only Torrin was mage enough to challenge the Ennead, and she had delivered them his destruction.

"Tolivar . . . I can't . . ."

He turned, irritated, then stopped when he saw her sink to the floor. He crouched painfully beside her, checking the passage with hunted eyes. "I have to go on, Liath. If my daughter's not at the old stewards' gate, I have to go back and get her."

"I know," she said. "Go on without me."

"I won't." He tried to smile. "All in the same boat."

"That's how it should be."

"That's how it is. Come on—arm around my shoulders, there's a girl. Now up. Ugh. We can go slow, so long as we go."

It wasn't far. The exit they'd chosen was the way Mellas had first brought her in—not much used, he'd said, and she remembered how startled the watchman had been. The inner gate was up, and there was no watchman now.

"Where is she?" Liath whispered. Her battered body could still feel the familiar caress of dread.

"Outside. Safer, more hiding places." Tolivar opened the ironbound door with care that might have been hesitation. He had not been outside the Holding since harvestmid or before. Cool air crept in, carrying a scent of thyme and hyssop, the sea and weathered stone, driving away, for one sweet breath, the reek of blood and the chill odor of the Holding. Tolivar blinked in the slanted light of afternoon or morning. Liath came up behind him, glimpsed weathered blackstone against a greenish sky—

Seldril stood smiling just past the swing of the door, her arms folded across her thin chest, her bloodred robes rippling in the breeze, garish in daylight. Her smile—a rictus that carved hard lines into chalky skin— was not for Tolivar but for Liath. She waved a finger toward them. Stewards in velvet livery advanced.

One sprouted a knife from his neck without Liath knowing she had thrown; Tolivar stared at his longblade, sunken in another's ribs. The man's mouth worked soundlessly, his eyes shocked, betrayed. Liath drove her elbow into the chin of the one coming around on the right, and groped at her belt for knives she had left behind as two more took hold of Tolivar, who had no more resistance in him. She put up a better fight, wielding the weapons they all forgot when they took up blades: bones, teeth, boots, head. But they had her in the end. So much of her was broken and used up. There was nothing left. These men were fresh.

"You released my stock," Seldril said, watching calmly. "I find I have a dearth of mages. The two of you should be adequate compensation. My brother and Gondril have handled this badly. But you are in my hands now."

Seldril swept the whetstone one last time along the curved, shining blade, then touched it lightly to the back of her hand. The thread of blood it produced was like a fine-inked line.

She could not have let Landril have the illuminator. Unsupervised, he could not be trusted to resist the more immediate gratification—and she had wanted this one for herself. Naive and trusting, so full of righteousness and loyalty and courage, she would last a long time on the table, and the moment of her breaking would release such pain and light and power as the Holding had never before contained. It would be the work of days, and Seldril could imagine no better preparation for the hein-na-fhin, no better meditation on her own imperatives, no better means of fueling herself for the battle to come.

Landril surfaced to awareness deep in the tunnels where the sewer led. The fall had not hurt him overmuch; his honed body had absorbed what impact the mire didn't. But something, some thing of magecraft, had hit him like a fist, plunged into his viscera and gripped and twisted and torn pieces of him out. His last memory was of a searing light, a sound like a mountain bursting—

His warding. They had broken his warding. He'd cast it using three good mages—wasted now, and the rest no doubt flown. It had been a thing of spirit, the woven spirits of triaded warders, but it had contained some of his spirit, too. Its breaking had nearly torn him apart.

But it had not. Neither fall nor breaking had broken him. There was a deadness at his core, as if someone had imperfectly sealed his light, but it was easing breath by breath, like circulation returning to a numb appendage.

Still stunned, he got to his feet and staggered on.

Gondril tightened his grip on the sweat-slicked hilt of his ritual blade. The climb to this junction had been both tiring and undignified. This was Landril's fault, Landril's failure. But he would set it right. It was an old score. As well to settle it now as later.

Disloyal stewards scurried through the interstices of the Holding like vermin, as if their little rebellion could hurt anyone but themselves. Gondril sighed, and checked the positions of his men. Always one more galling matter to attend to. He would put an end to this one now by lopping the head off it. Then the way would be clear to Luriel's reckoning, and his own bliss.

"They're coming, sir," his head steward whispered. The servants had taken to addressing them with these absurd honorifics—Lerissa's doing, he suspected. Deluded child. A scream of pain, a face devoid of hope, was the only obeisance that mattered.

The iron landing inside the junction chamber rattled in its brackets at the tread of many boots. The Holding was neglected; Lerissa would have her servants' work cut out for her, transforming it into a regal fastness. When the small band of men and one woman were gathered on the landing, debating which door to use, Gondril made a small gesture: Do it.

His private guard, in nine-colored velvet livery, sprang through the three doors and disarmed the unsuspecting band with little effort. They were bloody and battered from the fight down below—the fight that would have been the end of the uprising, if Landril had done his job. Gondril came onto the crowded landing and smiled at the slow recognition in the leader's eyes. They had not seen each other in half a lifetime. But the memories ran deep.

"Such betrayal, Brondarion, after all we shared. You and I, my sister and brother, poor lightless Wynn. We played in these passages—do you remember? Or have you been buried too long in horse manure and diapers?"

The Khinishman's eyes closed briefly.

"Your pathetic attempt on our lives failed, as did both your uprisings. I was certain Wynn was behind it, or that taciturn seamstress, but lo and behold it was Bron, affable Bron who played with ponies while we recast magecraft itself. I've got your fosterlings, you know. A dozen of them, from toddler to youth."

Oh, that was sweet, the expression in those pretty eyes.

"If I were my sister, what pleasure I would have of them in your presence! My brother will of course be given care of the girls in any event—"

A gob of phlegm took him directly in the eye. He drew out a hand-cloth with lazy nonchalance and wiped it away. "But," he continued, unperturbed, "I will content myself with the look I see on your face right now—and with this."

His ritual blade slid silken into the belly of the nearest of Bron's men. He twisted deftly, then pulled it out. The hooked end did its work. The smell was rank, the effect delightful.

"They were prepared to die for you, yes?" he said in a mild voice, not troubling to wipe the blade.

"Ai," Bron said softly, eyes locked on his man's, sharing his death. They believed this was a noble thing; they missed the point entirely. "As are a nonned others."

"The usual defiant claims," Gondril went on, calmly disemboweling another. There, Bron had flinched, despite himself. Good. "'This isn't over yet, you'll pay for this,'" he mocked.

"You will," Bron said. His voice was steady; quite a change from all those years ago, when he had flown at them in rages after they'd taken some pet or other. "But you won't believe that till you stare your own death in the face. I'll be there, Gondril."

The Khinishman's words were oddly disquieting. To cover, he dispensed with the woman, a small denial of Landril as well, who would have saved her for himself. Then the two remaining; let him share three deaths at once, if he could, or choose which to lend the empty solace of those deep brown eyes. This errand had wasted enough of his time. With practiced efficiency he thrust the blade into Bron, twisted, withdrew. Whatever brave words the man would have uttered came forth a gout of blood. As the light faded in the earthy depths of eyes Gondril had adored as a child, he said, "Go, then, and wait for me, Bron. I will savor our next meeting."

They left the carcasses for the bonefolk.

"The rebel host is coming, Wordsmith. We've captured a pigeon sent by one of Naeve's spies along their route. They'll be here by Ve Galandra, at the rate they're traveling."

Worilke sighed and laid down her quill, glancing forlornly at the history of Galandra so close to completion—the fine, even rows of glyphs, no embellishment, just clarity and truth. Must she leave off and put her quill to more immediate use? She looked up at the steward. "Are all the proxies in?"

"Yes, on your order, Wordsmith."

"Well, then. We will see to it as soon as they've made sufficient headway into the mountains." She had already seen to the destruction of Torrin; she had not trusted that to the triplets and whatever pathetic offering that illuminator child had brought them, but taken Freyn's tools and made certain of it herself. Nonetheless, the host was her triad's responsibility, as it was down to Naeve's balance triad to preserve the codices, leaving the triplets free to join in hein-na-fhin and rid her of both themselves and the threat that had hovered beyond the shield since the beginning of time. The obvious place to stop the host was the plateau; they would probably camp the night there, at the halfway point of their passage through the Aralinns, seduced by the sweet stream and early-flowering fruit groves, lulled by the waterfall. "Post some of our folk on the other side of the plateau. They're to send a bird when the host is half a day from there, then ride back here."

Her elderly steward shifted. "Wordsmith . . ."

Reticence was uncharacteristic of Valik. He'd been her family's steward since he and his pledgemate had come to the Holding, four nines of years past, all the way from the Weak Leg. They'd come with a child in tow, a girl of six so bright that reckoners had urged them to take her to the Holding rather than risk poor training from some local triad. Their family had been lightless for generations. They came ignorant, frightened, but not cowed, and would not give the child into the Ennead's care. It had been easier to retain them as private stewards, to avoid upsetting child or parents, and over the years the two families had merged into a semblance of one. Worilke had been nine then, and Freyn n'Eniya l'Valik had become a sister to her, Freyn's family her own extended. The distinction between light and lightless had remained—there was no question who was mage and who was steward—but they had always spoken frankly to each other.

"What is it, Valik? Tell me."

"There are mages with them too."

Worilke paused for a long moment. They were probably lapsed or untriaded. All bright and loyal proxies had returned safe to the Holding at her call. She could not save them all. If some mages insisted on sacrificing themselves for this misguided uprising, she couldn't stop them; and if they tried to ward against the host's destruction, they became antagonists, and would reap what they'd sown.

"No helping that," she said softly. "We cannot let ourselves be overrun. Post your sentries. Inform me when it's time." Her triad would bring the rocky walls down on their heads as they lay sleeping in perfumed blossoms. If there were strong magecrafted wardings, she would convene the Nine, but she did not anticipate difficulty. This was their mountain; it heeded them. It would smash any intruders they told it to.

Valik acknowledged the instructions and left her to her scribing, but she found it difficult to pick up the trail of her thoughts. Her mother's voice, teller's voice modulated into mage's, echoed in her mind: "*Tellers affect minds and hearts, while castings affect only tangible things.*"

"*Yes, Mother,*" she had said, weary of the old debate, "*but only for a few moments, or the hearer's lifetime. Words should last longer than that.*"

What she had scribed here would last forever—the canon of a new order, a return to Galandra's way. Magecraft had crippled itself, lost its way; the light was dying. Whole languages and symbologies had been forgotten. The division into triadic disciplines had made each mage a third of what she should have been. There should be no panicked search for illuminator or binder when three perfectly bright lights were within reach. Galandra's time had been a golden age. Each stroke of her quill brought the second coming of that age closer. She had manipulated the Ennead, husbanded the light, protected Eiden Myr as best she could. But without this chronicle to light the way, all was for naught.

hey hurt her, and then healed her. How long it went on she did not know. Breaths that could be days. Lifetimes passed between the beats of her heart. Sometimes it seemed the next beat would not come; she floated free of her body, free of the pain, then was yanked cruelly back. Sometimes they questioned her. She told them everything they wanted to know—the strength of the horde, the location, the names, Torrin's plans. She would do anything to stop what happened to her as she lay helpless on their carven tables. Sometimes they tired of her screams and sealed her mouth. Sometimes her sinuses clogged with blood or mucus and she began to suffocate. She tried not to let on. She tried to slip away. But the spirit had a will of its own, and the flesh clung to life even as the mind howled to get loose. The body would buck and spasm, and she would return to awareness, breathing again.

They were so tender when they healed her.

They never tired of Tolivar's screams. They let him scream for her. They penned them together, too weak to bequeath each other death, in order to torment them. It was the pen in the center chamber. The work was done in the innermost, where the stone cells were. That was to horrify too: more frightening what you couldn't see than what you could, what you only imagined as you listened to the screams. Liath didn't have to imagine, for they did the same to her; yet the difference between imagining and happening grew more significant as the line between reality and fantasy thinned. There was a very great difference indeed between imagining agony and experiencing it. Still she would at any moment have given herself for him. Inanely, she begged them to take her in his place, as if they hadn't all the time in the world to do them both. It was a terrible choice, yet time after time she made it, knowing she would not be able to endure what she offered, offering just the same. It seemed to amuse them. After a while she feared that they were keeping him alive because of it, and stopped. But each time they returned him to the cage she knew he still lived. He was not yet refuse for the foul sewer below. Each time he came back to her, she rejoiced even as she grieved.

They taunted her with blinding. To lose her eyes would be worse than losing her fingers, and they regularly came close to removing those. So far they had not cut off anything they could not grow back. But she knew they would. They blinded Tolivar. They had blinded Portriel. Poor 'Triel.

But that wasn't right. Portriel had blinded herself, in paroxysms of madness when they cut her off from her light. Liath tried to strangle herself, to dash her brains on the stone. But always the body rebelled, or gave out before she was finished. She hated her body. It was the source of pain. Better to be free of it. But they healed any damage she did to herself. There was nothing she could do, with bare hands and iron bars, that they could not undo.

Tolivar screamed and screamed. He broke his beautiful bindsman's voice in screaming for them. After that, the silence was ghastly. Then there was only her own heartbeat under the whispers, and the whispers spoke eternity. Heartbeat meant life, and life meant pain, and it would never end.

She could barely lift her head when they tossed him back into the cage, but something in the way his body hit the stone—some limp heaviness, the careless crack of his skull—roused her to crawl to him. To what was left of him. Rather than stuffing him down the slaughterhole, they'd given him back to her. To break her heart. Never knowing it was a gift.

She smoothed his skin back into place with care. It took a long time. There was a lot of blood; she found the rags of her shirt and wiped him, in short, gentle strokes. Then she drew the edge of a broken nail deeply across the soft hollow of her palm, between calluses, where veins branched close to the surface. With a fingertip dipped in fresh, warm blood, she began to paint him—illuminating him for the next life, caressing pattern across his sweet, smooth, cold flesh. He sailed other seas now. *May they be kinder seas than you've known, under clearer skies. May you find there all the ecstasy and light you craved in this world.* She didn't know if she'd spoken aloud; she didn't know how deeply into madness she had fallen.

"Dabrena's safe," she whispered to him. Somewhere, his haunt would hear her. "Dabrena and the child. She has your eyes, Tolivar. Your eyes remain in the world for her to look through, your wise, clear eyes, and when she sees things as they ought to be she'll have your smile to give." Her tears were running in the kadri she had scribed, changing the designs, blurring them into new shapes. "It's never over, Tolivar. Sweet Tolivar . . .

free of the rock now . . ." She kissed his bloodless lips, and his empty eyelids—one, then the other. Three kisses, for farewell.

She dreamed the bonefolk took his body into a strange greenish light. She dreamed that Mellas reached out to her through his dreams; she took his hand, and for one shining, terrible moment she was free . . . but she did not dream well enough, or believe hard enough, for he could not keep hold of her, and she slid back into agony's arms. She dreamed that Heff sang to her, in words she didn't know, his voice deep and rich and whole. Nole and Father lifted her and spun her, laughing. Keiler caught her when she stumbled and promised never to let go; Graefel praised her; Mother forgave her. Nerenyi explained it all, patiently, but her words whirled into disks of light, the three luminaries, too bright to look on. Torrin broke free of the bonefolk, come back from the realm of death itself to save her, or her light—but he was all in pieces, losing an arm here, a foot there, and by the time he'd gotten to her side he crumbled into a disjointed heap. She tried for a long time to reassemble him, but she couldn't make the parts fit, and she could never find the eyes.

Does that hurt, Illuminator?
—Yes.
Do you like it?
Yes.

The cornfields stretched as far as the eye could see. There were no mountains, no streams, no towns. The sky was silver. The light cast no shadow. She bent over the kadri scrawled in the dirt, her tongue sticking out of the side of her mouth. She must do her best or Hanla would be angry. She must do her best or Hanla would hurt her. She dug the stick hard into the soil, wounding the earth. It wasn't fair. It wasn't fair that Hanla would hurt her even though she was doing everything Hanla said.

Except that Hanla never really hurt her.

Does that hurt, Liath?

She nodded, not looking up.

It should hurt, Liath. When it works, it should hurt. It should hurt so much that you cannot stand it. Does it hurt, Liath?

Yes! I told you! Can't you hear me? What's wrong with you?

Outraged, she glared up through her bangs, and saw that she wasn't in the cornfield at all, but in the smokehouse. It was much bigger than it should be, as big as the greatroom, and they didn't have a smokehouse. Roiden always smelled of smoke. Now she knew why. That was a horrible smell. He made whiskey here and traded it for Finger wine. They traded him for it even though no one ever drank it except some proxies they didn't like, and they served it to them because they wanted to get rid of them. Mother was always getting rid of proxies. Mother hated proxies. Liath was supposed to hide from proxies. Pelkin had told her to. But he hadn't told her to hide from Roiden. Roiden brought her to the smoke-house. She didn't want to go. She didn't like him. He frightened her. He liked to frighten her. He wanted to frighten Keiler, too, but Keiler mocked him when Graefel couldn't hear. Keiler was brave. Keiler wouldn't have let Roiden take him to the smokehouse. Liath shouldn't have let him take her. Mother would be angry. A daughter of the Petrel's Rest was supposed to look out for herself. She knew that when he grabbed her, but he was big and she was small. He wrestled her inside. He barred the door. His face looked like aged parchment in the lamplight, parchment that a binder had left too long, the kind of parchment they practiced on because it was gone old and dry and bad, no use for castings.

The smell was awful. She couldn't breathe. *This is what it should feel like*, Roiden said. *And like this*. He hurt her. He hurt her! It hurt! No one hurt her, no one hurt anyone, not even Erl or Tarny or Sarse, not like this, he was really hurting her—

Stop! she cried, but his hand smothered it. She stamped on his insteps, kicked his shins. He laughed and took her by the hair and drowned her scream in a bucket of water. Again, and again, until there was no scream-ing left in her, only a quick desperate dripping gasp for air when he pulled her head out. *This is what it will feel like*, he said between dunkings. *When the guiders burn bright. When you hold all the world's colors. At the end of a brush. This is what it feels like. To me. All the time. Because they won't let me use my light. Does that hurt? Does it?*

Good. The light is pain. Pain is the absence of light. Never forget that. Never.

She came to in the cornfield and stumbled home soaking wet, half drowned, no memory of how she'd gotten that way. Mother would be so angry. She must have fallen in the river—when had she gone to the river? She was coming back from Hanla's, from her lessons, she was late for evening setup, she was so late, even Father wouldn't be able to get her out of this one . . .

Spirits, child, where have you been?

I don't know, Mother.

Oh, Liath . . . oh, my girl . . .

She staggered past Geara and into her father's arms, but all his hugs and soft words couldn't squeeze from her heart the smoky black thing that had gotten in there, that she couldn't explain, that she couldn't remember.

Where were you, Liath? What happened to you?

I don't remember, Father. I can't remember. . . .

. . .

"You don't have to remember, love," he said gently. "Best to forget. Come on, now. Up."

"No more," she begged. She couldn't see. They'd blinded her at last. There would be no healing that.

"No," he agreed. "No more. Come, love."

There had been bars. The bars had moved. But it had been her, moving past the bars. Flying. She had flown from her cage. Perhaps she would fly home, the storm petrel returned from her long journey over the sea. But home was gone. The only home for her now was death. "Let me die," she said.

"Only if you stand up. I can't carry you through here, it's too tight. Walk for me, love, and you can do all the dying your heart desires."

She had seen the bars. She had seen the stone cell, seen the carven table bouncing toward her, heard the bootsteps, felt the hand muffle her pleading cry, and gone black again. Striving for death before they could pour the potion down her throat, the smoky potion that denied release. Those were memories. Recent memories.

"Walk for me, love," he prompted, for she had already forgotten what he'd said. Walk, and they would let her die. It was a reasonable bargain. Probably a trap. But there was no wriggling out of traps. You did what they said. No matter what.

She put bare feet on stone and dragged one leg in front of the other. He was taking most of her weight. They squeezed tight through an orifice of rock, a chill scrape across her back. She barely felt it. Some skin rasped away. It was nothing. Then they were through. Like being born through stone.

Her vision was clearing. That was bad. It wasn't good to see what they were doing. Would they had blinded her. But that was bad too. It was bad not to know when the cuts were coming. But that was only in the beginning. After a while it didn't matter anymore. Even your own mind couldn't defend you. There was only searing pain. She had counted the cuts, once. That was bad. It was bad to know that there were three nines of cuts to go, two nines and eight, two nines and seven. But it was bad not to know when it would end. But it was bad when it ended, because then they would seal the cuts and start over. And sometimes they made fewer cuts, or more. They knew she'd counted. They knew everything.

She spasmed. "They'll know!" she hissed, questing blurrily for a glimpse of his face. "They'll know . . . you've taken me . . . sweet spirits . . . put me back . . ."

"What will they do to you if they find you that they will not do to you if we return?"

She didn't know. But she didn't have to know. It would be bad. "Let me die," she said.

"That's two. On three, I might consider it."

His tone startled her. Their voices were always reasonable, even kind. Relentlessly soothing.

"Who . . . *are* you?"

"Either a hero or a very great fool, and right now a frightened man who is cursing Torrin roundly. Not that I haven't been doing that for some time as it is."

She was trembling uncontrollably. She had been this cold, once. Perhaps she was still there, under the snow, and it was Torrin talking to her . . . but that was only her imagination, tormenting her, taking her away for a while only so they could bring her back. Fantasy was like hope. Hope was bad.

"All right, love, it's not far now. You were due for another dose of Freyn's brew, it's what kept you from dying of exposure lying naked in the cage. We'll get you warm. Three shakes of a lamb's tail. All right, maybe six."

What astonished her, as movement subsided into something she might have felt once as warmth, was that he wasn't lying.

"Let me sleep," she slurred, when she'd drunk as much of the drugged broth as she could.

Somewhere above her swam a smile with the charm of Mellas's, the wickedness of Tolivar's. "That's more like it."

She woke in a thrashing terror into darkness, and he was there to calm her. Flesh and blood. Real, not hallucination. "Who are you?" she asked, and he said, "Sleep, love. Sleep safe. Dream all the silver from behind your eyes."

When she woke again, she was mounded warm on a comfortable pallet across a soft-lit chamber from the proxy who had stopped her in the passageways the first time she tried to reach the Ennead.

"Did you ever find that trinket?" he asked, laying aside a bound sheaf of vellum like the one Torrin used to study.

She wanted to reward his rescue, his comfort, his smile with something brave or cheerful, but she said, "No. I only lost more of them, more precious than that."

He nodded as if he understood, and leaned forward into the light, and she drew her breath in sharply and recoiled.

"Evonder n'Vonche l'Naeve, Ennead binder," he confirmed, and rose, raking a hand through his sandy hair—a weary gesture Torrin had often made. A nineyear older than she'd thought, he looked nothing like the bored, resentful youth who'd sat with the Ennead only days ago. But it was the same face.

She fell back under a wave of nausea.

"I don't know how they expected you to live till Ve Galandra," he said, pouring her a cup of water. "You were hovering awfully close to the edge."

She ignored the proffered cup and huddled closer in the blankets, shaking too hard to speak.

"Liath," he said. "I've rescued you, love. It's real. It's not another trick. This won't be snatched away from you the moment you believe in it. You're safe. Not for long, but for now. I promise you." He sat on the pallet and offered the water again. "Drink. You've a lot of Freyn's philters in you still."

"Don't touch me."

"I'm only touching the cup. You can take it without brushing my hand at all."

Warily, she did. He sat very still as she slurped—she was desperately thirsty, she had been thirsty for days, a lifetime—and folded his hands in his lap when she was through. She set the cup on the floor beside the pallet. He returned it to the little table.

"I did not assist in your torture," he said quietly.

It had been Seldril, and sometimes Landril, aided by stewards who never spoke, some who had no eyes. "You sat by while it happened. To me, and dozens of others."

"Yes," he said. "I did."

She pressed her hands to her face as if it were a mask she could pull off. The scars were a strange, puckered tracery under her fingers. "I betrayed him," she said. "I told them everything."

"You don't know everything. Nor do I. Nor did they know what questions to ask. And I betrayed him too, once." He smiled, a soft smile of remembrance just like Torrin's. "We got over it."

"You . . ." But the ally had been a woman. Yet Torrin had never said that. She had filled the words in for him. She was so blasted bad at words.

"Your color's returning," Evonder said. "That's good, because you have to leave as soon as possible. I'll heal you, of course, but there's only so much magecraft can do. They hurt your spirit, too. Badly. I know that."

"What they did . . ." She took a deep breath. "They never—they never even did any castings, while they . . . They just cut me. And broke me. For the sake of it. And killed Tolivar and threw him back in the cage. And . . ."

Evonder raised a hand to halt her pained account. "They were trying to make you despair, Liath. That's what they're going to send through to the other side. They can't send arrows, or illness, or poison, or anything borne of matter, and they don't have any materials they can use to shake a continent to rubble. They're sending a plague of spirit."

"Why did you save me now?"

"I had intended to kill you. But I was asked to save you. So I did."

"Who . . ."

He smiled, and her heart melted a little. "It seems you have a number of advocates. The most proximate was a warder. My remaining people took a few toys away from Gondril. Among them were the warder and her child. She was mad with grief over betraying you and her binder—she'd told Seldril the gate where you were supposed to meet, when Seldril threatened the baby. She begged us to get you out."

"The binder's dead."

"His death bought her child's life."

"Bron . . ."

"He's been missing since Gondril took the fosterlings. But he and the triplets were childhood friends. Rumor has it that Gondril was enamored of him in their youth. Perhaps they spared him."

Bron was the only one who had not reached to save her in her dreams. Somehow she'd known. "No," she said. "No, he's gone."

"I'm sorry, Liath." And she saw that he was, though he lived in a world of pain and futility. Somehow he had hung on to compassion. She wondered how deeply he'd buried himself to preserve it—how many faces he had.

"In the passageway . . . you were a reckoner . . . older . . ."

"I find it expedient to be other than I am. Since Torrin left, I am not sure who I am. For these few breaths with you, I've remembered, and for restoring that trinket I thank you. Now let me heal you, so I can send you from here. I *will* kill you rather than let them use you."

She moved the muscles that should produce a wry grin. "I couldn't very well complain. I asked you three times to do it."

"Only twice." He grunted as he pulled an ornate chest from a corner and lifted the lid. She smelled ordinary binding materials, but the scent of the vellum and parchment made her queasy. "I can't promise much, let me warn you. I am only one. I can't smooth the flesh. But I can bring your strength back, and purge the last of the decoctions from your blood. You'll sweat, and go hot and cold. Wrap up tight, now."

"Maybe you shouldn't," she said, thinking of Heff, and binders' slaughtergrounds, and the value of the life that would be given to make her strong again.

"I can only imagine why you would say that," he began, smoothing parchment over a binding board and inking a goose quill. "But unless I do this, you'll be many ninedays recuperating, and your casting hand is a mangled mess. Do you consent?"

She nodded and lay quiet while he cast. Like Torrin, he worked quickly; like Torrin, he burned brighter when he cast. Not blinding bright, but fierce and beautiful, brighter than any nine proxies. She could not see what he scribed or drew, but his bindsong was a balm to the spirit, low and melodious. *I will be ever breaking my heart on bindsmen,* she thought, as he helped her rise out of the post-casting languor to bathe, then rubbed her dry.

She put her healed hand on him, molding her palm to the muscles under the loose shirt. A current of desire ran between them, surging as she touched him through the linen, felt his heartbeat. "Your friends are dead," he said, taking her hand to remove it from his chest. The contact of bare flesh only intensified the feeling. He faltered, then went on, "The body cannot grieve, so it defies death by asserting life."

"Tolivar would have wished such pleasure for me," she replied, stepping closer. "And Bron too, most like."

"There's often a surge of lust after mages heal a mage," he persisted, but his attention was not on what he was saying. His hand curved around her breast. "Light reaches out to light. . . ." A breath away from her mouth, he said, "Life is strong, and when it wins it exults intensely."

"Then let's exult," she said, pressing against his arousal and tasting his lips.

With a growl of frustration, he gave in to the kiss, working her mouth hard, his binder's hands tracing a line of fire down her spine. But when she reached between them to get at his trouser fastenings, he trapped her hand with his and broke away. "If that were all, and if there were time, then I would revel in it. You are very powerful, my dear. I'm enough a creature of Ennead to crave that for myself. But it isn't me you want. I remind you of him, I know; we grew so close we grew alike, over the years. One light, one dark, but the same voice, the same mannerisms. When I'm myself, I'm Torrin, without his brooding complexity, without the world on my shoulders." He set her away from him and reached toward a pile of clothes. "Save the rest for the right man."

"He's dead," she said softly, taking silks from him, a blowsy white shirt, black breeches. He had nothing plain.

"Then why does he cry so fiercely for you that his man Jhoss risked all our lives sending me a message to retrieve you?"

She pushed her battered heart down with little effort when it leapt at his words. "How long ago," she said, expecting nothing.

"A couple of days."

"How long was I in the . . ."

"A threeday."

The message had been sent after the casting had been done on him. Something had gone wrong. He was *alive* . . . "Were you there? When they used what I brought them?"

"No. I thought they'd killed him. They still think so."

"Perhaps Jhoss . . ." *Perhaps Jhoss is lying.*

"That is a risk you're going to have to take. You must leave the Holding in any event."

"Where is he?"

Evonder raised his brows, then set about rummaging for shoes. "The message didn't specify. Safer that way, yes?"

It was. She sat down to pull on the black boots he offered. They were loose. He handed her a thick pair of wool stockings to go over the silk. "I'll find him somehow."

"Good girl. But you'll have to be quick about it. Ve Galandra begins in a nineday. The triplets plan the scourge of Ollorawn for the balance day. I'm doing what I can, but chances are I can't stop it, or even hinder it much. Not alone."

"I could stay . . . I could help . . ."

You can't fight them from within. Someone's got to fight them from without.

"You can't cast here," he said gently.

"No," she said. "But I think I know why now."

"That's a start." He caressed her face, then regretfully let his hand drop. "Anyhow, Torrin has a use for you, if indeed he lives. You must be one leg of his prospective triad. I hope he's found the other, and I hope she's as bright as you, or we're lost."

"Won't removing me from here be enough?" If they did not have her to use in Portriel's stead . . .

Evonder shook his tawny head. "I don't know. We can't be sure they don't have another tucked away. Landril covers all contingencies; it's why he tried to keep you isolated to begin with, why he didn't just throw you down in the cage with the rest. He must have known Portriel was chancy. Above all, though, we have to stop the hein-na-fhin. Whether or not they punch through to deliver their plague, they'll be unassailably powerful once they're joined. If Landril is thwarted, he'll turn his rage on Eiden Myr. The others will turn their hunger on it no matter the outcome. That's one reason Worilke and Lerissa have been working so hard to support them in this. Better they should destroy the world outside than the world we live in." He shrugged. "It's a bad job no matter how you look at it, love, unless you get to Torrin in time. How do you feel?"

She stood and took a dove-gray cloak off a hook on the wall over the pallet. "It doesn't matter. Well enough to travel."

"Come on, then. I have some friends you should meet."

The chamber had not been his private quarters, but some nest kept secretly, for trysts or solitude. It was located high in the Holding, away from the Ennead's core, but deep in the back, where the passages were rough, unfinished, unlit. Though it was large, the Holding occupied only the face of the mountain. Leagues of solid stone lay behind it.

"I took you out through that new passage your folk made," Evonder explained, walking ahead of her in pitch darkness, as unerring as Portriel. There was no magestone here. "Handy thing, that, though it leads back into the Holding. Who cast it?"

"Mellas," she said. "He broke the warding too."

She felt Evonder's surprise through his hand. His hands were as smooth as Torrin's, as expressive as Heff's in their own way. There was so much she wanted to ask him, but her mind had not come fully back to her yet. "I thought one of us must have done that," he said. "I couldn't fathom why."

"He must have been afraid, or still tied here in his heart," she said. If the passage only led back inside, it was all for nothing. They'd probably recaptured them all, or killed them.

"Well, he's a canny lad. The thing branched endlessly. They'll never find all the forks and exits." His hand squeezed. "He got them out."

He couldn't know that for certain, but the words were kind.

She thought the memory of light must be playing behind her eyes, glints and sparkles that the mind conjured in total darkness, like metallic nightstone flecks sent dancing across the passageway. But as they went deeper, as the subliminal hum of magecraft subsided into an ancient still-ness and the unnoticed human scents of the Holding faded, the play of not-light increased. She could swear she felt it against her scarred flesh, like bubbles.

"Stop now," Evonder said. "Keep still. Don't be afraid."

What should I not be afraid of? came the wary, unvoiced question, but she obeyed him.

A marvel rewarded her. They were no longer in a passageway; they had come into a cavern. The space above them danced with blue-white motes of light, a misty scintillation. The air was still, but the minuscule lights swept into currents, braiding and unraveling, circling then flying apart. Gradually, they took on something like form—diaphanous streaks and shreds, fluttering up, then drifting back down. As if curious about the warm beings that had come into their domain. One settled on the back of her hand, gossamer and luminous; another brushed her hair. Exploring. Others came close, then flitted away, as if her breath had touched them, the flutter of her eyes blinking. "Oh . . ."

"Mountain wraiths," Evonder said, without startling them.

"Are they haunts?" she asked, sorry when the ones on her flew off. But in a moment they were back, a little braver this time, a little more sure of her.

"Elementals," he said. "Look."

Across the cavern, shreds and flutters combined into the vague form of a person. A body, a head, ragged arms; drooping holes where eyes and mouth would be. What ghosts looked like, in the teller's tales. But these spirits had never been human.

"That's hello," he said. "They try to look like something you'll un-derstand. The mountains are alive, Liath. The earth is alive, the air, the water. Alive, and aware."

And he reveled in it. He looked youthful, gentled—supremely happy to stand in the midst of the flitting spectres that had become his friends.

It was beautiful, and profoundly sad.

"They'll take you from here," he said.

She turned a full circle, scanning the cavern's walls. Solid nightstone, except for the deeper darkness of the passage they'd entered by. A flock of wraiths lifted off her when she moved, then settled again, adapting to her motions. She waved her arm back and forth, grinning at their attempts to cling to her. They were better at it by the third pass. She was spangled in bluish light. It was wondrous. But there was nowhere to take her.

"The mountain changes," Evonder said. His voice was dreamy, as if the touch of the wraiths relaxed him, drugged him. "The mountain will make way for you. It protected you before. It knows you now. It will show you the way."

"The labyrinth changes," Portriel said. "The labyrinth lies. The labyrinth tries to trick you. The stone dreams . . . and in its sleep it shifts, dreaming itself new."

"Trust it, Liath," Evonder said, and when he turned to her it seemed that motes of light danced in his eyes. "If you're meant to go through, it will take you." He reached out shining arms and kissed her through a shimmering sparkle. Where their mouths sank into each other, soft bubbles seemed to burst, tickling her palate—a kiss sweet as sowmid wine, sprinkled with light. She did not want it to end. She did not want to go alone through the leagues of cold stone. She did not want to leave this haunted, lonely man.

"We're none of us alone," he said. "Go quickly now. Tell Torrin it's to happen at noon on the balance day." He held her out to the length of his arms, then opened his hands and backed away. Wraiths closed around her, nudging. "Eiden guide you, Illuminator. He is more alive than you ever knew."

She let the wraiths shepherd her, swallowing her questions, swallowing light. Where they led, the stone yielded, passages opening where there had been no passages before. She glanced behind her; they did not close up. The way would always be open, somewhere. To go forward, or to go back.

Eiden was alive. The land was shaped in his image, the land was his body, the stars in the night sky were his light in the darkness. Human beings lived in harmony with the spirits—Eiden, Morlyrien, Sylfonwy, and all the lesser who were their children, the spirits of tree and stream, rock and field. Even Torrin did not dispute that, though the seekers tried to explain it. But still it awed her to see, to feel, the evidence. Eiden was alive. The mountain was alive. The mountain's light caressed her, perceived her. She was known, inside and out, all her flaws and all her goodness. Known and understood.

She was not alone.

The tunnel opened on changeable enormity. When the wraiths released her into the overwhelming odors and variable light and shifting air, and disappeared—invisible in daylight, or retracted back into the tunnel—the contrast drove her to her knees. The ordeal, behind her and below her in the rock, was over, yet inside her it would go on and on. The memory was unendurable. The world had turned inside out, and she had turned outside in, and the horror was not something she could brace herself against; the horror was inside her.

Now she was the horror.

She toppled forward onto her hands and retched up a thin stream of broth and bile, then groped away from it, into tufts of dormant mountain grass. She pressed her face into the clean, cold scent, turned her scarred cheek flat. If she could put new things inside her to bury it, a cat scratching sand over offal. If she could make new memories to drive it back. But she could not seem to move.

A foot away from her, looming large in her vision, tiny flowers fluttered in the crevices of tumbled black stone. Heartsfire and snowdrop and nodding purple neversee, dewed from recent rain. The delicate mauve lines in the neversee's petals, the spray of pollen-dusted crimson at the center of the heartsfire, the frill of leaf around the snowdrop's head . . . So intricate, so complex for their size. Somehow they came back, year after year, no matter how harsh the winters. She had forgotten their lesson.

She was tiny, stubborn. A hard little seed, blown by wraithwind to this fecund patch of earth among the stones. She lifted herself. There was no sun to stretch toward, but the sky was limitless, and free. There was no sky inside the Holding.

She was muscle and sinew, breath and heartbeat. She was spirit and heart and intellect; she knew herself.

She lived.

Sitting back on her haunches, snugging the gray cloak, she considered her options. The thick cover of clouds had a greenish tinge, a harbinger of storm, but she might be spared rain till she'd found shelter for the night. A faint deer trail led up through rocks and trees; down was not negotiable. Where to, once she found a road? He'd been headed up the Lowland coast. . . .

Think like a seeker, she told herself.

He was going to break Galandra's shield. The Ennead would strike on the balance day of Ve Galandra. That holiday and Ve Eiden were an ancient tradition. The balance days. The opposite of Longlight and Longdark. More important than spirit days, bonedays, or any of the myriad regional festivals. Ve Galandra and Ve Eiden had spirit names, and the solstices did not. There were reasons for names. Traditions recalled history. Something had happened on the sowmid equinox for folk to call it after Galandra.

Galandra's great achievement had been to rally the persecuted and bring them safely here. But her greatest casting had been the warding around Eiden Myr. That was the day the mages were truly safe at last. Of course they would celebrate it. But perhaps it was more necessity than happenstance. Perhaps Galandra's ambitious casting had to be done on a particular day. Wouldn't she have chosen an equinox, to best balance the elements inside and out?

Ve Galandra was the day the mage Galandra cast the warding. She had done it after shattering the strait. Where had she been standing? Where was the casting circle?

She banged her knuckles softly against her brow, trying to knock Torrin's words loose. He'd said so much. She'd tried so hard to dismiss it as lies. But something odd had caught her ear; she'd let it go by, distracted by the movements of his hands . . .

To the east, he'd said.

Of course.

East and west and north and south were designations so unhelpful that people rarely used them. What mattered was where you were bound, be it Legward or Neckward, upland or downland. One side of Eiden Myr was high, the other low. The Head was at one end, the Feet were at the other, the Arms to either side. The sun rose in the east, but never in the same place as the year turned, so "winterrise," say, was of more use than "east." Useful concepts came in threes. Up, down, sidewise. Highlands, Midlands, Lowlands. Four directions were too many. Norther and Midder and Souther were a climatic distinction—probably held over from those first refugees, she realized. They'd have been critically concerned with climate. But Ollorawn lay to the east, and long ago it had been connected to Eiden Myr by a strip of rocky land.

It was the Fist. The Fist was the stub of land left when the strait was broken. A clenched fist, forever extended toward those who had tried to destroy them.

That was where Galandra had stood, on the sowmid equinox, to cast her warding. That was where Torrin would go to break it.

Blisters formed fast inside the ill-fitting boots. As she came huffing and sweating up to the main trail, the terrain began to look familiar. Too familiar.

Stupid, she thought, when she knew where she was. *Stupid, stupid spirits.* The wraiths had listened to her heart, and her heart had cried out to go home. They had put her just below the Heartward trail. The trail she had taken a year ago. The trail that led back through the Neck.

"I have to get to the Fist!" she cried, smacking a tree trunk in frustration. "I have to get to Lobe and find a ship!" She was on foot. The Heartward route would take her too far out of the way to make the days up. She would never reach him in time.

She would never reach him at all if she stood here swearing. She struck off along the wide trail. The wraiths had saved her days, she had to give them that; she was past the flowering plateau, more than halfway to Clondel. Someone might ride by, someone she could beg or trick or overpower. Where was that blasted horde, with her good roan mare? Scattered dead in the Girdle, probably, felled by storm or flood; or drowned in the colored lakes of the Belt, or mired in Heartlands mud. The Ennead had to be running messages still, or even proxies now that their own warding was broken. Someone would come.

Very possibly someone sent to catch her. They didn't know for certain that she'd left the Holding, but they knew how badly she wanted to go home. This was the road to home.

Hoofbeats sounded. She hid behind a burled oak and hefted a rock. The hoofbeats slowed to a stop just around the bend in the trail, then resumed at a walk. He was cautious, whoever he was. Perhaps he'd caught a glimpse of dyed clothes. She cursed herself for walking so boldly, and tensed to throw.

He came around the turn, on foot, leading two horses, not the ones they'd started with. His clothes showed the wear of hard travel, and half his face was shadowed with beard. It was smiling.

I will always find you.

Considerate of them to put you on a trail where I could make good time, Heff said, striding directly toward her before she'd come out from behind the oak, his words slurred by the reins he held. You were up and down inside that mountain like a sowbug.

She stepped out from the tree shade, and his hands went still.

"They carved me up pretty good," she said quietly. When he did not reply, she added, "It's all right. It wasn't much of a face to begin with."

It is your face, and it is still beautiful, he said softly, his gestures subdued. I thank the spirits for your life.

"There are a few people you can thank as well." She took the reins of the smaller horse, busying herself with cinch and halter that would not need checking. "I hope you'll get to meet them someday. But we have to hurry now." She flinched as his gentle hand fell on her shoulder; then she froze, staring at the saddle.

She hadn't known. She hadn't known it would affect her like this. The healing passion was so powerful she hadn't realized. *Don't touch me,* she thought, and bit the inside of her cheek.

He lifted the hand and stepped back.

"I'm sorry." She couldn't look at him. But he couldn't talk if she didn't. She made herself turn. Every fiber of her strained toward his beloved arms. But her body was a wire strung tight.

Heff glanced down the trail, in the direction of the Holding, then made an ugly gesture.

"Yes," she said. "Yes, they are that."

You'll be wanting this, he said, and untied a straight bundle from alongside his saddle. She knew it was a longblade before he'd unwrapped it. The scabbard was designed to strap on the back, for riding, not at the side, as in the Holding. She shrugged into the harness and fastened her cloak over the sheath; the hood's folds bunched around the hilt, concealing it but not hindering access.

Heff mounted and said, He's in the Fist.

"I know," she said, managing a smile. Her cheeks didn't dimple right anymore, but she wouldn't let them take smiles away from her too.

Grant him life. Let it be true. Let him live.

Evonder stood for a long time in the cavern the mountain had opened for them, letting the misty iridescence wash through him. Then he turned and went back, taking a different route, feeling the passages shift in his wake. He was born of the mountain, as were his parents before him. Liath Illuminator was not; he was glad it had welcomed her. He had not been certain it would. Perhaps her little village, nestled at the Aralinns' base, was enough a part of the connecting bedrock for it to know her. The mountains were alive, but the mountains were not always kind. Perhaps that was something she never need learn.

Torrin must be mad for her, he thought with a chuckle. *Alive, and pining.* The last of the light danced around him, laughing too. Then it was gone. The wraiths did not exist in the Holding proper. Where the Holding was, the mountain was dead. Only the magestone offered a semblance of life, soaked in the memories of the race long lost, the race he had sought and never found; and the magestone was only an echo of what had been. Once, before the rise of darkcraft, the wraiths must have inhabited the Holding. What a wonder that would have been. The dance of wraithlight, the sparkle of mica in the nightstone walls by torchglare, the calm glow of the memory stone in the presence of good and decent mages. What a wonder the other Holdings must have been. Established in abandoned places like this, the fastnesses of those who had crafted this world before the mages came and crafted it again from ashes. What had destroyed those folk? They'd had the power to make *mountains*—white abutting black, granite at the foot of chalk, iron beside granite, copper below. Jet and chalk and smoke and mauve and gold and rust and blue and green. They had illuminated their world in stone, arranged it in their own likeness. What kind of beings wielded such glorious power, and what had been their downfall?

He would never know. If there were time, if things were different . . . But they were not. He must go back, again, into the dead places, the places of suffering and cruelty. He could not rescue them all. He could not even rescue himself.

You left me, his heart cried out, as it ever did when he returned to the lamplit darkness. *You left me alone!*

It was necessary. He knew that. He knew that Torrin's way was the only way. Even together they could not have defeated what generations had entrenched. Jaemlyn had tried, Maeryn, Portriel, all the wise and beautiful children of Niendre and Mathey, and died for it, one by one. Too late they recognized the black thing that had blossomed in the deep caverns of their Holding, the rot that deadened its base and crept upward. They made their stand, and failed, and left their children isolated, frightened, ignorant, too young to carry on the fight in any organized way. Somehow he and Torrin had found each other, and begun the long, secret work of discovery and subversion. Slowly they'd begun to shield the youngest and brightest, smuggling them out. Bron had helped; he'd been doing the same for years, fostering the lightless and seeing that the brightest runners never returned. But some of them were called. Some of them came back anyway. So few of them believed what they were told.

"*They won't believe you*," he'd told Torrin, the night he left. "*You can spew truth from here to Khine, and they'll only scoff at you. If you're fortunate.*"

"*The Nine are breaths from finding the trick of it*," Torrin had said, or something like. Torrin was the one who remembered words; Evonder was a bindsman, he spoke through his hands, through the molding of objects he could feel. It galled that, bright as he was, he was not bright enough a bindsman to serve. "*I need a triad*," Torrin had said "*They're out there, somewhere. Galandra willing, I'll find them in time. Meanwhile, I'll speak, and teach. What else can we do, Evonder? Tell me, and I'll do it.*"

There were a nonned things, all impossible. They were both argued out. Both stubborn. Torrin would go his own way; he always had. Evonder could not stop him.

Evonder would have given anything to go with him.

But one of them had to stay. One of them had to watch, and listen, and continue all the small, delicate work, lest the fragile resistance they had built here—such inadequate accomplishment, for a lifetime—fly apart like a frightened wraith.

It was not enough. It would never be enough. But one small, strategic failure, one insidious suggestion, might be sufficient to tip the balance toward Torrin, when the time came. He had to be here to do that. He might still maneuver some of them. Freyn, for instance. She was already half mad from some tragedy years past. General opinion held that a good bedding would set her right. Lerissa claimed she was frigid; Evonder sensed she was anything but. She merely transferred her passions to inanimate things that could not hurt her. He could sympathize with that. He could use that. Perhaps tonight he would approach her.

He had done well with Lerissa, over the years, husbanding what her arrogant father had planted. We'll rule the world, he'd told her. We'll be the new aristocracy. That's how it was meant to be: mages given their due, with the Ennead over all. Lerissa would protect Eiden Myr like a spitting cat; she considered it her realm to inherit. She would not let the triplets harm it, and formidable Worilke shared that goal with her. He'd teased her smoldering ambition to life as his hands teased climax from her flesh. As coldly pleasurable a task as it was nauseating— and he'd never known what happened to the child, that first year he took her, when she was nine-and-six. He'd had no way of knowing Worilke had never cast the first freedom on her. Her father was still alive then. He'd beaten Evonder nearly to death, told him to get rid of the thing the moment it was born, to the spirits with any light it might possess. A boy child, sable-haired like his mother. He'd found Bron, then. Fostered the child to warders whose names had died with Bron. That was the beginning of it.

He'd like to see the boy, before the end. It grieved him that he never would.

There'd been no children for Torrin, no accidents. Perhaps he'd had Lerissa, perhaps not; it had never mattered. Women had figured in neither of their lives. They'd had each other. There had been dalliances, of course, especially when they were young, just reawakening to life, emerging from dark childhoods to find that the world could, just conceivably, be a place of light and pleasure. Before the weight of secrecy and failure had settled on them. But he had always sensed that Torrin was waiting. Searching, and not finding. Evonder hoped he had found her, this time. But he envied even the search, even the wanting. There would be no one for him. Perhaps Torrin himself had been the one. He snorted softly as a thread of jealousy pulled tight inside him. Astonishing. But at least it meant he could still feel.

Lucky illuminator, he thought. *I wasn't mage enough for him.*

He wished Bron had warned him about the stewards' revolt. There was much he could have done—not least, cautioned against ill timing. They were good, brave souls. It was the right thing to do. But they had restrained themselves past all bearing. They could not wait any longer. And they had not waited long enough.

He had failed to save all the children. Bron would not thank him for that, if they met again. That warder had made the right decision, though guilt would probably destroy her. He hoped the babe shone bright. He hoped her world was light and safe.

As he came into the familiar, static corridors, he slumped, lowered his chin, angled his glances obliquely, softened his lips, turned the corners of his mouth down. He ran both hands through his tousled hair, smoothing it neat in an affectation of vanity. He straightened his clothes, but unlaced the top of his shirt in a show of roguish nonchalance, a small juvenile defiance. He was pleased with himself, just returned from some insignificant seduction; he rubbed his cheekbones to simulate the flush of satiety. He gnawed on the remains of a fingernail as he walked. He became the son they expected everything of and gave nothing of themselves to, neglected in the midst of cosseting. He became the second son, the shadow of the elder—Evrael, who had rejected them and flown to self-imposed exile on Khine, as far as he could get from the Holding. He became what they had to content themselves with. The runner-up. The one they bore late, in recompense for the golden one they'd lost. Smarmy, sardonic, and always that moment of blankness before he responded, always that vacancy in the eyes, the brief hesitation while he analyzed what had been said for tricks or slights and settled on which reaction to give. It wasn't a difficult transformation. It was as much his self as any other. He became the prince of mages, the bright, spoiled scion of the Holding, Lerissa's intended consort, the future ruler of Eiden Myr; while deep inside him, a lonely boy yearned to return to the deep labyrinths and the wraiths who were his playmates, and sleep safe and loved in the scintillating air.

Vonche grumbled at his absent son as he made his way by feel down the unlit passageway. Now, when there was finally some use for Evonder, when this delicate errand wanted doing and it would ill behoove Vonche to be discovered wandering, the lout was off bedding some laundress. He would never forgive the loss of Evrael. If Evrael were here, they could have dispensed with those three insufferable abominations and done it all themselves.

No helping it now. He came into the chambers—sweet spirits, what a stench—and turned the wick of his lamp up to illuminate the cluttered space. All piles of pillows, tasseled and fringed, pebbled and satiny. A blind illuminator's desperate attempt to inject texture into her blank world. Pathetic. Yet fascinating: the walls were filled with oddments. The woman had been a magpie. He saw himself in that. He collected bits of old lore in similar fashion, lined his own secret chambers with codices as this place was lined with the Holding's ephemera. She collected objects and he collected knowledge.

Well, there was no question of which packrat had accumulated more power. Portriel had been a clever girl, but distracted by foolishness. She had tried to read the sky, of all things, never understanding that nothing useful could come of the configurations of stars, only the configurations of glyphs on a leaf.

But she had been very beautiful when they were young. A sapphire in starglow. Naeve had detested her—sensing in her rival, no doubt, the stubborn passion for life that she believed she'd cornered all trade on.

How fitting that in the end the rival would herself pave the road to immortality.

He puttered around the complicated space. There had to be something—something intimate, something drenched in her spirit. They could not have cast passage for her. It had been done quickly, Landril said, with bare hands, and there was no casting circle, no scent of ink or pigment on the stale air. All natural fibers went with the bonefolk, but they left anything metal. Her killers would not have known enough to take . . .

There. He smiled very slowly, spying his prize across the chamber. Oh, how sweet, how unexpectedly perfect: both the ring and the triskele, draped there as if expecting him. The ring was strung somehow on the triskele's chain. A puzzle; he would enjoy solving it. She herself would tell him how she had done it.

She would tell him so much, before it was over.

He negotiated the treacherous cushions and lifted the chain from the dusty, cobwebbed wine jug. Considered, for a moment, bringing the jug along too; containers were powerful, and it might have some significance he would fathom only when she explained it to him. But the chambers would remain undisturbed. If the jug need be fetched, he would send that useless boy for it. Let him bring his whores here, if he chose. It was certainly well appointed for a lively tryst. He was so like his mother, in that respect.

Foolish, foolish Portriel, to think that death would free her.

Let them use that self-sealed illuminator as their conduit. He had grown adept at his binding rituals in the last months. He would bind Portriel's spirit as he'd captured his own bindsman's. That was a first attempt, no more. An experiment. He had come so far since then. He no longer even needed a triad—which was for the best, since Naeve had refused and he'd had to part with precious codices to buy Worilke's aid. It had made room for the boy, of course, which was half the reason he'd chosen his binder as his first subject. But the boy was a vast disappointment. Not worth the seed expended to father him. Bright, impeccably trained, but dissolute, and then there was the tainted association with Maeryn's get. At least he'd grown out of that.

Perhaps he might consider inviting the wastrel to redeem himself by helping to bind this haunt. Show his mettle as a bindsman. Yes, that might do very nicely.

Muttering to himself, intermittently laughing, Vonche left the chambers. The pewter triskele and gold ring dangled from his hand, swaying as he walked, flinging lanternlight in dull lozenges against the walls.

ith horses, they had a chance. But being mounted didn't lay a sidewise road to Shrug. It was too far and too dangerous to ride back and start again, and any ship they got from Nape would have to round the Head through the Sea of Storms. She gritted her teeth and rode down through the forests of childhood, toward the sedate confluence of Clon and Ianda, curving like borderwork amid the lazy swells of downs and meadows and furrows. There was a light in the triad's cottage, but she vowed to ignore the turning. The village was tiny, a little strip to either side of the road.

This is your home? Heff asked, giving his big gray mare her head to free his hands.

His sign for "home" was something carried within the chest. "I grew up here," she replied neutrally. She should have gone home when it was over, when she had found a secure place to put her memory of pain. This was no time for a word like "home." She could not stop. She could not rest. Not yet.

We should persuade them to abandon it, he said.

She looked at him sidelong, raising a brow.

This is the route the horde will take to the Holding, he said, and picked up the looped reins.

"There is no horde. They would have been and gone by now."

Heff shrugged, and gestured ahead with his chin, and she squinted through the dusk, frowning. Was her memory of the village replacing something she ought to see? It was getting dark, and they were still three leagues away. The road meandered through foothills, obscuring the view more often than affording one. But as they got closer, she saw torches burning, little lights scattered in farmland; closer still and she could make out the dark line of some kind of fortification in the fields, mounded earth or sacks of rocks. And they had barricaded the road to Heartward.

Spirits—the fools were going to make a stand.

As they came in past the outbuildings and crofts, past the path to Graefel's cottage, she saw people hurrying this way and that, some a bob of lanternlight as night came on, some lightless shadows moving purposefully across the road or beyond the cottages. The village teemed with people, far more than would gather even for a pledging. To hide her black-and white-dyed clothes, she fastened her cloak. She pulled her hood up—and Heff pulled his hat down, to better shade his face—but most of these folk would not have known her anyway.

Probably her own folk would not know her. Just as well.

Small tents lay scattered like fallen moths in the fields, inside what looked like a floodwall. There were dark snoring bundles in alleys, in front of cottages. Clondel had become Sauglin, overrun. The big lamp outside the Petrel's Rest was unlit, only the little lantern over the door to show there was still a tavern there at all, and its shingled three-story bulk rearing up black against the sky. The windows were shuttered against the chill, but bars of light escaped the louvers along the ground floor, and by the lantern she could see the pewter mug hung right side up. The tavern was open for business.

"What are you doing come in from that way?" a woman asked. "No point posting sentries Headward."

"No point posting sentries at all, unless it's to warn you when to run," Liath said. "Or when to die." The angling of Heff's shoulders told her that was not the way to go about it. But this was her village. These people were strangers. What did they think they were doing?

A man's eyes raked her up and down. "Know about that, do you? Why don't you go tell the boss her business, then?"

"That's just what I plan to do." It became true as she said it. "Where is she?"

"I'll show you!" said an eager boy little older than Mellas.

They dismounted and let him take their horses, followed him down the road, past the weavers' and the fullers', past the redolent bakery—baking at dusk, they must be trying to feed all these folk—and to the stable, which was full of people bedded down in straw, their mounts milling in overcrowded paddocks out back.

Disingenuous, she asked the boy, "Who are you going to fight?"

"The Darkmage," the boy said proudly. "And his horde."

"The Darkmage is a living shadow," said someone nearby, as if reciting a teller's tale, "with eyes of fire, riding a man-eating horse at the head of his legions." It was Nelis; Liath recognized the voice, though it was dreamy, almost lovelorn. "He's warded against blades; he's warded against death. Nothing can kill him. He is the man who could not die."

"His consort," said her sister Nin with relish, "has flaming hair and eyes with no color, and is protected by a monstrous halfman." Where Nelis was, Nin was never far, nor a pretty lad. They seemed to be trying to flirt with two strangers, but the lads were more interested in the sticks they were sharpening. "His horde is all great mouths with metal teeth to gnash us, and a pale haunt with eyes of blood whispers in his ear."

"They've killed reckoners," Nelis said, beside herself with delicious wickedness. "They cast flood and fire and quake. They've struck men dumb, quenched mages' lights—they've killed *babies!*"

"Oh, calm yourselves," one of the youths snapped, uneasy. His friend set to shaving his spearpoint with renewed vigor.

Liath closed her eyes. Half truths and fractured stories garbled into myth. It would break his heart to hear this. He was a gentle teacher. He was trying to give them back their past.

She could not tell them all they needed to know in time. She had to ride on. She had to get to the Fist. But they had to leave off this suicidal stand. . . .

The boy tethered the horses outside the stable and led them across to the Petrel's Rest, into the spill of light through the tavern door.

Liath's mother sat to one end of the greatroom table, moving stones on its surface as if engaged in some enormous game. Marough sat across from her, moving back whatever stones she moved. She thumped the table and the stones jumped like startled bugs. So did the wranglers and millers and strangers seated around her. Off to the side, two busty blondes sat drinking ale and making ribald comments loud enough to draw glares— Geara's sisters, come home from their merchant travels. Liath had not seen them in a year and a half. She bit her lip to keep from greeting them.

"You can't spread them so blasted thin," Marough said. "The road runs through the village. They have to come through the village. We have to hold tight right here!"

"There's an infestation of them out there—you couldn't spread them thin if you spread them to Khine," Geara said. "And what makes you think they'll stick to the road? They'll come over the fields and along the river. *This* is how we must deploy them—here and here and here." She stubbed stones back into place, and for a moment Liath's heart swelled: they had illuminated the greatroom table with objects to create a landscape of Clondel's environs. Spoons linked serpentine for the rivers. A thimble for the mill. Old bread for the mountains, tobacco pouches for the hills, scraps of felt for fields and meadows; spice pots lining end-to-end tallysticks were the village and the road. For common folk who had never studied rendering, they'd made a brilliant model. "Split them at Iandel, drive half against the hill forests where they can't regroup, send the rest where mud will mire their horses—"

Marough swept Geara's stones away with the flat of his hand. "This is what they'll do to your infestation, and then we'll have too few to hold them off." He drew breath and Geara said, "It's my decision," but Marough had finally noticed Liath and Heff, and Geara pivoted to see what he was staring at.

They had moved past the standing lamps by the door but stood at an angle to the hearth, their faces unlit. One tall figure cloaked in dove gray, one giant figure shadowed by a Lowland hat.

"Yes?" Geara was brusque, but she squinted at the dyed cloak.

"You've got to leave this place," Liath said in a low voice.

The frown deepened in Geara's flushed face. Wisps of strawberry blond hair had escaped confinement; she swiped them back in irritation. "And who are you when you're at home?" she said. "Six dozen proxies ride through here telling us we've got to make a stand, then leave us wondering how, what we'll face. Then the folk start coming, fleeing upland as they did in my mother's day before a Great Storm. But they aren't fleeing. They've come to fight. Proxies sent them here, they tell us. Ordered them to yield, to spare their fields and villages, to bring the defense where it can do some good. They come, so that our home can be laid waste instead of theirs. They come spoiling for a fight. They bear tales of ravening hordes, a darkmage born of shadow with eyes of flame. That is what is coming, they say, to tear the Holding down. That is what the proxies sent them to fight. But nary a proxy remains. They've left it to us, a town of farmers and hillwomen and herders. And now some new kind of proxy, some gray proxy, stands in the doorway of my tavern to tell us to leave. The horde is a day away. Wouldn't you say it's a little late?"

The proxies had stopped all resistance between here and the Girdle. The proxies had gone back to the Holding. Had they been called in? Had they been told to salvage the land and people by sending the fighters here? Or had they organized themselves?

Geara's speech had drawn Nole and Danor from the cookroom. Liath smelled lentil stew, the tavern's staple when there was a crowd to feed. The last time she'd smelled that was the night she took the triskele. She swallowed, waiting for her father to know her, but only Nole realized. He went very straight.

When she spoke again, Danor knew her too, and opened his mouth, but Nole's hand on his arm silenced him. "It's never too late to live," Liath said. "Fall back, and they won't harm your folk. But they are as many as you, and they're armed with the tools of death, and they *will* kill you if you get in their way."

"And are you their emissary?" Geara rose, displaying her formidable bulk. She knew her daughter's voice, a voice she hadn't heard in a dozen moons, and she made no move toward her, gave no smile or sigh, only asserted her authority and questioned Liath's allegiance.

"Not theirs, no," Liath said quietly, refusing to be baited. They had shifted from headwoman and proxy to mother and daughter; yet the terms of the debate were not changed.

"I would not have chosen this fight," Geara said. "But it's been handed to me, and I'll see it's done right." She did not glance back at Marough, but it was clear she meant that last for him. His eyes flashed and he shifted on his seat.

"Then see it's not done at all," Liath said. "Let them pass. Let them do what they have to do."

"Tear the Holding down?"

"If they have to. Stop the Ennead, if they can."

"Stop the Ennead!" Daughan roared. "Have you looked up lately, woman? Do you know what that green sky portends?"

As he said it, she did, though she had not before. A Great Storm. What would that mean? For a moment she was confused, and everyone at the table began speaking at once.

"Where is the triad?" Liath said. "Let Graefel sort this."

"How do you know of Graefel?" Marough demanded, as Sael Miller, Ferlin's father, said, "There is no triad. Keiler ran off to see the Darkmage—probably joined him, may he reap what he's sown. Graefel objects to resistance as much as you, Proxy, and sits brooding in his cottage. Hanla drills archers in the fields."

So they wanted to play with bows and arrows. They'd never been interested when it was a sport. Now they would have human targets. Was that all it took? All those folk, riding all those miles at the prospect of a battle. Maybe they deserved each other.

"It stops now," Liath said. "You don't know what the Ennead has become." Bitterly, she echoed Torrin's words—just another acolyte, speaking for him in his absence, a proxy Torrin: "Don't die for them until you know them for what they are."

"Who *are* you?" Marough asked, rising, eyes narrowed. Daughan moved up behind him, and Meira, and Sharra, and their brothers and sons, his formidable, tight-knit, unpredictable clan assembling itself around him.

"On whose authority do you speak?" said Meira.

"I've never seen a *gray* proxy before," said Sharra. "I've seen black ones and heard tell of white ones, but never gray."

"Show your face," Daughan demanded, coming around the table.

She saw now that they were armed—had all laid weapons close to hand, against the table's trestles or propped in corners. Spades, hoes, bale-hooks. Any tool could be a weapon. She had thought the longblades abominations, tools designed to kill. But these were worse—tools made for planting and harvesting and storing food, perverted. She unfastened her cloak for better access to her knives, then remembered she had none. It was longblade, fists, or nothing.

Geara interposed herself, and her sisters rose, no longer laughing. "This is my tavern," Geara said. "I give the orders here." Danor had moved a step to the side, putting himself behind Marough, and Nole was circling toward the center, though only Liath noticed it. They were so blind, the pugnacious wranglers, to subtleties of position, angles of attack. They could heft all the hoes and spades in the world and never defeat the freshest recruits to Verlein's horde. They would stride up to the enemy and be skewered with blades and arrows while they hauled off to punch it in the face, then wail that it wasn't fair.

Liath stepped into the light and shoved her hood back. "This is what your Ennead does," she said, staring hard at Marough and Daughan so as not to see her family's faces. From their shocked eyes, she knew Heff had doffed his hat as well. Why not? In its negligence, this Ennead was part cause of his burning too. "This is what you're so keen to protect."

"Monsters!" cried Meira, waving three fingers to ward herself.

"Yes," Liath said. "The Ennead are monsters. Bred by their forebears for evil acts." She looked at Daughan. "We have other mages, good mages, to turn the Great Storms," she said, with no idea if it could be done. "Don't die for this Ennead."

The room exploded into debate. Geara's sisters came to flank her; Danor was at Liath's side. "I'm all right, Father," she lied, smiling for him, forcing herself to hug him though he had not touched her, always able to sense what she couldn't say aloud. He smelled so good. He smelled like Father. She blinked the burning from her eyes. "I'm hard to kill nowadays." She brushed Nole's hand, winking to calm his helpless outrage. "Breida is safe?"

"We sent her to Drey yesterday on Small Basil," Nole said. Small Basil was one of their draft horses, gentle and reliable, and he knew the road to Drey in his sleep.

She nodded, then gave in and met Geara's unremitting stare.

"You left me," Geara said.

She'd left before dawn, without a word to mother or sister, craven. A flood of guilt angered her. "This isn't the time for this, Mother. But you were driving me out for years."

"And glad I'd have been to see the back of you, if you'd graced me with it." The words were too fierce to ring true, but still they cut. "You couldn't have told your father where you were going. You couldn't have sent word. Selfish, hateful girl—we had no idea what had become of you!"

He didn't ask, she thought miserably, *he didn't question me*— But it was true. She should have said. Her disrespect was reprehensible. Of course he hadn't asked. Just gave her leave to take the sorrel filly, and bade her come home safe to him. Enwrapped in her own troubles, she had never considered theirs.

"I was a child," she whispered—but Hanla had come in, followed by folk with short bows, among them Erl and Sarse, and Ferlin, who looked stricken when she saw her. The bakers' sons, swearing, tried to get trays of warm bread in out of the chill.

"I had them shooting in the dark, in case they come by night," Hanla said to Geara or Marough, though her eyes fixed on Liath. "I came to say they're as ready as they'll be, and to get them fed."

"If the horde's a whole day away," Liath said quietly, "you should have them unstring those bows."

Hanla cocked her head. "That's a very interesting thing for you to know," she said. "I heard some interesting things about you, from the proxies who were called back."

"I heard some things about you as well, Hanla Reckoner."

Heads turned toward Hanla. She did not deny the name. Perhaps she had only just assumed it again.

Danor had hustled a few of the boys along with Nole into the cook-room, and they emerged carrying steaming stewpots between them on poles, the smallest one at the rear balancing a stack of oak bowls. It was the millers' younger son, Liath realized, though he'd grown some. They marched out the front; Hanla leaned down to say something to the millers' boy, who nodded.

"How do you know so much?" Islia Miller said.

This was dangerous ground, but Liath gave a caustic laugh. "I've been to the Holding, Islia, and experienced it firsthand."

"No," she persisted. "How do you know the size of the Darkmage's horde? How do you know what weapons they carry?"

"What's that sticking out of your cloak?" said Marough.

Heff glanced warning at her.

"And who's your halfman friend?" said Sharra.

It hadn't taken them long to put it together. Flaming hair, colorless eyes, monstrous halfman. The Darkmage's consort had infiltrated their midst. It was their worst fear: one of their own, made monstrous, gone a year on unknown errands, come back just in time to prevent their last stand. They were already frightened, already confused, already worked up; a fighting fever simmered just below the surface. Heff had shifted almost imperceptibly to cover her back, then shifted again as Danor and Nole joined him. Aunts Eife and Seira stepped away from Geara to make it a rough circle.

This was the instinctive magecraft of the Petrel's Rest.

"She lured Keiler away!" Ferlin cried.

"She failed as a mage and only the dark one would have her."

"Look at her face! Look what he did to force her loyalty."

"Her own mother called her his emissary."

"His proxy!"

"It seems I am," Liath said softly. "And what I bring you is his plea for peace. Yield the road. Save yourselves. *Don't try to fight those people when they come.*"

"She's turning a fair cheek."

"She would disarm us for them."

"He marked her, with his dark craft."

"Look at that thing that protects her!"

"*I'm one of you!*" Liath shouted, goaded past all bearing—but she was not one of them anymore, nor had she ever been, mage among publicans, prentice among mages, and even Hanla was backing away, looking out the door, as if seeking escape—a crowd was trying to push in, there was no room and no egress—

She didn't see who broke first, though later she knew it had been Marough, taking the opportunity to wrest leadership from Geara. "Dark-mage whore!" came the vicious hiss, and the crowd of villagers and strangers rushed them.

Her aunts loved a brawl, and grappled, whooping, with the first attackers, their fierce glee startling the strangers into backing off. Bearlike Danor spun all comers and booted them away, while his son's quick fists darted at this nose, at that chin; no one had time to raise a weapon, and if they did a kick in the belly knocked the fight out of them. But Daughan had held back, making sure his folk were armed. The second wave came in earnest. A flail whistled at Geara's head and cracked against a stool she raised just in time. Heff wrested a prybar from Sharra and brought it up, a hand on either end, to block the sweep of a hoe aimed at Liath, all a flicker at the edge of sight as she sidestepped the downward arc of a shovel and brought her knee up into Sarse's groin. Someone near the door whirled the lid of a stewpot into the melee and flattened Erl by mistake; next it would be spears, or arrows badly aimed. Marough's clan was trying to kill them, and the ones they had knocked down were starting to get up.

People they'd traded and celebrated and grieved with all their lives, people she'd never seen before who could have nothing against them—fueled by wild rumor and fear, so primed for battle that they could not wait until the enemy arrived, but must create the enemy among them.

Brawls are all well and good, Liath's own voice said in her mind, as Nole brandished the leg of a smashed chair in the face of the scythe that Daughan raised two-handed, stepping toward her brother over his own sons, drawing back to strike. *But we don't draw blades in this tavern.* Nole could have him if he went inside the swing and struck or stabbed with the jagged wood—two steps in, *now*, and turn—but he was backing reflexively. Liath's hands, trained over long winter days, reached behind her of themselves. The longblade came free in a silver whisper, sang through the air and took Daughan's scythe at the outward apex of its sweep. The scythe jarred from his grip and sprang apart against the floor. *Finish him*, Kaẓhe hissed. Liath shifted the blade to her off hand, stepped in, and smashed her fisted casting hand into his scowl.

Meira and her brothers and Sharra's were still besetting Danor and Geara and her sisters. Liath made short work of their farmers' tools with her tempered, balanced weapon. The archers were gone. The others fell back in awe of the blade, and Heff and Danor and the aunts disarmed them as Geara, quick to smell injury on her children, set about binding a gash on Nole's thigh.

A flicker of yellow hair at the door caught her eye, then fox-colored beard as the crowd parted. Eirin the millers' boy had fetched Graefel. Hanla had been watching for him, not fleeing. Now she stood beside him. Keiler's absence diminished them.

"Come out of your sulk, Wordsmith?" Marough sneered, wiping blood from his mouth—then shut it hard when Graefel glanced at him. She had forgotten how piercing those ice-crystal eyes were.

She had forgotten how bright he was.

They stared at her sagging blade as if she'd found some astonishing formation of dung in a midden and dragged it inside her own house. She sheathed it and suppressed the mocking bow she wanted to give them. She needed their authority intact.

"Out," she said to wranglers and millers and Midlanders and Beltmen. Some of them obeyed. Ferlin spat at her as she passed, and Liath bestowed on her the fighters' feral grin. She'd lost Keiler all by herself. It was none of Liath's doing. The wranglers stayed, most of them, unwilling to leave her colluding with mages. She stepped in close and lowered her voice.

"Graefel, you have to make them understand that this is futile. They will die if they fight this horde."

"I have said as much for a nineday," he replied quietly. "Clearly to no effect."

"You know they're fighting for the wrong side. You must know that, Graefel. Explain it to them."

He cocked his head like the fox he resembled. "I know nothing of the sort. They're quite heroic, the more so for the hopelessness of it. You'd have done better to leave them to their planning. Ride on, Liath. Ride off to whatever unholy alliance you've forged with Torrin n'Maeryn."

"You knew him." She had never been able to hear it, the Holding refinement that flattened his good, thick Neck accent. She'd only thought he sounded erudite, wise.

"I never knew him. I met him briefly when he was a boy. A brooding boy with no respect for tradition. I met him, and I feared him, and I fear him still. But the Ennead will see to him."

She raked a hand wearily through her hair. What a proxy he sounded. Leave it to the Ennead. "You can't have been a vocate and a proxy in that Holding and not know what was happening there."

"A very high level of magecraft," he said. "I suspect that is what this horde wants to destroy. Anything too powerful is dangerous. Next they'll be trying to rid Eiden Myr of all its mages. Torrin n'Maeryn is not at the head of them, am I right? He has his own goals. But he has taught them to fear magecraft. The Ennead will deal with that."

"There are Storms coming," Hanla said. "The Ennead can't be distracted at a time like this. *We* must see to this."

"As their proxies, yes." He smiled a little. "Yet I forsook the black, and sent my ring back to them. I am no longer any proxy of theirs. I discharged my duty."

Liath put her last stone on the table. "They have mages," she said. "Nine for every one on the Ennead."

"Lapsed proxies and the untriaded."

"Strong reckoners and strong triads."

"And you are not among them."

Sniping at her. Did her failure still gall him so? "I know what blocked me now," she offered. "Who." She waited, then said, nearly in a whisper, "Don't you want to know?"

He regarded her with frosty indifference. "You failed. Excuses are irrelevant."

She almost said, *I was a vocate, Graefel. We earned the ring! I would have been a proxy too!* Still desperate to please him. Disaster on the doorstep, and nothing changed. "I humiliated you," she said. "The Ennead sent their runner on your word, and I failed and failed, all right in front of him. You failed them. *You* failed to see that I could have been redeemed. You failed to send me anyway. I went there, and they welcomed my light, and set me a great task, and I did it and came back to them, and this is what they thanked me with." She held her palm out to him, displaying the white-limned puckers that overlaid the kadri of natural lines. He looked away, expressionless, and she said, "You failed, Graefel. You failed to recognize their evil. You failed to remain a reckoner. You failed in calling me. You never trained a prentice. You lost both your sons. You've done nothing, Graefel. Nothing of value to anyone. Nothing but hide. *Stop hiding and help me.*"

Softly, he said, "There is so much you don't know. So much no illuminator can know." Like Torrin, he spoke without preamble, his crystalline eyes fixed on some far point. "All knowledge is encrypted in the ciphers we use. I've spent my life studying it. Watching the work of other wordsmiths, remembering their scribing, their phrasing, comparing it with others' in my mind's eye, distilling the commonalities. The vocates and proxies were useful to me, as journeyers have continued to be, but I needed solitude and quiet to do my work. In the end it was best I had no prentice. Our craft—my craft, the wordsmith's craft—is an ingenious code. Do you know what a code is? A system for embedding information inside something that appears to be other than what it is. Magecraft was peripheral.

The point was to preserve the code. Every scribing carries a piece of history in it. We have forgotten how to read between the lines, comprehend the allusions, the treble meanings, the clever twists of phrase, the patterns hidden within patterns. What is there, in a foliage of technique and rigid structure, has been buried in regional variations and the general decay of the craft. But I will have it soon. Then I will bring it to the Ennead, and it will be worth a nonned silver rings, a nonned vocates. I wanted you to remind them of me. I wanted you to be a message to them that soon I would have it, and I would come, and give all history back into their keeping."

Liath gaped. All this time, holed up in his roadside village, it was the Ennead he had been trying to please. Just as she had tried to please him. "Why not do that work in the Holding, where all the bound volumes are?"

His head jerked. He focused on her. His brows knit. "What?"

"The . . . codices. Bound sheaves of vellum with permanent scribings. Preserved since the time of the first mages. The things Galandra and her folk brought with them when—"

"Sacrilege!" he rasped—but she'd seen greed stir in the icy depths. Desire warring with the ethics of his tradition. It was sacrilege—yet it could be the key to his life's work.

Too late. She could not mend this for him. She could not make him see past the hidebound confines he worked in. If she could bring him to Torrin . . . if they could work together, these intellects so alike . . . but it was too late, too late. *Oh, why did we never speak truth to each other?*

"*If we had,*" Nerenyi's voice whispered forlornly from the flickering shadows, "*imagine what we might have learned.*"

"Is that what he teaches, this Torrin Darkmage?" Hanla said.

"Sacrilege?" Liath answered vaguely. "No. He's not a darkmage. He's trying to bring light back into the world." She looked at Heff. The night was wearing thin. A day closer to Ve Galandra. They had to go. Marough and Daughan were watching, waiting to see what the mages would do. She couldn't leave them in Verlein's path, not even if they wished her dead. But she had to reach Torrin. She didn't know what to do. Even Graefel couldn't make them yield.

Get your family out, Heff said. Take them and let's go.

She looked at the family she'd come home to a blade-bearing, incomprehensible, mutilated stranger. They were waiting too.

"Did we teach you so badly?" Hanla asked, stepping close. Barring her from Graefel. "Were you so easily turned?"

It took her a moment to come back to them, to their troubles. The betrayal of a prentice was insignificant here. It was difficult to care, anymore, what they thought of her. "No, Hanla," she said. "It was not easy. And the Ennead carved its kadri from one end of me to the other, lest I ever forget how hard it was."

In one vicious motion, Hanla had ripped the triskele from her neck. The chain burned a new line in her flesh. She barely felt it. The pewter pendant dropped to the floorboards with a soft clunk, disappearing in the rushes. Hanla ground it under her boot. Then her hand drew back. She was going to strike her. Liath stood calmly for the blow.

Geara's broad arm shot out and stopped the hand midway to Liath's face. Her body came in behind it, bearing Hanla back a step. "That's a daughter of the Petrel's Rest," Geara said. "Under this roof, you will show respect for her, or you will answer to me." With a shove, she sent Hanla out of reach, then bent to retrieve the triskele and the broken chain. Liath would have left them there. "Take it," Geara said. Liath closed her eyes, shook her head. Her eyes sprang open at the feel of the chain against her flesh. Geara was knotting it at the back of her neck with her thick publican's fingers. "I hate the forsaken things," she said, "but it's part of you. You wear it."

A second bestowing of the triskele. From her real mother, this time. Liath stood speechless.

Hanla turned on her heel and strode out of the tavern. Graefel lingered, stroking his beard; then he shook his head and followed his pledgemate, with a measured, indifferent stride. Liath was no longer of any consequence to him.

The mages had rejected their prentice.

It was the outcome Marough had awaited. He led the rush to the door. Geara's authority was shattered. They would do as they pleased now. There was no longer sense to them, or strategy. They would fight as they wished, and die.

Marough's voice shouted something outside. Rocks pelted the front of the tavern. They sounded like hail. Their own neighbors were the storm now.

Liath drew her blade without thinking. "Bar the door!"

Eife and Seira moved quickly, but the last of Marough's lot had not yet gone through. Meira's brother, Sharra's—then Melf n'Daughan, the youngest, who'd cowered in a corner during the brawl. He turned at the doorway with a smirk, then reached out and toppled one of the standing lamps.

The drink-soaked rushes, unchanged for days, caught with a whooshing crackle.

With an oath, Danor fetched the cookroom's washwater, but as he flung it on the blaze—to no effect, oil and alcohol were too potent—a big stone smashed through the shutters on one side, and a lit torch sailed in after it.

"The wardings will hold," Liath said, smothering the new blaze with Evonder's cloak, stamping on it, unable to comprehend that their own folk would *do* this to them.

"The wardings weren't renewed!" Eife said, trying to block the window with the stewpot lid.

Two more torches flew through the door before Seira and Heff got it closed. "Keiler was gone," Seira panted. "The proxies wouldn't stop to help."

They beat and stamped at the flames. They couldn't get them all. The dry rushes ignited too quickly. The flames spread out of control. Rocks still pounded the front of the tavern, then abruptly stopped, leaving only the hungry crackle of fire and the sounds of riot outside.

Heff's half face was entirely drained of blood as smoke collected in the low-raftered shadows. But he barred the door, with the wooden cross-bar and his own weight. He looked at Liath.

"It's the crowd out there or the flames in here," Danor said, eyes fixed on Geara. "I'm sorry, love."

They threw the door open and stumbled out coughing. Liath sought the mages and found them: Graefel walking, a lone figure, up the road back to his cottage; Hanla staring at the burning tavern.

Herders and hillwomen had forced the crowd back with crooks and quirts and their dogs. The rioting crowd was all strangers. It was their own folk holding them off. Coopers and fullers and tailors, potters and millers and drummers, cobblers and bakers and saddlers stood in the road with arms linked, a human barrier. Burly smiths and stablers and farmers harried the sides of the crowd, swearing and shoving, relieving them of their torches. Some black-haired Midlander let fly another rock and Den Weaver cuffed him. Marough's lot were halfway down the road to the barricade. Their own folk had not turned on them—it was these battle-mongers, come to eat their bread and stew and fight anything they saw, incited by the pure cussedness of Marough and Daughan and Meira and Sharra. Eiden strike the proxies who sent them!

The publicans stood in the dark road as their home burned.

The sight of it seemed to drain the bloodlust out of the crowd. Some ran, some stood and stared, most were booted off by farmers determined to clear the Neck of them. Orla Weaver said, "Form a line to the well. Move, Naragh. Move, Sael. *Now!* Porl, Nelis, Lisel, fetch all the buckets you can!"

It will not be enough, Heff said. His hazel eye was wild and white, the pupil contracted to nothing; sweat beaded half his face. He said, It will burn too fast.

"We have to try," she answered, but she was standing with her blade point down in the dirt, unable to move.

A piercing cry split the night. They looked around, then up as it came again, a shrill, desperate child's cry: "*Mama!*"

"Sweet spirits." Nole went ashen. "Breida."

— She was at the high round window of the attic. She'd gotten the shutters open and one arm out. Her face was a pale blur. Her hair blew forward like flame. "Mama!" she screamed again.

Geara started for the front door. It took three hillwomen to stop her. "I sent you to Drey!" she cried in helpless rage.

Buckets of water were coming along the line, from cottages, the river, the well. They beat the ground-floor flames back, but smoke came in gouts through the upstairs shutters. It had run up the walls. Were the stairs still clear?

Nole had run to the alley below the window, blood soaking his leg afresh, and was shouting to Breida to find an axe, there were old tools up there, hack her way through the wall, they'd catch her, she'd have to jump. Eife and Seira dragged mattresses out of the cobblers' cottage. Danor had found a ladder, and he shoved past them all to maneuver it against the wall; at the impact Breida fell back from the window. The ladder was too short. The sound of axe blows drifted down through the thunder of the flames, but stopped with a shriek—whatever Breida had been standing on had given way.

Liath realized that she'd been trying for long moments to get to the front door, that Heff was the reason she was making no progress. "Let me go," she said, "that's my *sister*. . . ." He grunted under the battering of her elbows but held tight.

Hanla was trying to move too, but up the road rather than across it. To fetch Graefel? To what end? They were only two. Geara took hold of her and forced her around. They were both stout women, muscled, one fair, one dark; though Geara was the taller, Hanla could have shrugged her off, but she went limp in her grasp. "You gave me that child," Geara snarled. "Your magecraft gave me a daughter for the one you took. You save her with it, now!"

Liath stared at her mother. What was she talking about? Breida a child of magecraft? There was no time to make sense of it.

"We have no binder," Hanla said weakly. She turned blinking to Liath and Heff. "Your bindsman," she said. "He must serve. Graefel! Get the binding—"

"Do you see a light there?" Liath snapped. "He's not a binder, you fool. *He's not a mage.*"

"Breida, come back to the window!" Nole shouted, as he and Danor staggered trying to jam the ladder on crates they'd stacked against the neighboring building. It was the coopers'. In moments it would be burning too. "I'm coming, Breida!" The ladder reached. He went to scale it and his leg gave out. Danor lifted him off and started up himself. A Midlander girl broke free of the farmers and ran to offer him a woods axe. He snatched it and went up. The ladder gave under his weight, but he didn't pause.

She's not at the window, she's fallen, they won't be able to get to her. Liath twisted in Heff's grip, then found herself flat on her back two threfts away, and scrambled up to see him lifting the rain barrel by the front door and upending it over himself. She was half the distance to him when he shoved two bucket-wielders aside and plunged into the burning tavern.

"*Heff! NO!*"

The foot of the ladder jammed behind the crates and pried them from the coopers' wall. Nole, bracing them, fell back. The ladder slipped down hard and cracked in half. The jagged ends just missed him. Danor tumbled heavily into the mattresses, which burst.

"Keep going," Orla said, moving up and down the brigade. "Faster." There was only thundering silence for long, heaving breaths. Hanla and Liath together just barely prevented Geara from following Heff. The doorway swirled orange and black and red, impassable. "He'll get her," Liath said, but she knew he wouldn't, this was his atonement, he had gone in there to die because he hadn't saved his brother, *Breida jump, Breida get up, Breida wake up, climb up and jump, Breida Breida Breida—*

The coopers' was beginning to burn, and the cobblers' on the other side. The ladder collapsed in flames. The water lines broke, people stumbling away as the fire spread, some running to their homes. It would have that whole side of the village.

"Rain!" Liath screamed at the swollen sky. "Rain, by all the benighted, forsaken spirits, *rain!*"

Morlyrien answered her. One small droplet plashed on her face. Too little. Too late. She sobbed, and her mother broke free, and Hanla ran to catch her, and the attic collapsed into itself as a liquid explosion of sparks blew out the upstairs shutters—and out of the alley, past the midden and the old copper vats and the path that led up into the hills to become the bindsman's road, a smoking hulk came staggering with a big wet-blanketed bundle over its shoulder, a smaller under its arm.

Heff went to his knees in the road just in front of Geara, released Breida soaked and sobbing into her arms, and bent to lay the other bundle on the ground. He unwrapped it as Liath got there. Growl the tavern cat was a wet ginger lump.

"You were meant to be in Drey!" Geara yelled into Breida's face as her hands ran over her body, checking for injury, burns, cuts. She'd have some good bruises and her hair was singed short, but she was all right.

Breida responded to the ministering hands instead of the angry voice. What Liath had always been unable to do. "I wanted to see the battle," she said. "I wanted to see Eirin n'Sael. I turned Sweet Basil around. He's in the paddock. He's all right."

"Ach, you stupid, *stupid* girl." Geara embraced her hard.

A pail of water up there, Heff said, dazed by the miracle of it. He stroked the cat's flat fur. And him, he said, gestures failing. Blankets to wrap. Water. Back stairs. Cellar.

His hands fell limp. He looked done in. Then Growl twisted to lift his shoulders, his rump. Heff sat up.

"The roof always leaked," Liath said. "It wasn't worth a casting but we could never quite get it mended." She was looking at the burning tavern, the burning cottages. People were driving oxen and horses and donkeys across the road into the fields. Another spatter of rain fell. In the mountains, thunder rumbled. Perhaps it would save the rest of the village.

Heff set the cat on its feet. It shook itself, staggered, then bunched its haunches and took off in a drunken zigzag.

"He'll be safe in the fields," she said. Heff nodded and got up. "Are you hurt?"

He rubbed his shin, then said, with a wry twist, *You should do something about those cellar steps. I nearly broke my neck.*

The smile died on her lips as the Petrel's Rest sank into itself with a great groan of surrendering timbers, sending a cascade of sparks into the misting rain. The smoke was thick. They had to move. They were too close. Heff went to find horses as Eife and Seira helped Geara and Breida through a crowd of stunned strangers, down past the tinkers' field to the grassy triangle where the road forked Heartward and Shrugward. Figures moved along the barricade, a dozen threfts along the Heartward tine. Sunrise was a dilute flush along the hilltops; the solstice stones cast faint shadows on the green. Geara would not let go of Breida. "We've got to get her inside," Liath said, kneeling. She touched her sister's shoulder. "It wasn't Galf n'Marough you stayed for, eh?" she said, smiling. "At least the millers' boy smells good."

Breida stared as if Liath had crawled from nightmare.

She'd forgotten her horrible face.

She reared back on her haunches, started to rise. Her family would pull themselves together. Danor was coming, a bulky bearded figure supporting his limping son. Where was the cart? Had it burned? Where were their draft horses? She'd fetch them and then go, see her family onto the Drey road and go—

Geara took her upper arm in a viselike grip. "She's only startled," she said. "She's had a fright. It's all right, Liath."

"I missed you," Breida said in a small voice. "You didn't say goodbye to me."

"It would have been too sad," Liath said. Her throat was closing up. It was raining now, not hard but steady. She had to get out of here. But her mother would not let go. The hand shifted from her arm to her face; she flinched, but Geara had her firmly by the jaw.

"They did this to you?" she said. "The Nine?"

Liath nodded. "Yes, Mother," she said.

Then, suddenly, the tears came.

It was her fifth summer. A year, still, before the light changed everything. Erl and Sarse yanked her braids, shoved her. A dispute over a treehouse. She would not give ground. They poked her. She poked back. They knocked her down, flung themselves on her. She was quick with elbows and knees and nails. But they were two, and she was one, and they were bigger, a little older. She only made them mad enough to hit her hard before they ran away. She would not cry. She got up, dusted in vain at her soiled, torn kirtle, then marched back to the tavern, defiant.

Her mother saw at once what had happened, and did not scold her. Just wiped her face, rebraided her hair, and straightened her clothes. It was the firm kindness that made her cry. Mother was strong. Mother loved her, even though she had lost.

"Mama," she said, crumbling. "Mama, they hurt me."

"I know, love," Mother said, and let her cry awhile. Then she sat her up straight and thumbed the tears from her cheeks. "But you gave them a good thump for it, didn't you, my girl?"

Liath nodded, awed. She had gotten in some good thumps. Could that be enough? Somehow, though she had lost, she was still a good, brave daughter of the Petrel's Rest. She followed her mother back to work, carrying the wine jugs that were the heaviest thing she could manage, while Mother lifted kegs in from the coolhouse. She had lost . . . but she'd given a good fight . . .

She could not stop the tears, they came and came, humiliating, and the choked, unstoppable words: "They hurt me, Mama."

Geara pulled her hard into the circle of her arms. There was room for two against that ample bosom. There always had been. Breida was shocked quiet to see Liath cry, and after a moment, in amazement, she put her arms around her too. For a moment the three women held tight, locked in an embrace they had never shared before. The aunts held watch. When the racking sobs eased, Liath sat up, and Geara thumbed the tears from her cheeks and said, "But we'll give them a good thumping for it, now, won't we, my girl?"

Liath coughed out a laugh, through the mask of tears and scars. "Yes, Mama," she said. "That's what we'll do."

"They're coming!" A young girl's piercing voice carried the alert through the rain and the last of the night's shadows.

Geara dragged her daughters up. "Nole!" she barked. "Take her, take a horse, it doesn't matter whose. Take her home to Megenna."

He looked toward the barricade. He did not want to leave them. His father took his shoulder. "We'll all go," he said. Eife and Seira nodded.

"Not me," Geara said. "This is my home. I stay."

"Mother!" Breida set herself, stubborn.

Liath smoothed the red-gold hair off her bruised and sooty brow and smiled into her pleading eyes. "Go with your brother," she said, "and dream of peace instead of battles." She pressed her firmly into Nole's hands. Nole had always had a way with her. If he went, she'd go. He should have seen her clear to Drey. His thigh would need mages' healing or he'd always have a limp.

Danor and the aunts took her brother and sister back into the smoky village, past the smoldering ruin of the Petrel's Rest.

"Now," Geara said. "How well do you know these rebels?"

"Well enough, I hope. What was Marough's plan?"

"He had no bloody plan. Stand at the barricade, like a fool."

They looked out past the earthworks at the swimming fields. "They're coming by the road," Liath said. No one had challenged them all the way from the Girdle. They had no reason to march through muddy fields.

"I was wrong." Geara huffed. "Eiden strike that Marough. I'm not a bloody battlemaster!"

In fact, her strategy had been sound. If they'd split them at Iandel, the earthworks would have been critical to the defense. If they'd had the day to prepare, if they'd rallied to Geara instead of arguing among themselves, they might have held them off. For a while. Till all the defenders were dead.

People were running wildly, directionless. Something had to be done with them. "Who put you over Marough?"

"A proxy. Jerize was her name. Sound woman. Said Hanla was to go to the Holding, and I was to lead the defense. Hanla stayed to help me. The Khinish . . . She seemed to know what she was about. We made the earthworks . . ." She swore at the chaos their plan had become. "Eiden's blood, I hate proxies."

Responsible Jerize had somehow caused Hanla and Geara to work together, two women who had fallen out over Liath years ago and never reconciled. "Invoke that name," Liath said. "See if Hanla will stand by you once I'm gone. Keep them out of harm's way."

"Where are you going?"

She clasped her mother's arm tight, forearm to forearm, the sign of respect. "To stop this, if I can. To go on, even if I can't. Oh, Mother . . ." Words failed her. "Spirits shield you."

"And you." Geara gripped her so hard it hurt. "I only ever feared to lose you, Liath."

"You'll never lose me." She glanced back to see Heff mounted, leading her horse. She gestured for him to stay, gestured again when he shook his head. I'll just have a look, her gesture said. I'll be right back. She set off through the rain to the barricade.

Built of jumbled furniture and junk wood, it stretched across the road and a dozen threfts to either side. The horde would flow around it. Marough *was* a fool. He marshaled the defenders, armed with pitchforks, stickles, dung drags, sheep shears, into a rough, inadequate formation, while Meira set the archers precariously on benches to shoot over the barricade. Their sons, nephews, and pledgebrothers were interspersed with two score Midlanders, a few dressed in the layered style of the Belt; no other villagers had joined them. Tarny and Galf looked like they had spent the night out here shaking from cold. When Tarny saw her, he looked away.

The heavy sky was lightening to pearl. Around the curve from Iandel came two dozen mounted figures. Shields, the bristle of longblade hilts and bows. No one on foot. They were moving at a jog, eating ground without hurrying. When they were sure of the barricade in the half-light, one broke off and rode back at a lope.

An advance guard. It wasn't the horde yet.

"That's it?" said Sarse.

"That's enough," said Liath quietly.

Marough whirled on her. "Haven't you had enough?"

She had. She was dazed with their cruel stupidity, drunk with it. In one fluid sweep she'd drawn her blade, hooked the tines of a Beltman's pitchfork, and levered it from his hands. He scrabbled after it, swearing. "That's only a party sent ahead to check. The rest of them will be along after. They all have these blades, Marough, and they've been learning to use them for moons. What chance will you have against two dozen of them, when you saw what this one could do?"

"*I will not yield,*" he said. "This is your bloody home we're risking our lives to—" He stopped and threw his hands up. It wasn't much of an appeal. His nephew had burned her home.

Liath sheathed the blade. She'd held naked iron in range of his sons' backs, after what his folk had done, and he never blinked. Now she knew what Torrin meant, when he'd told her he would grieve when her naive belief was shattered. The blind faith in good intent these people had, even when they played at battle. It was a precious thing to lose, that even cruel, careless men could trust so. "Let me talk to them."

Meira squinted at her. "Bring them in range of our bows?"

"No, Meira. Persuade them not to slaughter you."

Meira waved her off in disgust, and Marough shook his head.

"You can still live," she offered. "I know them. Isn't it worth a try?"

Muffled through the cloth he held to his broken nose, Daughan cursed her. It answered for all of them.

Liath shrugged. "Then die," she said, and walked back toward Clondel, out of bowshot, to watch, and see who led the guard.

The barricade wasn't wet through. Three flaming arrows set it smoldering, driving the archers off their benches before the attackers were in range of their short bows. Thinking their weapons useless now, the archers broke and fled, some flinging the bows away. The armed defenders staggered back, unable to see through the smoke pouring from the wet wood. In moments the guard had surrounded them. They tried to make use of their greater number to drag the horsemen down, but the horses danced away too easily, and now that they would have been useful their archers were gone. The spears they threw went wild. More of them ran. She could hear Marough shouting, but she couldn't make out faces. She winced as longblades glinted dully in the dawn. Her stomach clenched. *I tried,* she thought. But it wasn't enough. They didn't know. They were idiots, but they were afraid, they were defending themselves. They didn't all deserve to die. She took a step toward them. One guard miscalculated and came off his horse; two took hits. The unhorsed man came up swinging his blade. He didn't make it, but neither did the four who'd jumped him.

It wasn't long after that. They spared anyone who dropped a weapon and raised empty hands. Perhaps a dozen they left dead by the smoldering barricade. The rest they set to dismantling it. Five guards remained to supervise, while the main body continued up toward Clondel.

Lannan rode at the head of them.

Liath walked to meet him. "They yield," she said.

From somewhere off the road to the hill side came a creak. Before the twang followed, one of Lannan's women had nocked an arrow and let fly, and the roadside archer toppled dead, his arrow skidding through the dirt.

Liath raised her brows. "They yield like you do, apparently."

Lannan took her meaning and raised a hand to belay further response from his fighters. He didn't seem quite sure what to make of her. She'd been an enemy, yet she'd escaped Verlein the same night as Torrin and Kazhe and Jhoss. "You speak for them?"

Liath wasn't sure she wouldn't be sprouting an arrow herself in a moment, if there were any more like that one around. "If he lives," she said, "bring me the man with the broken nose, and we'll let them tell you themselves."

Lannan hesitated.

"Oh, go on, Lannan," said the woman with the quick ear and quicker aim. A Souther. "I saw her spare you. I saw her outlast Kazhe in a drunken brawl. She's all right."

With an oath he called the order, and Daughan was sent stumbling toward them. When he tried to run into the fields, one of the riders went back and collected him.

"Marough's dead," he hissed to her.

She cocked her head. "We're not on the same side, Daughan." She walked back to Clondel, trailed by the riders herding the wrangler. Where the saddlers' faced the chandlers', she stopped. Geara and Hanla waited in the road. The fires had died. The wounded village was ugly in the gray-green morning. The rain tailed off.

Hanla recognized the well-armed, disciplined forward guard for what it was and said, "We yield. Your people can pass."

Lannan looked at Liath, genuinely puzzled. "What is going on here? Did you come to rally farmers for a last stand and fail?"

"I live here," Liath said. "Or I did, once. I was hoping Verlein could refrain from killing my neighbors."

"She won't kill anyone if they don't get in her way."

"They'll trample our fields!" someone cried.

"Better your fields than your heads," Liath said.

"They'll burn our homes!" cried someone else.

Their allies had made a good start on that all by themselves. "You won't burn their homes, will you, Lannan?"

He shrugged, wary and impatient. "I won't burn anything if you let us pass. All I want is use of the road."

"That's settled, then," Liath said. "The battle's over. Everybody go home!"

A young man she didn't know stepped from the shadow of an alley, holding a bog harrow. "Where's Marough?" he demanded. "We said we'd go where he told us."

You can go to the spirits. "Marough led the defense at the barricade. These people just stepped over it like a stile. But we've got his brother here. Will he do?"

The young man shifted, uncertain.

"Tell them you yield, Daughan."

He spat blood. "I'll never—"

She flicked her fist backhanded into his nose. He doubled over with a muted howl. "Tell them you yield, Daughan."

"I yield," he moaned, barely intelligible.

"Hanla, could you fetch me some ink and sedgeweave?" Hanla squinted at her for a long moment, then started for her cottage. Geara, with a look hard to fathom, went back to the work of reorganizing. They would rebuild, or not; but it was time for the farmers and herders and hillwomen to go home, for the Midlanders to ride back to the Midlands. The battle *was* over.

She turned to Lannan. "I think the wind's knocked out of them, but you'd do well to wait here for Verlein, keep an eye on things. Proxies have been sending folk up here in a frenzy to fight you. They might get their courage back."

He rubbed his face. "We have a lot of ground to cover."

"There's nothing to stop you from here on," she said. "No villages, no homesteads tucked away in the trees."

"What about all those proxies? What's waiting for us on that trail?"

"It was clear yesterday. Today, I don't know." She shoved Daughan out of earshot and stepped in so that only the fighters could hear her. "But I have a better way for you. A back way they'll never suspect—not over the mountain, but through it, right inside to the Holding. You'll take them by surprise. But you'll have to go on foot for the last bit, and bring torches. And watch for stewards, the folk in plain clothes. Some of them will welcome you, some of them will try to kill you, and you can't tell them apart."

Hanla had returned with one of Keiler's bindsacks, an old one; he must have taken his good one. A soft pang went through her. She remembered when he stitched this. She could still see the spot of blood where he'd stabbed himself with the canvas needle. "You might want to dismount," she said. "This will take a few breaths."

"You've gone completely mad," Lannan said. "What in all the spirits *happened* to you?"

"The Ennead happened to me," she said. "Go on, have a rest. I'd invite you into my tavern for a meal and a good ale, but I'm afraid it's a bit of a mess. The bakers might be persuaded to feed you, if you promise not to burn them out."

Lannan's bay horse sidled, responding to his discomfort.

While she was speaking, she'd found and shaved a quill, unstoppered an ink jar, laid a sedgeweave offcut on a binding board on her lap. She was surprised at how difficult it was to draw without the preparation of a casting—one mage, sitting like a fool in the mud, wet through and shivering without cloak or coat. She was more surprised to see her guiders form; Daughan's pain was palpable. It didn't matter. Kadri and ornaments and borderwork were not her purpose here. It was more like a historiation, a picture of a physical scene, but a historiation of landscape, larger than what would fit in the triangle around an initial.

She was drawing the trail to the Holding, the landmarks, the particular formation of rock at a specific place. The entry to a tunnel. It would still be open. There was no reason to close it.

Hanla watched in fascinated outrage. "What have you done?" she said as Liath finished and got stiffly to her feet, waving the sedgeweave to dry the ink in the misty air. There should be something to sprinkle on it, to bind it. So much, so much she would have to learn. She could barely believe the leaf was still whole in her hand. It wasn't going anywhere. It was sedgeweave, and sedgeweave it would remain, until air and time decayed it. It felt curiously flat, neutral. Like the difference between her triskele and a pewter flagon. Yet this offcut held great power. As long as someone could look at this drawing and look at a landscape and recognize when they corresponded, the sedgeweave was her proxy: it would guide them to the secret entrance to the Holding, and see them safely under the dangerous trail.

"I don't know," she said to Hanla. "I don't have a name for what this is. It's a guider, I suppose." She handed it to Lannan.

He turned it sidewise and upside down and back. "Is this a joke?"

"Verlein will know what it is." She went to Heff at last, took the reins of the little black gelding. He handed her a dry cloak, good plain Neck wool. "Or she'll have an illuminator who'll suss it out. She has until the balance day of Ve Galandra. Then it will be too late." She mounted, and waved to her mother up the road. "This is Lannan!" she called. "I didn't kill him once! Twice, in fact. He'll mind his manners here, or he'll answer to me!" She grinned wolfishly at him.

He swore at her as the fighters around him laughed. "Why should Verlein trust in anything you give her?" he said.

Liath reined away from the destruction of her home. The barricade was almost down. Heff, quiet in the aftermath of conflagration, wary of the fighters, followed a length behind.

Without turning, she said, "Tell her the truth was drawn in my flesh, clearer than any scribing. Safe passage, Lannan."

"They disappeared. A whole host, gone. There was a scouting party, which doubled back, and then they came ahead a bit, and then they were just *gone*. Nonneds of them, in an eyeblink."

"Does Worilke know?" Naeve asked. The woman's triad had handled their exterior defense as badly as Gondril's had handled the uprising. Could it have been on purpose?

The steward shook his head. "Her sentries had already spotted them and left. Our man sent only one bird, his best, and I received it myself to be sure this one was not intercepted."

"Let's keep it that way. Send armed defenders into the back passage-ways, as deep into the mountain as they can go. Someone's found them a shortcut. We shall cut it even shorter." Naeve's voice had not modulated out of its customary gentle pitch, but her stewards snapped to obey. "Oh, Lenn," she said, as if on an afterthought, and smiled when the leader paused and turned back to her. "Keep an eye out for any chambers that have recently seen use. My beloved pledgemate has a cache of secrets somewhere that no one has been able to locate for me. If you happen to stumble over it, you will bring me any golden rings you find, won't you."

His answer was the bow she had taught him when he was younger. Lenn had been a beautiful boy, full of life. Years overseeing larders had not dulled him a whit, only left him hungry for action. A pity that the years had aged him too.

But she had outgrown such diversions, and wonders awaited her that would put fleshly pursuits to shame. The trick was to see that the triplets' joining proceeded as planned on the day of their birth. Portriel was dead, the penned mages flown, the young illuminator lost or dead; the brightest new reckoners had been sent foolishly into the field, for reasons she distrusted, and did not return with the rest. Landril claimed to have alternatives hidden away, but if they were adequate why had he not produced them? Something had to be done. As usual, the balance triad would have to see to it, and because Vonche was stingy with his playthings and Evonder had not yet outgrown his paramours, it came down to her.

Vonche could bind haunts. Nine-and-six years ago he had bound his first: their cousin and bindsman, Daivor. She had refused to participate, though she did not dispute that it was necessary to clear a space for Evonder, who had just taken the triskele, and to dispense with Daivor, whose ethics had become more than inconvenient. But the process of casting passage, even inward rather than onward, would have revealed too much. Neither Vonche nor Daivor knew the truth—that when she bedded Vonche she never came with child, and when she bedded Daivor at last, she did. The family resemblance ran strong, and she'd continued to service Vonche, who had offered certain pleasures then. Later, when it became necessary to conceive Evonder, when Evrael had taken the triskele and fled, she had bedded Vonche one last, distasteful time before she moved gratefully into Daivor's arms. Vonche had never known, and Daivor had assumed she'd taken precautions. All those years he trained Evonder, never knowing the boy was his own. But Vonche had no use for the dreamy, sensuous son she'd replaced their firstborn with; the only link between them was his paternity, the illusion of which she must preserve or her triad would crumble with ever-lasting life only a breath from their hands. She had always wondered which wordsmith had stepped in to bind Daivor, in her place—and what Vonche had traded for the service. Now she wondered why that mage had not stepped forward to reveal Vonche's secret. That too, it seemed, was down to her.

He had retrieved Portriel's ring. He must have; he'd been sated as a cat these last days. And he must have tucked it away where he kept Daivor. That band of magecast gold was the key to bet-jahr, with all else lost. The key to immortality, and Vonche would keep it as a toy. She would not let his greed deprive her of her destiny. Sending defenders into the back tunnels was the perfect excuse for a wholesale search. She would have that ring, and she would hand it on to Gondril's triad, and they would punch between the worlds, and she would ride their cloaks into forever.

She had only the one regret—the golden child she had lost. *Why did you fly from us, sweet Evrael?* Had they pushed him too much, or praised him too little, or denied him too many pleasures? Or had Daivor tainted him? They had pushed Evonder just as hard, but they'd indulged him, too, and limited Daivor's influence, and they had a competent and obedient bindsman to show for it now.

Well, there was no telling with boys, was there?

"You are charged with preparation of the vellum," the other binder whispered to Freyn, caressing her forearm with a light touch that raised hairs and made her shiver. "Think of the opportunity."

"To kill them?" she said, pretending to surprise. She knew what he wanted—to seduce her secrets from her. She might part with one or two, if his caresses were sweet.

"Must you put it so crudely?" He moved behind her, his breath raising small hairs behind her ear, his caress running up along her silken sleeve. "You know they scorn your lineage. You know they tolerate you only for your extraordinary light. What better way to show them that it was you who wielded the true power all along?"

It was all lineage to them. Arael's line, Luriel's line, this line, that line; the children of Niendre and Mathey, the children of Galandra. She had all but fostered with the venerable line of Loekli, and triaded its only daughter; she had pledged and triaded Rigael son of Portriel, a prince of the Holding; and none of it was enough. Still she was Freyn of the Weak Leg, Freyn of the swamps. She had long ago planned to kill them in their moment of triumph, but she permitted the binder's stroking to continue, even swayed back as his lips brushed the nape of her neck and his fingertips circled down her breast. If only Rigael had caressed her so gently, how different things would have been. There would be no sweet, spiced wine on Ve Galandra, no draught of death for those who believed themselves her betters. She and her pledgemate would have fled this place, or ruled it. But Rigael had used her cruelly, despising her for taking his lost love's place—the place *he* had offered her, but only that he might ingratiate himself with Worilke, join Arael's line with Loekli's by triading Worilke, who was like a sister. Instead the triplets used her coldly, used her light and her potions, took the concept of poison she gifted them with and returned not so much as a bow. Freyn, the spawn of the lightless. Freyn, the wildling light. Freyn, who is here on our sufferance. She was not Freyn to them at all, but only Freyn's light, Freyn's philters.

"They will know it," she said, removing his hand, turning, "on Ve Galandra. They will toast me with it, though they'll realize only after."

His brows arched into the forelock of sandy hair. "Wine? Surely you don't believe they'll drink any wine of yours."

She frowned. She had not considered that. Slowly, replacing his hand on her breast, stepping in closer, inviting the seduction to resume, she said, "What, then?"

"You are a binder. Bind them a very special vellum. There is still time, assuming you have some in preparation now. . . ." Leaning down to kiss her, he moved his binder's fingers to her face, touching her skin . . .

She smiled against his mouth and broke away. "Of course!" she breathed. Delight surged through her, far more intense than anything his hands could stimulate. "Of course . . ."

Quicksilver, minium—mages were poisoned by casting materials their lives long. Reckoners cast off the magesickness for them. But her banewort could produce such magesickness as they had never known and would have no time to purge. One touch of the root could kill, as its greedy poison slid through the barrier of skin and entered the blood. She had flirted with it for years, dancing ever closer, ever longer, until it could no longer harm her. But woven into mageflesh vellum, how greedily its flesh would cleave to theirs, as each touched the leaf in casting the hein-na-fhin. . . .

"But you too will die," she said softly, puzzled. "You too will touch the materials." Evonder shrugged, but she recognized the mixture of hunger and uncertainty in his eyes. "You're in love with death, aren't you," she said. "Haunts and wraiths and bonefolk." Rage flashed through her. Did he take her for one of his spectres? His eyes narrowed and he took a step back. She softened. She hadn't meant to frighten him. She forgot, sometimes, how imposing she could be when she angered. "Oh, it's all right, sweet," she said, and gave him a smile. "There is no need to seduce my flesh. I have another lover now, and you could never match him. But you have seduced my mind. Let me show my gratitude."

She went to the bonewood cabinet, unlocked a small drawer, and drew out a glazed pot the size of two thumbs. "A counterherbal," she said. She had given her tools away before, herbal and counterherbal—to dispense with Evonder's pesky friend, as it happened, Rigael's cousin Torrin, who had looked so like Rigael, except that he did not have the deep blue eyes of Arael's line. The same nose, the hard chin, the same angular planes of face. Evonder resembled them too, although he descended from Caithe's line. As she handed him the pot, she wondered if he knew what she had given Worilke in order to destroy his friend. *No*, she thought, *I won't tell him. His caresses were sweet, but not sweet enough.* She liked secrets. She liked to feel her secret smile touch her lips.

The counterherbal was an inert mixture of ginger root and resin, of course, sweetened with cane and maurmallow. Until tonight, this boy had shown no interest in her; he had cut a swath through the proxies over the years, not to mention the stewards, and it was Lerissa he had fathered a child on. Rigael had nearly killed him for interfering with her training. If only he had been so protective of her. To this boy, she had ever been Freyn of the lightless, unmoored to any ancient line. The triplets were the thirdborn children of a third child of a third child; their elder brother, Wynn the secondborn, was lightless, an abomination, made a steward and told to be grateful for it—they'd fostered the eldest to spiderkeeps. While she, who showed a light, was somehow less than those rejected children, because lightless or not they came from light, and she did not. Evonder came from light. No, she would not save him.

"Thank you," he said, but she waved it away, waved him from the chamber. She had preparations to make.

Her lover awaited her.

orrin's folk were camped on a rocky sward of green, cropped close by sheep and goats; beyond it a sheer drop to the Forgotten Sea, which chewed at the broken stub of land in a wild gnashing spray of spume and menace. The Sea of Sorrows had been no calmer, their passage from Shrug a heaving misery. Two dozen dog tents and three large ones were staked down tight, their canvas sides rippling like sail. Some mages were standing around a firepit in the center of the encampment, trying to get kindling to ignite.

Boroel spotted them first. The wind snatched at his call. But Kazhe heard it. Flying out of a tent as if bowshot, she vaulted onto a horse bareback, startling it into a gallop, sending the other horses milling. They flew over the corral ropes and thundered past wagons, up the road. The horse picked up speed, charging them; at the last moment Kazhe, a Girdler practically born ahorse, hopped up onto its back and let its next stride launch her at Liath. Liath's mount shied as Kazhe's raced past, but it was not enough to jerk her out of range, only to weaken the impact.

They slammed into the stony ground and rolled, then broke apart. Liath was only to her knees when Kazhe bounced up, knife in hand. Liath drew her longblade as Kazhe moved for the kill. Kazhe pulled up at the point, arms wide, knife hand low. Liath stumbled to her feet and backed away, protecting herself with the longer blade. With barely a flicker of an eye, Kazhe threw the knife—into the soil between Heff's feet. *Interfere, and the next one will be in your heart.* Her longblade cut the wind with a low whistle as it came free of its scabbard.

Their blades met with an arm-jarring crash. Neither yielded; Liath's height gave her leverage to match Kazhe's muscle. Iron slid on iron till the crossguards met. As the shriek of metal died in their ears, both sprang back. Liath flailed out and down with her blade as she moved. She was aiming for the shoulder and she knew that Kazhe would deflect the blow, but parrying kept Kazhe from thrusting, and Liath lived for another breath. She twisted the heavy blade up and over. Kazhe turned her blade with it and slipped free, then thrust hard and fast for Liath's gut. Liath knocked the point away and whirled to Kazhe's weak side, fighting the temptation to swing her blade around in an arc that Kazhe would only duck as she stepped in to kill her. Three steps took her out of Kazhe's shorter reach, but Kazhe drove forward, pounding at her, and it was all she could do to keep the blade at bay, to keep from tripping on her own feet as she backed over uneven ground. It was a matter of how long she could last.

But she had lasted for a long time, in the Holding. She had killed a lot of people for no more reason than that they were trying to kill her. She was so bloody tired of people trying to kill her. She drove forward again, fueled by something as intense as light, something that burned. Kazhe fell back, eyes narrowing.

I'm no longer the woman who trusted you to pick up your blade in the practice ring, Liath thought, and as if reading her mind, Kazhe growled, "I'm not Lannan," and swung hard.

Blocking, Liath said, "And I'm not Liath Publican anymore."

Kazhe would not be bent on murder if Torrin lived. Heff guided them by someone else's light. The triplets' casting had succeeded. Jhoss's message was a ruse. This flashed through her mind with the dull deadliness of iron under a roiling sky, as Kazhe beat her back. She should be dead already. Kazhe was punishing her. Kazhe would beat her into the ground before she killed her.

Gathering all her strength for one last offensive push, she got past Kazhe to take the high side of the slope, but that only made it harder to step back. Someone was shouting Kazhe's name as Liath lost her footing and went down. One sweep of Kazhe's longblade drove Liath's from her hand. The backsweep was angled for her neck.

Heff plummeted into her from the side. Kazhe's blade flew loose. They both rolled down the slope. Liath found her blade and stumbled after them. Mages and fighters were running to stop it. But Kazhe was up. Kazhe was the toy that would not stay down. Her knife was blooded.

Heff did not get up.

With a roar, Liath swung the blade. *Never swing in anger,* her father's voice murmured, *anger makes you stupid,* and Kazhe ducked and landed a boot in her ribs and drove her down, then took away her weapon. Liath tried to flop over from her prostrate sprawl, but only got her elbows under her and turned to look over her shoulder. Kazhe held death point-down over her heart. A face swam up the slope beyond her, her grandfather's face over a blur of black. Dead Pelkin, reaching to greet her from the other side.

"Never swing in anger," Kazhe said, her blue eyes an agony of murderous rage, and drove the blade down.

Agony exploded from her kidneys and swept her away, a fleck of ash in a searing white storm that screamed in her own voice.

A waste of vellum. We haven't enough to expend it healing the damage you do in a reckless fury.

A waste is right. Tell them to stop. I'd have saved them the trouble if that bleeding proxy hadn't fouled my aim.

She came back to finish him.

She came back because I sent for her.

And risked all our lives, including his!

He was calling for her.

He's smitten with her!

He needs her light. The alternatives are not bright enough.

She's the one who did this!

She's come to rectify it.

It can't be rectified. You tried. Spirits, I'll kill her, I'll kill her—

Back to your posts. Both of you. Now.

Why should I listen to you?

Because in his absence I command you. Go.

Life, it seemed, was an argument of voices. She had failed to find Pelkin, or Heff or Torrin, who should have been waiting for her too, or Gran Breida or Tolivar or Bron; there were so many folk she wanted to see. Why go back, if it was only to listen to the living yell at each other? People were *waiting* for her. But somewhere nearby was a flare of light. It tugged at hers, a swirl of familiar scents. Whose? She *knew* them . . . In the end, it was curiosity that drew her back into her body, made her open her eyes on the world again.

"Hello, child," said her grandfather.

She embraced him with a cry and inhaled the scent of linseed oil, acrid pigment, tallow soot, and the indefinable mix of flesh and light that was wholly Pelkin. He was thinner than she remembered, almost bony, and not so big, though he was a tall man; she had grown since she was seven. On the exhalation, she pulled back to arms' length and said, "You're not dead."

"Nor are you, thank the spirits and these good strong mages."

It was difficult to tear her gaze from him, her mother's eyes silvered under bushy blond brows and receding hair dulling to gray, the flat cheekbones and pointed chin, beloved familiarity rendered new and strange by separation. *I took the triskele, Gran. I took the triskele and was a vocate in the*

Holding since I was last with you. Behind her, she could feel the spill of light through the door of a tavern that existed only in memory. But behind her and beside her were the mages he was gesturing to, mages she had known as vocates, matured and hardened in the year since they had met. "Annina," she said. "Herne." They were beautiful, even Herne, even scowling. She recognized the swell of desire and dismissed it—though she had not noticed before how muscled Herne was, how broad his shoulders. It was a craving for his light. As they healed her, her light had reached up and mingled with theirs, and her body, newly alive, strove to follow.

"Don't be throwing yourself on your old gran, now," Pelkin said with a twinkle. "I'm far too old for the likes of you."

"I hate healing mages," Herne grumped. Annina punched him in the arm. Liath started to smile—they had not matured as much as she'd thought—but Herne looked sincerely chastised, and Pelkin's twinkle had vanished.

"Where's Torrin?" she said sharply.

They exchanged a look. "In another tent," Pelkin said. "Guarded by Kazhe, who will wound you past healing if you go near. I advise against it. Let us keep trying. We've nine mages with him now, and we'll increase it to two nines, three if we can."

"Trying what?"

"To heal him." It was Karanthe, coming through the entry flap with a dark mage Liath realized was Jimor; between them they supported Heff. Liath's surprise at seeing Karanthe alive, in black, fled at the sight of the blood-soaked linen bandaging Heff's middle. Kazhe's blade had taken him in the side. "Which this stubborn brute won't let us do for him, or even keep him abed," Karanthe continued, grunting under the weight. "He seemed to know where you were, and wouldn't keep still until we brought him."

Liath rushed to help ease him onto a crate. The tent was full of crates and tarps and stored things, binding materials and supplies; the casting circle had been chalked on the canvas groundcloth. "Are you daft? Let them heal you," she said, but he shook his head, his jaw set, his hands still. With an oath she turned to Pelkin. "Will this heal on its own?"

"I do not believe so."

"Heff, you bloody idiot." She crouched in front of him and clasped his hands, shaking them. They were limp. "Why? *Tell me.*"

"He can't speak," Karanthe said.

"He can speak to me." She searched his face, found only pain and stubborn, smoldering anger—against what, there was no telling. "But he won't, the benighted fool. I'll kill Kazhe. I'll *kill* her." She was on her feet, searching blindly for a longblade that wasn't there. Pelkin took her by the shoulders and said, "And she will kill you, and Torrin will have lost you both when he needs you most. Get ahold of yourself, child."

He shook enough sense into her to make her think. "Ve Galandra," she gasped. "Pelkin—how many days—"

"Ve Galandra begins tomorrow," he said. "The message Torrin received in the mountains claimed the Ennead would strike on Ve Galandra. We've been trying to plan some kind of defense, with the mages we have. But ignorance hinders us."

"They'll strike on the balance day." The light was waning. "There's still tomorrow," she said. "Torrin is alive."

"Barely." Herne spoke up bitterly, rising. "A consumptive disease. Eating him alive, from within. We can feel it when we cast on him, but we cannot halt it. We could not prevent it. Nine of us on the ship with him from Maur Gowra, nine of the brightest, and still our warding was breached."

"They got through the wardings of a nonned mages in the Blooded Mountains with a handful of dirt," Liath said.

"Then those mages were inattentive or tired or substituting materials," Karanthe said. "We were not."

"We did everything right," Annina said in her soft, shy voice.

"They're the Ennead," Liath said. "And I brought them enough to work with."

"Nothing should have been enough," Karanthe said. Trying to absolve her; trying to reconcile their friendship with Liath's unforgivable betrayal. "Not even darkcraft."

"They can work through wardings," Liath said. "They can work through the spirit world."

Karanthe looked to Pelkin. He sighed, and said, "We know that, Liath. We know what they plan to do. What we do not know is how Torrin planned to stop it. He trusted no one enough to confide it. Unless . . . ?"

She shook her head. "No. Not me. Me least of all. I told the Ennead everything I knew. As he knew I would." She looked at her grandfather through a sting of tears. "I'm sorry."

"From the look of those scars, I'd say you paid in full," Pelkin said quietly. "We had enough to do sealing the wound in your back. But we'll heal them, when this is over."

"Don't waste the vellum." She looked at Heff, looked at the five reckoners, the tent full of supplies. So much power gathered here, and all crippled, thwarted.

"Jhoss says he calls for you. Even Kazhe admits he calls for you, though she curses him for it." Pelkin moved close, and it startled her to feel the authority he brought to bear through the merest shift in stance. That childhood memory was augmented, not diminished by the years. She stood up straight, as if pulled by a thread. "You have the brightest light here. Brighter than mine by ninefold, as I told you a dozen years ago. You must heal him."

"He didn't call for me to heal him," she said. "He called for me to help him. He wants my help. My light. Not my healing." She would say anything to avoid the truth. But it was inevitable. "I can't heal him. I can't heal anyone. I can't cast through pain."

"Then we're lost," said Herne.

"Is that what it was?" said Karanthe. "The barrier I felt?"

Liath nodded. Pelkin busied himself lighting a lantern, filling the tent with illusory warmth. Distancing himself from her failure? She wanted to tell him what she'd remembered in the Holding, how Roiden had wrenched her casting hand behind her, gripped her flame-colored hair so hard he nearly tore it out, came just short of drowning her in a barrel, again and again, then left her unconscious by the river—how he'd tried to douse the light of a seven-year-old girl, half mad from being denied the use of his own. Compassion, Torrin had said, was the fundamental quality of mages, and if you didn't have it, your triad wouldn't bestow a triskele on you. Cruel Roiden hadn't passed his trial. He'd spent a lifetime tormented by a light he couldn't use. She'd shown a light at six. A year of watching her, smelling her, sensing her, a blazing testament to his failure—it must have been more than he could stand. So he'd crippled her. *This is what it will feel like*, he'd said, *when the guiders burn bright.* But it had twisted, somehow, and she'd associated pain with being helpless, lightless, drowning. She'd come to with no memory of what happened, unable to tell anyone where she'd been; they all assumed she fell in the river. She would never know whether Roiden left her for dead, or was sure she wouldn't remember, or just lucked out. Until the night she took the triskele, he'd glared loathing at her, and they'd ascribed it to an old man's bitterness. But he'd been biding his time, safe in her blanked memory, awaiting her failure, and when he'd witnessed it at last he'd faded into the shadows. She hadn't thought to look for him when she'd returned. Perhaps he'd left Clondel for good, the night she failed to heal Tarny. Perhaps that had been the great triumph in his life, and he'd gone to die.

She wanted to explain it all to Pelkin . . . but it would only be an excuse. Failure was failure. She couldn't cast through pain; what difference did the reason make?

Heff tapped her thigh weakly. Try, he said. Try now.

"Kazhe would kill me," she said, with a wry sorrow. They both knew that was not why. She simply could not bear to fail again. "And I'll kill you, if you don't allow yourself to be healed by those who can." For a moment they regarded each other, immovable, unable or unwilling to explain. Then Jimor, who had stood quietly to the side, said, "He's got to lie down, at any rate, and stop bleeding all over himself. I think I can make a poultice . . ." Abruptly Heff's hands moved, and Liath translated the complex instructions. Jimor's eyes lit up as she spoke, and he stared at Heff. "Yes," he said. "Yes, that might do it . . ."

They took him out of the materials tent, and Herne and Annina followed, not looking at Liath. They had healed her for Torrin's sake, or Pelkin's, but they did not forgive what she had done.

She sat heavily on the crate Heff had vacated and scrubbed her hands through her hair. "I wish I could see him," she said, though in truth she feared to see what her betrayal had wrought. She looked up at her grandfather. "Your mages *have* to heal him."

Your mages. She blinked as her own words registered, mixing with the echoes of other words, the echoes that had become a kind of shadow in her mind, the past running like a bindsong under her awareness. *Why should I listen to you?* Kazhe's voice said, and Pelkin's answered, *Because in his absence I command you.* And he did. Every mage in this tent had deferred to him, subtly.

What could possibly have been so important that he would abandon his own family? She had wondered that her whole life. You don't deny a proxy call, she'd been told. When the Holding calls, you go. But when Tolivar said he'd denied the call, she wondered why Pelkin hadn't. When the Ennead told her Graefel and Hanla had forsaken the ring, she wondered why Pelkin hadn't.

Torrin corrupted, working dark magecraft, the Ennead said. *Our head proxy lost, perhaps dead, in pursuit of him. . . .*

"*You* were the head proxy."

"The head reckoner." He sat wearily on a square of folded tents. "Pirra's triad were the last head warders, and they died nine years ago." His eyes glinted like pewter in a face that grew handsomer with age. He was bright, much brighter than she could have sensed as a child. Brighter than Graefel, brighter than Hanla, brighter than Yerby the false shining darkmage; brighter than anyone save the Ennead, and Torrin casting, and one or two of the vocates, who might have rivaled him for his position one day.

"Did you know what was practiced there?"

"Not as a vocate, no. Not even as a reckoner, not at first; it was the old Ennead then, and darkcraft was only simmering under the surface, where no ordinary proxies could see. Not when I called Graefel to the Holding, or even later, when I returned to cast him triad with his sister and pledgemate. But the last time I went back, when young Breida was born . . ." He sighed. "I suspected then, yes. I feared for you. I thought to take you with me, to foster you somewhere far from the Holding. Geara had another child; perhaps it would be enough for her, I thought. But I could not take you from her, not after what I'd already done. It meant leaving you to suffer Geara's bitterness. I knew she would favor the daughter Graefel's triad gave her to replace you. But neither could I take you from your father, who was blameless and who adored you." He stroked the corner of his mouth, an old gesture she had forgotten. "I thought perhaps the Ennead would overlook what was right under their noses. Hanla n'Geior was a fine, bright reckoner in her day; I knew she would train you well. And Graefel promised me he'd guard you from proxies."

"Graefel sent his proxy ring to the Holding so they would call me themselves."

Pelkin nodded, but seemed incapable of anger. He had abandoned his pledgemate and his daughters. Perhaps he, like Evonder, could not fault betrayal after having betrayed.

"I'm sorry, Liath," he said. His failure to shield her from the call; his failure to spare her the ordeal that scarred her. For a moment he was her grandfather again, not a proxy who had worn two cloaks for half a lifetime and now bore the burden of the world, with Torrin ailing. He gripped her by the shoulders, squeezing once, hard. "You've grown into a fine woman despite us."

He'd pledged so young . . . He and Breida had been childhood sweethearts, inseparable even though his family was in Drey; they'd all but fostered in each other's homes. Geara had just been born when he took the triskele; he returned from his year's journeying to father Eife, denying the call, and denied it again at Seira's birth. But there was no triad for him in Clondel, which had been served by the Drey triad that trained him. When the call came a third time, he went. "I thought I would serve them a nineyear," he said, looking off into the past. "I would visit home on each round of the proxy circle, then retire to Clondel for what was left of my daughters' childhood. But they sent me farther and farther afield. As if they were trying to estrange me from Brei, cut me off from the distraction of family. My light was dedicated entirely to their service, but that wasn't enough; they wanted my heart, too. I knew something was amiss. No compassionate Ennead would demand such a thing."

"You became head reckoner because you didn't like the Ennead?"

"I became head reckoner because I had the brightest light and Rontifer and Yelwyn believed they had broken me to harness. But I stayed a reckoner at all because they used me badly. Ironic, eh? Yet it allowed me to declare Clondel off-limits. No calls were made in my home village while I was head. I protected you as I could, Liath. I could not know Graefel would break his vow."

"Did Gran know?" she asked softly.

"I couldn't lay that darkness at our doorstep. I asked her to come with me, you know. When Seira was nine-and-seven and Geara was old enough to run the tavern. 'They're strong women,' I said. 'Leave the work to them. Travel with me.' At least we'd have been together. It was . . . intolerable to be away from her, even for a night. I loved her more than life. But the world was at stake. I couldn't risk one of Seldril's creatures taking my place and running my reckoners. Folk depended on me. And she wouldn't come. The Petrel's Rest was her strength, her body . . ."

"But you were her heart," Liath finished, because he couldn't. Gran

Breida had died when Liath was four—just died, sickened and died, and no casting could save her. Jolly, robust Breida. The heart had been ripped out of her, and she had simply stopped living.

When Liath showed a light, Geara had been grieving her mother for two years. It was no wonder she'd gone spare. "You said Graefel's triad gave my mother another daughter," Liath said. Across the camp, she could hear binders singing over Torrin, their voices weaving with the wind's. "Mother said something like that to Hanla. What did you mean? I knew she bore Breida to make up for me, I've always known that, I could count the truth on my fingers. But there's more to it, isn't there? Something to do with darkcraft."

"No," Pelkin said. "Never accuse your training triad of that—their fault was too much integrity, not too little. It was not darkcraft, not like what the shadow warders used to make the triplets. Just a casting, to nudge the child toward girlhood. All babes are both male and female in the womb, early on. Hanla insured that Geara bore another girl. It must have been quite a struggle, persuading her to do that—persuading Befre, and Graefel. It is not a thing that magecraft should be used for."

They are a creation of darkcraft themselves, identical triplets of different genders, Torrin had said. "Why make one of the triplets a girl?" she asked, frowning. "What good would that do?"

"From what would have been three girls or three boys, they made one boy, one girl, and one of both. That's the word, anyway—can't say I saw proof of it. Gondril is rumored to have loved a lightless boy, but that bespeaks no female parts; he grew heavy as he approached puberty, perhaps to camouflage breasts, but Ennead children are spoiled, it could have been sloth and overindulgence. Yet the stewards claim he bled, at nine-and-four."

"Didn't the proxies know what was happening? Not the reckoners, maybe, I was with them for a while, they're all gossip with no substance—" He raised a brow, but nodded for her to go on. "But the warders? Couldn't they have . . . ?"

"Some genuinely did not know. It was dangerous to tell anyone, even to seek help. Most kept speculation to themselves; those who didn't had a tendency to disappear. Some allied themselves with the Ennead, to stay alive or out of ambition. There was a cabal, you see—almost a shadow ennead, working to subvert the old Ennead. They were the ones who put Rontifer and Yelwyn in power. They were the ones who . . . created the triplets, you might say. But their creation turned on them; when the three triaded, at two nineyears of age, they cut their strings and the puppeteer's throats. Pirra and Alliol rallied the remaining warders, over time, but when they were killed the warders fragmented. There was no one strong enough to lead them anymore."

"You could have gone back."

"I did, to make reports, once a year or so. But I could not have returned to stay. They would not have had me. Reckoners don't become warders. Rontifer and Yelwyn wanted me in the field, where they believed I would remain at heel."

Portriel had mentioned those names. "Who were they?"

"The triplets' parents. The murderers of Niendre and Mathey and their children, all the good and decent line of Arael."

Liath struggled to remember the other one Portriel had stressed, found it as a shape in her mind. "Jaemlyn?"

Pelkin cocked his head, surprised to hear that name. "Jaemlyn and Maeryn were sons of theirs, Portriel their daughter. Maeryn was Torrin's father."

The strands of the world interlocked. "And Eilody?"

"His mother? I don't know." He got up stiffly and went to the tent flap. "They've made a fire," he said. "We'll be warmer there. Come."

She was still puzzling it out. "One woman, one man, one of both. To preserve symmetry . . ."

"Yes. To make a triad balanced in all qualities."

"How can we possibly defeat that?" Liath said. "Any triad we create will be two and one in some configuration."

"I don't know," Pelkin replied, looking out into the dusk. "He would not tell us. And now he can't."

"Unless we heal him." She got up with effort. The life and lust and energy after a healing were temporary. Her limbs were heavy, logy. But her light wasn't. Lights didn't get tired. He said she had the brightest light. What good was that, if she couldn't heal Torrin? Try, Heff had said. Try now. Why now? "I can't fight past Kazhe," she said. "Does she ever sleep?"

"She did, and Boroel watched. But I doubt that she will now, with you here." Pelkin gestured her through the flap.

"Jhoss might persuade her." As she said it, she knew it was useless. She'd heard them arguing, as she came back into herself. And Kazhe would fight off anyone who tried to subdue her. They'd have to kill her. Benkana and Boroel would not permit that. Perhaps an arrow . . .

She was appalled at what she had become. "She'll die to keep me from him, and I'll only fail."

The fire blazed high in the middle of the camp, whipped and torn by the wind; they had no fear of attack by force, not here in the middle of nowhere, with the fighting off to Headward. She felt mages casting—one group in the largest tent, a second in a smaller that must be Torrin's. There were at least three nines of lights here. She should tell Pelkin he needn't ward the camp, the Ennead believed Torrin was dead, there would be no darkcraft onslaught, they could set all their mages to healing him at once. But Pelkin was speaking stern words against self-pity. And standing over a smaller cookfire off to the side, her dark face reflecting flame, her pale hair shining, was Jonnula.

Karanthe came up next to them. "Oh, she's still a toad," she said, following Liath's gaze. "But she's a bright toad, and she knows where the power lies. She joined us moons ago."

"How many moons?" Liath said softly. Jonnula was ladling stew into a bowl, looking across at a tent lit by lantern and magelight.

"I don't . . ." Karanthe blinked at Liath's expression. "In late summer, I suppose. At Maur Gowra, we gathered there, she heard about it somehow. I didn't trust her either, but the worst thing about her now is her cooking. Everyone else is casting or nackered or we'd never have let her near the pot." When Liath didn't laugh, she said, "Jonnula would never ally herself with the weaker side, Liath. Now listen, there are some others you should meet, and I want to know how Tolivar is doing, and . . ."

Jonnula moved toward the tent. Liath launched herself before she was halfway there. Karanthe cried out after her. Boroel loomed from fireshadow and caught her up hard. Jonnula glanced at the commotion, saw Liath, and quickened her step. "Don't let her go in there!" Liath snarled at Boroel, who responded calmly, "He has to eat." She writhed in his iron grip; two fighters added their strength to his. Immobilized, she screamed past the startled reckoners, "Kazhe! *Don't let Jonnula near him!*"

"What is *wrong* with you?" Karanthe said, catching up, aging Pelkin still a few steps behind her.

"Look around you, Karanthe. A ragged band of killers and lapsed proxies, camped on a desolate headland, their untriaded leader dying before their eyes—what's that compared with a stone fastness full of colored silks and velvets and ninefold power? You said Jonnula would never ally herself with the weaker side. *We are the weaker side, Karanthe!*"

Karanthe stared at Pelkin. "She *was* on the ship . . . the warding . . ."

"Should not have failed." Pelkin moved fast, flinging a gesture back at Boroel. Released, Liath pounded after him, past him, Boroel at her side. The tent flap was fastened from within. Boroel's blade sliced down the center, and light spilled out.

Torrin's pain filled the space like a stench. He lay supine on a pallet, bones stark against chalky, pitted flesh, emaciated. Food stained his mouth. Jonnula half turned with the spoon in her hand and a faint smile on her lips. Startled reckoners were getting to their feet. Kazhe barred the way, centered behind her blade. "What's the fuss? I took her knife, I made her taste—"

Liath sprang for Jonnula. Kazhe lunged at her and met Boroel's blade. Jonnula dove for the back of the tent, one arm still stretched toward Torrin. A chain snapped and Torrin's body jerked. Liath flew past reckoners to tackle her, but her arms closed on air; someone had pulled the stakes up and freed a hole for Jonnula to roll through. Liath shimmied under the canvas on elbows and knees. Behind her she heard Kazhe's roar, heard Boroel say, "Go, I will watch," and then she was up and running through twilight after the fleet shadow. The moonlight hair was a beacon. Her boots snagged on rocks that Jonnula's slippered feet flew over. She knew the way. This was planned—not well, but planned. A horse whickered up ahead, past a thin stand of sourwood. Boots thudded behind her, but Kazhe was short-legged, she would not catch up, and Liath could not catch Jonnula. What did it matter? The damage was done. But still she ran, until a mounted rider loomed among the trees, hauling a second horse around for Jonnula to mount—

"*Down!*" Kazhe shouted, and Liath went down. The knife sang over her and sank into Jonnula's back. Jonnula went to her knees. The rider broke and fled into the dusk.

Kazhe ran past, and was yanking the knife out as Liath came up to them. Jonnula shrieked. It was a Souther blade.

"I made her taste it," Kazhe was saying between obscenities. "I made her bloody *taste* it first . . ."

Liath shoved in and grabbed Jonnula by the hair. Her pale eyes were glazing. "The Ennead sent you, just like me."

Jonnula gave a ghastly smile. "You were an ignorant tool," she said, past some kind of bubbles in her throat. "Worilke and Freyn sent *me*. To take action. Poison. Antidote. It couldn't harm me. I saved Herne and Annina. Took them with me, part of the bargain. That has to be worth something." She coughed foamy blood. "Heal me and I'll . . ."

"Let's see your antidote for *this*," Kazhe said, and drew the blade across her exposed throat in one deep, unhesitating stroke.

Liath let go in revulsion, and Jonnula's body flopped to the ground. "You idiot," she said softly. "She would have told us how to save him."

"A purgative," Kazhe said. They could already hear the sounds of retching—Torrin, and the others who'd had a few bites of stew before chaos broke loose.

"Then there was no need to kill her," Liath said, though she would have done it herself. "She could have told us—"

Kazhe was a blur of white-blond fury as she slammed Liath against a tree, her hand a breath from crushing Liath's throat. "I know how to save him now," she said. "*You* will save him."

"Or what?" Liath rasped. "You'll kill me again?"

Kazhe shoved away from her and walked back toward the tent, downhill, retrieving blades as she went.

I'll take that as an apology. Liath looked down at the pale-haired corpse. What Jonnula had done was no more than she herself had done. But Jonnula knew. If Jonnula believed that taking bright Herne and Annina for her own use was a rescue, she knew what was going on in the Holding.

"I hope you don't give the bonefolk indigestion," Liath said. She pried Torrin's triskele from the cooling fingers, and followed Kazhe back down to the camp.

· · ·

His beard had come in, a lush silver-black lying close along the jaw; probably Kazhe had been unwilling to keep him as clean-shaven as he kept himself, but would allow no one else near him with a blade. Beard and hair made a triangular frame around pallid skin, accented by charcoal slashes of brow and sooty lashes, and beard and mustache made a sensuous oval around bloodless lips. Even ravaged by disease, it was a striking face.

She had been sitting here for a nonned sleep breaths, as nine mages cast, then twice nine, to no effect. The remaining nine who could form threes sat around them now, quills scritching on parchment; she was barely aware of them. A circle of shadow—she had been circled by shadows for as long as she could remember, of one kind or another. Heff had come in some time ago, bleeding again. He would not be healed, but he would not lie dying alone. Jhoss sat copying from a bound volume onto slate, to pass the time. Kazhe sat with her magecrafted longblade across her knees, rocking from side to side; her blade could not protect him from this.

"Can you heal him with your earthcraft?" Liath had asked Heff.

I do not know what that word means, Heff had said. But no.

She laid her hand over Torrin's heartbeat, and sedgeweave crinkled inside his shirt—the message Evonder had sent, she saw as she drew it out and unfolded it. Their boyhood code, incomprehensible. She turned the leaf over and picked a crumbly stick of charcoal out of the cold brazier. Except for the thing she had made to guide Lannan, she had not drawn in a long time. Her hand itched to work. Her eye itched to render the waves of hair, the slashes of brow, the hooked nose, the crescent lashes . . . she was drawing them already, without thinking, as if perception and the motion of drawing were the same. What she saw appeared below her hand, sketched on sedgeweave in outline.

She began to fill it in—casting a private passage, too early as the one for Tolivar had been too late. The image of his face took shape on the surface of the leaf as she shaded the contours of brow and cheekbone, the hollows of eyes. Shadow cast depth; she had learned that from the mage-stone. It was his face as it should be, whole and hale, or at least his face as she had known it, though he'd been weary even then. It had his quiet authority even in repose, yet it frowned a little, concerned and uncertain, pained by some private grief.

She realized that her guiders had formed only when she began to draw a border of kadri around the picture. Though she remembered the shape of every glyph she'd ever seen, she did not know how to order them into words. She could not scribe. She could not cast on her own. But she could manipulate symbol; she had pulled kadri from deep within during long sessions without food or sleep. Kadri were the ancestors of glyphs, he'd said. She scribed her kadri around the edges of his shadow face, following the shimmering blue light in her mind.

You are casting, Heff said. She shrugged; she could not heal him by herself. She could feel his light responding to hers, a sluggish stirring in the depths, but she could not make a bridge to it alone. Yet Heff seemed agitated—eager, or frightened. What was to fear? Not failure—there was no hope of success. Not harm; Torrin lay dying, lapsed into a stupor as his body collapsed in on itself. She could only celebrate the man he had been, the ember of self still burning somewhere deep inside the failing flesh.

The flesh wanted to be whole. She tried to give it one last memory of wholeness, one last joyful glimpse of the proud, beautiful thing it had been. When Heff handed her a brush—where had he gotten it? from Jhoss? Jhoss was standing just beyond him, she couldn't imagine what he wanted—she took it resignedly. He had smeared it in blood. His own. She could no longer feel horror. She touched color to the outline of lips, then on a whim added a dab to each eye. Now they looked open, burn-ing—not in their own amber color, but it suited him to look awake, intense. The effect pleased her. It animated the features, brought an illusion of life to the flat image on the leaf. Funny; Heff had chosen a horsetail brush, as if he could have known one from another. The wooden end of it was blunt. She snapped it in two, and ran one jagged half down the hollow of her palm, as she had done for Tolivar. Blood congealed quickly, but working her hand gave her enough to ink the border in. Any color was better than none. His life had been a wash of ideas and knowledge, a vivid drive to prevent disaster. She painted a weave around the kadri framing the face, then laid the leaf with satisfaction on his chest. It almost seemed then that his light flared, but perhaps that was like the last breaths—perhaps he was slipping away even now—*Kazhe*, she tried to cry, but her throat was closed, and *Wait, Torrin, please, not yet!*—and in her spasm of panic she was only peripherally aware that Heff was croon-ing, that Heff had clasped the hands she had lifted to hold death at bay—

The swell of light took her broadside. The sun had risen in this corner of the canvas tent, eclipsing lamplight, eclipsing sight. A dam had broken and released a flood of radiance. Could she have connected somehow with Heff's earthcraft? Yet it was a *light*, it was light itself—it was Torrin's light, she knew the taste of it, the impossible blinding brightness, his light was reaching out of him to theirs, and she could feel the flesh repair-ing itself under their joined hands, and the charcoal lines she had drawn on sedgeweave were hovering above the leaf in a blaze of liquid flame, his face burning in the air, and the blood—the blood ran silver, molten silver—

For one timeless instant, she could *see*.

She could see what Heff's eyes saw, the flesh, the pulses, the hot, brief lives. There had never been a great love in Heff's life. It was an emptiness at the core of him. There had been a man, a mild, untroubled man who loved him, but he pushed him away, regretful but firm—too distracted by concerns of his own, by a shapeless darkness that haunted him. Serle found Folle, and they were happy together, for a brief span of sweet years, and Heff fed off that happiness, convincing himself that he could live on it, that as long as his brother was happy it was enough for him. He put into protecting Serle all the determination and love and energy and courage he would have put into protecting a lover and a fosterling, and there was nothing left. It was a kind of hiding. Serle had Folle now. Heff should have embraced his own life. But he hesitated. And Torrin came to find him, and his world went up in flames. Serle was dead. He was at fault. He had nowhere else to go. He had made no life for himself. And then Liath had rapped on the stable door, a beacon lost in the dark of night—

Shocked out of Heff's world by the sight of herself, in the next heartbeat she was looking through the luminous facets of Torrin's eyes, seeing the world as he saw it, flawed and wounded but profoundly, poignantly beautiful, every life a light—a world full of lights, like stars across the horizon, a shifting dazzling world of magelights. And in the midst of them, this blossoming unity, circle and bridge, sphere and gateway—

Torrin spasmed and cried out, and Heff's hands tore away from hers, and she was flesh again, and what she had seen was fading into gossamer memory. Kazhe was shouting for Jhoss, Jhoss was saying "I'm here, I see, I'm here," and Torrin was sitting up, groping at her, groping at Heff. Coming out of deep sleep into the midst of crisis. "What happened?" he demanded, looking around the tent. "What happened to the ship?"

Kazhe was laughing. "You're all right!" she cried, shaking Jhoss's shoulder hard. "Eiden's bloody balls, they've *healed* you!"

"You're in the Fist," Jhoss said, stumbling free as Kazhe danced to the entry to yell for Benkana. "The Ennead struck at you on the *Fairwind* and you fell ill. A flaw in the warding, a mage who was not what she claimed. You called for this one in your delirium. I sent to Evonder. He returned me these two."

"Evonder . . ." He groped at his shirt, for the sedgeweave that was the only tangible link to his friend.

"It's gone," Liath said. "I . . . seem to have used it as a casting leaf. Evonder's scribing . . ." She shook her head hard.

Torrin went still, taking in the situation. She saw the healing desire flare in him, felt it through the hand that gripped her upper arm, saw him recognize it, master it. He looked away, withdrew his hand. He did not want her to see it. He looked at Heff. His amber eyes burned. Was that it? Was it men he wanted, was the ally his lover after all, was Evonder more than brother and friend? Then she looked at Heff too, and it came to her that she was smelling two magelights, not one—then three, five, nine as she became aware of the lights that had surrounded them, supported them, and more as Pelkin and Karanthe and Jimor came in, but there was still another light, a taste and smell at once strange and utterly familiar. . . .

Heff shot Torrin a look of pure betrayal, lurched to his feet, and staggered away.

"We'll cast it again," Torrin called sharply after him. "Heff, I would not have done this to you . . . it wasn't me . . . you did it to yourself . . ." He swore and put a hand to his head. "Too much," he said. "It's too much."

"You were insensible for two sixdays," Jhoss said. "Tomorrow begins Ve Galandra, but Evonder sent further word that the Ennead will not strike until the balance day. There is time yet to prepare." He turned to Pelkin, who watched with something like awe. "You must cast them triad at the first opportunity."

No! Heff's gesture was a wildly flung arm.

Softly, Pelkin said, "I believe they have already cast that themselves. But we can enact the ritual, to be certain." He looked at Liath, and his eyes went sad. "Tomorrow," he said. "After they've rested. When the festival of Galandra has begun." As if he could no longer bear to look at her, he left the tent, herding Karanthe unwilling in front of him.

"Kazhe," said Torrin. "Jhoss. Leave us. Take the proxies."

For once it was Jhoss who was reluctant to go. Kazhe, exuberant, swept him from the tent, and Liath could hear her laughing as she posted herself guard, calling for Benkana and Boroel and for someone to bring her a bloody cup of bloody ale.

"He wants to fill you in, make plans," Liath said. Better trying to explain Jhoss than what had just happened, or admitting the rush of heat that made her too weak to stand.

"Pelkin has already made the plans in his mind," Torrin said. He was watching Heff, who stood with his back to them, his breathing ragged. "Jhoss knows it is more complicated than that."

Heff turned as if the movement were an agony. I don't know, his hands said. I have to think.

Torrin looked at Liath. She translated, uncomprehending. Heff's face was twisted horribly. Oh, Heff, her heart cried out, what is it? But she was afraid to know.

"I cored and sealed him," Torrin said. "We did, Evonder and Pelkin and I. In the Holding."

"In the what?" Liath whispered.

For three breaths, Torrin did not answer. Then Heff gave a curt nod. Permission.

"Heff and Serle were boys in the Holding when Evonder and I began to smuggle out the bright ones, to keep them out of the Ennead's hands. Heff was the stablemaster's favorite. Brondarion te Khine. A good man. He fosters children. The boys were the children of a reckoner who persisted in bearing children to her lovers, then fostering them when she lost interest in the men. Heff was considered lightless, but a light flared very suddenly in him when he was a dozen summers, like a banked ember he had tried to suppress and could no longer fight. Serle was seven at the time and lightless, and remained so. Bron would not split them up and could not bear to lose either; he kept Heff hidden for a year, working deep behind the stables in the smithy. But Serle was a quicksilver child, full of energy and mischief, and it was no life for either of them. By then Evonder had established a trust with Bron, and brought me in. I told him that I had been able to distinguish Heff's light from all the other lights in the Holding—he was that bright. We arranged to send them to the Haunch, where they would not look out of place; an ironsmith wanted prentices and would ask no questions." He scratched in annoyance at the beard that had grown on him in his absence. "Heff loathed his magelight," he said. "It was anathema to him, a cursed thing that rose up to ruin his life. He did not want to go into the world a mage. Reckoners would only call him back. He would never take a triskele. So we cored and sealed him, at his own request. Pelkin had been using his position to help Bron. He was illuminator for us. It required three; Heff's light did not want to be sealed off. His relief when it was done was profound. The only draw-back was that the moment he was sealed, he began to see magelights—all magelights, at any distance, just as I could. My own light is partially sealed, the result of an unfortunate childhood, and that, I believe, is what gives me the ability, which I lose when I am casting."

"Portriel had it," Liath said. She had not understood that before. It was part of how she navigated, blind, through the passageways. That and her illuminator's sense of path, and her fearless conviction that the stone would catch her if she fell.

Torrin nodded. "They sealed Portriel to punish her."

"But Portriel went mad. Heff's not mad."

"Portriel's light defines her. She *is* her light. Heff is nourished by other things."

Heff had sunk down onto a crate and put his forehead on his crossed arms. Liath started up, to go to him, but a light finger on her arm held her in place. She swallowed. She was so hideously scarred. Yet he had not seemed to notice it. *Fool*, came the bitter thought. *Selfish, foolish Liath.*

"I went to Gulbrid to ask him to be unsealed and triad me. I needed his light. I asked honestly, but it was a selfish request. And I made a grievous miscalculation regarding local sentiment toward the Ennead. Greedy for converts, I pushed them too hard. Serle's death is on my hands."

"Serle's death is on the hands of those who killed him."

Maybe, said the brief tilt of his head. He still would not look at her. He was holding himself on a tight rein.

"What now?" Liath asked.

"Your own return suggests that you are willing to be my illuminator.

Now either I have a triad, and the day after tomorrow we break the shield, or Heff asks me to core and seal him again, and I look for a binder strong enough to enable us to."

"You had a triad in the Blooded Mountains," Liath said, "and after we escaped. You had us then. Why did you let us go, Torrin?"

"I had no triad. I had a sealed, untrained bindsman who had dedicated his life to protecting the brightest mage he'd ever met, and an illuminator loyal to a tradition I planned to destroy. Words could not have broken the shields around either of you. You had to break them yourselves, or I had to do without you."

"But you couldn't."

"In the event, no." He smiled, still avoiding her eyes. She was sorry she'd looked. If anything could crack the shield around a heart, it was that smile. "But I never stop hoping."

"That's a precious thing," she said in a low voice, turning to the picture of despair that Heff's curled-over body painted.

Then Torrin did look at her—and touched her, tracing a fingertip over the white, puckered seams in her cheek, her neck. The triangular inscriptions of agony made her grotesque. She recoiled from the intimate examination, but the light touch was arousing, both caress and comprehension: he was reading her pain through his skin. Shame and desire washed over her. "Don't," she choked, then winced when the touch withdrew.

"You were a child when we met," he said. "Fierce and innocent and awkward and so full of light I could barely breathe for want of you. Now . . ." He paused, then said, "That was healing and triading and unsealing, all in one, just now. Clearly the most powerful things do come in threes. Perhaps when the healing passion has subsided, it will be easier."

Why must it be easier? Liath started to say, but Heff was rising, making for the tent flap. Reflexively she rose with him.

I won't make you wait long for an answer, he said, and left as Liath was saying the words aloud.

"He can be healed now," Torrin said. "He couldn't before. His light would have tried to reach out to the casting mages'. It's what happened when I tried, after the fire. He couldn't bear it. He stopped me halfway."

"I'll see that he is," she said, then stood stupidly for a moment. "I'll go now." She did not move.

"All right." Torrin got up, a little shaky but waving her off as she reached to help. "I will take the opportunity to boil some water and rid my face of this appalling growth."

She took a step away, then hesitated. She might never be alone with him again. She would not force herself on him; but she could ask, "Why did you leave the Holding, Torrin?"

This time the smile was only the small closemouthed curve of lips. "I was a prince of mages, Holding-reared. In my day the scions of the Ennead ceased to go journeying. Their fastness was steeped in craft, they believed, and their triads were determined from the day they showed a light. I wanted to triad outside what was decreed for me. So I went on a journey."

"You had nine nines of mages, in the mountains."

"I had only two triads I trusted with my life—Porick's and Sera-fad's—and neither of them was mine."

"You could have taken the brightest mages—"

"It doesn't work that way. A triad is not what three reckoners become when they cast together. A triad is a bonding. That flash of insight, that moment so much like casting passage—that was the triad forming. I had no idea it could happen of its own. That was remarkable. At any rate, it can't be two mages chosen for their light alone. It has to be the right people. I hadn't yet found them, or didn't know them if I had."

"Not even Evonder? And . . . Lerissa?"

He sighed. "Lerissa was never my lover," he said, answering her childish unspoken question, "and Evonder, though he was right, was not bright enough for what was needed." An old, barbed guilt.

"Heff is brighter?" She couldn't see it.

"He will be when we cast. If we cast. Heff was damaged by the Holding—like Evonder, like myself, like your runner boy. Lights learn to hide, sealed or not."

"Or to fail," she said, of her own.

"Your block is broken," Torrin said. "Did that happen just now as well? It was such a pretty conceit, with three."

"No, your three in one is safe," she said. "Seldril broke my block on a table in the Holding. I just didn't know it until now."

"*They will heal you,*" Portriel's voice said, "*but not the way you think, and you cannot ask them for it.*" Roiden hadn't known the truth of pain, when he tried to pass his on to her. But expert Seldril had taught her. Roiden was nothing, after that.

"I grieve for you," Torrin said. As he'd promised he would.

She was still only a step away from him. His cat's eyes burned golden in the lamplight. His arousal was obvious; he did not find her hideous. But he did not reach for her.

After the healing of the knife wound—he wouldn't let them heal the burns—Heff sat on the windswept cliffside, staring out at the sea. She found him by his silhouette against a brief ragged expanse of stars, and by the gentle warmth of his light.

I will not be able to find you anymore, he said as she sat. Not unless you are a ninefoot away from me.

His words came across quiet, as if the wind were drowning a sound with its mournful song, but it was only the dark. A moon hung over the sea, revealed by tears in the fast-moving cloudbanks. "Then I'll just have to stay within a ninefoot," she said. "At least now I can smell you."

I see it, he said. You smell it. Torrin tastes it.

She nodded, and cuddled in close to him; she'd lost her cloak in the fight with Kazhe. He opened his big cloak to include her, then withdrew the arm to say, I despise the light in me. I despise a craft that kills. And I can't *see*.

She remembered what he'd said about how some things were clearest only in the dark. No mage she knew could smell her own light. But somehow the shine of Heff's light diminished the world's light, for him. She nodded again, listening; the wind seemed to moan through his fingers as he spoke.

I couldn't tell you I'd seen your grandfather in the Hand without admitting where I came from. It was our great secret. He kept it when we arrived here. He is a good man.

"Is that why he left, after the Isle of Senana? Because you were there?"

I told him I would look after you. He had to arrange for a ship to be ready at Maur Gowra whenever Torrin required it. He had followed you too long.

"Oh, Heff," she said. "There's so much we should have told."

We could not, he said, simply.

They sat for a while longer, sharing warmth, watching the sky close up again over the sea. Then Heff, his gestures more felt than seen, said, Does Bron live?

"I don't think so," she said, her heart twisting.

I have missed him, these dozen years. But we still shared the same world, walked on the same ground.

Heff was alone now. Whatever had made him dedicate himself to her, she could not make up for what he had lost.

Or what he had never had. "Are you in love with Torrin?" she asked gently.

He shook his head. Then he said, I wish I were. I have desired, and I have coupled, but there has never been one person who took the breath from me, who captured my head and my heart *and* my flesh. I would like to be in love. Someday, perhaps . . . Then his hands opened wide, as if releasing an object held too close.

Ve Galandra, he said, sensing the passage of midnight.

"Is there a tent for us?"

Yes. The one where they healed me. We should go there.

They rose, and turned together from the Forgotten Sea, and started back up the slope. Torrin's tent still glowed from within, but his shadow crossed to the lantern, and the tent went dark.

"You have a sweet light," Liath said without thinking, already moving toward sleep. "I should have known."

He pulled away abruptly and halted. His hands moved, but she couldn't see them well. He was angry. He got angrier when she said, "I can't make that out, Heff, it's too dark," and strode to their tent, leaving her to pick her way. Inside, he lit a lantern, and she was able to find the flap and get in. "What?" she said, upset that the soft peace of the night had broken.

A sweet light, he said.

"Yes . . . I meant it as . . . I'm sorry, I—"

So now you think, Oh, I underestimated him, he said. Now that I show a magelight, I am no longer merely your trusty protector. Suddenly I matter. Suddenly I might be your bindsman. And I am no longer Heff at all, but this light inside me, this blinding, cursed thing. I can't see past it to do the work I love, and you can't see past it to me. This is how I win your respect—this thing I have no control over, can take no credit for, this thing that forced me into exile from the closest thing I had to a father.

He was shaking. It was horrible, not least because in a way he was right—she did see him differently now, with a kind of awe.

Even if he seals me up again, he said, his hands stabbing and slicing the air, you'll always look at me and think, There is a light in there, and so he matters now.

Someone had piled spare blankets for them and left a hoggin of water, and there was room to stretch out in the center where the casting circle was drawn. They were standing on a healing ground, perhaps even the spot where Galandra had stood to cast safety for Eiden Myr. The birthplace of the world they knew; the heart of the magecraft their world was built on. But he was not a mage, however bright his light might shine.

"You underestimate what you taught me," she said, keeping her voice very low, her hands very still. "Maybe you never knew you taught it to me at all. Earthcraft, someone called it. It was a marvel to me. I didn't know. I thought magecraft was the only true craft. But you showed me. Just by being what you are. You could blind me with your magelight and still I would see you, and your . . . your compassion, your connection to the earth and its creatures and its spirits. Eiden strike your bloody light. Seal it up!"

Her words hurt him more. He closed his arms around himself, pulling in tight as if to keep his big frame from flying apart.

"We'll seal you, Heff," she said, helpless before his anguish. "Spirits, if it hurts you so, we'll do it now, we'll wake them . . ."

He shook his head. His arms fell to his sides. Then he said, Did they ever play would-you when you were a child?

She winced. "Yes."

Would you swallow a slug or let your mama die? Would you suck a sheep's tail or let a Great Storm come?

Softly, she said, "Would you cut a lamb's throat or let the Ennead destroy a world?"

She had been the lamb on the slaughterground. When he refused the binder's way, it was her he was protecting, too.

He turned away, hands limp. She put her arms around him, laid her cheek on the ridge of spine below his neck. She rested there, breathing with him, her heart beating slow against the heartbeat through his back. He took her hands and held them tight.

"You matter," she said. "You always mattered."

When he felt her getting drowsy, he disengaged from her and said, I have to think. You have to sleep.

They set out the blankets and she curled into hers. "Don't go," she said. She meant for him not to leave the Fist, not to abandon them—as if that was something he would have done. It was what she would have done. He shook his head as he reached for the lantern. Before he turned it down he said, I'll stay by you.

She slipped into dreamless sleep. He knew she loved him. He was there. He would watch. Always.

older son, on Khine, and received promising messages in return. Gradually she had apprised him of events in the Holding, as it became clear that he concurred in her thinking. Khine had hardened him, taught him discipline that Vonche and Naeve could not. He would help her manage Evonder. He had been gone for three nineyears and seven; he'd left a year before Evonder was born, and it was well past time for him to return and claim his legacy. On Ve Galandra, she would meet him at last, and he would become her support in the new rulership of Eiden Myr.

Worilke and Freyn made the base of her triangle. She needed the cachet they would carry as members of the former Ennead, she needed their light, and she needed Worilke's strength of purpose, although it would have to bend to her own designs. But one corner of the base had remained empty until she went trolling through the proxies and found her man.

Loris, a wordsmith from the Strong Leg. Short, with a crooked nose and an endearing eagerness to be seduced. His light was bright but would not outshine her own. He was ambitious. He was grateful. He would do. She'd tucked him in her chambers, showered him in luxuries, a prisoner of repletion held in reserve. He was amusing, a competent lover, and beautiful in colors.

All she needed now was some way to insure Evonder's cooperation. She had nothing to hold over him, not even the child her father had made him take from her. She would have liked to retrieve the child—aristocracy relied on lineage, and she had a dynasty to consider—but she could make other children. She would have liked to triad Torrin and Evonder, and that wasn't possible either. The triplets had killed Torrin, and if they hadn't then Worilke had certainly managed it—she would not abide his dissidence in the world she planned to run. Lerissa would have liked more opportunity to forge an alliance with him, but he'd wanted little to do with her—a frustrating man, immune to seduction. And the illuminator was gone—dead, according to Seldril, although Lerissa suspected that someone had taken her for himself. She'd have been a tasty morsel for either Landril or Gondril, and Landril had warned Lerissa off viciously enough, but she could not imagine either of them working against Seldril this close to the hein-na-fhin. She had the unsettling thought that Worilke might have spirited the illuminator away in case Lerissa Illuminator betrayed her, but that wasn't Worilke's style—she dealt directly with threats. That left Naeve's triad. But what could they possibly have made of her? Worilke had had some dealing with Vonche, she knew that much—Worilke had done him some service, to come by the codices she pored over, the dusty old accounts of Galandra's life, as if Galandra, dead these long ages, could possibly have any importance. What could Naeve's triad have wanted with the girl's bright light?

Her father would have known. She had needed him, these last years. She had wished often for his death if she could not have his approval, but when death came it robbed her of her best advisor. He had taught her that light and power were the only things that mattered. He had pledged Freyn out of ambition, and acquired the position he wanted for Lerissa in turn: Ennead illuminator, replacing Worilke's father when he passed, as Freyn replaced Worilke's mother. How could such a man have loved the light-less, common woman who bore her? He had spoken of her only once. "She was beautiful, your mother," he'd said, drunk and maudlin and guilt-ridden, the day Lerissa took the triskele. "Lessa was sweetness itself, the most gentle of women. You are the image of her, Lerissa. . . ." He'd reached out to her, and it was terrifying, her stern, rigorous father acting the lovelorn fool, she could not endure it. She'd smacked his hand away in revulsion. "Recall your position, Rigael!" she'd snapped, and left him sobbing, broken. The next day she'd found him in his bed, colder and stiffer in death than he'd been in life. Dead of a cracked heart, when she'd never known he had a heart at all.

She'd ascended to the Ennead, and he had not been there to see it. She would rule all Eiden Myr, and he would not be there to congratulate her.

Bloody fool. She could have used him.

A knock at the outer door startled her. She checked that Loris's chamber was locked, then received her visitor. "Bofric," she said with some surprise. "You were not to come to me here."

"It may be important, my lady," the bulb-nosed steward said.

"Enter, then, but if my triad stops by I'll have to hide you, and the image of you in my bedchamber is not one I wish to entertain so close on suppertime."

He took her gibes with a distracted look that told her it *was* important, then pulled from his robes a triskele-sized object wrapped in purple silk. Her eyes brightened with interest—she had taught him to use that wrapping for anything that she might potentially use in a casting. "Naeve's steward Lenn found Portriel's ring and triskele in a private chamber of Vonche's, after a search for a rebel host that has thus far failed to materialize," he said. Lenn worked with Bofric on the vocates' levels, though most stewards there were more than they seemed. Lerissa reached hungrily for the object, but he held it away—a liberty he would not have taken for a triviality. "That triskele and ring he took and presumably delivered to his mistress. But I'd contrived for one of the searchers to be my own man, and he noticed this lying discarded on the floor of the chamber. I do not know whose it is, but I am quite certain it will be of value to you."

She reached for it again, and still he held back—always hoping for some scrap of reward, some new volume to read or another lesson in one of the old tongues. "Hein-na-fhin approaches, Bofric. There'll be ample time for learning when we've established the new arrangement, yes?" Grudgingly, he surrendered it.

It was a triskele. She held it for a moment on the palm of her left hand, the silk flung back to reveal ordinary pewter tarnished by time and damp. Then she touched it lightly, in the center, with her pointing finger.

"Oh, my," she gasped after nine breaths, curling the finger away. "My, my, my."

It was Daivor's shade. When she touched the magecrafted metal, she could sense him with the clarity of casting passage. She hadn't yet lived two nineyears when he disappeared, but she remembered his rugged blond-ness, his gray-green eyes at once merry and wise, his ready smile. He'd been the most accessible member of Naeve's triad, and she hadn't understood why Naeve had pledged Vonche rather than him. She understood now. Daivor had detested Naeve's ruthlessness, Vonche had shared it. But Daivor could never resist her bed, though he always felt soiled afterward, sick and wrung-out. She had thought Daivor old, and he'd been a bound haunt for years, but his shade was that of a raging young man.

He was Evonder's father. Naeve believed Daivor hadn't known. Was he Evrael's, as well? Daivor suspected it but wasn't certain. Evrael now would be just a little younger than Daivor was when he was murdered. She wondered how he'd take the news, and whether he would share his sire's rugged vitality. But she knew how Evonder would take the news. She knew how badly Evonder would want this triskele. "I'll be in Evon-der's chambers," she said to Bofric, smiling. "Stay here and see that no one disturbs Loris."

The last stone had fit into place. Evrael was coming to add his light to hers; she had Loris tucked away, bright and eager and compliant; mad Freyn should be easy enough to manage; and now she would have Evonder on the chain of his father's triskele. That left only Worilke. Worilke was formidable, her bond to Freyn unbreakable. But Lerissa's will was stronger. Lerissa's determination had been forged by Rigael her father, and now all the stones were on her side of the table.

Two nineyears in training, three nineyears in power. All culminating in this festival of Galandra, and its balance day: the day of their birth, five nineyears ago. They prepared themselves by retreating to a dark chamber, locked away as they had so often been during the first dozen years of life. The casting materials had been prepared by subordinates and approved. The old man had bound Portriel, their parents' nemesis, the tool they had thought lost, with her own chained triskele and ring, and by locating and delivering those the old woman had delivered Portriel to them.

They meditated on the great wrong that had been done in the shadowed past, when the world conspired to extinguish all magelight. Flesh and light had grappled, and for one breath of the ages flesh had prevailed. The light had retreated to a dark chamber. But the light had matured in its cask. The light had distilled itself, through the long tunnel of years.

The light had produced them.

They were its culmination and quintessence. Balanced, edged like a fine weapon. They clasped hands; their hands were the same hands, the same flesh split into three. Their independent wills had conceived discrete imperatives, but in this act their minds were united. They would emerge from their dark chamber of one mind, one heart, one spirit, to become one flesh again.

Jeff Farrier of Gulbrid was unhappy in the casting circle that Annina Reckoner had carved into the frosted grass with a hawthorn stick; he could never arrange his thick legs comfortably on the ground, and he did not like being the subject of a casting. Torrin n'Maeryn sat cross-legged, hands draped over his knees, relaxed and centered. Facing them, Liath n'Geara hugged her shins and watched Pelkin n'Rolf accept the inscribed sedgeweave from Herne Reckoner. She had never seen her grandfather draw.

She had woken thinking she was home—that she had fallen asleep in the attic, among the old stored things. It had made sense to see Pelkin first upon leaving the tent. Sleep had taken her back years, back before her birth and her mother's, to when Pelkin was home, where he belonged, where he would be the first person that Breida n'Onofre would see upon rising.

It was not quite dawn, the gray time between night and day. All ritual castings, the most powerful castings, were done at twilight, either dawn or dusk. The gray time, the transition time, was more powerful than day or night. "In the early times," Pelkin had said, handing her a gray wool cloak, "the enneads wore only gray, a symbol of power and humility. Gray is the color of betweenness, of potential. Gray can go to either black or white."

As he went to prepare, Karanthe had handed her a cup of steaming tea and said, "I envy you. The way I've chosen, we never triad. But I've cast triads, and I know. You touch the light in a way the untriaded can never dream. Spirits bless you, Liath."

The spirits had blessed her. She had dreamed of being cast triad by her grandfather. Though the times were hard and the circumstances strange, it was nice to have one dream come true.

Pelkin's illumination was a marvel. There was a touch of the archaic to his patterning, and his tonal choice surprised her—thick, vibrant pigments, magenta against viridian, uncomplementary colors that drew strength from opposition. His borders were thick plaitwork, and he was a long time working them; they filled the edge of the leaf to three solid finger widths. Between Herne's lines were step patterns and key patterns and squared spirals, and his kadri were embedded in a triangular knotwork at the bottom, a knot like something a sailor would fashion, turning in on itself with no loose ends. Unification kadri predominated, with holding kadri, warding kadri, and augmenting kadri added at intervals that themselves formed a pattern.

It was the work of a master patterner, with no historiations at all. He had not even tried to include their likenesses in the illumination. The opening ciphers were treated as angular objects, absorbed into the design. His casting was a thing of power and manipulation, crafted to effect a result, not to reflect essences. She realized that she was looking on the Neck style of illumination for the very first time. Her teacher had trained her in the traditions of Khine. This was the technique of her homeland.

The leaf, laid between herself and Heff and Torrin, the triad within the triad, thinned and spread as the binder sang. It reached toward them, stretching into points as it sank into the ground—holy ground, Galandra's ground. This was a powerful place to be cast triad. Annina's song braided into the wind's song, the forlorn lament of this lonely headland, and made it a thing of beauty. Wind, like surf, was both changeless and ever-changing. So should magecraft be. So should each triad.

Coaxed by the bindsong, the reckoners' light merged into an unbroken circle around them—a shield meant to guard the first tenuous joining of her light with her binder's and wordsmith's. But their light had already joined, in a climactic blaze in the night. There was no vertiginous rush of insight now, only consolidation. She closed her eyes and basked in the glow of unity, Heff's meaty, blunt fingers in one hand, Torrin's long smooth hand in the other. There would be only one more joining for them, after this. That knowledge, ringing clear inside her, startled her eyes open: there had been insight after all. But not one she had expected. Torrin and Heff looked equally startled, but she would never know what they had seen. The reckoners had told them that it was traditional to keep one's casting insight to oneself—a small privacy within the intimate union.

She had smiled as Pelkin gave them the speech about compassion, thinking she knew it all already, thinking that Heff could show him a thing or two about compassion. But she did not know it all. She rose chastened from the casting circle.

· · ·

"Dabrena and Tolivar named a child for you."

Karanthe laughed. "I'm not dead yet! Or a great-gran—" She pulled up when she saw that Liath wasn't smiling, and her own expression flattened into a proxy's neutrality. "Tell me the rest."

"He's gone."

"How?" When no answer came, she drew breath deeply and looked away. "No. Better not to know."

Liath had meant to give the account like a reckoner, in a calm, clear voice, but she found herself saying, "I tried to cast passage for him. The only way I could. It was too late, I think, but . . . The bonefolk came. I dreamed it, but I think it was true. They came and . . . and made him into light . . ." She realized she was crying when she heard the stammering echo of her own words and felt Karanthe's arms go around her. Karanthe was crying too.

They would be a lifetime grieving sweet, wicked Tolivar, and all he should have been.

"The tavern burned."

Pelkin went still, and stared into the pale flames of the fire the reckoners had tended through the night and all the day, for warmth and cheer, for balance. "We are all wanderers now."

"Why did they call it the Petrel's Rest?" she asked. "Do you know? A petrel is a seabird. Clondel is landlocked."

"The storm petrel, yes. As Breida told it, it was a bird blown inland on one of the Great Storms. The Ennead must not have split the storm high enough, and it came down over the Aralinns. It was nesting season, and the bird was half dead, exhausted and storm-battered. They had only just built the tavern, a little one-story cottage, and the chimney made a nice warm spot for a nest. In a few moons the birds were gone, flown back to the Sea of Storms. But their brief visit was remembered in the name of the place."

"There's an island off the Hand," she said quietly. "A tiny spit of a place, it's where I was going when you saw me getting into that coracle. The Isle of Senana. There are three mages there who should be cast triad. Reckoners haven't gone there in a long time. If you could . . . when this is over . . ."

The inexplicable sadness crossed his face again. "I'll go there," he said. "It must be quite a place."

"It's the people who make a place," she said. He understood that she meant Clondel, and their family. Wherever their folk were was home. No matter how many buildings burned to the ground, no matter how far they strayed, there would always be a place for them—safe haven from the storm.

• • •

As she sat watching the death of the day, Torrin sat beside her at the cliff's edge, stretching his long limbs with relish. A roil of black clouds had risen from the Sea of Sorrows and was crossing toward the Dreaming Sea. "Is it a Great Storm?" she said.

"Not yet, I don't think. But I have never been able to read the sky. Or the sea." He drew from his battered pack the bound volume he always kept with him. "I wanted to show you this, before the light went."

She took it gingerly. The velvet binding was stained and dented, though he kept it wrapped in waxed canvas.

"It's the private book of a little mage girl named Luriel. Her thoughts and dreams, her love for a scribe who was too old for her. It is addressed to him—a song of love and binding. No one thought it was important, scribed before the sundering and exile. But it explains a great deal. Luriel was Galandra's daughter."

Liath examined the first leaf. The words of a living girl speaking across the ages. Her hands had touched this parchment, her tears had fallen on it, there and there. "I wish I could read it," she said.

"Someday you will."

"Did she live? Or did someone else bring this over?"

"Both," Torrin said. "She left this behind for the scribe to look after. They could not carry all the codices, in the last rush to escape. Scribes then were not always mages; some were slaves, keeping records for the powerful. He meant to preserve the abandoned codices. But in the end he followed the mages. This is his scribing, here, on the back of the last leaf. He was frightened, trying to scribe quickly. It is the wrong side, rough under a quill, and the glyphs are the Ghardic of his day, not a system used in magecraft. It took me years to make sense of it. But the other scribing, there, the brief annotation below his words—a mage scribed that, a mage we'll never know. A woman whose life he saved. She says he died in the breaking of the Serpentback, preserving that last sackful of codices. This volume was among them. It appears that it never found its way back to Luriel. But from the words that fill this volume, from Luriel's own story, we know who she was: the mage who would never forgive what was done to the mages in Ollorawn."

"Galandra's daughter . . ."

"Her father, a soldier turned pacifist mage, had been murdered in front of her. Her family lived in terror of the purges. From what the scribe says, she fled the city as her home was about to burn. She would not have been the only one to bring rage with her into exile. But hers was so intense that it survived the ages. The result of it is Landril and Gondril and Seldril, descendants of her line, magecrafted children bred to vengeance. Because of a little girl so badly hurt that she could not forgive."

"If they're descendants of her line, then they're descendants of Galandra."

"Yes. We are all one, in the end."

Liath touched the parchment edge. It was hard as the nail on her finger. She turned it to reveal the next leaf. Time had faded the colors, but the girl's work was lovely. She seemed to be an accomplished scribe, her ciphers even and flowing and sure. Her drawings were simple but nicely balanced. "How did you come by this?" she asked, though she already knew.

"It was the codex I was copying when Evonder tattled on me. The volume I stole and hid in my chamber."

"Thank you for showing me," she said.

"I thought you would like it."

"No. You wanted me to see it. You don't know what I like, or don't like. You don't know me at all." When he had sat down, she had still been thinking of Pelkin, of what happened in Clondel, of all the places she had been. Torrin did not know about Roiden, or Hanla, or Keiler or Graefel or the vocates or the stewards, none of it. Her story was as unreadable to him as Luriel's was to her.

"I've seen through your eyes," he said. "In the joining."

"It's not the same. I saw through yours too. And Heff's. And I hardly remember what I saw, only that I saw it."

"It remains inside you nonetheless."

"That's not enough." Her voice broke. "There isn't time. Who are you, Torrin? Who have you loved, what have you seen, what kind of life did you lead for three nineyears and five?"

"I have loved you." He lifted a hand to touch her hair, then let it fall. "It was unwise of me."

What was it that stopped him? It could only be that when he reached for her light, he came up against the barrier of her flesh and her self. "You love my light, just like the rest of them, from that journeyer to Tolivar to Evonder. Even Heff, the bloody hypocrite. You know nothing about me. Perhaps there's nothing to know. A publican from the Neck. I haven't lived long enough to count, yet. A child, you said. You were right. Yet in this last year, the things I've seen, and learned . . . Every moment of it mattered. Every person I touched was a *world*. I barely knew it. I wish I could do it again, knowing that, knowing what to look for. What to savor. I want to tell you, Torrin. I want you to know. I want to see you understand. But a lifetime would not be enough."

"No," he agreed softly. He pulled his pack over and said, "But look at this." He drew out another volume, unwrapping it and handing it to her before he took back Luriel's codex. This one was bound in wood, deeply graven with a pattern of leaves and florets. She had never seen patterning on wood. It added dimension, but it was so blasphemous that she could hardly bring herself to touch it.

"Open it," he said, rewrapping the velvet-bound volume and returning it to his pack. "It is a window on another world."

She lifted the wooden panel, turned it on iron hinges to reveal the first leaf bound inside, and drew her breath in sharply.

The likenesses of men and women, garbed in a rich complexity of fabric and ornament, gathered around the severe angularity of glyphs. They were captured in daily tasks, but with a vividness and detail that rendered the ordinary beautiful. Circlets around their heads, their arms, their ankles were pressed in gold. Their expressions and gestures were animated— alive on the flat parchment. Every creamy fold of satin, every crinkle of linen was reproduced, light and shadow used so expertly to simulate depth that she felt distance, not dimension, made them small: if her arm were long enough, she could reach through the leaf and mold her hand to any object and find it whole. Droplets of condensation glistened on a jug of water; a highlight in the eye of a woman's face reflected the window near where she sat knitting.

The following leaves showed other places, other activities, richer clothes, finer surroundings.

"That is what Ollorawn looked like, at its height."

Another world. Yet what amazed her was not the glimpse of a time and place she could never visit. It was the craft. Each leaf represented a nineday's effort, or more.

"I could never do work like this," she said. "No illuminator I know could do work like this."

"Of course you could, given time and materials. This is what our craft can be. This and so much more."

Yet what was the point? It lay static, affecting nothing, changing nothing. What was the use of leaves that could not heal, or ward? Their power was real—the power to remember, the power to record. Their beauty went beyond words. But compared with magelight, compared with the power of a casting, all their gilded patterns and paints were as flat and dull as a pewter flagon.

"It is such a world as you describe," he said. "There is a lifetime preserved in those leaves. A mind, and a soul, and a heart, burning as bright now in that pigment and ink and gilding as ever a magelight did in a living mage."

"I wouldn't trade magecraft for this," she said.

He did not reply. He was staring at the sea, at the curtain of night the sun's setting behind them drew up over the horizon toward them. She pulled her cloak tighter, though the air was no colder than it had been. "Why don't you tell me what you plan to do, Torrin. You have your triad now. The Nine will strike at noon tomorrow, the balance of the balance day. I can't scribe a message to tie to some bird's leg and send off to them to betray you."

He rewrapped the book and stowed it, then settled the pack between his legs. "Will it never be 'we' for you, Illuminator? Always 'you' and 'they'?"

She drew breath for a caustic rejoinder, but his mouth silenced her—his thin, curved lips cool and dry, yet seeming to burn where they touched hers. She went very still, then opened her mouth, sought his tongue, but he drew back and pressed a finger to her lips. "You will regret it, after what I'm going to tell you. Best not."

She waited. If one last revelation was all that separated them, she would endure it, whatever it was, and have done with it.

"I cannot break the warding. You and Heff and I together could not break the warding. Only the triplets, enhanced by darkcraft and supported by Worilke's triad and Naeve's, have the power. That is not how they plan to use it; they plan to work through the warding. But once they meld into hein-na-fhin, the one-of-three, they become a weapon. A tool. An arrow, long sharpened, fletched by two triads. The trick is to aim the arrow. Once it's been let fly, we three will deflect it into the warding."

"That wasn't so hard," she said, watching his lips. Twice she had felt them against hers, and it was not enough. Now nothing stood between them . . . "See? I'm not even angry at you, now that you've told me."

"How will that put an end on darkcraft?" he asked, with the persistent, leading patience of the teacher.

She frowned. She was not a pupil any longer. "Gondril's triad will be destroyed."

"Perhaps. But the others will remain."

"Verlein will kill them—"

"Is that what you want? Is that why you raised your blade to me in salute, each day in the Blooded Mountains?"

I want you, just you, can't you shut up and understand that? "No, of course not, but . . ."

"Breaking Galandra's warding will put an end on magecraft."

Muddled with longing, insulted by his pedantry, she could not make sense of what he'd said.

"It will stun the magelight dark, in all of us. Not a sealing. A burning-out. There will be no more magelight when this is done."

Betrayal jabbed her. "You said that teaching scribing wouldn't undermine the craft."

"The craft is the craft. But the light will go out when the warding breaks."

Without magelight, the craft was only scribing, only painting. What would she be without her light? She would go mad, like Portriel, like Roiden. Yet they had never been without their light. The light had always been there. It was denial of its use that drove mages mad. If there was no light at all . . .

"That's—absurd," she said. "That's killing a man with a sore to stop it festering."

"The darkcraft this Ennead has unleashed can never be put safely away again. Verlein could slaughter every living creature in the Holding, and somewhere there would still be someone to plant the seed of it again."

"Then we'll keep fighting it." She was reeling as if from a blow, the sting of it only beginning to reach her conscious mind. "We'll reinstate the Triennead. We'll reconfirm the rule of compassion. We'll stop using vellum, and parchment, and tallow, just sedgeweave and— You can't . . . you can't just . . ." Words failed her, again. She groaned. Why couldn't she make him see what she was seeing? "There are ways. We'll make a way."

"It would have happened anyway. The magelight is dying. Worilke's breeding schemes have done nothing but weaken good bloodlines. It would have happened in a nonned years, or a—"

"Then let us have those nonned years! Spirits, are you daft, to think I would help you do such a thing? What will ward us? What will heal us? Magelight is . . ."

"Everything? What did you say to me, not three ninebreaths past? That all I wanted was your light?"

"You can't do this. I won't do this."

"Then darkcraft cannot be stopped. It will destroy the world outside us, and our own world will sink into oblivion as the magelight fails within the warding. Break the warding, and we have a chance to live by our wits and our skills. Leave the warding intact, and eventually there will be no mages to divert the Great Storms any longer. What's left of us will be swept away, and Eiden Myr will return to wasteland."

It was a game of would-you. But the only child who ever won a would-you match was the one keen enough or brave enough to say, *I would do neither*.

"In the meantime, your nonned years would be spent in a vain attempt to block mages from the most powerful use of their craft. Somewhere there would always be suffering, somewhere there would always be cruelty. It could be a very unpleasant nonned years. Is that what you wish for Eiden Myr?"

"You'll be coring and sealing an entire world."

"It's already sealed. We have been living inside Eiden's light. But we can do so no longer."

"You can't make this decision."

"No. But we can."

"Heff won't . . ." She stopped herself. Would he?

Some things can be seen clearest only in the dark.

"Heff will," Torrin said. "Despite his opinion of magecraft, he resisted; but in triading us he agreed to do what must be done. We spoke of it at great length in Gulbrid. Heff is the only one who has known, all along, what I planned to do."

The world was an onion, and each layer peeled back revealed another, and another, until there was only a pile of peelings that made you cry.

"How can you know what breaking Galandra's shield will do?"

He tapped the pack between his knees. "I read it. When you can read, you will read it too."

It was completely dark now, night fallen in thick layers that the unceasing wind could not shift. Behind them, the fighters and proxies were burning all the fuel they had gathered, in a festival bonfire, to keep the night and the fear at bay. Until the fuel ran out. It cast their shadows off the edge of the cliff, into nothing.

"They found darkcraft in those codices, didn't they," she said. "That's why they were sealed up. Because they were dangerous."

"Perhaps." He pulled in closer to himself. "But the codices were unsealed in Vonche's lifetime, and the craft of pain was practiced long before that. You cannot place the blame there."

"You're a breaker of worlds. You, and them. All of you. You justify in words everything you do, but in the end it's all destruction. We've lived in peace. We never killed each other, we never hurt things."

"We killed, no matter how kindly. Now we have blades. And darkcraft."

"We always had blades. We just used them properly. We can use magecraft properly."

"Can we? A blade confers limited power. Darkcraft—bloodcraft, paincraft—offers unlimited power. We might forget the use of longblades again, if left to ourselves. But the potential of anguish has only barely been tapped. If we do not stop it now, think what it will grow into. Don't you remember the dazzling exhilaration of your first casting? *With this power, we might do anything!*"

"We could heal the very spirit of Eiden Myr, should it ever fall ill." It had been only a year ago. She remembered very well.

"It has fallen gravely ill, and we must heal it."

"By amputation!"

"We can live without magelight. As long as there is magelight to actuate it, the craft of pain will be irresistible. Galandra's vision was very beautiful, the foundation she built was strong. But Luriel's pain was stronger. What choice do we have? What else can we do? Tell me, and we'll do it."

He had turned her after all. The Ennead was right. His tongue was silvered, but with truth, and truth had a taste so bitter she would rather have swallowed lies.

"I only wanted a kiss," she said, so softly that the wind took the words away.

"I wanted a good deal more than that," he replied, reading her lips. "But the next kiss would be three, and that would promise you a lifetime."

"No." She got to her knees, planted one foot on the ground. "I don't plan on dying tomorrow. I won't put an end on magecraft and then conveniently evade the consequences."

"Yet in a moment you will stalk off and leave me here on the precipice because our conversation has become inconvenient."

She hesitated. "I saw it, this morning. That we would only cast to-gether once. I didn't like it. I don't accept it."

"You're not supposed to tell me what you saw," he said, trying a smile. Then, as she sat again, "All right. You don't accept it. Yet you have spent the day saying farewell."

She was not fool enough to think they would not be risking their lives. But she understood Pelkin's sad looks now. *Good on you, pet,* he'd said once. *Never agree to a trade until it's clear.* In triading with them, in agreeing to this plan whose cost she hadn't known, she had committed her life to the end of their craft. And Pelkin had known it would be her death.

"Kazhe will go spare," she said randomly, helplessly.

"Kazhe will have her hands full as the self-appointed bodyguard of Eiden Myr. And as you say, perhaps it won't come to that. We make a strong triad. Perhaps we will be strong enough."

They sat for a long while in silence. Waves pounded the rocks below them, flinging spray into the firelight. In her mind she saw the Petrel's Rest, her family's home for generations, collapsing in flames. Beside her sat a stranger, a lean dark man with eyes of light, clutching a battered pack full of words. Was he the fire, or the warding that should not be permitted to fail?

"I'm a child of harvestmid," he said.

It was an offering.

"I was born at harvestmid," she replied. "Toward the middle, after the leaves had turned but before they fell."

"I came a little later than that. The leaves were drifted in banks and colored the ground, and the trees were bare and wet and the wind was chill. A gusty, stormy time of year. My mother was a creature of storm. It must have suited her."

"What was she like?"

"What little I remember is not worth the breath it would take to tell you."

"You're doing it again. How can you be so passionate about the for-gotten history of Eiden Myr and have no interest in the worlds of history carried by every living person?"

"It is not theirs I have no interest in," he said. "My adult life has been an attempt to redeem the past with the present. The world of history inside me is not a world I want to visit. It is a black rock veined with terror and cruelty."

"It made you who you are."

On a bitter laugh, he said, "Yes. A flawed, weary man who has erred grievously, so frightened of what he will lose that he cannot bear to have it at all." He rose and stepped away from the cliff, slinging his pack as if for a long journey. "Sweet dreams, Illuminator. I wish you had found the man you sought."

Supper was in the making, on a cookfire Benkana had built, fresh goat's-milk-and-mushroom soup to make up for the travel rations they'd been living on. Heff and Pelkin left her to her musings, but Kazhe, flushed with drink, came over as she was rinsing her bowl to stack it on the rest.

"Leave me alone, Kazhe," she said, scrubbing at a stubborn gob of soup. "We both only ever tried to keep what we loved alive. For you it was a man, for me it was a way of life. There's no difference between us now."

"He's a fool," Kazhe said.

"Yes," Liath replied, drying her hands. "He is that."

"But you're not."

Liath looked up into the flat face. It might have been pretty once, pert, before the nose was broken and rebroken, never healed by magecraft, before hard drink and hard drilling and watchful nights had hollowed the eyes. Liath rose as Heff came over, and laid a hand on his arm. No more fighting. Not tonight.

Kazhe held her eyes a moment longer, then nodded and went off with Benkana's arm around her, leaning wearily into his side. She had guarded Torrin for a long time.

His tent was dark, the lantern's flame blown out, but his amber eyes caught the firelight like an animal's, betraying his presence. He stood at the tent flap, a shadow within shadow, like a haunt of himself. Watching to see that she returned safe to the tent she shared with Heff; brooding on what might have been.

Drumbeats had started, on logs, on cups and bowls, a slow rhythmic paean to Galandra. It was a somber sound, but it grew in complexity as counterrhythms wove in and out, making pattern of the air itself. There would be no dancing this night. Only the drums, and the flames, and the darkness beyond the firelight, and what camaraderie they could find within it.

"Good night, Heff," she said softly, and walked back past the fire, past the tense fighters and reckoners joking and tale-telling to stretch the night out, past Karanthe and her grandfather sitting close and speaking in low tones; past Boroel, who would wait and watch until morning, his longblade his only companion.

He was no longer at the entry when she got there. The ties had been repaired, but not fastened from within. She went through.

"It's the end of the world," she said into the darkness.

"Yes. The end of the world we knew."

. . .

At first he would not yield to her, only tolerating her lips, her hands; then he lifted her as if she weighed nothing, swung her around and low-ered her onto the pallet. The aired blankets smelled of forest and winter; his mouth tasted of spiced wine, some last indulgence before the end. His mage's hands were deft, removing her clothes as he kissed the corners of her mouth and the pulse at her throat, unfastening his trousers; she had barely opened his linen shirt when he entered her, in one silken move-ment. The darkness burst instantly into glittering splendor, and she muffled her voice in his shoulder, sobbing half with relief and half with terror that this was all she would have of him, this quick bright moment; but he did not withdraw, he had held back his release, and her cries were drowned out by the drumbeats. They were alone within the sound, within the canvas walls lapped by firelight. He thrust gently, speaking low in her ear, his breath hot; he stroked her, prompted her, and this time when the spasms started he drove his head down and cried out her name, as if that were as much release as the one that convulsed his body.

After a moment he shifted aside, making even withdrawal a prolonged caress, and gathered a loose fold of blanket around her. The arm underneath held her close, but with some care, as if it was something he was unac-customed to. Their triskeles had tangled on their chains. He ran a finger lightly around her neck to free hers, and she shivered and reached to feel for herself: the knotted chain was whole. As was his, where she had knotted it around his neck while he lay ill. "They heal themselves," he said quietly. "I don't know what it means."

She laid her casting hand over the fine, dark hair on his chest, and felt him breathe, felt his pounding heartbeat slow.

He covered her hand with his, moved it to his cheek; turned to kiss the palm, eyes shutting. She imagined she could see their fierce glow through the pale lids, like the firelight through the tent wall.

"You asked who I am," he said into her hand. "I couldn't answer." He opened his eyes, turned the golden stare on her. "I don't know who I am, Liath, not really, not anymore, after all the years of—purpose, of single-mindedness. Someone who would very much like to be brave for you. To live for you."

"Then that's who you are, and that's what you'll do," she said, and after that there were no words for a long time, until long after the drum-beats had died and those who could find sleep had done so. She had drifted off to the sounds of sorrow and celebration for nearly her whole life. Now sleep was a thief that would rob her of him, and she fought it like a small death. These were arms she would have called home, in a safer time. Dreams were no match for what she had found here.

"You are exhausted, love," he said softly, "and so am I."

"It's not enough," she protested, and his practiced, accommodating hands drew her to him again, filled her with him, rocking her with a deep intensity. He probed her mouth, swallowing her cry when it came, then broke away, threw his head back and groaned raggedly into the dark air. She clutched his hips as his climax pulled another from her. She was still thrusting at him when his hands stilled her. It was not enough. It would never be enough.

Dazed with repletion and weariness, she let him turn her, pull her into the curve of his body, cover them both warmly enough for sleep. He embraced her with a hunger he seemed to be trying to comprehend, holding her tight against him in the darkness, fitting her rump to his groin, finding a comfortable way to twine his legs with hers. His cheek rested against her hair. It came to her drowsily that for all his skill, he had never slept with another person. No brother or sister warm and mumbling beside him; no vocates sprawled together; no lover he'd been willing to entrust his nights to. One hand lay under her thigh, curving to its shape; she clasped the other between her breasts. *I won't let you let go.*

The voice he had used to arouse her murmured soft against her ear. "I fear I am only the breaker of worlds, now. But what I've felt for you . . ." He pressed his face close, breathing in the scent of her hair. "Perhaps there is still something of me left. If there is, my love, I give it into your keeping."

The words merged into her dreams, and she dreamed of him, and when she roused, and roused again, the dream was still true, until she slept deeply, believing it; she woke at last to find the pallet still warm but newly empty, and his clothes gone from where he'd flung them, and full light glaring harsh against the canvas walls.

In her sleep, she had let go.

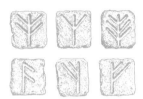

The balance day of Ve Galandra dawned invisible outside the walls of the Ennead's Holding. Veins of memory stone glowed softly as six mages filed into the presence chamber and turned to receive the ones who would be cast hein-na-fhin this day.

Great powers are assembled here, Lerissa thought with satisfaction. A fitting inauguration of her new reign.

Freyn moved with Evonder to present the casting materials to Seldril, the binder bound for hein-na-fhin, the one-of-three. She smiled as she chalked her arc of the casting circle and joined it to theirs. Lines, it was all lines to them, lines on stone and lines on vellum and lines of descent. A line was such a thin thing, to hang a life on.

Worilke watched with some concern as the layered, trebled casting began with the first touch of Gondril's quill to vellum. She had brought stone crashing down on a flowered plateau to disperse a human storm, but in her bones she felt the gathering of another storm, a Great Storm. Her triad was the weather triad. What if she had to choose?

They look serene, Evonder thought, watching Landril take the inscribed vellum from Gondril and illuminate the foundation. *And my mother and Vonche look newly pledged, betrayal the resin that binds them.* He could not defeat that combination. The other binders would make up for any intentional shoddiness in his craft. He was still reeling from what Lerissa's trinket had revealed to him. She wore it around her neck, a second triskele, a mockery, just as Landril wore Portriel's. Accompanied and supported by the shades of their dead. Who would have imagined that Vonche would manage to bind a spirit whose flesh was gone? He had trapped the spirits of the dying, tethering them to the flesh that Freyn's potions kept viable; it was not so great a leap from that casting to one in which the spirit was tethered to another form of matter. But binding the unpassaged . . . He felt a shameful stab of eagerness at the notion. They could cast passage for them after all—collect their haunts in objects or containers, then cast on those and send them on. If only the collecting did not require a death. Oh, seductive darkcraft. He had fought its temptations all his life. He must fight them just a little longer.

On behalf of her balance triad, Naeve accepted the vellum as Seldril's rasping song trailed off, binding her triad into the casting, leaving them free to act. She would have to watch them closely, gauging her moment. Vonche would go ahead of her, and no doubt try to block her entry, but better to let him test the waters of eternity. She planned to take her body with her; his was disposable. She inscribed her section with care, following the instructions Vonche had unearthed, following the structure of Gondril's scribing. Then she passed the leaf to her illuminator.

Vonche reveled in the swell of power in the chamber, the magestone illuminating the rock itself, absorbing and reflecting their light. He painted light itself into the leaf, twining quicksilver in echo of the dark knotwork Landril had filled his corner with. His was the balance triad; this was a balance day. Already he could feel this world balancing against the next. He passed the leaf to his son and binder. The boy sang well; his bindings were always too sweet, too melodic, but here they were the ideal complement to Seldril's coarse, dark song. The balance triad had done their part. Just three mages left between himself and eternal insight. Worilke frowned as if plagued by some private concern, and Vonche frowned, too, fearing her distracted; but the light continued to swell as Lerissa received the leaf and filled the last blank spaces with her characteristic lush swirls and jewel-like ornaments. *Yes, oh yes,* he thought as Freyn's eerie song filled the chamber and the triplets rose as one to move into the center of the circle. *This is it . . . it will happen now . . .*

The balance triad and the weather triad watched in awe as the leading triad crossed arms before themselves and clasped hands in an unbroken link of flesh and light. They circled slowly at first, then faster, like dancers in a set, though the throb of pulses was the only drumbeat. Faster, then faster still, bodies canted out, a picture of tension in release. They became a blur of light and motion, each indistinguishable from the next, until the light was so bright the six mages had to squint against it. It filled the chamber, then contracted abruptly into a pillar of radiance.

The weather triad and the balance triad gasped. As one, uncoached, compelled by echoes of traditions instilled from childhood, they breathed, "And three become one."

The membrane between the worlds parted, and the joined triad was transported into light.

I see. I see. I see it all, I understand . . . I can see forever . . .

Incredible! The energy, the vitality, the power! I will live forever!

Just a few more moments, now, and they will begin to feel it. Oh, my sweet lover, what a marvel we have wrought! All their light, all their lineage cannot save them now!

Sweet spirits—they have entirely merged. Who would have thought it could actually be done? Astonishing. But I wonder how long this bloody thing will take. I have a realm to inherit, and I'd like to get started.

She's there. I can feel her. On the other side of the light. I have only to reach in, and I will touch the very face of Galandra . . .

I failed you, Torrin. I failed to stop this. Forgive me, my old friend.

We . . .

are . . .

one.

he end came to her in images, in shapes.

Torrin Wordsmith at the precipice, head flung back, arms spread, leaning into the wind with hair and cloak streaming behind him. The sky a rage of chartreuse and charcoal and the angry purple of a bruise; the sea boiling white below. Heff on one knee, three fingertips on the first stirrings of sowmid in the hard ground, eye shut. Their triad, a tight ring within the ring of reckoners inside the ring of fighters. Local mages who had arrived during the night, huddling by their mounts, well back—Ailanna and her triad, the phlegmatic mage who claimed he could talk to haunts, the prenticemonger with melting smile and emerald eyes. Beyond them, up the slope, at the edge of bare trees just fuzzing green, the spindly figures of bonefolk, waiting. The wind whipped their tatters; the storm sky lit their parchment flesh a glaucous white.

Someone would die here.

She had traveled the length and breadth of Eiden Myr in her journey year, traveling backward into the past. History had been illuminated, as by a torch carried ever deeper into a cave. Her own past. Graefel and Hanla's. Her mother's. The Holding's. The past of Eiden Myr itself. Every motion had a consequence, every life was a world. The past settled like yeast; you drank the ale, but what you tasted was the story of its making.

How bitter to die with so much only just discovered.

Jhoss handed Heff a bindsack and stepped back. He had been all night preparing the materials, with the proxy binders. He had been a beekeeper, before he met and followed Torrin. Like Heff, he was a new kind of bindsman, bringing other talents and other lore into the craft that had sustained them for twice nine nonned years.

They knew, now, that that was how long it had been. When she'd come out at daybreak, she'd found Torrin at a cairn of solstice stones that Heff had discovered, back toward the woods. The stones were mossy, undisturbed for long years, but a mound of earth behind them sported only a year's growth. Heff was the one who began digging. Soon all three of them were sifting through the damp earth, hands closing on stone after stone, unable to stop although they did not know what they had found. When the hole was deeper than the cairn was high and they were still finding the buried stones, a voice had stopped them. They'd looked up as one.

"Archis," Liath had said, amazed to see the wizened old woman. With her was a child of perhaps six, with large eyes of velvet black, a cap of raven hair, and the shy beginnings of a magelight. "Archis the spider-keep."

"Archis the stonekeep," she'd said. "No need to dig them all up. Too much trouble to put them back. My folk have tended this cache since the beginning. A stone for every year, lest we forget, though I no longer know what it is we were supposed to remember. But I'm a fosterling. Perhaps it's not in my blood." She'd laid her hand on the child's dark head. "I'm glad it's been discovered. This one's just shown a light. My grand-daughter. She would have tended it, when I'm gone. Now she'll prentice to mages."

"How many are there?" Torrin had asked.

"Twice nine nonned, less one. We came here to add the one." She'd gestured to the child, who displayed it on the palm of her hand. A stone like the others: green marble, smoothed and rounded as by a river, with three circles graven deep, each within the next. "These are Galandra's stones. This is where Galandra began, twice nine nonned years ago. Now you are here. I suppose that means the end has come."

"It must be a deep hole." Torrin had bestowed on her one of his rare, dazzling smiles—avoiding the question. "Twice nine nonned is a lot of stones."

"Indeed it is," she said. "A weight of stones. A weight of years. Will we start a new pile, now?"

"If you like," he'd said, rising. "But put that last one in, before we seal the hole up again. The year is gone."

"And quite a year it was," she said, taking the carven rock from her granddaughter and kneeling with difficulty to lay it atop the others. "That's my job done. Someone else will have to tend the new."

Torrin had looked long on the pale, dark-haired child, as if he might have known her. "Perhaps it will be this one, after all."

They had returned to the swatch of rocky grass that would be their casting ground, and Liath had tried not to think about the little girl whose light would be extinguished just as it began to shine.

There was no telling the moment of noon, or when the Ennead would make its own approximation of it. They sat on the circle Heff had awkwardly delved in the grass. Liath centered herself, preparing for the guiders. Heff weighted sedgeweave down with an ordinary rock, set out pigment pots, arranged quills and reeds easy to hand within the windshelter of the bindsack. He worked frowning, surprised at how easily it came to him, not liking it.

An arrow pierced the sedgeweave as if it had sprouted from the hallowed earth.

Heff moved to shield Liath as Torrin twisted to see the arrow's source. There was a twang from somewhere in the thin ranks of fighters, and a distant cry from the wooded hill. Kazhe was already halfway there, her longblade drawn. She came back leading the brown horse with a white leg which Jonnula's fleeing accomplice had ridden. A man lay over the blood-smeared saddle, dead arms swinging. Kazhe hauled the body down to flop at Benkana's feet. The arrow was lodged in the ribs, shaft broken off; Kazhe's blade had left a hole in the heart.

"Good shot," she said. "But he was still alive."

"Are there more where he came from?"

"It doesn't look like it."

"We'll post sentries higher up, to be sure."

Liath recognized the man, though it took her a moment to remember why; he'd been one of the Ennead's aides, a Khinishman like Bron, the steward who'd put Amaranth's reins in her hand the morning she left on her quest to find Torrin.

The strands of the world, interweaving like knotwork.

Pelkin no longer trusted in the fighters to shield them. He set his reckoners in a semicircle around the outcropping. The warding they cast shimmered like a heat mirage, unaffected by the buffeting wind. Within it the air went still, warming with the heat of their bodies.

They were alone, now, to do what they must.

Heff handed a fresh leaf of sedgeweave to Torrin. Perhaps vellum would have been better, or parchment, but Heff would work with neither, and that must be part of it, that his preferences would choose the right materials for them. This was a casting of spirit, not of flesh. Sedgeweave *was* the correct material.

Torrin spoke while he scribed. The words were foreign; they had the shape of Mellas's nightspeech but the structure of Torrin's intellect. He could only be guessing at how the words he scribed should sound. No one had spoken these languages since the earliest times. His scribing was like nothing she had ever seen, the glyphs unfamiliar, curled in on themselves in ornate swirls. He was drawing on some memory of magecraft immensely old, some system of glyphs culled from years poring over the old codices. Copying them, steeping in them, until their lore and languages suffused his mind. Bringing them out, now, from the silence of ages, from the darkness of the ancient cave into the light of the present.

She was awed and humbled, watching him. She was a child again, in the company of a master. *Pelkin should have been his illuminator,* she thought. *I cannot match this level of craft.* But Pelkin's craft was the epitome of the old. She was charged with the creation of something new. Something so strong and certain that it would have the power to deflect apocalypse.

Torrin handed her the leaf.

She felt them coming. Torrin's scribing had opened a link to their own casting. "Is there time?" she said. It couldn't be noon yet. What she sensed had to be their preparation. Such a casting as theirs would take time to gather itself.

Torrin said, "I don't know."

She chose a slim length of bonewood from the selection Heff offered. She dipped its sanded point in a mixture of copper water, catsclaw sap, the wounds that birthing wasps inflict on oak. She inked the outlines of knots and weaves. The One-of-Three was a shimmer at the edge of vision, as if space itself were a penetrable weave of air and belief. She did not look up. The triangle of flexible sedgeweave became her field of vision, and on it, subsuming and augmenting the glyphs of power her wordsmith had inscribed, she created a world.

It was the world as it should have been. It was Tolivar's world, where believing in the best was enough to make it so. It was Heff's world, where kindness was all. It was a world of light, of peace, of simplicity. It was the Eiden Myr of her childhood, before she learned that the safety of home is not enough and is not forever. She twined it in the drowsy, intricate foliage of dreams, and locked it into place with a three-strand knotwork border, interlaced left-handed on the right, right-handed on the left. Among the blocks of glyphs, an exuberant riot of twists and spirals. She historiated the initials with memory and wishes.

She drew a stick of charcoal from the bindsack, another tool new to her, and began the task of shadows. Shadow imparted depth; shadow implied substance. Shadows were a thing of power. Gondril's triad were creatures of darkness, and they had put into her such darkness as would make mountains malleable in her hands. Her bright light cast shadows profoundly dark. But after charcoal came chalk, and highlights: the surge of hope, the spike of courage, the glint of dauntless determination in an eye harrowed by grief. She had not realized she had drawn a face, in the center of the leaf, or even that Torrin had left room for one, his glyphs scribed in triangular blocks that formed a border of their own. She had drawn a woman, strong of cheek and brow, sharp of chin, with defiance in the turn of her head but compassion in the lines of her eyes. When she took brushes and pigments from Heff at last, the hair became a mane of red curls, the eyes the green of a sky about to storm.

Evonder had Galandra's eyes.

She filled the knotwork, the ornaments, the leaves and blossoms in the foliage, with malachite and viridian and cerulean and vermilion and saffron, the vibrant colors of life that returned year after year, no matter how harsh the winters. She brought the historiations to vivid life. The world was color. Life was color. The emotions swelling in her were all roiling, raging color. She was in love, she was in mourning, she was afraid; she was exulting in her craft. And she was brave. Eiden Myr was brave. Eiden Myr would be brave enough to go on. Together, they would face the end of the world, and begin a new one.

She added the intensity of kadri almost as an afterthought. She tucked Integrity here, Empathy there, put transformation and material kadri around the face; she drew a string of increase kadri at the bottom, linked augmenting and warding kadri up the sides like chains to hold the casting fast. At the top she placed Endurance.

What she had done was unassailable. It was the culmination of a lifetime; it was the greatest and the last illumination she would ever do. She laid the leaf in the center of the casting circle, laid the memory of Galandra on Galandra's ground, and raised her eyes in triumph to her wordsmith and her bindsman.

They took her hands. Past Torrin, she could see the shimmer twisting in resistance. It did not want to be drawn here. It did not want to be pulled from its path. But it could not resist what they had wrought. It could not work past them now.

Heff, at last, began to sing. It was only his earthcraft, the product of a seared, ruined throat, but it was *him*: the sound of his soul. His light had been sealed off for a lifetime, his magevoice silenced. In the vibration of the air, in the vibration through his hand, she felt all his pain and grief and abiding love. The world had harmed him grievously, but somehow he loved it still. As he sang his song of binding, which was a song of healing, the only song he knew, the leaf began to shine. Just a paleness around the edges of the glyphs and the illumination, at first; then a silvered luminescence. The patterns rose above the leaf, casting themselves in the air, formed of light. The leaf itself subsided into the ground with a sigh, but the scribing and illumination hovered before their eyes. Galandra's ghostly face, swimming in words and pattern. A picture of her mage's mind, absorbed with symbol, dedicated to rendering the world anew through this most arcane and powerful of crafts. It seemed to shudder, and split, two other faces forming behind it, then becoming clearer as they took their places beside it. One light, one dark.

Her triad, Liath realized.

The world outside them had gone dark. Storm battered the warding the reckoners had made, black rain lashing at the shield, but it held, and within it the light of Galandra's triad grew, making a bright sphere of their casting circle.

"It is a Storm," she said, as Heff's bindsong faded into echoes and was gone. "It is a Great Storm——"

"Yes," Torrin said into the charged silence. The air went opaque; she could no longer see him, only feel his hand in hers. His human hand, that had caressed her, that had bespoken love his wordsmith's lips could not speak aloud. Her bindsman's hand was slipping away, and she groped to retrieve it, in vain. Everything outside their circle would be destroyed, swept lifeless by the Storm, they should have diverted the Storm, not the Ennead, what blind fools they had been, what use in saving a world that would be wasteland——

"Don't let go," Torrin snapped. Her hand tightened reflexively, but he wasn't talking to her. After a brief hesitation, Heff submitted the fleshly link to be restored, though she could feel him straining away. He did not want to be in this sweltering bubble. He wanted to be in the world, to live or die with the rest. "You can't get through the warding now," Torrin said. "It will release us only if we succeed."

Their combined light filled the space like a substance. She drank it, inhaled it. She could no longer feel the ground under her. The hands that gripped hers were made of light, their pressure a charged hum. It was like being in Mellas's dream. Perhaps they were no longer in the world at all; perhaps from outside they had appeared to merge, and wink out, like a midderbug after its brief bright arc. But in the center of them the leaf's inscriptions still danced, a scintillation in the milky air. Faces could no longer be distinguished in the shifting patterns. This was more than magecraft. Magecraft connected with the spirits, but an illuminated leaf was a thing of matter which acted on matter. What they had done here had propelled them into some other realm—she felt Heff writhe in it, unwilling, agonized——

"Where are they?" she cried. If they'd followed the triplets into the warding, or through it, they were lost.

"They're here. Can't you feel them?"

Your eyes are no good here. Darkness demands more of you.

She saw them without sight, with the clarity of vigil. Three in one, a creature so bright it could not exist on this plane. A bridge of immense power, stretching from the Holding, and through them, and beyond them, out to sea and beyond it. Threading between the layers of matter and spirit. Only half-perceived, but even that half was too much light to bear. It was hatred, pure and vicious; and hunger, and cruelty. It was tainted—and yet there was something, something at the heart of it——

They were here. And they were winning. Her casting, their casting, would not be enough. They had slipped free of the world the warding shielded, knocked spinning into the place of light, the place she'd glimpsed through Werka's dying eyes. That meant they were dying. Their spirits had come unmoored. Why hadn't her body fought harder to hold on to hers? It had fought so hard to stay whole when they cut her. She hadn't had a chance, she hadn't felt it happening, it wasn't fair!

"Hold on," Torrin said softly.

The words were meant to give them strength, but she knew that low voice too well now. She heard the doubt in it. They had not deflected the arrow. They had merely slowed it. Jumped in its way and snagged on it and slowed it down. She felt cored by the power that was flowing through her.

Heff knew. Heff knew they had failed and was mad to break free, to save what he could. His worst fear had come to pass: he was trapped, blind, inside his own light. He was trying to bring them back, to anchor them in the world again. To bind them, lest they slip any farther into pethyar. But all his weight and strength could not hold them. They were speared helpless on the Ennead's blade, while outside them, or behind them in the place they had left, the Storm was destroying the world.

The marsh folk and their haunts and their belching furnaces. Girdlers in their fragile huts. Beltmen flinging their gentle insults. Oriel riverfolk eating their boiled barnacles. Geara, Danor, Nole . . . Breida. Eife and Seira, Oriane and Taemar, the weavers and drummers and hillwomen and farmers and cottars, all the good folk of Clondel and Orendel and Iandel and Drey. Megenna, the new sister she'd barely known. Graefel and Hanla, Keiler wherever he was. Nerenyi and her uncast triad and Gisela her uncast pledgemate. Korelan and Artesal. Folle and Beilor and Charvisk—what had happened to his poor son Jann? Had he gone for vellum, gone for a scrying? Pelkin and Karanthe and Jimor and Laren, Jhoss and Kazhe and Benkana. The Holding itself would be ravaged—Dabrena and her babe, the stewards who had fought so hard; Oreg, Jerize, Ronim, Wynn, old Knobface, all of them. Even the horde. Verlein and Lannan. All the fighting for nothing, all the effort, all the pain, all the courage, all for nothing, because the Ennead had chosen to harrow Ollorawn instead of divert the Storm, because she and Torrin and Heff had failed.

"*No!*" she cried, into the blinding silence, at the same moment that she heard Heff roar—a hideous, broken sound, a bindsong truer than the one he could not sing.

In a place of opalescent radiance, the twisted shadow-thing writhed. Agony racked it, and though it had left its body far behind, it felt the tremors in its memory of flesh, and knew the flesh was poisoned, dying. Its twined spirits fought to return to the flesh, but something prevented them. Something blue and silver as starlight, something that yearned toward the stars themselves . . .

They had been pushed off the correct path. One writhing thread of shadow reached to consume the others and was bucked away. They could not extract the parts from the whole, though one of them tried, sensing itself hindered in its blind, driving imperative. It tried, and failed, to break free, to complete its trajectory, to find its target, and shrieked in rage and frustration.

The remaining thread writhed in pleasure.

The undulating glyphs and kadri exploded in a deafening, searing burst, straight up in a spouting wake of sparks. She ducked, and came hard against Heff's shoulder, and looked up blinking to find that he and Torrin were flesh again, and outside them a calm night under a blazing canopy of stars that paled toward sunrise in the direction of Ollorawn.

"What . . . ?" she began. Torrin and Heff rose to their feet, pulling her with them. Stunned reckoners were picking themselves off the ground. Kazhe stood battered and dissheveled, as if she had been hurling herself against the casting-circle warding. That warding was still there, a thin, liquid barrier. "What happened?"

"Heff completed the casting, I think." Torrin was blinking, trying to make sense of it. "Someone diverted the Storm—the warders must have organized themselves—but—"

Arcing into the blush of dawn was a trail of light like a ship's wake, tinged with smoky crimson at the edges, a pure luminous silver-blue at the center. Like starlight.

Look with mind and heart, not eyes. Your eyes are no good here. Darkness demands more of you. Portriel demands more of you.

"Who are they using for a sealed mage?" she asked in a whisper. Torrin stared at her. They had not bothered to wonder. If not her, it would have had to be someone else Landril had tucked away . . . and yet there was no other light so bright . . .

"It's Portriel," Liath breathed. She knew that light. The sweet purity and anguish at the center of the current of power, the contained magelight the Ennead required to punch between the worlds. "It's *Portriel* . . ."

"Portriel is dead," Torrin said, a strange shocked light in his eyes as he stared at her, realizing what she had done. He had come by it with the vision only casting passage could bestow. He knew—just as she now knew, with the calm understanding of something always known, how much Portriel, his aunt, had meant to him.

Portriel was dead; yet somehow the Nine had bound her. What they had seen, with the clarity of vigil, was what Portriel saw. They had not been casting a deflection of the hein-na-fhin at all.

"We just cast passage for her," she said.

Torrin stared at the incomprehensible sky. "They were not the arrow . . . they were merely the bow . . . and we became the archers . . ."

Heff wrenched free of their grip and said, It's not over. She was not the only one.

Liath felt bubbling laughter that was not her own well up inside her. A wild, fierce glee. She followed Heff's gaze upward. Still disoriented from the unmooring, half bewildered at being in her body again, she felt she could fall into the sky, fall upward, fall forever. *I'll haunt the stars . . .*

The sky cracked open. The blazing stars twisted on their fabric of night; the fabric *unfolded*, rolling back and away like a vast tide receding, returning the blue of day to the bowl of sky, a clear cloudless blue in which the sun blazed at its zenith.

The arcing ribbon of magelight faded from Headward, cut off at its base. Somewhere over the Forgotten Sea, it simply ceased to exist. The rippling trace left by a finger trailing through water: there, and then gone.

"It *is* over," Liath said. "It's over, Heff! *We did it!*"

Reckoners and fighters outside the warding were hugging each other, dancing in twos and threes. She smiled at them, only faltering a moment to see Kazhe bashing wildly at the warding with her longblade. Of course she would be desperate to get through, to see for herself that Torrin was all right. But he was fine, they were all fine, they had succeeded, they had saved the world—and if the reckoners' warding was intact, it meant the magelight hadn't gone, they would have that too. No tragedy, no price to pay. It was too much joy to bear. She wanted to embrace Heff, but he was frowning, still dazed and hurt by the casting, they would have to seal him, he had done his part, she wanted to tell him that but she was too full of triumph to speak, so she turned back to Torrin, moved to hold him, to taste the sweetness of victory and safety on his lips.

Heff snatched her back as a great wind swept through, flattening reckoners and fighters, flattening tents, knocking horses over. Inside their warding, they stood unaffected. Confused, she struggled in his grip, still trying to reach Torrin, but Heff hauled her around and for a moment all she could see was Kazhe, scrambling to her feet, diving headlong at the warding, hacking at it with her useless blade, her mouth open in a soundless scream.

Then something went through her a nonned times brighter, a nonned times more powerful than the thread of light the Ennead had launched. As if every magelight in Eiden Myr had been concentrated and thrust into her, all at once. She cried out, convulsing in Heff's arms, which clenched her tight against the pain. Torrin staggered, let out a deep groan. The searing light was completely alien; it contained the light of no one she knew. She was charred from within by something that had no malice, no taint, but so much intensity that it could not keep from doing harm. A white-hot poker had been rammed down her throat and through her heart and gut, through the very core of her.

It is Galandra's triad. The shield was made of them.

Their spirits, joined in hein-na-fhin—their magelights, their souls, their wills—had formed the shield around Eiden Myr for twice nine nonned years. And now they had been passaged, too.

She screamed, writhing in Heff's grip; across the shimmer of the warding, like a silent reflection in a pool, Kazhe screamed back. Abruptly she could hear it, a shrieking wail—and then she was lifted, raised high in the air by Heff's arms, the blacksmith's arms whose true strength she had never known. She dipped again, queasily, as his knees bent. She tried to flip over, tried to get free, tried to find Torrin, to snag some piece of him and hold on. But with a grunt Heff's great body launched her headlong through the air, tumbling through the unraveling woven place that had been the reckoners' warding. Through ordinary air.

She hit hard, rolled back, and dug her hands into the rocky soil, tearing flesh as she braked. She staggered to her feet, coming up next to Kazhe. Together they stumbled down the slope toward Heff and Torrin.

The two men, driven to their knees, regarded each other in silence.

With an earsplitting crack, the tip of headland burst apart. Jagged boulders that had been solid rock fell with a roar into the sea. The outcropping was demolished in a single breath.

Liath went sprawling just shy of the edge. Kazhe, still screaming, tumbled over. Her hand caught Liath's. Liath gripped the wrist, held on, shimmied closer to get the leverage to haul her up. Sections of rock were still crumbling away. They scrabbled back as the place where they had been sank three feet and cracked off. They sat staring at empty space and the ocean beyond.

Torrin and Heff were gone.

As the hein-na-fhin dissolved, leaving abomination and a shattered triskele in the center of the broken casting circle, Vonche and Naeve, who had stepped into the pillar of light, crumpled to the stone—still breathing, but unresponsive, their eyes fixed on a far point.

Worilke sat on the chalked line of the casting circle, hugging her knees, rocking back and forth, mumbling incoherently.

Freyn stared at Worilke and thought, *Why aren't you dying? Didn't you trust me?*

Lerissa bit down on a cry of triumph. The triplets were gone, Vonche and Naeve would be gone in moments, she had gotten precisely what she wanted, but why was Evonder doubled over pale and sweating? "No last kiss for me, sweet Lerissa?" he said with a ghastly smile, the light dimming in his green eyes. Green as the glow of bonefolk feeding . . .

Realization came to her, cold as a cold bright stone. She and Worilke had had themselves warded against Freyn's poisons long ago—they could not have remained triaded with her otherwise, working day after day with materials they could not trust. But Evonder had not. Someone must take his place beneath her in the triangle. She leaned down and pressed her cool lips to his. "Where is the child?" she whispered. "Tell me, Evonder, and I'll see you healed."

"It's long past time for healing," he replied, and drew a glazed pot from his pocket. He pressed it into her hands. "The counterherbal," he said.

She was blinking at the pot, her hands occupied, as his fingers closed on the triskele that was not her own and ripped it burning from her neck.

Evonder staggered to the binding table, already drawing tools from the back of his belt. He laid a chisel point on the heart of the triskele and smashed the mallet down with one last effort of will as the banewort leached sensation from his limbs. The fading magestone flared, bathing them in silver, casting, for an eyeblink, one shadow in the chamber, then three, then none. Evonder sagged to his knees, jammed his elbows against the tabletop to keep from sliding to the floor, but he was laughing too hard to hold on, and he sprawled back on the cold, dead stone. Daivor, imprisoned for nine years and six, would not let his triad savor any joys of the spirit realm. One glimpse of forever was all they'd have, one taste of omniscience, immortality, before their thwarted, unpassaged spirits took permanent residence in the black rock that had borne them all.

He was still laughing as he began to die. It was only in the last paroxysms that the laughter turned to sobs. Evonder n'Vonche l'Naeve had never cried, even as a child. He died keening the sunlight he had never seen, the life and love he would never know.

He was dead before he knew his magelight had gone.

Worilke felt the magelight go dead inside her. *Of course*, she thought. *Of course. This is my punishment.*

Freyn ignored Lerissa's outcry, pawing distractedly at her chest as if she could brush away the discomfort of the light's passing. Good riddance, spirits take the light—she still had her potions and her plants, those would command respect in a lightless world. The Ennead was broken. The venerable Holding lineages were only names, now, dusty memories, powerless. Now she and Worilke were equals. She kneeled next to the woman who had been like a sister and tried to make her drink the correct counterherbal.

Worilke just sat there. "I saw her," she said. "I *saw* her. I was wrong. Every word I scribed, every belief I held, all wrong, all of it . . ."

Freyn slapped her. Worilke was hard as sculpted blackstone and could have broken her arm without effort, but she just *sat* there. "You're only a little sick," Freyn said. "Drink this, Worilke, and it will all come right—"

"Oh, leave her alone, Freyn, what's wrong with you?" Lerissa said, gasping as if the loss of her light had knocked her insides loose. "Don't you understand, you daft imbecile? The light has gone. Worilke is the last of our worries. She was warded against you! Everyone with any sense was warded against your forsaken philters!"

Freyn did not look at the jumbled lump of flesh that had been Gondril's triad, or the corpses of Vonche and Naeve, twisted from their death throes, or the corpse of Evonder. She looked at Lerissa, the only thing besides his lost love that Rigael had ever cared for, and said, in a soft voice, "Your father never did have any sense."

Color returned with a rush to Lerissa's cheeks. "What?"

"I said I killed your father. I killed your father as he lay in a drunken stupor in the bed he should have shared with me. Isn't that what you wanted to hear, Lerissa? All the years I mothered you, wasn't that the admission you sought? It was only what you wanted yourself. You should be happy now! I cleared the way for you, you wretched girl. You joined our triad because of *me*. You should *thank* me!"

Sounds of battle penetrated the thick wood of the main door. Freyn turned her back on Lerissa; the ungrateful creature was of no value, and she must attend to Worilke, who was rousing a little from her shock, looking toward the faraway clash of blades. "They're coming, Worilke. You must get up now. . . ."

Worilke focused for a moment on Freyn, then past her. The main door opened, admitting a lean figure and a pungent whiff of burning. It was Valik, Freyn's elderly father, Worilke's loyal steward. He looked at them in a panic, mouth opening, as if a cry was stuck in his throat, and waved his arms. He tried to run toward them, but he hadn't been able to run in years. What had frightened him? Worilke shifted her gaze to Lerissa with no particular interest, her eye drawn by the glint of a blade in the smoke-tinged air. Lerissa was standing behind Freyn, holding a knife low. *Mind yourself, Freyn,* Worilke thought. It was too much effort to say aloud.

"We're all lightless now," Freyn was explaining patiently, "but it doesn't matter, I'll care for you, we'll—"

A curved red smile opened below her chin as Lerissa reached around and cut Freyn's throat. "Thank you," Lerissa said.

Valik reached them only in time to take his newly lightless daughter in his arms as she died. His cry came forth at last, a thin keening. Worilke watched him without seeing. Her mind's eye was full of the vision of Galandra, the communion she had sought for a lifetime, the unbearable truths it had illuminated. She had created her own construct of Galandra, and forced the inscribed histories to conform to her construct, that she might bring Eiden Myr back to the path from which it had strayed, purge the taint of lightlessness, make the world a place of pure magecraft. But that was not what Galandra had meant. That was not at all what Galandra had meant.

Lerissa eeled out the door and past other stewards, wiping the blade on her robes. Where in the bloody spirits was Evrael? She had to get to his ship, get away from here, get into plain clothes, reconsider her options. The Khinishmen he had promised to bring her would be her wisest alliance now. If she and golden Evrael could forge the natural discipline of the Khinish into a rigorous loyalty, they might still salvage their realm. She began to run, as if to drive her mind faster. Leadership would be needed, she did not know who still lived or who her adversaries were but Evrael would give her sanctuary while she devised a new strategy, there were always options, Father had taught her that, Father had taught her to be adaptable and never give up, never give in, never—

She swayed to a halt at the Crownside gate, shocked by the sea air. She had never been outside the Holding. It was all she could do to force her foot over the threshold. At least they'd raised the gate. The gatekeeper lay dead. She spied the tawny hair and beard like a beacon among the swarthy Khinish, and pushed herself toward it. "Evrael!" she cried. "Evrael, it's me!"

"Lerissa?" he said, catching her up as she hurtled into him.

"Hush," she said, "I must not be Lerissa for a little time, until we've devised a new plan—"

"Hush indeed." He pushed her back to arms' length and surveyed her with cool green eyes. He looked remarkably like her father, though he was fair. The stamp of the Holding was so clear on its children. She began to smile—and then he put her in the grip of one of his Khinish sailors, while another found her blade and a third bound her wrists. She opened her mouth to protest, but he had already turned from her, as if she were no more than a larder steward caught loitering about. "Find out if any others escaped," he called over his shoulder as he strode toward the gate. "We're not so late that we can't clean up whatever's left."

Lerissa stared after her ally and her rescuer. "Your messages!" she cried, blinking furiously.

He paused long enough to say, "A creature of this Ennead—how could you overlook the power of words to deceive, little girl?" Then he was inside, and his Khinishmen hustled her away.

Worilke sat in the corpse of the Ennead, drenched in Freyn's blood, though Valik had carried Freyn off. Cradling his firstborn, he'd begged Worilke to come with him. The horde had found a back way in, he said— the horde she'd crushed—and Khinish had fought the Storm to land in Crown with golden Evrael at their head. They were on their way up. She must come with him. "Get out," she'd said. "Get away from me, cursed, lightless steward." At last he had gone, and left her with the blood and the poisonings and the grotesque three-faced, six-limbed thing the triplets had become.

She sat among the grisly remains, her mind's eye looking on the transformed visage of Galandra. Along the passageway, like the inward rush of surf, came the sounds of triumph, the cries of victory, the demand for spoils; then someone shouting, "It's not over until we count the bodies!" A woman with long black hair and olive skin and green eyes. She burst in, surveyed the carnage, whistled. Then her eyes fell on Worilke.

"One left," she said.

Worilke did not move.

I t was the remnants of the breaking," Jhoss explained patiently. To her? To someone else? What did it matter? She wasn't listening. "Galandra's triad were breaking the Serpentback when they cast themselves hein-na-fhin to create the warding. The warding subsumed them, but the casting was unfinished. Its own suspended energy was part of what maintained the warding over the generations. That, and their strength of will. They loved their vision of Eiden Myr so well that even time could not decay the shield they had made. But when they were freed, the casting completed itself. A casting older than memory, hanging there, awaiting completion. Extraordinary."

Extraordinary. If she could have opened her eyes or moved her limbs, she would have killed him.

"Not both of them," she cried, in her delirium, into darkness. No one heard, no one came; perhaps she cried out only in her mind. "*Not both of them!*"

She woke in a tent. A gaunt shadow stood at the foot of her pallet. All a dream, then, and Torrin just come in from relieving himself or taking the air. The tent was softly lamplit. The bonfire had gone out, but the strangest sound was coming from outside. She tried to sit up to ask Torrin what it was, to pull him down beside her for the slender hours until day broke and they had to save the world. But something was wrong with her body.

She could not sit up. Something was wrong with the shadow too—it was stunted, not Torrin's shape. It raised a longblade; lamplight ran red along the polished iron above the blood groove. It was death, come for her at last, because the night was over, and noon had come and gone and taken Torrin from her. He would never return to pull her warm into the curve of his body, sink his face into her hair. She tried to lift her arms, to welcome death. But it let its weapon sag. The thread of crimson was swallowed by darkness.

When she roused again, Kazhe was seated at the foot of the pallet with knees drawn up and longblade across them, as she had sat for long nights to guard Torrin. In the light diffused through canvas, her face, caked with old blood, was grayed, harrowed.

"We both only ever tried to keep what we loved alive," she said softly, and levered herself up with the longblade, and limped off into the glare of day.

"I'm a healer," said the bindsman as the fever cleared. He replaced on her brow the cool, damp cloth that her waking had dislodged, and returned to stitching a gash in her arm as if mending a torn shirt. "The lore and skills of binders will have many different uses in these new times. I'm not sure if this is the one I'll choose, but it's a start."

It was Keiler. He looked travel-worn, but his bright enthusiasm was undimmed. She turned her face from it as if burned.

"Father will finally be able to record all those scribings he kept in his head," he said, finishing the last stitch and bending to break the thread with his teeth. "He probably doesn't know it yet, but this will be the best thing that ever happened to him."

He was lightless. So was she. Her magelight was gone. The deadness at the heart of her was worse than pain. She was cored; she would never be whole again. *This is what it would have felt like, if I'd lost it before,* she thought.

Better to be that bright, blocked, anguished illuminator, than whatever empty thing she was now.

"I can't believe I missed the casting," Keiler said, retrieving the fallen rag again and dropping it in the basin of water. "You'll have to tell me all about it and make me jealous. Liath n'Geara, Torrin's illuminator! I'm so proud of you, Li."

Perhaps he didn't see the tears leaking from her eyes down her temples. Perhaps he took them for drops of water left by the compress. "At least your fever's broken," he said, "and I think your ankle and ribs will set all right. You took a beating in that quake. But you'll be right in no time."

He was so young.

"Listen to that," he said, perking up.

It was the strange sound she had thought a product of fever.

"Human voices, raised in song, with words and all. I dreamed my whole life of a day when I could sing with other people, but I thought it would only be mages, and only if I was called to the Holding. The songs are pretty bad. I don't know who thought to put words to them—someone said that's what binders used to do, a long time ago. I guess we'll find out, as all the truths the Ennead hid from us come into the light, eh?"

She did not respond.

"Oh, come on, Li, admit it. Isn't it beautiful? Isn't it the most beautiful thing you ever heard?"

Liath thought, *And so it begins.*

She stared out across the Forgotten Sea, at the dark ribbon of land on the horizon. How long would it take to notice them? How long before the ships came, and what would they bring?

"We'll be ready," Jhoss said.

Liath snorted. He'd begged Kazhe to ride to the Holding, to summon Verlein here, where a human shield might be needed. But Kazhe was off drowning in a barrel of ale, and Verlein, from the fractured reports, seemed too busy ransacking the Holding.

"Verlein will preserve the codices," Jhoss said. "Torrin made it clear to her, before we left the Blooded Mountains. That they must be salvaged at all costs."

Liath had given Verlein's horde a way into the Holding. If they'd gotten through, the Holding would be a smoking husk by now. Verlein had no respect for scribing and no reason to abide by Torrin's instructions. He had stopped the Ennead with magecraft. He'd made good on his promise to do that. But Verlein had no way of knowing it, unless she'd come across all the Nine lying dead in a chamber somewhere. All she knew was that Torrin had run out on her. She wouldn't even know, yet, that he was dead.

The keening cry in her mind rose to an unbearable pitch. "Leave me alone, Jhoss."

"We will need teachers," he said. "We will need a place of safety to keep the codices. A center of learning that is difficult to find, but not inaccessible. A new Holding, if you will."

"Go build it," she said. "I wish you joy of it."

"You were with him. You were his illuminator, in the last triad. You will be listened to, as I will not."

She grinned at him, and he backed away.

Night came clear and moonless, and with it a spangling of stars more numerous than she'd ever seen before. Perhaps that was what had become of all the magelights. Just lights in the sky, now, forever out of reach.

She stared at them, unblinking, for a long time. Tears swam along her lower lids. Then, as if her eyes had adjusted to a dark place, as if she had *opened* her eyes after a long time asleep, the stars came into focus—the stars abruptly made sense. In awe, she blinked the tears away, and what she had glimpsed was still there.

"I see them, Portriel," she whispered. "I see the kadri in the sky."

She dreamed Heff held her tight in the darkness. In the dream, she wished he would croon to her as he had crooned to struggling and terrified animals; she yearned for just one touch of his soothing earthcraft. He merely held her safe, in wordless comfort, until dawn came and the dream lifted clear of her.

Then, at last, she cried.

Not both of them, she begged the unheeding spirits. Too late—far too late—but the cry bubbled up again and again, she could not squeeze it down. *Not both of them!*

Either one could have seen her through to the far side of grief for the other. But she lay alone in the dark tent. Shadows cobwebbed the corners; the walls drew a nacreous glow from the first touch of day. She was the last of the wounded.

She roused herself, fumbled into clothes, made her way out into sweet dawn air. The other tents were gone, and the horses, and the wagons. The reckoners who had not been injured in the breaking had gone off under Pelkin's command, to see what they could salvage of their proxy chain; others had been taken into homes in the nearest villages. She did not know what they would reckon now. They were at the mercy of the weather from here on. There would be no warding, no diversions. There was no longer an ennead to be proxy for. A few fighters remained, as if stationed here, waiting. She did not know them, and they did not speak.

She walked down to the precipice. It was not so long a walk now. The headland was blunted, diminished. If there had been bodies to find, down in the jagged mound of rocks, the bonefolk had them days ago. There was nothing left here. Nothing but the combing fingers of the sea.

Not even haunts. They had cast passage for Portriel; they had cast passage for Galandra's triad; and they had cast passage for themselves. She was supposed to go with them, but Heff had promised to protect her, and so he did. *I will always find you,* he had said. How would he find her now?

She returned to the tent, gathered her pack and the other two that Pelkin had left for her, hefted them on one shoulder—none of them had carried much, except for Torrin. She found her saddle on a rock and her little black gelding tethered to a tree behind her tent, which had been Torrin's.

She fastened a lead to Heff's rangy gray mare, mounted, and reined upland. She did not look back. There was no one left to say goodbye to.

I t was hard, in the first moments after. Time meant nothing, and he had no breaths to count with. All the years of maneuvering and secrecy sloughed off him, leaving emptiness, desolation, an aching loneliness. He had become no more than his secrets and imperatives, his flesh, his light, his pain. Now those were gone, and he reeled, solitary and disoriented. A small boy wandering lost in the labyrinth. Cold and frightened, unable to find his way back, unsure if he even wanted to.

Then he heard the song of memory that the veins of magestone sang. He'd been a bindsman once. He had sung songs. Now the rock sang to him, and in its song he began to comprehend the ages.

He could no longer see, but he could sense, and he sensed the wraiths he had loved. He'd had a light once. The wraiths had come to him as light. Now he felt them, felt the deep spirit of stone as he never could in life. The gentle scintillation welcomed him home.

He freely roved the shadowed interstices of the nightstone mountain. Here and there small fires still blazed, human battles still raged; large sections would be silent and dead, steeped in the effluents of agony, for a long while. But the stone would endure. The stone would heal. It was alive, and aware; it knew him. It had always known him simply for what he was—no more, no less.

There were no more disguises. Evonder n'Daivor was himself at last.

Tꝏe ISLe

Sunset through the cottage window set the air aflame. Liath n'Geara l'Danor sat on a driftwood chair, drawing idle designs on its sea-smoothed arm with the tip of her finger, watching the glow of the peat fire deepen as night came on.

Unable to find Mellas, or Heff's horses, or Amaranth, she'd turned toward home—then veered Armward, toward the high coast. She had come back to Nerenyi, and told her everything. It had freed her. Nerenyi the seeker would know how to put the pieces of knowledge together. Nerenyi the illuminator would preserve them, disseminate them. Nerenyi would know what to do.

The women who had been mages saw her through grief by pushing her to conquer fear. They taught her to swim, then taught her to sail. Then she and Korelan had set about building a boat.

It had taken two full turns of the moon. She had to earn what lumber she could not cut herself, and all had to be rowed over from the mainland, then painstakingly carved and cut and joined. An old shipbuilder had supervised—able to direct them, though her aged hands could no longer work the wood or bend the sails. It was a beautiful craft, small and maneuverable, with a deep draft, and good solid Senana stone for ballast. It would hold three ninedays' freshwater and provisions: one turn of the moon.

Jhoss had found her here by following Pelkin, who'd come as he'd promised to. There would be no casting triad now, but he'd cast Nerenyi and Gisela's pledge nonetheless. Ritual had significance still. Jhoss had sent for the Holding codices, drafted workers for the laborious construction of a shelter for them. Perhaps, in building their stone walls, they would use up all the isle's rocks after all. She could think of worse uses for them.

What had happened on Galandra's ground was wilding magecraft, unfocused. They had cast at each other blind, cast their own imperatives on the table like stones and then groped to feel how they had fallen. It was what someone in the Blooded Mountains had told her of heavy blade-work: *"Just two fighters coming at each other, and one in better position to begin with—one chop and it's over, and on to the next."* No finesse, no strategy. One all-out burst of power from the Ennead, one from them. They had won because Portriel was there, because Portriel would break through the warding to haunt the stars. They had won because they had instinctively invoked Galandra's triad.

They had won by accident, or luck—or the spirits' will.

The magewar, folk were calling it, but it had been no more war than the scuffle in Clondel. The clash of blades, the clash of power, was an afterthought; the outcome was determined by the angle of attack, by the set of their feet, by the weight and strength of what they'd brought to bear.

The Khinish had joined forces with the warders Dabrena had rallied to divert the Storm. Verlein, after a brief struggle with their leader, had taken her horde to the Fist, where ships would make landing when they came. If they came.

"Teach," Jhoss had begged her. "Keep his memory alive."

Already there was a backlash. Torrin Martyr had become Torrin Light-breaker, the man who extinguished the magelight in Eiden Myr. Some venerated the Ennead that was gone; scattered battles broke out, plain folk against the rebel fighters they blamed for weather they could no longer control, illness and injury they could no longer heal, crops they could no longer rely on. They had been safe in the world they knew. Now the unknown lay all around them.

Echoing Torrin in a faint voice, she had said, "I'm ill suited to be a figurehead." She knew what a figurehead was, now: her little sailboat had one, mounted on the prow just under the bowsprit, after a drawing they'd seen in Torrin's ancient illuminated volume. She'd carved it herself, over long days of learning to turn wood under her hands as she had turned lines on parchment. It was the image of Galandra.

They'd named her *Stormwind*. It would have been an unlucky name, in another time. But times were different now.

Liath looked out the window at the dusting of sowmid stars across the fabric of sky. It would take her the turn of a year, perhaps two, to learn their seasonal configurations, but she was fairly certain she could steer by them. Her little boat waited in the harbor. Only one more task remained, before she went.

She took ink and quill and sedgeweave from the supply that Imma had given her.

Jhoss's prentices were already swarming here, to this hive of new learning. She had even learned, a little. Not enough to read Ghardic, which was becoming the language of messages, of records, of trade; but a little Celyrian, the language of healing. She could not yet read Luriel's story, or the frightened words that Seblik the scribe had appended, or the words of the magewoman he had saved. But she knew enough to scribe a message home, in the strange archaic tongue that all but wordsmiths had lost. *I shall be some while a-journeying. I shall return to you. I love you all.* She knew enough, now, to inscribe her name beneath it.

In Ghardic, her name was as Torrin had shown her, three glyphs with a mark indicating the breath of aspiration, of contraction, of silence. But in Celyrian it was composed of five: three for her, and two others, the silent glyphs, the ones she would carry always, a hidden part of herself, like her innermost thoughts. The ones that represented the two men who had made her whole.

Torrin and Heff were the shadow ciphers in her name.

She rolled the leaf up, bound it with string, and set it aside for Korelan. He would find some Neckward traveler to take it. Then she blew out the single oil lamp and settled by the hearth.

On a wistful impulse, she drew out a glowing brand and raised it to trace a figure overhead. Where the embers passed, they left an illusory trail of flame in their wake. She inscribed Torrin's name in the dark air, seeing its beginnings dissolve into shadow even as her movements produced its ending. She inscribed Heff's name; shorter, it hung complete in her vision for nearly a breath, and remained behind her lids even when she closed them. Then she drew a kadra, a thing constructed as much of motion as of shape, a fleeting thing, the arc of a midderbug through the night, flaring and then gone: the resonance that was herself.

Some things could be seen clearest only in the dark.

LIST OF NAMES

CLONDEL:

Liath n'Geara l'Danor
Geara n'Breida l'Pelkin, publican, Liath's mother; daughter of Breida
    n'Onofre l'Nole and Pelkin n'Rolf l'Liath
Danor n'Taemar l'Oriane, publican, Liath's father
Breida n'Geara l'Danor, Liath's younger sister
Nole n'Danor l'Geara, Liath's older brother
Megenna, crafter from Orendel, Nole's intended
Eife n'Breida l'Pelkin, traveling brandy merchant, Geara's middle sister
Seira n'Breida l'Pelkin, traveling brandy merchant, Geara's youngest sister
Graefel n'Traeyen l'Brenlyn, wordsmith of local triad, pledged to Hanla
Hanla n'Geior, illuminator of local triad, pledged to Graefel (Hanlariel
    n'Geior ti Khine)
Keiler n'Graefel l'Hanla, bindsman of local triad
Marough, wrangler
Daughan, wrangler, Marough's brother
Meira Farrier, Marough's pledgemate
Sharra Farrier, Daughan's pledgemate
Tarny n'Marough l'Meira, wrangler, Marough's middle son
Galf n'Marough l'Meira, Tarny's younger brother
Sarse n'Marough l'Meira, Tarny's older brother
Erl n'Daughan l'Sharra, Tarny's cousin, Daughan's eldest
Rolf n'Daughan l'Sharra, Daughan's middle son
Melf n'Daughan l'Sharra, Daughan's youngest
Sael Miller, Ferlin's father
Islia Miller, Ferlin's mother

Ferlin n'Islia l'Sael, the millers' eldest child
Eirin n'Sael l'Islia, the millers' youngest child
Demick Smith and his sister
Porl Carpenter
Den Weaver
Orla Weaver
Naragh Cobbler
Nelis and Nin, the fullers' daughters
Roiden
Lisel Drummer
Drolno Teller
Taemar and Oriane, Danor's parents, visiting from Iandel
Danor's two brothers, visiting from Iandel, and their families

VOCATES:

Dabrena Wordsmith, former cottar from the Fingers
Karanthe Illuminator, from Elingar, in the Belt (Karanthe n'Farine l'Jebb)
Tolivar Binder, former sailor from the Knee
Jonnula Illuminator (Jonnula n'Devra l'Jonnel)
Herne Wordsmith
Annina Binder
Eltarion te Khine
Corle
Ronim
Jerize
Selen
Terrell
Dontra
Garran
Loris

HOLDING STEWARDS:

Wynn Steward, the vocates' materials steward
Bofric Steward, the vocates' lessons steward (old Knobface)
Lenn Steward, the vocates' larder steward
Bron Steward, head of the runners' stable (Brondarion te Khine)
Valik Steward, personal steward to Worilke's family; from the Weak Leg;
    Freyn's father
Seamstress (unnamed) who was an organizer of the stewards' uprising
Oreg Steward, loyal to Bron

The ennead:

Gondril n'Rontifer l'Yelwyn, wordsmith of the leading triad; of Luriel's
   line; Landril and Seldril are his twins
Landril n'Rontifer l'Yelwyn, illuminator of the leading triad
Seldril n'Yelwyn l'Rontifer, binder of the leading triad
Naeve n'Bevriel l'Sonder, wordsmith of the balance triad, pledged to her
   cousin Vonche; of Caithe's line
Vonche n'Reiff l'Aerion, illuminator of the balance triad, pledged to his
   cousin Naeve; of Caithe's line
Evonder n'Vonche l'Naeve, bindsman of the balance triad, son of Naeve
   and Vonche; of Caithe's line
Worilke n'Karad l'Geidek, wordsmith of the weather triad; of Loekli's line
Lerissa n'Lessa l'Rigael, illuminator of the weather triad; of Arael's line
   through her father
Freyn n'Eniya l'Valik, bindswoman of the weather triad

Also in the holding:

Beadrin and Tazzi, stablegirls
Portriel n'Niendre l'Mathey, of Arael's line
Kara, baby girl

Gulbrid:

Folle, a stablemaster
Heff Farrier
Serle Ironsmith, Folle's dead pledgemate, Heff's younger brother
Beilor, a tavernkeep
Daglor, a pining youth
Charvisk, an angry father
Leskana, Charvisk's daughter
Jann, a mage, Charvisk's lost son

Isle of Senana:

Gisela Wordsmith
Imma Binder, Gisela's mother

Werka, an elderly dying oyster diver (Werkarel n'Dalrien)
Werka's sister
Korelan, Werka's grandson
Artesal, a concerned mainlander

ÞORÒE IN TÞE BLOOÒEÒ ꟿOUNTAINS:

Verlein, former harvestmaster, founder and leader of the horde
Kazhe, once Verlein's closest friend, now a bodyguard
Benkana, Kazhe's lover, a high-placed fighter in Verlein's horde
Jhoss, former beekeeper
Eshadri, a fighter and brandy smuggler
Auda, a bladesmith
Serafad, a mage
Lannan, a guard
Boroel, former assassin, child of Holding warders, fosterling from Crown

OTÞER CÞARACTERS:

Mellas, an Ennead runner boy
Torbik, Gadiya, and Ontas, companions of Verlein and Benkana
Jimor Proxy, a reckoner
Laren Proxy, a reckoner
Porick Wordsmith
Jolia Binder, of Porick's triad
Mirellin Illuminator, of Porick's triad
Gill
Coll
Yerby, a wordsmith
Kael, Yerby's binder
Ashara and Indar, fighters
Evrael n'Vonche l'Naeve, Evonder's older brother, who fled to Khine
    when he was two nineyears old
Nerenyi t'Galandra Illuminator, a seeker from mining folk in the Heel
    (born Nerenyi n'Jheel l'Corlin)
Pelkin Reckoner (Pelkin n'Rolf l'Liath), Liath's grandfather, an illuminator
Torrin n'Maeryn l'Eilody, estranged scion of the Ennead's Holding

OThERS (DENTIONED:

Befre n'Brenlyn l'Traeyen, Graefel's sister and former binder, journeymage bindswoman

Galandra, legendary mother of all magecraft (Galandra na Caille le Serith)

Luriel, Galandra's daughter

Eiden, spirit of earth

Morlyrien, spirit of water

Sylfonwy, spirit of air and wind

Jaemlyn and Maeryn, Portriel's brothers

Rigael, Portriel's son, Lerissa's father

Lessa, Rigael's lost love, Lerissa's mother

Arael, Luriel, Caithe, Loekli, ancient Holding lineages

GLOSSARY

bonedays: Three days a year (one in each season) when the dead are remembered and offerings are left for the bonefolk. Observances differ regionally. Binders often choose bonedays to harvest skins for vellum and parchment.

bonefolk: Mysterious fringe folk who dispose of the carcasses of people and animals, leaving nothing behind but any metal or stone.

Eiden Myr: The world. Eiden is its animating spirit.

Ennead: Nine mages, in three triads, bound to protect Eiden Myr from the Great Storms and other catastrophes. Also called the Nine, the Three of Threes. Live and work in the Ennead's Holding.

harvestmid: Autumn (one side of midder). The three seasons are winter, summer, and midder.

hein-na-fhin: "One of three." A dangerous, powerful casting in which three mages combine into one being.

kadra: An ideographic symbol enclosed in a triangle. Plural kadri.

Longdark: The winter solstice.

Longlight: The summer solstice.

midder: Considered one season, though it occurs in part between winter and summer and in part between summer and winter, midder is the time between the other two seasons.

moon: A month, which is twenty-seven days, or three ninedays.

nonned: Nine nines (81). Twice nine nonned is 1458 (Eiden Myr's equivalent of our 2000).

parchment: The skin of a sheep, lamb, goat, or kid used as a writing material.

pethyar, also *bet-jahr*: The spirit world.

proxy: A mage who works on behalf of the Ennead, either as a reckoner in the field or a warder in the Holding.

reckoner: A proxy, trained in the Holding, sent into the field to manage other mages and report to the Holding (through the proxy chain) on weather conditions. Reckoners cast in threes but do not form permanent triads.

sedgeweave: Papyrus-like writing material made of laid strips of reeds.

seekers: Itinerant folk, suspicious of superstition and convention, who try to discern large truths by applying rigorous logical inquiry to stories, legends, and empirical observations. Considered crackpots. Associate loosely with each other, usually arguing a lot. Put a silence on themselves when they need time to think.

sheddown: Down collected where it's fallen.

sowmid: Spring (the other side of midder).

spirit days: The dark of the moon; corresponds to no phase of the moon (the moon's three phases are waxing, full, and waning).

stewards: Non-mage support staff in the Holding.

stones: A game, something like a cross between marbles, Go, and table croquet. Played without a grid, using pretty colored stones that would be called jewels elsewhere.

threft: A yard; contraction of "threefoot."

triad: Three mages (wordsmith, illuminator, and binder) who form a threesome to do a casting; also, three mages who are cast triad by reckoners, to make their threesome permanent.

Ve Eiden: The autumnal equinox.

Ve Galandra: The vernal equinox.

vellum: The skin of a cow or calf used as a writing material.

warder: A proxy, trained in the Holding, who remains in the Holding to assist the Ennead in managing the weather and maintaining the physical premises of the Holding itself. Warders form permanent triads.

Special thanks to: Bob Stacy, Steven desJardins, and Russell Handelman, for reading it; Rob Stauffer, for copyediting it, and Becky Maines, for proofing it; Fiorella deLima and Tom Finnegan, for shepherding it; Gary Ruddell, Carol Russo, and Ellen Cipriano, for garbing it; Teresa Nielsen Hayden and Patrick Nielsen Hayden, for taking it on at a difficult time; Russell Galen and Kevin Broderick; and my mother, for the fantasy reading that seeded it, and for being the finest example I know of compassionate intellect.